MW01480555

The Volga Flows Forever ~ Book Three

From Gulag
to Freedom

The Indomitable Spirit
of the Volga Germans

Sigrid Weidenweber

Center for Volga German Studies
at Concordia University
Portland, Oregon

From Gulag to Freedom

The Volga Flows Forever - Book Three

FIRST EDITION

Typography by Lori A. McKee.

Weidenweber, Sigrid, 1941-

From gulag to freedom : the indomitable spirit of the Volga Germans / Sigrid Weidenweber.

p. cm. – (The Volga Flows Forever ; 3)

Summary: A novel, drawn on historical material, about growing up in a Volga German colony and surviving the hardships of Soviet collectivization, deportation and imprisonment in a Siberian gulag. Katharina, the heroine, with the help of a native Komi tribesman, escapes from the gulag and makes her way to the San Joaquin Valley of Central California where she becomes part of the Volga German community that had been established there decades earlier.

1. Russian Germans – History. 2. Germans – Russia (Federation) – Volga River region. 3. Forced labor – Soviet Union – History. 4. Immigrants – United States – Economic conditions. I. Title. II. Weidenweber, Sigrid, 1941-. The Volga flows forever ; 3.

HV8964 .S65W45 2009   635'.45'094709043 – dc21

Library of Congress Control Number: 2009929678

ISBN(10): 1-934961-03-5

ISBN(13): 978-1-934961-03-2

Printed in the United States of America.

To Anne, my daughter,
ever loving, ever faithful.

S.I.W.

In Appreciation

During the years of researching and writing the trilogy "The Volga Flows Forever," I was sustained by the support I received from my husband and John Van Diest. Their belief in my work elevated my mood when I tired, their promotion of my books spurred me to greater effort, and their excellent humor cheered me.

I must mention that aside from books and materials available to me, the Internet, Google and Wikipedia, the free encyclopedia, made finding the small details enriching a story much easier. I was amazed that, upon crosschecking, Wikipedia's facts were correct. I, at least, never came upon egregious errors. This useful tool has been a blessing.

Most helpful in promoting my understanding of Stalin and his inner circle was Dmitri Shostakovich's book *Testimony* and the answers to my questions directed at Vadim Yakovlev, who had personally known "The man."

I am very thankful for Kate Joseph's intelligent, erudite treatment of my book. To my amazement, few subjects introduced in the book were foreign to her. I marvel at her astounding wealth of facts concerning WWII, and I marvel at my fortune to have her for my editor. How she came into my life is another story; a story I have to accredit to my husband Donald who knew Kate, and thought she would be perfect for the task.

Lori McKee has produced once again a cover that does the story justice. She is also responsible for the layout of the book, a beautiful continuation of the trilogy.

My grateful thanks to the people who helped with the publication of this and previous works, their labor did not go unnoticed.

Thanks and blessings upon the head of David Henson, my son-in-law, who, with his knowledge, has saved my work countless times from falling victim to ruthless hackers.

Furthermore, I have to thank my loving family for the support that has enabled me to keep monastic hours and still be part of a rich life.

S.I.W.

Preface

As I was researching and writing the story of Katharina Grushova, a Volga German woman, I was eerily reminded of the fact that, in parts, I had lived in East Germany the very life I was describing.

There are so many parallels to lives lived in communist countries that to this day, when we "former inmates from behind the Iron Curtain" meet, we soon begin to compare those details of communist life we experienced that were the same and those that were culture-specific.

With a few notable exceptions—Romania and Albania come instantly to mind—none of the communist satellites were quite as gruesome and ruthless in the treatment of their citizens as were the Russians. Russian communism was made utterly dreadful and inhumane through sheer class-envy expressed in violent hatred and murder. The savagery loosed upon their own people is comparable in recent history only to the exploits of Hitler, Mao Tse-tung and Pol Pot.

Stalin created an artificial famine of devastating proportions designed to eliminate classes of people he and his henchmen designated "enemies of the Party." In this endeavor he had millions of willing executioners who robbed the people at gunpoint of their last grain of wheat. They shot those showing the slightest resistance. By such means the starvation of close to fourteen million people was accomplished. Most of the victims resided in the Ukraine, in the North Caucasus, Kazakhstan, along the Volga and other regions deemed recalcitrant in their resistance to collectivization.

Stalin and his communist ilk killed altogether over twenty-two million people, innocents labeled kulaks who had the misfortune to have worked hard, lived without debt and perhaps owned a horse or a cow.

In the words of Mao Tse-tung: "Classes struggle, some classes triumph, others are eliminated. Such is history; such is the history of civilization for thousands of years." Yes, he is correct. History does show this pattern. However, history also documents that people involved in the extermination of another class become barbaric and set civilization back by centuries. Furthermore, the psychopathic elimination of another class clearly shows that when man usurps the role of God, by assuming power over the life and death of groups, all hope for humanity to attain a higher spiritual ground is driven underground.

It is embarrassing, no, shameful, that today, seventy years later, the world at large overlooks the cataclysmic Russian tragedy. Few monuments have been erected to the victims, and the world media, with certain exceptions, seems to have neglected exposing Stalin's atrocities. I wrote this book to shine light on these gross injustices.

As I went through the editing process, I relived part of my childhood, which was often painful and daunting, and left me with a lifelong paranoiac concern about governmental powers.

But now that it is accomplished, I feel relieved. I am glad that I told the story of the Volga German victims and, within the documentation of one woman's life, a bit of my own life's tale.

The most powerful tool of any totalitarian regime is the extermination of all opposition. If a government silences its critics and forbids ideas contrary to its ideology, labeling such ideas "hate speech," that is the end of freedom. Stalin, Hitler and Mao are frightening examples of such oligarchic dictatorships.

And may we never forget how quickly a nation can lose its precious freedom and fall under the aegis of fear and the power of ruthless demagogues. This moving story has implications for our lives in this complex world today. Readers will draw their own conclusions. The book speaks for itself.

S. I. W.

Cast of Characters

KATHARINA (KATYA) ALEXEYEVNA GRUSHOVA—*heroine*
ALBINA GRUSHOVA—*her mother*
ALEXANDER PETROVICH GRUSHOV—*her father*
VICTORIA AND HOLGER HILDEBRANDT—*her grandparents*
MARTIN—*her uncle*
GUDRUN—*her aunt*
MICHAEL AND PETER—*her brothers*
SOPHIA ANDREYEVNA PESTOVICH—*Soviet teacher*
ANASTAS SERGEYEVICH PELKOV—*Soviet teacher*
JOSEPH BAUMGARTNER—*adopted brother*
    MARIA BAUMGARTNER—*his mother*
    ARKADY SEMYONOV—*his friend*

ANDREY STEPANOVICH VERONTZEV—*Kolkhoz commissar*
KARL—*neighbor*
ALYOSHA SEMYONOVICH KULOV—*gulag commander*
    MARYONNA IVANOVNA KULOVA—*his mother*
TIMOTEO BEROKODZE—*Stalin's valet and body guard*
ANGELA HUBER—*Schaffhausen neighbor and gulag camp-mate*
BARBARA HUBER—*camp-mate*
HANNA MÜLLER—*camp-mate*
VASYA—*young soldier and camp guard*
GENADY MARKOV—*camp sergeant*
YEVGENY ANDREYEVICH KHOLSTININ—*train commandant*
PROKOFIEV—*camp sergeant*
ANTON PETROVICH BELUSKOV—*Ukrainian camp cook and survivor of three gulags*
DEMYAN KROPATKIN—*convict shoemaker*
ILYA GRIGORIEVICH—*adjutant to Kulov*
IVANKA—*convict woman*
KALACHNIK BOGDANOVICH MATVEYEV (IVAN THE TERRIBLE)—*new gulag commander*
SUOMO—*Komi native*
    PAVEL—*his brother*
    SAMEA—*his mother*
    KORYA—*his friend, Katya's guide and protector*
AMUTA—*Nenets native woman*
EVGENY OKRUG—*Nenets elder in Arkhangelsk*
    MARIA VASSILYEVNA—*his wife*
ANTON ANTONOVICH DEREVNIKOV—*merchant*
ROBERT HOWARD—*captain of the destroyer* HMS Intrepid
ELLIOT BROMFIELD—*ensign*
HERBERT BAUMEISTER—*American pilot*
CORA BLACKWELL—*boarding house owner*
HARRY PILLMANN—*druggist*
CARY MCKENNA—*husband*
FIONA—*her daughter*
KEENAN—*her son*

From Gulag to Freedom

The Indomitable Spirit
of the Volga Germans

Prologue

My people once resided on the east bank of the Volga River where the Kazakh steppe begins and stretches seemingly to the end of the earth. On this bank, just a few kilometers removed from the great Volga, six villages were strung together along her side, like beads on a ribbon. The largest, Katharinenstadt, was closest to other settlements while my village, Schaffhausen, was the lone bead at the end of the ribbon. Beyond our houses began the open land, fields, meadows, a few copses, and then—the vast steppe.

Closest to Schaffhausen was Basel, then Zug, Orlovskaya and Ober-Monjou. When I was born, our village was quite large—about five thousand people. Our houses were clustered, almost melting into each other, along a broad road and straight side streets. Because most houses had roofs fashioned from straw or reed bundles, we feared fires as much as we feared the devil.

Our houses were constructed from wood that was sometimes left unpainted, weathering to a silvery gray. But, houses inhabited by proud owners were painted a deep blue, a blue that I call to this day "Russian-blue." Different colors were used for the trim around the windows and artful designs embellished the shutters and doors. Each small house possessed a minuscule porch, a kitchen garden, an orchard, a barn and stables. Our fences, protecting the gardens and orchards, were mostly made from brush and wattle. Looking at Schaffhausen from afar, I always marveled how a place of many people could be so stark, so monochrome. Thus it looked, especially in early spring and before the onset of winter.

The Podstepnaya Creek, dry for most of the year, creased the land surrounding us. And, of course, there was the Volga, the blessed. Her mists cooled the heated land about us on summer evenings, and her waters saved us in years of drought. Forever I will remember my misty, mystic morning walks up high on her banks, looking into her slate-gray, seemingly placid depth.

1

My village owned more saline and sandy land than arable acreage. We cursed this barren ground when we had bad harvests. The best of the soil could barely sustain us in a good year.

Yet, although our lives were drab, hard and desperate at times, we loved this small spot in Russia's vastness, for it was ours—had been for generations. We were born to this soil, and our blood, sweat and tears had enriched the barren earth and tamed the wilderness.

A New Life

RUSSIA
VOLGA VILLAGE SCHAFFHAUSEN
JULY 1921

Baptismal water dribbled over the baby's head into the font. In his traditional Lutheran garb, a simple black robe with a worked-in stole decorated with Christian symbols that was worn over a black shirt with white tabs, the pastor pronounced in the ancient sonorous singsong: "In the name of the Father, the Son and the Holy Ghost, I name thee Katharina Alexeyevna Grushova." I, the small person sound asleep on the white, silken pillow did not deign to acknowledge the rite with so much as a blink of the eye.

Content in the world of dreams, my failure to acknowledge the few drops of water was an indication of how I would handle the problems presented to me by the world in the future. And the problems would be countless.

I had chosen a most unhappy time to make my entry into a world plagued by a miserable succession of wars. In addition to world upheaval, this particular spot on the planet was not auspicious for a child's birth either. Russia, in the throes of the Bolshevik Revolution, was not a place guaranteed to nurture and shelter a small girl whose fate had placed her into the womb of a Volga German mother. My father, a Russian, gave me his name, but that was almost all he could give me. However, he vested in me enough courage with which to live an entire life.

2

The Russian Revolution had been in full swing since March 1917. In its very early antecedents, it had been an event, stimulating ideas of greater freedom for minorities. Anticipation of *Mitbestimmung* was raised; having a voice in government was significant especially for my people, the Germans, who had cultivated the wilds of the Lower Volga. However, their hopes were placed into shifting political sands. For, not long thereafter, Lenin decided that the philosophy giving impetus to the Revolution, a bourgeois state with a socialist agenda and a parliamentary system of government, was not going to provide him with the power he craved. Under such a system the Bolsheviks would have to parlay and bargain with other parties and be forced to forge compromise; otherwise they would have been an ineffective opposition, for they could never hope to become the majority in a Russian parliament.

And so, Lenin with Trotsky's help—a man well respected by the masses— began to isolate and destroy all opposition to the Communist movement. Only four months prior to my arrival on July 20, 1921, the communists had put down a mutiny by the fractious sailors of the naval base in Kronstadt, with rivers of blood and human sacrifice. History will remember the slaughter of good Russian men and credit the massacre, absolutely and imperatively so, to Field Marshal Tukhachevsky of the Red Army.

The sailors in Kronstadt had clamored for free elections and access to the soviets and rejected the total domination and staffing of the determining committees by the Communist Party. The Revolution that was to have been the saving grace of all disenfranchised Russian peoples had turned, as it often happens with such peculiar notions, into a search for the singular power of a particular group. What began as a revolution of all Russian Marxist Socialists, Bolsheviks and Mensheviks alike, became a venue for Lenin and his Bolshevik Soviets to assume power, ridding themselves of all interference from their "brothers in revolution" by killing and intimidating them. This was the bloody path they would follow throughout their entire reign.

I knew neither that our village of five thousand people was in the throes of a famine caused by the Bolsheviks, nor did I know that, between the day of my birth and the same day in July two years later, 1,965 people would have died of starvation in our small village. Later I would learn that one of Russia's greatest writers, the incomparable Maxim Gorky, had in July 1921, movingly appealed to then Secretary of Commerce, Herbert Hoover, begging for famine relief. Hoover responded by founding the American relief agency responsible for saving over half a million lives of Russian Germans and Ukrainians.

But I, the baptismal object, knew nothing of my country's woes. My mother and other villagers filled in much detail as I matured. As early as I can remember, I knew that I was special, German. Why that was so special, I acquired laboriously by and by. Even my Russian papa, I recalled in my later years, made me aware of the fact that it was a good thing to be German and live in our Lutheran village of Schaffhausen.

Yet before I was old enough to figure out what the good thing was, at age four, in 1925, the Red henchmen came. They came after the noon meal, during which only a little bread and milk had been consumed because we were in the second year of a famine. They looked like uniformed bandits, these soldiers allied with the communists. Their uniforms were dirty; their hair matted; their boots encrusted with mud; their eyes wild and drunk with power. They rode filthy horses and ponies geared with dirty tack and swung grimy rifles over their heads in their headlong approach.

We heard them from a mile away. The thunder of hoof-beats, their shouts and yells traveled as one mighty sound wave across the flat land, bringing us running from our homes. Wide-eyed and frightened, we stood in the doorways, as if our huts and houses could protect us from this massive onslaught. We heard tales that they had been to other villages before. So far, we had been left unmolested, perhaps because our village was small, one of the poorest in the region.

My papa had pushed my mother halfway behind his broad frame. My grandfather, grim-faced, stood beside Papa, Grandmother was next to him. I squeezed between Father and Grandfather, for I was a nosy, precocious child that, like the proverbial cat surveying the hot stew, needed to know everything that was going on. To my emotional peril I was soon to find out.

There were perhaps thirty riders who descended upon our village. The moment they reached the village center, marked by the church, they stopped their horses short with great bravura. Looking on, I was breathlessly excited and impressed by their riding skills. Stopped short, some of the steeds reared until they stood vertical on their hind legs. Some horses slid to a halt, sinking back onto their haunches, but the riders, looking like bandits, sat solid and straight-backed in the saddles.

Their leader, an unshaven giant, as unwashed as the rest of them, was distinguished by a red armband sporting a yellow hammer and sickle and a white stallion, a much more handsome horse than the rabble under his command. How would a four-year-old snot nose, especially a girl, know about horses you ask? Well, I had been on horseback since age two. Papa had been an officer in a cavalry regiment and the manager of one of the greatest stud farms in all of Russia before he married my mother. We had the best horses in the village and our stud, Borodin, was the sire of a considerable herd of horses in the area. Before I was born, Papa owned a small breeding business, but the soldiers had come and confiscated most of the horses for service in the Army.

From the moment I began to understand language, Papa taught me the anatomy of the horse. Repeatedly, he mentioned that the withers must be high and the hocks broad, so tendons and muscles have a good hold on the bone; chests must be wide and barrels deep for the lungs to be able to expand when the horse ran. "Never buy a horse with a narrow chest," he admonished. "They always have lung problems."

The giant on his powerful stallion grimly mustered the assembled Germans and then, after a moment of silence, he bellowed with stentorian might that he was appointed by the Supreme Soviet as commandant of the Saratov region; that under this dictate he was to appropriate the properties of all counterrevolutionary propagandists, their followers, and all kulaks. Under this designation we were all enemies of the state, for kulak meant wealthy peasant and, compared to many Russian farmers, we were prosperous. Furthermore, he declared that all families designated as counterrevolutionaries had five hours in which to collect their belongings and leave their properties for deportation and detainment in Siberia. Their land and holdings would be given to deserving families of revolutionaries. I grappled with the content of his directives, but only discerned there were dire consequences for the village once they were put into practice.

He came prepared. From the depth of his ill-used leather riding coat, he pulled a paper, much like the dreaded *ukase* of the Tsar and just as arbitrary as these writs of old. He read from the parchment what he had proclaimed already, followed by the names of the unlucky victims of Bolshevik persecution.

The first name rolling from his lips was the name of our saintly pastor, Paul Eisenherr. At that time the village had been the sheep in this good shepherd's fold for thirty years. It had been declared a miracle that our pastor somehow survived the great purge of church leaders, allowing him to remain with us until then.

He answered strong in voice: "I am Pastor Eisenherr, and I am here."

Slightly bent, he was after all close to seventy, silver-haired, his cheeks reddened by rosacea, giving him the ruddy, healthy look of so many Germans in late life, he stood in front of his small church. It was not much of an edifice, nothing but a weathered, planked building with matching two-story tower. His slight, mild-looking wife, Anna, her gray hair braided and pinned around her gentle, creased face, stood beside him. She raised her childlike blue eyes to the giant on the horse.

"*Babushka*," he bellowed, "why are you not shaking at my words? I said loud enough for you to hear that your husband is a traitor."

"Ah, but I fear only one thing, and that would be the wrath of my Lord," said the old woman in a surprisingly strong voice. "And, by God, I know we have not done a thing against man or God that we need to fear His anger. The small trespasses He will forgive us. As for you calling my Paul a traitor, I know that is wrong. He has loved this country ever since he was born on its soil, and he would not betray it."

I saw that the giant commandant was not comfortable. He looked as if his skin was itching and he could not scratch. His eyes were restless and unhappy. A good man, a brave man, never liked to do the dirty work of the mighty, and he was no exception. He was caught up in the natural perversity of his fate. In agitation, he smacked his boot with his riding crop and then yelled at the pastor.

"You, what kind of man are you to let your gray, old wife speak for you? Have you nothing to say for yourself?"

"What is there to say?" Pastor Paul spoke loud and clear, the way he did on Sundays when he wanted to reach the sleepy last row in the church. "My wife ably said what there is to say. I am no traitor. I serve God and He will judge and protect me. There is no more."

Perhaps the giant wanted him to put up a better defense, perhaps he grew impatient, but he jumped off his horse, and all those with him dismounted also.

"Where is your house?" he asked, twirling the riding crop irritably between his hands. The imperturbable Pastor Eisenherr led the way to his small, immaculate, blue wooden house, with an open porch facing the main street. There he sat every evening in good weather with those parishioners in need of counsel. At one time or another all the souls of his parish had joined him there. Sometimes, even insignificant persons, such as I, had sat there. If I felt like it, I skipped to his house, past the poplars planted long before I arrived in my parents' life. I skipped along on the unpaved, barely raised and graveled road until I reached his porch and the safety of his presence. Yes, he and his sweet, dear wife, they always made children feel welcome and safe.

The pastor could not keep up with the rabble of Soviet goons, and they half-dragged and half-carried him the rest of the way to his house.

Not long after they disappeared inside, as the village watched in painful silence, the door of the pastor's house opened. The disgruntled giant strode angrily across the porch, into the street, and shouted something, in disgust. I was close enough to hear, although I did not understand the meaning of his words.

"Who made this insane mistake? This is a house worth nothing, with nothing worth taking inside. So, who gave me the information that this is the house of an important man who needs to be disowned. Damned Dogs! This old fart heads the top of the damned list. How could this be?"

"He is a pastor, that's why." A young Mongol soldier spit the words together with a wad of *machorka* from his lips. "You know what they say at the Soviet: 'The church is finished and God is dead'."

There was a strange look of pity in the commander's eyes. Nevertheless, he told the pastor and his wife that they would have to take what they could carry; they were leaving for the train in Saratov. At the end of this cruel pronouncement, the congregation—the entire population of our village—broke out in a loud, heartbreaking lament.

"Have mercy, man! Not these dear, old people."

And shouts of "Take us. Take all of us, but not the pastor and his wife."

I looked around. The grown women were crying while calling for the Russians to have pity on the pastor and his wife, while their children, scared by their mothers' despair, were bawling and clinging to their thighs. The men looked somber and unhappy. I wonder why no one stopped the giant and his rabble. I pulled my father's hand: "Why don't you stop him, *Papushka?*"

My father was strong. Together with the other men he could resist. But the German men, sworn to their God not to kill, stood like sheep in the pasture. Their heads were hanging as if their necks had lost all muscle; their eyes scanned the dirt. What were they looking for—a sign? Did their heads hang in humility or in shame? I did not understand then that a fight would have availed my people nothing. We were a minority in a vast country and any kind of resistance was put down with bloody force, as in other villages, where psychopathic commissars provoked resistance.

Moments later, the commandant was much happier at the home of the next name on the list. This home belonged to Christian Unterhalter, the village smith. Christian was a man of the same stature as the Bolshevik giant. He shod our horses and made and repaired the iron implements used throughout the area around Schaffhausen. Christian, unlike our pastor, was well-off. His house was also made of wood, but the front advertised prosperity with its brick façade. Inside, the furnishings were beautiful and solid.

There were paintings on the walls of the sitting room, the *gute Stube*. Moreover, Christian had beautiful Astrakhan carpets on his wooden floors. The shelves in the kitchen were filled with items of chased copper and polished brass. Gleaming pots and pans hung from an iron device shaped like an eight-hooked anchor above the huge stove. His beds were dressed in fine linen and soft down bedding. Well-crafted nightstands, wardrobes and chairs filled his bedrooms.

Yes, that was a house worth taking. "Go pack what you will need in exile, you kulak," the giant bellowed and proceeded with the reading of the next name. Christian found himself instantly surrounded by a pack of soldiers. For a moment he stood like a giant moose surrounded by a yipping pack of dogs. Then they pushed him into the house. His wife, Carolina, blond, plump and pretty, followed the group. Her body seemed stricken by horrific pain, the hem of her apron was raised to her face as she was dabbing at her eyes. Their three small children toddled behind her in bewilderment.

The reading of names went on and on. Farber, Erzmann, Baumgartner, Krüger, Waldmeier, Eggers, Wohlheim, Brenner, Salzmann, Erdinger, Schuster, Schneider, Kramer, Hellman. The list seemed endless. Like Christian Unterhalter, those chosen for deportation had one thing in common—they owned the best farms and houses. Those called forth by the Soviet commandant had a short time to collect what they could carry during the exodus. The rest of us remained standing—ashamed, astonished, impotent and, in the case of most children at least, without understanding why this awful, monumental change was happening in our lives.

Our name was never called. Mother and Grandmother pulled me forcefully into the house. I was disinclined to leave my post between Papa and Grandfather, despite the hurtful, anguished drama unfolding before us. When the monstrous reality of their position registered, some women of the afflicted families again broke into heartrending lament. Others faced their fate with a pitiful, aching stoicism, pulling stronger on my heartstrings than the laments and tears. Many of the men, about to lose the fruit of their life's work, crossed themselves against the evil permeating the village center. They squared their shoulders, gathered their offspring, and entered their homes for the last time.

Crying and sulking, I was deposited by Mother onto a chair at the kitchen table. A soft knock on the back door, leading into the garden, both startled and frightened us. Taking heart, Grandmother Victoria opened the door and discovered Maria Baumgartner and her seven-year-old son

Joseph. Frau Baumgartner had been created with Valkyrian proportions. Corresponding to her figure, she possessed the spirit of Valhalla. She pushed the half-opened door to accommodate herself, slipping, Joseph in tow, into our kitchen.

"I got away from the soldiers," she said, dry-eyed. "I don't think anyone saw us." She set her eyes on my mother. Her glance was not so much beseeching as willing Mother to do her bidding.

"Albina," she half sobbed, "they are taking us to God only knows where. It looks that most likely it will be Siberia. You know, I have five more to look after. How am I going to feed them in the barrens of Siberia? How am I going to clothe them? I just don't know. God put it in my mind that you might keep my youngest for me, seeing that you get to stay."

Now she was on her knees in front of my mother. "Please, Albina, for the love of God, keep him for me. I could not bear to have him freeze to death in hell's own garden. The others are older. We will cope. They can help themselves better, but Joseph? He is too sweet, too dreamy, he would be doomed."

Grandmother Victoria suddenly pointed her forefinger at me in a way that brooked no disobedience. "Take Joseph into the *gute Stube*, and show him your father's trophies." Dutifully, I took Joseph's cold hand and pulled him into the parlor, the usually forbidden room. In this sanctum, which only saw human faces for funerals, births, high visitations, and on Sunday afternoons for coffee and *Kuchen*, I showed a bewildered, teary-eyed Joseph the trophies of horses my father had trained to become champions in their divisions. Yet, while I explained with four-year-old zeal the wondrous feats of hunting, racing and dressage steeds, his attention was woefully directed toward the kitchen. His ears seemed to turn toward the slightest sound emanating from there.

"What is it, Joseph? Why are you so worried?" I asked. Without hesitation he answered, "My mama wants to get rid of me. She does not like me anymore and now she wants your mother to take me."

Here his coherence broke and the slim, tow-headed boy with large gray eyes just bawled as if his heart was breaking. He stood before me in his high-water pants, hand-me-downs from his older brothers, in his checked shirt, well mended but too short in the sleeve, looking like a small, frightened scarecrow.

I had no clue what do with him. I was, after all, only four, and did not know about these things. In place of something better, I took his hanging hands in mine. I knew that his big, powerful mother loved him. She would not give him away. I had seen her sail through town like a brig in rough waters firmly clasping Joseph's small hand in hers. Nothing could break that bond. Therefore, even I could sense, her reason for bringing Joseph here must be of enormous importance.

I wiped his tears away with my hand and beckoned him to follow me. We put our ears to the kitchen door and listened intently. I heard mother's voice: "Don't cry Maria, *Liebchen*. If you think that they do not know he is yours, I will gladly raise Joseph like my own. Katharina could use an older brother to tone her down a bit. But are you sure you can bear to part with the dear boy?"

Outside a commotion ensued. The voice of the commandant demanded of my father that he open the door. "I must have an account of all heads in your household," he shouted gruffly. "You have to vouch for everyone there and identify their relationship to you."

"Maria, you must go. I promise I will keep him as my own," swore my mother, tears in her eyes. Then, louder, she begged: "They are coming, Maria. You must leave. Now!"

Listening behind the door we heard a heartrending sob and the closing of the back door. My grandmother rushed into the *gute Stube* knocking us backward with the door. She gathered Joseph in her arms and while she wiped his tears with her apron, whispered, "*Bubele*, when the men ask your name, you must say Joseph Grushov. Katharina is your sister and I am your *Oma*. Do you understand? If you don't do this, they will send you to the coldest place on earth. Your mama does not want you to go there. She wants to save you. So, be good, and do as I ask. I will explain all later."

She quickly pulled both of us into the kitchen, only a second before the front door opened. Papa entered, followed by the giant commandant. The moment Mother saw Father, she flew to him, kissing his face, saying something in German. Fleetingly, Father looked perplexed, then stunned. Scanning the room, his face assumed his normal father-look.

God was watching over Joseph that day. Bewildered, and frightened by the giant man, he stopped his crying, clinging to Grandmother's hand.

"Who are these people?"

"They are my family," answered Papa. Pointing at my mother he explained, "This is my wife, Albina Grushov, my mother- and father-in-law, Victoria and Holger Hildebrandt, and my children, Katharina and Joseph. This is my whole family."

We were standing almost in a circle. Papa and the giant, looking us over sharply, were standing at the door. Grandfather and Mother stood by the kitchen table. I stood in front of the window while Joseph and Grandmother closed the circle. Joseph's eyes were huge. It seemed as if he drew understanding through these orbs. Grandmother Victoria stood very straight, one hand under her apron, the other attached to the boy.

People mentioned often how much I looked like my mother. I was tall for my age, skinny, oval faced, with silvery-brown hair, just like Mother's. I was quick, sure-footed and had nimble fingers. Grandmother Victoria, who was not born to farm work, liked my nimbleness when we worked together in the house and the garden.

It had been hard and bitter for my grandmother to adjust to the miserable life on a small, communist-restricted farm. She, who once supervised a staff of servants in her house and garden, had to kneel in the dirt, bend and *schlep* like the least person in the village, now that she was old and frail. She and Grandfather had been robbed by the Reds of every possession they had acquired through many years of hard work. Now, they were among the poorest in the village. I adored her, for she lived even her new, deprived life with the dignity of a queen. She and Grandfather praised God every morning and were able to joke about their predicament.

All in the family circle, except me, had assumed defensive poses under the scrutiny of the commandant. Only I, unable to understand the gravity of the situation, was not intimidated. Looking from one face to the next, I smiled happily. No one smiled back. The solemnity of the others dampened my natural exuberance.

A sudden movement of the commandant's hand startled me back to the state of affairs. After a moment of silence the commandant eyed me expectantly and said, "What is your name, *dyevochka*?"

"My papa just told you, Katharina Grushova. You should listen when people talk to you."

The commandant grinned broadly, exposing *machorka*-stained teeth. "Who says I should listen better?"

"My mama. She always tells me that when I don't listen."

"*Ochen horosho*," he said, petting my head, whereupon he left with a hearty, "*Do svidanya*."

For a moment the adults talked in high German. I understood little. Something about "sparing the children *das Austreiben*." I knew they meant the deportation going on outside. Grandmother herded us into the parlor once more, where she praised Joseph. "You behaved like a good, smart boy," she told him. "Your mama would be very pleased with you. She feels very good that you can stay safely here with us, when your brothers have to leave for a bad place." Promptly Joseph began to cry again, keeping Grandmother busy, murmuring sweetly and drying tears.

I was entertaining myself by kneeling on the back on the sofa and leaning against the window. This way, I could see the scene in the street. The white lace curtain hung over my head and my back. I think, from the outside, I must have looked like a miniature bride. Hanging onto the window, I could see what was going on in most of the village.

The soldiers had begun to load the richest of our neighbors onto open trucks, much the same way the farmers loaded cattle for the market. Most women cried, clutching children and bundles. The men were stone-faced, stoic. But there were exceptions. I could tell by their eyes, a few would gladly have fought. They were barely able to contain their anger and seething fury. But how could they have fought a well-armed enemy with their bare hands? So they forcefully heaved the bundles and cases onto the trucks that would take them, like animals to slaughter, to a miserable fate. They had, of course, heard of Stalin's slave-labor camps.

Stalin, the self-declared man of steel, had become the head of the Soviets. He had managed a meteoric rise among the Red revolutionaries, displacing and crushing every opposition. It was Stalin who emulated Ivan the Terrible. It was Stalin who, even then, in the infancy of his powers, became a terrible visionary, who dreamed of electrification for all of Russia, of a steel industry unrivaled in the world. For this man had plans to become the head of a super-power. Everyone knew it was impossible to turn his dreams into reality unless one ruthlessly sacrificed human lives, for Russia was poor, backward, underdeveloped, and overextended with the expenses of a war. Only cheap labor could realize his dreams and so he did as Ivan did, as every ambitious Tsar had done; he sacrificed humans. He had at his disposal the minorities. Germans, Kalmyks, Chechens, Ukrainians, and Tartars as well as rebellious Mongol ethnicities, Cossacks and prisoners of war, were dispensable and without advocates.

By evening, all of those named on the lists had been driven away to Saratov's railway station. Arriving there, all Germans were dispossessed by edict and herded into trains to Siberia. Reports came back to the village, describing how families were torn asunder, by herding the people, with baton-blows, crushing them into different cattle cars.

Village in Turmoil

Our family was left unmolested by the Reds because my father was Russian and the farm was not one of the best. I was busy all the time. I had a lot to learn, and so did poor Joseph. He cried for days for his departed family. He felt lost, abandoned, unwanted and hopeless. That he finally calmed and accepted his lot was due only to Mother's patient love and care and Grandmother's logical sermons.

Where Mother hugged and petted, cosseting with little tidbits and sweet words, Grandmother took a different tack. She would engage him in a task and while they were weeding the garden or washing dishes she preached logic.

"See, Joseph," she would say, "it is like this. These bad men took your family to a place far away, where the winter lasts many months more than here, and you know how harsh our winter is. There, the rivers do not thaw until May, and they do not have fields with grain. It is a cold, hungry place. Your brothers have to work in the freezing cold, day and night. Your mother wanted you to be safe, warm, and loved, and that is why she gave you to us."

To assuage his feelings of abandonment, she read to him again and again the only note his mother had been able to smuggle out of the forbidden wilderness. Only a desperate mother would have found a way to send a message from this closed-off hell. Maria Baumgartner's messenger, an itinerant, half-crazed mystic, had traveled mostly on foot across frozen wasteland to bring us the note. My family marveled at this choice of messenger—a miracle surely, for only so marginalized a person as this wild-haired, dirty, old man would have been left unmolested by everyone. No one paid him any mind. And so we received the only sign that I remember testifying to the survival of a few deported villagers.

> *Dearest, beloved Son, dear Grushovs!*
> *I hope that you are well and living happily with the Grushovs.*
> *I want you to know that your mother did not forget you—nor will I ever. When you grow up you will understand that my love for you was greater than my selfish wish to keep you with me.*

13

We were shipped across the Ural mountain range and pushed into barren land that has no name. Things are unbearably hard. We are starving, freezing and working harder than the oxen we once owned.

Our oldest three boys were taken from us together with Christian Unterhalter and other younger men. We don't know where they are. Christian's wife is with us. We weep; we pray unceasingly and think of you.

I hope this note will reach you. Father Myznik promised he would find you.

Pray for us!

Your mother,

Maria

The man Maria called Father Myznik stayed with us for a week. While with us, he had to remain in hiding because we were scrutinized, watched at all times. Strangers were not tolerated for they might carry tales of the truth, spreading the seeds of rebellion. We fed and cared for the strange old mystic until he wanted to be on his way again, carrying messages. My grandmother, of course, had been itching to clean and groom the old man, to which he objected, gently pointing out that she would destroy the better part of his disguise.

In time Joseph got over his grief, but he clung to me like a burr. Sometimes his clinging was hard to take, and I found gentle ways to lose him. The other Germans had never denounced him to the authorities, although we, too, had communists in the village. The local Russians did not know any better, and so Joseph became my brother.

The farms, so ruthlessly stripped from the possession of the prosperous among us, were given to communist leaders who had excelled in devotion and zeal in promoting the soviets. Oh, what people they were. When they arrived, moved by their handlers in army trucks, we stood shy and ashamed behind our curtained windows and watched. I know Grandmother was ashamed because no one had stood up for the dispossessed.

"It gives me a heartache to see how these strangers walk into others' homes. They have no right to take what they did not earn," said Grandmother.

But the newcomers thought they had all the rights in the world. Had they not served the party in every way? And had they not been told a thousand times that the Germans were eternal enemies with no natural right to the soil of Mother Russia? It was Russian soil that had fed the kulaks and made them rich. Nay, even worse, the Germans had sucked the very essence from the precious Russian loam.

Oh, deep in their hearts they knew the injustice. In the past they had experienced injustice themselves, and they knew deep in their gut how hot evil burns. They had often heard the saying that begrudgingly praised German industriousness and fortitude: "You can transplant a German anywhere and he will prosper and grow like an oak."

Our elders watched, indignant eyes filled with pity and disgust as the city men and women pulled their belongings from the trucks with hardly a helping hand from their handlers. It was an inferior array of beat-up, ramshackle household goods. They dragged mattresses, stained and torn by years of harsh living, into houses left pristine by grieving former owners, only to throw the selfsame mattresses from the windows into the street or the yard. For in their new homes they found exceedingly superior things, the furnishings the deported were not able to take with them. Much of their former sad and seedy lives were thus discarded.

Our watching villagers were aghast by their customs. "Did you see this? Out of the window—into the street," gasped my incredulous, aristocratic grandfather. Grandmother, besides a great sense of humor, had a well-developed, practical streak. Now she laughed out loud.

"It saves them running up and down the stairs, and these things are not worth saving anyway." It tickled her humorous side, as it did mine, how someone could do such a thing, so totally foreign to the sober, fastidious mindset of Germanism, Lutheranism.

Later in life, I thought of the burden that Papa patiently carried for many years. He lived a well-ordered, tightly controlled life among persnickety Germans, who, apart from their own precise mentality, were even more regulated by their religious laws. As I looked into his face that day, his eyes were twinkling and the corners of his mouth decidedly curved upward. Dear Papa. He had courted Mother when he was an officer in the Tsar's elite regiment, the Preobrazhensky. Before his service in this regiment, he had managed one of Russia's grandest horse farms belonging to a Count or Duke whose name I never consigned to memory when Father told his tales. He would tell them in the kitchen after the evening meal, holding me on his knee while Mother did dishes in a large metal tub. He had an endearing way, spinning his tales, speaking straight at me, while at the same time shooting smiling looks at my mother, filled with a deep meaning that only they knew.

Mother would be standing at the sink, tilted a quarter turn in our direction, her face pert and prim, yet smiling. Every so often, when the yarn was not spun to her liking, she would roll her eyes at Father, but she never rebuked him. Father was the best looking man I knew. However, whenever I would state this belief, he laughed out loud and roared, "Yes, I am a fine example of what Mother Russia can produce in a man." Whereupon he would snatch me, calling me his best girl, tossing me into the air, catching me upon my return. But I knew I was right. He was great looking.

In retrospect, I think he was about six feet three inches tall, hitting his head occasionally on a doorframe while ducking into the next room. It did not hurt his appearance one bit that he had blue-gray eyes, a Slavic face with broad cheekbones, and heavy, wavy brown hair, so often found in Muscovites and Ukrainians. Best of all, I liked his well-shaped mouth, presenting two solid rows of teeth which sometimes oddly shone like mother-of-pearl. I loved the way he smiled.

In our village of staid though happy people, who mostly behaved in a subdued fashion, Father was like a smart breeze stirring the curtains and blowing about the hay-wisps. When he laughed, he did it with gusto, loudly from his belly. Yes, when I looked at my father, I knew why my mother had married him. I would have done so, too. He was the best Russia had to give.

However, many of our new, forced-upon-us villagers were examples of Russia's worst people. Often, after learning of their past lives, one could not help but feel sorry for them. Without loving arms to hold them as children and responsible parents to teach them, they embraced the familiar. As we watched them, it soon became apparent that many had a problem with regular work. Most of them had never owned anything before they were foisted upon us. Now, in their well-made houses they saw themselves as rich kulaks, protected by the party. This misconception led them to live as they had imagined rich farmers to live. Some even came to the village with the mistaken belief that they would have German servants. Most drank vodka to excess every night. Our people were dismayed. We had rarely seen someone terribly tipsy, never mind so drunk that they would vomit on their own front stoop, falling asleep where they collapsed.

Our new citizens often had headaches at mid-morning when they finally arose from wherever they had fallen last night, a circumstance that aroused in them murderous moods and led them to beat their wives and children. The cows, which they inherited by their party's theft, were not milked on time. The bellows and screams of their animals brought tears to our eyes. Their horses and pigs joined into the cacophony of tortured bellows because, with few exceptions, no one fed them regularly.

My father could not stand animal neglect. After a few days he called everyone, Germans and Russians, to an evening assembly. For obvious reasons, the Russians were unwilling to enter our church; he held the meeting in the open, in a meadow not far from the village. God must have been instructing my father, for the meeting went rather well. The evening was mild, the wild flowers in the meadow scented the air, and everyone seemed to feel mellow, friendly.

Surprisingly, quite a few of the Russians showed up. With gentle coaxing and a lot of patience, our men explained that the new farmers must do certain things to retain their wealth. Not all the blame for their terrible husbandry resided with them. Most of them were city folks. They had no idea what to do, nor did they understand how hard the life of the envied kulak was. There were those who truly believed that owning land meant no work. They had thought that servants and hired hands would do their work.

When they came to understand that in only a few short months the collectors would come for their taxes, and that they were required to take milk and butter to a collection point daily, their eyes almost popped from their sockets. Our men continued to explain that, furthermore, each time they butchered a pig the state got more than half. And the grain harvest as well as other crops could only be sold to the state's collectives. It was the way in which the soviet insured a controlled, beggarly remittance to the farmers. A free market with competitive prices was forbidden. No one would do well—no one would get rich. Such recitals of reality threw some of the new villagers into a state of turmoil, confusion and sorrow. Life as a kulak was suddenly not so glamorous anymore.

For the next few weeks things were better. Their women began to visit the neighbors and learned, by example, how to milk a cow. They came not only to learn but also to borrow. They were only a few short weeks among us and yet had squandered already the wealth of the cupboards and pantries they inherited. "Please—a cup of sugar!" "Have you got a little tea?" "I have no flour for bread. You must have some, neighbor. Give a little."

At first, when the begging began, our impoverished people gave because they had to live with these people from now until God only knew when. However, after a few weeks, with no end in sight to their mendicant ways, their constant whining requests hardened the hearts of our people. Soon, when we saw the Russians coming, container in hand, we refused to answer the knocks on our doors, although some of the scroungers banged away so forcefully, that it would have awakened the dead.

There were those who seemed to believe it was their right to be supported by us villagers because they were true Russians. To them, we were nothing but tolerated newcomers. These were the troublemakers, standing in the road, screaming abuse after having been refused more contributions to support their sloth.

In the end, after weeks of refusals and agitation, everyone learned what was acceptable and what was not. Since my father was a Russian, he often interceded, reminding everyone that we were all toiling in front of the same cart, belonging to the regional soviet. He refreshed the Russians' memories, we, of course had never forgotten, recalling the famine of 1921 and the horror the lower Volga had lived through. This famine was so horrific that thousands of starving people fled the Volga region, seeking refuge and sustenance in the Ukraine. Little did they know that the Ukraine had already been plundered of resources. Once there, the people had no homes, no food, nothing to sustain them. Many dug caves, practically with their bare hands, into any small hill they could find. (Years later, in 1928, when collectivism robbed most farmers of their possessions and land, moving hundreds of thousands to Siberia, a few fled to the Ukraine. There, they found the victims of this horrific famine still living in their unspeakable mud holes.)

Mother told me later how she had feared throughout her pregnancy that I would be born deficient, because she had been starving for nine months. At that time she also told me about my brothers, Michael and Peter, living in Germany with her brother Martin. I sobbed, as she described how she had smuggled the boys out of the country during a time when no one was allowed to leave.

It dawned on me then that I might have been an unexpected guest in this world. My parents, thinking that they had protected their living children from the Revolution had not planned to have more. When I needled my mother with piercing questions, she admitted they had hoped to spare another child the terrors of the Revolution's aftermath.

"But, when we knew that you would come into the world, we were happy despite our misgivings. God sent you to us for reasons yet unknown. We do not know his plans and must accept what is given to us."

Mother hugged me, and we cried a bit. I was old enough to understand the reasoning behind my parents' actions, and strongly felt wanted and loved. With this realization, my world was well again. Yet all these revelations would come at a later time. Meanwhile, my father tried to keep peace in the village, making everyone pull the same plow, in order to fulfill the demands of the soviet. This endeavor was a tall order at times, for the two village factions were cleaved by deep twin chasms of culture and religion, or the lack thereof.

Some of the Russians had been raised in Orthodoxy and had, therefore, at least an inkling of divine oversight. The others, of course, did not believe in God—their god was the party. They did not believe in the commandments; they believed in the power of physical force and sought release from travail in vodka. Their children were true reflections of their values.

Since our pastor had been deported and our church was sealed shut, we had no means of showing the Russians the communal strength we gained from our church services. We were forbidden to proselytize, which meant we could not even talk about our faith. Instead of church services, we began to hold small prayer sessions in one another's houses, but soon, even that was forbidden. An edict about the assemblage of too large a group was read, forbidding families to come together for prayer.

This edict was circumvented by celebrating even the smallest events in our lives, such as name days and birthdays, which had never been made a fuss over. Now they gave us much needed excuses to get together and worship as a group. Soon, however, the party instituted Sunday afternoon amusements. They sponsored picnics and dances where a large part of the time was dedicated to indoctrination, with speeches about the new Russian spirit and the important role we played in the new country.

These affairs were ill-attended. So they were made mandatory. "What do you think they are trying to do with these Sunday affairs?" asked Mother.

"They are supposed to become a substitute for our church services," answered Grandfather. "If you take away an important part of life from people, even more if you take their faith, their beliefs, you leave a vacuum, which they try to fill with the deity they worship—Stalin, enshrined in their party, and they pray their own communist litanies."

Grandfather was prophetic. Henceforth, their cries went up, "Do this work for the Party! Sing this song, praising the Party! Sacrifice, for the Party."

As time went on, Party-worship became more common and more pronounced. And, on top of the Party hierarchy sat comrade Stalin. Soon his pictures would overshadow all the icons of Russia; hover over every market; cover every wall of any size; and fly overhead on banners.

In the meantime Russia's children grew up without guidance, without love and without hope. Most of the Russian children, unlike the large flock of German youth that received affection mingled with birchings, grew up without grandparents and the benefits of extra love, spoiling and teaching. Seeing how little attention they received from their families made me very aware of the care lavished upon Joseph and me.

Life with Grandmother

When in doubt, consult your grandmother.
—WOODROW WILSON

Our cemetery lay to the east of the village, a goodly but pleasant walk away from our home. It was Grandmother's custom to visit there on warm summer evenings, just about a half hour before sunset. She would fill the large metal watering can and place her set of gardening tools in a small basket. All assembled, she would call for me, for she knew that I loved to accompany her. These peaceful strolls to the resting place of our dear departed, as she called them, were our times to renew the special bond we shared.

For Grandmother, it was a time to pass onto me the truths she had discovered in her lifetime. Her wisdom was not to be found in books. In her lifetime few women's thoughts were recorded, because women were not thought to be invested with great wisdom. And yet, my grandmother was wise. Approaching the end of life, Grandmother had the patience and kind love of a saint. Always pleasant, always calm, she plucked her truths from the Bible or her book of Apocrypha, from which she read to me sometimes. Once she had gathered the profound, she measured it against the reality of her life. Only morsels surviving the test of reality became her treasure to be passed onto me.

For me, these evening walks were my opportunity to discover what kind of tree I sprang from, what my core consisted of, and who I might become. When we walked in the mild, waning light, first along the main road in the village, crossing onto a path through the dry Podstepnaya Creek, I always felt

happy and blessed. The air was stilled, sweetened with the breath of wildflow-
ers, or, perhaps the bloom of the few fruit trees cultivated in the three orchards
of the village. It was the time when night-creatures gently ventured forth and
day-creatures and birds hastened to find their shelter for the night. Small bats
fluttered about and nighthawks darted after moths. Cows were lowing in
the pastures; their udders filled, they eagerly waited to be milked. From the
village, snatches of conversation wafted across the fields, but were quite subdued, as if the approaching night filtered the sound through cotton.

"*Oma*, how do I become wise?" I asked often, because I knew that
was her pet subject. Grandmother laughed, and the tools in her basket
jingled and clanked.

"A good question. A question worthy of old Solomon," she would
smile. "And you know, *mein Goldstück*, my piece of gold, Solomon knew
how to become wise." Whereupon she told me that King Solomon
thought, "The fear of the Lord is the beginning of all wisdom." Out of this
obedience would follow the sincere desire for learning and instruction. He
believed that love of learning brought men's souls closer to immortality
and thus closer to God.

"You see," she said, "I think he knew that to be wise and follow the
laws of wisdom you must keep the commands of God. That is the way to
become holy."

I sighed, because what Grandmother told me sounded grave and
seemed connected with much tedious work. But, because I loved her, I
decided I should at least try to become learned and perhaps wise in the
process, a weighty proposition for a six-year-old.

When we reached the simple cemetery and strode across the soft,
cut grass between the graves, we always followed the same path. The small
plots on either side of the path were lovingly cared for. Freshly planted
greenery or cut flower offerings covered the spaces before the humble stone
markers. Grandmother always headed straight for a rather large assemblage
of graves in the middle of the cemetery.

"Today we will take care of Kurt's grave," she would decide when we
reached a gray granite stone, displaying the inscription:

HIER LIEGT IN GOTTES HAND UND FRIEDEN
KURT MEININGER
GEBOREN AM 15. MAI 1775
GESTORBEN AM 7. SEPTEMBER 1818
EIN TREUER SOHN UNSERER *GEMEINDE*

At the grave, Grandmother sank to her knees and crossed herself. I followed her moves and after a short prayer we began to weed the grave with nimble fingers. "Kurt Meininger was a great-great-grandfather of yours." As Grandmother dug with her small trowel and planted a few sprigs of forget-me-not—transplants she brought in a pot, roots, soil and all—it was hard for me to imagine that she was the same person I had seen in her youth in pictures. Nor did the humble image of the kneeling old woman fit the tales I had heard about her.

Educated, opinionated, elegant, proud and strong—these were the words my parents used to describe her to me. As a young woman she desired the tall, good-looking Holger Hildebrandt, the Sarpinka King, and, of course, he married her. Anything she had wanted in the days of former prosperity, she had received. She had been waited on by servants, traveled in Europe, been invited to the homes of the country's most illustrious families, run charities—yet, here she was, her frayed, black dress enveloping her thin, bony frame, her knees buried in steppe dirt, her face sweet, serene—happy.

I was told how she could have escaped the Revolution's tidal wave. She and Holger had many opportunities to leave the miseries of the new Russia; but they declined to leave without their youngest child, Albina. Yes, it was Mother's love for Alexander Grushov and for Russia, this crazy, vast quilt of extremes, that had kept all of us anchored on the Volga. Now, having been plundered a few times, we were all poor like church mice and Victoria had become a saint.

While she worked, her fingers as quick as my own, she talked about the Germans who had wrung a living from the harsh steppe, civilizing a world still living in a time hundreds of years removed from the fast-ticking clocks of Europe, an ancient world, studded with cultures stuck in antiquity.

Sometimes she talked about Kurt's father, Christoph, the first one to settle over on the Bergsite, in Norka.

"Imagine, the poor boy fled because he feared being pressed into the Hessian Army. He was tall and handsome they say. Had he stayed in Germany, he probably would have fought for the British in the American colonies, because the Hessian prince looked for *Lange Kerle*, men six feet tall and more, to fill his army."

Grandmother never missed a chance, such as this occasion, to teach me my heritage. In the process, I also learned geography effortlessly. When I asked where America was, she decided that we should seek out the atlas in the remnants of the library to find out. For some reason, the Reds had taken most books but left us the atlas, as if they wanted us to pine over the rest of the world we could not visit. In this way I learned that Germany was the heart of Europe. At least that was what Grandmother and Holger liked to think. I trailed with my finger the long, arduous trek of the first settlers, who had come so long ago to Schaffhausen. From their home village my ancestors had traveled overland to the port city of Lübeck. There, or in Hamburg, they had to wait until enough bodies had congregated, to be sufficient for a full ship's load. Then they boarded sailing ships.

Once on the ships, crowded and ill-fed, they sailed for weeks to Oranienbaum, where they were sworn in as Russian subjects. From Saint Petersburg, the grand Russian capital and port, they traveled on over land, forever it seemed, through Russia's interior to Tver on the Volga. From Tver they traveled by boat to Saratov. In Saratov officials dispersed them to the villages of their destination. Some hardy souls found their way across Poland, the Ukraine and Russia to Saratov, traveling in horse- and ox-carts, braving death by illness, malnutrition, bad weather or attacks by bandits.

"Why would they travel so far and suffer so much?" I had once asked. Her answer was, "*Ach, mein Goldstück*, the Tsarina offered the Germans *das Himmelreich*, the heaven: land to purchase and loans to do so, exemption from military service, freedom to worship as we wished, self-administration and few taxes. Where else in the world would people have had it so good? When people suffer; when they see their children die of hunger and their young carted off to war; when they cannot worship their God and live by his commandments; then, they will do anything to change their lives. Some people fight to live free and righteous, but we cannot fight, because we are forbidden to kill—we love our fellow men no matter their nature."

I knew then what it was that made us special. To refuse to fight, even in self-defense, is to honor God's commandment in a way that overcomes all self-interest. I thought about that often. What would I do? Although I was a girl, I had fought already, and my family, even more, the whole congregation had been ashamed for me. Yet, I knew, I would have done it again. If Pjotr Chabarovsky had ever whipped my horse again I should have pummeled him with the same fury I unleashed on him before. Secretly the result of that tussle pleases me to this day, although I had to repent in front of the whole congregation.

"How could you do this to the boy?" asked my grandmother. "His nose was bloody and one eye was closed. You should have talked to him."

"We don't solve our problems with violence," said Mother, with the cool rationale that founded every act in her life. "At six you are old enough to know better."

Yes, I did know better, but Pjotr was eight and much taller than I was. Everyone knew he was smarter than my horse, so why had they not held him responsible for his actions? Why had they not punished him for torment-ing my beloved, blameless colt? He was an animal so sweet that he had not defended himself, although I think, he could have killed the little heathen.

My father and grandfather said nothing at all during the day of my disgrace. Later, in the evening, when I had scrubbed the dirt off my body and combed out the strands of hair that Pjotr had torn from my scalp, Father walked me down the river path. We liked to visit the spot, where a gangway for the rowboats of the fishermen stuck into the Volga bank like a straw into a dike. When we were comfortably seated at the very end of the plank, our feet dangling just above the water, Father patted my shoulder and said, "He made your blood boil, didn't he?"

I looked up into Father's eyes, and knew that he understood. "Mother does not understand that talking does not help with some children," I explained. "They don't listen. In their houses no one preaches peace. They do not love God, at least not the way we do."

"Don't tell Mother," Father smiled. "I love her too much to argue with her about things she holds sacred, but I believe that God looks favor-ably on the righteous fight, the good and honorable fight. Killing is wrong. However, sometimes we have to fight for what we believe or lose our souls. So, tell me, why did you beat the stuffing from his hide?" I laughed loudly because Papa referred to Pjotr as if he were a straw mattress.

"The nogoodnik ran around our horse pasture with a whip, lashing my poor beast after cornering him. The horse had no place to go."

"So what did you do?"

"There was no time to talk. *Voron* already had welts all over his barrel. I jumped on Pjotr from the top of the fence. He lost the whip, and then we fought." Papa's arm snaked around me; he bent over me and kissed my hair. "I forgive you," he said, "It was a fight for an honorable cause. You protected innocence."

Suddenly, for the first time that day, I felt very good. My eyes moist-ened; a few tears washed away the tension and shame of the day. I wished fervently that someone would always be in my life who would understand and forgive. It was then that I knew God would always be there to under-stand and to forgive, as my father did.

My grandmother's voice brought me back into the night's stillness and the cemetery.

"Why so quiet all of a sudden?" she asked.

"I am still thinking about the great-great-grand folks," said I, not wishing to speak of my fighting disgrace. Grandmother, still on her knees, loosened the roots of pesky weeds with her trowel and asked me, as I was kneeling next to her, to pull them out with my nimble fingers and throw them into the tool basket.

She pointed to the roots of a moss rose where a weed had grown for weeks to astonishing proportions, sheltered from our prying eyes by the pretty plant. The moss rose was one of the few blooming plants that withstood the drought conditions of the steppe. But in fall Grandmother had to dig them up, storing them well covered in the barn.

"Look closely, *Hascherl*. The strongest weed will be the one sheltered by a useful plant. You will find in life that often well-meaning, good people protect the greatest sinners from discovery. For evil to cease it must be exposed, brought into the light."

I loved my grandmother, because she helped me see things that explained confounding experiences.

When it was already quite dark we finished our chores, gathered the implements in the basket, now emptied of plucked weeds, and walked back to the house.

The Evil in Children

Tolerating evil leads to more evil.
And when good people do nothing,
their communities will be consumed.
—Bob Riley

By the time I became cognizant of differences in children and their behaviors, I noted which children in the village one had to know in exacting detail in order to get along. There were no simple games in the sand box, with perhaps a dispute over a toy, for the mixed lot of children in our village. We grew up caught between the fragmented factions of a divided village. Where before, in almost beatific Lutheran unity, children toddled

barefoot among their elders and assorted livestock, watched over by the
alert eyes of an entire village, we now had to be aware of our farms' boundaries. We learned early the divisive lessons of class, culture and religion in
a microcosm of the new Russia. Already at age six, I came to believe that
the Reds, the Bolsheviks, were bad. Everything terrible befalling the village was visited upon us by "them." I was not alone in my belief. I shared
my experiences with Joseph, who was older and should have known if my
perceptions were wrong; he, too, saw things I did. Together we worked on
a picture of our reality.

On one hand we had the teachings of our family and church; on the
other, we had daily encounters of another kind with the children of the
privileged Russians. Many were mean, hurtful children. They did not know
God—that they were accountable to him for their deeds. We watched a
few of these children with the same intensity the devil bestows upon a soul
he wants to snatch. They were vile. They used some of the smaller children
in experiments. For example, they wanted to know how long they could
hold a child under water before he went limp.

They killed three-year-old Pjotr Dimanov that way. Of course, nothing
happened to the murderous wretches because they were only children. The
inquiry by the police and a judge led, time and again, to questions probing if
German children had been involved in the assault on Dimanov. Fortunately,
none of us could be connected to the crime. In the end, it was decided that
the episode had been nothing but a tragic accident. Accident—ha! If only
the adults could have seen these children and heard them talk the way we
did. They, too, would have known that these boys fully understood what
they were doing. Eight-year-old village children know about drowning—
they have seen it done to kittens—they know about death.

I told Papa what I knew. He looked at me so sadly that I cried, and
then he said, "Do you remember Volodya, the horse I brought home one
evening?"

"Yes, Volodya the kicking, biting brut. I remember him."

"Well, then you also must remember how I turned him around in
one year to be a beautiful, useful riding horse."

"Do you remember what I did to him? Did I beat him, kick or whip
him?"

"No! You were nice to him and you fed him well."

"That is true. But most of all I taught him. I never allowed him to be
mean. I had punishments for that—not beatings though. But most of all I
taught him to trust me."

"What does that have to do with the little brutes in the village?"

"They are mean because they are taught nastiness. Their parents beat them, starve them, and do not teach them goodness—rudeness and terror is all they know. Let us try to give them an example of goodness. Remember, Katya, these are not ordinary Russian children who also have good families, but they stem from families who, in all probability, lived before in the slums of Moscow. They are living here only because their fathers maimed and killed for the Revolution. Their parents never owned a home before."

I was just about to walk away and leave the house when he called me back. "I meant what I said, Katya, but that does not mean that you allow them to torment you. Avoid them, to be safe, but in school you can teach them goodness by example whenever you get a chance."

Not all the Russian children were monsters. Some were friendly but subdued, tormented by the others. They would shyly smile when I met them apart from the cliques of the brats. Whenever I talked to them, they responded and were nice. However, whenever one of the evil ones came within sight, their faces would shut, as if a curtain were drawn over a window, and they would melt into the background. Yet every day the meek and the monsters would meet in school where torments of another kind would befall the meek.

On the whole, I was left unmolested because Father was a big man and a well-known presence in the village. He never had the power and esteem of the *Vorsteher* and the elders, but was given a different kind of respect because he exuded the power and force of a military officer. It was as if the bad boys knew, by inhaling his scent, that he would break their necks if they hurt me.

We were schooled, grades one through eight, in a modest schoolhouse. From the beginning, fifty years earlier, it was too small. Forty to forty-five children were crowded into one room. Sometimes first and second grades were combined. After eighth grade most children left school to be apprenticed in a trade, or to farm full time with their families. A few bright, gifted children would go to other towns, often Katharinenstadt, on their way to higher education. But intelligent children, wishing to learn, had many obstacles to overcome. Often the stones in the road were their own parents, denying them the means and permission to leave.

Every schoolroom was furnished with small desks and chairs and a large blackboard. The walls were painted pea-green. Joseph said the walls looked like pea-soup vomit. There was truth in this awful simile, for, over time, ugly, dark patches from the rubbing of countless small bodies against the walls appeared and small chunks of plaster were missing where chairs had scraped and scratched the surface, creating the look of mashed yellow and green peas.

School became very different when the Reds removed most of our German teachers. The teachers were taken away in a car. No one knew where they had been sent. We were reduced to tears. We had been taught a different curriculum than the Russians. Now we had to adjust to lessons delivered mostly in Russian, with a totally different content. Of course, every sign or mention of God was banned from the classroom.

Although they removed the simple wooden crosses high up on the front wall, they could not erase the lighter images beneath. Oh, they had tried to make the crosses disappear, by blending them into the wall, washing with moist cloths around the outline, achieving to our delight and subdued laughter a wonderful halo effect that enlarged and emphasized the humble crosses. So the crosses had to remain until the government of the oblast would find enough money to paint—perhaps never.

Compared to the new teachings, ours had been superior. We were ahead in mathematics, geography and history. We knew German history as well as the history of Russia, and knew every Tsar beginning with Ivan the Terrible. We also were bilingual and could tell each other secret things in German, infuriating the Russian kids who could not understand. Their reading and writing skills were not very good either. Papa blamed it on the Moscow slums.

The new curriculum was strongly laced with praise of Bolshevik power—the power of the worker and agrarians to forge a new society. We had to learn about Lenin and Stalin—about their dream to mechanize our farms with combines and tractors—integrating all people in the great design of the Union of Soviet Republics, making us all equal citizens of Russia. Among the new teachers, Anastas Sergeyevich Pelkov, and a woman, Sofia Andreyevna Pestovich, went from classroom to classroom denouncing the Tsars and their ilk. My parents called Pelkov an agit-prop-man. Agitprop was party speak for Agitation Propaganda—political enlightenment.

Sofia Andreyevna actually never went anywhere. She remained in the room with the first through third graders, while Pelkov preached for half an hour in one class, half an hour in another. At that time I was in second grade. Sofia Andreyevna showed us pictures of the Tsar's family. The girls were attired in beautiful, frilly gowns and looked sylph-like, airy and unreal. "Ha!" screamed the Pestovich woman. "Look how fine, how angelic they appear in their expensive rags. But take them out of that fine, expensive finery and they, like everyone else, look no better than beggars."

Then she showed us other pictures. In the new set, the elfin daughters of the Tsar were transported to their exile, a word Sophia Andreyevna had to explain. "Where they are going they cannot harm the Russian people anymore," she exclaimed excitedly as if the fairy creatures in their white, silken finery could have harmed anyone. In the new pictures their precious, fanciful clothes had disappeared. Instead, they had been stuck into bulky, drab, olive-green or blue pants and tunics. Miserable round hats hid their long, shiny tresses. It was obvious to us, even before the teacher evidenced the fact: stuck into formless sacks, even sylphs and angels look like common street urchins.

"You can see that the pampered little women of the Tsar look just like washer women when deprived of their pretty outfits," shrieked Pestovich, almost with glee, as she pointed out the hapless girls, cowering before the photographer while armed guards threatened them with guns.

"No one looks like an icon angel when sacks hang from our frames." Suddenly she had made a transition into the personal sphere. "Hang from our frames." Even at seven I understood that this woman must be consumed by jealousy. I understood that she took being born into an inferior station as an insult, and that she hated the royal family with a passion inconceivable to us in the village. We got the message: she, Sofia Alexeyevna, should have had a chance to look like an icon.

We knew little about Sophia Andreyevna. She had been brought to the Volga from Moscow, where she had belonged to a Bolshevik student group involved in revolutionary activism. With her background of brilliant, early revolutionary organization, she should have been highly rewarded by the new Soviet government. Instead, she had been shoved into the backwaters of Schaffhausen.

Much later, it became clear to me that only her obvious sexual frigidity could have terminated her advancement in a climate where it was the duty and delight of the female revolutionaries to gratify the desires of their fellow conspirators. One had to be a part of the socialist spirit of openness. By promiscuity women displayed total rejection of bourgeois culture and renounced its religious tenets. I saw later how clever females used their sexuality, mixed with shrewd understanding of the party's inner workings, to successfully advance their careers. Sophia Andreyevna was not of that persuasion.

She was ascetically slender, of medium height, with black hair that fell straight to her shoulder where it was cut blunt and straight. Her dark eyes, almond shaped, hinted of Tartar blood mixed with that of Slavs.

Her clothes looked like military uniforms. She wore drab, greenish-brown, straight skirts made from poor material that had not accepted the dye evenly. Over these skirts she wore long, loose, military tunics, which she pulled into her waist with a broad belt adorned by a huge steel buckle.

As her olive skin was flawless, her mouth well-shaped and generous, she could have looked very pretty, enticing even. However, a look of constant worry pinched her features. She accentuated this look with a huge pair of tortoise-shell glasses, which for some reason added anger and fury into the mixture.

God only knows who had shaped her early years. She was seething with hatred for the rich kulaks, the nobles, the Boyars. But she reserved even more hatred for the disgusting, depraved bourgeoisie. When she taught geography and spoke of Moscow, she peppered her lecture with chastisement of the greedy grain merchants who had kept everyone hungry while selling grain all over Europe. "They starved us, let us die like dogs, to make greater profit," she hissed at us, as if we had been the responsible party.

I too thought what the grain merchants had done was terrible and sympathized with her feelings until I talked to Grandfather Holger.

"Life is never quite as simple as demagogues make it, Katya. Yes, there were undoubtedly unscrupulous merchants who squeezed the last kopek out of a *pud* of grain; but there is more to commerce than the simple transactions. If you deal on the European market—and I know how it works for the tobacco business—things are often determined a long time ahead. Sometimes, when I needed money to expand the factory, or for new machinery, I would sell an entire crop ahead of harvest."

"You mean someone would give your money and then wait a long time for the tobacco?"

"Yes, that is exactly how it works. Doing a deal this way is often disadvantageous for the seller, because the sale is based on the yield of an average year. Should the total crop be spare, with little tobacco on the market, one could have received a much higher price and profit by waiting."

Grandfather also told me of agreements made years ahead of delivery of goods, which when broken, would result in penalties and future lost business. "So you see, things are never quite what they seem. The fault really lay with the government. You know that our villages had grain silos in Saratov, and even a few in Katharinenstadt, where we saved grain for our people in bad times. The Russian government should have done the same. Or they should have had large cash reserves to purchase grain. Instead they came and robbed our silos and our private people of every kernel of grain, letting us starve. For in the end, we were worse off than all the other citizens."

Before Grandfather let me leave the horse-stalls, where we had convened, he admonished me, much as all the adults around us did when they talked about serious things. "Now Katyusha, not a word in school about what I told you or they will brand us reactionaries, anti-revolutionaries, and send us to Siberia." There had been no need to remind me. By now the warning about Siberia was ingrained in my mind. Those were the days when I learned to mistrust strangers and weigh my words carefully.

Although my name was Katharina, no one ever called me that. Father had started calling me by the Russian diminutives, Katya and Katyusha, when I was a toddler and everyone had followed suit.

I remember that Joseph usually called me Katya or Katrinka. When he was serious he called me Katya; when he wanted to agitate or excite me he used Katrinka. On the day he came home from school, with his hands swollen and bleeding, he called for me. "Katya, Katya!" he yelled with urgency in his voice, pulling me from the stall where I tended to my love, my horse Raven. He wanted no one but me to see his hands, see his humiliation and pain. So he came to me. Hidden from adult views behind the barn, he turned up his palms to show me his hurt.

"Who did this to you?" I screamed, horrified. His hands looked more like the huge bleeding paws of an animal—not like the hands of an eleven-year-old boy. As if my scream had doubled his pain, his crying rose to loud sobbing. He stuttered as he spoke the name of Anastas Sergeyevich.

"Your teacher did this? Why? This is abominable!" Before he could stop me, I screamed at the top of my lungs, "Papa, Papa, help, help! I need help!"

Papa came running. So did Grandfather. While Joseph blushed with embarrassment, I held his wrists, turning his mutilated hands upward for the men to see.

"Dear God," exclaimed both men as one, "who did this to you?" Crying, sniffing up snot, Joseph told the story of a small wrongdoing—he had whispered a funny joke to his neighbor, who burst out laughing. Pelkov had assumed the joke was about him and flew into an insane rage. He had dragged Joseph to the front of the classroom, where he beat his hands unmercifully with a thin riding crop, which he always carried in his boot.

Pelkov was a redhead with fiery, copper-red hair and milk-white skin like a girl's. He was slender, of medium height, with a face so sharp, it seemed it had been carved from wood. His green eyes looked at everyone with piercing suspicion, making a student quake the moment he focused on one of them. He was very strict, with a reputation for flying into rages when annoyed. An ardent Bolshevik, he disliked us "German kulaks" with a passion. Twice before, he had been reprimanded for sadistic punishment of a student. One incident involved a rude Russian boy who had repeatedly provoked him.

When Father saw Joseph's mangled hands he became suffused with hot anger. I saw the color rise in his face, rising upward—straight into the roots of his hair. "Holger, please take Joseph to Albina so she can take care of the boy. I will see to Pelkov." He walked with powerful strides away from the barn, past the house and into the street. I saw him walking toward the schoolhouse.

Later that week, we heard the story of Father's encounter with Pelkov. Papa walked into the schoolhouse where the two Bolshevik teachers were grading papers. In a small village news flies on the swift wings of a swallow. By the time Father arrived at the schoolhouse, a building as gray and uncared for as any in the village—who had the means of restoring or painting anything—a Russian and two German parents were striding behind him. They had not hailed him. Nor had they inquired into his business; nay, they followed him like wolves follow their leader for a kill.

Papa found Pelkov without a problem. There was, after all, only a small anteroom where the teachers left their coats and where they could get a drink of water and eat their food at noon, when we were sent home for an hour to eat the main meal of the day.

As Mitja Koslov told the story later, Father charged into the classroom where the teachers sat. His small entourage filed in behind him. In the bare room, filled with minuscule desks, Papa looked like a monolith as he stood before the surprised teachers.

"Comrade Pelkov," he bellowed, "Please explain to me what terrible crime your student Joseph Grushov committed. For what did you punish him so severely that he might be unable to use his hands for months—or ever again? Tell me, what devilish prank did this innocent, shy young boy perform, causing you to exact such terrible punishment?"

Mitya Koslov said Father looked like a terrible God unloading his wrath upon small, red Pelkov. Like all cowards, faced with one larger than those they usually torment, feeling the wrath of an avenging force, Pelkov had shrunk to diminutive stature. However, like a cockroach cornered, he managed to hiss at his attacker in the hope that false courage might save him. Pelkov straightened his spine and spit at Father, "So you are the father of the misbehaved, laughing delinquent? Why have you not brought him up properly? Taught him not to make his teacher the laughing stock of the classroom?" Yet he miscalculated. Father was not to be trifled with.

Mitya Koslov reported with obvious glee what happened next. "Oh, it was too comical to watch without laughing. Grushov raised himself up in front of the creature, as the bear rises on his hind legs when confronted by a threat. He became almost twice his size and then, without saying a word, he grabbed Pelkov by his upper arms and lifted him two feet in the air. When they were eye to eye, he said in a mordant voice, "Pelkov, I heard Joseph's tale and I heard yours, and I believe the boy. Even if you had been the butt of the boy's joke, you had no right to smash his hands. If you ever touch my children again, you will not live to see the next day. Do you understand me?"

"Are you threatening me?" screamed Pelkov, who had gone first red and then blue in the face. "I am here representing the Party, you reactionary! You threaten me—you threaten the Party. I will have you deported to Siberia, you kulak, you Tsarist swine."

Before Papa could react to the man's outburst, Mitya and the other men came forward surrounding Papa and Pelkov. They shouted angrily that they would tell their own tales at an inquiry conducted by the Soviet officials. Mitya trumped all the others by shouting, "I belong to the Party just as you do. Believe me, you will be alone before the tribunal. The rest of us will stand against you. I have not forgotten what you did to my boy—sadist."

Henceforth, Pelkov remained subdued. In time, when he discovered that the boys were just boys and no one was out to ridicule him, he settled down and became almost human. We believed he had put his anger aside and carried no grudge. Joseph's hands healed, but slowly. For a good while, I wrote his homework for him. Mother ensured that it was by his dictation and that he read his own material, answering questions himself.

And so we lived in Schaffhausen, cheek-to-jowl with the Russian transplants. Hunger, taxation, obligatory payments of grain, meat and milk—whatever one raised on one's farm, in our case horses—evened out the differences to a point where we could survive together. A year slipped by and then a new wrong was perpetrated upon us.

The Institution of Collectivism

> Government is an association of men
> who do violence to the rest of us.
> —LEO TOLSTOY

In the summer of 1928 the small local peace on which we had managed to base our lives was violently destroyed. Sun parched the village, fields and meadows, and the road was dusty gray. We heard the roar of engines before we saw the cavalcade of trucks coming toward our village. It was mid-morning and few people were in the village. Most people had left for the fields at dawn and were not expected back until evening. Joseph and I were in school. Only *Oma* Victoria and *Opa* Holger were at home. Father had taken a horse to the smithy, to have his shoes reset, and Mother was somewhere in the orchard.

The trucks stopped in the middle of the village amid a dust cloud hiding most of their vehicles. The motors ceased their roaring. When the dust settled, we saw that the Reds had arrived with many vehicles and men.

In the schoolhouse the lessons came to a halt. The teachers hastened into the street, after admonishing us to sit quietly until their return. However, they did not return. After a good while, we got up, peeking through the windows first. When we were unable to see anything, we, too, snuck outside.

The few old people left in the village had departed their homes. They stood on their stoops or in the road, talking fearfully, while assessing the military force that had arrived. The armed men—they could have been soldiers, police or NKVD, it was hard to tell what they were—organized themselves into purposeful groups around a uniformed, decorated man. Apparently this war hero had fallen afoul of the party and was being punished with this assignment. He gave commands, in a voice loud enough to be heard at the schoolhouse.

At one point their leader shouted for the mayor, the *Vorsteher*, but that good man was out in the fields with the rest of the men. At that moment Papa came, riding up on the newly shod *Schimmel*, the white horse, which had worn down its shoes. The moment the leader spied Father, he ordered him to approach, and then he questioned him in great detail.

Later still, men on horseback were dispatched into the fields and ordered to bring back every soul belonging to the village.

During the time it took to retrieve the householders of Schaffhausen, the curious bystanders were commandeered, providing water for the soldiers and for the overheated engines. There were even requests for tobacco, for food, and beer—all these requests were studiously ignored by our people.

When at last, herding us like cattle in a meadow, the men gathered the entire village population around their leader, they confronted us with the reason of their coming. The meadow was instantly churned to dust. Trampled by hundreds of feet, dry grass and soil turned to powder. Yet, never mind the mess; they made us sit so everyone could see their leader.

Families huddled closely together although the closeness made the late afternoon heat unbearable. Some of the soldiers had carried wooden boxes into the middle of the large circle made up of our people. Father said that their leader, who had climbed upon the piled boxes, was a major of sorts according to his epaulets and other decorations.

The major in his dark mustard uniform, with a round conductor's hat, stretched out his arm. At this command the murmur among us ceased. It had become quite apparent that the soldiers brooked no interference with their mission, and would beat anyone disobeying their orders into submission with their clubs and bayonets. As we had experienced numerous times before, the major pulled out a voluminous document, and began to read from it. He shouted page after page of orders at our hapless people.

The major was an ordinary-looking man of medium height with a fat, ruddy-complected, round face. As he read, sweat streamed over his face and soaked the collar, the back and the front of his army shirt, creating interesting maps. Next he shed the jacket, which completed his uniform. His voice began to crack after few pages, whereupon one of the soldiers handed him a metal water-cup, which he emptied as one draught.

I could not understand all he read, but from the looks on the faces surrounding me, I knew that hell had come among us, and that life, as we had known it, was over. The moment he finished reading, the people, Russians and Germans alike, broke out in a soul-shattering lament.

"Dear God! What shall we do now?" "How can we survive?" "How can they take everything we worked for, generation after generation?" The clamor rose to such a pitch that it drowned out individual voices, becoming a united, agonized scream of horror and violation.

People forgot themselves and advanced with raised fists against the major and his minions, screaming their hatred and fury. Joseph and I had been holding hands, for we were afraid—mortally afraid, because this was worse than the deportation we had witnessed before. This was the end of the Volga German villages—the end of life, as we knew it. Everyone was standing. The surging mass of people swept us forward toward the major, crushing us. For a moment I thought I would fall and be trampled. I managed, however, to remain upright. Then shots rang out. The bullets whizzed over our heads, stopping people in mid-stride. A moment later the people were driven back by the soldiers, lashing out at those closest to the center.

Again the soldiers fired into the air. All became quiet, whereupon the major could be heard once more, telling everyone to go home and await confiscation of their farms. As we walked home many were crying. Especially the women were sobbing as if their hearts were breaking. Some of the men said powerful prayers, asking God for protection, while those of little faith cursed abominably, disparaging the Reds in German and in Russian.

Bit, by bit, Joseph and I pasted together parts of the speech, deciphering what had befallen the village. Stalin's communist-inspired vision for all agricultural lands was collectivization—uniting every last parcel of the farmlands in Soviet hands. The *kolkhoz* was to be farmed by the new form of serf—one who owned nothing, yet was bound to the land, forced to fulfill the crop-expectation-yields of functionaries who knew nothing of farming.

On the way home Father groaned with worry. He knew Russia and its inner workings well. I heard him tell Grandfather Holger that the new dictates would reduce the people to a state worse than serfdom. "At least the nobles who owned serfs knew when their peasants had a bad harvest, and left them enough grain and other foods to make it through the winter. Also, serfs had their own plots of land to grow food. They had their cow, their pigs and chickens, food sources that belonged to them. Now, they take from us any and all resources to live on. The Reds do not care if we all die of starvation as long as their expectations are met."

By the time we arrived home, I was astonished that my mother's beautiful face was stony. She had not cried, nor had Victoria. They were holding their despair within, looking for strength in faith, sustaining themselves through prayer. As if nothing upsetting had happened, they set about preparing the night meal, *das Abendbrot*. Mother sliced bread, sausage and meat with her huge kitchen knife, while *Oma* Victoria set the table, putting out pitchers of milk, buttermilk and beer for the men.

As we were wont to do, Joseph and I did our usual chores. Joseph slopped the hogs and carried water for the animals; I measured grain into the cribs and Father pitched hay to the horses and the cows, Grandfather Holger sat in the parlor, the *gute Stube*, a strong drink in his hand. You could tell that he was deep in thought.

We sat down for the last meal of the day, filled our glasses with the drink of our choice, filled our plates with bread, meat and pickles. Grandfather said the prayer over the food, but instead of allowing us to eat, he said, "I want all of you to think during dinner of what we can do to lighten our load under the new edict."

"Do you also mean for me and Joseph to think? Do you believe we could find a way?" I asked. "Yes, even you should think what we could do." As we ate and drank, the adults talked.

"That is the end then for all of us, Russians and Germans alike—the end of farming. First they are going to steal us blind, then they condemn us to slave labor."

"So what are we going to do now?" asked Grandmother Victoria. Father looked around the table and said, "I have been thinking about that. We will discuss it when the children have gone to bed."

"You said we, too, should think of ways to help, and now you shunt us off to bed," I demurred. My voice vibrated with protest.

"That is true," agreed Father soothingly, "But bedtime must be observed, and you can think in bed about solutions." The adults said nothing more on the matter, quietly concentrating on their drinks. Joseph looked meaningfully at me. His glance said clearly, "They do not want us to hear. Things must be bad." Moments later, Mother sent us off to bed. I slept in a little alcove in the living room, while Joseph had graduated to the small room in the barn that once was Timur's.

I had never known Timur the Tartar, but I had heard many tales about him. He had been a very brave man who had risked his life to save Father's; a man of convictions, who, despite threats to his life, had changed from his Muslim religion to ours. Alas, he died before I was born. Mother's eyes still welled up with tears when she talked about his death. "He had been so hale; such a strong man, and then he died within two days of pneumonia. He said one day, "I am very tired today and my body aches." Lo, before we could get the doctor from Katharinenstadt, where he was fighting a diphtheria epidemic, Timur had died. Doctors were still rare in the countryside. A single doctor was responsible for the health of several villages. Often the patient died before the doctor could be located.

Years ago, when Mother's parents were forced from their holding at Katharina's Gate, they had come to live with us and inherited the second bedroom. For the longest time, Joseph and I slept in the kitchen where it was warm in winter. Then one day the adults said we were too old and needed our own space. They moved me into the alcove and Joseph into Timur's room.

Joseph did not mind. It was a place of his own, warm and cozy. He could lock the door and be undisturbed. He was not alone out there, away from the house. One of the stable boys, a child of too large a family, had a room next to Joseph's and when he got lonely he could talk to this boy through the wooden partition.

That night, when everyone thought I was settled in my bed in the alcove, I quietly crept in my bare feet from the house. I held my slippers, which would be a scratchy give-away, in my hand as I slipped outside. It still was very warm although a thin fog crept in from the Volga. I snuck by the stalls of the cows, the pigpen, and the chicken coup where small rustling noises announced the presence of living beings.

Passing the horses in their boxes, I gave a carrot to my own darling horse, Raven, and then knocked on Joseph's door. He opened his door without asking who was knocking.

"Are you not supposed to ask who is there?"

"Yes, but I knew that you were knocking and so it was all right."

"How did you know it was me?"

"Footsteps like a cat. The mares did not nicker, and the stallion did not snort—a dead give away. Could be only you or your father."

"What about Karl? It could have been him."

"He is with his family tonight until later. Seems everyone is talking about losing our farms."

After I had slipped into his room, Joseph closed and locked the door. He had been told, often enough, that the door must be locked when he was inside. If an intruder tried to break in, the locked door would give him time to grab the revolver Father had given him to defend himself. Joseph was a good shot and very sure of his aim. Papa had taught both of us to shoot. "You never know when you might have to use a gun," he always said. In this respect he was different from most Volga Germans who abhorred violence and wanted nothing to do with guns.

We both sat on his bed. It was a simple platform on stilts, holding a lambs-wool mattress covered by blankets and white-and-blue-checked sheets. That was good enough for summer. In winter he had furs and a feather bed to stay warm, for although the two rooms were heated by a wood stove, it got terribly cold if you forgot to feed the stove at night. As we sat there, our legs dangling, I looked about the barren room. Wooden, brown plank walls, beaten, marked wood flooring, and a wooden closet where he kept his school clothes, was all there was. The rest of his belongings, his few toys, Sunday clothes, a picture of his family, were kept in the house with my things.

"What are they saying at our house?" asked Joseph. For just a moment his thin boy's face looked worried and old.

"I heard Father saying—he spoke louder than the others—that we must try to leave for Germany. I have never heard him speak so forcefully, so worriedly. He said that the new government is proceeding in criminal fashion. That the acts of the Reds are against every law civilized man has lived by. He even said Stalin must be criminally insane."

We both knew from the constant chatter among the adults that Lenin, the driving force behind the Bolshevik takeover, had died in January 1924. A vicious struggle between Stalin and Trotsky for the leadership of the party had ended in Trotsky's ouster and exile. Trotsky, highly intelligent and educated—his father had enrolled him in the famous German school in Odessa—had tried to forestall Stalin's criminal subversion of the Revolution. For this attempt, and his continuing opposition to Stalinism, he paid with his life. Stalin's long arm reached into Mexico where the communist agent Ramon Mercader would assassinate Leon Trotsky on August 21, 1940. Trotsky's had been the last effort to save Russia from the monster. We were now all subjects to Stalin. My family feared him like the devil.

"So, what will we do? If they take the land and the horses, we will starve," said Joseph. "We have nothing else. Horses, a few beef cows, the milk cow and a couple of pigs. What can you grow around Schaffhausen? Nothing—the land produces little. "

At one time or another everyone in the village had experienced hunger to the point of starvation. We both knew what hunger was.

"I do not know what they will decide. Perhaps we can leave and live in Germany with Uncle Martin and Aunt Gudrun."

"I would not give a kopek, betting on that," said Joseph dismissively. "I have listened carefully when the *Vorsteher* talked with the men in the *Gemeinde*. They are saying that the Bolsheviks will not allow us to leave— something about keeping everybody in Russia for slave labor."

"Stop it! Perhaps Papa will get us out. Perhaps *Opa* Holger can do it. He has so many friends that might be able to help." I was terribly upset that Joseph should give up so easily on the idea of leaving. After all, I was seven and believed in miracles and fairytales. The idea of leaving, of going to Germany where my brothers lived, was so tempting that it hurt to think we could not go there.

I crept back into the house, long before Karl returned from his family. Sliding in, I heard the adults still talking in the living room. That in itself was an unusual occurrence, because most of the time we lived in the kitchen. By now I was tired, too tired to spy on their conversation. I crawled into my bed.

The Serpent's Revenge

Poisonous snakes always strike;
it is their nature.
—S. I. W.

I never knew what they had decided to do, for the next morning, right after breakfast, a knock on the door and a booming voice ended our peace. A complement of soldiers was standing outside, their guns at the ready. They asked for Father to come out and accompany them. Father asked what this was about, but they said they knew nothing. They had been ordered to bring him to the major.

As Father pulled on his boots, Mother stood by him like a grieving widow. Her eyes were wide with a wild, fearful look. She was wringing her hands, saying over and over in Russian, "Not again, Alexander, not again. Oh my love, what now? What now?"

Father rose from his bent position, boots in place, and took Mother into an embrace. "It will be nothing. Questions perhaps, horse talk. Do not worry, Albushka." Albushka was his pet name for Mother. I liked it better than Albina. Those were his last words before he left.

My mother was suddenly in a frenzy. Usually composed and calm, she had lost her deliberate mien. "I must know what they want from him," she shouted. She put on her shoes and wound her loose hanging hair into a knot at the nape of her neck, fastening it with a clasp. She grabbed a shawl, for the morning fog had perversely cooled the air.

"Perhaps you should wait here for him," suggested Grandmother, "maybe you are too hasty, following him."

"No, I know that I have to go and see for myself." With that she was out the door, fairly running down the road. The next few hours were interminably long. Not much was accomplished because all of us could be seen staring down the road in hopes of seeing my parents returning.

Joseph reverted back to his long forgotten mode of insecurity and fear. He sat beside me on the stoop, where I had stationed myself for the best overview of the road. I placed my hand in his rough boy-paw, pressing it fiercely. Hours passed, as we silently kept vigil until we finally saw Father striding toward our house. Mother, hanging on to his arm, tried unsuccessfully to match his long steps. Our parents were closely followed by a detachment of soldiers, holding guns across their chests.

As Father and Mother approached, we saw that she was in tears and Father's face was a mask composed of hurt and fury. Mother flew right by us, up the steps and into the house without giving us a glance. Father shouted for Holger and Karl. As the two came running, having never heard him shout like this before, we saw a convoy of trucks approaching.

The soldiers, stone-faced, had formed a semi-circle around our house. "What is going on, Alex?" asked Grandfather. "Why the soldiers? Why the trucks?" In a voice choked with anger, Father said, "They have come to begin their robbery with our holding. It seems someone has complained to the soviet in Katharinenstadt that I am a tsaristic, reactionary element in the village and must be punished."

Father breathed shallowly, stenotic, as if his air passages were closing. He was shaking with anger and rage. I pulled my hand from Joseph's grip and stood up. I walked to Father and took his hand, holding it between my hands. He looked down into my eyes, and for a moment he breathed easier.

"Who would malign you? They love you in the village; no one would speak such lies about you."

"Some did. Perhaps Anastas Sergeyevich did. He was there when they read me my sentence, and he seemed to be exceedingly pleased."

"What sentence? What crime?"

"Without a hearing, I have been sentenced to slave labor in a re-education camp in Siberia."

"Dear *Gott. Mein armer Junge.* Is there nothing that can be done about it? Should you not be able to confront your accuser?" Grandfather's face had turned ashen upon hearing Siberia. They had spoken in German and now one of the soldiers, apparently more powerful than the others, shouted, "*Nemezkiy svynia*, speak Russian so we can know what you two are hiding."

Neither Father nor Holger deigned to acknowledge him with as much as a glance, but they continued in Russian. "They will take the horses, Holger, the beef cows and the pigs too. The major has promised they will leave the milk cow. However, she will be dry soon. She will produce nothing and will consume feed." Father sighed heavily. He rubbed his forehead, as if this would help him think. His face looked fallen, drawn down with worry.

"I need to gather as much stuff as I can carry, because where they take me I will need every rag in winter to keep me alive. Someone mentioned the Pechora."

Grandfather gasped. Everyone had heard of the horrid, small camps just north of the Arctic Circle. There were rumors that coal had been discovered in the Pechora basin, years earlier, under the Tsar; however, this coal was hard to mine. From inside our house I heard the high-pitched voices of my mother and grandmother, alternating between hot outrage and dark, tearstained lament.

The round-faced major arrived, ordering the soldiers to search the premises. They went into the barn, the orchard and the garden. A detail of four—the major in the lead—entered our house, herding the rest of us ahead of them into the small entry and into the kitchen. I held onto Joseph, who was violently shaking. It seemed as if he relived the day they took his parents away. And that, indeed, was happening again. They were taking away the man who had been his father, his defender and friend.

The soldiers found little of what they were looking for in our house. No money, no precious jewels, no gorgeous, oriental carpets or statuary—nothing they had hoped for was present. Hah, too late! We had been robbed twice before in grand fashion—nothing left to steal. They cleaned out the pantry in lieu. A few smoked hams, sausages, a barrel of beer, the long loaves of fresh bread Mother and *Oma* had baked the day before—all of it was carried by greedy, grubby hands to a truck.

In the bedroom, the major noticed Mother's famous, quilted feather bedspread, and waved to one of the knaves to lift it, roll it up and wrap it in a blanket. Finished with the house, they went out to see to the horses, which had been pulled from their stalls and paddocks. They danced excitedly on their makeshift leads, snorting in fear because they disliked the smell of the men pulling on their necks.

I knew these men were bad: no one had to tell me that. First they took the docile beef cows. The stupid animals marched sedately up the truck ramps—onward to certain slaughter. Among the horses they took from our farm was my own dear, *Voron*, the raven, a black gelding with a white scimitar on his forehead. Somehow I had believed they would leave him, because he was mine. As they led him to the truck-ramp, reality sank in, and I fell apart. I ran to my horse and I clung to his hind leg, screaming so loud that I thought my lungs would burst. My screams were cut short; a swift kick, delivered by a soldier sent me sailing several feet. Raven's crazed whinnies as another soldier pulled on his lead turned my heart to stone. My horse must have known what awaited him, in all probability a horrible death from neglect and abuse.

I lay sobbing in the dirt, in front of the house. Tears and snot mingled with the dust of the road. For me, small creature that I was, snot and dust were the metaphors of what life had become. Strangely enough, years earlier, when the Communists had taken away our people, Joseph's family and others, I had not understood the finality of their leaving. Yet, when they came for the horses, I knew with certainty that I would never see Raven again. And at this moment, I understood clearly that I might never see my father again.

And where were the adults during this horror? My mother, Albina, delicate and pretty, had fled crying into the house unable to witness our fleecing—because what they did to us was nothing less than state-sanctioned robbery.

My father, a gun trained on his body, did his best to calm his stallion, Borodin, so named after the Georgian composer. The horse was Father's pride and joy. Father had carefully selected an Arabian mare and a *Trakehner* thoroughbred stallion, bred them, and reared the resulting foal. Thereafter, he trained the astonishing young stallion with the same patience he expended teaching me, ending up with a horse like none other. Borodin had sired more foals in the region than any other stallion. Working, he outperformed all others decisively. You could tell his foals from far away—they had what horse breeders call presence. They, like their famous father, had an attitude. They knew they were gorgeous. Out of their mother's bellies they came, and a few hours later they stalked about, their little necks stretched in a curve, their eyes alert, their tails arched. Most of them sported the color of their sire, a deep dark bay coat with black stockings, manes, tails and muzzles. Their eyes were enormous, their heads chiseled, their backs straight and short-coupled, their hocks powerful, necks long, barrels deep. Yet, their best feature was the sweetness of their disposition.

My heart was breaking because now they took Borodin too. They pushed and pulled him up a ramp into a ramshackle truck. Borodin was a gentle stallion, but he had just about enough of the treatment the soldiers were dishing out. He would have walked the plank had they asked him gently, would have walked calmly and with panache; manhandled, however, he resisted powerfully. As they could not control the horse, they turned Father into Judas, requiring him, with guns trained on him, to load his love, his pet, onto a truck that would take him to ignominy—perhaps death.

He had been the first horse my father had put me on when I was just a mite. He had walked me about, gentle as a kitten, when Papa wanted me out of harm's way. Seeing my father taken prisoner and Borodin prodded onto the truck was too much for me. I had seen enough horror for one day. I could watch no more. I slunk into the house, where I buried my head in Mother's apron folds and cried my eyes out.

Grandmother came to gently disengage me from Mother, while murmuring that Mother had to look after Father, for the soldiers were pushing him to get ready to leave. Holding onto each other, my parents went into their desecrated bedroom where they began to assemble the most important items needed for a man to survive in Siberia. Siberia, the mere word chilled us to the bone. We, used to extremely cold temperatures, shuddered at the thought of living there.

I learned later that the Siberia used by the tsars to banish the rebellious was quite a different place from the Siberia of the Communists. The tsars' banished lived in well-built, heated houses. If they had money, they could have their servants, their cooks and valets accompany them into exile. They had commerce with exiled friends, had parties, had their books and were not required to work. Lenin's mother sent boxes of books and materials to him. She also sent furs, clothing and delicacies. Years later my blood boiled, when I read of Lenin's exile. How loftily, spoiled even, he had been allowed to spend his exile days, for by then I had experienced communist Siberia myself.

Time, which seemingly had stood still in the morning, now flew on the wings of eagles. Father's kit had been packed. Mother clung to him, as if she could keep him here in her presence, if she just held on tightly enough. And for the first time ever—I saw Father cry. Huge tears fell from his eyes, as he desperately tried to maintain composure so Mother and the rest of us would not fall apart.

He disengaged himself from Mother's embrace. He hugged *Oma* Victoria, thanking her for treating him as her true son. He shook *Opa*

Holger's hand until I thought it would break, saying nothing. He picked me off the floor, holding my face to his and whispered, "Never forget who you are, never forget this moment. Remember who they are, what they do to us, and recount it, if you ever see them before a tribunal. These men are terrorists, criminals—history must bring them to justice one day."

He put me down on the planked kitchen floor and told me in Russian, for everyone to hear, to look after my mother. Then he picked up Joseph, much the same way he had held me, and told him, "Be strong, son. You now are a man among men, and you must behave like a man. Take care of the women; help Holger. He will need your help." He put Joseph down, slapped him on the back, and picked up his pack, which Mother had prepared. He left, abruptly, before anyone could break down and undermine his strength.

We ran after him, only to see that two soldiers had grabbed his arms, manhandling him into a truck. For a moment the picture of a great Russian bear came to my mind, hounds snapping at his heels. He could have killed a few with his bare hands, but there were too many dogs in the pack. As the trucks left, Papa waved to us while we stood in a huddle in the middle of the road.

Holger and Joseph held Mother upright. All strength had left her. She hung in their grip, limp like a ragdoll. Victoria's face was old and inscrutable. Her eyes had turned black and unmoving, seeming to looking inward. She held my hand, almost breaking it, gripping it so tightly.

"One day, before God, they will have to account for their evil deeds and they will be made to pay." Victoria seemed to be very sure that her pronouncement would come to pass. She stood erect, statuesque, her eyes aflame with a secret fire of certainty, as if God had promised her revenge.

Grandfather and Joseph had taken Mother into the house a long time ago, but Grandmother and I still stood in the darkening street. "*Mauseken*," she used her favorite pet name for me, "I want you to know something about people. You can go all over the world and whenever you meet truly good people you will be able to know them by the light in their eyes. You will be able to trust them—no matter their culture or creed. God has put this light into their eyes and courage into their hearts. God has his hand on them, and you will know them." She looked fiercely into my eyes and said, "Your father is one of the blessed. There are many more out in this world. I hope you will find them when you need them." In time, her prophetic pronouncements were surrounded by the shining halo of truth.

That night Grandmother put Mother to bed like an injured child. No one noticed that we had not eaten our night meal—no one was hungry. Joseph reverted back to old fears and insecurities, while I discovered a new depth of hurt. In one short moment of this day I had profoundly changed. From a happy, carefree childhood I had been viciously thrown into the painful reality of the adult world.

While the grandparents were busy with my shocked mother, Joseph had gone to his room in the barn. He returned; his skinny arms filled with pillows and blankets. Answering my questioning eyes, he said, "I can not sleep there anymore. I know they will come for me next and drag me away." I understood and nodded my head.

"You can sleep here in the living room with me. I am scared too."

"Will you come with me and help me carry the mattress? I could not carry it by myself."

"Of course, I will. Let us get it now while they are busy with Mother."

We made Joseph a bed on the floor, a few feet away from my alcove, and without being told we washed and crawled into our beds. As we lay under our covers, without speaking to each other, the day's terror was visited upon me once more. Again I saw in my mind how they pulled my father onto the truck, and I began to cry. The inevitability of his leaving sank into my innermost being—I began to know that the horrifying pictures were real.

Wrapped up in my grief, I had not noticed at first the tormented, stifled sounds coming from Joseph's pallet. His anguish was doubly my own, for he relived the loss of his entire family all over again. I climbed from my high alcove bed and went to where he lay. I curved my body around his bony back and snaked an arm over his chest and so, softly crying and warming each other, we fell asleep.

We did not go to school the next morning. The ugly devastation, a pogrom really, went on unhindered by considerations of right or reason. House by house was taken apart, stripped of all the soldiers were told to take. Barn after barn was emptied of livestock; every cellar and silo was depleted of grain, foods, beer and tobacco.

Truck upon truck left the village filled with the means of winter survival. Besides Father, other people, too, were removed by force from the village. They even took two of our Russian neighbors—God only knows what they had done to deserve this treatment. Had they not been, only a short while ago, the favorites of the party officials and been rewarded for their socialist zeal with German homes?

"Who can figure out the Reds? They hate their own as much as they hate us," said Grandfather scornfully. Once, Grandfather had been Russia's greatest Sarpinka dealer—the Sarpinka King. By the combination of great-grandfather Alexander's fortune, which Victoria had inherited, he had been one of the richest men in the triangle between the Volga, Moscow and St. Petersburg. Now, the great, sweet man had become a poor cynic. I was to remember his words later, when I saw with my own eyes how the Revolution devoured her own children with the same appetite as she had devoured us.

It took an entire week for the enormous theft to be completed. People screamed heartbreakingly as their favorite animals were led away. Especially the woman lamented grievously when their milk cows were driven up the truck ramps. They had special bonds with these creatures, making life possible, feeding their babies and children, putting butter and cheese on an otherwise frugal table.

"You will be provided with new animals and seed grain as soon as the commune is established," said the commissars.

"Why not leave us our own then?" asked our men. "We would rather care for our own animals then other folks' decrepit stock!"

"That's the reason why things must be changed. As long as you look at the animals as your own, there will never be a commune. Your attachment to things and animals must be broken for you to think socially responsibly."

"*Scheiss, verfluchte Räuber,*" said the men behind their backs.

"*Lügende mist Kerle, vom Teufel geschickte,*" said others. Yet their curses helped them not—all was lost during this one week.

Pursuing Escape

At home life had returned to an altered normalcy. Mother had come out of her bedroom after three days. Her face was wan, her eyes dead, yet her mind worked. She asked for me and Joseph, searching our faces as if our emotional trauma would be recorded there. That very same evening, as we sat down for our meal, right after the prayer, Mother spoke up.

"I have been thinking and thinking for the last three days, and here is the conclusion I have come to. Dear Mother, dear Father, there is no other way, but you must go to Moscow and ask for permission for us to leave the country. I have resisted my entire life the urge to desert my birthplace. Now I know we must go. Before they led him away, Alexander told me that I should take the children and leave for Germany. If he ever gets away from their prison he would come and find us in Germany—one way or another."

For a moment, stunned silence reigned. Then the discussion began. After an hour we children were sent to bed. "You will be going back to school tomorrow," said Mother. "We must appear as normal as possible; nothing must be out of the ordinary."

In the following days, my family prepared for my grandparents' trip. The last of our money was scraped together, for no one knew how long they would have to remain in Moscow in the long lines of bureaucracy.

One week later my grandparents left for Saratov, where they took the train to Moscow. It was telling that the Soviets had once again invested Moscow as the capital city, the same city abhorred by the tsars for its sloth, decay and corruption—the vile embodiment of the Eastern system filled with nepotism, *baksheesh* and assassins.

As they stepped into the carriage, taking them to Katharinenstadt, they looked frail and worn. In the city they would take the ferry, crossing the Volga to Saratov. Mother and *Oma* Victoria had searched their few belongings for the best of their outfits, mending them, making them fit thinner frames. Grandmother laughed, "Well, it is easier taking them in than letting them out. There, that is a good reason to be slender."

They looked outdated but respectable and carried valises, which only days ago had sported the decals of grand hotels and shipping lines. It was Joseph's and my job to remove these labels, for they would have marked my grandparents as kulaks, suffocating the effort for emigration in its infancy.

We waved them on in their quest to secure our freedom, saying many prayers while we waved. Joseph and I were back in school. Overnight we had become branded children, marked by the label slapped upon Father by the soldiers—reactionary. This label seemed to convey upon our teachers the power to punish us severely for the smallest mistakes and to heap jeering remarks upon us. Of this treatment Joseph got the worst.

At night, before we would fall asleep he would often tell me how Anastas Pelkov was grinning at him, "Now, little German rat, you have no one to save your fingers, do you? No Russian officer to frighten teachers." And then

Pelkov would let him know in subtle ways that, through his "good offices," Father had been identified as the tsarist remnant in the village.

Sophia Andreyevna was easier on me. She saw me as the innocent product of reactionary parents, an object still worthy of re-education, an education she would provide. Although she never let me forget my flawed parentage and therefore my defective upbringing, she zealously tried to make me into a little girl in the image of the party.

The first things she revolutionized, perhaps because it was the easiest to accomplish, were my clothes. I was wearing the standard dress of a Lutheran girl—the simple, straight, ankle-length dress, long-sleeved in the winter, elbow-sleeved in the summer. These dresses had few adornments. Sometimes they had a diminutive ruffle around the neck, the bottom and the cuff, but little else. Some were gathered under imaginary breasts or around non-existent waists. Most were made from Sarpinka, the chintz-calico fabric woven in the homes of the region.

Soon the Pestovich woman insisted that I join the ranks of modern Russian children. One day she had me stay after school and "freed" me from my kulak-Lutheran roots by cutting off my current dress just below the knees.

"Oh, Sophia Andreyevna, this is not good. My mother will be angry. She will not like this at all," I moaned as she snipped away at the garment.

"Nonsense! I will personally explain to her the benefits of modern dress."

It was not enough that she cut my dress to pieces at the bottom. She then attacked the bourgeois ruffle at the neck. It fell, as the lower part my dress had fallen, to the floor.

"Much better," said Pestovich, as she eyed her creation, and then she walked home with me to confront Mother. I had told her that Mother would be working in the calving barn that day, but she insisted that we get the confrontation over with in that moment. We found Mother in a small separation unit, a stall for sick calves, where she tended to a small, brown creature. Mother had a knack for healing sick people and animals. Here she was engaged in drenching the calf with medicine—probably just a tea brewed from local herbs. Most of our medicines, for animals and people alike, were folk remedies.

Mother's pupils enlarged to their full extent when she saw us coming into the stall. Pestovich shoved me ahead of herself. Before Mother could say a word, Pestovich held forth with a squall of verbiage that robbed her of breath. Now she, too, heard all the propaganda I had endured for days, while she was kneeling in dirty straw beside a half-dead calf. At the end of Pestovich's oratory Mother got to her feet. Looking me firmly in the eye while suppressing laughter, she said, "We have to thank Sophia Andreyevna for taking time and care to help you become a better Russian citizen. Please thank her right now for doing this. And I thank you too, dear teacher."

I nearly dropped in a dead faint when I heard Mother speaking thus. Dear God in heaven—she sounded already like one of them. Later, alone at home, as Mother was preparing our food, she said, "I almost burst out laughing when I saw you there looking like an orphan in throwaway clothes; however, it was better to go along with the crazy plot than to burst out in righteous anger. The nerve of the woman to ruin your pretty dress."

When I pressed her on her non-reaction to this intrusion into our personal lives, she just said, "These people are ruthless. They are killers and robbers. I have decided in order to stay alive, I will placate them as often as I can and choose my battles with care." That was the end of that. I wore the Pestovic-improved dress the next day and the next. The kids laughed, making fun of the ugly thing, and I laughed with them, telling them that my finery was the work of Sophia Andreyevna; she deserved all the credit. I called it my revolutionary Russian dress and we had much fun with it.

For one thing, the short *Fummel*, a great Polish term for an awkward, ill-put-together garment, was good for running. It gave me much freedom to move around, climb over fences and run through ditches. I had begun to think that, perhaps, there was something very good about the improved garment, until my mother stuck me into a pair of bloomers that were nearly as long as the dress. This ugliness dampened the freedom idea.

As the weeks dragged on, more and more people were pulled from their homes and disappeared. Our little church, in which it had been forbidden to worship God, was desecrated by becoming the new storehouse and kitchen for the commune. Henceforth, everyone would receive the same amount of food. There would be designated women working as cooks and food servers, feeding us communally. Thus every village woman would be freed to work her full eight-hour day along side the men. Bread would be apportioned by weight. Men, of course, were to receive larger portions than women doing the same jobs. Milk would be dispensed to children first.

Behind the backs of our prison warders—because that was what the village had become, a prison that we could only leave with permission— the people laughed.

"They will pay us for eight hours work, making us into factory workers. How stupid can they be? In the past we worked most days for ten, even twelve hours a day, because that is what it takes to run a farm. But if they pay only for eight hours and say that this is the time we shall work—we will, of course, obey."

Others quipped that perhaps, "The new functionaries will be the ones sitting up at night for a calving, for the cows now belong to the state and so maybe the state will take care of them after hours."

However, we had not reached this idyllic stage of communal living yet. Winter was coming and dread settled upon the village. How would we survive the frozen months of horror without food? Meanwhile we had no news from Holger and Victoria. Perhaps the long silence was an indication that they had been able to set things in motion? Could it be that through incredible luck—a miracle really—we might escape the deprivations of this winter?

As we waited the days grew shorter and colder. Joseph and Karl stealthily dug up the entryway to the root cellar, which, ever since the first invasion by revolutionary workers from the city of Volsk, we always kept covered with manure. We still had some potatoes, carrots, beets and other roots hidden down there, together with some grain. A little flour and some salted meat were contained below in sealed urns. Grandfather had started the storing in urns because our only good hiding place, the root cellar, was moist.

It was always problematic to retrieve our supplies from the bowels of the earth, for no one's eyes could be trusted. Some Germans, too, had turned communist in hopes of material benefits. They were the worst, for before they became known we trusted them, while they secretly reported us for rewards. Therefore, Karl and Joseph would dig at dusk and bring a week's supply of food up to the kitchen, whereupon they carefully erased all traces of their work. Karl's family and ours had shared food and resources during hard times before, but it got harder and harder to know what we could afford to share.

After the first great freeze, Mother rationed the little wood we still owned. Instead of using precious wood we burned the leftover bedding of our confiscated cattle. It was a mixture of dried cow pies, straw and reeds—a smoldering, smelly kind of fuel but it was the only other fuel we had. Mother made fires only in the kitchen stove; and soon, as the cold settled in, we carried our bedding into the kitchen, where the three of us slept—Mother in the middle—in front of the stove. She often held our hands before we fell asleep, saying prayers for Father, the grandparents, and all the poor German folk along the Volga.

Somehow we survived the winter. We were thin, hungry, cold, but saved, while a few village people never saw spring. Joseph and I missed many days of school because the cold brought life to a standstill. Strangely enough, during the winter months Anastas Pelkov had seemingly forgotten to torment Joseph. It was as if the cold and the hunger, which even he with his enlarged government rations must have felt, had robbed him of his inborn meanness. Yet, as soon as the ice burst apart on the Volga, the nasty sap rose again in his veins. Soon Joseph complained again about verbal and physical abuse.

He never said anything to Mother, for he did not want to worry her. But he told me about the cuffs, the smacks on the head, and the twisted ears. I am afraid that other than listening and petting his hand or his arm, I was of little help. Sometimes I got mad and planned revenge. Yet, whatever childish plan I developed, Joseph instantly negated my ideas, insisting that he would just have to endure.

"Whenever I get angry, I think of Father and the kind of things he might have to endure." He sounded very grown up and manly when he said such things, making me docile by example.

Trapped

One rainy night in April there was a knock on our door. Instinctively we looked at each other, fright and suspicion in our eyes. The knock came again, and then we heard Holger's voice, "Albina, Joseph, Katya! Someone please open the door." The next moment we all scrambled, but I got there first. I slipped the bolt back, opening the door wide, and there they were, my own sweet grandparents.

They looked oddly unfamiliar in their travel clothes, a bit worn but overall well. What hugging and kissing there was in our house. Even shy, awkward Joseph was swept up in the moment. Mother put on the samovar to make tea. "Are you hungry? I can make some potatoes and eggs," she offered, "We are lucky; the chickens just began laying again and so I can offer you something nice."

The grandparents, however, did not want food, and so we all sat around the kitchen table and drank Mother's tea. The grandparents told about Moscow—a place infested with a new, mad officialdom, lording

their new, superior power over the masses. Every day they had been standing in another line, only to be sent away again. Until, after many months,
someone had decided to act on their behalf.

"There must have been up to fifteen thousand Germans from all over
Russia in Moscow trying to get emigration papers. You cannot imagine the
lines and the problems to get food." Holger smiled proudly, "It was hard,
but Mother and I managed." Victoria nodded, smiling consent.

After a while, Mother elicited, in fits and starts, from her parents the
sad news that our request to emigrate had been denied—but not in totality.
The Soviets, in their calculating way, had looked upon my grandparents as
useless, a drain on resources, and granted their request to leave. Of course,
nothing they still owned could leave with them. Anything of value had to
remain in the country.

Victoria cried, as she was telling us the sad news. "We cannot go to
Germany and leave you here all alone," she sobbed. "Yes, we have decided
to stay," said Holger in a strong voice. For a moment we were taken aback.
It took a while for the fact to sink in that the grandparents had the desired
documents and could, in fact, leave tomorrow if they wanted.

Mother broke the silence, "I do not have to think about this very
long," she said. "It is very simple. You must leave, as soon as possible. Before they can change their mind again, you must be out of the country."

"But, but Albina, *mein liebes Kind*, what about the three of you?" Grandfather positively stuttered. "You will need us to survive." Mother left her seat.
She walked to her father with outstretched arms. Entwining him, putting
her cheek to his, she said, "Papa, darling, I never thought I would say such a
terrible thing, but now I must." She was crying and laughing, saying, "Dearest
parents, I cannot afford to keep you here anymore. You must leave."

Looking into their hurt, perplexed faces she began to explain the new,
changed world we were about to face. Eight-hour days with pay, communal
living, communal eating, the most food going to the strongest with little left
for those unable to earn a day's pay—this was the new reality they faced.

"Do you see now how foolish it would be to keep you here, when
I will be able to earn barely enough to keep myself and the children fed?
They will have no work to give to the elderly—not on eight-hour days.
I have been lying sleepless for weeks, thinking what we would do if our
emigration would be denied." Tears streamed down Mother's cheeks, as
she said, "God has answered my prayers, allowing you to leave. Do you see
now? You must leave. You will be safe in Germany, and I do not have to
worry about you anymore."

As the adults argued back and forth, Joseph and I discerned Mother's feelings of crushing guilt; her monumental fear of being the reason for her parents' predicament. What could be worse than being trapped in a country ruled by evidently soulless people? My grandparents tried to convince Mother that they could help her, could work, could be a part of the new *kolkhoz* workforce, but Mother was adamant. The final reason for changing our grandparents' mind arrived in the form of the commissar in charge of work details. Approached by Holger, he told him in no uncertain terms that there was neither work nor bread for old *babas* and *batiushkas*.

One week after this fateful night, accompanied by tears, sighs and prayers, my grandparents left for Germany. *Oma* Voctoria told me, as she walked with me one last time along the dry bed of Podstepnaya Creek, it was the most agonizing thing for her to contemplate, that now she would die in Germany and I could never come and tend her grave.

"But I will, Grandmother. One day I will get out of Russia, and I will find your grave. I promise." *Oma* Victoria smiled and squeezed me, saying, "I almost believe you will be able to do that, you strong-willed young lady." And then we parted.

The Kolkhoz

The historical experience of socialist countries has sadly demonstrated that collectivism does not do away with alienation, but rather increases it, adding to it a lack of basic necessities and economic inefficiency.
—POPE JOHN PAUL II

During the next two years, 1930 and 1931, collectivism was perfected in the Volga German villages. The men in our village had to enlarge the best barns to house the communal animals. To no one's surprise, the commissars decided that our horse barn was one of the best and largest buildings and, enlarged, would hold all the dairy cows and calves. Of course, like most of the decisions made from afar by the bureaucrats in Moscow, nothing worked out once their plan was implemented.

Even the severely reduced amount of livestock returned to our village did not fit into the buildings as Moscow had planned. With haggling, threats and tears, the original orders were compromised and changed as soon as the overseers left. In any case, my family was settled with an abnormal amount of livestock. Most of the cows and the calves were installed on our property. The party bureaucrat in charge of job assignments quickly spotted Mother. Knowing that she lived close to the cows which he had assigned to our barns was sufficient ground for him to decide willy-nilly that she should be in charge of the calves.

Mother tried to gently direct him to another assignment, by telling him she knew very little about raising calves but that she was a very good cook and could organize a large kitchen. The former was a bald-faced lie because Mother was great with livestock, but, of course, like most of the Volga German women, she was a wonderful cook.

"You will learn, comrade Grushova. We all must learn new things for a better, brighter life. Comrade Stalin has dreamed new, better lives for us. These plans we must execute."

During the subsequent months our *kolkhoz* implemented the mass feedings planned for the whole commune. That idea, as so many others, turned into a devastating failure. The cooks had never planned and prepared meals for a multitude and poorly estimated the amounts needed, with the result that only the first wave arriving at the kitchen got properly fed. Half the village walked away hungry from the feeding station, seething with anger. Recrimination, shouts, and pushing in the lines insured that the venture was judged a failure—even in the eyes of the commissar sent to make us a successful *kolkhoz*.

Henceforth, evening meetings for every adult in the village were ordered, during which the commissars discussed how to make the impossible workable. After a few meetings the number of commissars was reduced until only one powerful person remained in charge. This reduction alone removed many duplications and errors in the workings of the super farm. The meetings, however, went on unabated. Sometimes we accompanied Mother to these boring speech marathons.

At one of the first meetings, my quiet, reserved Mother spoke up and made suggestions. Mother was educated, intelligent, and spoke three languages fluently—Russian, German and French. She also could think quicker than most people I knew.

"Comrades, it seems that part of the problem is connected to the inadequacies of the building. It was built as a church, after all, and not as a kitchen." How cleverly Mother already used the party-speak and how cleverly she inserted a dig about our desecrated church.

"Although I am not trained in the organization of mass food production, I think we could work out the problem more equitably if we rationed out food portions per week for each family. Then they could cook and eat at home. That would eliminate the kitchen and seating problem. It also would free up the food workers for other services, as they would weigh the rations only once a week. But, most of all, the children would be fed at times appropriate for their integration into the school hours. Thank you for listening to me, comrades. I hope these ideas give you food for discussion."

This was the liveliest discussion ever witnessed at out *kolkhoz*. People asked Mother questions in Russian and German; even the commissar got into the fray. Mother calmly and competently answered, and by the end of the night, it was decided that the food problem would be taken care of exactly as she had suggested.

As we walked home with Mother that night, Joseph and I told her how proud we were of the intelligence of her suggestions. "We never got enough to eat," we complained.

"I know. That is why I wanted the system changed. I know major theft occurred in the kitchen. That might not change totally; however, people weighing and rationing food while working in a group, can be more easily controlled than people in a kitchen, working alone at different stations."

"What else did you dislike about the communal kitchen?" asked Joseph.

"The way food was wasted through spoilage and improper cooking methods, and of course, I missed not eating with you after blessing our food."

Henceforth, Mother sent us into the countryside in search of edible roots, wild onions, and herbs in the steppe. Since no one had time to garden anymore—the garden plots were communalized anyway—gathering of wild vegetation was the only way to subsidize our table. No one would lift a hand for unpaid extra work in a communal garden that would not benefit their own family. The slackers never did their fair share; therefore, the communal gardens died, becoming matted with weeds. That kind of selfish thinking had become pervasive—the new system asked, nay begged for it. We all saw soon enough that people worked only the eight hours for which they were paid. The minute their hours were concluded, they dropped whatever their hands held. Whether it was a hoe, a shovel or a trowel, it fell to the ground, with luck to be found again in the morrow.

At first, our German villagers could not function with such a mind-set. A tool was precious to them—it must be treated properly. However, our Russian neighbors taught us in a hurry that nothing was worth anything when you did not own it. In the first days of the *kolkhoz* our men did their time in the fields and then, religiously, put away the tack. They bedded the animals for the night, and fed and watered the livestock.

It took only a few weeks of experience to change their ways. The Russians, much more clever and used to dealing with tyrants, took a clock into the fields. They knew it would take at least an hour to put things away. So, depending how far away from the village they had worked, they left the fields early; no one paid them overtime.

"Why comrade, should I work for nothing?" they would say. "Who is going to give me anything?" And so it was. There were times when the village was filled with a cacophony of squealing and mooing. The animals, fed or milked too late, made their discomfort and hunger known. For weeks the beasts' torture went on, until finally a system was worked out by which people worked in shifts instead of entirely from eight to five, with an hour for lunch.

Kolkhoz Children

It was hard to remain a child in our village. The world of the adults had become so harsh, so unbearably filled with pressures, that they filtered down upon the young, aging our minds in the process. Although the Communists' manifestos all said that there should be no child labor in the new workers' state, within the new *kolkhoz* children worked harder than before. Sunday had been the village's primary day of rest. No one worked, with the exception of feeding and milking the stock. Families worshipped together, had their wonderful Sunday dinners, and went for walks along Podstepnaya Creek, in the cemetery, or even through the fields into the meadows, which were uncultivated, grazed steppe.

Although in the past Joseph and I always had work chores, we had found time between assignments for a quick run through the village; found time to jump into the hay from the rafters in the barn; found enough time and friends for a game of hide-and-seek. Without fail, our parents corralled us much too soon again, but we had had our fun.

Now things changed drastically. Mother worked so hard to sustain the three of us that we felt guilty having fun. A few months after establishing the *kolkhoz*, a new torment was inflicted upon us. After people were given their work assignments, they were informed of their expected achievements for the day—the norm. The norm hung over the village like a gray cloud. The norm required the cows to give pre-qualified amounts of milk—never mind how much food went into their stomachs. The norm expected one calf per cow per year. No one checked or cared whether the cow was a barren animal, whether insemination had taken place at the breeding, or whether the cow had aborted in the middle of a very cold winter, a common occurrence when it was too cold and there was too little food. Often the animals just re-absorbed the fetuses, thereby sustaining themselves to breed another time. The officials in Moscow were as ignorant of animal husbandry as they were of most things in real life.

Our mother was much too dutiful, too respectful of life in any form, to perform her work the way the rest of the village did. She still treated the animals in her care the way she had cared for her own. Therefore, she spent much more time in the stalls than anyone else would have. She schlepped many buckets of water and feed, long after the rest of her crew had left. Seeing her in abject travail, Joseph and I tried to help out. Many hours that by rights should have been ours to enjoy in childhood were spent helping Mother.

We were not the only children helping out. There was one Russian boy, Arkady Semyonov, who performed almost all of his father's duties. His father had injured his leg and now limped painfully about the village, unable to perform the work required to fulfill his norm. Arkady was a tall, raw-boned, strong boy with broad shoulders and a deep chest. At fourteen he had the physique of a grown man. He had a pleasing face with broad features, blue eyes, and dishwater-colored hair. He could handle the town's big Holstein bull and plow with the best of the men.

Perhaps it was for these reasons that Anastas Pelkov hated him almost as much as he hated my brother. Arkady bore his harassment with the patience of an ox. He believed that he deserved to be upbraided for falling asleep in class, a thing he would do often after having worked his father's night shift. I adored Arkady. After Father was arrested, we became defenseless, and he had saved me from a mob of children, ready to beat me up for lack of better entertainment. Seeing me in trouble, Arkady had ripped a respectable stick from a nearby fence and placed himself before me, taking on the mob.

Hidden behind his large frame I felt safe and protected. He handled the pack of children as he handled everything. All he said was, "Leave her alone, or I will show you what it means to fight," and that was the end of the affair. The children backed off and ran home. Arkady turned to me and said, "Run, little one! They are gone." I could barely breathe my, "Thank you, Arkady. I will not forget this," yet he was already leaving. Henceforth, Arkady had a special place in my heart, and I made it my business to know what was going on his life. The norm became a monstrous burden for him, because his father could never fulfill the expected workload.

Under the norm, the state expected a per-acre yield of grain, hay or oats no matter the condition of the fields. The village had been built upon a part of the steppe where only 420 *desyatinas* of allocated acreage were considered arable. The remainder, much larger part of the village acreage, 600 *desyatinas*, was considered too sandy and saline and, in a few places, lay submerged under shallow lakes. But never mind reality; the officials in Moscow looked upon their maps and expected normal crop yields from 1,020 *desyatinas* of acreage.

The villagers of Schaffhausen had traditionally coaxed tobacco crops from some of the questionable fields, which they assiduously fertilized with manure to raise a cash crop. They had sold the resulting inferior product to the local Kalmyk nomadic population. Yet the planners in Moscow not only expected grains, like wheat, oats and millet, but also turnips, rape, beet-root and potatoes to be planted everywhere. More even, they told our farmers when to plant and where to do it.

At first, drawing on their experience, the men firmly told the commissars what could be expected when harvest time arrived. However, the new breed of agronomists made it clear they were not interested in their knowledge. Thereupon the villagers shook their heads—and spoke no more. Who were they anyway? These German men of the fields, consigned to the ground for centuries, ignorant of modern science—what would such as they know? Were they better equipped to judge the Volga soils than the new breed of scientists in Moscow?

The new agronomists did not understand that the sites designated "meadows" were nothing but raw steppe. They were only used for grazing, growing wild grasses that could not be made into hay to sustain livestock through the winter. The state agronomists just assumed that because meadows were included in the village maps that hay could be had from those areas. They wanted potatoes planted in the few fields capable of producing great crops of wheat and asked for wheat to be sown in saline, sandy soils that instantly killed the germinating wheat.

In addition to the fields belonging to the village, we had always rented acreage to sustain our population. Despite the yields from this extra acreage, we had often barely survived the winter to live another year. Our colony was miserably poor compared to the larger villages like Norka, Warenburg and Katharinenstadt. Wherever colonists had embraced home-industries, as in Sarpinka weaving, pipe- or implement-making, their living standard had increased. Sadly, we had been left out of the loop of these developments.

However, despite the known history that our village could barely sustain its own population, it was robbed of the crops, the milk, and the meat heretofore feeding us—feeding now the party adherents in Moscow.

The next few winters were hard on my people but bearable. Not every one of the Soviets' outrageous plans had yet been implemented. The winters had not been unusually hard and the harvests had come in at medium yield. By 1930, another wave of mass-deportation swept German families from our village. Once again, more Russians replaced them.

This time, even our Russian neighbors were appalled. Over time, suffering the same hardships, they had come to like the way things were and did not wish for change. The new crop of villagers was even less equipped for farm life than the first wave had been. At the same time that our *kolkhoz* was torn apart and restocked, the rest of the norms were put into place.

What my mother had foretold came finally to pass. Between 1932 and 1933, the weather, combined with the many illogical, downright idiotic edicts put upon my people, produced Russia's greatest famine. Uncounted Germans along the Volga died hunger's death. Although the harvest had been execrably poor, the Soviet bandits from Saratov came and took practically the entire harvest "to sustain our workers in the cities."

Mother had lived through famine before. She knew the signs of nature and had begun to worry long before many others in the village caught on to the threat. Already in spring, when the wild geese came to the Volga, she had excused us from school with fabricated illnesses. Instead, she had sent us off to scrounge around the shallow lakes and ponds where the birds nested, to collect their eggs.

This was not an easy undertaking. The geese defended their nests ferociously. Coming at us with outstretched necks and flailing wings, they were a formidable force. Joseph, now fifteen, was a tall, strong well-grown boy. I rather liked the looks of my foster brother. His hair had darkened, but, strangely, his eyes had remained deep blue. He had the clear, clean skin that many of us open-air children possessed, and his face showed the world a calm, patient mien. This was not to say that mischief played no role in his life. Oh, yes, Joseph could be quite devilish on occasion.

As we poached goose eggs, we employed a method developed after a few contentious encounters. Joseph would carry a stout stick and a long-handled net, while I carried a basket and the same sort of net. As he boldly approached a nest, drawing the parents to him, I circled behind their backs toward the nest and extracted the eggs. I never took the entire clutch, for we had been taught never to deplete a resource.

Father had explained that often it took twelve goslings for one or two to survive. The life of a goose is perilous, he had preached. So, battling a pair of parents at each nest, we filled our basket, sneaking home with our loot.

Mother boiled the eggs and preserved them in a heavy salt solution—storing them in large, ugly crocks, which we buried in the dirt under the house—a most uncomfortable and dirty undertaking. There were a few floorboards in Mother's bedroom, which could be pried loose with a great amount of effort to give access to the space below. In all the years we had lived there, no one had ever found this space below her bed.

In addition to the egg hunts, Mother made us comb our small forest for mushrooms. The forest consisted mostly of willows—only good for basket making, tea and wattle. Yet a part of the forest contained poplar, birch and oak. It was there, among the oaks and the birches, that one could find mushrooms—some in spring, some in autumn.

I hated the mushrooms, because it was my job to clean them, fix a part for dinner and slice the rest of them to be dried. After the tedium of cleaning and slicing, I then had to pierce the slices with a needle, fastening them in an orderly array on a thread, whereupon, like decorations, they were hung to dry from the ceiling. I was going on thirteen then and hated the boredom of the operation, although I loved the aromatic, earthy smell of the drying fungus. After this harvest dried, Mother placed it in brown paper bags, hiding the bags between the boards surrounding her bed and the mattress.

Ever since the grandparents had left, Joseph had been given their bedroom. He had grown so tall that he needed more room than a pallet. I did not mind. I liked my alcove just fine, and when it got really cold we all slept on mattresses in front of the kitchen stove anyway. I remember many of these nights with great fondness, for Mother would tell us Russian folktales she had learned from my father. Or, perhaps, she would recite poetry in German and Russian or teach us history until, warm and drowsy, we fell asleep.

The Fire

Early in the summer of 1932—from the massive continental spread of the East—heat wafted over our land in waves, each wave more searing than the next. I remember that I was still in school, but Joseph had come home from boarding school in Katharinenstadt. Mother had insisted that he continue his education there, because he was bright, patient, and eager to learn. She made enormous sacrifices for him to go on. Boarding him with a family we knew was part of that outlay, along with expensive books and the other supplies.

A while earlier, I, too, had graduated—straight into Anastas Sergeyevich's classes. As long as Joseph had been a pupil he had ignored me, venting his seething class-anger on my hapless brother and other more worthy objects of derision. Yet, the moment Joseph left the school Pelkov transferred his rage and ire from the absent Joseph to present-in-class Katharina.

He never called me by my name, preferring the appellations Katya or Grushova. He began to smack my head with a ruler at the slightest hesitation on my part when called upon—sometimes so hard it gave me a headache. As the year went on he became meaner and I, anticipating torment, made more mistakes, which gave him in turn more reasons to hurt me.

For the longest time I said nothing to anyone. Joseph had so bravely carried his cross and survived, triumphed even, that I tried to follow his example. I did break down, however, and told him some of the things Pelkov did to me when he came home for the summer break. After Joseph's return, I was still in class for two more weeks.

It was during this time that the terrible heat wave descended upon us. There was an instant shortage of water. Much of our water in the village came from wells. Water had to be pulled up from considerable depth in buckets for all the functions of the farm and the house. Joseph helped Mother all day long. Sometimes, when things became pressing, I had to leave class to carry water for Mother's charges, the calves. My absences were a newfound reason for Pelkov to torment me.

His newest instrument of torture was a willow switch which, soaked in water, became an exquisite tormentor's tool. Whenever Joseph came, calling for me to come home, Pelkov would cry, "*Dura, dura, tui durak.*

Fool, fool, you are a simpleton. Yet you go home instead of learning," and he would smack my bare legs with his switch. One day he did this so savagely that I escaped with bleeding welts.

Joseph saw the swelling marks when I came into the bright sunlight and a few red drops rolled down my legs. I tried valiantly not to cry, but the pain and Joseph's look, filled with pity, brought tears to my eyes.

"That animal must be punished. Something has to happen. This is too much."

"There is nothing we can do, Joseph. They have all the power. The Reds have the power to commit crimes unchallenged. I know, compared to what they have done to many of us, my welts are nothing."

"Yes, yes, yes! I know. That does not make it right though, and it does not mean he cannot be touched."

"Oh, Joseph! Don't even think of it."

However, my brother was not to be deterred. For him, it was one thing to be tormented himself yet quite another to see me endure the same punishments. The very same evening Arkady came to our house, summoned, somehow, by Joseph. The two disappeared into the depth of the cow barn—our old horse barn. Intrigued, I followed them clandestinely.

Arkady had become a man. He was alone in the world now, working in the machine depot of the *kolkhoz*. The grand term "machine depot" required an enormous stretch of the imagination, for the old barn they were using as their "depot" was even more decrepit than the one old tractor, the two trucks, and the commissar's car that made up its inventory. Arkady's father, the crippled man, had died in an accident. His mother had followed her husband soon thereafter, carried off by tuberculosis, which ran rampant through Russian cities.

At eighteen, the promise we had seen in Arkady the boy had been fulfilled—he was gorgeous. I had always had a crush on him, my hero and protector, following him and my brother like a puppy on a lead. Usually they did not know that I trailed them. In the current instance, into the barn they went, straight to the old monster, the iron stove, which was sometimes still used to heat the barn when the cold threatened to kill the livestock.

Joseph had inherited the secret of this beast from Father, who told him how his friend and helper, Timur, had not only moved the stove but also created beneath the monstrous entity a heavenly place of concealment. At some point, I also overheard that the cavernous space had once sheltered the father of General Vladimir Antonovitch Tumachevsky, who had found refuge there from pursuing Reds.

I had followed the boys, watching them closely. Having detached the stovepipe they used a trick, a mat of straw, to slide the old stove away from the hiding place. I saw them lift the floorboards and descend underground. Oh, God, I worried about these careless boys. What if someone came into the barn for a calving? What if a nosy commissar merely came to inspect the premises?

I wondered, could I possibly push the stove into place and connect the stovepipe to make things seem right? No, I was quite clear in my mind that I could do nothing of the sort. Unable to influence fate in any way, I decided to be the lookout for the careless boys. I marveled that in my mind one poor decision could take away the appellation "man" from an overgrown boy. However, I now viewed Arkady with the same measure of deprecation that I applied to my brother's follies. And, therefore, I sat above their hideout and listened to the bits of their conversation floating up to me.

Punishment was a frequently repeated word; burning the animal out of his lair, was also a recurring phrase. I became terribly frightened. The two men in the village I cared most about had set their feet upon a most dangerous path. What was I to do? On one hand, I could not tell anyone. If I told Mother, she would worry and perhaps tell someone to get help to stop them. Then the boys would know of my tattling and never include me in any of their adventures. They had been kind to me, taking me along when they went night fishing.

Even mere conspiracy to harm a Soviet official would be brutally punished. On the other hand, I could not allow them to go on without supervision. I prayed and prayed and the answer I received, or thought I received, was: protect them and leave them be. After their meeting below ground, they heaved themselves up through the narrow passage onto the floor of the barn. Arkady and Joseph slipped away into the darkness and I, too, crept back toward the house.

Joseph, hearing a noise behind his back, lunged, tackling me, and pressed me to the ground. When he saw whom he had caught he hissed angrily, "What are you doing, Katya? Are you spying on me?"

"Yes," I cried, for there was no reason to deny the obvious, "I think you and Arkady are fools."

By now we were both sitting on the moistened soil of Mother's garden. Not much was growing here anymore. Yet, every day, as she had always done in past years, she splashed the wastewater onto the ground, encouraging self-seeding plants to emerge. Joseph scratched his head in frustration. "You have no right to follow a man around. You are just a girl and should mind your own business."

"I know what you two are up to and I do not want you to do it," I cried. "I can stand what Pelkov dishes out. I do not want him to have the pleasure of seeing the two of you go to prison."

We argued for a good while without any clear resolution. I threatened that I would tell Mother if he would not give up the idea. That threat tamed him a little and I thought, that for the moment, I had won the battle. In the end we left the garden angry and hurt. Joseph had even called me a despicable traitor. But, I could live with this slur—if only he were to give up his plan.

On closer examination, I did not believe that Joseph had given up on the Pelkov revenge. I knew him too well. Joseph was slow to be aroused to anger, but when he reached his boiling point his anger could simmer for a long time. And so I watched him with the extreme caution with which a hen watches her chicks. Of course, I did not tell Mother anything. She had worries far beyond our childish concerns, or that was what I thought. In reality she must have worried hour by hour about our very existence.

Only a few days later, the boys were ready to execute their plan. They had picked a dark, moonless night to get their revenge. I had hardly been sleeping since the day of their first meeting. In half slumber I constantly listened for my brother to leave the house. When I finally heard him sneak from his bedroom, I blessed the creaky bedroom door. Mother heard nothing: working two jobs, the *kolkhoz* during the day and our household in the evening, tired her beyond hearing creaky doors.

Joseph had not been gone a minute when I followed him. I had been sleeping in an ugly pair of black cotton pants and a gray undershirt belonging to Joseph. Attired thus I needed no blankets because it was always stifling hot. I slipped into my rope-plaited house shoes. They were well broken in, cradling my feet, noiseless when I crept.

I caught up with Joseph in the now neglected orchard of a neighbor, one well-remembered Johann Friedrich. Herr Friedrich, much too successful for our village, had been deported for being a kulak, together with every member in his family. His untrimmed trees had not produced well lately, but they provided great cover for conspirators. My cat eyes spied Arkady, waiting under a tree for Joseph's arrival. Immediately they were engaged in intense discussion. Throughout their talk I remained motionlessly wrapped around the trunk of an apple tree, raptly listening. I was only about fifteen feet from the boys, amazed that they had not spotted me.

Arkady had a candle, which he lit. In the sparse light of this waxy source, they manufactured a weapon. I heard Arkady say that this was a

weapon of the Revolution that revolutionaries against the tsarist bourgeoisie had successfully used. I saw them bending over a bottle, temporarily
gleaming green in the candlelight. They poured liquid from a metal container into the green glass. Joseph's back obscured what they did next.

Clinging to the tree trunk, I felt like dying. I was tired. I was scared—
for myself and for both the avenging fools. Strangely though, the strongest
sensation I felt was of freezing cold. How could I be cold? The night was
very warm. Joseph and Arkady wore light clothing; dark, long cotton pants
and black sleeveless undershirts, blending into the night's shadows. This
was the moment I should have acted—intercepted them. But I did nothing. Mesmerized—as if wishing the drama to continue to unfold—I stood
and gawked.

Next the conspirators crept through the orchard toward Anastas
Sergeyevich's house. I wondered whether he was sleeping inside. They stopped
at a respectful distance from the house. I saw Arkady bending, depositing
something on the ground. A moment later, I saw a light flash, igniting a fuse.
In a second, a brightly burning, flaming object arced through the air, landing
on Pelkov's straw-covered roof. Instantly the fire spread as if riding on fumes
in all directions. While my eyes were riveted on the horror unfolding, a second
missile hit another part of the roof, spreading more flames.

As if linked by chains, both boys suddenly began to run as one body
from the conflagration. They were fast, gone in a moment. I, however, was
still rooted in place. People began stirring in the houses close by. I heard
fearful cries and became suddenly aware of my vulnerability. How perilous
if I were to be discovered in flagrante delicto.

Slowly, silently I began to move away from the Pelkov's house as it
turned quickly into an inferno. Then I remembered that Arkady had put
something on the ground and left it behind. Whatever it was, it could
mark Arkady and Joseph as arsonists. I had never prayed as much in my
life as I prayed then. Fervent requests to my maker passed my lips. The
most prevalent, "Save me, save the boys, help! Oh, help the people contain
the fire. Please save my village! Please forgive my inaction."

I found the gasoline can without any problem. Thank God, it was
almost empty and therefore quite light. I grabbed the handle and moved,
half running, away from the house. I kept on running toward the Volga
until I stepped onto a patch of soft sand. Without thinking I fell to my
knees. Like a badger, using my hands as shovels, I dug and scraped until
my fingers ached and I had a hole deep enough to swallow the gasoline
can. I buried the dangerous object deep under the sand.

I said a little prayer of thanks and got up to go home. By now my eyes were well adjusted to the darkness. I had no problem finding my way back to our house. From afar, I saw that the flames on Pelkov's roof had been extinguished; sighing deeply I exhaled a small prayer of thanks.

Not anticipating any trouble, I crept through the yard and stumbled upon Joseph. He was kneeling behind the house, retching terribly. I collided with him, scaring him nearly to death. His nausea was instantly cured. He stopped his futile offerings to the god of disquietude, a term coined by Mother, who hated coarse speech. She always disguised the functions and failings of the body in flowery words or phrases that made one think.

"Katya, you idiot, what are you doing here? You nearly frightened me to death."

"I am returning from a mission of sheer mercy, dear Joseph," I mocked. "If it were not for your dear sister, someone would soon have connected two young morons to a certain gasoline canister behind Pelkov's house. Thanks to me, you both will be safe. There is nothing to connect you to the crime now."

"You mean Arkady left the gas can?"

"He most certainly did. But don't worry. I carried it away—a good long way, and buried it in sand. What were you idiots thinking? You could have burned the whole village down if Pelkov's neighbors had not instantly begun to douse the fire."

"I know! I know!" he groaned. "The thought of the village burning made me vomit—I was so scared."

"Why did you not think of it before you set the fire? And what about Arkady? He should know better."

"We did not think at all; we just wanted revenge. As for Arkady, he had been tormented so badly by Pelkov in the past that he could have strangled him with his bare hands." Joseph sighed softly. "After Arkady's parents died, he wanted to revenge himself on the teacher. I talked him out of it then. But when he heard about your legs he became livid." With wonderment and a certain glow of importance, I listened to Joseph's explanation. I felt touched and a little bit grand that Joseph and my friend cared so much about my hurts that they would take terrible risks, avenging me, while they had denied themselves revenge for their own pains.

"Why did you not stop us—you paragon of vitue?" Joseph mocked, "I know you wanted to."

"I don't know! Perhaps, deep down, I, too, wished for revenge. I stood, as if paralyzed, watching the drama unfold."

Joseph thanked me many times. He even gave me a furtive hug—not something he did often. At last we crept into the house and our beds. I don't know if Joseph slept soundly that night; I know I did.

The Grand Inquisition and the Commissar's Passion

As usual, Mother woke us at six in the morning. Upon becoming members of a *kolkhoz,* we had gained one hour of sleep in the morning. As private landowners the entire family had risen at five and put in two hours of hard work before breakfast. At the *kolkhoz* the day began at seven or eight, depending on the shift. On this day, however, even six, our normal time to rise, was much too early. Our nighttime adventure had cost us valuable sleep.

As I washed, dressed and did my hair in Mother's bedroom, I heard a grand commotion. I detected amid the neighbor's familiar German voices the guttural Russian voice of the commissar. What was he doing here? I heard him giving orders to soldiers. "Find the boy, Joseph. Pelkov accuses him of burning down his house."

"Oh, woe and pain. What to do now? They will question me, of course." Those thoughts and others raced through my mind. I made up answers to some, and found reasons laying a foundation for others. Of course, I would lie for Joseph. Not only would I lie, but I also begged God with all my heart to help me lie with the greatest sincerity. "They are just stupid boys, Lord! Forgive them, and please let me save them."

When I came out of the bedroom I could barely walk into the living room. From the front door, through the kitchen, and into the living room, the house was packed with people, angry people. Because, as I found out later, they had worked hard most of the night to contain the fire. By the grace of our Lord only Pelkov's house burned to the ground.

The soldiers found Joseph in the bedroom, and pulled him before the *kolkhoz* commissar. Mother had dressed long ago and was ready for the day. She was already returning from her morning duties in the stalls. She pushed her way into the living room where she remained, rooted at the spot, looking about in utter disbelief.

Her face clearly expressed what she thought, "What on earth is going on here in my house? What are these people doing here?"

Mother had always had a flair to look noble no matter what she wore. She had a way of fixing her lush hair in a simple twist atop her head, where she caught it with a tortoise-shell comb. Of medium size, she still rose above the crowd, because she carried herself erect. Clothes worked to her advantage. The offspring of new Volga German aristocrats, she had a style all of her own that made her stand out.

On that fateful day she was dressed in a straight, long, light-gray skirt and a white, long-sleeved blouse, over which she wore a dark blue quilted vest. Such attire was standard fare for women. She, however, had transformed her vest into a work of art by stitching a vine with flowers and leaves on both sides of the vest with a heavy white silk threat. She looked lovely in this most everyday outfit. It seemed that dirt did not attach to Mother, for she had labored in the kitchen and barn and yet looked prim and fresh as if protected by an eggshell.

Joseph was held by two soldiers against the wall of the living room, a plain, white surface. He looked dazed but defiant; his eyes searched the crowd for a friendly face. The commissar, a new one, had been in the village for only a few weeks. The old one had been recalled and imprisoned—a fact trumpeted about with vigor—because he, a corrupt member of the party, had stolen from the people and worse, from the local Soviet. The party had made a great example of him, announcing to everyone that betrayal ended, without trial, in death or exile to Siberian labor camps.

Andrey Stepanovich Verontzev was the replacement for the thief who had been removed. Verontzev was an interesting fellow. He was commanding but approachable, almost jovial in the way he allowed people into his inner sphere. He had a straightforward, problem-solving manner with which he had managed to pacify our discontented, seething village. He was a man of medium height with erect carriage. He had a narrow face with high cheekbones, dark eyes, and tough, iron gray hair, cut so short that it stood stiffly on its own, like cut wheat in a field.

He was about five years older than my mother, who had passed the zenith of womanhood and was now forty-six-years old. Somehow, despite famines, hard work, and childbirth Mother had managed to look pretty and young. One had to look closely to see that many fine lines in her face betrayed her years. They said then that I looked a lot like my mother. I am built upon her long, slender lines, and I own her narrow face, dark blue eyes and silver brown hair.

I parted the people like a swimmer parts water—I needed Mother. Clawing my way to reach Mother must have impressed the commissar, because he watched me closely. I stood beside Mother, assuming a calm face. I was up for a fight. Joseph was my brother; stupid or not, I would defend him against all the communists in the world.

"Would someone explain to me what is going on in my own house?" Mother asked sharply. She had drawn herself up to a new height. I knew that she must have been afraid and terribly worried for Joseph when she saw him between the soldiers. And yet, she allowed no other emotion to show except disbelief.

"Are you the mother of Joseph Grushov?" asked the commissar.

"Yes, what is the problem?"

"He has been accused of arson by Anastas Sergeyevich Pelkov."

"Impossible!" snapped Mother. "How could he have committed such a thing? He works with me all day and I know that at night he sleeps here in my house. I know where he is almost every minute."

"Well, Anastas Sergeyevich seems to be pretty sure that it was your son who set fire to his house last night."

"What proof does he have? On what kind of fact or reason does he base such a horrible accusation?" Mother's eyes were blazing and her voice was sharp, cutting like a knife.

The commissar observed Mother with great interest, as if she represented a strange new human specimen. He now fastened his eyes on her face and said, "Pelkov claims that Joseph did this to take revenge, because he, Pelkov, had to discipline Joseph's sister."

At that point Joseph could not contain himself anymore. Straining in the grip of the soldiers, he burst out with an acid-laced voice. "Is that his evidence? Well, then we might accuse every child in the village because he has abused all of us severely. Everybody has a grudge against him, everybody hates him."

The neighbors, who only minutes ago would gladly have thrown Joseph to the wolves, suddenly grumbled, agreeing with him. Every child had complained about Pelkov—every parent knew of his "German-kulak" hate.

Commissar Verontzev felt his authority slipping. The mood of the crowd was shifting, turning ugly. He stepped forward and, motioning to Mother, he said, "This is not the place to conduct an inquiry. We will reconvene at the community center, a proper forum."

We all knew what he meant by the community center. It was nothing but our old beloved church. Verontzev had the men set up a table in front for himself in the role of judge and for a few Russian party members as advisory committee. With some chairs and benches placed opposite this table for the crowd, the courtroom was ready. The place was so crowded that many people did not find a seat, but leaned against the walls, or stood outside, far beyond the open doors.

I had known upon awakening that this day would be terribly trying for all of us—the commissar, my family and all the villagers. It had been broiling hot for days. Even the cool well water had done nothing to revive me from sweat-soaked sleep. For days now Mother repeated ominously and ever more strongly her warnings of a poor harvest—perhaps the misery of famine. She still used every opportunity to hide bits of dried fruit, herbs and roots. Heeding all the morning's signs I had mentally prepared for a long, tortuous day. In this I was not disappointed.

The commissar had placed Mother, Joseph and me in the front row. From there I had a straight view of the spot where the altar had been. I gasped. They had tried so hard to banish God from this house of worship, and yet he would remain here forever. For on the wooden wall, above where the altar had been, was the clear, bright image of the cross. The cross had hung there so long that the wood beneath, sheltered from light, dirt and oxidation, shone forth clean and light.

A smile crossed my face. I sank back quickly in my seat with the certain promise that all would be right.

Commissar Verontzev wasted no time in opening the meeting. Anastas Sergeyevich Pelkov had arrived and was seated to our right, two places removed. Verontzev called him first to testify. Pelkov rose from his seat and, half turning, faced the commissar and the audience in the back. He was shaking with the excitement of importance. He began speaking in a high, squeaky voice, which he tried to control by rasping out an occasional harrumph.

"Comrade Verontzev," he began, couching his speech in formality, "I am here before you, the victim of a murderous crime. Murderous in its intent to cause me physical harm or even to inflict death upon me."

He paused, drawing breath to lunge into greater oratory, but that was a tactical mistake, for the commissar instantly interrupted what Pelkov had surely intended to be a grand soliloquy.

"Comrade Pelkov, as I explained when I called upon you to testify, this is not a formal inquiry but an informal hearing. So please just state with the greatest brevity what happened last night, what you heard and saw, not what you assume happened."

His verbal fire quashed, Pelkov recounted how he had awakened, about two in the morning, to the horrifying sound of crackling fire overhead and loud screams from outside. "I pulled on my pants and immediately ran outside where a crowd was already forming a water brigade."

"When you left your house were there flames already coming through the roof? Was there smoke in the house?"

"No, I don't think there was yet."

"Why then did you not take any of your belongings with you? You must have had something you valued?"

Having been revealed as a coward, for any other man would have tried to save as much as possible, Pelkov had the grace to blush furiously.

"I did not think of anything, your grace," he stammered.

"We do not address people as graces anymore, comrade. Anything else you want add about the situation outside your house?" Pelkov thought for a moment and wisely decided to end his testimony.

Next the commissar questioned, one by one, those neighbors who had arrived at the fire first. They all agreed that Maria Hinterwald, who had seen the roof aflame on her way to the privy, had called them from their homes—perhaps only moments after the blaze had started.

At first, they had tried with long, hooked poles to pull the afflicted roof into the barren street, where it could have been safely doused. In that endeavor they had been hindered by Pelkov, who screamed that he did not want his house destroyed.

"So, comrade Verontzev, we tried to douse the fire. A water brigade armed with buckets was already in place. Some fellows with long flails and pitch forks pushed in the burning walls, away from other buildings, and that was how we contained the fire," reported Martin Heidegger, the foreman of the machine depot.

"Did anyone see or hear anything suspicious before the fire broke out? A person running? A sparking chimney? Anything at all?"

To all his questions the answer was negative. It was a blessing that the night had been still, without a breeze; therefore, with the exception of Pelkov's house, which, of course, had been expropriated from an exiled German family, nothing had been destroyed.

The temperature in our old church had risen noticeably during these proceedings. People fanned themselves with odd pieces of material and dabbed frequently at the copious sweat upon their brows with huge white and blue kerchiefs.

The commissar, having removed his coat, suffered like the rest of us and rolled up the sleeves of his gray peasant blouse, looking infinitely more appropriately attired for harvest than a hearing. He now asked Pelkov, "What leads you to believe that the boy, Joseph, is the culprit?"

Pelkov hesitated for a moment. Then he said, "This boy—this German kulak child—carries a grudge, because I had to discipline him often when he was my student. He was obstinate and recalcitrant."

"As I understand it, comrade, the boy has not been your student for over a year? Why should he act now so violently when he is well removed from your power?"

Pelkov seemed stumped for a moment but then went on with renewed fervor.

"Perhaps he did it because I switched his sister, Katya Grushova. I just know in my gut that he did it."

"So, his sister is obstinate and recalcitrant also?" The commissar seemed amused.

Pelkove hesitated, caught in a quandary, but then he said, "Yes, she is also a problem." At that, the commissar called Sophia Andreyevna Pestovich: "You also have taught the girl, Katya. Was she a problem in your class?"

Torn, obviously pained, Sophia Andreyevna hesitated for a moment. She had feelings for Pelkov, in whom she thought she detected a fellow idealist, a maker of the grand, new, good Russia, but then she answered truthfully, "No, she was never a problem in my class." Called upon, other teachers also testified to my good conduct.

Commissar Verontzev looked thoughtful as he perused the notes he had taken. He then called upon a soldier, an expert in pyrotechnics, to speak to the cause of the fire and the manner in which it had started. The soldier, a man in his forties with the hungry, wolfish look of one forever on the prowl, stated his observations thus, "I believe the fire was set with the help of gasoline. It raced too quickly across the roof to have begun from a spark. Furthermore, I found two bottles so badly burned the glass had begun to melt. I found other bottles too, but these two were different."

Did you find any containers filled with gasoline in the vicinity? Anything to directly indicate its use?"

"No, comrade Commissar, there was nothing else." As the soldier's testimony was finished, my mother raised her hand. The excitement of the morning had driven blood into her lately pale cheeks and she looked very young. Most of our German women were very pretty in their youth, before hard labor, childbirth and hunger drained their health.

Called upon, Mother began to speak in a forthright, almost daring manner.

"Comrade Verontzev, I must respectfully submit that it seems there is little fact and even less veracity in Anastas Sergeyevich's accusations."

Mother wrung her hands as if she could squeeze the truth from her palms. "First, Pelkov reasons that Joseph carries a grudge against him because he was a cruel teacher. That reason can be dismissed instantly, because any of a hundred mistreated students have the same motives and opportunities he ascribes to Joseph." Mother looked pleased with her argument and continued undaunted.

"Second, if the fire was started with gasoline, pray tell where would Joseph get it? He has no access to cars, gasoline, or any machinery for that matter." Mother was now in grand flight and the words just poured from her well-shaped mouth, "Thirdly, I know with certainty that my son and daughter can never leave my house without my knowledge, and I certify that both children were in their beds last night."

Depleted by her testimony, Mother sat down exhausted. I had been watching the commissar with great interest, intrigued by what I discerned in his demeanor. To my astonishment, he looked at Mother the entire time as if mesmerized. His former officious, detached manner had given way to the absorbed look I had seen in my father's eyes when he gazed upon Mother. I realized then, with horror and fascination, that the commissar was more interested in my intrepid Mother than the case before him.

I was still dealing with the shock of my discovery, when a loud scream from Pelkov shook the room. He had bounded to his feet, expelling words like balls from a cannon.

"I know how he got the gasoline. He got it from his friend Arkady who works in the motor depot. That is how it must be."

With the intuition of a malicious fiend, Pelkov had unerringly detected the evil in others and put it all together according to his own demonic mind.

His uncalled-for outburst set the crowd to grumble ominously.

"Is it not enough that Albina Grushova counters all his accusations, making them moot—now he must attack yet another person." Arkady was liked by most people in the village.

"He attacks an orphan boy without a family to defend him. Foul!"

Since no one in the village liked Pelkov, with the exception of Sophia Pestovich who believed him to be a pure soul like herself, his situation had suddenly worsened immensely.

The grumbling of the villagers, the Germans and now even the Russians because one of their own was accused, swelled to a roar. From far in the back of the room a strong Russian voice cried out, "Sver, Beast. Not enough that out of jealousy he destroyed Joseph's father, a good Russian man and soldier, by denouncing him as a tsarist reactionary; no, now he must destroy the son as well."

Upon this man's outburst the roar became a furor. The commissar, rudely torn from his contemplations of my mother, had a revolt on his hands. He banged his hammer, which he used as substitute for a worthier, but unavailable, gavel and bellowed with stentorian might, "Order! Order! This is not a trial. This is a fact-finding inquiry—so we will be finding facts!"

For a moment Verontzev consulted with the men at his table who, until now, had been sitting like immobile scarecrows, swayed in their thinking by the mood of the crowd. Having consulted for the record and being confirmed in his opinion, he called the foreman of the machine depot, Martin Heidegger, to stand. Questioned, Heidegger, a man short on words and long on patience, ascertained that the depot had four gas cans. The commissar dispatched a soldier to the depot who came back, reporting that there were only two gas cans at hand. One of the missing cans was accompanying a truck in transit to Saratov; the other one missing was temporarily displaced, probably lost in the field while supplying the tractor. Nothing to worry about as they would find it soon enough.

"Ha!" screamed Pelkov, having jumped to his feet once more, his face beet red. "Just follow Joseph around and sooner or later he will you lead you to it. A good whipping might beat the truth out of him!"

"Enough!" roared Andrey Stepanovich Verontzev, "Enough, comrade Pelkov! There will be no beating; there will be nothing other than what has been established here!"

I remembered that upon hearing of Pelkov's denunciation of my father, the commissar's face had fleetingly shown a disgusted look. It was obvious that he had become exceedingly ill disposed toward the odious man. To top off the flaring tempers, the temperature in the room had risen sharply, leaving everyone short on patience and good behavior.

The commissar, I noted with great satisfaction, sweated with the best of us. His face had reddened while streamlets of sweat ran from his forehead, finding the channels of his face. He halfheartedly swiped at them with a checkered kerchief, already soaked and dripping. Finally he resorted to the demeaning task of wringing it out, watering the floor.

Even my prim mother had divested herself of her quilted vest, revealing sweat stains all over her formerly pristine white blouse. The different exudations wafting through the church, although the double doors were wide open, had coalesced into an indescribable pong.

From the door rose the cry, "Who knows, maybe Pelkov set his own fire to blame some of us?"

"Yes," cried another, "he came out of his house with amazing speed, as if he knew how fast that fire would spread."

"Let us question him closely and see what his answers will be." Those cries, getting louder and more clamorous with every passing second, motivated the commissar to act expeditiously. Once again he banged his ugly hammer on the table before him and called for order. Having achieved it, he intoned, "I find that you comrade, Pelkov, are a person capable of arousing great adversity. I discern that you yourself are in danger of being hurt. Therefore, I am placing you in protective custody until the proper authorities in Saratov can hear this case. Hereby, the hearing is concluded!"

He then called for soldiers to lead Pelkov away. One of the houses taken from a German had been turned into the town's temporary hold for drunks and misbehaving individuals. Now the commissar relegated Pelkov, the accuser, to this facility. Pelkov violently objected to what to him seemed unwarranted treatment, "You are turning me into the criminal!" he shouted. But Verontzev, looking dangerously agitated, bellowed, "You are becoming a nuisance, comrade! You have disturbed the peace of this village by making false accusations. I will have your case investigated by the judge of the Soviet in Saratov—he shall render a verdict after making his own inquiry into this affair. In the meantime, I must protect you in any way I can from the wrath of an angry populace."

I was not the only one astonished by Andrey Verontzev's actions. Usually, whenever a German was involved in even the slightest unpleasantness, the judgment and general tone of a proceeding was shamelessly prejudiced towards the Russian, whether he be the accuser or the accused. We therefore were left wondering about the motive of the commissar.

Later, much later, I was to learn what differentiated Andrey Verontzev from the other Soviet administrators. Verontzev had at one time been a professor of economics and a highly valued organizer for the Communist Party at Moscow University. An idealist, he had worked tirelessly for the overthrow of the Tsar.

However, soon after Lenin's death, Verontzev became disenchanted, nay, downright appalled by the means with which change was accomplished. As his feelings of abhorrence grew, he observed with an ever-sharper eye that the methods used to establish compliance with the radical new goals, especially those enforced by the NKVD, became gruesome.

Helplessly, he watched one day as the NKVD rounded up university staff deemed to be politically unreliable, marching the professors toward the entrance hall from their department floors. Taken aback at first, then aghast, he observed from a window on the third floor, which provided a full view of the hall, how two of his colleagues suddenly ran, hoping to get away. They obviously believed, as anyone would have, that the NKVD would refrain from violent intercesion in a university hall.

How fallacious their thinking had been! Rapid gunfire mowed all of them down, even the compliant academics, standing still. In an instant the murder of ten men had been accomplished. Blood was sprayed everywhere—living, vital men of great intellect only minutes before lay as dead bodies on the ground.

Strangely enough, the rest of the students and faculty had vanished, dispersed as quickly and quietly as feathers on the wind. Two NKVD-men, standing among the fallen, raised their eyes and trained their guns on the windows above. They slowly scanned the windowed floors above for any sign of prying eyes.

Verontzev had slumped to the floor below the windowsill at the first motion by the two men and lay now on the dirty marble tiles, silently screaming with horror. Was that what had become of his ideals? Was that what he had fought for, risking his life for? How could he condone this savagery and still call himself human? He had heard of incidents such as the one witnessed. There had been rumors, disbelieved by him. Now these rumors were confirmed, leaving all hope moribund.

Henceforth, his life changed. The very constructs of his mind collapsed and were slowly replaced by former philosophical and ethical concepts, harkening back to his childhood. His wife and daughter had died of tuberculosis during the time he had been fighting Wrangel's White Russian Army in the Crimea from 1920 to 1921. No one then thought that this Baron Wrangel, who had never commandeered more than a four-thousand-man army, would hold on for an incredible seven months. He maintained his force in the face of unbelievable odds before finally being overwhelmed and driven out to Turkey in an immense sea-born evacuation.

While Verontzev fought for the Reds, the two people he loved most had died alone, without the comfort of his presence. What a tremendous price he had paid—for what, this horror before his eyes? Henceforth, during night after sleepless night he thought of a way to gain distance from the center of evil, so he would not be a part of it anymore. At last, it came to him. It had to be an escape to an unprepossessing village far away from Moscow—from the center of Stalin's spider web.

Time and again he had heard at party indoctrination sessions that establishment of the communes required people with economic acumen. Well, he was qualified, in more than one way. He had commandeered squadrons and supply trains, had organized economic structures in Moscow, and knew how to lead men.

He waited for exactly the right moment during one of the after-hour planning meetings to present his proposal. "Comrades, I have heard the Party's call to instill the ideas of communism in the population. Often I have heard that kulak resistance to the socialism plagues our new *kolkhozes*. I have begun to think that, perhaps, I can be helpful in the implementation of the Party's goals. Please avail yourselves of me, if you think I can be helpful. Send me to where you believe I can be most effective for the Party."

As a professor with rhetorical skills, he had carefully gauged the meter and tenor of speech most probable to induce a favorable reaction from the functionaries. He was not disappointed. No one in the mid- to upperechelon wanted to leave Moscow or Leningrad to go to the Volga, or for that matter, to the Ukraine, to Bessarabia or even to Samara Province. If there was such an idealistic fool willing to go, well, send him quickly before he could change his mind and become obstreperous. This kind of duty equated consignment to Siberia. In the end, no one seemed to know, least of all Verontzev, how he got an assignment to Schaffhausen, of all places.

"Perhaps someone wishes me well," Verontzev thought when he heard the news. And this is how he arrived in our village.

As the days passed, we heard from Verontzev's driver that the commissar had dumped Pelkov into the lap of Saratov's judicial offices, together with a stern remark that he had to fulfill a norm during an extremely difficult year and could not be expected to solve crimes as well. He branded Pelkov a malcontent who had almost stirred the population to riot. "If the damned gas can is found the case will be closed for me," he had opined in front of the judge.

The Gas Can

Behavior in a human being is sometimes a defense,
a way of concealing motives.
—Abraham Maslow

A few days after the inquiry, driven by guilt and fear during a rather too brightly moonlit night, I arose from my bed and left the house. I wore the short dress, which Sophia Andreyevna had butchered in her zeal to bring me from German Lutheranism into modern communism, making me look like an ill-dressed orphan. It was now much too small for me, but I thought it would serve me well because it left my legs unrestricted. I had put it into my head that it was my duty to save Joseph and Arkady from further accusations. To establish their lack of involvement in the fire, it was necessary to return the missing gasoline can to the machine depot.

My task was not that hard, given that we now had few dogs and cats in the village. Most pets had been eaten in the last famine and were never replaced because people did not have enough food for themselves. Therefore, no barks or howls would give me away. I took the shortest route to the sandy plot where I thought the gas can was buried. The night was so bright that I encountered no obstacles or surprises, but it was much harder to find the burial spot than I had imagined.

The night was warm. From the Volga, despite its distance of a few kilometers, the dank, earthy-fishy smell of river water, enveloped in mild fog, stole across the land. Bright silvery moonlight bathed the steppe. Grasses shimmered and the few trees reflected mild silver, yet our gray houses absorbed the silvery shine and looked as indistinct and unprepossessing as ever. Dare I admit such a reprobate statement, but I, a girl supposed to be safely ensconced in my bed, was deliriously happy to be about on a clandestine mission.

After searching like a bloodhound for the gas can, I finally found the spot. The ground in the moonlight revealed a slight disturbance of the sand. I dug, using my hands as before like little shovels, and soon laid the can bare. After the exhumation, I immediately began to carefully rub the sand from the metal, because sand on the can might lead to unwanted suppositions. It was a blessing that I was not hindered by my usual long dress and I loped along toward the abandoned tractor, which I had seen in a field not too far away.

As usual, it had broken down after plowing barely half a field. The tractor was ancient, worn and in constant need of repair. Arkady and Martin Heidegger apparently held it together with wire, curses, magic, and Martin's prayers. When I found the old heap of machinery, I deposited the gas can close to a wheel so no one would see it too easily. I was a good ways away from the tractor, entering the *kolkhoz* orchard, once Karl Seifert's pride, when I heard a noise behind me. For a moment I panicked—to be discovered by anyone meant big trouble! To meet up with the occasional wolf, still plaguing the realm, could be extremely dangerous.

Suddenly I was afraid. My heart pounded, driving blood through my body's vessels so hard and fast that I felt the pulse in my neck beating like a hammer. I froze in mid-step—listening. Nothing. Ever so cautiously I turned around. Nothing! But the moment I stepped out again, there it was—the rustling noise. This time I turned around quickly, and from behind a tree emerged Andrey Verontzev—the commissar.

I was so afraid, I wanted to die. What was he doing here? How long had he been following me? Had he seen the gas can replacement? What was he going to do to me? In the moonlight his face looked grave and sad.

"You are Katya, are you not? Joseph is your brother?"

"*Da*, commissar."

"What are you doing out here all alone?"

I gathered my wits and stupidly blurted out, "I am taking a walk. I could not sleep."

"So, you are walking in the moonlight, eh? Does your mother know you are about?"

"No. She does not know. She is too tired to have heard me leave." Maybe I only imagined it, but I saw a smile cross the man's face. He thoughtfully studied me for awhile, and then he said, "What is this you are wearing? I have never seen such a dress in the village." Suddenly I forgot my fear and laughed ringingly.

"Sophia Andreyevna altered it with a pair of scissors—to make it modern in the new Soviet style for girls."

"Ah, I see. Well, I will not ask you again the real reason for your night walk. What I do not know, I do not have to act upon."

The commissar seemed suddenly very pleased—satisfied, as if he had come to a great decision. "Are you finished walking and willing to go home?"

"Yes," I answered quickly, pleased that I got off so easily.

"In that case, I will walk you home, and see to it that no harm comes to you," said the strange commissar. Then he walked me home—slowly, sedately, enjoying the moonlight. As if pleased with himself, he hummed the tune of the little field, "*Polyushka, polya,*" until he suddenly asked me about Papa. I told him all I knew—how my father had been an officer, a lover of horses who wanted to have his own stud farm and breed the perfect horse. And then, of course, I told him how they had first taken away our horses, and then Father.

"We have not heard from him since they took him away. We think he is in Siberia. Mother says that he must be far away in a bad place or he would send word to us. We pray for him constantly, for only God can return him to us."

In front of our house the commissar petted my hair and said, "Sleep well, little Katyusha, and do not worry, all will be well."

He was right. All was well after that; especially after the Russian tractor driver, who was always drunk on vodka, rediscovered the gasoline can by the tractor where he reasoned he had left it. The judges in Saratov had bigger fish to fry than pay attention to the gripes of a difficult, unpleasant schoolmaster—and so the matter died.

Starvation

By mid-August everybody knew that the harvest would be execrably poor. The commissar could hold off norm delivery only to the middle of October. Norm was what the Germans called *das Soll,* meaning that which must be given. Unlike the tithes they gladly gave to their churches, constituting 10% of their earnings for the year, *das Soll* consisted of arbitrary amounts construed by the party from the first and best of our production. It consisted of an enormous amount of farm products to be delivered promptly at harvest time.

It was laid upon our backs that the party expected so many pigs, cows, calves, goats, pounds of grain, flour, potatoes, beets and, of course, butter and milk to be delivered to a central station in Katharinenstadt, the town they had rudely re-named Marx in honor of Karl Marx, the German communist philosopher. Many of the functionaries, who willy-nilly decided the production figures to be met by our poor *kolkhoz,* had never seen a village, never mind assessed the amount of work associated with growing food. They knew nothing of soils, climate, fertilizer, fertility, re-absorption of fetuses during famine, knew nothing of diseases of livestock such as hoof-and-mouth disease.

So, when October came and *das Soll* was due, the commissar sent to the Great Central Collection Point the production he thought we could do without, accompanied by a letter stating the reasons why our village was unable to fulfill the norm. Mother, who read the content of the letter, praised him, calling him a reasonable man. According to her account, he had written: "We will barely survive without the products I am forwarding to the Central Collection; however, we will try to make it through the winter. I have withheld enough grain as seed for next year's harvest. On livestock, I kept all bred animals with enough feed to sustain them through the winter. We shall make up for the shortfall of meat in spring by sending a new crop of slaughter animals."

No matter how well worded and reasonable the commissar's report, scarcely two weeks passed before the inspectors came to the village. They did not come alone. Surrounded by a bevy of soldiers and NKVD men, they invaded the office of the commissar. They put him up against a wall and trained their weapons on him. Then, like pigs, they rooted through his desk, his files and every other thing belonging to his office.

Dissatisfied with their office search, they began to search the village, leaving the commissar sitting at his desk, holding his head between his hands. Of course, they found the granary first, filling their trucks and lorries with the grain meant to sustain us through the winter and seed our fields the next year. Next, they took all the pregnant sows and herded them into their trucks. The phlegmatic, brooding sows reacted to the horrid treatment with squeals, screams and great stress, which sent them, in a few cases, into early labor. Upon which, to the consternation of the functionaries, the distressed mothers proceeded to consume their premature offspring. Not a gram of protein was ever wasted on the steppe.

They cleaned Mother's barn of cows, leaving only the heaviest pregnant animals behind. They took almost all of the calves—but, worst of all, they carried off every bit of animal feed, consigning the animals they deigned unworthy to remove, to the certain death of starvation.

I was there to hear with my own ears how our commissar fought for subsistence leavings—something for the village to get by on. However, his cruel masters did not listen. They ridiculed him, calling him an egg-headed academic, a dreamer and coddler of German kulaks. "They will have food hidden somewhere! They are clever these *Nemezkiy svynia*," they laughed.

"You don't understand!" roared Verontzev. "This is a mixed village. Russians, Ukrainians and Germans live here!" He was so upset, he sputtered. "You took almost all of the village's horses, giving them a decrepit tractor instead. We could not till the entire acreage because we had no draft animals. Now you take all the seed and our food for the winter. What do you suppose will happen in two months?"

"Why should you care? Why should they care? Don't they get their salaries? Go and buy food, like everybody else."

"Where?" screamed the commissar, "where can we buy food? The next store is a hundred kilometers away and its shelves are empty! How do you expect this village to produce anything at all next year? I will be amazed if you will find anyone left here next year."

"Who cares if your rabble survives! They are superfluous in our design. So what does it matter if they starve!"

Especially the NKVD men laughed until they almost burst, and then they drove off with all of our grain, our animals, our milk, butter and cheese. These evil purveyors for the Party carried off everything we had prepared for plain survival. They had gone from house to house ripping from cupboards the odd egg, a bowl of sugar, a loaf of bread—anything resembling food. They had examined the gardens, the orchards—every inch of cultivated ground in their quest to find hidden food, and then they left—to feed the Moscow spider and his privileged ilk.

The hunger hit us in November with the force of a blow to the stomach. Somehow until then we had hung on by collecting the seeds of steppe-grasses, digging for roots and eating the last of the hidden morsels everyone had managed to conceal. But with the first overpowering blizzard, the steppe's few resources became unavailable to us.

Crying and begging, we prevailed upon Mother to break out the dried mushrooms, the dried apples, and the hidden goose eggs—all to no avail. "If you think we are hungry now, just wait until December and January," she chided. She would know. She had seen us through another of these Bolshevik government-induced famines before, and remembered the famines of her youth.

There were times when Joseph and I drank cup after cup of herbal tea, for no other reason but for the special moment when it temporarily spread a feeling of satiation and warmth through our bodies. Joseph's school in Katharinenstadt, no, they now called it Marx, had closed for the winter. As it was a Lutheran boarding school, the Communists had cut off all fuel supplies and thus closed the school as efficiently as if ordered by edict.

I was glad that my adopted brother was home with us again. I had missed him very much. I had few friends in the village. My best friend, Friedel, had been sent to Siberia with her parents. I grieved for her and, thereafter, did not seek out another girl friend. Joseph had become my friend, confidant and fellow bearer of sorrow. Children worked as hard as their parents and had little time to play and socialize. When we did play, however, we were a loosely organized group, which temporarily followed the rules of one of the older boys, until dispersing like a scattering flock of sparrows at the call of a parent.

Mother's assessment of our fate was proven right in December. Winter had come early, taking a firm grip on our land. Many people ran out of wood fuel early and resorted to burning dried cow manure, straw and the smelly bedding of animals. When frozen fog lay upon the village, holding the smoke from the chimneys close to the ground, the village was enveloped in an incredibly smoky stench.

Mother finally cracked. Seeing us suffer with begging eyes, she rationed out small amounts of dried fruit. We soaked that dry pittance for hours in hot water, slurping the resulting mush with almost holy appreciation. She concocted soups, made from water, salt, and dried mushrooms which, when finally consumed, allowed us to feel full for an hour. At last she dug up the sole eggs in their crocks from below the floorboards.

One by one she rationed out the precious source of protein. One of these eggs could lie in our shrunken stomachs for hours, giving us the illusion of having been nourished. I do not know how they fared in other homes. Hunger had ended social visits.

Mother, as well as all other adults, had to report every morning for work, even though they were barely able to go through the motions. Beneath voluminous clothes walked skeletons, held together by prayer, iron will and deep anger against the state oppressors.

Karl, from next door, said to Mother with venom-laced voice, "I will not die and give these murderous criminals the satisfaction of having been eliminated by their cupidity."

He was not the only one who felt this way. The stoicism bred into our hardy people kept many alive against all odds. There were many others though, the old ones and the young children, who could not sustain themselves with the pittance of food available to us—they gave up the fight and died. Our dear, humble, old church was put to a different use once more. It now became the mortuary. In the thrall of the deep-freeze it had become impossible to bury the bodies. The ground was frozen solid, and those who would have prepared the graves were too weak to raise a shovel. Wrapped in sheets and cloth, the frozen bodies were stored in the church. They would be preserved there, frozen stiff, until spring.

The ridiculous indoctrination sessions had stopped completely. Even if the commissar had called for them—no one would have gone. I remember asking my mother, "Mama, why torment yourself? Why do you leave your bed so early to tend to animals that do not belong to us and will be dead of starvation soon, like the rest of us?"

"Because they have an even harder time than we do, love. We understand why things are bad; they do not. I could not live with myself if I did not try to make things easier for them."

And so, sharing her plight, we trudged beside her to the stalls in the deadly morning cold. We carried water, and the pittance of available hay, and stirred their bedding around so they would not stand in a deep muck of their own dung. After only a few hours in the barn, we returned to our home, totally spent, in desperate need of warmth and rest.

But the house was cold for most of the day. Mother only fueled the stove to warm water and to heat the river stones we put into our beds for comfort—the only incentive to crawl beneath the ice-cold sheets. I had found a way to keep myself sane, refusing to allow the hunger roiling my guts to also dominate my brain. I knew that Mother achieved this state of temporary bliss, by reciting her favorite prayers over and over again, like an endless mantra. I was not disciplined enough to do this.

Therefore, I resorted to the stratagem of recalling in minute detail the stages of my life. I imagined that one day I would be freed from the yoke of Soviet Russia. For that day, I had to remember what had happened to my people on the Volga—so I could shout it to the world. And so I would lie in my cold bedding in front of the cooling kitchen stove, recalling the minutes of my life. Joseph had confided to me that he also used a strategy to keep from going berserk with hunger. He solved mathematical equations and puzzles in his head. "If I did not have this distraction, I could attack a cow or a calf and commit the felony of cow murder." He smiled; savoring his sardonic joke, for the Reds had declared it a crime for the starving populace to slaughter the few animals left in the village.

I had seen the commissar walk through the village a few times, looking gray and grim. He kept his eyes focused on the treacherous road, away from people, as if he could not bear to look into their gaunt faces, their cavernous eyes. He visited Mother in the calf barn a few times, and asked how she was faring. He told her that he had been promised that the village would soon receive rations. "I do not believe it," he said looking at the ground, kicking the dirt.

In January, when I thought I would surely die soon, because I could hardly rise from bed in the morning and my head had become a strange muddle of voices, of moving pictures and fantasies—miracles occurred. As always Mother had dragged herself to the barn and found a calving cow. Sensing trouble, and wishing to place responsibility for the animal in other hands, she sent Joseph to find the commissar.

He arrived at the moment of birth—the very same moment when the starved cow died, having spent her last energy expelling her calf. A moment later the small newborn creature, emaciated and weak, drew her last breath in the icy stall.

"What now, commissar? Two animals dead of starvation. However, they are not sick or diseased. Could we have your permission to cut them up and feed them to the village?" asked Mother. She asked this silly question because a ridiculous party edict prevented fallen animals to be consumed. The Party worried that the starving people would make certain that many animals met with fatal accidents.

The commissar tiredly nodded his head, giving consent to the plan. "I take full responsibility for the slaughter," he said, and then, laughing a false, grim laugh, he said, "I will count these bodies toward the supplies they promised the village."

Within two hours the animals had been carved up. There had not been much meat in their carcasses, but there were bones and the hides. Yes, at that desperate juncture we gnawed on hide and leather, if we could find it; but even with these hides there was not enough to go around for everyone in the village.

And here we received another miracle. While the excited people were still in the barn with the commissar, a second cow expired and a third. It was as if the animals, deprived of almost all edible substances—and cows can survive on garbage if necessary—were drawn to follow the first cow into death.

By evening the cooking pots were ready with a heavenly smelling soup. Everyone had received at least a few morsels of flesh, sinew and bone. Boiled all day, every bit of sustenance was now in the soup. At one point during the weighing of the portions the commissar said to Mother, "Comrade Albina, I make you a proposition. If I cook my small portion of the spoils it will yield little; however, if I give it to you it will make a better soup. So please, invite me to eat with you."

For a moment Mother's face was inscrutable. To share the little we had with a virtual stranger, a Communist official to boot, was not to her liking. But, always generous and kind, she collected herself, saying, "It will be our pleasure, Andrey Stepanovich, to see you at our table."

Whereupon Verontzev handed her his small amount of bone and gristle, saying, "I will be back with something for the soup." A while later he returned with three potatoes.

"Here, I have saved these for a special occasion and this is such a one." Mother blushed as if he had given her a bouquet of roses. This was truly a princely gift. "Oh, Andrey Stepanovich, you are too generous. You already gave your meat for the meal!"

Behind Verontzev's back, Joseph waved his hands at Mother and rolled his eyes greedily. "For God's sake," he seemed to scream. "Keep the potatoes!"

"It is good so," said Verontzev. "This will be the first time I will not be eating alone in months."

Mother washed the tubers well and chopped them into very small pieces. "This way they will lend strength to the broth," she announced. It is hard to imagine—we were starving after all—but Mother insisted that we eat the miraculous bounty of this meal in a festive setting. She handed me a white tablecloth, telling me to set the table with the good china. She sent Joseph to the well for fresh water and put our last candle into a silver holder she magically retrieved from a hiding place even we did not know.

When we were seated, the commissar between Mother and me, she served our large bowls of steaming, heavenly soup with great ceremony. Every bowl contained exactly the same amount of soup, as I saw with one quick glance. We had no bread to go with this soup, but Mother had thrown caution to the wind and thrown a good measure of our dried mushrooms into the pot, thereby enriching the stock immeasurably.

Mother prolonged the agony of waiting for the food with a prayer that was much too long for my stomach. I prayed silently for God to forgive me my impatience. At last we dipped our spoons into the soup and began to eat.

"Excellent, Albina Grushova, you have taken scraps of nothing and turned it into a magical dish. I don't think I ever ate better in Moscow's finest restaurants."

"You flatter me, Andrey Stepanovich," smiled Mother gently, but secretly pleased that the soup tasted good.

Joseph and I said nothing at all at the table. We spooned soup into our mouths so fast that Mother admonished us to stop for a moment. "If you eat so fast after fasting for months you will get sick and throw up your food." Oh, heavens, that was not what we wanted to do. No, every morsel, every drop had to remain within our bodies to give us warmth and strength, enabling us to make it through another day.

After the meal I felt warm, wonderful, content, and a bit drowsy. Mother noticed and sent us to bed. "Don't forget to take your hot stones to bed," she reminded us. It did not seem at all strange to me that the commissar lingered, although the food had been consumed a while ago.

From Mother's bed in the kitchen, where I had been sleeping with her and Joseph ever since the onset of the cold, I heard snatches of their conversation. The door was left ajar to let the little warm air emanating from the kitchen penetrate the room. I was asleep the moment my feet touched one of the hot stones wrapped in felt cloth, with another pressed against my chest.

Later Mother told me that the commissar told her of the family he had lost to the war; of the positions he had held, of his academic career and the fact that he was glad to have escaped his past. I think she told him our family story. They must have been thankful to be able to unburden their hearts for a moment.

Only days later, the commissar came to tell Mother that he would be gone for a while. He felt he could not watch the horror of starvation any longer. In an hour he would be on his way to Moscow. There he intended to petition old friends, party greats—anyone he deemed capable of being moved by his story, who might be willing to alleviate the suffering.

The effects of the one good meal we had eaten left us all too soon. Within a day the hunger was gnawing again. I sometimes had hours when I was not hungry anymore, hours when I walked without knowing where I was going or what I was doing. Awakening from these strange somnolent episodes, I was filled with the overwhelming fear that I was losing my mind and would soon be completely insane.

Mother found me sitting on the edge of her bed one day, crying in despair. I confided my fears and she comforted me, consoling me, "It is natural what you experience, love. When the body needs to preserve vital parts it shuts off the energy needed to run the head. Whenever you find yourself in this state, you must go to bed immediately, rest and stay warm. I have experienced these states myself and can assure you that they will cease when you get good food again."

The commissar was gone more than two weeks—those were the most dreadful, terrifying days I remember of that winter. Every time I was outside in the road, I saw moribund people carrying, half dragging, the body of a dead family member to the wagons collecting the dead. This wagon was an ordinary cart pulled by a horse and an ox, two skeletal, unlikely companion beasts. Both were hardly able to pull the cart to the church without men pushing from behind. One by one, whole families disappeared, having deserted this place of starvation and death. They sought to find sustenance in the larger towns, in Norka, Marx and Saratov.

Little did they know that Stalin's curse covered most of country with equally awful misery. You could not run from the hunger, could not outrun death. I was to learn later that the Ukraine suffered as much as the German villages did, because the Russians looked upon them as nothing more than conquered, ignorant, dispensable peasants—another expendable minority to be exploited.

On the day I was ready to meet God, I had pleaded with Him to take me away from this village. "Release me from the pain, Lord," I whimpered. At that moment Mother came into the bedroom where I lay ready to die. She looked at me and knew. "Not yet," she said. "Andrey Stapanovich has returned with food. I have some right here."

On a plate she proffered a piece of bread that she had softened with tea and sprinkled with salt and oil. Oil! I saw it shimmer and wanted to taste it. Mother fed me slowly, bite by little bite, and let me sleep when I had consumed all of it. From that day forward we had regular portions of bread and oil, sometimes even a piece of meat. To my amazement I recovered. It took a long time to get any strength back—but I had survived.

Joseph too made it through the famine. Forever I will marvel at the strength of my mother. What held her together; kept her upright during those days? I know the answer. Nothing but her faith and prayer—God sustained her when death was all around her. Somehow, who knows at what cost, the commissar had procured for us bread, oil and sugar for our tea. Those who had lasted until the commissar's return lived to see spring. No one ever bothered to count the Germans, Ukrainians and Russians who died hunger's death that winter. Later estimates were just that, estimates in a long calculus of deaths throughout the Communists' reign.

The years following the famine were marked by great changes. The empty houses were soon restocked with Ukrainians, whom Stalin's henchmen had torn from their homes and resettled among us. This was done to make another of his dreams become reality, for now he could settle many hundreds of thousands of Russians in the Ukraine, and through their sizeable presence rule and totally control these people so different in their culture from the Russians.

Cautiously, ever so cautiously, the village returned to the *kolkhoz* way of life. We had enough food—enough not to starve. The powers in Moscow supplied the *kolkhoz* with new cows and horses—but not too many. God only knows from whom they had stolen these animals.

A store had opened in the village, a small market in a formerly private home. Here the Reds sold us what they wanted us to buy—not necessarily what we needed or wished for. The store was stocked with crabmeat cans from one of their factory combinates on the Black Sea, which had overproduced for its region, with hair oil from another factory, and of all things, plastic sandals from another of their failing enterprises. Who in our village, with its rutted streets and its dirt and dust, would have been foolish enough to wear these things? So they stayed in the store, gathering dust, losing their color, until one day they were thrown out and burned. A similar fate befell the crabmeat, a food that we did not like and was much too expensive for us. It bulged in its cans, having been improperly sterilized, and some cans exploded to the dismay of the store clerk.

They sold us brown "Mako" cotton stockings that fell apart with little wear, while usually Mako was the finest, strongest Egyptian cotton. They sold us canned tomatoes in summer when we raised our own, and not in winter when we would have been glad to have them; sold us toothpaste that blackened our teeth and pots that could not withstand any wear. What they did not sell was good meat, the sausages we so loved, good bread—their bread was laced with sawdust and rancid butter. They sold two things we prized, but were not always able to buy: sugar and sunflower oil. Of course, we paid dearly with our hard-won rubles—in this way our pelts were shorn twice. First we raised the food with our labor, and then, after taking it away from us, they sold it back to us.

Father's Death

*It is not flesh and blood but the heart
that makes us father and son.*
—JOHANN FRIEDRICH VON SCHILLER

I went back to school. Another teacher had been brought in to replace the horrid Pelkov. Joseph was dispatched to Marx to finish *Oberschule*, and the commissar had started a search for my father. The report returned to him was the saddest letter I ever read. Even today, so many years later, the name "Vorkuta" chills the peoples of Russia to the bone. What is Vorkuta? To all of us—intelligentsia, farmers, minorities, and simple citizens alike— the name to this day means death!

At the turn of the century, huge deposits of coal had been discovered 1,500 miles beyond Moscow, just north of the Arctic Circle in the Pechora basin. The surrounding mountains drain their snowmelt into this basin, forming the source of the Pechora River.

Coal was precious—black gold. The problem was how to mine the black gold in this most inhospitable place, which no man would inhabit by choice. Therefore, from the moment of discovery, it became the favorite place of confinement for political opponents of the government. Without the bare necessities of warm shelter, a stable food supply, proper clothing against the cold, and without appropriate tools, these "convicts" were made to claw the coal from the frozen earth. They were given a norm—in this case, an amount to be produced every day—and without the norm's fulfillment their starvation rations were cut in half or withheld.

Vorkuta thus became hell on earth to those castigated, rejected people, whom a powerful elite sent there to be worked, starved, and frozen to death. It was to this special part of damnation they had sent my father. Here is the report of the commissar's agent:

Commissar Andrey Stepanovitch Verontzev   May 15, 1934
Podstepnaya Kolkhoz

Greetings, comrade Verontzev:
   According to your instructions I visited Vorkuta labor camp and inquired about the prisoner Alexander Petrovich Grushov. As he was not among the living, I asked permission from the camp commander to examine the daily records of the camp. Fortunately the commander, newly appointed to the job, voiced no suspicions and employed an impeccable secretary. Therefore, I soon found the report stating that in December 1928 Grushov had been shot to death by two guards. The records detailed Grushov's part in a detail of men pushing and pulling a cart overflowing with coal from one of the shallow mine shafts, when a wheel on said cart broke and coal spilled all over the track. Here I must explain that the entire operation is very primitive. No tracks for lorries have been laid, and the loads of coal are pulled by means of primitive handcarts over the frozen, deeply grooved, and potholed ground. Seeing the spilled coal, which delayed the operation, a detail of overseers approached the cart and the men. One of the overseers, cursing and screaming, began to lash the prisoners with a long whip, the well-known nagaika. Suddenly Grushov had enough. He grabbed the end of the whip, pulling his tormentor within the range of his arms, and proceeded to strangle the man. He broke his neck in an instant. When the lifeless body fell to the ground, two of the guards killed Grushov in a hail of bullets. There was a remark by the old commander included in the record, stating that he regretted the rashness of his guards. Because Grushov had been one of his best and strongest men, exemplified by the fact that he was able to break a man's neck in the blink of an eye. He mentioned that one could have punished him with a good beating and still used him as the ox he was.
   This is the end of my report. I hope it proves helpful and satisfactory to you.
   Respectfully,
    Vladislav Markovich Starkovsky

The commissar had brought the letter during the midday meal. His hair seemed to be even grayer than before, and his face looked so sad that the gravity of his visit was broadly recorded there. Mother read the letter dry-eyed, but then she went to her room and stayed there for the rest of the day. So they would not dock her pay for the entire day, I asked if I could finish her shift and the commissar gave me permission to fill in for her.

As I performed every one of a hundred familiar motions, I thought about my father's death. Vorkuta explained why we had never heard from him. No news came out of this camp. It was hermetically sealed off from the world, for the *Bonzen* in Moscow did not want the truth of their murderous ways to be known.

Later I was to read that beginning in 1933, Stalin's wave of terror swept every one of his opponents to death, to exile or into labor camps. At that time, Vorkuta grew into a camp of truly enormous proportions. The total physical liquidation of the Trotskyite Left opposition was accomplished in Vorkuta. What had been a primitive beginning of forced coal mining had been established by 1932 into a Gulag with the capacity to kill thousands, after first squeezing every last drop of blood from their bodies. Of course, once the victims arrived by the thousands, their deaths were no longer recorded, except as numbers missing from a work force that never lacked replacements.

Stalin's enemies, or those he perceived as enemies, were legion. At the 1934 Party Congress the members wanted to elect Kirov secretary general instead of Stalin. Kirov was a beloved party figure who would have led the Party in a much more benign manner. The wish of the congressional members to elect him sealed Kirov's fate. Three shots ended his life. To avenge himself on what he perceived to be his enemies, the congress was purged by Stalin—1,100 were consigned to the gulags. Many were killed.

Lifting buckets and forking hay in the calving barn, I remembered Father as I had experienced him. Larger than life, filled with good humor and good will, helpful, protecting the weak, bursting with kindness and fun—that is how I remembered him. He was just the kind of man who would not tolerate being whipped like a dog, for he would never whip a dog or raise his hand against a person weaker than he was.

I saw the picture in my mind: I saw the overturned cart; saw the guard whipping the men, cursing and angry; saw how the anger rose in Father, upward to the head coming deep from the gut. I imagined what he looked like during his last minutes. And I saw before me St. George, the dragon slayer, whom the Catholics revered. Standing tall—ready to meet his end—Father faced the guard and finished him, as St. George had finished the dragon.

But unlike St. George, Father faced not one dragon but a hydra of monsters, forfeiting his life for valor. As much as I had wanted to see my father come home alive, I almost felt better that he had not allowed them to whip him, humiliate him. He died like a man—not a tortured beast—he had taken the cross upon himself.

Late in the evening, Mother said, echoing my own thoughts, "Now we know why we never heard from him. I am glad his torment was cut short." She wiped a few tears from her eyes. "God answered my prayers. If he had lived much longer, his torments would have been unimaginable. His soul would have cried out against fate and he might have doubted his Maker. This way, he died like a man—and his suffering was short."

Joseph said little, but ever since he had read the letter a strange fire burned in his eyes. At sixteen he was as tall and as slim as a birch tree; he had clean, strong limbs and, from afar, the look of a handsome, soft-faced young man. However, close up one detect a few hard lines in his countenance, uncommon in one so young. He had taken an after-school job in Marx, stocking the shelves in a government store. Whenever he came home, he proudly gave Mother his earnings, but more importantly he brought her food and other items that we never saw in the stores near our village.

He told me he thought the store manager stole from the enterprise. I warned him that he would be blamed one day for shortages of goods. "Quit the job, nothing good can come from this," I prophesied.

"No, no! I was extremely lucky to get this plum. I cannot get better paying work anywhere. At least I am always inside, especially in winter when others freeze their toes off outside."

"But you are a German and the thief is a Russian—when the commissars from the NKVD come, you will be blamed."

"I don't think so. I know where he stores the loot and I can turn him in."

"In that case, you better be careful that he does not silence you by killing you," I said cynically.

"You have become a biting misanthrope, Katya. How could you lose your faith in mankind at such a tender age?" he laughed. It was a bitter sarcastic laugh and I knew its meaning exactly. Oh, yes, Russia had molded us with rough hands into cynics as if we were already hoary old men and women.

The antidote to our acidic, distrustful minds, the Church, had been banished into private homes, where a few families still clung to their faith. One had to be careful to worship even in this very private way, because there were spies everywhere noting how many people congregated in any home and, besides that, most homes could not possibly hold many people.

Not long after the fateful letter arrived, the neighbors began to notice how often the commissar sought out our home for a plethora of unrelated reasons. At first, Mother did not react kindly to his visits; but then, after Verontzev persuaded her to walk with him along Podstepnaya Creek one evening, her outlook on these visits changed.

He would always bring her things, courting her in a way few women in the village had ever been attended to. I have to add here that women generally were not treated very well. Their men dictated everything to be done in the home and the field. If a woman objected, there were those men who would not hesitate, striking their wives, beating them, as if they were mindless automatons. The best a disagreeing woman could expect was cold disdain, being ignored.

My father had not been such an authoritarian man. He had adored Mother and treated her with such overarching kindness that she was the envy of the village women. I do not know what it was about Mother that she attracted kind, thoughtful men. Perhaps it was the light of goodness shining from her eyes, surrounding her with an aura of magic, drawing only the best people to her.

Whatever it was, the commissar responded to it. He often brought her food and stayed for dinner. Once, he magically procured a very old wonderful wine, which we were allowed to taste. The two of them drank the rest of the bottle slowly and reverently. It seemed inevitable when, after two years of this courtship, Verontzev proposed marriage to my mother.

I had been sitting on the little front porch on a mild evening in June. The windows stood wide open, and so I heard how, inside, this kind man begged my mother to marry him. "I can make life easier for you and your children, Albina Grushova. I love you dearly and, becoming my wife, you would make me so happy."

Mother stewed over his proposal for days. At that time I was becoming a romantic, and I wanted Mother to have a companion when, inevitably, Joseph and I went into the world. I had decided that I would not stay in the village but would try to escape the drudge of the *kolkhoz* through education, a plan Mother approved wholeheartedly. To that purpose I had enrolled in a school of higher learning for girls in Marx. I had been a good student to begin with but had greatly enlarged my intellectual horizon with Mother's and Joseph's help.

The latter carried uncounted numbers of books for me in his satchel when he visited us. Mother drilled me in French, Russian and geography. She read and recited poetry for me, sharpening my memory skills by insisting that I learn many poems by heart. Joseph drilled me in mathematics, a subject at which he excelled, and history. From all this I was well on my way to compete one day at university.

Having this goal firmly fixed in mind, I was concerned for Mother and therefore strongly advocated for marriage to the commissar. "You are still young, Mama, with many years ahead of you. It would be nice if you had a man to look after you, help you and even spoil you a little. Verontzev is a good man. I know that. He is worthy of you."

"How would you know such a thing? You are a young girl dreaming romantic dreams."

"No, I am not. I am basing my words on reason and facts." And then I told Mother with bold candor about the night the commissar had caught me returning the gasoline can to the tractor. Mother was horrified, hearing of my exploit. She was even more agitated when she realized that Joseph had indeed torched Pelkov's house.

Calming her and extracting a vow of silence cost me the best part of an evening. "You cannot ruin four dear people with misplaced honesty," I said. "Would you have all of us cast into Siberia? Joseph and Arkady committed arson to punish this man for sending Father to the gulag. He deserved his fate!" After this outburst Mother had no more arguments left and folded her sails. However, hearing that the commissar had protected her children began to weigh heavily in his favor.

Romance Is in the Air

Love is patient and kind; love is not jealous or boastful;
it is not arrogant or rude; it does not rejoice at wrong,
but rejoices in the right.
—1 CORINTHIANS 13:4

The next time he asked her for her hand, she said yes. They set the date for July of the following year. Of course, the commissar wished the ceremony to take place as soon as possible, but Mother, perhaps plagued by premonitions, insisted on the delay. On a personal note, I remember that 1936 was the best year of my teen years. I turned fifteen during that summer and finally attracted some attention when I came home from Marx for vacation. The few young men left in the village always seemed to know when I went walking with Mother. We would meet some of them as if by accident in awkward-looking groups of two or three.

At Kirmes, the thanksgiving for the harvest, there was a dance. We had been lucky. The weather had held and stayed dry, keeping the temperature bearable for an outdoor event. Everyone, whether they were Russian, Ukrainian or German, enjoyed dances. These people, thrown together by the powers in Moscow, had learned to make the best of it. They joined each others' dances, giving it their all on the dance floor.

Arkady, now a young man, came and asked me to dance with him. I was flattered, for he was by far the best dancer present and the most handsome of the young men's crop. I danced every dance until the music stopped. Catching my breath between fast-paced whirling and high stepping, I thought that for this small moment in time I had been transformed into a light, sylph-like creature, able to fly effortlessly through the air and glide high above the rough surface of reality.

It was nice to flirt with Arkady, knowing the other girls watched with envy. It was even more gratifying that he looked at me as an equal, as a grown woman. It was tingly-pleasant to feel his hands on mine during a round dance, feel his strength when he swung me about, and see his dark, hot eyes in his smiling face shine down upon me. We did not dance exclusively with one another, because a few times I was asked by other men first and had to oblige; yet he always came back to me as soon as he could.

At last the musicians played their last song, a slow waltz. Arkady came and asked me for the dance.

"Ah, little Katya, how you have grown: into a very wonderful, pretty woman who makes one forget the precocious, daring, nosy girl that saved Joseph and me from years in prison," he said, when we were slowly waltzing at the edge of the crowd.

"What do you mean?" I asked cautiously.

"I know who hid the gas can and then made it reappear."

"What are you implying?" I pretended not to understand.

"I saw you the night when you dug out the gas can in your short little dress. I saw you take it to the tractor, and I saw the commissar, who came upon the scene just as I wanted to approach you. He took you home, and I was behind you all the way, making sure he would not hurt you."

"But how did you know what I would be doing that particular night?" I asked nonplussed.

"I did not know anything, but it was such a beautiful night that I was on my way to your house to pick up Joseph for a hike to the Volga. The mighty one is magical during the silvery nights. Instead of finding Joseph,

I saw you slip from your house. Of course I was very curious. More even, I became concerned for you and decided to be your shadow."

"Oh, Lord, so you have known all along? Did you tell Joseph?"

"Yes, I did, but we decided to keep silent. It was too dangerous to talk, even to you. But we were very grateful and very proud of you."

Just then the music stopped, our movements slowed, and Arkady bent down and kissed my forehead. He led me back to Mother who sat between the commissar and her friend Anna Baumeister. Arkady bade us a good night, and walked into the night like a prince without a country— proud and a little sad. Mother wrapped a warm shawl around me because the night had become rather cold. On the walk home she said cryptically, "Forget Arkady for a good while, *mein Kind*. You are much too young yet for romance and you must concentrate on school."

I knew the truth of her words only too well. And yet, this evening had been enchantingly wonderful with its paper lanterns, its campfire, starlight and the fiery music. So delightfully magical that no one had noticed the clay-stamped ground and the dust we had stirred up, staining our shoes and stockings! This evening was proof that the human soul needs more than just fulfillment of basic physical needs. We need sheer exaltation and joy to sustain us. I fervently believe that innocent joy brings us closer to God.

A few days later I returned to Marx and my studies without having seen Arkady again. I enjoyed my years at the high school very much. We had only one Russian teacher, a quiet dreamer of a man, teaching us the subtleties of the Russian language. His soul was filled with the beauty of Russian poetry.

When he read from the works of Lermontov, Pushkin, and Shcherbatova he could bring us to tears. We all liked him—had crushes on him— because, besides being a romantic, he was also a handsome man in a tall, velvety-dark way.

The other teachers—Germans all—were intelligent and surprisingly well educated. I say surprising with emphasis, for generally not much learning was credited to educators of our remote region.

Somehow the director of the school, an energetic, large, hefty man, had managed to keep the school operating and undisturbed through Soviet conflicts and purges. How he had accomplished these feats, I cannot imagine to this day. Perhaps the credit was due some of the star pupils who had become established in government circles.

I did not board at school but was lucky enough to be taken in by the same family that had cared for Joseph in earlier years. Joseph, with the help of the commissar, had advanced to university and gone away to study in Saratov.

The past few years of our lives could have been called almost normal. If it had not been for the constant balancing act on the edge of the abyss, one could have believed that all would be well one day. I, however, could not convince myself that such hope would become reality. In my mind, I always saw our village and its people in the total eclipse of traumatic, evil events. I was never disabused of my gloomy outlook for as long as I lived in Russia.

No Wedding for Mother

Another year passed, and the day for Mother's wedding came closer. The date had been set for the second of July. It was the beginning of June and I had just returned for summer vacation. We were having a mild, pleasant summer for a change. The *kolkhoz*, which had been named *Prekrasniy Mir*, "wonderful peace," had planned a grand party.

It was meant to honor the outstanding workers of the commune with medals, awards, food, and a dance. The event was to take place on a sandy flat outside the village. For weeks the men had put up benches, set up tables, and had worked to produce a plank floor. As progress was being made the sand flat began to look so inviting that the commissar told Mother this was the place where their wedding should be celebrated.

Shy at first, disdaining an ostentatious display of happiness and good fortune, Mother fought the idea, until he marched her to the place and said, "Look—this way the people might get two festivities instead of one. You are giving them a blessing." Convinced, Mother agreed.

Two days later, a black limousine arrived in the village, disgorging four ugly, hard-faced men. I saw them come toward the office, because I was inside, sitting on a desk, adding figures for the *kolkhoz* secretary. Verontzev had given me this summer job—a plum if ever there was one—and I tried to acquit myself well. I was actually of help, for the secretary, Sonja Vertayev, was an unfit accountant. Because of this circumstance I sat in the center of the brewing storm.

The four men perambulated more than walked toward the office, turning about frequently, scanning the street and the houses. They entered the office without knocking, as if they were expected. They neither introduced themselves nor stated the purpose of their appearance. I had seen men such as they were a few times before, and thought, "Dear God, preserve us! NKVD—whom are they here for?"

Despite the warm weather they all wore long, light jackets, almost reaching to their knees. However, the looseness of their jackets could not quite hide the telltale bulges of weapons. One of the men, short, but very broad shouldered, with a pockmarked face and cold fish eyes, slouched into a chair across from the desk which Sonya and I shared. He casually pulled a gun from his jacket pocket and, pointing it, said, "Put your hands on the desk, and don't move until I say you can."

The other men had disappeared into Verontzev's office. We heard a few dispassionate, calm words float through the open door—much too low to understand. Moments later the commissar walked out ahead of the three men, his face a drawn scape of despair. The NKVD men behind him seemed to be blocks of carved ice.

Verontzev stopped before our desk. Looking deep into my eyes, as if conveying an important message, he said, "Something unavoidable has just come up. I must leave and attend to it. Please tell your mother that the wedding has been put off, Katya." I saw that he blinked back tears, and I heard tears in his voice. He faced Sonya, "Goodbye, Sonya Vertayev, you were a great help to me. Goodbye, Katya."

At that, the group left the office and casually walked to the waiting limousine. Sonya and I, our hands still frozen on the desktop, watched how they pushed the commissar into the back seat between two of them and then, cold as Volga ice in the deepest of winter, they drove away.

For the longest time Sonya and I sat there, incapable of movement, until I jumped up, stung by the horrible thought that I would have to tell Mother the awful news about poor, dear—yes, beloved Andrey Stepanovich Verontzev. Suddenly I screamed. How could I tell Mother what I had just witnessed? How could I look into her eyes and tell her?

I looked through the window and saw a group of men in the street, shaking angry, impotent fists in the direction of the car's disappearance. Everyone liked Verontzev, especially after having experienced other commissars before. They mourned him already. I now was cold and calm. I touched my cheek and felt no tears. I had not cried, had no more tears—only screams.

I left Sonya crying in the office. She was a fortyish, red haired, freckled, plump mother of three who had been transplanted here from some small town in Ukraine. She had never gotten over the shock of having been made homeless and mistreated by the Communists.

Bad news and death travel with the same lightening speed. When I reached our house I found Mother inside, sitting crying at the kitchen table. She had already heard from a neighbor that the NKVD had picked up Andrey.

"They will not rest, Katya, until every good *Mensch* has been eliminated. They will exterminate all of us until only monsters and ghouls inhabit Russia," she cried, rent by a terrible pain. When she spoke her voice was as sharp and shrill as that of a fury, not like my mother's at all.

"He was a good man. Why would they take him away?"

"Why did they take Papa? They need no reasons—they make up their facts as they need them." For a moment we were silent. I was thinking of my father who had been torn from us for no other cause than the evil denunciations by a jealous man.

"Perhaps our people were too happy with him?" I ventured. "Maybe he did not flog us, punish, or starve us often enough? Who knows? I doubt that even they know why they came for him."

Mother stilled her tears, "I am thinking of the poor man, what he must have felt when they came, what he must feel right now." She raised her ravaged face to countenance mine. "You saw it, didn't you? Saw how they came and led him away. You must tell me every detail—I want to know all."

I told her every horrible detail from beginning to the end. "His last words, his thoughts and concerns were for you. He burned into my eyes the message that it killed him to leave you. His voice was laced with tears; he barely could contain himself."

"The poor, decent man will be consigned to hell by these tyrants," said Mother, "We must begin to pray for him right now. Perhaps God will be gracious and help him to clear himself of whatever they accuse him."

I think Mother's words adumbrated his fate. God granted him release from an awful fate, for three days after his disappearance, Arkady found the commissar's dead body in a remote part of the *kolkhoz*, far, far out in the steppe. The killers had shot him through the head, even before they had left the boundaries of the village. The land where they threw his body was remote. Usually no one would have gone into this wild corner of our land except to pasture livestock there the following spring. I believe God wanted Andrey Stepanovich found, sending Arkady on a tractor to look for a lost cow.

We prepared Andrey's body for a proper burial in the way we did for our own. We did not know whether he was an Orthodox believer, an atheist, or if he had his own covenant with God. In sheer defiance of the murderous NKVD and their handlers, we gave Andrey Stepanovich

Verontzev the biggest funeral we ever had in the village. They had expected him to decay in anonymity—forgotten, erased from the minds of our people, deprived of loving thoughts and remembrances. Their malicious design, however, was foiled. With a large head stone praising his goodness, he would be forever with us in the village. No matter how many of us were killed or died, there would always be someone left to remember him.

Life continued sadly, besieging us with well-worn slogans and party pronouncements. A huge painting of Stalin—"Father of the Country"—was hoisted between two tree trunks and permanently put in place right beside our beloved old church. Our people, eclipsed by grief and horror, expressed their suppressed fury by spitting at the ground when walking by the picture. It was not long before the new commissar forbade spitting within a hundred meters of Stalin's icon.

Soon, the people began to make the sign of the cross when walking by the picture. You know already what I am about to tell you now. Yes, crossing oneself also was forbidden. As soon as the commissar, a true obedient apparatchik of the Moscow autocracy, saw what the people did he posted a warning, threatening two days confinement in the jail. He could not forbid, however, that henceforth the people smiled at the picture.

Preparing for War

In 1939, a Non-Aggression Pact was signed by the ministers of foreign affairs, Molotov for Russia and Ribbentrop for Germany. Momentarily the German hatred cooled. I was in my last year of high school in Marx. Because of my exceptional grades and the quality of my work during the socialist activities I had been forced to absolve—I was supposed to follow in Joseph's footsteps, who at twenty-one was an outstanding mathematician at university.

The German minority did not trust the momentary appeasement arising from the Non-Aggression Pact. Many, taking advantage of the opportunity of temporary German-Russian unity, left Russia. In 1940, 80,000 Germans left Bessarabia for the Warthegau in Germany. Mother tried to get papers for the three of us to leave also. Yet our commissar and the authorities along the Volga did not want to lose their slaves. Therefore, Mother could never attain the papers necessary for us to leave, no matter how hard she tried. There was worse to come for me.

Despite my grades and achievements I had been denied a study opportunity at Saratov University and was living once again in the village. At first the new commissar was bent on breaking me, the "arrogant" academic overachiever, by placing me into the horse barn. He could not have done me a greater favor. I loved the creatures with a passion and rejoiced being removed from the designs of fickle, mean people. I could relax around the creatures, enjoying myself in a simple fashion.

However, it was not long before he needed my help. His books did not show the *kolkhoz* to advantage. In truth, they showed him to be an abysmally incapable person. He had picked me to doctor his pages of incompetent documentation, wishing me to turn them in a favorable light. I struggled mightily, not knowing what to do. On one hand, I wanted the truth about him to get out loud and clear—for he tormented the people— on the other hand, I could not risk defying him. With the stroke of his pen he could eliminate Mother, Joseph and me.

Fate intervened once more, in the middle of my dilemma, when I was trying to manipulate numbers in the most favorable yet honest way. On June 22, 1941, Germany attacked Russia. The war began with an assault on the Black Sea city of Odessa, which was besieged by Romanian and German troops. When this news arrived on the Volga, the slumbering hate against Germans exploded once more, turning into a raging fire. Stalin, lacking any military qualification, immediately assumed the command of Soviet Commissar for Defense and thereby became commander of the entire Red Army.

Within weeks, most young men, but especially Germans and Ukrainians, were inducted into the army. Joseph was never even allowed to come home to pack his kit. We got word that he was with his regiment already and Mother could bring his necessities to the barracks. Hastily, before they could move him out, we packed his kit with what we thought he needed. We were so concerned with his physical needs that the awful truth of Joseph going to war, having to kill or be killed, had not yet fully been driven into our consciousness. We went to Saratov with the commissar's special permission.

On the ferry from Marx we met Arkady. He, too, was being deployed. Although he was older than the group generally inducted, the fact that he was still unmarried made him a perfect target. I had never seen Arkady looking better. Tanned, strong, white teeth shining in a smiling mouth, he seemed invincible.

He perceived our worries, our pain of sending beloved people into the killing fields, but made light of it. He had not been raised in the church or with much spiritual teaching. So, here he was laughing, "Not to worry, sweet ladies. The Almighty has already decided if we live or die. If he favors us with life, we will come back to you." He bit into a piece of black bread married to an enormous slab of bacon, and flashed his strong teeth.

He crushed us to his chest as if he could take us with him when we parted in Saratov, grinning endearingly at me, while saying, "Wait for me, my princess—I am coming back for you." A moment later, he was swallowed up among a throng of men reporting for duty.

We found Joseph in the midst of chaos and were given ten minutes to say goodbye. Joseph was sad, not to say depressed. Like most Russian soldiers he had internalized the belief that one did not easily come back from war. He shared Arkady's view that his fate had already been decided. It pained him not to know how his life would play out—he liked to be prepared. Mother spent our last minutes with him, reminding him of God's grace and mercy and the power of prayer. "Remember the only important thing is to live righteously. Do what you must according to your own convictions, which are not always those of your superiors."

Her talk strengthened him, fortified him with a new outlook on what he would encounter on the battlefield. The camp guards rudely ended our goodbyes, roughly escorting us from the camp's enclosure.

Back home, Mother and I were all alone, and we were afraid. The news coming from the front documented Stalin's ignorance. The Germans advanced with frightening strength and unbelievable speed. On August 28, 1941, the Germans took Dnjepropetrovsk. The Russian-Germans in that region escaped in droves to Germany.

On the same day, the Upper Soviet of the Soviet Union released the infamous order to dissolve the Republic of the Volga German minority and ordered the deportation of all Russian-German citizens to Siberia and Middle-Asia.

Satellite to the Sun

MOSCOW
KRASNODARSKAYA ULITZA, #425, 3RD FLOOR
APARTMENT OF MARYONNA IVANOVNA KULOVA
MARCH 30, 1939

Maryonna Kulova, at 65, gray-haired, rotund, with a wrinkled apple-face, embodied the Russian woman of the working class. Motherly, tired, worn by heavy work and never-ending worry, she nonetheless stood in her small kitchen and with deft hands prepared the dishes her son, Alyosha, preferred above all others. Her swollen ankles and misshapen feet were the direct result of 45 years of standing and walking slowly back and forth, tending a machine in a meat-and-sausage factory.

Her hands and fingers were not plump by nature, but fluid filled, and the joints were blown up by arthritis. And yet, she hummed, like a twenty-year-old, '*Raszvetaly yablony y grushy*,' an ancient folk song, because soon her one and only treasure in life, Alyosha, would come and have a meal with her, as he did once a week.

The last of her bliny came golden-brown out of her frying pan; the borscht, hot and smelling sweetly of beets, simmered in her largest pot. The piece of pork in the oven filled the kitchen with the smell of roast and garlic—oh, yes, she was ready. "What incredible luck I had today to get pork," she thought to herself, for meat was hard to come by. Often when she found meat, she didn't have enough money to buy it.

She remarked to herself that things had been better lately, because now Alyosha had a position as an aid to a high-ranking Soviet official. Disturbing her was the secrecy that went along with this job. He would not tell her the name of the official, nor would he say what his job entailed. At first, he had been very happy and excited, but lately he had always been depressed when he visited. A few times he had even cancelled his visits, throwing her into deep despair, for he was all she lived for. Since she had divorced his father, a mean drunk who would have killed her and her small boy eventually, Alyosha was all the family she had. For the most part, she was self-sufficient and content with the way things were.

For a fact, since Alyosha's promotion, their money situation had been much improved. With such thoughts, she moved from the miniscule kitchen, endowed with one small counter, an open shelf for pots and dishes, a two-burner stove, sink and small oven, to an area that served as eating and living space. On the far end of the room was the only window, a medium-sized opening, adorned with a grayish lace drape that remembered better days. Try as she might Maryonna had never succeeded in whitening this precious piece of lace, although she soaked it for hours in soda water and applied those appropriate chemicals she was able to get in the poorly stocked pharmacy.

As she removed a bottle of vodka from a shelf, where it was hidden between an old atlas and a volume of Karl Marx, a special knock on her door announced Alyosha. He had trained her long ago never to open the door to any other knock. Young no-goodniks, thugs roamed Moscow at will, and one had to be careful. "One of these days," so he assured her, "the Party will clean up the lawless ilk, and decent people will fear no more."

"Alyosha," she called out, "is that you?"

"*Da*, Mama." Satisfied by his voice, Maryonna opened the door by pushing aside a bolt, opening the lock.

The moment she laid eyes on her boy, she began to worry. He was pale, thinner than last time. There was a haunted look around his eyes. Maryonna contained herself, drawing her worries in. There would be time to probe later. Now he had to eat, relax, and let go of that which bothered him. She stood on tiptoes, getting her usual kiss on the forehead and a bear hug, for Alyosha was a tall, broad fellow with powerful arms and great strength.

"Come, Alyosha, let me feed you some borscht and bliny to start with. Eat something, *lyubko*, and you will feel better."

"No, Mother. I can't eat right now. Just give me some vodka. I need a strong drink."

"Alyosha, what's wrong? You never drink before you eat."

Her son, blond, blue-eyed, with heavy brows that almost joined over the bridge of the nose, rubbed the square chin of his high-cheeked, Slavic face. His well-defined, generous mouth softened the otherwise strong, masculine features. He closed his eyes and rubbed his face some more, as if to erase a clinging unpleasantness. She gazed at her child adoringly. Scrutinizing his tired features, eyes closed, skin drawn and tense, she realized that at this moment he looked much older than his 32 years.

His mother handed him a well-filled water glass of vodka. *Sto gram*, 100 ml, that was how the men liked to drink their vodka. As the former wife of a drunk, she did not approve of liquor, but in this case she deemed it medicine.

"If it would only loosen his tongue so he could unburden himself," she thought to herself. She firmly believed, like most mothers, that she could help her child if only she were consulted.

Alyosha drank deeply and put the half-empty glass on the table. For a moment they sat in deep silence across from each other at the set table. Maryonna looked down upon her miserable table coverlet. Instead of her fine cloth, she was reduced to using this waxed covering because washing had become a terrible chore for her. Soap was hard to come by, as was toilet paper, heating and cooking fuel, fresh fruit, butter and oil, together with almost anything else. "It was better under the Tsar," she thought, and then berated herself for such treason. "I was one of those clamoring for the Revolution, and now I don't like it much. Nothing much has changed, except for the ones on top skimming off the cream. For me—it remains all the same."

Alyosha tossed back the rest of the drink, sighing deeply. A moment thereafter he said: "I can eat now, Mother."

Maryonna ambled painfully into the kitchen. There was always a sharp, painful stiffness in her joints after sitting down for a while, but she ignored the torment she lived with every day of her life. She ladled the borscht into two soup plates, dainty relics of another time. She finished the soup by adding two large dollops of sour cream to each bowl. She smiled, remembering how she had obtained the sour cream. It had cost her a lipstick, for which she had paid double the price at the druggist, just so she would have a trading item for the store girls. Nowadays it was not enough to pay for food; no, to attain something a little better, you had to bribe the clerks who hid the best, the special things under the counters or in the back of the store. She served the borscht, and limped back for the platter of bliny.

For a while they ate in companionable silence. When she served the roast, smelling deliciously decadent and rich, accompanied by potatoes, exuding the aroma of the bacon and onions they were fried with, Alyosha again filled his glass from the vodka bottle and drank.

"*Ochen horosho, Mamochka*, very good, Mom," he acknowledged. Then, having mulled his dilemma over and again in his mind, he decided to confide in her.

"I will tell you a secret, Mother, that you must guard with your life. You can never talk about it to anyone, for my life depends on silence."

"Alyosha, of course, you know me. I would die before I would hurt you. I know it will help you if you can talk to me. You know what they say: 'Two heads are better than one'."

"Well then," sighed Alyosha. "You know that six months ago I was offered a promotion. I told you that I became aide-de-camp to an important person." He drank more from the water glass, gazing meaningfully into his mother's eyes.

"Well, the important person is none other than Josef Vissarionovich Stalin."

His mother's fork clattered onto her plate. "Joseph and Mary," her cry was almost a moan, reaching far back into her Orthodox upbringing.

"Oh, son, such honor; our wonderful leader—your boss."

"Don't say that, Mama. Wonderful leader! Comrade Stalin! Oh, how they love him, the idiots. They just do not know. The man is a monster, the devil incarnate, and I am doomed."

"Alyosha, dearest, don't say such things. You will kill me with such frightful pronouncements. It cannot be so bad. I am a simple woman; tell me all so I can understand. And what of Stalin? I have never heard a bad word about him. To the contrary, they praise him at my factory all day long."

Alyosha's face was cloudy with worry. Now, Maryonna noticed for the first time the dark circles under his eyes and a slight tick high on the left cheek, as he concentrated on the task of how to explain his predicament to her.

Ages ago, before the Communists had ordered him to report for officer's training, he had been a happy scholar working on his Ph.D. He was teaching while studying Russian literature; he delighted in the word. For a moment he was lost in reverie. Snatches of verses and philosophical quotes rose in his mind. Suddenly he quoted from Goethe's drama *Faust*: "The devil is a sophist…", and added, "Stalin is such a one. He is a sophist. There is no evil that he can not explain away with a rationale."

"What is a sophist?" a lost Maryonna wanted to know.

"Someone who uses clever, specious reasoning. Reasoning that has the ring of truth, but is far from truth, righteousness and goodness. It is a way of explaining with deceptive and fallacious terms that which leads good people to do bad things."

He sighed, "Oh, Mother, if you only knew. Do you remember how happy I was when they selected me to become an officer? How I thought that now I could truly serve our people, that I would defend our new nation and help build better lives. Hah, I was enthralled by damned, stupid idealism! I believed all that Marxist mush of workers' rights and freedom, education for the deprived; the blather of serfs emancipated, their burdens lifted. I followed all of Lenin's speeches, swallowing with pleasure the poisonous broth the Reds served; together with the rest of my comrades, I believed it all."

Agitated, Alyosha walked about the cramped room, his vodka glass filled once again. He stopped, looked into Mayonna's face and begged: "Do not let them pick me up while I am drunk. Lie to them if they come, and let me sleep it off first."

She promised, and he slumped down upon the well-worn sofa and its green, velvet-covered plushness. He reclined, closed his eyes and began telling his story.

He had to go way back to the time when he began to disbelieve the tales of the Bolsheviks. They were the days of officer's training. Everyone selected for officer's training was imbued with similar attributes. The chosen were as physically fit as they were mentally bright. They had been as dedicated to the Revolution and an end to tsarism as they had been capable of inspiring and leading others.

And then, long before receiving his commission, Alyosha had observed with anguish that some of the best and brightest of his classmates were culled from the ranks and disappeared. First to go was Jossy Mandelovsky. Jossy's Jewish name had long been adapted to the Russian form by adding the "ovsky." He was one of the few truly scientific scholars in the program, and their commander had been grooming him to become an important part of military intelligence. Jossy seemed eminently suited to this task until the day the Politburo heavies and the NKVD came to do evaluations and examinations of the cadets. The next thing the cadets knew, Jossy was gone and with him a few other men Alyosha had not known as well as Jossy.

Alyosha groaned as if in pain, the vodka having loosened the tight control he usually exercised over his emotions. He continued his tale, his voice strained and animated by the excruciating subject and drink.

"Later that year, again after a visit from the Politburo, more of our classmates packed their belongings. They told everyone that they had been ordered to serve in special units. Petka Kovalsky, a teacher of languages from Moscow; Pavel Kamilov, an engineer from Kiev; Vladimir Bukovsky, who had been a historian in St. Petersburg before being ordered to attend the academy, and many more left in this manner. Strangely enough, no one heard from them again, which was most surprising for we had been a very close-knit group. When news finally arrived, it was of their deaths, passed along to us in friends' secretive reports."

Alyosha then told his mother how brave men, risking their lives, had documented how the cream of Russia's youth had been thrown, undeservedly and unprepared, into war situations guaranteed to kill large numbers of them.

"Stalin was then the political commissar of the Red Army. Mother, he personally supervised military actions in the civil war where our troops fought the Whites on three fronts. The great generals, Kolchak, Denikin, and Pyotr Wrangel, led the Whites. In an incredible slaughter, thousands of young Russian men had been killed on both sides. Especially our troops were decimated because an incompetent led them fighting a war against proven, savvy generals and troops. For a while, it looked as if the Whites were going to win the internal struggle. However, our 'beloved Stalin' who was neither bound by feelings for the Russian people (he was after all Georgian) nor troubled by a conscience—what were lives compared to his power—found ways to turn the tide." Alyosha's voice dripped with sarcasm.

Maryonna's round, rough, wrinkled face mirrored the horror she felt, hearing her son's terrible tale. If another person had told her such things, she would have called for his arrest—but this was her son. He was the good boy who had always told the truth even when it was to his disadvantage, the one who had always been loving and kind to her, the only man she could trust completely.

"Alyosha, my child, why don't we hear about these things? Why is it not written in the papers?"

"I will tell you, Mama. By now Stalin has complete control of the newspapers. Nothing gets printed without the approval of the Party. Anyone with knowledge of atrocities has averted their eyes, has been either silenced or been killed."

"On Stalin's orders, the NKVD entered the battlefield, and stood without scruples behind all officers. They instantly executed officers who showed reluctance to throw their men into a hopeless battle. We call these fights a meat grinder. Furthermore, your beloved leader devilishly ordered all grains and other foods confiscated. Thereby, he starved the peasants, the kulaks, the Cossacks, in short those supporting the Whites, because they discerned in us the menace to democracy that we were. Stalin personally ordered anyone disagreeing with the plans of the Bolsheviks brutally tortured, imprisoned and killed."

"Of course, it took many months before reports of such treachery seeped back into the academy, but before long it was obvious even to the densest of cadets that young men stemming from academic and bourgeoisie families were sent to lose their lives in situations deemed futile by their leaders. They were as faithful to the Party as you and I, but Stalin killed them anyway."

Alyosha had been speaking nonstop. Now he reached for his great-coat and pulled from its pocket a small leather pouch, some thin pieces of paper and a matchbox. By stuffing *machorka* from the pouch into a v-shape of paper, he dexterously rolled up a cigarette, which he closed by licking the paper edges. Maryonna watched him indulgently as he brushed a piece of tobacco from his lips. She hated the cigarettes, she hated the smell, but what was she to do? He did not smoke enough to warrant complaints from her; and so she just pushed a saucer across the table for his ashes. The smoke from his cigarette formed tender, gray clouds above his head, and with his eyes closed, he returned to his narrative.

"So, you see Mama, the horrible truth is prevented from riding home fast in a troika. No, it has to walk slowly on its own legs, avoiding pitfalls. This is why few people know about the killings, about the exiles to Siberian gulags, to Vorkuta and the other torture chambers." Alyosha sighed, as if he alone carried the burden, the secret.

"Life became frightening and strange then, Mother." He recalled how a little poem written on a toilet wall had caused a firestorm of hysteria at the academy. It was political disaster in the making, controlled only by the cool head of the academy commander. He swore to secrecy those men who had seen the offensive ditty, threatening to hurt loose mouths; then he had the offending wall painted. The offending poem had extolled the interesting fact that Stalin, political commissar of the army, had blundered with his war decisions against Poland. It had decried the lives lost because of his vanity.

The moment Alyosha fully understood the treachery that had befallen his classmates, he had at first felt tremendous relief to be safe. After all, he was one of the cherished worker-serf children. Oh, yes, he more than others qualified for party favors. In contrast, Mother's education, if six years of grade school counted as such, had made employment other than menial work impossible.

For as long as he could remember, she had slaved in that stinking meat factory. Her hair and her clothes reeked forever of blood and offal; her legs, varicose-veined and always burning with pain, could be relieved as little by warm water footbaths as her hair could be cleansed of the smell by washing with chamomile.

Oh, yes, he was a worker's child. Yet, after feeling the passing relief of being one of the chosen, there had come the enormous wave of self-disgust. Curses upon him! What kind of a human was he that he had rejoiced in the fickle safety bestowed on him by birth? No fault, flaw or rumor of treason could have been laid upon the heads of the poor fellows that had been shunted off—sacrificial lambs to communist expediency. They had been as idealistic and fervent in their zeal for the Revolution as the rest of their cohorts, perhaps more so, especially those chaps from academic families. Their backgrounds, for those still alive, predicted a most ominous future. Steeped early in life in the beliefs of secular humanism, they had clamored louder, more forcefully, for change than fellows like Alyosha, who had to study long and hard before they could connect other tenets and theories to the dictates of Marx and Engels.

The reasons for the extermination of these young men who were condemned by their "counterrevolutionary backgrounds" became apparent later, when rumors of the struggles between Lenin and his protégé Stalin surfaced. Stalin, born to Russian Orthodox parents and destined for the priesthood, became a rabid iconoclast and hater of the middle class. That was the point where he parted from Lenin's view of Russia's future. Lenin by no means wanted to destroy the underpinnings of the entire social order; he wanted to excise unwanted portions of classes selectively. Stalin, however, the "man of steel," a name the former Josef Vissarionovich Dzugashvili had chosen for himself, strove viciously to eradicate those people, who, whether by inheritance or the work of their hands and minds, had more material wealth than he had known in his childhood.

Alyosha, idealistic, romantic, and good by nature and upbringing, had observed more and more the glaring moral flaws in his leaders and teachers—the injustices they perpetrated in the name of the Party. His confidence shaken, he eyed with suspicion even the most commonplace occurrences and detected a politically correct lawlessness, a ruthlessness to further communist goals even when they ran counter to every dictate of humanism. He began to fear for classmates' lives, prayed for the lives of outspoken teachers and then, as if his treasonous thoughts could be read, he began to fear for himself.

At times, he felt as if he had been cast into Dante's Inferno and was condemned to descend daily into the chasm of hell. Upon perceiving demotions, defamations and lives lost or destroyed, all in the fierce struggle of a few men to assume supreme power, he suffered the agonies of a righteous man cast among psychopaths.

Soon, his predicament fixed in his mind an image of himself as the proverbial Russian dancing bear. He felt that, like the bear—proud symbol of Russia's significance—he, too, once captured, was made to dance on hot metal plates, performing to the tunes played by his tormentors. For months he agonized over ways to extricate himself from this torturous net he was caught in. However, as he turned the facts over in his mind, the only option open seemed to commit suicide. A decent human being at heart, he contemplated the thought with gravity. In the end, his youth and the thoughts of his lonely mother and all her sacrifice for him had won out. He berated himself as spineless, cursed himself with appellations such as coward, rotten dog, and worthless scum, and yet he lived. And so, unable to remove himself from his situation, he did as he was told. He kept his discontent and despair to himself, and worked ceaselessly to become the most inconspicuous of cadets. A fisherman's proverb was foremost in his mind: Always swim in the middle of the school; on top the seabirds catch the fish, on the bottom the sharks.

He graduated fourth in his class, good enough to show application, but not with the excellence required for a top commission. He had planned it this way. They could not fault him for being a slacker, neither could they send him on fast-track assignments where he would be forced to make life and death decisions on a daily base, perhaps kill innocent civilians and, by such feats, rise quickly through the ranks.

"You see, Mother, even then, I doubted and worried. Later, came my service on the front. One quickly finds the best and the worst qualities in one's fellow men on the front lines. Fortunately for me, my commander, Alexander Tolkovsky, was a great man; a man of courage and conviction, whose orders I could follow willingly. He was a man of reason, allowing for initiative, and so I could distinguish myself. Because I was prudent, I refused to sacrifice men when stealth and wiliness would serve."

Alyosha had fallen silent, reminiscing. He drank more vodka. Maryonna noticed that by now he should have been quite drunk, but that the alcohol had not affected him at all. He was totally lucid, slightly agitated perhaps, but not impaired.

Sitting upright once more across from his mother, he peered into her eyes and asked: "Do you remember when I came home from the hospital after the bomb blast got me?"

"How could I forget? My fear, the sheer terror, thinking that you might have died. Then came the note, the blessed relief that you were alive and unharmed."

"Unharmed, yes. Except for the temporary deafness. That became the problem, and is my cursed dilemma still."

"What do you mean? The deafness was temporary only, and your hearing is fully restored."

"Oh, Mother! If only you knew. Do you know how I got my promotion? It was neither my sterling performance on the front, nor my academic achievement. No, I was promoted because I was deaf. My commander received a directive from Stalin to furnish him with an adjutant. Tolkovsky allowed me to read the order. It stated therein that a bright, young officer of good disposition should be sent to the Kremlin, preferably one with a hearing problem. I seemed to be the only one fitting the bill."

Alyosha eyed his mother glumly. His short silvery blond hair, tousled by his restless hands, stood in spiky islands upon his head, and his eyes were reddened. It seemed as if speaking caused him emotional pain, but he pulled up the thread of his story once more.

"Tolkovsky was almost grieving when he told me, 'I have to send you, Alyosha. I have no one else. You know I love you like my son, but that does not matter. For the Cheka, no, now they call it the NKVD, knows of course, of your existence and that is why they sent the directive to me.' Alexander Tolkovsky is a good man, Mother. He warned me that I would walk into dangerous territory. 'Stalin is paranoid,' he said. 'His aides never last long. Some whom we knew were sent to Siberia; others died strangely. So many accidents happen to people close to Stalin. Watch your back and your front, my friend, and trust no one'."

Proceeding with his tale, Alyosha unnerved Maryonna with discoveries about the man who insisted being called "Leader and Teacher."

"Ha, the teacher hates the arts—they are decadent. He hates Shakespeare—he cannot understand him—and he despises the best music composed in Russia."

"Did you know that Shakespeare once said those who dislike music should not be trusted? He said it as if he knew about Stalin, a man so afraid of his true image that he is consumed with privacy. No one is to know the details of his life—perhaps to prevent us from drawing conclusions about his character. The man is nothing but a façade evocative of the devil. And just as the devil's doings are carefully concealed, Stalin's loves, his hates, his family, his food and his drink are all hidden in obscurity. Only one man knows his secrets. That is his servant, a moronic being who serves him like a dog."

Drawing smoke from his cigarette deep into his lungs, Alyosha nodded his head as if to strengthen his point. "Most of all, he worries that his private conversations could be repeated. Therefore, I was perfect to be at his service yet unable to hear what was being spoken in his apartment. Would you believe that the odious, suspicious man tested me himself? For days on end, he called my name loudly. I, of course, could not respond to anything. Then, suddenly, at odd moments, he tried to startle me with sharp noises. All to no avail for I was truly deaf."

Maryonna, totally unnerved by now, had been following her own train of thoughts.

"But Alyosha," she interrupted, "why did you never tell me about Stalin. All that time you were with him and I never knew."

"I am, of course, forbidden to relate this to anyone, even my mother. Right now I am breaking an oath and I am under the threat of death. Yet, speak I must, or choke to death."

The tick under his left eye had grown stronger, and he rubbed his cheek vigorously.

"To my horror and despair I noted that, bit by imperceptible bit, my ability to hear increased. Soon, I heard snatches of conversations, secrets—vile secrets. I heard orders to bring him in the deep of night a woman he obsessed about. He later married her. I heard of men he wanted eliminated or sent to Siberia, and I heard about those whose reputation he wanted destroyed. It is so easy for him. Often he suggests only daintily that a play, a concert, or an artist's work is too daunting, and, magically, the play will not open, the concert is never heard, the artist's work disappears into obscurity."

Alyosha ground the last of his cigarette vehemently into the saucer. Agitated, he rose and paced. The diminutive room, cluttered with a solid, carved sideboard and a couch and dining table did not allow for great mobility. Therefore, he paced as in an agitated, monotonous dance. Two steps forward, two steps back, moving hypnotically like one of the great Russian brown bears behind the bars of his cage.

Above the sideboard hung a painting. It was a still life in oil, and rather too large for the room. It dominated the living space with its imposition, its subject a study in ferocity. Depicting a hunt's bounty, one viewed a brace of pheasants, their heads drooping over a rough country table's edge, blood dripping gorily onto the floor. A rabbit, with crimson chest, wide-open eyes, and despondently drooping ears, touched the pheasants in communal death. A woodcock, his neck tied to a long, bronze candlestick was sadly hanging over the table corner draped by a red cloth. It, together with an assortment of garden vegetables, completed the drama before a dark dramatic background.

The painting was a relic from Alyosha's university days, when he had known the new crop of young Russian artists ready to supplant the old guard. This painting was the work of a young talented painter who had usually painted abstracts. Forced to make money to feed a wife and child, he agreed to do commissioned works, real things, "art" that the elite paid for. In the end, this work meant for the dacha of a functionary who supplied the gory photograph for the theme, had been rejected, and Alyosha bought it for a pittance compared to its real worth. Maryonna had been overjoyed.

Not only had her Alyosha been able to place her into this small apartment, where she could live in privacy and dignity at a time when often three bodies would have to share such a space; but he had also given her the first and only piece of real art. As far as the imposing presence and the bloody theme of the work was concerned, Maryonna could not have cared less. Did not her whole life deal with such matters? A few drops of blood, as in the picture, added color and meaning to life, particularly her life that unfolded daily to more blood and slaughter. But a look at the blood pooling below the table in the picture reminded Alyosha once more of his own dilemma, and he continued his tale.

"It was then that I began to play a role more difficult than any role an actor ever played on stage. I will have to play the deaf servant forever. Stalin writes out his questions and commands—and I, the officer-puppet, read and speak." Alyosha's hand ran furiously through his hair, as if he could comb Stalin out of it like a bothersome nit.

"The worst is keeping a straight face when he plots death with Kaganovich, his foul party leader and brother-in-law. However, the hardest is not to laugh when his fawning sycophants tell him the most hilarious jokes. Some jokes are hysterically funny, and it takes all my willpower to cast my face into a mask."

He threw up his hands in despair, "Ah, *Mamochka*, you cannot imagine how it feels if you want to howl with laughter, yet must constrain yourself. I hear of horror and instantly my face goes dead, unmoved as the stones of a crypt. It seems horror and sorrow are our closest companions, so we learn early not to emote. Laughter, however, is a different thing. We learn to laugh with our mothers in our language, our heritage, and we like to laugh so very much."

He reflected on the different aspects of cultural humor. "People all over the world laugh about the same things. Humor eases the hardship of our condition. It is the way in which we all express our view of the world and our choices of words and our phrases spice the humor."

He fell silent, remembering a professor at Moscow University who lectured on the peculiarities of expressions. "German jokes," the man had expounded, "are precisely constructed, Americans love puns, Britons delight in obscured meanings, the French love a flamboyant, piquant finish, and we the people of winter-depression take a club to end our jokes, a club to bring down heavily upon our prey, making our comic kill."

Alyosha recalled a story widely circulated about the conductor Alexander Vasilyevich Gauk and his wife, the ballerina Elizaveta Gerdt, upon being named honored artists of the Russian Soviet Federated Socialist Republic. After receiving so great an honor they celebrated extensively, giving a series of soirées. The musicologist and intellectual, Sollertinsky, possessed of razor-sharp wit, attended one such soirée. To amuse himself and his friends he stood, glass in hand, congratulating his hosts on the tremendous honor that had been bestowed upon them. Then he wondered—as if in passing—had they already passed the test needed to confirm the honor? "What test are you speaking of?" Gauk inquired.

"Oh, the test on Marxism-Leninism," replied the amused Sollertinsky, leaving the party. His hosts, bereft of hopes to ever pass such a test, were devastated for days until they discovered "the club"—there was no test they had to take in order to receive the honor.

Reminiscing, Alyosha smiled at his old teacher's poignant remark, "We like the poetry of the Germans, the fashion of the French, and Polish composers; and we need Russian artists to cry with." He explained to his mother how an irresistible force overcame him each time he heard an outrageous joke, a well-turned word play, a piercing arrow of humorous precision.

"Without our will, laughter arises someplace from our middle, we shake, and our face contracts into the widest grin. Ah, it is the most impossible urge to resist. I had to develop a technique to keep my face inscrutable," he said. "So far they have not found me out. However, I think I am going crazy."

Maryonna cried softly. "Alyosha, son, this is terrible, unendurable. No man should have to live like that. Pretending to be deaf will make you sick. Yes, it will make you crazy. Alyosha, *lyubko,* if you could only explain your predicament to Stalin himself. He is a good man. Read in the paper what they write about him. They praise him daily at the factory."

Hearing his mother's demented whine, Alyosha's tenuous hold on self broke. Forgetting himself, he snapped at his mother from the depth of his personal hell. "*Dura!* Fool! Idiot! Is it possible that you are this stupid? Have you understood nothing? Have you not listened to anything I have said? How can you still believe in the drivel the Party puts out? For weeks I have been hinting at things. You yourself told me of neighbors disappearing. Remember what happened when the plan was not fulfilled at your meat-combinat? It was you who told me that the director was held responsible, and then he disappeared. Have you not wondered where they sent him?

Siberia, Mother! Wake up! What I have told you can send me to the gulags or have me killed, and you still believe Stalin is a nice man? If you want to kill me, go tell him that I can hear and see what will happen!"

Alyosha sank onto the edge of the couch and buried his face in his hands. Shaken to the core, his mother looked at her son with a mixture of anguish and hurt. Tears were beginning to drip over her round, wrinkled cheeks. Her hands shook with small tremors.

"Yoshi, of course I believe you. I will not tell. No one. I promise. I was just thinking of how one could help you. Forgive me. Of course, I am a stupid person. Look at me. What have I learned? Nothing. Meat factory, that is all I am good for."

She painfully rose to her feet, limped around the table and enfolded her son in her arms, pressing him against her ample bosom like an un-happy child.

"I am sorry, Mama. Sorry that I exploded, sorry for me, for you and all of unhappy, cursed Russia."

"What to do, what to do?" murmured Maryonna, sinking beside him onto the saggy sofa. Her son just shook his head in helpless negation. In a suffocating, powerless silence they sat beside each other, holding hands. The picture of an artist couple condemned to death by Stalin for "treason," came to his mind. "We sit just as they sat, holding hands—hopeless."

Suddenly he sprang to attention. He consulted his watch, an ancient timepiece, a present from his grandfather. Although ancient, the old watch kept time impeccably and he liked it for the heavy, rounded comfort it imparted to his hand.

"Eleven o'clock. I must be gone, Mother. I have to be within the Kremlin walls by midnight, and I still have to find my driver. Hope to God he is in the car and only half drunk. If you can pray, Mother, then pray for me, for I know of nothing else that can help me."

He scrambled off the sofa, kissed his mother on the forehead as he had done a thousand times before, and grabbing his army great coat and round hat, he rushed out the door. As Maryonna locked and bolted her door, she heard him fumble with the door of the communal bathroom in the hall, a terrible smelly place, containing a bathtub and sink, besides the toilet. The door slamming minutes later indicated that he had finished. His rushing footsteps were growing fainter, telling her he had left her floor.

She dragged herself to the table, beginning to clear the remains of their meal. Working, she contemplated her life, which had become a hor-ror. Her mind and soul deeply wounded, she wondered about her child's fate. "Who would wish this life on a dog?" she thought, "and yet we live like dogs every day." Finally she was through with denials. There was no workers' paradise, and those in charge of Mother Russia were criminals and exploiters. For the common man, there was no difference between the Tsar's governance and the reign of the Red elite. No, after all the blood and tears—nothing had changed. She saw the samovar at the sideboard. It had been ready for tea after the meal. Although tea, with the ensuing ceremony beforehand, was an integral part of their dinners, she had totally forgotten the existence of the exquisite old tea maker. Yet, why would she not forget all else, especially so trivial a thing as tea, in the face of her child's deplorable predicament? As he had poured out his troubles, her soul cried with him, because once again another dream she had dreamed was destroyed.

She was a simple person who had hoped for little in life—oh, so very little. A small apartment, a good husband, a few healthy children—that had been all. Education was a thing she never contemplated. During the Tsar's reign, the child of a streetcar conductor could not hope for schooling. When the family needed more resources, she had left school after the sixth grade, beginning her lifelong toil before the sewing machine of a furrier. To this day, she could not think of anything as hard as sewing fur pieces together with those ancient, temperamental machines. For all the world to see, she still had the scars on her hands to prove how difficult it had been to fashion glamorous coats for the rich. She had never complained, asked for nothing. Therefore, it now galled her doubly that even her one and only treasure might be taken from her.

Maryonna remembered the suffering of poor Russians under Tsar Nicholas II. Although a personable, mild-mannered man, the Tsar could not conceive of modifying his government, abdicating some of his absolute powers, and thereby easing the tensions within his domain. Russia had eroded from the inside, ruined by a multitude of divergent interests. Aspirations of the rising business class often ran counter to the interests of landowners and bureaucrats. The latter, having held power and influence for centuries, felt threatened by the new political players who were interested in ties and trade with the West.

They represented a threatening new force, gathering power within the establishment. Nicholas had been able to impose the gold standard on Russia. With this progressive stroke of leadership he brought foreign interest and capital into the country, with the result that the industrial working class grew enormously. It had been unavoidable that this new class of workers, much more sophisticated than the serfs on land holdings,

envisioned a better role for themselves in the new Russia. But Nicholas'
policy of Russification, a continuation from the reign of Alexander III, had
continued the discrimination against all Jewish interests; it had pressured
the Muslim Tartars and the Finno-Ugrians to convert to Russian Orthodoxy. Furthermore, this policy enforced the Russification of the German
schools in the Baltic provinces, a continuation of pressured assimila-
tion that had begun in the villages on the Volga. To add insult to injury,
Nicholas had alienated the faithful Armenian population by robbing the
Armenian Christian Church fund of its monies, transferring them to
Russian administration. Furthermore, he infuriated the Finns by placing
imperial decrees over Finnish laws.

Such counterproductive policies, combined with the nobility's and
the militia's contempt for the people, which they called the plebeian rabble, negated his progress. His militia killed the common poor like rabid
dogs for the slightest offences, some only perceived or imagined. Then,
along came the Bolsheviks with their promises. Maryonna, like so many of
her class, had fervently hoped that the great Lenin, and with him Stalin,
"the Teacher," would open to them the portals of the promised workers'
paradise.

With most of her impoverished cohorts she had marched for the Bolsheviks. She had fetched and carried, unpaid, for the cause, and lent her support
whenever the party called on her group. Unable to stop the endless flow of
facts and thoughts, she now faced up to the greatest betrayal in her life. Somehow, despite the evidence to the contrary—the cold, the hunger, her miserable
hole of a home—shared with three other women before Alyosha intervened—
she had fooled herself into believing that better days lay ahead.

Yet, only a short while ago her son, afraid and exhausted, had sat
here at her table, dealing with eerie surety the death knell to her wishful
beliefs. Oh, she had heard rumors about Stalin's brutality and had angrily
shrugged them off as slander; worse yet, she had turned on such traitorous
voices with fanatical viciousness. It could not be so—damn them all—it
just could not be so.

By what measure, however, could she dismiss Alyosha's factual in-
dictments? Enemies and friends alike had been disappearing. They were
found dead or ended in the gulags of Siberia.

Deep inside her a small flame of truth flared, burning ever more
fiercely, engulfing her in pain. It was all true. She sensed with almost physical certainty that after this night's frightening revelations she would live in
denial no longer.

What had Alyosha said? Stalin's aides had turned up dead or missing? Was this to be the fate of her boy? For him, she would have to think of something to save him, make a plan of sorts. Tired, despondent, she lurched to and fro, from table to sink, until the table was cleared. She had decided to leave the dishes for the morrow. It was almost midnight, and the thought of waiting for the water to heat on her miserable little burner to wash dishes had been too much for her even to contemplate. Painfully she hobbled a short way down the drab, gray, concrete hallway to the communal toilet and bathroom. Soon she was entering her cubicle of a bedroom, locking and bolting the door securely. Hooligans had become a plague in the city. Everyone knew that, while the police vigorously pursued trumped-up charges against ordinary citizens, they only occasionally swept the city for criminals despite complaints flooding the departments.

After undressing, she sat on her bedside for a moment, massaging her varicose veins. Stroking upward from the ankle to the knee she mulled over her son's predicament. Imagining the complexity of the role he played, she shuddered. He was an honest, open, loving young man, now faking most deceitfully the existence of a deaf, admiring and dutiful servant. And then, as she stretched out on her lumpy, yet comforting bed, she did something she'd given up as an eighteen-year-old when she had joined the Reds; she began to say prayers for her son's life. Yet, she prayed even more fervently that God might hear her.

The Lair of the Monster

Meanwhile, Alyosha found to his delight that his driver, Slava, was asleep in the staff car. Whatever he had imbibed earlier, he had slept off by now. Slava, like most Russians, drank vodka like a smelter inhales iron ore and, perhaps, that was what fueled him. Alyosha could report him for his drinking; the consequences would be harsh. Many times he had asked himself the question: "Why sacrifice a man when he would not learn from the experience and when, furthermore, the next driver would have exactly the same predilection?"

Slava drove a bit too fast through the empty streets to the Kremlin. They passed seven different sentries. Each checked the car with exceedingly excruciating scrutiny, for the teacher and leader had a magnificent case of paranoia. But, after making so many enemies, his paranoia was justifiable. Alyosha checked his watch and was pleased that they had arrived with fifteen minutes to spare. He reminded the forgetful Slava to be ready for duty at nine in the morning, and then departed.

It was quiet in the halls of the Kremlin as Alyosha rushed, coattails flying, footsteps clacking sharply on the marble floor, to the duty room where he had to check in. It was imperative that he sign in before midnight with a countersignature from the duty officer, a precise recording of the exact minute he was back in the Kremlin. Stalin demanded it that way—no exceptions.

The duty room was a plain, square affair with a wooden desk covered with duty rosters, forms, files, and the duty book. There were a side desk, upon which a typewriter resided, several uncomfortable looking metal chairs for guests, and an upholstered, leather swivel chair for the officer on duty. A few metal filing cabinets completed the room's accoutrements. The oil paintings of Stalin and Lenin in elaborate, handsome frames were the only expensive items in the room. There was Stalin, trying to embody the role of the teacher. By striking a pose, big book in left hand with the right below in support, he was trying to convey his sincere studiousness. His dark, red-cast hair always had so healthy a sheen that visitors often mused whether the makeup person used linseed oil on it—used it, much as the cavalry officers did on their horses, making the manes and tails silky and flowing, making their eyes appear larger by surrounding them with a circle of oil.

Like Alyosha, all who met Stalin in person knew very well that he looked nothing like his pictures, paintings or the person portrayed in films. A vain, conceited creature, he was obsessed with his looks. Many people had ceaselessly labored to elaborately design for him a heroic, handsome, tall look. Their labors had been inconceivably difficult, based on the material they had to work with. Short, chubby, one arm shorter then the other, Stalin was arduous clay to mold. The portraits could only be completed to his liking with the utmost trickery.

The book he held in the painting made it appear that both his hands and arms were of equal size. Another way to accomplish this feat had been to paint him in Napoleonic pose, with the hand of the shorter arm hidden in his army jacket, while he carried a sword or implement in the other. Filmmakers had found their own way to accomplish the impossible. All camera shots of him came from the perspective of a lowly, cowering creature, the cameramen on their bellies in the dirt. At that angle a midget could become a giant.

By comparison Lenin looked in his pictures like a thoughtful business-man in a sober gray suit, white shirt, and claret red tie. A powerful domed head, large rounded forehead and a strongly receding hairline distinguished him. His features were of the plebeian German-Kalmyk type, with thick, sensual lips and deep, piercing eyes. He was below medium height, but like Stalin, he was powerfully and strongly built. And, like Stalin, he insisted that he appear in any kind of portrayal in preternatural size. Depending on the artist, one could detect a solid streak of ruthlessness in his features. Sometimes he appeared clean-shaven, at other times mustached. Simplicity in bearing gave him distinction. The pair looked to be well-fed and unused to deprivation, so different from the suffering population.

Alyosha pondered the lives of Stalin and Lenin often. What kind of ex-periences had forged these people into the fearsome giants they had become? Of their personal lives little was known. They had wives, but no real families. Stalin begat a daughter, Svetlana, who was being raised entirely by his second wife. Stalin's first wife, a deeply religious young girl, had died shortly after giving birth to a son. Unfortunately the little boy grew into a sensitive, intro-spective young man, perceived as worthless and weak by his cruel, unnatural father. For the unforgivable defect—being soulful—he had been sent during the war to the front lines, where he was promptly captured.

Lenin had a wife, Nadezhda Krupskaya; but the only picture of her known to Alyosha was an archive photograph of her and Lenin outside their dacha in Gorki. Krupskaya looked sweet, motherly, and dumpy in the picture, belying her intellectual prowess.

During her lifetime she established the Russian library system, and long before she married Lenin she had been a professional revolutionary with a strong academic background. Like Lenin, whom she met as a mem-ber of an intellectual Marxist group and married in exile in Siberia, she too came from a bourgeoisie family with humanistic pretensions.

Wryly, Alyosha remarked to himself that the world of the terrible Tsar had been much more humane than the revolutionaries replacing that regime. As it stood now, the Communists just killed their opposition. Any-one agitating against the Communists the way Lenin had acted against the Tsar was shot without trial. Instead of killing him, the Tsar's government had allowed his girlfriend and fellow revolutionary to join and marry him in exile. This had been a much more humane treatment of an adversary than the Communists would ever grant.

How amusing, thought Alyosha, that the Tsar allowed the same poisonous adders to be put into one bed in Siberia, enabling them to hatch out the very plan that eventually destroyed the empire. He sighed, acknowledging that the present powers were incapable of such a humane, yet stupid gesture. Comparing the old and new political system in his slightly impaired mind, he was brought back to the present by the voice of the duty officer, Petka Fyodorovitch. Petka was a vile creature, harassing those below him, vexing with insolence his equals, fawning at his superiors. He now smacked a paper on the desk, pushing it in front of tired, red-eyed Alyosha.

"That's for you, milk-face," he snarled sarcastically, looking challenging into Alyosha's face. "Comrade Stalin wants you in the small dining room, the sooner the better. Hurry, where have you been anyway, slacker?"

They both knew, of course, were Alyosha to complain about his insolence, he would talk himself into the clear by saying that he had only been joshing, no harm meant. No one could touch him. He was a member of the Party, and an officer handpicked by Stalin for Kremlin duty. Suppressing his irritation, Alyosha said politely, "*Spacibo*," leaving the room quickly, thereby avoiding punching Petka's face. He had been longing for months to physically punish the creature, beating him to a pulp in a fistfight.

Half running, taking the stairs two at a time because the elevator was stuck somewhere above, he reached the upper floors. Suddenly he stopped at a landing silently cursing in German and French, for a new anger blinded him with its fury. "*Scheisse! Merde! Verfluchter Mist!*" He collected himself, trying to stay calm, thinking superfluously, "Why does our mother tongue seem to be inadequate when great anger makes us curse? Is it that being overly familiar with our own obscenities makes us choose the stronger, more expressive curses of others?" He stopped his musings, returning to the reason of his being incensed. He knew, all too well, what was in store for him. There was no other reason for his call to attend Stalin but one: The illustrious teacher had once again given in to his whims for late-night, impromptu suppers. Often these suppers were misbegotten affairs conceived in Stalin's mind in the middle of a late night meeting. Alyosha knew from experience that, whenever Stalin's Georgian nature bubbled forth from beneath the artificial ice, he began feeling mellow, curious or lonely. In the grip of the Southland's sentiments, he would command a bevy of his underlings to attend him at supper. Sometimes it was amusing to observe how cleverly he directed his dinner guests to perform like trained seals in a circus. At other times it was gut-wrenching to watch how he played on their fears and abject terrors.

"*Gott verdammt. Merde, merde!*" He flew up to his room—only two doors away from Stalin's suite. They had given him a large, comfortably furnished room with a private bath. That in itself was a great honor, but far beyond that he had more square footage to himself than eighty percent of the people in Moscow. A thick, flowery Chinese carpet, presented to Stalin by one of the Chinese envoys, covered most of the room's floor. Such carpets, but a hundred times more exquisite, covered the floors of Stalin's suite. Alyosha grinned sarcastically, "If the Russian people only knew how the man really lived!"

The propaganda machine portrayed Stalin as living in a sparse, almost monastic style. To buttress this image, visitors were shown into a small room complete with a rolltop desk; he liked the hidden and locked compartments, simple, wooden chairs and bare wooden floors. The real apartment lay behind a plain, but solid, steel-reinforced door, through which most people never walked. The mighty one was not consumed with opulence, but he immensely liked his comfort. Besides the Kremlin apartment, Stalin had been given or, better phrased, had taken for himself, a house in Moscow. This was the domicile of his wife, Nadezhda Alliluyevna, and his daughter Svetlana, whom he rarely saw. Furthermore, Stalin owned numerous dachas in different parts of Russia, all in exceptionally beautiful rural settings.

Although Alyosha had been dead tired only moments ago, the summons so infuriated him that, charged with the adrenalin of anger, he changed with lightening speed into a clean uniform and military blouse, rubbed his face with a moist cloth, swished cologne through his mouth instead of unavailable mouthwash, and ran a comb through his hair.

Minutes later he opened the side door to the smaller of the dining rooms and, without hesitation, strode quickly to the head of the table. The small dining room was a study in socialist splendor. Instead of the Tsar's flowery damask panels, wood frames now surrounded red velvet. The old crystal chandeliers, designed to hold hundreds of burning candles, had been replaced with electric chandeliers of much simpler design. Except for the serving buffets, a few pictures and flower arrangements, the only worthy, truly grand item in the room was the dining table for forty, dressed in immaculate white and beset with white, gold-edged china.

Stalin already sat at the head of the table with his ogre manservant, Timoteo Berokodze, behind him. The thirty-odd guests were crowded close about him, leaving a gaping hole at the other end of the table. Striding toward Stalin, Alyosha stopped a few paces behind him, to Stalin's right. He stood at attention while Stalin's man scrutinized him, inch by inch, with the concentrated gaze of a lizard watching prey.

Stalin, laughing at a witticism dropped by the secretary of higher education, knew full well that Alyosha had arrived. As a matter of fact, he had been informed of Alyosha's presence the minute he walked through the Kremlin's door. Someone said of Stalin that, in a different era, he could have been a great hunter, for nothing escaped his attention, a fact of which those around him were well aware. Anything displeasing him in their behavior was recorded in his mind and would be retrieved from memory when it suited him to build a case against them.

For the hundredth time, Alyosha covertly observed the short, stocky body of his nemesis; his swarthy, pockmarked face, his fierce glance, the heavy, black brows and the thick mustache. Amazing, that so small a man could have such presence and command such rapt attention! His reputation for ruthlessness had preceded him in party circles before his arrival in Moscow. Furthermore, he was physically strong and endowed with a prodigious will. But his willpower and cunning were his most extraordinary attributes, turning him into an implacable foe when combined with his patient timing for the execution of his plans. As Alyosha knew only too well, everyone who had offended Stalin even in the slightest way faced severe retribution.

A small wave of Stalin's hand directed Alyosha to approach. A soldier, who only moments ago had been standing motionless beside the door, brought a chair and placed it to Stalin's right, noticeably back from the table. Alyosha was tall, placed next to Stalin he would have dwarfed the "teacher." Placed back slightly, he looked to be Stalin's equal in height.

Each of the three large doors opening into the room was manned by a complement of two guards, leading to the secret joke among the initiated that "it was easier to get to the food than away from it." Without being obsequious, Alyosha smiled a greeting at Stalin. He placed a notepad and pen within Stalin's easy reach. He had learned by now that he was not to stand on formality or talk with him when the great man was involved in social situations. If Stalin wanted to acknowledge him he would do so, otherwise Alyosha was to act the silent attendant. With surreptitious, quick glances Alyosha attempted to inform himself about the present company. It was vitally important for him to identify as many of the attendees as possible to be able to gauge what Stalin would expect of him.

Three seats to his right, he noted Anastas Ivanovich Mikoyan and his mousy, shrill-voiced wife. Molotov, too, was present; beside him a theater actress who had become famous for her portrayal of Lady Macbeth—a play now forbidden by Stalin, because, perhaps, it reminded people too much of a certain power-hungry killer. He could not recall her name and was annoyed with his memory. Stalin was sure to ask him her name.

Akhmatova, the poetess, sat across from him. Perhaps she, too, had been summoned to recite poetry earlier in the evening. A whole flock of artists had been assembled here, and he hardly knew any of their names. Even worse, he had not heard, read or seen any of their work. Some faces were familiar from his daily perusal of *Pravda*, but otherwise he had not been able to keep up with the arts—no time. Stalin consumed every minute of his day, draining him of energy. After a day with the "teacher" he was just glad to be allowed to fall into bed.

Attached to the more prominent men were beautiful girls hoping to escape the dreariness of their lives by landing a role in a movie. And thinking of movies, he spotted the great director, Sergey Mikhailovich Eisenstein, seated close to Anna Akhmatova. That name was a pseudonym for Anna Andreyevna Gorenko. Sergei Mikhailovich operated under a burden of strikes against him. To begin with, he had been born in Latvia and, therefore, was not Russian enough. In addition, he was of Jewish descent and not pure enough for the Jew-haters in the Party. So far, his saving grace had been that he was a truly great director and inventor of new cinematic techniques. Stalin had been pleased with his work, especially "Battleship Potemkin," for this spectacular work had legitimized the Russian movie industry.

Alyosha scrutinized the great director. He came in contact with many great people, none whom he admired like this man. Suddenly he feared that he would never see Eisenstein again. Stalin was fickle—tomorrow the man might be banished to Siberia. For now, however, Eisenstein was gesticulating energetically, as he explained his technique of a montage to a man later to be identified as a German film director. Eisenstein was a lively man, tall, broad in the shoulders, with a strongly receding line of dark hair and brown, intelligent eyes. These eyes were now fastened on the sharp features of the blond German, who had consumed the vodka served with a capacity equal to the Russians. Yet, amazingly, the man still followed Eisenstein's difficult explanations. An architect by training, Sergei Michailovich believed that cinema was a synthesis of art and science and that, with machines, film cameras and cutting techniques, psychological portraits could be painted. And, of course, he had shown how this could be done.

As Eisenstein was Russia's greatest filmmaker, so Akhmatova was thought by many to be Russia's greatest poet. A tragic figure, she was haunted by the wrath of the Communist Party. For most of the time, she had been ostracized for her style of poetry. Although how anyone could disagree with her pure, compact and exquisite art was impossible to imagine—unimaginable, at least to Alyosha, who in his former happy poetic life had immersed himself in her spirit-soothing poems as in a clear, sweet pond. Nevertheless she had displeased the mighty, been declared by the Party to be bourgeois-aristocratic, and was at times forbidden to be published.

"What is she doing here?" wondered Alyosha. Not too long ago he had heard she had been banished from Moscow. Perhaps it had been nothing but a rumor. Then, suddenly, it all made sense. Grouped around Eisenstein and the poetess, sat a gaggle of foreign dignitaries. He heard German spoken, and instantly understood that these were artists from the German UFA Film studio. That explained Eisenstein's presence. Then he heard that a prominent member of this group had wanted to meet Akhmatova. Clearly, that wish explained her command performance at the table. By tomorrow, she would be banished again from the art scene.

Lately, it had become a common phenomenon to see persons paraded about in front of the public for just one performance. This was done to establish the living presence of the particular artist or scientist for the liberal visitors of the West, reassuring them that all was well in Mother Russia. Thus Stalin allowed them their infantile delusions of the developing perfect, socialist state. Alyosha, however, knew only too well that in the morrow it would be impossible to find the very person the western emoters had come to see.

How fervently the liberal humanitarians of the West embraced the dream of a perfect land where the common man had been exalted; and how little they understood of the horrid reality. However, this German delegation—one could rest assured—had no such distorted views of Stalin and his empire. Alyosha sniggered to himself, "They have a monster of equal proportions and, therefore, they know better."

His glance returned to Akhmatova. Poor woman, her face was deadly serious, almost suffering; her eyes looked downward as if concentrating on the dinnerware. Stalin had executed her first husband, Nikolai Stepanovich Gumilyov. Zoshchenko, her second husband, a writer, was thoroughly hated by Stalin and, through him, by the entire Communist Party. They treated Zoshchenko with an even greater aggregate of venom than they had reserved for Akhmatova.

Yet, observed Alyosha, despite all her problems Akhmatova was magnificent. It was easy to see why they called her the aristocrat poetess. She was beautiful, possessed of a rare refined beauty that arose from within, from the beauty of the mind. Her eyes were enormous and dark, and she carried herself regally. Her clothes, all black, were of a fine cut, setting off her elegant limbs, had been selected with great thought for the occasion. Her blouse, simple, opening in a narrow V, accentuated her slender neck and the long sleeves exposed beautiful hands, and long, tapered fingers.

No wonder the proletarians hated her! She was the opposite of who they were and what they represented. They had become coarse and brutal, for the Party obliterated the ethics and spiritual values they had once cradled in their souls, which had sustained them during the Tsar's reign. Those ennobling tenets had been replaced with greed, fear and the wish to soil and degrade all that was magnificent.

Two places to the left of Stalin sat Lavrenti Pavlovich Beria, the Commissar for Internal Affairs. "Surprise," thought Alyosha, "another Georgian is present." All of Russia feared Beria, Stalin's right hand, master executioner of the purges and spectacular show trials during the 1930s. Having pleased the mighty one, he had been called to Moscow. Now they shared a gruesome bond—the bond was death. Understandably, he was a man of whom Alyosha was deathly afraid. He was loath to run afoul of Beria.

After receiving his post, perhaps the most powerful position after Stalin's own, Beria commenced to execute his unlucky predecessor. This tremendous act of horror set the tone for Beria's leadership. So far there had been no one who had attempted to challenge him. Two, slightly tipsy, blond girls flanked Beria, here tonight without his wife. Simple and dizzy, they were marked sacrifices. "Poor girls," reflected Alyosha, "life could be very short for you. Any misstep, any annoyance to the mighty men assembled, and you might never be seen again." Hiding his subversive thoughts behind dead eyes, he looked around and saw the waiters approaching with soup tureens.

"Damn," he thought, "I am out of luck tonight. It is midnight and they are just serving the soup." Just then Stalin pushed the pad with a note toward him. Alyosha gently reached, and without attracting attention to the interlude, he covered the note with his hand. He covertly read the message. In small, precise Cyrillic letters, Stalin had expressed this order: "Drink to Mikoyan. Toast him and empty your glass, so he will have to do the same."

"Oh, hell," thought Alyosha, "he is playing one of his favorite games again, getting all of them drunk." He did not want to drink any more vodka, but could by no means refuse the command. Mikoyan was a member of the Communist Party's Central Committee. Therefore, Stalin looked upon him at times as a threat to his supremacy.

Alyosha recalled from Mikoyan's dossier that he had been an active Party Member since 1915. He was an old Bolshevik who had rallied to the red flag early on. Unscrupulous by nature, he had managed to garner important cabinet posts and lucrative positions in the food industry and in international trade. A joke circulated through Moscow, explaining how anyone could grow fat, in body and bank account, under the red flag. The punch line was that one had to wave the flag over one's head just right. It implied, that the flag, like a magic wand, made prosperity come true for those who knew how to use it. The joke was directly aimed at Mikoyan.

Alyosha rose and raised his glass, filled to the brim by Stalin's man at the mere raised eyebrow of his master. Berokodze, soldier-servant and fellow Georgian to Stalin, was a veteran of many skirmishes. He was a dull-witted individual, but loyal as a dog, and perhaps the only human being invested with Stalin's trust. There were those who speculated that their common bond was rooted in their Georgian heritage and culture.

Stalin had been born in the provincial Georgian town of Gori in the Caucasus. Although he allowed his fondness for all things Georgian to show through, favoring Georgian wine, songs, et cetera, his fondness did not extend to loyalty to Georgian compatriots who either became a threat or tried to restrain him. A clear demonstration was the example of Gregory Konstantinovich Ordzhonikidze. Ordzonikidze had been an adherent of the Communist Party since 1903. Later, he became commissar extraordinary for the Ukraine and later still, for the South of Russia and the Caucasus. He had been a close friend of Stalin's who supported him and, in turn, had been served well by his friend. Still, Stalin never hesitated, impelling him to commit suicide when this political comrade tried to stem his murderous excesses.

"A toast to your incomparable stewardship of our food combinat, comrade Mikoyan. May you enjoy the dinner our illustrious host Josef Vissarionovich has prepared for us," Alyosha intoned, raising the glass to his lips. With profound relief his nose detected that his glass contained only water, upon which he downed it in one gulp.

An exceedingly surprised Mikoyan could do nothing but follow suit, saying, "Thank you for your courtesy, Alyosha Kulov," and gulp his drink, also. So surprised and nervous was the man, he spilled some of his drink on his shirt, a thing greatly frowned upon. Real men do not spill their vodka—they drink it. Mikoyan sensed that there was deviltry afoot.

Waiters materialized ghostlike, as if stepping out of the paneling. They made the rounds, immediately filling the empty glasses. Some of the assembled company drank only wine, particularly the women, but a few of the beautiful girls drank vodka with the men to show that they were good company, willing to go a few extra *versts*. Alyosha looked with amusement at the gorgeous, revealing dresses of these girls. They were not vulgar. Stalin frowned on harlotry. His favorite image to convey was that of a staunchly moral family man. Yet even he—he was male after all—could not object to stylish, accentuating gowns, revealing alluring bodies.

Beria, probably cued by Stalin, raised his glass and toasted Mikoyan, who responded unenthusiastically. His face had become as colorless as his dishwater gray hair. After he painfully emptied his glass, his eyes began to tear. Sitting down, he fished clumsily in his pants pockets for a kerchief. Mikoyan's wife tried valiantly to control her inner turmoil. She sensed that this was a game played with her husband. A dangerous game, which could cost not only one's position but also one's head. Avoiding her husband's eyes, she concentrated on the exuberant Germans across the table, who had become ever more animated as the evening progressed.

Alyosha had to sharply remind himself that the Mikoyans were despicable carpetbaggers before he was able to control a spontaneous flow of pity for the miserable couple. How many people had suffered because of their extortionate enterprise? Who could count them, in the hundreds of thousands?

Now, to stoke the fire ever more, Stalin rose. He seldom stood for a toast, but here, mustache quivering, eyes twinkling with restrained mirth, he stood, toasting his faithful comrade on the road to socialism. "How are you, friend Anastas," he asked kindly, and then downed his drink, which Alyosha knew to be water. Stalin liked to drink, but alone. In company he would never allow himself to get even slightly tipsy.

The waiters carried huge, heavily laden trays of food to the table, schlepping into the room wave after wave of delicacies. Suddenly, two of the men valiantly trying to serve all guests at the same time, collided. Their massive silver trays overloaded with platters crashed to the floor with the sound of an explosion. Everyone's heads turned, conversation stopped, embarrassed silence reigned. The terrified waiters, with the faces of scared, snared rabbits, apologized profusely before falling to the ground in an effort to remove the carnage.

Stalin smiled with great benevolence, "Accidents happen, comrades," and turned back to his guests, after giving Alyosha a deeply probing, significant look.

"I am doomed. Oh God, I am doomed!" thought Alyosha. "I turned my head and Stalin saw it." He covertly observed Stalin's manservant, Timoteo, and knew from the man's look that he had seen it too.

From that moment forth the evening dragged on in slow motion. Somehow Alyosha performed; somehow he carried on, while his mind was reeling with thoughts of having been discovered. After eating his fill, Stalin abruptly got to his feet, telling everyone to continue having a good time. He, however, had more work to finish before the night was over and, therefore, had to take his leave.

Stalin left the room, his factotum Timoteo Berokodze and Alyosha in tow. He dismissed the tormented, internally quaking Alyosha almost kindly. "Have a good night, Alyosha. Long day again."

Alone in his room, the tormented young officer fell to his knees, shaking with fright and the anticipation of the terror that was sure to follow. "If there is a God in heaven as they say there is, then please God help me now. Oh God, help me now!"

At last, his shaking subsided, and he stood. "Must not do anything different. Everything must be the same," he thought. He undressed and fulfilled his ablutions as always, put on his pajamas and lay down in his bed with a book in his hand that he did not read. "Help me, Mother, God help," were the only thoughts coursing through his mind.

When they came, they did not burst through his door, having of course had a key to this room. Stalin had sent three of his best operatives. Alyosha pretended not to hear that they had entered. Two of them rushed to his bed, pulling him out by his arms. One of them hit him across the face.

"Speak, swine, since when can you hear? You are supposed to be deaf yet your head turning tonight gave you away." As they spoke straight to his face, he answered.

"I am deaf, but I heard a noise today for the first time. What can I say? The doctors said there was a chance that eventually my hearing might return."

"We will find out how much you are able to hear," said a man of bullish appearance with a scar running across his cheek. The three wore long leather jackets—easier to clean the blood off, quipped the young wits among the elite. The second man who had laid hands on him was as bullish and square as the first, but the third was different. He was a slight, tall, sinewy figure with the ascetic look of an icon—fanatic eyes, large and burning. He looked at Alyosha with those bored, yet inquisitive eyes and said, "Yes, let us find out how much he can hear."

That had been the start of the most hellish torment Alyosha could ever have imagined. They pummeled him with their fists and kicked him in stages that were interspersed with "trials of his hearing." He could have endured their brutality, the blows, the rib-shattering kicks. The true torment, however, came from the insidious, sadistic games they had prepared for him. They would turn him from their presence, facing the window and one would whisper, "Now, push him through the window, it will be a suicide."

It had taken all his will power to relax his muscles, standing unmoving, quiet like a dumb ox in a field. A quiet voice in his head kept whispering, "They do not know how much you can hear. They are here to find our how much of Stalin's secrets you have heard. You have played the deaf man for months now—successfully. Play it a while longer. You can do it. Trust me!"

Following the voice's lead, he stood stoic, as if carved from rock. Soon they began another test. This one involved a revolver being held behind his head. Then, the trigger being pulled repeatedly. He heard the distinct clicks. If they were playing Russian roulette, the bullet would finish him any minute now.

"No," said the quiet voice in his head. "They are not going to kill you until they know what you know. If you convince them of your innocence, they do not have to kill you."

Alyosha never moved a muscle, but kept up his prayers for deliverance. Blows rained upon him once more, assuaging their anger following the failure to break him. Not to worry, they had other tools at their disposal. On and on they went. They tried to break him with the threat of burning, of drowning and an arsenal of less potent threats.

After hours of torment, they shot off a gun behind Alyosha's back. The blast was horrific, the sound deafening. Alyosha turned, facing the trio, and said, "I heard something! What was it?" A punch to his shoulder turned him back immediately, facing the wall.

"Damn, could he really be deaf and just on the brink of coming back from his injury?" asked the scar-faced man.

"Possible! Or a very good actor," offered the tall man with the iconic face. "Yet, I do not think so. We have put him through hell and he never reacted. He could not have heard anything."

Hearing them talk this way, a miniscule amount of Alyosha's confidence returned. He felt almost no pain; his tissues had swelled from the blows to the point where the nerve impulses were suppressed. Blood obscured one eye. It slowly coursed down from his nose over his chin and his neck into the collar of his army-blouse, fresh and clean only hours ago.

While they decided his fate, he stood stolidly with closed eyes. He felt his teeth with his tongue. They were loose, but would mend—none were knocked out. He slightly tensed his body, and almost screamed. Yes, some of the ribs were broken. A few punches to his kidneys, received earlier, were beginning to hurt excruciatingly. Despite the pain he never moved. "Become like the animals in the stable," said his internal guiding voice.

"We will let the teacher decide if he has to die," said Icon Face. "I will not have him killed if the teacher has other plans."

The three NKVD men left the room suddenly. Alyosha, having heard the exchange and their leaving, was faced with a decision. He could drag himself to the bathroom and take care of his injured body or stay exactly where he was, intrepid, implacable—in pain. He stood, praying, "Let it pass. Let them pass me by." They came back with Stalin moments later.

"Look comrade, Stalin," said Icon Face, "he still stands the same way we left him. He did not know we left. He hears nothing except the most violent noises. Although his hearing is returning, it will be months before he can hear voices. Watch!"

He pulled his revolver from his holster and shot into the ceiling. The blast rocked the room; plaster fell from above. A plaster piece struck Alyosha, and he turned. Seeing Stalin he called out, "Comrade Stalin. What luck! You came to rescue me from these men. They insist that I can hear, when I cannot."

"You heard the shot," said Stalin, "and you turned around to find out what happened."

"I heard a hum, then something struck me." Stalin looked at Alyosha, whose eyes, swelling shut amid his bloody face, were fastened on his. Stalin's visage, as usual, was an unreadable masque. It was the same countenance crowds saw when he stood high on a podium, the face he showed at party sessions, the face reserved for party demonstrations on Red Square. Who knew what went through the mind of this murdering tyrant? However, at the end of his silent deliberations he fancied himself in the role of the merciful father of the nation. Alyosha had fallen to his knees before him, and so he said, "These men have been hard on you. They did not know better. They were much too severe for what should have been nothing but a casual conversation. I think you should check yourself into the infirmary." He looked at Alyosha with feigned concern and left.

"Yes," thought the beaten man kneeling in agony on the floor, "much too hard for a casual conversation." However, deep inside he rejoiced. "Saved! Could it be that I am saved to live another day? They seemed to have believed his playacting. Thank you, Lord."

While still on his knees, he heard the head interrogator tell the other goons to help Alyosha to the infirmary. Then he also left. Although the thought of being touched by his tormentors once more sent shivers of fright down his spine, when the goons gripped him by the arms and pulled him upright, he knew he needed their rough assistance. To Alyosha the trip to the doctors, down two floors, seemed to last an eternity. Every step threw agonizing waves of agony over his body. In his pained, muddled mind a record played over and over, "Oh God, let me pass out."

In the bland, pea-green room of the infirmary the men pushed him into a cold metal chair, to the surprise of a young medic whose eyes had grown enormous.

"Comrade doctor, here is a patient for you who carelessly walked down the narrow staircase and fell. We found him at the bottom of the stairs," said the NKVD man with the scar face, without blinking. As if this sentence represented a reasonable explanation to cover the condition of the beaten man, and a reason, nay order, for the doctors to act, the two left.

The young medic's face showed clearly that he was new to the Kremlin's emergency room. He pulled Alyosha into an upright position, eyeing him with mounting dismay. The moment the goons had left, he said, "You must be in great pain."

"I am," murmured the hapless patient.

The medic called for reinforcements. Soon a smiling, young doctor appeared with a female nurse, who looked to Alyosha suspiciously like the aged grandmother Baba Yaga from the witch's fairy tale. She was monstrously large with a wart on her chin, gray hair pulled into a bun on the back of her head, and the cold eyes of a predator.

Inwardly Alyosha quaked; would she, too, torture him? Was there to be no end to his travails?

"Stairs?" the terrifying woman grinned facetiously upon hearing the patient's story. She reached for Alyosha's other arm, guiding him with the help of the medic to an operating table. As the nurse and the medic stripped Alyosha's clothes off his swollen body, the young doctor's face was grim. Baba Yaga—that's what Alyosha called the nurse in his mind—looked upon his broken torso with the jaded eyes of one never to be surprised again and said, "Morphine! A lot! Get the syringes ready, Boris."

Sprawled on the cold operating table, Alyosha looked into the searching eyes of the young doctor. The man's face was serious and drawn as he examined Alyosha, pushing on his painful ribcage with a stethoscope. Baba Yaga delivered morphine into his veins. Minutes later, the unlovely woman looked to him like a beautiful angel. He could suddenly breathe, almost without pain. The world about him, the green walls of the room, the bright lights above him, and the three people had become unreal. They were far away in a nebulous cloud. He heard them as they enumerated the damage of his body.

"Six broken ribs; broken ulna; bruised thigh, kidneys and back; cracked cheekbone and nose. Strange fall that one had!" Subdued laughter followed the latter remark. They slowly pulled him into a sitting position. With the medic's help, the doctor wrapped his torso tightly in cold plaster. "That should stabilize the rib cage for healing," said the doctor, satisfied with his handiwork.

Then they worked on his nose, filling the nostrils with cotton. They salved and bandaged until he was half asleep, then pulled him off the table and walked him slowly down an empty, dingy hall into a small room where they put him to bed on a narrow army cot. They covered him with a sheet and heavy, rough blankets. He was almost asleep—barely hearing the voices of the medic and the nurse.

"They almost finished this one."

"Yes, had the ribs penetrated his lungs he would have bled to death."

"I know! They are getting more brutal every day. I cannot wait to be sent elsewhere, someplace where the patients have real injuries."

"Oh," said Baba Yaga, "these wounds are real enough." They snickered. Silence fell. That was the last Alyosha remembered of that day.

Departure

Volga German folksong, "*Nach Sibirien muss ich reisen*"

Nach Sibirien muss ich jetzt reisen	*Now I must journey to Siberia*
Muss verlassen die blühende Welt	*Leave behind the world in bloom*
Schwer beladen mit sklavischem Eisen	*Heavily burdened with slavish chains*
Harret meiner nur Elend und Kält	*Awaiting me are cold and doom.*
Oh Sibirien, du eiskalte Zone	*Oh Siberia, you icy domain,*
Wo kein Schiffer die Fluten durchzieht	*Where no zephyr gladdens the meadows*
Wo kein Funken der Menschheit mehr wohnt	*And no spark of humanity glows*
Und das Aug' keine Rettung mehr sieht.	*And the eye sees no salvation.*

(Translation S.I.W.)

The doctor released Alyosha two days after his admission. On his way to his old room, accompanied by the young medic, they came close to Stalin's apartment. Suddenly the now familiar NKVD men appeared, filling the narrow corridor, in effect blocking it.

"Do you have family, Kulov?"

"My mother—no one else."

"Good! In that case we will take you straight to your next assignment. You have received new orders."

"What orders? I know nothing of new orders. I am assigned to comrade Stalin."

"No matter what you know," said the leader of the trio, sneering. "I have your new orders. You have been reassigned. Until you ship out you will be staying in barracks."

Alyosha knew better than to ask any more questions and the vile trio volunteered nothing else. They had brought with them his few possessions, stuffed into a valise and a round, long leather kit. They ordered him to dress in the infirmary while they waited. He was forbidden to enter his old room. He painfully squeezed himself into his uniform, slung his greatcoat over his shoulders, and donned his hat.

The goons told him to pick up his gear and follow. He lifted the valise and the kit, groaning as his sore body screamed in agony. The ice-faced NKVD men laughed disparagingly, expressing well-worn sadism. Somehow Alyosha managed to follow them out into the street where they directed him to enter a waiting car. Someone must have been watching over Alyosha, because two of the pugs were about to leave with him in the black sedan when a sharp command by their leader called them away. A violent commotion had ensued in the entry, requiring the full attention of the trio.

One of the men returned momentarily, shouted instructions to the driver and left the scene the moment the car moved out.

Peering myopically out of the darkened window, Alyosha saw the guard at the gate wave them through onto Red Square. The driver half-turned.

"Is that you, Colonel Kulov?" asked a familiar voice, filled with surprise.

"Damnation! Is this you, Slava?"

"Yes, Colonel! What happened to you? You do not look so good."

"You don't want to know, good man." Alyosha now knew that heaven had provided him with this one and only opportunity to let his fate be known to his mother.

"Slava, I must ask you a great favor. Can you promise on the grave of your mother to keep a secret?"

"I promise. What is it, Colonel?"

"I would like for you, on one of your off-duty days when you are sure not to be followed, to go to the address where you have taken me often. It is my mother's address. Her name is Maryonna Kulova, and she lives on the third floor. Please tell her that I have been sent to Siberia."

"You, colonel, to Siberia? Why?"

"I do not know, Slava. Someone wants me to go there."

"I will do it, Colonel, and I will pray for you. In Siberia you will need prayers to all of our saints."

"Thank you, Slava!" They fell silent, each following his own thoughts. Alyosha was still thanking heaven for sending him Slava and keeping the NKVD away. He had known Slava for two years. He knew that the man was not a communist but a drafted soldier who had somehow been chosen for duty at the Kremlin. Reliability and attention to his duties may have been the attributes that had qualified him. Alyosha knew that other drivers were staunch communists, who had received the driving jobs as plums for party activity. As an afterthought he said, "Slava, when anyone asks—we did not talk at all! I was deadly silent."

"I understand, Colonel."

For a fortnight Alyosha remained confined to the barracks of what had once been the Moscow headquarters of the old tsarist Ismailovsky Regiment, an installation situated on the outskirts of the city. After this respite he was ordered onto a train leaving for Kotlas in the Siberian taiga. It came as no surprise to him—he had known for a long time now that his fate was leading him to Siberia. The gulag he was going to had a name holding no recognition or meaning for him—it did not matter anyway. His life was over. The rest of his life would be spent in despair.

Home Torn Asunder

SARATOV REGION
AUGUST 28, 1941

A formal Decree of Banishment by direct order of Josef Vissarion-ovich Stalin was posted in all public places and offices. The order also abolished the Autonomous Socialist Soviet Republic of the Volga Germans. My people, or more precisely, what was left of them, had lived since the establishment of this republic much like other ethnicities of the newly established Soviet Union in the 1920s. Through this new decree we became, instantly, another repressed ethnic group. The Chechens, the Crimean Tartars and the Kalmyks shared our fate of dissolution.

The true meaning of the decree was quickly revealed to us in September 1941. The Soviets, not satisfied with the takeover of our best farms, now wanted the rest. Although our properties, livestock, private implements, houses, barns, stalls—everything—had been thrown into the hodgepodge of collective super-farms, our German collective farms were still more productive and better organized than most others. Therefore, they now needed to be cleaned of our presence. Our religion had already been declared counterrevolutionary, and we worshipped only with the greatest secrecy in small groups in each other's houses. Our churches looked as if stricken with plague. Blotched and broken-down, they were beyond repair—doomed to die.

It was during this bleak, heartbreaking moment in history that Stalin's henchmen came again and proclaimed the evacuation. On September 1, 1941, under the blue sky of the Russian steppe, another Russian commandant loudly delighted in the fact that the hated Germans were punished. He announced that we had ten days grace to collect necessities, whereupon we would be resettled. He had told a lie—there was to be no resettlement for most of us.

Ten days later we were rounded up like cattle. Everyone carried as much as they were able. A rumor had been circulated that we are all destined for the icy hell of Siberia.

Siberia, the name alone froze my blood. My father had already perished there. Mother shared my fear. Doing our evening chores, milking the cows in the *kolkhoz* and feeding the calves, we were thankful for God's grace. It gave us peace of mind that my grandparents had been removed from this uncertain, destructive future. It was impossible for us to imagine what exile to Siberia would have meant for them. We had not heard from Joseph since his induction into the Red Army. We prayed every night for him and his friend, Arkady.

I demurred when our elders asked us to continue some of the *kolkhoz* work, despite the fact that we were branded enemies of the state and disowned of all that was ours. They had begged us in the name of our Redeemer to continue the care of the living creatures until, at last, some responsible people would take over. Yet no replacements arrived while we were there. The political creatures removing us had come motivated by hate and zealotry. Unprepared, without plan, they were willing to inherit what our industrious hands and nimble minds had created. But they were incapable, or, I think too lazy, to inherit the work.

I saw the Red zealots moving about the village, counting the cows, the calves, the horses and pigs; recording on tablets all implements, tools, bales of hay, barns, pens and paddocks. They were functionaries. They knew how to spend and consume; yet they could not create, could not make anything. I marveled that they could walk right by an ailing horse; that they ignored the sores and scabs on a cow and closed their ears to the hungry bellows of young bulls. From morning till night they did nothing to keep the farm going. We only tended to the most basic needs of the most distressed animals, for we had little time to spare from our preparation to be exiled.

The Bible forbids me to hate. I was to love my neighbors as I love myself. My new neighbors, however, were nothing like myself or like the people of the village I grew up in. Oh, I admit it, I hated them! May God forgive me, I despised them, I wanted to hurt them when they mindlessly walked by an aching creature that had never before known neglect; a creature well-tended all its life by people who loved life itself, loved their work, as a grace they were allowed to perform.

Indifference, sloth and mindless greed reigned in a village that had known joy, prosperity and goodness. I railed at Mother. Why would God allow this? Again? Had we as a religious community not suffered enough the first time, before coming to Russia?

"I have no answer, *Liebchen*, who knows what God has in mind for us to discover?" she said. She did not say this in the milksop way some of our Lutheran brethren mouthed religious platitudes. From her, it was a plain statement of fact. She had conviction, and yet, it was not a satisfying answer.

"I hate these people, Mother. Yes, hate, hate, hate, and I can't help it," I acted like a brat, stamping my foot to release my inner tension. "I am trying not to do so, but anger against them rises up in me, bloating me like yeast bulges dough." As an afterthought, I added, "And don't ask me to overcome it with prayer. I have prayed and prayed, and still I want to drive them from the village, if necessary with guns."

Mother's blue eyes grew dark; her face grew serious, sharp, until her nose looked like the tip of a rapier.

"You don't want to become as they are. Speaking like you do will get you there. I can understand your anger. You are young and hurt and you want to make everything right and good. But you know better. You know God gives every man free will. Yet that leaves mankind in a quandary because man is imperfect and therefore unable to live in peace and goodness. We cannot dictate the ultimate fate even with guns. Everyone is responsible for his own actions. The evil deeds of others must be endured, for they will have to account to their Maker."

My mother was an enigma to most people. Always a fragile, dainty figure, she astonished and perplexed people with inner strength and iron will. Her delicate porcelain face, now run through with the telltale spider lines of worry and sadness, revealed nothing of the steel in her core.

Not satisfied by her pacifism, I asked the elders. I was desperately searching for a chink in their spiritual armor that would allow me resistance to brutality and meanness. But the old, saintly men spoke like Mother, offering only prayer as a remedy against oppression, leading to verisimilitude—suspension of thoughts and belief.

"We are not the only people tormented and oppressed," they said. "Look, Katya, and see what they do to Kalmyks, the Chechens and the Crimean Tartars. Pray for them, child, they need prayer as much as we do."

I walked away and prayed. Yet I could not pray for the Soviets who had killed my father. I cursed those who had taken Joseph with hundreds of thousands of our young men, pushing them into the front lines of the war, sparing their own cowardly hides. Few of these men, forcefully removed, were ever heard from again. I fought against the violent thoughts in my heart, but could not reconcile the preached concept of Christian love with my reality until I learned a vital truth much later in life. And yet, it is a concept blindingly brilliant in its simplicity: One must not give up righteousness, standing up against evil, fighting the good fight—no, to the contrary—one must fight, while still wishing and praying that one's enemies may reach spiritual clarity, receive goodness and grace, and thereby reach their full human potential.

Breaking the Ties—Gathering Things

We spent every day of the grace period searching through the remnants of our plundered wardrobes and old cases in the attic. Our search was rewarded in a wondrous way. My mother remembered an old trunk my father had left especially for me. The spiderweb-covered, seemingly vilely abused object had never roused anyone's curiosity. When I opened the ancient trunk, leather-covered, vestmentally adorned, I found a treasure. Stored there, almost on top, gently wrapped in tissue, spiked with naphthalene balls, lay a great coat of surprising worth. Although the rich brown outer cloth was worn in places, slightly moth-eaten in others, it still attracted attention for its softness and fine work. As I pulled out this marvel, lined with karakul lamb, a letter fell to the ground. I read in wonderment what my father had meant for me to know:

> *Lyuba, Katharina:*
> *I know when your hands touch this coat, you will have been driven to search this trunk either by curiosity or by dire need. I hope with all my heart that curiosity, not need, will bring you to open its lid. I told your mother, before I had to leave for Siberia, that every item contained therein is for you. These things are a part of my heritage. Now they will be a part of yours. For the two of us much meaning is contained herein. These things don't mean the same to your mother. She understands that for her the leavings of my life have only sentimental value, whereas for you, they are the symbols and metaphors of our lives and those who have gone before us.*
> *The coat is ancient, and should by rights have joined the bones of the man who wore it. I know that the name Grigori Potemkin is very familiar to you. What would Russian history be without him? It is unimaginable, for he was larger than life. Without Catherine the Great and Potemkin, her faithful vassal, today's Russia would be just a backwater of Europe, inconsequential in the global view. The Tsarina and Potemkin fashioned Russia into a country with culture and power. I know you learned our history well, but you cannot know that you are, by blood, directly connected to those who shaped the destiny of our nation.*

I have never revealed, even to your mother, that I am a direct descendant of Potemkin, albeit through a byline. Those mean of spirit would call the man, my great-great grandfather, born to a then prominent noble woman, a bastard. They are welcome to the appellation, but I assure you that this wonderful woman was happy to have Potemkin's child, and was provided with the means and care for them both. Their life was filled with joy, devoid of notoriety or disrespect. The child grew to be a man of learning and political influence, inheriting later in life his mother's estate. Out of respect for his mother, no claim was ever made on the name Potemkin by his descendants.

I hope that the very spirit of this man, bred into our line, will help us to endure the fire in the crucible of Stalinism. I fear Stalin, for he is a man lacking a soul; I fear the future that will be ours. Stalin is a man capable of smilingly killing millions to achieve his goals, capable of killing for nothing but the sheer exertion of power. I have known men like him before. They were like the walking dead, devoid of all feeling, but none had the power structure of this Stalin at their disposal. Therefore, I fear that terror will reign in this country, the blood of our own people will flow and injustice will triumph.

As I am powerless to protect my family, my only hope is prayer. I pray that you will be strong, able to hold onto God, capable of action with righteousness and conviction.

With my blessings and great love for you,
your father Alexander Petrovich Grushov

My tears were falling upon the pages as I read. Papa, taken to die in Vorkuta, had been gone for a long time, and yet I felt as if he was standing beside me in the attic. His love and concern for me were almost palpable. A second sheet of paper was filled with explanations of the items he had left for me. In addition to the broadtail coat—I knew that broadtail was the finest of the karakul furs, consisting of the pelts of prematurely born lambs, harvested in a horrible process that often killed the ewes and the lambs—I found an engraved, jewel-encrusted gold watch, and a small leather bag, once white but now yellowed. I gently shook the content of this bag into my open hand, and lo, it contained loose gemstones. Like blood drops, three rubies the size of robin's eggs lay in my palm; five emeralds of different sizes, flawlessly cut, contrasted with a few pearls and two diamonds. I immediately realized that I held a great fortune in my hand.

I was astonished. Through good times and bad, this fortune had been concealed here in a trunk. Father, all of us, had lived sober, frugal lives while the jewels had slumbered in their white, soft bag. I called for Mother. There was no doubt in my mind that, of course, I had to share the knowledge of this fortune with my mother.

Mother, prematurely aged by worry, tiredly glanced at my hand and smiled. "I knew they were there, he told me they were for your future the day you were born. The true miracle is that they were never discovered. Twice the Reds had looked into this trunk and had looked no further, not knowing the true value of the old coat with its naphtha smell and moth-eaten fringes.

Amazing grace, I was rich. Good thing the Soviets did not know about this stash, they would have killed me as a traitor in a minute. I thought hard. What would Father have advised me to do in this situation? About to be deported, we would have need of the treasure. At the same time, I understood the terrible risk of carrying such a fortune around on one's person. Never mind the problems we would be facing, changing the cold stones into necessities. What would happen if we were to be separated? I did not trust anything the Bolsheviks said. So far, our experience with the new Russian power had consisted of acts of brutality, theft, murder, lies and unwarranted force.

Therefore, I said to Mother, "Here, *Mamochka*. We are the only two left in this family. Let us share this fortune just in case they should separate us." I had divided the stones evenly and offered her half of the treasure in my outstretched hand.

"*Ach, Kindchen*, don't say such a thing. We will stick together and it doesn't matter who carries the stones."

"No, no, Mama. We must split them up and think of every possibility. We also need to devise a sure way of hiding these stones so they can't be found in even the most intimate searches."

Mother was not convinced that such measures would be necessary; therefore, we argued for a while. I, however, was extremely persuasive. At last, she gave in, taking half of the stones. All night long I tossed and turned, trying to imagine the safest spot on my body to carry the stones. Sewing them into items of clothing seemed a sure bet at first. Yet, I reject that possibility when the idea of theft entered my mind. Anyone could steal a garment while you bathed or slept. The experiences of my short life had led me to believe that the people of the Revolution had no morals, no ethics. They seemed devoid of feelings for anyone, never mind those they could label counterrevolutionary or enemy of the state. All German citizens had become enemies of the state, allowing all of "them" to steal from us with impunity. But I was not whining. Lord, look at what they did to their own people!

It was obvious that clothing or other belongings were worthless as hiding places. Excluding all other items, I was left with my body. But how and where on my person was I to stash the gems? That was the question. Toward morning the answer came to me. I said a prayer of thanks and slept deeply.

"I know how to hide the stones safely on our bodies," was my greeting to Mother the next morning. When I explained, she thought it would work well.

Exodus to Siberia

No State can build prosperity on the bones of its own citizens,
and if all who have eyes to see are tortured and killed,
then the rest will live in a kingdom of the blind for a very long time.
—Excerpt from "Excursion to Gulag, photos of labor prison camps"
[judicial-inc.biz/excursion_to_gulag.htm]

On the morning of our ouster from Schaffhausen we ate a meager meal of *kasha*, a swallow of milk and an apple. Our bundles and cases were packed. We were not allowed to take much, and had spent considerable time carefully evaluating each item for its usefulness before choosing it to be packed. Some choices were heartbreaking. Mother's old family Bible, brought to Russia by Christoph Meininger when he was just a boy, was an article we could not take. Over the years it had grown exceedingly large in volume, as each child born into the family had a personal section, handwritten, added to the book. Inspired, profound sermons from visiting pastors, in their entirety, had also joined the pages, and so had special prayers and events, enlarging the book enormously. Rebound, Mother's Bible had become a weighty tome and, moistened by her tears, had to be left behind.

Today, on what I had named in my mind the morning of infamy, we washed our dishes until I said: "Why on earth are we washing the dishes. Who cares that they are dirty. Those taking our home from us will not thank us for our labor, nor will they give one single thought to our fate."

"Perish the thought," came Mother's rebuke. "If all would think like that, human societies would fall apart." And so we finished the dishes.

We heard the trucks pull into the village; heard rough, harsh voices, shouting for us to assemble; then, we left our home for the last time, carrying what we hoped would sustain us through the worst. Outside we comforted each other; proclaiming righteously that, with God's grace and our love for each other we would survive, nay, triumph—wherever they sent us. And as we stood in the drab morning light, under a gray sky, we helped each other with the array of our burdens.

One by one, they filled the trucks with our neighbors. Everyone, without distinction, was herded like cattle into the open trucks. As the morning wore on, the sun burst through the light cloud cover and soon the morning became odiously hot.

"*Davai, davai!* Faster, faster!" shouted the Red soldier, shooing us up a ramp. Encased in his uniform, in broken-down, slant-heeled boots, covered by his felt great-coat, rifle slung over his right shoulder, the pimple-faced manling was a picture of fury and unhappiness. His sweaty brow was crowned by the ubiquitous gray, round cap of the foot soldier, sporting above the forehead in a red-circled field the insignia of hammer and sickle. The insignia was new, denoting the victory of the Bolsheviks over the intelligentsia and all things bourgeois.

The pasty-faced guard tried herding us up a cattle walk into an open truck. Meanwhile the heat of the day became oppressive. Perhaps, later in the day, the Russians who had been left in the village would see thunder and lightening. For us, crowded together before the trucks, the heat was as unfortunate as it was for the hapless soldier for we carried on our bodies many items we could not bundle into the cases they allowed us to take. Trundled together, old and young alike, we clumsily bumped each other with our cases and bundles.

Along with the pimple-faced soldier, a red-faced, rotund sergeant with the manners and the visage of a Kazakh peasant shouted his *davais, davais.* Great eructations emanated from his stomach, tinging the surrounding air with vodka fumes. I stood close enough to him to be inundated by the cloud and imagined vividly how a precocious child, igniting a match, could set this scene afire. However, my temporary impious and hilarious musings were instantly extinguished by the plight of our people. Surrounding Mother and me, they pushed and shoved like cattle for the best places on the truck, exhorted by the Soviet soldiers.

The truck, I would swear, was a conveyance the army had used to transport cattle and horses to the front lines during the war. The cattle walk, pockmarked with cloven imprints of hooves in the planking and the sharp odor of cattle dung, reminded us of previous uses. Two benches, so rough that the old people given the seats snagged their clothes on long slivers, had been added to the wretched, dilapidated lorries. Not wanted anymore in the war effort, they made a despairing pretense at serviceability for humans.

It was interesting to observe that even in life-altering situations our basic character traits did not change. I noticed that we all behaved very much according to the formula we had employed during our previous life. Angela Huber, the angel of our village, eighteen and holy, stepped into the cattle truck in a manner befitting an angel passing through the gates of hell. Her pretty head, crowned by a broad braid of shining chestnut hair, was raised high, held up by a slender neck encircled by a black velvet band holding a jade cameo. Her large, brown eyes expressed the same fear I had seen in doe's eyes when cornered. She stepped high, as if fearing her feet would be mired in morass, and her right hand pressed a bundle to her small breasts while the other clutched a case so hard that her knuckles shone white.

Barbara Bauer, voluptuous, twenty-four and still unmarried, flirted shamelessly with the eructatious sergeant to be given quick entry onto the truck, gaining a good seat there. Frau Fröhlich, seventy-five, clinging to her octogenarian husband, limped up the plank looking up toward heaven, a lifelong trait of hers. The comfort she derived from above was palpable.

Mother and I clambered up the ramp. I found a seat for her on one of the two benches running along either side, and remained standing because there weren't enough seats for those in need of support. The truck was almost filled when a loud shout stopped the proceedings. A messenger had arrived. Moments later, a shout ordered all unmarried young people from fifteen to thirty to disembark the truck.

"I won't go without you," said Mother, clutching my hand. And true to her words she rose, picked up her bundles and walked off the ramp with me.

"*Nyet! Nyet!* You can't get off!" shouted the soldier who had been the enforcer of all orders so far. Not knowing what to do with two non-compliant women, he called for re-enforcement. A military officer, apparently of high rank for he fairly shone with glittering medals and epaulets, approached and grimly questioned the low-ranking youngster. He frantically pointed to us and explained in a high-pitched voice that these two unruly women refused to separate as he had ordered.

Mother and I stood side-by-side, hands linked, surrounded by our bundles. I imagined Mother's face was showing the same defiant look set upon mine. Behind us, huddled together like sheep, stood a flock of teenage girls and young women.

"What's this disobedience?" shouted the officer once he understood the situation. "You have been given clear orders. Older women must be on the truck, young women down here. So up with you, Mother."

"I am not leaving without my daughter. I will go where she goes and do what she does."

"You will go into the truck!" shouted the officer, pulling his pistol from its holster. Without warning he struck Mother across the face. Her nose, and a gash on her cheek, bled ferociously. I had been about to throw myself at the officer and pummel him with my bare fists, when Mother, sensing my move, threw her arms about me, screaming, "No! No! It is useless; do as he bids. We have no power. We have no rights. We must bend—not break."

"Listen to your mother," laughed the officer gleefully, while the young soldier, perhaps thinking of his own mother, looked on terrified. "Come, come, Mother," he said soothingly, "come back into the truck."

As the young soldier was already pulling her up the ramp, I hugged and kissed my mother one last time. "I will pray for you," Mother called to me, as our separation widened. "God will keep you. I know you will survive."

"Stand back, you!" shouted the officer, and I stood back. I did not know that I was crying. My eyes were riveted on Mother's sweet, bleeding face—her eyes huge, and so incredibly sad. With one fell swoop, fate had robbed me of my last family member. I watched as they pulled up the cattle ramp, closed the truck's tailgate and drove away.

Mother and I looked at each other, as if our eyes were pulling the essence from one another into our being; looked passionately, until a hand touched mine and a female voice said, "Pick up your things, Katharina! Or the officer will leave them behind."

I looked around me and saw that the young women and girls were walking down the road, led by the terrifying officer. Struggling, they carried their bundles, some let their bags drag along the ground as they toiled under the burning sun. Except for Angela Huber, I was standing alone in the street. "Komm, we must follow or he will get angry and punish us," said the sweet girl, pulling on my arm.

It was for her that I moved. I picked up my bundles and walked beside her toward a new truck, which had just arrived. The imperious officer stopped the vehicle with outstretched hands. Angela and I reached the group of village women as the first girls walked up the plank. I was numb. Searing pain had killed something inside me. Automatically I did what Angela did. I walked onto the truck and sat upon my bundles as everyone did. Soon, the truck drove through Schaffhausen. The houses and cottages of the village passed before my eyes one last time.

With dull eyes I looked upon our mutilated, sweet, old church, and thought that by now, we all looked as hurt and abused as the dear old building. Out on the road I looked to where the steppe meets the horizon. Somehow I knew that I would miss the vastness of this landscape terribly. The steppe's emptiness had crept into my soul, to be locked up in there forever.

At some point during the journey, my mind left my body for another place. To this day, I cannot remember what happened along the way. I remember that at the Saratov train station we were herded into a rickety railroad car. At that time, I noted German girls and women from many other villages being loaded onto this very same train.

Someone had asked a passing official where the train would take us. "Moscow!" had been the snide answer. "You Germans will all be domestic servants for our Russian ladies."

Train to the Taiga

When the soldiers locked the doors behind us, the rail car was tightly filled with our bodies. We barely had enough room to sit on our few, balled-up bundles and belongings. To stretch one's legs was impossible. Soon the enclosed compartment became so hot that some women fainted. The very air became polluted—toxic to breath. Some of the women, especially those still in their teens, were gripped by hysteria. They attacked the doors, pummeling the heavy planks with their feet and bare fists to no response—no one listened, no one cared.

Benumbed, I leaned against a wall. Sweat oozed from every pore, flowing in rivulets, seemingly from the roots of my hair straight into my shoes. I, too, began feeling faint. At the point of swooning, I was saved by the car jerking forward as the train began to move. As the wheels rolled faster and faster, fresh air poured through the many cracks in the floor and the planks of the sides. Soon we felt better.

Among us were a few young girls. The youngest was Hanna Müller, fifteen, who cried pitifully, consumed by a nameless dread—a mixture of uncertainty, a loss of family and impending doom. We all felt the dread of uncertainty, of not knowing where we were going, what would become of us, whether we would be allowed to live or were consigned to die. In the midst of our despair a strong voice rose in prayer. Angela Huber recited the Lord's Prayer with such strength and conviction that, joining her, our voices soon broke free of the railcar prison, raising prayers in the cars following ours.

Night came soon. Exhausted we sank onto our bundles, trying to find a position allowing us to sleep. In the middle of the night a commotion ensued. Until now we had patiently, excruciatingly, held onto our bodily excretions. Now, however, the restraint had become torture for some. They cringed with modesty. What to do? There was no privacy, no designated area for relief.

We talked, searching for a solution, and decided that one particular corner where the cracks in the floor were exceptionally large would serve the purpose. By morning the air in the car had become fetid.

Grayish light, creeping through the cracks, announced the dawn. It had been very cold during the night. The plummeting temperatures had chilled our sweat-soaked bodies making us shake and shiver until we were able to pull warm clothing from our packs. Yet, soon, in the daylight, we shed these things as the car heated up once more.

We were plagued by ferocious hunger pangs. Few of us had thought to bring food, but more than anything else we were tormented by terrible thirst. The thirst overwhelmed us; it was driving us mad. The vocal among us, obsessed with insane repetition over the lack of water, aggravated the situation.

The train stopped, and we thought: "now the soldiers must allow us to drink." I peered through a crack, spying brush and trees close to the rails. Others reported seeing a railway station, a small place, dreary and desolate.

As before, we pounded on the doors and screamed for water—to no avail. It seemed that, once loaded onto the train, we had been deserted by the soldiers. When someone uttered this terrible thought, panic set in. Loud screams emanated from every car, and panic fed upon more panic. Women's voices, high with suffering and madness rent the air, but there was no one listening.

The train rolled on again. The women around me sat in hopeless stupor, knees to their chests, faces buried in their arms. Some wept, some prayed, some were dazed, staring mindlessly into the void, while still others rocked as if deriving comfort from the motion. Futilely I thought about the morrow, how to attain release from bondage, wasted thoughts, for the future could not be discerned through reflection.

For no particular reason the jewels I carried came to my mind. I had them with me—but they could buy me nothing. Mother and I had agreed that the best way to keep them on our person would be in an innocuous, everyday item, an item so revoltingly personal that no one would steal it even if given a chance. We had agreed that the most personal item many German women possessed was *ein Falsches*, a falsie. Women made these props from their own, combed-out hair, using them as the centers of their buns. Wrapping their long hair around this ball, they created a tidy hairdo.

Accordingly, we had baked our jewels into a ball made from water, flour and salt. The salt insured that the ball that would not mold with time. These two balls had then become the centers of our "falsies." These thoughts drove me even deeper into melancholy. I wondered where Mother was now, if she suffered as awfully as we did. Would she be able to use her jewels to gain favors? Would they gain her life when others had to perish? Only God knew the answers to my thoughts.

Like caged beasts, we survived in the train car for two days and two nights. They were days filled with insanity, despair, hunger, thirst and filth. When the third morning dawned the train stopped. We all remained silent, listening intently. We heard voices, raising our hopes for deliverance. Soon thereafter, the car door was thrown open and shouted commands told us to leave the car in good order or suffer severe consequences.

Although we desperately desired to rush out into the light and find water, our legs hardly carried us at first. We stepped cautiously. When I walked out the door onto a narrow boardwalk, the view before me took my breath away. Except for a narrow clearing, I saw trees wherever I looked. Birch, alder, beech and trees I had no name for were all around the train. Balancing along the platform with my bags was difficult. We walked with the gait of the old and frail. But we were young, and after our cramped legs straightened, walking became easier.

There were accidents. Some of the women, anxious to leave the awful cars, tumbled off the all-too narrow ledge, falling down a few feet into a watery muck, a result of the thawed upper layer of permafrost. We learned about the intricacies of permafrost later.

From the platform, we stepped onto solid ground, and painfully maneuvered on unsteady legs. Shouting guards herded us in groups toward waiting trucks. Beyond the train station, in the background, I saw a drab encampment. Barracks, surrounded by high fences and guard towers, stood out threateningly against the hazy sky. We had heard that this might be Kotlas, the gulag by the Northern Dvina.

I knew Russian geography well and understood why the Soviets would set up a large gulag by this river. The Northern Dvina wound through this part of Siberia all the way to Arkhangelsk, where it joined the White Sea. It was clear to me that the river could be used to transport wood, goods—and prisoners.

However, we were not to see the river. Instead, we were shoved and pushed into the waiting trucks, while being flogged with curses and sticks. Aboard, we did not have to wait long for the vehicles set out on the road as soon as every truck was loaded. There were benches only on each side of the canvas-covered vehicles. Therefore, most of us were left standing in the middle swaying dangerously as the truck bounced over the seldom-tended road, which looked as if eruptions of the soil created daily more craters. Our bundles, our sole possessions, were stored between our feet and a great hindrance as we tried to balance, keeping from falling.

The Gulag

They were informed by all the camp authorities that they had been abandoned by the world; they were beggars and lucky to receive the daily soup of starvation.
—MARTHA GELHORN

I think we traveled in this unpleasant mode for twenty kilometers—a distance covered in stunned silence. When the trucks stopped, the two guards sitting in the back threw open the tailgate and again we clambered down the cattle ramp they had attached to the truck. We were so tired and thirsty we could hardly be prevented from kneeling beside the puddle in the road, to drink the muddy water.

"*Davai, davai!* Faster, faster!" they shouted, unhappy with our disembarkation. *Davai*, we learned, was the most beloved word in the language of the guards, for they used it constantly to verbally whip the prisoners, all of whom they considered intransigent and uncooperative. I looked around and we were standing in the middle of a clearing in a beautiful forest. As it was about the 13th of September, autumn was already clearly present in the golden leaves of the birches, the reddish-gold of the maples and beeches.

Here, in Siberia, the days of warmth were numbered. I had heard that henceforth a snowstorm could arrive unannounced at any time. Then deep frost would follow shortly.

Assembled as a group, we were once again herded like cattle down a raised road into another, greater clearing. There, upon trampled grass and ugly, dried mud, stood a forbidding array of gray, ugly, almost windowless barracks. Central to the compound, a large building denoted its administrative status by the flagpole before it, flying the red hammer and sickle flag.

The few soldiers who had brought us here tried unsuccessfully to arrange us in formal rows before this building. We, however, had been pushed beyond endurance and were clamoring for water. Some of the women had fallen; some knelt, some howled with demented fervor. I felt faint, swaying, barely able to stay upright.

Into this bedlam stepped what seemed to be the commanding officer of the camp. If he had intended to address us, it was not to be. To my surprise, nay to my amazement, the commandant looked at us with something amounting to pity.

"Bring water!" he shouted to the soldiers. "They left these women in the train without water." I was astonished—he understood German, for our women had been shouting in German.

"Sit down," he yelled at us, "save your strength."

The soldiers brought buckets of water and birch dippers. The officer avoided anarchy and chaos, firing his gun into the air when some women ran for the water, trying to intercept the soldiers in their effort to drink first. With order restored, we took turns around the buckets, dipping in the birch cups, drinking the life-giving liquid, and were revived.

The worst of our thirst quenched, the soldiers ordered us to stand in rows before the flagged building, counting us as they arrayed us. The camp commander appeared again and addressed us:

"You have now become inmates of the taiga camp Berezovka. You have been sent here to fulfill your duty as Soviet citizens, to fulfill the grand vision of our leaders for a victorious Soviet Union. You will be felling the trees, which are sorely needed for the construction of a railroad, which will be connecting the workers' camps of Siberia; a railroad, bringing iron, coal and wood fuel to the front and to the cities of our great Union."

The commandant, a fairly young man, thirty-two to thirty-five perhaps, seemed uncomfortable while making his cheering, patriotic speech, as if he did not believe one word of it. He had a pleasant, sad face beneath a thick thatch of brown hair crowned by his round army hat. Perhaps I imagined things, but I thought I detected deep sadness in his face and in his voice.

He announced that the soldiers were not here to guard us, but were protection against attacks by bears and wolves. "You can wander off, if you wish," he said tiredly, "but, although there are no fences around camp, escape is futile. For if the wolves will not get you, the bears and the wolverines will, or, perhaps, the swamps will swallow you."

One by one the camp commander enumerated the Party's grand expectations of us. This was followed by the camp rules, those things permitted for us to do at camp and those forbidden. The Party insisted on a norm of ten felled and limbed trees per day. Hypothetically, that might have been possible to accomplish for a man in a temperate climate, with good tools and proper nutrition. But here, in a frozen wasteland with miserable tools and abominable food? I wondered from the beginning if women could possibly achieve such a norm. We were unused to such labor, such dire circumstances.

For the fulfillment of the prescribed norm, we would receive a few slices of bread, a bowl of *kasha*, and perhaps potatoes and vegetables each day—sometimes even a bit of meat whenever possible. What did possible mean? Where did meat come from? Was this camp not supplied with food? Did they have to hunt game to feed us? I wondered!

"Whatever we get—you will receive," said the commandant as if he had heard my question. "You will have to work every day except Sunday," he went on, promising us, "Then you can bathe and wash your clothes."

He talked about the difficult, permanently frozen ground, which only thawed a foot on top during the summer, leaving water standing in pools, creating bogs and runnels.

"You will have to learn how to cut the trees, because they are shallowly rooted and have a tendency to fall upon the crews if not properly handled," he said. Moments later he threatened that non-fulfillment of the norm would result in an according cut in our rations—two-hundred less grams of bread for every tree left standing. I listened carefully to his words—they sent chills up my spine. I feared already that I would be unable, even with another woman's help, to cut ten trees and turn them into logs in one day.

I was young and healthy, but I had never performed this kind of hard physical work at a steady rate. Furthermore, I knew nothing of sawing, limbing and the other tasks he talked about. And what would our life be like in winter? From all I knew of Siberia, in just another few weeks the camp could experience its first frost and snow. What then? How could one work in temperatures freezing your very breath? Suddenly I was cold— chilled to the core of my being. A monstrous fear gripped me—fear for myself, and the innocent young women around me.

Meanwhile, the commandant droned on, "There will be no fraterniza- tion with the soldiers. They are only here to protect you, so don't approach them in the hopes of getting better conditions." However, fraternization, with its sexual overtones, was not on our minds. I tried to overcome the deadening fear that rendered me helpless and frozen by concentrating on his words.

He spoke of hygiene—delousing! What was he talking about? We had no lice or bed bugs—supposedly the camp was clean. A soldier standing close by said under his breath to a comrade, "The camp is pristine. The bed bugs froze to death last winter." He spoke in Russian, thinking no one would understand. The soldiers grinned conspiratorially—the leer of the initiated.

The commandant droned on incessantly: there was a camp doctor who would get rid of vermin. There were toilets—screened outdoor pits. "Don't go there at night. At night wild animals sometimes search the camp for an easy meal."

At last, we were dismissed and led in groups to the barracks where we would be supposedly cleansed of vermin. Our belongings were taken to one hut where men in rubber suits and gas masks presumably sprayed them with DDT. In another hut, with the doctor in attendance, we had to divest ourselves of our clothes until we stood naked in the late afternoon gloom.

Our distraught, clamorous protests against this rude, brutal and completely unnecessary treatment were instantly extinguished by a group of soldiers called in by the doctor. With the full force of their batons falling on the bodies nearest to them, they stopped all resistance. We disrobed, humiliated and ashamed, as we stood naked before the grinning soldiers and the perversely leering doctor. I had a full view of the man who suppos- edly had sworn the oath of Hippocrates yet looked nothing like a sacred healer. Rather, he appeared to be a round-faced, brutal butcher, seeking victims among lambs. With the greatest pleasure he watched our shame, our cringing discomfort, taking an unholy, disgusting interest in our bare bodies. When the last stitch of clothing had fallen to the floor, our garments were taken from us for "decontamination."

Surrounding me, the chaste women and girls from my village exhibited every form of humiliation and loathing. Their crossed legs, their arms shielding their breasts, clearly showed their anguish. Never in their life had they displayed their naked body for a man other than a husband. Even the few married, childless women had never faced an event so traumatic and personally invasive.

The worst, however, was still to come. A complement of soldiers rolled hoses and barrels into the bare wooden room, and after fitting these components together, they hosed us down like inanimate objects. From head to toe we were doused with an abominable, evil-smelling spray that burned our eyes and the tender parts of the skin. "Rub, rub, under arms—everywhere," they exhorted, and we, encouraged by the clubs, did as we were bidden.

After what seemed to last forever, they sprayed us with clean water—freezing cold—and allowed us to dry ourselves with the wretched, dirty looking rags they threw at us. At last, we were given some long, gray convict shirts to cover our nakedness and marched to the huts that would now be our home. That day, the squalid, bare huts presented themselves in the very best light we would ever see them. The afternoon sun, shining through a few windows, imparted the illusion of warmth upon the bare, planked floor and the miserable, narrow, wooden cots. They were outfitted with sawdust-filled, spotted, greasy mattresses and frayed, dingy blankets.

How I rejoiced then, knowing that I carried a warm fur coat in my baggage. I would not have to suffer the indignity of having these blankets touch my body. At the present, however, we were shivering from the awful treatment we had endured. We were shaking with endured debasement, fright and abuse, as we trod upon the wooden planks to find a place to fall onto and retreat into nothingness. Looking at our bundles of clothing, it dawned on me: the enforced cleansing had been nothing but a sham meant to demean us. Any vermin attached to our bodies would also be living in our bundles, yet none of that had been fumigated.

In the barrack's middle stood a steel-gray, partially blackened, iron stove. Beside it, someone had built a receptacle for fuel, consisting of branches, stumps and splintered wood. Apart from these necessary items, the room was bare. The planked floor was raised high off the ground, because water stood in puddles throughout the camp and below the huts.

Despite our horrific ordeal, upon entering the dreadful barracks, everyone rushed to take possession of one of the awful cots, to establish ownership. The women in my group were not stupid—everyone sought a bed close to the stove. However, those finding such a bed enjoyed only temporary victory, for soon, with the onset of winter, a system of weekly change was instituted, allowing those on the outside a turn at the stove.

Experience proved that sleeping close to the stove was a mixed blessing—you were warmer close by, but you had to feed the maw of the iron beast periodically. Such crucial details, however, we would learn later. At present, we cared only about resting our abused bodies while trying not to think of the gnawing hunger in our stomachs.

I pulled my precious coat from my valise, wrapped myself in it, and fell soundly asleep atop the lumpy sawdust bag. My rest did not last very long. Whistles and shouts announced that we could go to the kitchen and, arrayed in orderly rows, receive a ration of bread. As we stood in a long line, I marveled at the beauty of the forest. Trees were growing in thick profusion only a hundred meters away from the camp boundary.

We heard that the tree-felling site was further from camp, in ancient stands. A tree had to grow forever in this forbidding land to reach stately size. The timber cut in summer was left on location, awaiting removal in winter, when the frozen ground allowed tractors to pull the logs onto the trucks that drove them away.

Finally it was my turn to receive my bread ration. I almost cried, beholding what I held in my hand. It was black rye bread. But the bakers, leaving them with flour to sell on the black-market and us with little nutrition, had stretched the flour with sawdust. Nevertheless, I was as hungry as a peasant during a famine and bit with gusto into the black piece. At least the bakers had the good grace to leaven and salt the dough, and so I forgave them—temporarily.

We had to pull our water up in a bucket from a well. The well was probably contaminated with runoff melt, because the cement coping was, to my eye, not high enough to keep high water out. Nevertheless, I drank my fill and lay on my bed. Around me women cried, prayed, arranged their few possessions, and talked about their lost homes; talked about their families and the misery of our circumstance.

I was numb and tried to shut out the world by closing my eyes. Having lost my mother, the last and closest part of my family, I felt like an abandoned orphan. Two months ago I had turned twenty. By the customs of our village, I should have been a married woman with my own family.

Now, I recognized that I was blessed. Fate had been good to me. For in the horrific turmoil of this country, I did not have worry about a man on the front or starving children by my side. I could selfishly concentrate on my own emotional pain and physical misery, escaping into childhood, the happy days, the free, stolen moments at large with Joseph and Arkady.

After a while of this indulgence, the soft sobbing in the next bunk seeped into my consciousness. It disturbed me, tugged on my heart. Opening my eyes, I noticed for the first time that on the cot next to me lay young Hanna Müller. Immediately I felt remorse for wallowing in self-pity while ignoring the angst and pain in those around me. How could I have missed, wrapped in self-absorption, that there were others with greater despair.

Chastened, I left my cot and sat beside Hanna. I knew not what to say to the fifteen-year-old—for my heart was filled with sadness and terrors of its own. Not knowing how to comfort, I reached out and pulled her to my breast, saying nothing. Her sobbing shook my body—shook murmured words from my core. I spoke to her as I had spoken in the past to dumb, injured beasts: calves with dead mothers, fledgling birds fallen from nests, a grieving mare standing over her dead foal. However simple and trite my murmur, it seemed to go straight to Hanna's soul, comforting her. Slowly her sobbing eased.

"Where did they send our mothers?" she asked. "Why did they separate us?"

"I do not know. Only God has the answers. I have heard different rumors. Some say they were sent to Moscow to become domestics for the newly rich Bolshevik bigwigs; others say, and I do not know what is true, that they were sent deep into Kazakhstan to labor in newly created *kolkhoz.*"

She thought about this and was quiet. I had agonized over these choices, arriving at the conclusion that I rather wished for Mother to be a Moscow domestic than a Kazakh farmer. I believed that in Moscow, at least, she would have enough food to survive no matter the treatment. There was no guarantee of that in Kazakhstan.

"Do you think we will ever see them again?" asked Hanna. "I mean all of the—my mother, my father, my brothers and sisters, your brother and mother?"

"I don't know, Hanna, *Liebchen.* But I do know that in order to reunite with them we must stay strong and survive—no matter what the camp commander will force us to do. We must persevere, bend under their yoke and live."

My speech calmed her and she fell asleep in my arms. It was perhaps her first rest in days. I nestled her among her own things, covering her with her jacket and the ragged blankets I would also have to get used to, and crawled onto my own miserable pallet. Night had fallen. The warmth of the day left with the last rays of sunshine. Within minutes the sterile barracks room became bitter cold. Soon all talk ceased and even breathing filled the room.

Henceforth, Hanna claimed me as her family. We were lucky, because the next day was a Saturday, giving us two days of respite and a chance to get acquainted with the camp. Every barracks in camp was filled with young German women. Among them, we found friends and relatives from other villages. Standing in the breadline, I came across two of my cousins from Norka, Hildegard Bauer, age seventeen, and Heidemarie Feldman, age twenty. Although closely related, we were but fleetingly acquainted, for the distances between our villages discouraged socializing. But here in the wilderness of the taiga, we suddenly felt a bond—much stronger than before on the Volga. Now, we were twined doubly, by blood and by terrible fate. We had hopes of living together in the same barracks, but these wishes never came to fruition. Instead of living with my blood relatives, I had to room with the camp officer's choices.

After breakfast—a slab of black bread, a watery wheat *kasha*, and a cup of execrable tea, consumed in a large, plain, rough-sided building furnished with crude, homemade tables and benches constructed from birchwood and branches—I decided to stretch my legs and get to know the camp. Hanna had been following me, the way a lamb follows her ewe. She now wanted to come along for the walk I had planned to take by myself. Although I desperately wanted to be alone, to follow my thoughts uninterruptedly, I could not deny her. However, I ruthlessly decided that I would have to find a way to make her independent, granting myself privacy.

On our walk along the camp's border we came upon a young guard—a boy more than a man. He looked forlorn in his ill-fitting, drab uniform. He held his gun across his chest with visible discomfort and eyed us with a mixture of suspicion and interest. His child's face most prominently revealed boredom. Despite the commandant's ominous warning against fraternization, I hailed him in Russian, salving my conscience by prevaricating with the thought that asking questions did not constitute fraternization.

To soften him up, I asked him his name. He hesitated. Then, shyly, he said, "Vasya."

"Vasya, a nice, sweet name. Your mama must love you." He reddened, and his eyes grew soft.

I gave him a moment to recover. Then I asked him where in Siberia Berezovka camp was situated. "We are close to the Kotlas railroad," he said, verifying the information I had collected. Oh, dear God! Kotlas—a gulag as famous as Vorkuta. We had heard rumors about these camps that had sprung up around Vorkuta and Kotlas. They were camps peopled by both criminals and ordinary innocent people who had somehow fallen afoul of the government. How had we annoyed the Party? Had we been too perfect, too successful, creating envy among those performing less? Or was it just enough to have German blood in one's veins to become an enemy?

I tried to hide my horror from Hanna and bravely asked more questions. "Do you know why we are to fell trees out here in nowhere?" He looked proud as he answered, delighted to be an insider.

"They are building a railroad line from Vorkuta to Kotlas, and from here to Konosha. For that mighty undertaking, they need wood—lots of wood."

"Who is building the railroad? You need engineers and planners for such a thing—not a bunch of young women," I mocked. He took the bait and revealed more than I had imagined he would.

"Not far from here, about fifty *versts* away, there is a camp where they hold men confined. Russians, Germans, Poles—all very bright—intelligentsia, you know. They do the planning and the supervision of the work crews."

I was pleased that the soldier was so forthcoming and would have asked more questions, but a deep basso voice boomed behind our backs. Moments later a sergeant approached, cursing at the three of us. Had we not been warned against fraternization? Did he have to beat the rules into our worthless hides? Hanna shrunk behind my back. Vasya looked as if doused with ice water. I was scared to death. However, my father's courage and defiance was my birthright. Gathering my wits, I said, "Forgive us. We did not fraternize. I only asked one question."

"What was it," growled the large, harassed-looking man, staring at us.

"I wanted to know where we were in Siberia."

"And now you know?"

"Yes," I said softly.

"Good! So go back to your barracks and ask no more foolish questions." As Hanna and I crept away from the men, we heard a storm of evil curses break over the hapless Vasya. We felt sorry for the boy. Later, we learned that we all had come away lightly from this affair. There were dreadfully cruel overseers in the camp, who were only too glad to punish the slightest infraction with a hail of lashes.

On Sunday we awoke before sunrise to the clanging of two iron pieces repeatedly struck together—a sound reminiscent of a broken bell—harsh, shrill, demanding. A guard announced that our group of forty women, henceforth named the 102nd, had the use of the washroom for exactly ten minutes. Any ablutions we desired had to be made in this space of time.

The guard led us to the washroom in an orderly line. Like the other buildings, it was another hastily thrown up barracks with a water tank and a heater in the back. Outside were two huge metal tanks, which, we learned the very moment before entering the washroom, we would have to fill every evening after work. Along two rows of wooden slats, holding metal washbasins, the women from the barrack next to ours, the one hundred, were already scrubbing their faces and brushing their teeth. After a night of sleep, a little food and cleansing water, some of their spirit had revived and they smiled at us as we marched in.

The guard shouted for us to line up the way we had marched in and to stop before a basin. He instructed to us to take the basin to the water tank, fill it, return, and begin cleaning. We had barely filled our basins and begun to wash when the women from the next two barracks were led in. Although the water was cold, the soap harsh and alkaline, and the towel a shredded rag, I felt better for the wash—ready to face the day.

Throughout the proceedings we were urged to hurry, for the women of other barracks had yet to arrive. Back in our barrack, we were told by a bored guard, who was obviously annoyed to have to perform this duty, to choose a leader for our group of forty. He commented to us that we had been fortunate in the assignment of our hut, because it was the only one without bunk beds—a circumstance that might yet change. He claimed we were lucky, for whatever might happen in the future, right now we only had to cope with half the bodies.

We stood in a circle, more asking for than choosing a leader. The guard had enumerated the duties of the group leader and they were considerable. It was immediately apparent that such a person could be a tremendous boon or a considerable detriment to the group. It had to be a person with the inner strength to stand up to authority for the group. Shrewdness would be a preferred attribute in a leader, for we had noticed already that the sharpest, fastest and most aggressive women got the best in this place.

The one to appropriate our hut had been Barbara Bauer. She had pushed by the young soldiers guarding us and chosen the nicest-looking of the barracks; the rest of us had followed her like sheep. She had also managed to get the best bunk—close to a window and the stove, and had been first in the bread line. It followed inevitably, we chose her to lead us. In the back of our minds resided the thought that one so capable of finding the greatest advantages for herself would undoubtedly do well for us, because anything benefiting the group also served her interest.

We had barely chosen Barbara, when the guard returned. Having been informed of our choice he smiled, and told her to line us up and lead us to the mess.

We received bread, a hard-boiled egg, tea and a tablespoon of sugar. Here I must mention that, although the mess was stocked with tin plates and cups, it afforded no cutlery. We had been warned to bring our own spoons and knives or eat with bare fingers and slurp *kasha* from the bowl. Even domestics had to bring their own cutlery. My brother Joseph had told me that soldiers always carried a spoon and a knife in their boots, guarding them at all times, because the army was notoriously lacking silverware. Since the Tsar's time men had to bring their own utensils because small table items were always stolen, shipped home and sold.

By sheer chance I had taken a set of silverware because Mother told me it was solid silver and worth good money. Knowing that, I had sown the set into the side seams of my long underskirt. There, I found, they bothered me the least. The next time I was in the latrine, I would pull out the spoon and use it.

Even in the mess, the guards intruded with their *"Davai! Davai!"* for the room did not accommodate the inmates of even one barrack. Barbara, growing by the minute in her role of overseer, did her best to hustle us from the cantina into the square before the office.

On the ground, barely elevated by wooden pallets, lay bundled, olive-brown uniforms. Before the bundles stood the unpleasant sergeant whose acquaintance we had made the day before. Several guards stood ready at his beck and call. On his order they began to dismantle the bundles by first cutting their binding strings, then they held up single garments in their outstretched arms, showing their sizes.

The sergeant, the soldiers addressed him as comrade Genady Markov, explained in Russian, which I translated for the women, that these garments were henceforth our work uniforms. The soldiers tossed the uniforms into our group. We were to hand them on to the next woman until we could find one that approximately would fit us. As they all were made for small men's bodies, nothing fitted well. The girls complained, groaned, and moaned, because the pants especially were an atrocious fit.

"What are they griping about," asked sergeant Markov. I translated and he laughed, "Tell them they will be glad in winter when they have room to fit other garments beneath." He admitted, sheepishly, "This is the first time we have women in camp. Always had men before." Under his breath, just for me to hear, he grumbled, "I can't imagine what work these girls can do in the woods." He sighed and shouted *"Davai, Davai!"* and hurried us off to have numbers painted on the backs of our shirts and long quilted vests.

From the piles of clothing we were led to a shack in the back of the camp, which was filled with worn, dirty leather boots, the pairs tied together by their laces. We were instructed to choose a pair of these rejects or wear our own boots, if we had them, into the muck of the taiga.

Looking at this terrible footgear, I thought of the people who had worn them. Where were they? Why had they left without their boots? Did they die here in camp? Did they starve or freeze to death, overworked and underfed? By now I had already formed a picture of what life would be like in this camp. The norm, the felling of trees, combined with a diet devoid of meat and fat did not bode well for survival.

"*Dyevochka, dyevochka*, girl, come here," shouted Markov. A squabble over a pair of boots had turned ugly. A guard belabored two of my barrack mates with his baton. I walked quickly to Markov's side. His face was angry, red with annoyance, "Tell them, tell all of them, that I do not tolerate riot and disorder. I will punish such severely—solitary confinement and little food."

I did my best, shouting out his threats with fervor, because I was furious that it took so little for us to turn on each other. I could foresee greater travails, which would cost us dearly if we did not stand together.

I suddenly noticed that, distracted, I had still not found a pair of even halfway-fitting boots. The moment I bent down for a closer look I heard the order to return to barracks. Depressed, I turned to leave with the others. I was worried, because I had no footwear capable of withstanding the muck we were sure to find. To my surprise, Genady Markov called me back and I learned an important camp lesson.

"Take your time and pick good boots," he told me. To the guards he said, "Let her stay here, if she has to, until the next group leaves. She is helpful and I will need her to translate again."

Back in our hut, I found that I had not done too badly with the uniform. It fit loosely and the pants could be held at my waist with the stout piece of cord holding one of my bundles together. I tried on the boots I had found in the pile—not too bad a pair—and thought that with my heavy wool socks and foot wraps I should have a decent fit. I was still contemplating what Markov had said, namely, that being helpful brought rewards. Interesting. I would remember.

Suddenly I heard Angela Huber scream. Everyone rushed toward her cot, where she stood lamenting the theft of some of her belongings. "My warm, woolen dress, the one I wanted to wear during cold nights—it is gone. I had a locket hidden beneath the mattress—it is gone, too." She was wringing her hands, mentioning other missing items—underwear, warm stockings and a precious piece of good soap.

"Who would do such a thing?" she cried! "Are we now going to rob each other?"

"Hush! For God's sake, hush!" I screamed. "It must be someone belonging to the camp staff. It can't be one of our own!" The last word barely left my lips when other women cried out in dismay. Searching their belongings, they, too, found things missing. It seemed that only the best and the prettiest of items had been taken.

Incited by these dismaying revelations, each woman rushed to her bed, leaving poor Angela to deal with her loss. I found my things undisturbed. Everything was still there. The women in my area, Hanna and Barbara among them, had lost nothing. It appeared the thief had filched only from the beds closest to the door, systematically going from one bed to the next. Our return to the hut must have caught whoever it was, in the process of pilfering.

A tragic scene ensued, fraught insanely with distrust. Those women who had lost items, doubly precious for we had so little, insisted on checking every bed. I protested vociferously against the hideous idea that one of us would steal from the others. However, they were not to be denied and a painful search began, during which the most personal details of our poor lives were dragged into plain sight of everyone.

There, before our greedy eyes, lay a stash of delicious cookies. These had been hidden all the time while some of us fainted from hunger. In another bed lay a hard sausage, gnawed on one end; in still another, eager hands pulled from a small bag homemade sanitary napkins, making the owner blush furiously. The demeaning search went on and on. Despite the furor, nothing sinister was found. Thank God, because it would have made life in the same room unbearable, nay impossible.

"It could be that someone from the camp administration steals from new arrivals, taking the good, valuable things—items they might not get here," I suggested.

"Yes," chimed in Barbara. "That is how it must be. But what shall we do about it?"

"We have no rights! We are prisoners!" wailed the married women despondently. Fathers, husbands and the *kolkhoz* commandant had dominated them and they had little spirit left.

"What can we do? Nothing," cried others.

"We will have to take the abuse like all the times when the Reds came and plundered our villages."

Our women had grown up in a male-dominated culture, where their fathers and the elders as patriarchs determined all things in their life. So they easily fell prey to power plays and domination. They were ready to accept what was to them the inevitable—giving up their possessions. To protest meant to be beaten and hurt.

But I had been brought up in a different way—in an almost patrician milieu where women had value. My father and grandparents had encouraged my hackles to rise when I encountered injustice and instilled in me the urge to defend what was mine. I had heard enough. I knew that we could not allow this egregious act to go unremarked. If we did, more theft, humiliation and power plays would follow.

Therefore, I now spoke up with a vengeance. "If we do nothing we shall be at their mercy forever. We will be slaves to all their wishes and desires. We must take a stand. A stand fraught with strength and profound meaning, backed by our willingness to die for it."

The room was deathly silent. The women's faces were stark with fear; their eyes looked upon me with disbelief.

"What do you mean?" asked young Hanna Müller. "Why should we die?" Others, outraged, called, "Why should we want to die for a few stolen things."

"It is like this," I said, "I have seen this before. If we let the theft go unchallenged, without a fight, they will steal with impunity every last little thing we have. But here, in the taiga, we will need every thread to survive. Furthermore, if we stand like lambs to be shorn they will treat us like dirt—turning us into everyone's slaves. They will use us without rules and regulations. This is why we have to protest. But powerfully so—putting our lives on the line."

"What do you propose to do?" asked Barbara, pragmatically. She was shrewd—astute in the assessment of our position.

"We will choose a committee and go before the commandant. We will protest the theft and tell him that we will not work if we are to be robbed of our last few possessions. We must tell him that we would rather just be killed than submit to theft. We are not convicts with a sentence. Therefore, our time will never be over here until we are dead or Stalin dies, and it looks as if he will live a long time. So what do we have to lose?"

"You believe this can work? What if they beat us? Torture us?"

"Then we will endure it or die, but without trying we are as good as dead already. I think the commandant possesses at least a shred of humanity and might protect us."

At long last, after further persuasion, everyone agreed that we must not allow the violation. We did not have lockers to keep things safe, not even a crate to store our belongings.

Barbara, our oldest, had grown in her role as leader already. Although flighty and flirtatious before, the camp had shaken her to the core; survival had become her main goal. "We have to report this," she now said, "and we must make it clear that we have been robbed of too much already. From now on, we will not be victimized anymore."

It was decided that Barbara, Bertha Krause, a married woman with her husband on the front, and I, were to go before the commandant and protest the outrage. We agreed on the content of the complaint. Then the women elected me speaker.

The Protest

In the most comfortable room of the administrative building of Berezovka Camp sat Alyosha Semyonovich Kulov before his plain wooden desk. It was a large room with windows appropriate to its size. His head, rested in his hands, hiding his troubled eyes. He groaned as if in agony. Standing up, he shook himself as if he could rid himself of his discomfort like a dog shakes off water.

Why on earth had fate visited upon him this travail, this torment? A camp in Siberia filled with women! Young, beautiful, innocent women! Why him? He would have to send them into the forest in the depth of winter and torment them with hunger when they failed to fulfill the norm.

He would daily see them in their misery—unable to help them, no worse, be complicit in their torture. He thought of his old mother and the misery his banishment must cause her. How did she fare now that the small flame of her hopes and dreams had been cruelly extinguished?

As he contemplated the past year, it seemed impossible that his life should have taken so many convoluted turns—some deadly, some incredibly lucky. Removed from Stalin's presence, the NKVD had sent him off on a train destined to a convict's camp near Vorkuta. He had believed then that his life was not worth a kopek. If the camp's conditions would not kill him outright, a convict might do him in if word ever got out that he had been on Stalin's personal staff.

While he sat on his bundle of clothes in the overflowing train compartment, a witness to Stalin's propensity to keep Siberia filled with slave labor, a young lieutenant had feverishly combed every part of the train, anxiously calling his name. The train had begun rolling when he finally found Alyosha. Sighing with relief, he thrust a package of papers into Alyosha's hand, requesting him to go to the window for instructions, whereupon the fresh-faced lieutenant fled the compartment.

Alyosha was mystified by the episode. Yet he fought his way through the crush of convicts to the window. Outside, the young lieutenant was running, his greatcoat flying like wings behind him, beside the dirty, gray compartments as the train slowly gathered speed. He saw Alyosha and shouted, "The package. It's from friends—new orders. You are not going to Vorkuta."

Consternation filled Alyosha's brain. What the devil was going on? He had a hundred questions, which he began to shout at the bravely, futilely running man. "See the train commander!" was part of the lieutenant's answer. Alyosha could not understand the rest.

By now however, the train was rolling along at good speed and the force of the wind carried the man's words, as his own shouts were drowned out by the clacking of the wheels. Finally, the young man's lungs gave out. He fell back, standing still at last, waving madly until the train went into a turn and blocked him from sight.

How had this young officer gotten on a heavily guarded prisoner train? Who were the friends who had affected a change in his orders? Alyosha's curiosity was burning so strongly that he was tempted to tear into the papers, enabling him to find an answer to this puzzle. But he did not dare give in to his burning wish and squelched the desire. Every convict in the rail car had questioning eyes upon him. A few, breaking the unspoken rule that forbade invasion of another man's privacy, asked outright, "Good news, comrade? Did they give you a reprieve?"

"I don't know. I have to read this carefully. Maybe good, maybe bad? Who knows?"

"The young officer went to a lot of trouble to get that package to you." This from a pig-nosed con who just would not give up and had to keep on grilling Alyosha.

"Yes," spat Alyosha sharply, putting an end to the inquiry.

He pushed the small paper bundle into the inner pocket of his great coat and thought. Who were they? What friends did he still have left? Who would dare to change Stalin's orders; change the orders of the butcher who would without hesitation kill anyone who undermined his will? "And it is Stalin's will to see me rot in a prison camp in the coldest place on earth," he thought.

After a while, when Alyosha believed the prisoners' attention to be concentrated on a man's tobacco pouch, he pushed his way through to the toilet. In the stink of the filthy dump-toilet compartment, under the miserable light of a fly-speckled light bulb, he laboriously deciphered the meaning of the papers. Although the orders came from the highest command in the army, they did not reveal the responsible person, for the signature under every document was illegible. That, however, mattered little to Alyosha, because the orders with all the stamps and affixtures were official, stemming directly from the high command of the 11th Mechanized Corps, a tank brigade.

He laughed to himself. Nicely done, deflect away from the real thing. He, of course, had nothing to do with the 11th. Instead, in the past, he had been assigned to the 34th Guards in Moscow, an artillery division. He spent a fitful night balancing his body on his belongings as the train rolled and lurched through Russia.

The next morning, maneuvering painfully through the crowded train, harassed by many guards, he sought out the commander of the prison train, a man by the name of Yevgeny Andreyevich Kholstinin. The commander had already been advised that new orders had arrived for Alyosha, saving him from the abysmal fate of imprisonment at Vorkuta.

"You must have powerful friends, Kulov," said commander Kholstinin. "Some influential and mighty people have pulled strings for you. Of course, I will have to check that everything is as it appears. If it does, I shall send you on to Kotlas."

The large, moon-faced commander looked bored and disgusted at Alyosha, as if sickened by his miserable assignment. He had been a combat man, who had trod upon someone's more influential foot and been reassigned to chaperon convicts, malcontents, and innocents to Siberia. He had an enormous staff at his disposal, for Stalin ensured that everybody caught in the NKVD's net would be safely delivered to the gulags to be worked to the edge of endurance.

"Thank you, comrade Commander," said Alyosha, "I have been assigned to car *nomer vosyem*."

"I know, I told my secretary to put you there. You are an officer no matter what. In your car, you will find only soldiers caught between fronts and escapees from the Germans, who have been branded deserters, whether they were or not. The rest are innocents who ran afoul of some petty official and were convicted without trial."

The commander shook his mighty shoulders as if ridding them of vermin. He obviously did not like his involvement in the sordid business of government slavery. A young, clean-cut soldier entered the compartment, carrying a tray with glasses and a bottle. The compartment was pleasantly warm. Alyosha felt almost relaxed for the first time in days. Upon seeing the soldier, the commander growled in a deep basso voice, "*Nakonyetz*, finally!" He dismissed the soldier with a wave of his hand.

"I asked for a drink two hours ago. The requisition officer wants everything in triplicate. Soviet bureaucrats! Ha! Worse than the Tsar's!"

"You are not afraid that I will report your critique of our new bureaucracy?" asked Alyosha, grinning sarcastically.

"I doubt very much that I should be. You and I have both been shat upon by the butchers." He pulled the tray closer with his huge hands. Cradling the bottle like a precious grail he said, "Will you join me in a drink, Kulov? By necessity I often must drink alone; less pleasure—alone."

Alyosha had mentally already waded through the implications of drinking with the powerful man and decided to take him at face value—a good, honest man raked over the coals for nothing, much like he himself. And so he said now, without hesitation, "It will be an honor to drink a glass with you, Yevgeny Andreyevich."

The commander pored the clear liquid into two cut-crystal water glasses, each capable of holding more than sto gramm, a hundred grams. The commander neatly pored sto gramm. "*Na sdorovye*," they clinked their glasses, drinking deeply.

"Very fine, goes down like water," said Alyosha, weak with appreciation.

"*Da, ochen horosho*," came the echo from Kholstinin. "There is no better drink in the world than a fine vodka," he remarked. Alyosha agreed.

They drank in silent enjoyment, feeling pleasurable apprehension right before the vodka bit their throats and warmed their gut. Suddenly Kholstinin bellowed for his aide and the man came running. For a moment Alyosha was disconcerted. "What is going on here?" he thought, anticipating the worst. "Am I going to be arrested? Did I misjudge the man?"

A simple explanation followed instantly. "What kind of a host am I?" smiled Kholstinin. "I give you strong drink and you must not have eaten in a long time."

"That is true, Comrade Commander," agreed Alyosha. Promptly, Kholstinin ordered food to be brought and moments later the smart-looking aide presented a tray with platters of fatty smoked ham, smoked sturgeon, butter, black bread, salt-pickled cucumbers and pickled green tomatoes.

The men fell heartily upon the food. For a while nothing could be heard other than their devoted delight, expressed in chewing and swallowing. Sated, they sat back, relaxing. The glasses were filled again. Now, mellow and imbued with the friendliest emotions, they began a personal conversation, exchanging names of army people they knew and had known in the past. They spoke of their families—Kholstinin had a wife and four daughters living in a village outside Moscow. They told fantastic war and hunting stories; in short they had a great time, enjoying each others company. At last they turned to a Russian's favorite subjects: poetry, song and again vodka.

"I confess, I was in the past somewhat of a poet," laughed Alyosha, made brave by alcohol.

"So, you are a poet, eh? So recite one."

Alyosha thought for a moment, laughed with embarrassment, and said, "All right, here is one for our present situation. It is called, 'In Praise of Vodka'." With the vodka kindling his poetic flame, Alyosha recited:

> For me, the Vodka.
> Not the sweet, insipid wine of Crimea.
> Or the thick beer of Germany
> That sends me to piss.
> Nor the girlish champagne of France.
>
> No, for me the Vodka.
> The drink of Russia.
> Clean as the birch—its birth maid,
> Vodka dispels the numbing cold.
> Only Vodka warms my soul.

"*Ochen horosho*, very, very good, Kulov! You must write it down for me. It says what I want to say about vodka." Yevgeny Andreyevich could not contain his pleasure, praising the poem's Russian flavor, "How clever of you to relate it to the birch, our favored tree," and on and on he went.

When they parted, Alyosha had become the commander's new favorite. Henceforth, things proceeded with splendid ease for Alyosha. He was fed better than anyone on the train; was invited to imbibe at regular intervals, and his transfer to a Kotlas camp became reality. Needless to say, he parted with the warmest regards expressed by Yevgeny Andreyevich Kholstinin.

Slowly, Alyosha's thoughts returned to the present. He looked around and sighed deeply. He was still confined in Siberia, still the warden of helpless women.

Rethinking the incredible stroke of luck that saved his life had put Alyosha in a vulnerable, mellow mood. He saw the people of Russia were now naught but poor devils, ready to be sacrificed if Stalin's finger pointed at them. He thought of his mother—what had they done to her after his arrest? He thought of Kholstinin and the simple, honest soldiers in the prison train who were consigned to slave labor because human error was not allowed in the new system. Just being in the wrong place at the wrong time could draw a lengthy prison term.

For his first year in Siberia he had been in charge of Yagnodnaya, a prison camp for men. It was a much larger complex surrounded by an enormous barbed wire fence. The wire was tightly strung between concrete posts and guard towers, high above ground, shot up skyward every few hundred feet. At night the place was lit so brightly by searchlights that one night, in summer, a disoriented snowshoe hare racing across the ground became the target of the guards, whose incessant firing caused a panic.

At Yagnodnaya he had seen with his own eyes what was being done to the innocent people of the nation. He could not countenance the unnecessary brutality of the guards, the inhumane conditions, the theft, the age-old Russian propensity for graft and greasing of palms. He had been doing his best to institute new, fairer rules, giving the men—most of them innocent as his perusal of their papers and sentences revealed—a slight respite from their drudgery.

The prisoners had appreciated his efforts, shown their pleasure by working harder and made him look good. The old staff, however, revolted. Unable to run the camp in their haphazard way, lazy, slothful, corrupt and brutal, they sent unfavorable reports up the chain of command. They cleverly insinuated that their commandant was too soft on the prisoners, making their lives too easy.

At first, they did not succeed because the work record proved otherwise. Nonetheless, as more and more such reports accumulated, the decision was made to transfer him to a camp that had been impossible to run—Berezovka—the camp without boundaries. That is how he came to be here.

Suddenly, disturbing his reflections, the sounds of a commotion reached the commandant. He called for his orderly, but before the man could make an entrance Sergeant Prokofyev burst upon the scene, shouting obscenities. Of all the sergeants, twenty of them, Alyosha most disliked Prokofyev. Privately, Alyosha called him the zealot priest, for he ran his assignments as Orthodox zealots ran the churches on the outside.

Prokofyev never allowed even the smallest infraction to go unpunished. He saw everything, and everything he saw was a wrong in need of savage rectification. Alyosha had had a chance to observe him for a few months when the camp was occupied by men and had come to resent—nay hate—the man. Hearing Prokofyev's voice, his body tensed.

Pushing through the door, Prokofyev was still shouting. "The audacity! You have no rights. You are prisoners. You shall be beaten and be punished harshly."

Suddenly Genady Markov's voice could be heard booming above the awful noise of Prokofyev's screams. "Calm down, comrade Prokofyev. It is nothing. They just want to talk to the commandant."

Still shouting, both men bounded into the room. Markov gained his composure. "Forgive the intrusion, comrade commandant, but we have a situation."

"Ha," screamed Prokofyev, "there is no situation! If we just locked them up without bread for a day, they'd soon forget their protests."

"What is it, Markov? I still have no idea what this is about."

"There are three women outside. They want to talk to you, actually they are complaining about theft—and they want to be heard. Prokofyev tried to remove them, but they screamed and resisted, creating an uproar. Once aroused, other women came from their huts and began screaming too."

"Just give me a couple of guards with batons and we shall have order soon enough," whined Prokovyev.

"Bring them in, Markov, and you, Prokofyev, go inspect the kitchen. It will be feeding time soon."

Prokofyev stomped out in a cloud of angry misgiving, while Markov called in the women. Alyosha dismissed him, too, and then gave his full attention to the women before him. They were young—in their early twenties or less, he guessed. To his left stood a tall, dark-haired one with lovely, creamy skin, dark eyes and a fine figure. To his right, a blond, blue-eyed, slip of a woman tried to make herself appear taller by standing very erect.

But the one that caught his interest was the one in the middle. She was of medium height, slender, with the most unusual hair. It was medium brown, overlaid with a silvery cast. She had an oval, narrow face, high cheekbones, and large gray green eyes, overshadowed by dark brows.

"You wanted to see me? So speak. What is it about?"

To his surprise it was the intriguing girl who spoke up. He had thought the tall one would be the leader. In fluent Russian, she said, "Comrade Commandant, we have come to you that you might help us by correcting a terrible wrong that has been done us. You see, before being deported to this camp, we were deprived of our families, our homes and our possessions. We are the saddest of the sad, the poorest of the poor. The little we were allowed to bring must sustain us through Siberia's winter, and yet someone in the camp has entered our barrack and stolen from us." The girl's eyes bored into his with almost painful intensity. She wrung her hands, in a gesture of woebegone helplessness that touched his heart.

"We are defenseless. Our huts stand open to every thief. We have no lockers to safe-keep our few possessions. The things stolen from us will be the difference between dying and living, and therefore, we beg you to protect us. We have suffered unspeakably already. Please, please do not allow for us to be victims once more."

The girl's intelligent, searching eyes continued to be fastened on Alyosha's with burning intensity, touching his soul. Her gaze was beseeching, pleading, yet there was more in her eyes—steel. For a moment, after her words faded away, silence reigned. Alyosha thought. How could he help these women without stirring up a hornet's nest of vicious backlash from the camp's communist adherents, the designated, institutionalized overseers, guards and workers? Many of them had been sent here as punishment for falling short of Party rules. He knew that a great lot of them were ruthless scoundrels.

He had come across their kind before. They were the people who stole flour in the bakery and substituted sawdust instead, they stole from each other at every opportunity. They shorted the ration of the prisoners, and savagely punched and beat every prisoner who tried to withstand their camp tyranny. He felt, however, impelled to ask, "Are you certain that the theft was not from one of your own?"

"Yes, we checked everyone's bed and their bundles," said the tall, dark-haired woman.

"What was taken?" The women itemized, as well as they remembered. Alyosha had a fair idea who the culprits were—the same miserable camp-grown ilk he could not rid himself of—for they reported to the party *bonzes* in Kotlas. He could see that the missing possessions were important to the women's survival, but at the same time he wanted to avoid a clash with the Red camp mob, for they could hurt him. Procrastinating, he said, "I will see what I can do." With that remark, for the women had aired their grievance, he hoped the problem would go away. He was wrong. The disconcertingly beautiful young woman's face had become hard. Her lips, so soft and pliant only moments before, had become tight, pressed into narrow lines of bitterness, and her voice was clear and cold.

"I mean no disrespect, Commandant. But that will not be enough. We want this solved and the thief or thieves punished. This cannot be allowed to happen a second time. You see, we are expected to go to work tomorrow, leaving the little we have open to theft. We will not work without protection."

An amazing change had occurred in the demeanor of the group's speaker. Whereas before she had been a pleasant, interesting young girl, she now had metamorphosized into a woman with power—seemingly equal to him—at battle stance. Her eyes had darkened with powerful emotions until they were almost black, and when she spoke, her voice was sharp as a knife.

Now he was intrigued. She had awakened in him that which had been suppressed for years—feeling like a man. As a trabant who orbited Stalin, the sun, he had lost the essence of self, of manliness, and had been naught but a slave. Looking at her—his self had returned. He felt like testing her, taunting her, and so he feigned to be another. He assumed the role of the almighty commandant, "I can send you to work with one word. The guards can make you go to work with their truncheons. A few good blows and you will change your mind."

"Good," said the girl with deadly emphasis, "then go and tell them to kill us all, for we will not go."

Again her eyes fastened on his. Her voice vibrated with deep emotion as she hurled at him, "A few years ago I had a family. Your people killed my father in Vorkuta, you robbed me of brothers, of grandparents, and, just days ago, of my mother. I am all alone in this world, in this horrible camp, while the likes of you live in our houses and sit on our land. So kill me then! Kill us all! In the end that is what your camps are for, are they not?"

Tears streamed down her quiet face in which nothing moved. It seemed as if her eyes never blinked as she looked at him. The women beside her also were weeping statues. When she had spoken of the certainty of death, their eyes had darkened with the same fanaticism.

Alyosha was suddenly neither the exiled convict nor the cynical commandant of a small gulag, but a young man, a poet, a philosopher who once had had hope of a life of truth, beauty and goodness. He felt helpless, overcome by empathy. He heard himself speaking, and knew what he was saying was all wrong. Yet, he said it anyway.

"I will protect your belongings. I will look after you."

The Miracle

The moment he said, "I will look after you," I knew that a miracle had occurred. God had set before us a man with a soul. He would help, for he was not intrinsically evil. I don't know how the commandant did it, but after the evening meal—thin cabbage soup with threads of something indefinable and a ration of bread—Genady Markov came to our hut, leading two soldiers who held the stolen items.

Markov gave me a long, strange look and said, "Here is the stuff. See that it gets to the right people." He turned on his heel and left. Of course, restitution was not complete; not everything was returned. Angela's locket and other small, precious items—such as the soap—were lost. However, we were glad for the things we got back. I was reassured. We could work—he would put guards on our huts or lock them.

So much had happened during this day that my head was spinning when I finally lay down upon the ugly, spotted, sawdust-filled mattress. The bed even had a pillow now, a canvas roll stuffed with wood shavings. Surprising me, a fresh woodsy smell emanated from the awkward roll when my head touched it. Perhaps someone had recently filled it. I said my prayers and, exhausted, I slept.

In the coming days we learned much about camp life and the work in the woods. Every morning the clanking of irons and the shouts of guards awakened us. We had been arbitrarily sectioned off into squads of ten, which had a significance all its own. Our squads, of which mine included young Hanna Müller and Angela Huber, were to do all things as a unit: appear together in the washroom, the mess hall, the drying hut where the boots were dried, and of course work together. And herein lay the significance of the squad. No slave driver was needed to keep an eye every moment on the workers. No, the squad itself performed that job, because rations were cut for every member of the squad if the norm was not reached.

We all pushed each other to greater effort when working, for our hungry bellies allowed no slackers. In the woods the guards gave us a section to work on after allocating the tools, which were counted and signed for by the squad leader—me. Relinquishing their responsibility to the squad leaders, the guards relaxed against convenient trees, smoking while perusing the clouds. Often a few of them joined ranks around a fire, paying no attention to us. Why should they? There was no place we could run to. The only way out was the road, which was strictly controlled. Around us, by three hundred fifty degrees, there was nothing but wilderness.

Within the squad of ten we were paired. We were given long, large-toothed saws that looked as if only a giant could use them, a notion the guards quickly dispelled by putting one of us on each end of the monstrous tool. They yelled at us to push and pull it across a tree trunk, and lo—we made a cut. In time we learned to guide the monster, forcing it to chew the tree until it fell.

I could have cried for the arboreal beauty we were forced to destroy. Since we came from the treeless steppe, we were awed by the forest's beauty. This infatuation did not last long though. After a few days of hard labor we seldom noticed the forest's beauty. Daily these trees consumed our strength—they refused to fall—dying only through our greatest exertion.

The guards forced us to cut each tree low at the base. Thus, we almost knelt at the ends of the saw, for the trunk's greatest thickness was close to the ground. Every work performed by people is imbued with its own art when it is done right, and this held true for felling trees. In time we learned to cut or hew a cleft into the trunk into which we set the saw. We learned to insert wedges when our saws were stuck in very hard wood, and we learned to respect falling trees. We learned to survive.

I was sawing with Hanna that first day when one of the almost severed trees began to twist, falling toward us. By sheer chance and God's providence we were saved from being crushed. I don't know why, but instead of running we threw ourselves forward, on each side of the trunk, into the very direction we had intended the tree to fall. By that simple act we were saved.

While four of us, sometimes even six squad members, felled trees, it was the task of the rest of the group to limb the fallen trees. Some women with small handsaws cleaned the trunks of vestigial branches, while others used clippers and axes on stronger limbs. None of these jobs were easy. The hacking and slashing was just as hard on hands, backs and legs as the felling. We changed work positions often to make it easier on our bodies, but it seemed to matter little which job we were performing—the exertion was enormous. The rotations taught us, though, that we had different aptitudes for performing these tasks. Some women had a knack for sawing, others for skillfully using an axe.

After a few days of logging work, our bodies ached so terribly that we thought the pain would stay with us forever. Straggly branches snagged our clothing, scratched our skin and poked holes into our flesh. A few women had the misfortune to be cut by their own axes. At first it had been impossible to gage the force needed to sever a branch from the trunk. Often a hard strike with the axe at a limb would glance off, injuring the worker.

The instability of the ground added another difficulty to the imponderable hazards of the work. We trod upon the strangest, most unstable surface—ground underpinned by permafrost. Fortunately, it was late in the year and conditions were ideal for this area of Siberia, the ground was as dry as we would ever see it. Most thawed snow and frost-water had drained off into streamlets and bogs. Still, among the trees plenty of deep pools were left with standing water. Small bogs abounded throughout the work area—mosquito-breeding grounds.

Despite our most cautious efforts we came home every night with wet pants and muddy boots. We dried our footwear overnight in the drying shed, receiving it back in the morning baked rock-hard.

Furthermore, in these miasmic miniature bogs resided the most virulent carriers of illness known to man. This was wild territory. Animals crisscrossed the taiga, leaving behind fecal matter and the rotting leftovers of successful kills. In my squad, several women died of septicemia. Angela Huber cut into the muscle of her lower leg with her axe and died three months later of an incurable infection.

The camp doctor had little with which to combat the infections in our wounds. He used yellow soapy waters and alcohol washes to bathe infected wounds, without much efficacy. I found for myself that the terrible gray lye-soap that circulated around camp was more effective in keeping infections at bay than any of the doctor's antibacterial solutions.

We were lucky that the beginning of our camp term fell in a very benign September. Thus we were the beneficiaries of fourteen initiation days before the full horror struck. We learned some valuable lessons the taiga had to impart. We got to know the capability of our tools, got to know the ground, the peculiarities of the guards; and we knew the rules.

Or so we thought. During the first days of October the first frost arrived. We woke up one day—sore, hungry and anxious—to find outside a silvery world of icy cold. Every drop of water had frozen in position the moment the cold had touched it. Small icicles hung from the barrack's roofs. Solid sheets of ice filled the puddles. The inside of our windows were covered with an etched design of frozen flowers, and the small porch in front of our hut had become a white, slippery hazard.

As I moved my squad to the washroom and from there to mess barracks, we quickly became aware of the new problems presented by the frost. Henceforth, we would have to wear heavier clothes and different boots. In our leather boots, our toes would freeze off. We would also need heavier gloves.

Sergeant Markov hailed me, as I led my small group to the mess. "Katya Alexeyevna," he greeted me, "bring your squad after breakfast to the drying shed. Quickly, before the others are aware of it. There will be *valenki*—felt boots, into which one can pull heavy socks and rags. Get there soon, so you can get the best for your squad."

I thanked Genady Markov profusely, letting him know how much I valued him. He had taken a liking to me, which I attributed to my good knowledge of the Russian language. My patron had numerous times before benefited my squad and did so again this time. We got the best boots, well fitting, in perfect condition, which we immediately numbered with our personal camp numbers to make them our own for our term in camp.

Scarcely had we outfitted ourselves with the precious *valenki*, when Sergeant Prokofyiev arrived, leading a group of women from a rival barrack. My curiosity was instantly aroused. What was this harsh, punitive man doing promoting barrack number 201? What was his involvement in a competition between Volga German women?

It took me a few days, but I discovered the cause of what troubled me. The women in all barracks agreed and were unanimous in their disapproval of the sergeant's sexual involvement with one of us. The woman was the wife of a German soldier serving on the German front. She hailed from the village of Schilling. The women around her, in her barrack, disapproved of her—her character and her conduct. They were ashamed that one of us would forget herself so much and consort with the vilest man in camp. Yet she was not alone. Yes, there were among us those who sold their bodies, their souls and every Christian principle for a temporary easing of our difficult conditions.

However, our women's moral condition was not my problem. I worried about many more important problems. Angela Huber was laid up with an infection impossible to conquer. Early one morning while we worked, Hanna Müller broke through a sheet of ice and fell into a deep pool of frigid water from which we laughingly, chidingly pulled her. Yet, nothing in Siberia was ever a laughing matter. As she stood there, sheepish, wet and freezing, my heart went out to the girl who had valiantly tried to act like a grown woman. In recent days, she had tirelessly worked to fulfill the norm. She did not want to be a burden to the squad and had pushed herself to the very edge of her endurance. We gave her whatever items of clothing we felt we could do without, allowing her to shed some of her wet clothes, but we could not find substitutes for her socks, pants and shoes. I begged the guards to allow her a spot by the fire, to let her dry her freezing, wet clothes.

But that was not to be. Beastly Prokofyiev, feeling attacked, for the whole camp either impishly grinned into his face or accusingly avoided his eyes, knew his secret was out. To make up for the humiliation of being caught in something approaching emotional entanglement, he acted more vicious than ever. He beat the guards who had allowed Hanna to stand by the fire with his club and threatened their removal from camp, which would make prisoners of them also.

He savagely pushed Hanna away from the puny fire and ordered her back to work. Hanna began to work even harder than before as a way of staying warm. Soon her face was flushed bright red. A short while later she said in her uncomplaining way that she could not feel her feet anymore. We waited until Prokofieyev left for another squad, then quickly removed her frozen, stiff shoes and socks and rubbed her feet. First, we rubbed them with snow, then with warmed gloves, until feeling returned to her feet. Returning sensation made her cry out with the agonizing pain of returning circulation to what had nearly become dead flesh.

By evening in the barrack, the girl shook with cold even though we had put her to bed, heaping all manner of blankets on top of her. We warmed round river stones in our puny stove, and placed them around her feet. We brought her the ration of food due her, and fed her the warm soup, for which I had begged a container from the cook, spoonful by spoonful. She could not eat the bread and gave it to me, saying, "You eat it, please. You carried me home. I can't eat it anyway—it repels me."

By midnight Hanna had a raging fever. Next morning I half carried, half dragged her because she was delirious, to the dispensary, where the miserable doctor gave her a few white pills and prescribed tea and bed rest. We left her weak and feverish in her bed as we set out for the woods, envying her the respite in bed.

By mid-morning, Genady Markov, in charge of the guards that day, sent to my squad the odd eleventh member from another barrack to help out. "If your girl has pneumonia she will not be back soon," he said ominously, "and you will need the extra help." The old camp hound was right. Hanna developed pneumonia. In the evening we stood beside her bed and watched helplessly as she writhed in pain with every breath she drew. We cooled her feverish head with moist, cold cloths and spoon-fed her *kasha* in the morning, watery soup and warm tea at night, whatever we could get for her.

There were days when an enormous machine of a woman supervised the kitchen; she would not allow us to remove even a bowl from the mess for the sick girl. In desperation I would seek out Genady Markov and beg him to help. More often than not he would provide the food for me. I realized that my requests indebted me to him, and sometimes I wondered how that debt would have to be repaid.

As the days passed, Hanna became a small bundle of pain. We watched her enduring, fighting the disease, when, suddenly, she succumbed. We had made her as comfortable as possible one morning before leaving for work, and still held hopes that she might recover—but at nightfall, when we returned, Hanna was still and cold.

I did not cry when I found her, for deep inside me there was a part that longed to go where she had gone. I knew that little Hanna was in a better place than we were. It would be restful, peaceful and warm where she had gone. Here in the camp we had no peace, no rest, no warmth, and no love. Here, we lived in constant worry, nay frenzy, about the norm. We lived in slavering anticipation over the size of bread morsels dispensed morning and evening and the amount of glutinous *kasha* dumped into our bowls. Did another woman receive more of the ration than I? Were others better at fulfilling the norm and, therefore, getting better rations than my squad?

Was I a good enough squad leader—working out the best deals for my women? Getting them soon enough in the washroom line? Insuring them the best and earliest meals? Everyone knew that the little bit of fat in the pot swam to the top and went into the first bowls. Such questions haunted me at night until my tormented body gave out, leaving me dull and dead asleep.

We prayed for Hanna, and had a funeral service in our hut, although she would not yet be buried. Not long thereafter the guards carried Hanna's stiff body away to the barrack of the dead—there would be no burials until late in spring.

Angela Huber died of gangrene from the cut on her leg. The doctor had not even made the effort to amputate when putrefaction of the wound set in. We reflected cynically upon the terrible truth that an amputee would be unproductive, and therefore, there was no reason to keep Angela alive. When Angela died, I noticed that none of us cried anymore. We were like dried stalks of wheat. What else could happen to us? Whatever it would be would put us into the death-shed, removing us from our merciless reality.

As we sat bemoaning our harsh life, I felt that our position had to be clarified even to the densest girls. I decided to be rudely honest, and said, "Here we are not valued for the kind of person we are, for our potentials, for what we could do if we were allowed to live free. Here we are nothing but robotic machines felling trees. We are as disposable as the trees we cut," I paused to let my words sink in deep, and continued, "Since no one protects us in this camp, we must look after our bodies carefully. We must not take unnecessary chances when felling trees, must take our time when clambering over hard, sharp branches, must do our utmost to stay warm. We cannot allow anyone to get injured or fall ill—because it means certain death."

"Can't you talk to the commandant the way you did when the thefts occurred?" asked Anna Schrenk, a small, dry woman with a round, knobby, red nose.

"Yes, yes, talk to the commandant," shrilled a few others.

"That won't do us any good!" Barbara cut them off. "Volodya was lonely awhile ago and talked to us. He told us that Alyosha Kulov has fallen on the bottle. He is drowning his sorrows in vodka, reciting poetry as he walks the floor of his office." She reiterated my warnings once more, adding that we would have to look after each other and treat our bodies as well as we could.

The Taiga's Essence

Soon after the first hard frosts fell upon the camp, winter blanketed the taiga with a vengeance. The first morning of true winter arrived with a blinding blizzard so strong it obscured the very buildings in camp, the trees, the flag pole—everything. I thought I had overslept, that I had not heard the clanging of the irons and the shouting of guards, but that was not the case. As I stepped on the small porch before our hut, I felt lost. Before me was nothing but swirling white. Although I squinted, screwing my eyes into focus, I could not make out the barracks next to ours. All was smothered in grayish white, obliterating even the camp's strong searchlights.

Behind me, Barbara approached. "What is going on? No guards, no noise?" she questioned.

"No, I cannot see a thing out there."

"Whatever you do, do not go a step further," admonished Barbara, "you'd be instantly lost in this." The cold on the porch penetrated us to the marrow and we retreated into the hut. I called to the women on fire duty to throw more wood into the stove.

"Not much left," they shouted back.

So, here were my brand new dilemmas. We had no wood to keep the hut warm and could not get more. How were we to reach the mess hut in this snowstorm? Just thinking about food made my stomach contract with agony. Where were the guards? If the snow was too daunting for them, it would be catastrophic for us to leave the safety of the hut.

Standing beside Barbara, I said, "We must tell the women something, but what? We cannot go to the mess hut, cannot go to wash, but we must keep warm. How?"

"Good question," she said. Then, looking sideways at me, she grinned lopsidedly, "We can take apart the porch for fuel."

"Sure, without tools, with our bare hands?" She did not deign to answer that question; instead she said, "Go ahead, announce something. The women are milling about like sick cattle—full of anxiety."

Shivering, I returned to the hut. After first calming the excited women, I said, "Barbara and I have discovered that a snow storm makes it impossible to go outside right now. We cannot see anything and apparently the guards cannot find us either. So, for the moment we must stay put. There might be no work today. We will wait and see what happens."

Immediately following my announcement, a firestorm of questions broke over our heads. What about tea and food? Can we go to the mess hall? We, however, had no answers. A few of the women, doubting Thomases, poked their noses out the door to see for themselves and provoked shouts of anger. "Keep the door closed! Shut the door, it is freezing in here."

The room settled into its regular hum and buzz. Some of the women pragmatically settled into their beds and fell instantly asleep. Others, unable to rest, fidgeted with their belongings, while a few lay on their beds and stared at the wood ceiling. We had no books—so reading was out of the question. Worried and disturbed, I prowled the hut, taking inventory. If the storm lasted for a few days, what were we to do then?

At last, I too, lay on my back and stared into the void. I must have fallen asleep, for I was awakened by a commotion. It was already dark. I knew it had to be, because the three naked light bulbs, dangling from distended wires, already dispensed a sad, miserable light, and they were never lit unless it was fully dark outside. The cause for the disturbance was the raging thirst that plagued all of us. The women had been sneaking out to eat the snow and thereby alleviated their thirst a little. However, every time they opened the door the hut got colder and we had no more wood. Anything dispensable, very little, indeed, had been burned already.

Reluctantly I left my bed and sought out Barbara. Somehow, her role had evolved twofold. First, she was the leader for our entire hut, yet that did not save her from also having to lead a squad and work full days alongside us. Now I said to her, "From now on we must bring even more fuel from the woods than before. Henceforth, we must have a surplus of wood, because this snowstorm will not be the only occurrence which will keep us stuck in here without water and wood."

She agreed. We silenced the squabbling women and told them that from now on everyone had to carry double loads for the stove. "We have to prepare heftier chunks to carry home," said Lina Meier, "They burn longer than the small branches we usually take."

"You are right," said Barbara, "but that will take more effort, because we will have to chop and saw pieces off the upper trunk or the stump left standing. More work in the same amount of time."

"If only we did not have to share our wood with guards we would be fine, but they are too lazy to carry their own and then they steal from us," complained Margaretha Andreas. Sadly, she spoke the truth. Although the

guards received rations of coal for their stoves, they stole our wood whenever possible for kindling and to stretch their meager rations of coal. We
could rest assured that their barracks were always warm.

"If we could carry a goodly amount hidden under our clothes, we
might escape their robbery," suggested a voice from the edge of the circle
surrounding us.

"Impossible, they search us to make sure we don't carry knives and
axes off and start a camp revolution with weapons."

"Then we will have to grab what we can at the last moment as always,
but we can make sure that there is good stuff to be taken."

The next day, early in the morning, with no letup from the storm, the
indoor latrine—a cubby with two wooden stools and buckets—reached
overflowing. As much as we hated to befoul the immediate environs of
our hut, the moment came when the two women slated for the unpleasant
duty that day put on their gloves and emptied the foul containers over the
porch railing. We hoped the frost would kill the odor. We also brought the
ugly aluminum samovar into the hut filled with snow and saw to it that
eventually everyone got a few mouthfuls of water.

By now hunger tormented us relentlessly. We had been hungry when
we had gone to bed two nights ago. The wretched, watery stew concocted
from small fish, shredded cabbage and salt that they had served us at that
time had only whetted our appetite for the more that never came. Now our
thin bodies screamed insistently for food.

Finally, around noon the snow stopped falling and although the
wind still blew ferociously we could see the mess hut. Barbara was in the
"latrine corner." I, therefore, called to our women, "102nd! Get ready! Get
ready to fall out!"

Never had I observed such quick compliance with my orders. Our
women were dressed in their warmest clothes, their *valenki* were stuffed,
and their heavy overcoats, were secured around their middles with string
or cord—whatever we had. We moved out, pounding paths through the
freshly fallen snow. A few times we had to breach snowdrifts, high-piled
obstacles—but the hunger forced us to break through. In this way, miserably cold and hungry, we arrived at the mess.

Since we were first, we sat down close to the kitchen counter, where I
requested food for our barracks. We were lucky. The cook on duty was Anton Petrovitch Beluskov, a Ukrainian who had experienced the worst forms
of abuse from the Russians. Petrovich had survived three previous camps.
He had survived by guile, cooperation, deceit, his wits, and an overall ability

to emote smart friendliness. Today he had gone into the kitchen early. He had left his warm quarters and prepared warm food because of his feelings of kinship for us. He had wanted to be ready for the starving Volga German women-wretches. Ukrainians had been accorded the same abysmal terror meted out to the Volga Germans, a terror that united us.

Both of our cultural groups had objected to Bolshevism, and had lost; both of our ethnicities had violently objected to enforced collectivism, and had lost again. For those efforts we were condemned to starvation, forced labor and forced relocation into the wastelands of Kazakhstan, Siberia and any lands deemed too sterile for cultivation.

The bowls of hot *kasha* Beluskov handed us, real oatmeal, not the oatcake cooked for days into a gelatinous mass, tasted doubly delicious for the hunger we brought with us. Beluskov, even kinder than usual, handed out sugar rations and a cup of milk with the *kasha*. Soon, as we sat upon the rough-cut benches, we were devouring the delicious treat. Even the lukewarm tea tasted wonderful after our ordeal. And the bread—the adulterated, black bread—it, too, was a special treat.

There was not much time to savor flavors and the fleeting feeling of fullness, because the next squads from another hut pushed their way in. They had to push us out, for we obstinately lingered in the warm room. We stole as much coal and wood as we could from the big steel barrel which served as fuel receptacle without being observed and retreated back into our hut. We started a fire with the filched fuel and began to dry our wet *valenki* because the drying room was closed.

I had avoided arousing interest in my warm coat by allowing it to shine forth in full neglected shabbiness. I had trimmed roughly ten inches off its bottom with a slashing knife at the worksite. Now it did not pick up snow and ice anymore to sling the frozen weight against my feet and *valenki*. However, the coat's outside with many tears, had become bizarre-looking because the pretty karakul had begun to shine through. This was an impossible state of affairs. Alerted, I performed repairs. Purposely, I sewed the rips with big, uncouth stitches, making the coat look even more abused, old and worthless. I had to admit with glee that after my repair the old worn garment neither invited envy nor created interest. To the contrary, I was teased and relegated to the cast of the poorest. Thank God, no one had seen its gorgeous, perfect lining. The poorly repaired woolen shell looked worse than an unclaimed beggar's garment.

However, I benefited greatly from the miserable piece of goods. I wrapped it around me before going to sleep and it kept me almost warm through the coldest night. I wore it belted around my waist into the forest and it warmed me to my ankles. Many were the nights when I fondly envisioned Gregori Potemkin and his love of exceptional furs. I wondered how much of his indomitable blood flowed in my veins, blood that would keep me alive despite the camp's adversity. I prayed that the Russian guards would never discover the treasure of the coat's lining. If they found out, they would rob me in an instant, shouting, "Kulak! Kulak!" which entitled the screamer to steal from the thus labeled victim.

Speaking of treasure, I still carried my small fortune of stones in my falsie, the hairball. Every morning, after combing my hair, which had become quite long, I twisted it around the falsie and pinned it tight. So the treasure and the coat were always with me, were so much a part of me that at times I forgot they were there, that they were precious.

After a few months in camp we had lost track of time. We had no writing materials, no calendars, newspapers and clocks, nothing by which to measure time. We were totally controlled by guard's shouts, clanging irons and the count of seven. Seven was Sunday, the day to rest and clean, the day allowing us to prepare for another miserable week in the forest. At first I had kept a stick by my bedside, a branch, stripped of bark, which I had marked daily with a slit to count the passing days. Alas, someone, not realizing its importance, had used the stick to fuel the stove and thus destroyed the record of our imprisonment.

Seven was also the number of hours we slaved in the forest. One hour of our day was spent transporting us back and forth from the felling ground. Seven were the hours we were permitted to sleep, and another seven were spent in the pursuit of food, the drying of *valenki*, the cleaning of the night pots and the latrines, the washing and mending of garments, standing in lines to wait for food or for water to wash, and being of service to the guards when called to do their chores.

We would ask the guards what month it was. Sometimes they answered truthfully, at other times they liked to confuse us with lies. When I estimated Christmas to be near, I stalked the innocent Vasya until I could I ask him what date it was. "Five days away from your most sacred holy day," was his answer. It would be a sad day, for our head count of forty women had been reduced by illness and eventual death to thirty-five. The five empty beds had instantly been filled by extras from other barracks where women slept in bunk beds, three atop one another.

In January we lost, camp-wide, ten women to an outbreak of enteritis. It was possible more deaths had occurred. Ten, however, was the number I could ascertain. I surmised that the effluent from our overflowing night vessels, which we were forced to empty into nature, had somehow found its way into the well. I preached fervently to all who would listen that our drinking water had to be boiled. Once more Barbara and I tried to get permission to see Alyosha Kulov, the commandant whom we felt to be sympathetic to our plight. But even Markov said that this would be impossible.

"If that is impossible, then perhaps you will insure that the kitchen staff boils tea and drinking water for five minutes at least, or we will all die. Even the guards can fall ill, because you are drinking the same tea, the same water as we do," I warned.

"I will see what I can do," said Markov.

But within days, more people succumbed. We re-boiled the tea from the kitchen in our hut, which took forever on the miserable stove, but no one in our group fell ill. Finally, after some soldiers and guards also took ill and died, an order from the doctor started a strict regimen in the kitchen. Even better, our lazy, uncaring camp physician somehow managed to get water purification tablets, solving the problem.

We celebrated Christmas with hot tea and a sugar ration, procured by Beluskov our favorite cook. Later, in the hut, we knelt around the stove and prayed for our families. We prayed for every soul tormented in a prison or work camp, the men in the war, and the sad, helpless women and children deported into the wilderness without homes or means to sustain themselves.

By February, the temperature had sunk several times below minus 30 Celsius, the cutoff-temperature for work. The amount of food provided during non-productive days was barely life-sustaining. The onset of winter had changed our lives dramatically. Within a few days of frost's onset, the frozen ground beneath our felt-boots had become as hard as concrete. At first I thought we could not last in the icy forest even a day—but somehow we did.

Soon we wore every garment we could layer one over the other. We were so thin that no matter what we wore our coats could still be tied around our waists. We had no breasts, yet we wore the halters that had once contained our breasts. Although every one of us had experienced severe weight loss, we looked fat and cumbersome in our work clothes—yet, our faces gave away the state of our emaciation. The camp provided heavy work-gloves to pull over our woolen ones, but our fingers were always in danger of frostbite.

Our feet, atop icy, snowy ground all day, were always aching with cold. But we learned to value the hurt. The guards had cruelly made us aware of taiga reality, "No feeling—no toes," meaning that frostbitten toes needed to be amputated. We became inventive, spotting in an instant every useful rag or old bit of garment to wrap around our socks. Everyone wore *valenki* two sizes too large. Any larger and one could barely walk. Yes, those were the vicissitudes of camp life—constant change and adaptation.

To withstand the biting cold, we pulled our fur caps—yes, we still owned the hats that had been so useful during the Lower Volga winters—deep into our foreheads, covering our faces with scarves or woolen shawls so that our eyes barely showed. Blink often, they warned us, or your eyeballs will freeze. At first we believed the guards were playing jokes on us—unfortunately their warnings were correct. We knew they were not joking when our very breath froze the scarves in front of our mouths, leaving our faces chafed, rough and burned. After a while the frost thickened on the scarves so that we had to reposition them, for breathing became impossible.

Another great change had arrived with winter. The frozen ground finally allowed heavy machinery to enter the taiga. Huge tractor-trailers invaded the clearings we had made, seeking out the piles of tree trunks for removal. With them, came front-loaders with their gripping iron claws.

Now, the silent forest resounded with the low rumble, the high-pitched whine, and the clanking and creaking of machinery and torqued wood. For us, the machines represented an added danger, for they moved about without paying the slightest attention to us as we were bent over the most recently felled trees. The masters of these monsters saw us as nothing but lowly pedestrians who should scramble and run before their might.

If it had not been for my fast reflexes, one of these behemoths would have crushed me beneath its rolling iron grippers. I flung myself away at the last moment as the machine rolled straight at me. I rose, ambling away as fast as my large *valenki* allowed. I was shaking, terrified.

"What kind of a man is sitting in the cab of that machine?" I asked Barbara with tears in my voice the moment I realized I was safe. "He saw me! He surely saw me and yet he kept coming, knowing that I, my back turned to him, could not see him. What kind of human would do such a thing?" I was outraged, and thoroughly terrorized.

"A young *Komsomol* member would," said a firm male voice behind me. It was Genady Markov, who had observed the drama.

"Watch out for them, girls. They are a new breed of man. They only serve the Party—no one else matters." We stared at him wide-eyed and silent. What a thing to say out loud! He could become a prisoner himself for such treasonous words, if reported. He must have trusted us implicitly—or thought that no one would believe us were we to betray him. We were still eyeing him with amazement when he turned and left.

Genady Markov was an enigma to all of us. He took care to protect us from the wrath of the camp officers. He fudged reports in our favor—taking great risks—and was kind in his fashion. Barbara and I talked about him at length, trying to fathom why he was so different than the other camp guards. We surmised that, maybe, he had experienced a great loss because of Soviet barbarism. We imagined him to be a secret Christian, or perhaps that he was a gentle man by nature, bred of a kind family. No one knew much about him. Even sweet Vasya—privy to many secrets, for no one bothered to keep anything from him—knew nothing about Markov's past.

Scarcely three days had passed since my reflexes saved me from certain death when the unimaginable happened. As it turned on its axis, one of the massive tractors plowed into a tree. The tree splintered, broke, and crashed down upon two women from the 108th, bent over while limbing a felled tree.

They never knew what happened. They had no time to cry out before they died. Their squad members rushed to their aid—too late. Freed from the load of branches and the tree trunk—they lay crumpled, unmoving. The blood gushing from their mouths—their chests had been crushed—had already frozen to a frothy, red foam. Our squad watched the scene in disbelief from afar.

Prokofiev was on duty that day for our section. He screamed like a banshee, "Work, work! Back to work everyone!" He flogged the stunned women kneeling in the snow beside their dead sisters as he bellowed, "Away with you! We will take care of them. Professionals will do the job. There is nothing you can do! They should have looked out for the machines. Maybe this will teach you to pay attention."

And so the work never stopped, not even for a moment of silence for the dead. The bodies were removed—carried onto a truck bed and covered with a tarp.

On the way home that evening the women of the 108th bemoaned the outrage. They painted a detailed picture of their sisters' death, which we, being too far away, had not been able to observe. Telling the horror tale, the women could finally release their terror and grief—could finally weep and mourn.

"Are we beetles or vermin?" asked Susanna Griess, a tall sturdily-built woman who hailed from Norka. "They starve and work us to death and yet they must crush us?" Tears gushed from her eyes, turning to ice as the wool shawl covering her mouth caught them. Wordless, the women of her squad held her—what was there to say?

The 108th did not reach its norm that day and their bread rations were cut. For the first time ever, we all broke off a bite of our own precious ration, collected the bites in an upturned hat, and delivered the gift to their barracks. That night every woman in camp felt that she, too, had been crushed.

As I lay on my lumpy mattress, on my narrow, hard cot, I thought of the day's events. What had my poor, brave ancestors ever done to deserve such hellish hate as was heaped upon us—their innocent, helpless off-spring? How could a cast of lowly farmers, leaning for generations to the hoe and the plow—humble beyond imagining—how could such paragons of goodness inspire such ire and wrath that their contemporaries, their fellow countrymen, could extinguish their lives without regard in so cruel, so purposeless a fashion?

But as I mulled the facts over and over in my poor, burning head, little emerged to make a picture that would explain the cold hate I had witnessed countless times. Could it be, perhaps, that the old panslavistic jingoism was alive, mixing well to xenophobic result with the new communist teaching?

Perhaps if one replaced God—an uncomfortable, unfathomable God, holding the believer accountable for thoughts and deeds—with the racist ideas that only Slavs deserved to exist in a Slavic country, one could explain a mindset as that we witnessed. This also would explain the insane Russian hatred of Ukrainians, Kalmuks, Koreans, Chechens and the other minorities.

And if one then enlarged the concept and added the totalitarianism of communism into the mix, then one could breed young men and women who would kill in cold blood, totally detached, without pleasure, without passion—squashing humans like bugs for no other reason but racial disdain.

Here my thoughts took another turn. It was as if I had been riding a horse in a straight line, when, suddenly startled by a lonely wolf, my steed flew in a new direction.

Yes, yes! That was it. I had forgotten the jealousy. My people had always worked harder, smarter, more ceaselessly and deliberately than any Russian farmers. Besides farming, my forbearers had supplemented their income with cottage industries. Weaving Sarpinka—the colorful chintz—famous in all of Russia and beyond its borders; inventing, perfecting, and making new farm tools, carving pipes, and wooden implements; thus my people had prospered.

Not that the Russian farmers were lazy—no, just deprived. Serfs until recent history, their very blood had been drained from their bodies in bondage. Released, they began to enjoy achievement for the first time. They did not envy us. They lived beside us and knew the hardships. However, their new delight in ownership had been short-lived, for the Communists made no distinction between Russian and German farmers who owned the land. To implement Stalin's idea of government farms, everyone needed to be robbed.

If you owned anything in the countryside, you were a kulak. If you resisted their theft and extortion, you were a kulak, and if you dared to hide what you had earned with the sweat of your brow, you were a kulak who had to be killed instantly.

This is how I came to make sense of it all: the new godless, communist crop—fed on Marx, Engel and Lenin's doctrines, willing to eradicate everyone who might, even passively, resist the new order—had grown up. Whereas the old, the first, revolutionaries had killed in hot blood, fired with zeal, the new guard killed for expediency—for we were meant to die here in frozen taiga anyway.

All at once my swirling thoughts stopped. I had my explanation, all the parts in the puzzle fit—we meant nothing, were nothing to the new Russia; like a used tool we could be thrown away to rot in the field. The knowledge of total hopelessness made me feel empty, like a drained flagon. My head, whirling with thoughts only moments ago, felt dull and useless.

I was overcome by deathly tiredness. My limbs felt heavy, as if filled with lead. Strangely, I did not feel the ever-present cold, for the cold was within me.

Days of Darkness

During these bitter cold and dark days, the work could only be performed with the help of petrol-powered generators, which provided electricity for enormous floodlights. Machinists used tractors to pull the lumbering stations to the edge of the work perimeter. From there the floodlights filled the worksite with bright rays they emitted like suns.

The sun was barely visible for the few hours during midday. Without the generators, work would have been impossible during the early morning and late afternoon hours. Sometimes we could barely see the tree limbs even with the power of the floodlights.

On one of these gray mornings the lights came on just as we arrived and were stepping from the trucks. As the first rays struck the tree trunks, I noticed a silvery flash, halfway up, in a wide-branched tree. There, in the crack of a branch, something silvery was hidden. I was instantly curious. No man-made object was to be found in this wilderness, unless it had been placed there by design.

What was the thing I had spied? Who had placed the thing in the tree—to hide it? I carefully recorded the position of the tree in my mind. I had learned that its smooth, tight-knit bark and the profusion of curly branches proclaimed it to be a beech tree. Two birches, their silver-white bark flecked with dark, rough patches, flanked it.

I determined that I would direct our work in such a way, that we would cut the beech first, giving me a chance to find what I already had come to think of as a hidden treasure. Could an escaping prisoner have placed the silver there? Or, had a native herdsman placed something there for safekeeping? Perhaps, but how could the native ever expect to find the thing again?

One by one we received our tools. I was given an axe. Under normal circumstances I would have traded it for a position on a long-saw because I had become proficient with this instrument. Many women did not like the long-saw and would gladly trade for the axe. Today, however, an axe was perfect for what I had in mind.

The guards never cared what we did after the tools were distributed. As long as we worked, no one gave a kopek how and which trees we felled. Having to guard us in this icy place was perceived by soldiers and civilians alike as punishment. Therefore, they did as little as possible at the work site.

Just as soon as the guards were safely occupied by the fire, I took my squad straight to my tree between the birches. The guards stood around the only glowing, warm spot in this freezing misery, tending their fire and a large can of tea. Rubbing their hands over the flames, they stamped their *valenki* into the frozen ground; they talked and cursed while the ones lucky enough to have tobacco smoked. Yes, if they bent close enough to the fire they could smoke, relieved of their heavy, fur outer-gloves, which otherwise prevented holding a cigarette.

I struck at the beech. It was hard as iron. It seemed to take us forever to take the tree down, but finally the beech fell. I had kept my eyes on the shiny spot and the tree fell nicely, leaving the branch in question in front ready for my perusal. I approached the branch, axe at the ready, pretending to be eager to chop off the branch, and then I saw it. Contraband! The most forbidden of all things in camp: a knife! The handle was exposed enough for me to know.

I bent, trying to pull the knife from the wood, all the while shielding the area with my body. But, however hard I tried, the knife would not budge. It was solidly fused with the wood. I took the axe and began delicately chopping at the branch. I did not want to destroy the object of my desire. Chipping closer to the knife, I suddenly heard a Russian curse followed by, "Hit the damned branch, don't pet it! Is this how you work here? Making a mockery of all of us condemned to be here with you?"

Prokofiev's voice was biting. I panicked. If he saw the knife, he would instantly assume that I had hidden it and was now retrieving it for nefarious reasons. With this evidence he could have me confined in the solitary hut, a miserable shed without a stove, in which I would freeze to death during the first night.

So far, no one had committed what the camp guards construed to be a crime heinous enough to be placed there. But if found, this knife would likely make me the first. My first inkling was to turn and look at him. Instead I reacted, powerfully whacking the branch above the one shielding the knife.

Prokofiev's laugh was a deprecating, wolfish howl, "Look how she can use the axe if watched by her superiors. Suddenly she can chop a branch off with one stroke." After his performance, he thankfully moved on to another group of unlucky women. I finally could breathe again, and the flush of terror receded from my cheeks.

Markov rarely checked on us when on duty. He counted the felled and limbed trees in the evening, managing often enough to satisfy the norm, even when we had come up short. How he did this, I don't know. But with him about, we seldom lost any of our bread. Prokofiev, however, was another matter. With him present we often went breadless—even if we had closely approximated the norm.

As soon as Prokofiev was far away, I gently cut away on my special branch. "What are you doing?" called Martha Landauer, "Prokofiev is right! You are just playing with that axe."

"I have come upon a knot," I answered sharply, "I am not going to strike it hard and injure myself just to please Prokofiev. He will not give a damn when the axe springs back slicing me. So mind your own work." Then, for good measure I added, "You know that I don't shirk or hold back—ever!" Martha did not dare challenge me again.

My last strike released the knife's blade. Shielding my doings by turning my back on the squad, I retrieved a truly great knife. Cradling its heft in my hand, I sighed, "Oh Lord, what contraband!" It was the most serious knife imaginable—a deadly weapon. Forged from the best tempered steel it gleamed even in the artificial half-light of the worksite. There it was—six inches of perfectly shaped handle—ten inches of long, sharp blade.

The mystery was killing me. Who had hidden this knife here in this frozen, ice-coated forest and expected to ever find it again? However, I could work on this puzzle later. Now I had to make the knife disappear. I slipped it into the sleeve of my coat, and although there was a layer of wool between my arm and the steel, its cold hit me as if hot coal burned the skin of my arm. I winced, yet carried on.

"I need a break to relieve myself," calling this, I went into the forest. Oh, how we tried to avoid these functions of our bodies. For hours we held waste until the discomfort could not be borne any longer. We took terrific pains to avoid exposure to the frost, the unmerciful cold. Even a few moments of exposure could cause skin damage, resulting in blisters that refused to heal. We had learned unmentionable techniques to avoid even a few seconds exposure to the full blast of the elements. We squatted and made a small tent about us with our coats, never removing the undergarments, but gently pulling them aside. Not a safe, sanitary method, but at minus 30 degrees your eyeballs would freeze if you forgot to blink enough and shield your eyes.

When I reached a likely spot I assumed the position—as if… By now the knife had warmed enough to be transferred to my safe place—my bosom. I took off my outer glove, opened the front of the coat a slit, pulled the knife from my sleeve, and, struggling, slipped the knife through the welter of odd garments I wore from my neck down into the front of my bra.

Safe! At last! My weapon was safely ensconced. My chances of keeping it were actually very good. When we had arrived in camp, months ago, anything that could have been used to construct a weapon had been removed from our belongings. Forks, dinner knives, small paring knives—all were confiscated—leaving us always in need; biting the threads when sewing; using the unwieldy, heavy work knives and clippers if anything needed to be cut.

The guards seldom performed body searches. If the tool count was correct in the evening, a thing we attended to assiduously, there would be no search. Where would we find weapons in the wilderness? Unless implements were missing, the guards could rest easy.

I could not understand why this knife had already become so important to me that I was willing to risk my life to keep it. I could not use it because no one must know and it was a constant danger to me if found. Yet, I had to have it!

That night I slept with the knife between my breasts. I felt its steely weight and wondered again why it meant so much to me. Somehow, it was reassuring to possess a weapon, a thing that could hurt, even kill. I marveled that I, brought up in a most pacifist community by a mother who abhorred violence, carried within me a savage desire to protect myself. How, when and why such protection would be necessary I did not know, but I wanted to be able to act if necessary. Was my life that important to me? Perhaps not my life—perhaps I would be called upon to protect another.

Only a day later, I found the ideal spot to hide my knife. Right under my bed was a slightly decayed floorboard. Coming back early from the mess hall one day, I scraped out enough rot to make a hollow large enough for the knife. I carefully covered the knife with the pieces of rotten wood, pressing them firmly into the hollow. Hidden under the bed, my cache was not too obvious. For the moment, I might get by with this makeshift cover.

The thought had formed in my mind that with a bit of glue I could make the wooden scraps look like solid wood again. The problem was that there was only one place in camp where glue was used—the *valenki* and boot repair place. In a warm hut, behind the drying shed, lived and worked Demyan Krapotkin, an older convict left over from a previous population. He repaired shoes and leather equipment. The walls of the hut were decorated by odd felt pieces, mostly gray, and an assortment of cured hides. From these materials he chose the patches for the repairs.

Krapotkin was a short, broad-shouldered, dwarfish man, with a deeply creased, permanently leering face, in which two lively, bird eyes flitted about. His skin, his clothes, and his hair were gray, and so he reminded one of a ghostly gnome. Demyan—the name means to kill—and I wondered if in his former life he had been just that—a killer. He made me cringe every time I had to go to his hut.

The women hated to take their shoes to his hut because the perverted man would only fix something for us if we were willing to expose a body part to him. He was not particularly choosy what one exposed; a naked arm excited him as much as a calf. However, for a difficult repair he insisted that a thigh or breast be shown. We had talked to the officers on duty, complaining about this sort of harassment.

"Well," they said, "Demyan is doing you a favor by repairing your boots. He does not have to do anything for you. He has served his sentence, and we keep him because he has nowhere to go and here he does needed services. We pay in rubles, cigarettes and vodka for the work he does for us, and you can do the same. You are lucky that you can pay with a look at your wretched bodies."

And so it came that the strangest deals were arranged among the women in all the huts. Some, modest to a fault, would agree to carry pots filled with night soil for a few days, while another, untroubled by shame, would take the modest ones' shoes, and in exchange, expose for Demyan. There were those who did the deed laughing loudly, as if performing on stage.

I, unfortunately, could not trade away my disgust to be ogled by him, for I had ulterior designs, which demanded that I excite him into forgetting his usually vigilant ways.

The exposure of most of my leg, allowed me a moment during which I stole a small metal pot filled with glue. Fortuitously, the demeaning act set him shaking with desirous want and he buried his head between his hands, allowing the theft. But more, it gave me an inside look into men, which I would later use to advantage.

Depleted Bodies

Once a month my squad was entitled to use the washroom for an hour. We used this precious time to clean ourselves thoroughly, sometimes even wash our hair. Two stoves stood at each end of the wash barracks. They were crude, black monsters, which heated caldrons of water. In order to enjoy the monthly treat, we had to haul water the night before and fill the huge boilers. Others brought in the allotment of coal and the wood we were required to carry into camp from the worksite.

At first call, long before the morning mess call, we would begin to feed the monsters and heat the water. A few dented aluminum basins, a little hot water and a cake of hard, gray soap that would not foam was all that stood between us and smelly decay. After filling a basin with hot water, we stood in front of a high bench, rubbing our bodies down with water and soap. Thereafter, a friend or workmate would rinse us with a few splashes of clean water, whereupon we dried with off with the gray, frayed remnants of what had once been towels. The room was never warm enough to feel comfortable when standing there naked. We shivered and shook throughout the procedure. Yet, we would not have foregone the ritual for anything, for it made us feel human, feel like women, for a while. Although we had been condemned to slave labor, domesticity prevailed. Our inbred instinct for cleanliness and civility was satisfied by the primitive procedure.

I figured it was mid-February when my squad was entitled to a cleansing once more. I saw the women standing naked before their basins, rubbing their flaccid skin. For the first time I saw with conscious eyes how terribly thin they had become. My body, too, had lost every ounce of fat. My breasts had shrunk until only two small bumps with brown aureoles remained. The problem of menstruation, the horribly delicate thing we had to deal with monthly—without sanitary napkins or other provisions—had stopped being an ordeal. For, we, one and all, did not menstruate anymore. Our bodies were incapable of shedding even one drop of blood—we had none to spare.

The women's once proud bottoms had become small, hard and muscular, and were covered by wrinkled skin. As I looked at them, in their sad, shrunken earthliness—their loveliness and appealing youth faded—tears came to my eyes. "If I am truly their leader here in this purgatory, then I must do something for them," I thought. But what could I do? "We must have more food," I thought, but that was easier thought than done. Perhaps I could go to the commandant and make him increase the rations?

I thought and thought about how I could make him pay attention to such a plea. When at last, I asked Genady Markov to take me to see commandant Kulov, he answered cryptically, "It will be of little use to reason with a vodka-soaked poet."

"What do you mean?" I asked stupidly.

"Just that. He drinks, recites poetry and walks the floor in his office. Something haunts him, and this is how he tries to forget."

I did not care what haunted Kulov. We were starving and were still required to work. He had to do something. The longer I thought, the more convinced I became that he must help us, save us. He was one of the few powerful people in camp who seemed to possess a degree of kindness. Who else could help us? Genady Markov would, but could not. Beluskov did his best to help by giving us extra rations whenever he could. Behind his back, the kitchen slaves stole from the supplies meant for us whenever they could, while the sergeants and officers received the best of the food arriving in camp. The management staff, consisting of supply officers, recording and accounting personnel, shaved off a goodly percentage of the supplies for themselves. They controlled Beluskov, leaving him with little to give us.

These men and one woman were the worst profiteering scum. Party darlings, they had been placed in positions where they could practice Russia's age-old custom of graft and theft. Corruption and the extraction of *baksheesh* were alive and well in Stalin's new farmers' and workers' paradise. Compared to the new crop of thieves and swindlers, the old tsarist guard had been childishly incompetent.

For a week I thought night and day of what I could do to change things. Someone had to tell the commandant how bad conditions were. This problem preoccupied me so much that I paid little attention to my work, almost severing my hand. That accident finally convinced me that I had to proceed with my plan.

I had come to the conclusion that to make a profound impression on Kulov I needed a drastic, dramatic, shocking statement, a picture that would speak louder than my small voice. I sidled up to Markov one evening after mess, when I believed the yard to be free of hateful eyes. As usual, the yard was lit by the powerful searchlights, and so we stood concealed in the shadow of the mess barracks.

"Please, Sergeant Markov, get me a hearing with the commandant. I must see him—my women are starving, any small illness will kill them," I begged. "I know we have already received much kindness from you, more than we can ever make up for. But I still… I must ask," I faltered, fell silent and stared at the frozen, dirty ground.

For a long while he remained silent. He remained quiet so long that I raised my eyes, looking fully into his face. He looked sad and old beneath his sheep-fur hat. I knew he was only about forty-five and yet, at this moment, he looked sixty and more.

"*Dochka,*" he surprised me, calling me daughter. "I know that you suffer. Give me a little time. I will come and get you when the time is right."

We parted and I hastened back to my barrack before the evening count. I was certain that Markov would be true to his word. Now I only had to wait for his call. My plan was firmly embedded in my head. I would act accordingly.

A week went by, hard, cold and dull. Suddenly, overnight the temperature dropped below minus thirty degrees Celsius, the point where all work ceased. It was not for our benefit that work came to a halt when the thermometer dropped. No, I am sure that our comfort was never of consideration. They would have driven us to work no matter the weather. The guards and the camp staff, however, refused to be outside when the low temperature and added wind-chill could freeze a man in a short time.

We lingered in the warm mess barracks until the cook's detail physically pushed us out. Keeping the wood stove fed, we occupied ourselves by trying to mend clothing and by sanitizing our foot rags, submerging them in fresh sawdust. This was another thing we lugged to the camp from the worksite. Sanitizing was perhaps too overblown a term for the process. However, after leaving the rags buried for a while in the freshly shaved wood, they smelled of the living forest—a great improvement over their previous condition.

Through the bed rotation, it had been my bad luck to end up in a bed far away from the stove. Presently, my bed was close to the outside wall. Only the night before a warm spot had been mine and now, with the temperature dropping and a chill wind finding the holes in the chinks, I was on the outside. We were constantly occupied repairing the walls. The guards sometimes gave us something akin to caulk, which we spread into the cracks and holes.

Often enough, though, we stuffed fabric and any other pliable thing we could find into the miserable breaches. Barbara even invented a paste, cleverly composed of sawdust and stolen machine oil, which froze into place if used like caulk.

I tried to sleep rolled up in my coat—to no avail. It was much too cold to sleep on the outside of the room while the wind was howling. Upon my thin frame I wore every garment I possessed—and still I was cold. I got up from my cot and joined other women huddled around the stove. Here, too, we rotated from the inner positions to the outer.

We braved the howling wind for our dinner rations, returning colder still. At noon we had sent a delegation for buckets of hot tea and a piece of bread. Outside, it had been totally dark for hours. It was a darkness barely defied by the searchlights shaking in the wind, as they dispensed their rays like a palsied man trying to light his way with a flashlight.

I was still trying to gain a spot by the stove, when the door was violently torn open. Genady Markov entered amid a great, horrid gust of icy wind. Everyone fiercely shouted, while shaking spastically, for him to shut the door.

Markov, too, shuddered. He pulled his facemask off, and shook himself like a large dog. Removing his outer fur glove, he rubbed his face to restore feeling, while he scanned us intently. His eyes fell upon me, and he smiled.

He waved for me to join him and I hastened to oblige. He spoke softly, insuring that only I could understand his words, "Today, of all miserable days, the commandant wants to see you. He is sober—as far as I can tell—and he should be able to comprehend what you tell him."

"Oh God, it is so cold. He had to choose the worst of all days for my meeting."

"Quit complaining and be thankful that you get to see him at all."

"I am! Oh, but I am, Genady Markov! I am very grateful to you."

"All right then. I will go with you and make sure the wind does not blow you away."

I wound the rest of my foot rags about my feet, pulled on my *valenki* and followed Markov out of the hut. Behind us, the women complained loudly again about the draft. This sudden call to see the commander was ruining my plan. I would have to improvise now. How could I make my strong, shocking statement without preparation? I did not know how I would pull off my surprise. However, nothing mattered now—I was going.

Outside, the wind sprang upon us like a tiger, ripping and tearing at our clothes, trying to strip our faces bare, assaulting our gloved hands, which unsuccessfully tried to prevent the fronts of our coats from flying open.

The walk to the administration building, which also housed the commandant, was short but difficult, and I doubt I could have made it there without Markov. He had taken hold of my arm, pressing it against his side, which steadied me and shielded me from the worst of the wind's assault.

Holding on to one another, we climbed the steps to the administration building, where Markov and I combined forces to open the door. The anteroom was empty but warm—much better insulated than our hut. A few abused chairs bearing the scars of rough, uncaring customers and a small wooden table carrying ancient copies of the magazine *Trud* and *Pravda* outfitted the anteroom. *Pravda*—the Truth, Verity—ha, no greater lie was ever perpetrated on the Russian people than *Pravda*.

"You go in through this door." Markov pointed at a side door, which supposedly led to the commandant's private quarters. He had taken his facecloth off and looked at me searchingly.

"Are you afraid? No? Good! I will be right here and take you back when you have finished your business." He looked at me meaningfully, fiercely. I took his big, gloved hand in mine and, rising up on my toes, I lightly kissed his ice-cold, bristly cheek. Turning quickly I went to the door he had pointed out and knocked.

"Enter!" came the strong reply.

Inside it was cozy warm. A stove, much like the iron thing we had in our hut was glowing—surely stuffed with good coal. I stepped deeper into the room. Alyosha, the commandant, leaned against the opposite wall with an open book in his hand. For a man who supposedly had been drinking his life away, he looked remarkably well. He had an open, pleasant face, dominated by intelligent—dare I say, kindly, blue-gray eyes. Brown hair, cut short, looked like a helmet placed above his high forehead. He was well over medium height, broad-shouldered—the figure of a sportsman, a fighter.

"So you wanted to see me?" he asked.

"Yes," I answered bravely, "your name means defender, and I come to you for defense." He laughed, ending in a little snort, "Hah, so you speak Russian so well that you even know the meaning of names."

"Why shouldn't I know the language and the meaning?" I asked, impertinently raising my voice a bit. "I am as Russian as you are. I would bet my bloodline is older than yours and nobler, perhaps." Somehow a tinge of arrogance had crept into my demeanor. I sensed that it would not hurt me to be confident, confrontational even. Things were developing satisfactorily, when a knock on the anteroom door interrupted what had looked so promising.

"What is it?" called the commandant.

"I have a problem with the coal accounts, comrade commandant, and need you to look at these papers before you sign them," came the answer from the other room.

"My adjutant," whispered Alyosha Semyonovich, as if we were involved in a secret assignation. "Go in there until he is gone." He waved me through a door into a small windowless library, calling to the man beyond, "Just a moment, Ilya," and a second later, "Come in, come in, Ilya Gregorievich!"

Alone in the charmless storage room for account books, I begged God hurriedly to send me grace to enable me to do what I was ordained to perform. I acted with the greatest of haste—and that was well—for soon the commandant called for me to return to his office. He once again stood, leaning against the wall, book in hand. Without pause he returned to our discussion.

"So you are Russian, eh? What then are you doing amid the Volga German women in camp?"

"My mother is German. My family has lived in Russia since 1764. I know no other country and, until recently, we loved Russia dearly." Taken aback, he let this information sink in. At last, he said, "What is your full name?"

"Katharina Alexeyevna Grushova. My father was an officer—like you," I spit. "They killed him, Alexander Petrovich Grushov, an innocent man, in Vorkuta." I paused, and then, as if prodded by the devil, I added, "Just like they sent you into our purgatory."

For a while the only sounds heard were our deep breaths. Suddenly he said, "Do you like poetry?"

"I love poetry. My mother always recited poems while preparing dinner. She would shell peas, and every pea became a profound word."

"You speak poetic lines," he smiled. I had been standing before him for a long while, holding my arms across my body. I was tired. The deep cold was leaving my body at last, and I began to shake as the frost departed.

"I am sorry. I am keeping you and you still have not been able to tell me why you wanted to see me."

As if performing on stage, this was my cue. I opened my arms wide. All the clothes I had been holding tight to my belly fell to the floor. I shrugged off the coat, and stood naked before the man.

"What does this mean?" he stammered perplexed.

"Look at me," I commanded him. "Look at every inch of my body! Do you see now why I am here? We are starving to death. All my women look like I do. We are young and look like ancient skeletons. Note that I have no breasts, not the last bit of fat or flesh on my thighs. I am dying— twenty years old and dying of overwork and starvation." I stopped, for the adrenalin that had carried me along, stopped flowing. Instead, tears streamed from my eyes.

"I beg of you, you have the power, to make them give us a little fat, a little meat, a little more bread. We work so hard in the merciless cold. Look at my frostbitten hands, my toes! For that, we get nothing to eat but watery gruel, watery cabbage soup with perhaps a few sardines thrown in, and a piece of bread enriched with sawdust. That is our life."

The commandant had lowered his eyes to the ground. My emaciated body must have appalled him. I stopped speaking. I stood there in frozen silence for minutes, and yet he would not look at me. Frustrated and ashamed, I gathered my clothes and fled into the dreary library-archive room, where I dressed in hysterical haste. Put together, I returned to his office and stammered, "I am sorry I offended you. I thought, if you saw a real body you would understand and help us. I was wrong. However, I want you to know that even the slightest illness will kill the women in this camp and you will be responsible before God, because he put you in charge."

Genady Markov was waiting for me. Outside, as the terrible wind tore on our clothes, he shouted, "What did he say? Will he help?"

"The lousy coward said nothing—nothing at all. And I begged him with every fiber of my body!" How true, I had put every fiber of my ill-looking, emaciated body into the fight.

"Don't give up yet!" Markov consoled. "Give him a little time to think about what you said. Give him a chance to find out what he can do." Thus, the lowly sergeant-guard nobly defended the almighty commandant.

"His life is hard, too. We do not know the reason why one so obviously educated and intelligent should have ended up in Siberia. So forgive him—and wait."

Frozen to the core I reclined on the lumpy sawdust. By now it smelled stale from absorbing the odors of many different bodies. The dim lights were shut off on the guard's last round. Moments later, the darkness and deep silence allowed the pictures of my visit to penetrate my conscious mind. I saw myself standing naked before the commandant—naked, ashamed, humiliated—my soul exposed—to what purpose? I had accomplished nothing.

My intent to arouse pity and concern in him had backfired. He had not even looked at me, evidently disgusted by my indecent display. His eyes had hugged the floor as if he could not bear to look at my stringy figure. I had made a spectacle of myself to no avail and devalued my cause. I felt so despondent that I could not even cry, to get release from my disgrace.

Alleviation

For a week nothing happened. The temperature remained below the acceptable and we did not work. Barbara closely interrogated me about my "adventure." I confessed to my utter failure, calling Kulov a cold fish, which, admittedly, made me feel a tiny bit better.

On the last evening of that hungry, cold, but restful week, I called the squad to the mess and walked them across the frosty grounds to the warm mess barrack. Already upon entry we smelled a difference. Instead of the all-pervasive smell of cabbage and old fish, the savory, mouthwatering smell of fried meat excited our noses.

We lined up, our expectations sky high. And there it was! A plate filled with potatoes, a piece of chicken and a portion of fried onions was passed across the counter and landed in the lucky hands of Maria Brill. We almost had a riot that very moment. Everyone began shoving and pushing, for no one believed that this miracle would occur twice.

I called out sharply, commandingly, for order and threatened that I would withhold the food from every woman leaving the line or causing disorder. As plate after plate cleared the counter, into greedily reaching hands, I began to believe that a miracle had happened.

Barbara brought her plate over to my table and sat next to me. She did not talk at first, devouring the heavenly food like the rest of us. It was not as if we had received the most wonderful sustenance. Under ordinary circumstances, one would not have given this food a second thought. But here it was like manna from heaven. Everyone was gifted with one whole potato, cut into six pieces, fried in oil, a half an onion—also fried in real fat and a small piece of chicken.

We ate with the feverish attention of starving dogs. Not one crumb was lost to our keen eyes, and then we wiped the aluminum plates clean with the small piece of real, unadulterated bread we'd been given. Almost sated, we stood, bowed our heads, and quietly gave thanks. All outward signs of faith were, of course, strictly forbidden; however, we had to make an exception, for a miracle had just occurred.

When Barbara had licked her lips for the last time, she looked into my eyes with profound meaning and said, "Whatever you did to the commandant, you did well. God's blessing must have been on you when you spoke and he laid the right words on your heart. Just look at the result."

I smiled sheepishly. For I will forever wonder if God approved of my forward ways—perhaps He blessed my desperation.

The Invitation

Henceforth our rations were larger, of better quality, and almost satisfying at times. A little more fat, sometimes a little meat, we began to feel a little better. Work began once more, for temperatures were rising. Markov joked one morning that soon we might reach minus ten Celsius and strip off our coats.

As life became easier, we worked harder. We all realized that we had to make the commandant look good for he had improved our condition. Barbara and I put out word that it was important to fulfill the norm whenever possible.

Markov entered the hut as I sat late one evening repairing my long, woolen stockings, the heavy, hand-knit ones, worn over cotton stockings, because they itched so terribly if worn on the skin. He came directly to my bed on the outside of the room, still far removed from the warm stove, and said in a low voice, "Put on your coat and boots. You have been summoned to see the commandant."

My heart pounded. What kind of trouble awaited me in the office? I thought Kulov had listened to my appeal, changed our circumstances, and that would be the end of it. Why was I called so late at night for a hearing? The lights would be extinguished in a few minutes; it felt as if it was ten o'clock. What did he want from me?

Markov read these questions on my face. "Don't worry," he murmured, "I will wait for you."

As we walked clandestinely to the administration building, among the shadows, I finally dared ask the question that had plagued me for months.

"Sergeant Markov, will you allow me to ask you a very personal question?" I began.

He chortled, "Why not? You always do what you want anyway."

I rushed on. "You know that in this camp you are my beacon of light and hope, for you are good to us. Why are you one of the very few in camp who does not hate us, does not torment us, but instead treats us kindly? What is your reason? Goodness? Christianity? Please tell me. I must know."

He muttered something about pesky, nosy women who cannot leave things alone, and fell silent for a moment. Then he said, "Perhaps I will tell you another time."

When we reached the office the protocol seemed to be a duplication of my earlier visit. Markov waited in the anteroom. I entered the commandant's office, and again he leaned against the wall, a book in hand.

"Ah, there you are, Katharina Alexeyevna. Tell me, how is the food?"

"Oh, thank you, thank you, it's so much better." The words of thanks gushed from my lips, as water spills over a fall, and then all of a sudden I became bashful, timid. The commandant did not allow the silence to continue.

"Good, I will see what I can do so it stays that way." When he noticed me awkwardly twirling my double gloves in my hands, he became aware of my discomfort standing at attention. "He pointed at a wooden chair close to his desk, and said, "Sit, sit, Katharina!" I noticed that he did not say comrade Katharina anymore—just Katharina.

I was barely seated when he came toward me, leading with the large book. "You said that you know poetry," he said, almost accusatory.

"I do. German and Russian, but I only retained my favorites."

"Who do you like best?"

"Hard to say. Lermontov, Akhmatova, Pushkin, Goethe, Schiller, Eichendorf," I named a few favorites. Without hesitation he began to recite Akhmatova:

> As a white stone in the well's cool deepness,
> There lies in me one wonderful remembrance.

Cutting him off in mid-breath, I chimed,

> I am not able and don't want to miss this:
> this is my torture and utter gladness.

"If the Moon On the Skies," he put forth the name of one poem.

"The Gray-Eyed King," I answered.

"The Death of Sophocles," said he.

"I Don't Like Flowers," I trumped.

"So you know Akhmatova," said Alyosha.

"How about my favorite, Lermontov," I countered, and I declaimed,

The glen of Daghestan, at noon, was hot and gleaming;
I lay on sand with lead sent to my heart;
My deadly wound was deep and easily streaming;
And drop by drop, my blood was oozing from the wound.

He came back,

Under the same star, I am sure,
We both crossed the worldly rims.

"I know that one," I called out. "To the Countess Rostopchin." I continued in German, "*Es war, als hätt' der Himmel die Erde still geküsst.*" I never finished the verse before he completed it for me in fine German.

We were both smiling. I could not remember a time in the last year that had given me more pleasure. "You do know poetry," he said, with obvious fondness. "Once, a long time ago, in a better life, I taught Russian literature and poetry." He sighed, "What a good life that was."

With a flush of guilt I became aware that much time had gone by while I enjoyed myself. Out in the foyer, sat faithful sergeant Markov waiting for me. I still had to creep through the dark barrack room to my bed. I had to end the pleasant visit presently before it got any later.

"Thank you for everything commandant. I enjoyed this visit very much, but I must leave. Sergeant Markov is waiting for me and all the barracks must be dark already. In the name of all the women, I thank you for the extra food." Then bravely, I added, "May God bless you."

The commandant smiled at me, looking very young and kind. "Good night, Katharina Alexeyevna," was all he said.

I left quickly. Markov had fallen asleep in one of the uncomfortable, ill-used chairs. He blinked, rose to his feet, and rushed me to my barrack. Halfway back, a suspicious guard with a gun slung across his chest intercepted us, who rudely questioned Markov. Finally, Markov had enough, "If you don't believe my word, go and interrogate the commandant. He will set you right."

Unconvinced, the guard, growled, "I might just do that. Watch your step Markov, you are much too sure of yourself. Prokofiev has an eye on you and will catch you sooner or later."

"I hate this damned camp," Markov spit through his teeth. "I follow the given orders of one, and the next one wants to destroy me for doing my duty."

He began to walk again and I followed like a lamb. Moments later, safely ensconced in my bed, I recalled with elation every minute of my meeting with the strange poet. I assumed it was the narrowness of camp life so ruthlessly imposed upon us that made even the smallest diversion a notable, a high event. It must be that the longing for a mental life made me giddy with joy when given a break from tedium. For we were forever consumed by constantly unfulfilled basic needs and fears.

In secrecy I visited the commandant a few more times, each a sweet respite from reality. There was between the man Alyosha and me a deep understanding, an unspoken feeling of deep mutual attraction, of tenderness and utter delight to be in each other's company.

During one visit, Alyosha came and sat beside me, ostensibly to share his book with me. He held the book between us and then his cheek imperceptibly touched mine—as if accidentally. But I knew, I was sure in my innermost being that he had meant it, so subtly and curiously, to happen. I knew that at this moment we both succumbed to an abundance of sensation. For his voice, as he read to me, fell to a murmur so low that I could hardly hear him.

When he finally finished reading and withdrew his cheek his voice was raw with suppressed passion and he rose, harshly twisting his fingers. The book lay forgotten before me. I kept my eyes glued to the open pages, but I could not tell you what was written there. I knew I had to leave this instant or we would cross a bridge that we could not, dare not cross.

"I must leave, Alyosha," I said softly, and he, with his back turned to me, said, "Yes, you must!"

Genady Markov worried fatherly about me. "Do not allow him to make love to you, *dochka*. In a camp like this, everyone knows everything. Soon tongues will wag and someone will try to harm you."

"You know me well enough, dear man, to be certain that nothing improper occurs during these visits."

"I know, and I believe. They however, all of them, do not."

My dilemma, that I craved these visits of the mind and the spirit, craved the presence of that kind man, was resolved in the end by trouble and sadness.

The last time I saw Alyosha, my poet, my commandant, the man who had become so dear to me, he drew me to him and stroked my hair. He held me for a while, not saying a word. He kissed me on the lips, and murmured, "Another time, another place, and we could be happy. Yet we were born to blood and destruction. For us, there will be no happiness."

The Plague

By mid-April milder weather brought thawing of the upper layer of permafrost. The temperatures hovered around three degrees Celsius, making it seem warm. In the taiga, however, even the slightest pleasure contains within it discomfort and unpleasantness. The newly thawed ground, a soggy mess, required new adjustments.

In the woods, the small bogs began their new lifecycle. The mosses looked vibrant green and gray, and formed small red spores on tiny stalks. The ground was squishy mud, making sucking sounds as we walked among the trees. Rivulets formed and ran in the direction of the river, which flowed not far from the worksite.

Our section of the taiga was of mixed forest. Stands of conifers, pine and juniper, were interspersed with stretches of deciduous maple, linden, ash, oak and birch forest. The sap of the deciduous trees rose, visibly expressed in the swelling of their buds. A fresh, clean smell pervaded the realm, to which the birds returned in small, but daily increasing, flocks.

The big machines, which loaded the tree trunks onto the trucks for their journey to the railroad project, churned the soil into vast, brown patches of morass, splattered and drenched everything within twenty feet. The churned, abused forest soil made me feel as if the men and machines raped mother earth with the same careless disdain they showed toward us. At last, the trucks, which before had frivolously, carelessly, cut their way throughout the worksite, were restricted to the raised tarmac.

The sun shone for longer periods, curbing the need for the searchlights. We felt happier—relieved that the foggy darkness had ended. Everyone reacted to spring in their own fashion. On the way to the woods, our women, bunched together in the open trucks, talked busily, and reminded one of the flocks of birds alighting in the trees.

I recited spring poems in my mind, thought of Alyosha, and smiled. Young Vasya hummed *polyushka, polya*, the song of the little field, and sometimes Markov joined in with his booming bass.

In the winter we had never seen animals in the forest. The horrific noise created by the machines had prevented the animals from coming close. We had, however, seen the tracks of creatures, made during nightly incursions. Now, as the machines fell silent, unable to maneuver in the morass, we saw the occasional fox slink by, saw the dark wolf skirt the perimeter's edge and once noticed, at a good distance a shaggy, huge animal ambling through the trees, unafraid, despite our presence.

The days of the *valenki* were over, or the mud would have sucked them off our feet. We gladly shed the foot rags as the temperature rose. The ground, soft and squishy, once more was treacherous. We had to be extra careful as we worked. Slipping and sliding led to injuries. Still, we rejoiced. The cold receded a bit more day by day.

Like oxen in the yoke we had adapted to our lot and performed, as we must. And yet we found small joys again in life, and a bird, a fern, the clear, blue sky inspired us. We were, after all, young women still at the beginning of life. "One cannot cry every day," was a saying, and so we smiled in the midst of slavery.

As if the levity, the bit of lightness we had allowed to arise, needed repression, or more even, serious punishment, the camp was struck by illness. In the barrack farthest from ours, thirty women fell ill from one day to the next. The dread word, striking fear in all of us, was cholera.

"It's the water," pronounced Barbara. She made us boil and re-boil the drinking water and even boil the tea from the kitchen. Markov confided in passing that he thought the latrine was the point of dispersion for the illness. "These latrines were not properly dug, lined or often enough disinfected," he said, with such certainty that I believed him.

"Don't go there, Katya," he advised me, "go into the woods during work time." The dread disease spread through camp like wildfire. The leaders of barrack after barrack reported sick women, unable to go to work, every morning. The infirmary was full. Therefore, the sick women were left in their own beds, thereby contaminating entire barracks.

In the face of the terrifying epidemic, the doctor behaved with abominable nonchalance. His measures to disinfect the latrines with quicklime came days too late. His orders to segregate the stricken barracks and quarantine the infected came even later, when almost the whole camp was engulfed. He provided few medications for the stricken women, who suffered immeasurably. Those who had observed the ill women, told me that they suffered incredible abdominal pains. The worst symptom of the illness was unstoppable diarrhea.

The first victims died quickly of dehydration. Because of ignorance and neglect no one supplied enough liquids to replace their losses. Finally, the doctor commandeered a group of our women to nurse the patients.

The coerced nurses were horrified. We thought that they would catch the cholera and die too. Poor things! They had no training, no linens to replace the befouled bedding, and no disinfectants. Some of these girls did get sick, but strangely, most of them survived, leading us to believe that the cholera was spread through water or food. Only because of their dedicated care did many victims survive.

Among the first to die were Barbara's two cousins from Norka. Barbara was struck to the core. She did not cry, showed no emotions, but she lost her voice. Like most of us, she was now all alone. The cousins had been the last link, the last connectedness to her deported family, who were now God only knows where. I tried to comfort her. At night I held her in my arms, singing to her. At work, I talked about the things we had to do, the simple, plodding routines in an effort to lead her mind away from death. To no avail. She remained as if sleepwalking. She performed her work, dressed herself and ate when she saw food; yet, she did not speak and did not seem to hear us.

I must admit that, like a coward, I thanked God every day that I was able to leave the foul camp and go into the fresh woods. There we worked and prayed nonstop for our stricken sisters. So far, my squad was blessed with good health—a most gracious gift, for which we thanked our Maker.

Epidemic disease makes no distinction between kings and paupers, guards and inmates—it likes every body equally well to propagate itself. Therefore no one was surprised when a few guards fell ill. Then the kitchen staff was decimated. Some administrators fled.

The norm had not been fulfilled in days. At this crucial point of dissolution, the miserable doctor finally realized the seriousness of the outbreak. He ordered the mattresses and the blankets of the dead and the sick to be removed and burned on an enormous pyre. That fire burned for a day, belching black, stinking smoke into the clean air. Quicklime purified the latrines. A large trench was dug by machine, wherein the dead bodies were consigned to be buried, but not before they, too, were covered with quicklime. He also had the water purified. Alas, too late! Too late for our dead, too late for my friend's relatives.

Upon returning from the forest one evening, we saw a convoy of cars and trucks. A flock of white-coated people, led by Alyosha, bustled about. In groups, they went from barrack to barrack. The food was very good that night, because the strangers also ate in the mess. We benefited, since so many strangers could by no means have been fed separately.

In the following days, work came to a complete standstill. The white-coated groups of men took charge of everything. All hands were set to empty and clean the affected barracks. The remaining patients were put on hydration, such a simple, life-saving measure, a measure our own inmate nurses had found effective to save lives. After new outhouses had been constructed, the latrines were shut down. Within days two brand-new, shining, large units purified our drinking water.

As soon as one task was finished, another began. Once the barracks had been disinfected and cleaned, a number of us were employed stuffing canvas bags with fresh sawdust—we had plenty of that—to make new mattresses.

When the newly refurbished barracks were reassigned, we counted eighty women dead. Eighty young, beautiful women were thrown into mass graves before they had a chance to taste the good things life had to offer.

Our souls were mourning, while our minds churned the facts of their demise over and over again. Barbara still performed automatically. I wondered if any of the daily events registered in her mind. I wondered if the pain that drove us to despair when we carried our dead to the horrible trenches that swallowed their sallow, thin bodies, if the abhorrence dealing with the cholera's aftermath, left any recognition in her mind.

There were moments when I envied her this retreat into nothingness. What bliss it would be to retreat and feel nothing! We, however, did not enjoy this luxury and dealt with our anguish as always with prayer. At night after lights out, we murmured a litany of familiar, soothing verses that produced deep comforting sounds, which in monastic monotony almost lovingly lulled us to asleep.

During this difficult time my inability to touch Alyosha when I beheld him caused me agonies. I saw him daily as he led groups of outsiders hither and yon. Each time I saw him, my heart contracted, skipping beats and I was reminded once more of our last, bittersweet meeting. He was my peoples' enemy, and yet how dear he had become to me. Oh, how valiantly I combated the flush that rose in my cheeks each time I saw him, how strongly I kept a rein on my roving eyes, and how powerfully I controlled my voice that would surely have given me away.

At times, the new officials, bureaucrats or functionaries—whatever they were—provoked loud disputes with the camp staff and the commandant on one side and the newcomers on the other. The first casualty of the functionaries was the doctor. He was instantly replaced with a new, young doctor in an olive-brown uniform, a red star on the shirt-collar, a red star on his hat.

Whenever we observed such disputes, always from afar, I noted that Alyosha kept a cool head and demeanor. Often the functionaries walked by one of our groups, arguing loudly. From the comments I overheard, everyone supposed the new officials were set upon finding fault, and ascertaining bad leadership. Within two weeks they seemed to have accomplished their goal, stripping the camp of most of its staff.

We awoke one morning to spring rain sweetly drumming upon the metal roof of the porch. Outside, the new officials busily filled several trucks with guards, soldiers and office staff. At first, it gave me great satisfaction that they, too, had to ride in the same discomfort we experienced every day.

Then, however, my heart stood still, and I turned so pale that the woman next to me thought I was going to faint. I had noticed a black sedan at the end of the small convoy. I knew that it would be reserved for the commandant—Alyosha. I cringed, when I saw Genady Markov and sweet Vasya among the men in the last truck.

We stood before our hut as still as the trees in the forest, our faces set and somber. "Oh, Lord," I said, "what will become of us now?" We knew these men. We knew who was good, bad and indifferent, knew how to manipulate some, knew to implicitly comply with the orders of others, and to keep still others at arm's length.

What kind of men or women would replace our familiars? Who would protect us now, with Markov and Alyosha gone? What would we do without Vasya's gossip and information?

Oh, unhappy guards and officials who had overall been tolerable, where were they going? We ventured that wherever they went, would be a wretched, punitive exile. One might ask, 'How could there be a place worse than our camp,' I assure you we had heard of camps much more dreadful than ours. All along the new railroad were camps so atrociously horrid that men said, "Under each end of a railroad tie rests a dead man's head." And then there was Vorkuta—never forget Vorkuta!

Alyosha's car was the last to leave. He left the administration building followed by his secretary and his adjutant—each carrying two large bags. They entered the dark car, and moments later the car pulled away. It was as if a stone fell upon my heart—the last bit of joy in my life had left.

Who would care about us now? Who would advise and protect us as Markov had done? We stood outside in the rain far too long and suddenly realized that we were wet and cold. Dispirited, we walked to the mess. Anton Petrovich Beluskov greeted us with a sad smile. I was glad to see him—a small ray of hope. His kitchen staff was—with few exceptions—intact. Breakfast was good: oatmeal, bread, one egg and tea, almost enough to fill our ever-hungry stomachs.

After breakfast, like rudderless ships, we drifted back to our barracks. The unusual idleness was nerve-wracking. We sat on our cots and talked about the terrifying changes in camp. It was remarkable that not even one of us believed the change in staff would be for the better. No, without exception, we believed that things could only get worse.

As if we had forsworn our luck, change was immediate and bad. We were called out into the steadily falling rain and made to line up. Our numbers were verified. Having finished their lists, the bureaucrats announced that our new commandant would arrive presently. Upon this pronouncement we were reassigned to fill some of the decimated barracks to capacity, leaving others empty. Our building remained the same, for the cholera had passed us by. Perhaps Barbara's boiling and re-boiling of tea and water had saved us.

Although re-assigned to new quarters, we were not allowed to enter our huts to dry ourselves. Instead, a drill master marched us in as good an order as he could effect to the administration building, where he arrayed us in squads of forty. Barely had he accomplished this feat—for we had never stood in formation, except at our arrival—when a caravan of trucks arrived and disgorged about a hundred women.

"Dear, God!" cried Emma Wiesner with disbelief. She was a small slip of a woman with clear skin and huge blue eyes, which she now turned up to me. "Do you see what I see?"

"I do! Oh, I do!" I retorted with emphasis. All of us stared with incredulity at the new arrivals. It seemed as if Stalin's henchmen had emptied Moscow's brothels and jails to assemble the astonishing flock before us. From copper-red-headed, milk-white beauties in extravagant, modish outfits to the coarsest, ugliest, toothless troll—every kind of Russian woman was present.

Among them was a group of large, mean-looking women, tough enough even to intimidate the guards. But we did not know then the caliber of the new guards. We did, however, finally understand why we had been required to dig holes and set posts around the camp's perimeter for the last few days. Now it became clear to us why the guards had strung multiple wires from post to post.

We now lived in an enclosed camp, for the new prisoners, among them lifers, murderers and robbers, might try to escape from an open camp—with help waiting on the outside. These new women still had families in the places where they had been apprehended. They were not in our hopeless, orphaned position. We were still gawking, when the guards who had accompanied these women, marched them to the two empty barracks to the right of the mess hut.

As they trickled into their buildings, a smart staff car pulled up to the flagpole in front of the administration building. Two uniformed men jumped out. One opened the right front door and stood at attention, while the other retrieved baggage from the trunk.

The rain still poured down on us, steadily, unavoidably, and cold. Finally, the new camp commander emerged. He stepped from the car, stretching to his full height. I heard a sharp intake of breath from many of the women surrounding me, for the man was enormous. He was above six feet; he had a square body with a short, muscular neck, a round bullet head, short pig-blond hair and massive shoulders. He reminded me, terrifyingly so, of the prize boar we once had in our village; a boar, which finally had been shot because he had killed a man and devoured him. Now, the picture of this boar was vividly before my eyes—a big, hulking, ferocious thing.

Ivan's Regime

The new commander gave us a cursory glance and dismissed us. A new adjutant, who looked sharply put together in his brand new outfit, performed this task. How precisely an impression I had formed, assessing the new commander, was revealed the next day. The moment the last inmates had been fed, we were called to stand in formation. The last, of course, were the new convict inmates, who did not yet conform to a regimen that had not changed. The clanging of irons at five in the morning was still the standard wake-up call.

The rain had not stopped for a moment. In its dreary drizzle we lined up in formation in front of the flagpole, its flag hanging down sloppily and bedraggled in the still air. The door of the administration building opened and the new man stepped onto the raised porch.

From there, sheltered by the overhanging roof, he assumed a stance meant to impress upon us with whom, henceforth, we would have to deal. He spread his legs wide, as if only thus could he support his bulk, and ran his eyes over our lines. It seemed to me that his glance came to rest on certain women in a curious, probing, interested way.

As I studied him, his narrow, sharply sloping forehead registered unfavorably. Below blond, bristly brows sat pale, round, small, piggish eyes, set apart by a big, fleshy nose. He had a wide mouth with large, sensuous lips that he licked lasciviously before even uttering a word.

Then he spoke. His mouth was cavernous. The teeth at its entry were large and wide-spaced. His face appeared flushed although the day was cool. Suddenly I knew why this face seemed so familiar—it was the visage of the man-eating giant in my childhood storybook.

"Woe is us!" I thought. "This man is evil incarnate. He will torment us." We had been standing at attention and total silence all this time. Now he broke the fearful spell. Sonorous, pronouncing each syllable, he made the following speech:

"I am Kalachnik Bogdanovich Matveyev, the new commandant. The officials sent here to deal with the outbreak of the cholera found serious breaches of camp policy, non-performance, general laxness, and a breakdown of camp order!" The new commandant stretched his arms upward and, attaining full height, looked more like a bear clawing a tree than a man.

"I have been sent to establish order. Under my command, the norm will be fulfilled by one hundred ten percent. The general slovenliness I have observed will cease." He looked around and his gaze fell upon the women convicts. In the early gray morning light, drenched and bedraggled by the rain, they looked not much different from our lot.

I have found that women's beauty is easily destroyed by misery and external circumstance. Men, made of more rugged stuff, hold up much better. Matveyev addressed the convicts by sharpening his demeanor. His eyes became more piercing and the veins of his neck became pronounced.

"You," he pointed at them, "filthy dregs of our new Soviet society, you especially must follow orders and work harder to convince us that you can be changed into new productive citizens of our magnificent country."

He then proceeded to read a litany of extraordinary commands— so many that we forgot them instantly. Everything seemed to be forbidden. No talking to and fraternizing with guards was a familiar taboo. This was followed by punctual embarkation for work in the morning, punctual appearance for meals and the washroom—no exceptions. No malingering! From now on only the doctor would decide fitness for work...on and on he went.

Every rule was laid down with its own special, harsh punishment following. There was to be solitary confinement for fraternization, reduced or no rations for failing to fulfill the daily plan, and flogging for repeat offenses. It was obvious that, henceforth, an unmerciful tyrant would rule us. We glanced at each other, covertly, with baleful looks of dismay.

By nighttime, we had dubbed him "Ivan the Terrible." The moment he finished his recital of the monumental work of laws, an *ukase* worse than any of the tsar's, the guards herded us into the trucks and shipped us off to work. We had been wet to begin with—by noon we were soaked to the bone. Our sodden clothes slowed us down severely. That day we did not even come close to making the enlarged "norm," and by evening our rations were reduced by half.

The nagging hunger kept me awake. My own misery under the new regime brought home, with renewed force, the suppressed worries about my family. As I lay shivering on my cot that night, I though of Joseph, my sweet adopted brother. How did he fare at the front?

An odd, strange thought, tinged with almost obscene jealousy, crossed my mind. "Could it perhaps be better to fight on the front?" There, at least, would be every so often a break in the fight, leaving you free to your own bidding—time to read, to write a letter, or to stretch out in the sun. Here, none of that was possible. Every minute of life was regimented—allotted to specific tasks. And as for death, it would come quickly with a bullet, while here, it was slow starvation as we toiled like oxen in the yoke.

I thought of my mother. Where had the new regime imprisoned her? Was she, too, toiling in a gulag? Or had she been sent with the other families into a wilderness without food, tools, shelters, or any supplies to survive even one winter?

I thought about gorgeous Arkady, the splendid survivor of a dreadful childhood. Was he dead? Or was he fighting with Joseph on the German front? I wondered if they could escape. Did they have enough food? I mused they might get much better rations than we did. Generals knew that men did not shoot straight when their stomachs contracted with pain.

And what had become of my grandparents and my older brothers in Germany? Living in my own troubled world, I had almost forgotten them. And what, oh, what had happened to gentle, beloved Alyosha? My eyes were wet each time I thought of him.

Why had God permitted for us to be confined, to be treated worse than cattle? Why? I knew Mother would say, "What happens to us is ordained by other people's free will. If they choose evil, we suffer." I had always hated that reply, because it implied that good people would suffer forever from the free will of evil people. My faith broke under the inevitability of this daunting logic.

The next morning I felt sick. I was shaky and weak. I surmised that the cause of my condition was being wet and hungry while driven on to the utmost effort. I do not know how I lived through that day. My squad mates did not look any better than I did. Again, on this day and the following three, we were incapable of making the new "norm."

Everyone, including the guards who watched us, knew it was an illusory goal set by a bureaucrat, who himself had never worked for even one day with his hands and body. Our food rations were reduced even more, until they were nothing at all.

Soon every barracks reported whole groups of women stricken with illness in the morning. Nonetheless, the new doctor dispatched all of them back to work, declaring them to be malingerers. Henceforth, at the worksite, the guards stood over us shouting commands to a faster pace, while they flogged us with their belts. It was to no avail—we could not make the norm. Predictably, after a few days of this regimen, we stumbled about dead-eyed. We trembled as if palsied, were prone to injure ourselves and others. The next few mornings some women could not get out of bed, flogging them brought little response, for they lay as dead. Some rose to escape the pain, only to fall to the ground after a few steps.

We were experienced enough to know that even under better conditions we had not been able to cut half of the ordered amount of trees. Now, however, our performance was much worse than during Alyosha's days. The new railroad consumed trees at a faster rate than had been hauled out during the winter months. Therefore the trucks and the mud-churning caterpillar loaders were back every day, almost tearing each finished tree from our hands. Yet, there were fewer and fewer trees to carry off.

I was so hungry that I gnawed on a piece of leather, which had broken off my belt. I staggered at the site, falling at times, but I managed somehow to get up each time. The particular stand of trees we were slaying, as I had come to think of it, was a mixed forest of maple, alder and oak. As soon as a tree fell to the ground, we swooped upon its branches to tear off the newly opened buds where fresh green leaves showed invitingly. We shoved them into our mouths as quickly as we could strip them off, gorging ourselves. The fresh greens filled us temporarily, but caused us the most terrible stomach pains a few hours later.

The guards cursed and yelled. They beat us with their batons and belts, but the hunger was more painful than the pain they inflicted with their weapons. The torment continued for weeks. The convict women, much tougher then we were, combated the guards. They fought them with their bare hands and screamed at them, for which they were beaten senseless, thrown into confinement, and chained to the flagpole, by way of example. Yet no matter the punishment, the norm was never fulfilled.

Early one morning an important looking car arrived at the head of a small caravan. A bevy of officers exited from the lead car. The most senior of them must have been at least a general, based on the number of medals dripping from his chest and the lametta, tassels and cords draping from his shoulders. He and his entourage were ushered into the administration building, where they remained for long time.

He was still there when we were hauled off to the woods. That evening, we received full rations. In the morning, the norm was dropped to the old level, and the bedlam with its irrational punishment ceased.

On Sunday, we buried five of our women, deceased, they said, from enteritis. I thought otherwise and others held the same view. We believed these women were killed by hunger and abuse—that, in the end, they had given up hope and allowed their spirit to leave the world.

Before going to bed each night, I would sit beside Barbara for a while, holding her, talking to her. She had lived through this last upheaval unscathed, untouched by it all. She had worked as if the hunger did not contort her stomach; had slept, as if untroubled by our pain. But when I went to her after the funerals and took her hand in mine, she suddenly spoke.

"The new commandant killed them," she said simply, as if we had been conversing.

She looked at me and then prophesied, "I have the dread feeling that I will die in this camp."

"No, dear, we will survive, we will fight, bend not break!" I cheered. What else was I to say? I was depressed, too.

"That, perhaps, will be your fate," Barbara answered, "I know that for me the shadows draw near. Pray for me," she sighed heavily.

What did she mean by the shadows drawing near? Was she losing her mind or did she wish to end her life? These questions kept my mind in a swirl long after the room darkened.

For a while, the weather at least was a cause of joy. Spring had fully engulfed the taiga. In the sweet little grass patches, flowers bloomed in profusion. Primulae, golden and white, pushed their stems toward heaven. Pink and purple, the flowers blossomed and compelled with sensuous splendor myriads of insects to come hither, much as the maidens had done in our villages each spring, attracting young men with colorful dresses and blossom crowns in their hair.

Oh, yes, balmy spring with dulcet sounds had arrived, painting the taiga beautiful. Bright green, dainty shoots and leaves graced every tree. Birds plaited nests and swooped at their flying fare. The water in the little brooks, so clear and clean, murmured and gurgled. If the pervasive noise of our operations subsided during the noon break, one could partake, for a moment, of God's marvelous creation.

A poem came to my mind:

> *Oh, fresh scent! Oh, new ringing sound!*
> *Now all must turn for the better!*

The poem reminded me of Alyosha. I thought of him as mine, as beloved, for I could have been happy with him. Perhaps I was deluding myself while shut away in a monastic labor camp, but it was nice to believe in love, in life.

Now that it was warmer, we changed our previously formless apparel into dresses made from rough-treated cotton and coarse linen. Although not beautiful, the dresses made us appear feminine again. However, having left the heavy chrysalis of winter behind had its own disadvantages. For now the guards and the commandant noticed our bodies, decimated though they were. The men could neither hide the light in their eyes nor the swagger in their step when they saw an attractive woman walk by. They forgot their strict admonitions and betrayed their code. They were, after all, only men who would stage whisper to us or low-whistle after some of us.

Suddenly, even the commandant stalked about camp—his eyes were everywhere. Foremost of those attracting his attention was a redheaded convict they called Ivanka. Her hair alone, an abundant titian-red mane, paired with a milk-white complexion, caused heads to turn. Yet she had still other charms to offer. Her figure, not yet starved to the bone, was sleek and supple. She still had curves, where we had corners. When the guards called to her she would shamelessly send back saucy retorts.

Rumors circulated among our women that she had been a high-class tart. I had my doubts and I hated nasty rumors. Therefore, intrigued, I asked her one day what unhappy circumstance had landed her here in camp. At first, she was standoffish and disdained to even acknowledge me. But my sincere manner and questions, combined with my flawless Russian, persuaded her finally to be affable.

She looked into my eyes as if to find my soul and then, satisfied, said, "My gentleman friend, a man so high I do not dare to say his name and give his rank, fell to the axe." She looked penetratingly at me, saying, "You know whose axe?" I nodded, violently, affirmatively.

"The man who killed him wanted to take me, as he had taken all my friend's possessions. When I demurred, he sent me with a herd of harlots to this camp." Ivanka clicked her white teeth in disgust, adding, "The harlots are better company than he is by far!"

Her experienced eyes slid over my face and body, "What brought you here? You are not exactly the enemy I expected. Are you the enemy?"

"No, I am not! Neither are the women in camp with me the enemy. We have lived in the villages on the Lower Volga since 1764. We love Russia, our motherland. Now we have been declared to be enemies. How? Why? We have never done anything wrong."

A guard shouted. No more words were exchanged. We belonged to different units and were not allowed to converse. Ivanka laughed, "He thinks we make conspiracy!" she winked at me. Tossing her hair, smiling broadly at the guard and swinging her hips, she walked away.

Except for me, no one noticed during the next few days that Ivanka was not among us anymore. We were too preoccupied with our hardships, our daily terrors. The guards relentlessly kept up the work pace. They even insisted that the minutes be counted when we relieved ourselves. They followed us, standing back, measuring time.

"Turn around at least if you must accompany me!" I cried the first time I was followed in this way. Most guards complied with such wishes and those who did not we avoided.

During one of the changes at the mess hall, a squad of prisoners came out as our squad moved in. A mousy-looking woman approached me and said, "You, Lower Volga, Ivanka made me promise I tell you—she is prisoner of commandant."

Before I could ask why I was to be informed of this, the guards moved her group away, off the mess hall porch. Why would Ivanka send me this message? Was it a cry for help? A warning? What did she want me to do? Whatever her reason, the frightening message disturbed me profoundly.

I could see why the commandant would make her his "personal" prisoner. She was a most desirable woman and he was a ruthless man, enamoured with power. How better to prove his manhood and power than to carry off the prize of the camp and keep her sequestered.

We never saw Ivanka again, neither dead nor alive. Rumors circulated that her bloody, bruised face had been visible at a window a few times, and then, nothing! I for one believed without a doubt that Ivan the Terrible had killed her. She would have rebelled against him, resisted him and not have been the pliable toy he believed her to be. God only knew what he had been doing to her. She would have fought him, too feisty to give in to slavery.

Slavery! How extraordinary, how curious a word. The word stems from the Latin and Greek *sclavus-sclabos* for various enslaved peoples of Europe, some of them Slavonic races. The Slavs captured in cross-border raids, however, were the most traded by the Muslims in the Middle East. These hapless victims were brought and sold in the Town of Caffa, the capital of the mediaeval slave trade. The Caliphate of Cordoba, too, received its Slavs from Kiev. And, here we were, the slaves of Slavs, the new order turned their own people into slaves.

A few weeks passed. The taiga reverted to its former self once more—it became hell. In the shallow bogs myriads of mosquitoes had bred, turning out swarms of bloodsucking, monstrous tormentors, which descended upon us each day. We wore kerchiefs over our noses and mouths and tied our long-sleeved dresses shut on the neck and wrists. Yet, despite these measures the beasts found each ever so slightly exposed spot. They crawled, as a final insult, beneath our headscarves and attacked our eyelids. As if these pests were not enough torment, large deer flies, seemingly dispatched by the devil himself, joined the effort to maximize our misery.

The guards burned smudge fires, which helped if you were close by. Elsewhere, the insects tormented us so much that we would set dry grasses on fire in an effort to get relief. To this purpose we had to steal the fire from the guards. Problematic always! A small fire could become an inferno at the change of the wind.

Days passed. The same mousy prostitute who had given me Ivanka's warning approached me again. This time I was crossing what one might call the "commons" in a village—the ground between the buildings. "The commandant is walking away from the camp every evening with another red-headed woman," she said, looking meaningfully at me.

"Oh, God!" the sigh escaped my mouth before I could control it.

"So you, too, think Ivanka is dead?" asked the mousy one, her face as dead as an iconic masque.

"Yes," I said, although I thought I should not venture such a surmise.

"The one he walks out with is called Valentina," the small woman told me. "We must watch and see what happens to her."

When I told the story from the mouth of the little gray prostitute in the barracks, one of our older women said, "Women of that trade look out for each other. They know trouble in any fashion. We can trust what she reports."

Weeks passed. No one saw Valentina again as the mousy girl reminded me on at least two occasions. Why did she tell me? I did not know, but I cared! I cared passionately and I wondered. But what could I do? Then came the evening I had feared, intuited, anticipated with dread.

As we walked in a group to the mess—we were always supposed to be with our squad—the commandant appeared. He looked over my squad as if checking our formation and then he waved Barbara out of the line. "You," he called out, "you come with me!" Stunned, unsure, with hesitating steps, she followed his orders.

She turned her head back to me and said in German, "*Die Schatten haben mich gefangen.*" As I stared at her with horror, I was reminded, that beneath her scarf, there, too, was a redhead.

Our faces must have spoken volumes of undisguised fear, because Kalachnik—his name appropriately meaning Cossack—roared at us, "Stupid, meddlesome German geese, prying eyes forward! Forward, march— go where you must go!"

He took Barbara's arm and led her off to the end of the commons, where a gate watched by two guards allowed access to the forest. Further ahead, where we had sometimes walked in the beginning when the camp was still open, one came upon the river. Many miles further downstream, this placid water flowed not far from the site where we worked.

I was sick to my stomach. The food I had forced myself to eat—I dared not save it, someone would sling it down the moment my back was turned— sat in the pit of my stomach. My mind churned. One thought raced the other. What did he want from Barbara? Why take her into the forest? Superfluous questions, we knew what he wanted; we just did not want to admit the horrible truth. I gathered a few trusted women around me. On the way back to our hut we promised one another to keep our eyes open at all times. We alerted the women in the other barracks that Barbara had been taken by Matveyev. I myself told the little prostitute convict what the commandant had done, and she promised that her women, too, would look for signs of our girl.

Barbara did not come back that night. It rained in the morning with the same mind-numbing, steady monotony as before, but by now we almost welcomed rain because it kept the stinging pests away from us at work. During breakfast, we decided that we had to act. Scared to death and yet rebellious, about twenty of us marched to the administration building. A guard saw us coming and went inside for orders. By the time we arrived at the front porch an adjutant, in freshly pressed and laundered uniform, appeared to intercept us.

"What do you want?" he asked without preamble, looking upon us as if we were vermin—rats and mice gnawing on his porch.

"We want to know where our squad-mate Barbara Bauer is. She walked off with commandant last evening and never returned. So, where is she?"

The adjutant had been briefed. His answer came fast and slick, "She has been released from camp. The commandant was kind enough to give her the good news." He stared haughtily upon our bedraggled lot and, after a sufficiently long and poignant pause, said, "You should be getting ready for work! Should you not? *Davai, davai.* Off with you!"

What were we to do? We were lucky to be let off easy. He could have called the guards and had us flogged. We moved back to the hut and reported the questionable tale to the others. "They are lying!" was the consensus. "They are protecting the commandant's vice, whatever it is." What could we do? The new commandant had proven already in many ways that we were helpless— clearly he killed! We hoped that Barbara was still alive, captive, but alive.

Forced from the building, by the guards with their guns drawn, we were driven into the forest. Days later, as we were cutting stands of trees close to the river, we heard a guard's shout. His voice was filled with dread and then we heard him retching. Premonition made us drop our tools. Moments later we were running toward the river. Two other guards got there ahead of us. Both of them, surrounded by heavy brush, were trying to pull an object from the river with the hooked spikes, which we used to turn tree trunks.

When they heard us they stopped their effort, turned, and shouted at us to leave. Of course, we did not budge, for a few of us, having parted the brush saw that, caught among the branches growing into the water amid flotsam and debris was the naked, white body of a woman. I knew instantly that it was Barbara. She had sensed her fate—the shadows had closed in on her.

Kneeling by the bank, his head held in his hands, was the first man at the scene. He was an older man who had always acted with calm deliberation. Now the other two mean, burly fellows barked at him to pull his gun and drive us away. We were suddenly keenly aware that their effort directed to untangle the body from the branches, was not to land it, but to push it into deeper water so it might float away. I screamed to the women from my squad that Barbara was in the water.

All at once, as one body, our women rushed to the river's edge, pushing the guards aside. We screamed like mad women as we waded into the shallow water and dragged the body of our dead sister on land.

Barbara lay upon a carpet of new green grass. Her naked body was as white and pure as if she slept, except for gruesome marks on her thighs and her belly. The fleeting illusion of sleep disappeared as one's glance moved along her body. Powerful hands, as vicious dark marks proclaimed, had mangled her neck. Her left cheek was a colorful bruise of green and blue—the eye swelled shut.

As we stood looking at Barbara's corpse, unwilling to accept the truth of her murder, the full bevy of guards set upon us. "Back to work!" They shouted. "*Davai, davai! Rabota, rabota!*" We did not obey. We picked up the body of our slain sister, preparing to take her with us. The guards became frantic. Using their batons and shooting into the air they drove us away from the body, back to the worksite.

They kept us from taking the body with us, but the knowledge of the killing was ours. Within minutes of our return, we had spread the ghastly news among every inmate group. I don't know how we finished work that day, how we returned to camp, how I got into my bed. My head was filled with terrible visions, fearful scenes, and dreadful premonitions.

There would be no inquiry into Barbara's death, nor Ivanka's, nor any of the other disappearances. What could we prove? The obvious? That the commandant had been the last person to see the women alive? Who would accuse him? Who would judge the case and where were the witnesses for the prosecution?

Henceforth, I could no longer rest. I saw the tortured bodies of the three women everywhere, and although I had not one red hair on my head, I knew he would come for me. To my own detriment, I had become too prominent. I had led the delegation to the river when we found her body—the guards would have already testified to that. And, as a squad leader, I had been noticed before. I knew I was a marked target. Red hair or not, he had to kill me.

The first time the barrack was empty of the other women I went to my hiding spot. With a hairpin I dug out the sawdust covering my knife. From that moment on, I wore the weapon tightly strapped to my right thigh.

I owned a dress and a work skirt, both were most unfeminine garments made from brown, rough, wool and linen cloth woven at home, which had served in the village to do milking chores. Now, I opened the seam in each garment on the right side and made a false pocket, which allowed me access to the knife. Having taken these precautions, however, did not ease my fears.

Fate ordained that my trial was not yet to be. In our barrack, five women came down with pneumonia. Their undernourished bodies, hot at work, cold in the rain, made them the perfect host for bacteria. We reasoned that one could have infected the rest, because they slept and worked together.

The new doctor, reminded by administrators of his predecessor's fate, promptly quarantined the five and had their sleeping area sprayed with a milky, watery substance. Finally, the rain subsided, and the weather became quite warm and humid again. Three of our women, Elisabeth Meier, eighteen, Margaretha Andreas, twenty, and Sibilla Barth, nineteen, the latter two married with husbands somewhere on the front, survived the pneumonia and came back to our hut. The other two, Anna Katharina Melchior and Grete Huber, also married, died quickly as if they had not wished to live any longer.

We desperately wanted to bury our own. No trench for these women who had shared our torment for so long. Barbara's murder left me the only spokesperson for the hut. When we tried to elect a new leader for the barrack, everyone had carefully declined to assume any kind of prominence. I understood! We had a German saying: "When crossing the river don't be the first or the last." Meaning that the first could be caught unawares in undertows and eddies, which followers could avoid. But the last one had no one to help him if he got into trouble.

As far as I was concerned, nothing mattered anymore. My face was known. The guards acknowledged me as the barrack's leader. I had inherited Barbara's position by default. I asked two women to accompany me. This time I would approach the doctor and ask for his permission to hold a burial. Margaretha Andreas, tall, dark and gaunt from her illness, and Sibilla Barth, a small woman with huge, blue eyes in a child's face, agreed to go with me. The doctor knew them, had cured them. Therefore they thought he might be better disposed toward them.

After receiving our rations, we ate quickly and left for the dispensary. As luck would have it, the doctor met us halfway, walking to the infirmary. He was a gaunt, gray-eyed man of medium height with longish, black hair and an ever-present shadow of dark stubble. Between his thin lips dangled a fat *machorka*-cigarette, seemingly glued there.

Margaretha and Sibilla thanked him for saving their lives. I translated. Then, I presented our request, speaking movingly and respectfully. Throughout the encounter, he had not spoken once. He measured us as one would regard specimens in a laboratory. Inhaling, the tip of his cigarette glowed; exhaling, bluish smoke left his nostrils. I had finished my request, and in uncomfortable silence, we remained standing.

Suddenly, his lips parted. I watched with unveiled fascination how the cigarette remained glued to his lower lip as he laconically said, "I will see what I can do." The next day he sent a guard to our hut with a message. After mess that evening, we could have a burial at the fence in the northeast corner of the camp. Restrictions were attached, however, to the exceptional permission: Only members of our hut were allowed to be present, there was to be no singing or prayer.

We arrived in twilight. The bodies were already there, wrapped in sackcloth. Under the watchful eyes of the guards, we had to dig the graves. Someone had brought shovels. As we dug the grave in turn, I unobtrusively, carefully removed the cloth at the women's heads to insure that they were ours—we did not trust appearances anymore. It got so dark that we could not see to dig. Unexpectedly—we were ready to give up on a burial that night—some of the guards lit torches.

The torchlight lent eerie warmth to our macabre funeral. Flickering light, which made moving shadows, contrasted with inky deep blackness beyond, creating a sensation of unreality. By the time we were carefully lowering the bodies into the grave, the doctor appeared. He stood at the end of the grave, cigarette lit, blowing smoke. He listened as I said a few words in German about our sisters' lives, as if he understood. We stood silent for a moment, with lowered heads, praying silently.

"Cover the bodies," came a command that destroyed our reverie. Black earth fell upon the shrouded bodies; of course there were no caskets. As we covered them, we silently said a litany for them—they were going to a better place.

Life somehow went on. I believe that every woman in camp knew of Barbara's fate, walked with fear in her heart, and knew that the murderer among us could strike with impunity, because we were helpless as lambs stalked by the wolf.

Summer had arrived, warm and humid, although the nights could still be very cold. We were healthier, supplementing our diet with forest products.

A few of the Russian girls knew just what flowers to pick for a snack. Sometimes we found mushrooms, their stems white- and black-patched like the birches, their caps deep brown. There were grasses and leaves we could chew for minerals and vitamins. The temporary peace did not last.

On a Sunday as we showered and laundered clothes, sat in the sun and mended things, Herta, a woman from the barrack next to ours, went missing. She was tall, blond, with a certain, sure aura, and pleasing features. Her friends sought her among us, but we had not seen her. She left to go to the latrine and had never returned.

In groups of threes and fours we searched the camp, as inconspicuously as we could make it look. No one had seen her. By mess time she still had not returned. Everyone knew that no one, but no one, would willingly miss a meal. So where was she? It was as if the earth had swallowed her.

I had always slept the deep sleep of the righteous worker. My body was always tired—my mind at peace. Now, I had trouble falling asleep. I do not know how I knew, but I felt that Ivan the Terrible had taken Herta, killed her. I knew with certainty he would seek me out, if only because I knew too much and intuited more. In my dreams I was set upon by a bear, chased by wolves, and sometimes followed by an enormous pig. I always awoke bathed in sweat, unable to sink back into oblivion.

The Murder

After everything—the dreams, the dread, the anticipation—when the assault happened, for just one moment, it was anticlimactic. "So," I thought stupidly, "this is it?" And in that moment, I felt no fear. I almost felt relief that the tension of waiting was broken.

It happened in the simplest, the most banal, manner. We had agreed never to go anywhere alone: that, henceforth, all of our activities would be performed by committee. We went to the washroom early in the morning between the hours of five and six in groups of forty. A squad of that size had about five to six minutes to wash and clean teeth, before the next squad moved in. We brushed our hair in the barracks because it was too time-consuming to be performed in the washroom, which was always overcrowded. Tired women would shove and push to garner a few extra inches. Accidents happened, tempers flared. Often, those finished would escape and wait outside for the rest of the squad, thereby avoiding the crush. I, too, gladly waited outside in summer's dawning day after rushing through my ablutions.

Mornings were always fresh, brisk and invigorating. One could quietly stand, leaning against the gray wooden planks, and pretend to be alone for a moment. The hardest thing for me was the unavoidable reality of never being alone. Of course, even standing there in the open I was not alone. Groups of women came and went; guards circled them, like watchful shadows or planets around the sun.

I had finished washing fast that fateful morning—an unimaginable morning that drastically changed my life forever. As usual I had given up the space containing my basin and gone outside where I stationed myself ten paces from the porch and the crush of the next group.

There I was, in full view of everyone, leaning against the gray wooden building—or so I thought—when I felt a body next to mine. In an instant, a large hand covered my mouth, while an arm, sliding around my waist, grabbed my left wrist, and pulled my arm so high that I thought I would black out.

In a second I was engulfed in a mass of fabric, and was marched off toward the still dark edge of the camp. I knew instantly who was powerfully forcing me to walk onward. There was no question in my mind. Looking upward out of the corner of my eye, for he held my head immobile, I saw the square pink jaw, the snout-like nose. Casting my eyes down, I saw that the commandant's greatcoat completely shielded me from view. No one had taken any notice of my capture.

"Don't even think of resisting me," Ivan the Terrible said softly, propelling me along, almost lifting me off the ground.

Walking helplessly beside what I knew to be death awakened such fear in me that I would have fallen. But he held me so tightly pressed against his body that it was impossible to even stumble as he pushed me forward. There was no strength left in me to resist.

My soul quaked deep within me. I did not want to die, did not want to drink my cup. I thought of our Lord on his way to the cross, how he had patiently born the certain knowledge of torture and death, and was calmed. Yet, such calm was fleeting comfort. It left me when the daunting question flashed through my mind, "What will he do to you before you die?"

Dawn's first rosy light outlined the treetops in the east as we approached the gate. The guards looked upon us as if we were an apparition. The hand was lifted from my mouth to make me seem a willing participant in the macabre game. "Scream and I tear your arm from its socket," the terrible one said, before uncovering my mouth.

"The guards will not help you, even if you scream!" I knew they would not. They had not helped the other women. As the guards opened the gate they averted their eyes and faces. Wrapped in his greatcoat, we walked like devoted lovers through a clearing in the direction of the river. Out of what seemed at first glance to be a dewy meadow, rose countless tree stumps, evidence of an earlier clear-cut.

The clearing presented a mystical scene in its pre-dawn brightness. Swatches of fog drifted in from the river, obscuring first one and then another view. Once I had felt so brave, so capable of resistance, but now I was but a small child in the hands of a monster.

The terrible Kalachnik never relaxed his painful grip on my arms until we were close to the river, its banks denoted by the lush growth of willows and alder brush. Most Siberian rivers flow calmly, placidly, as stately as matrons and dowagers stride. Only an occasional splash or gurgle announced the presence of flowing water.

Suddenly, the commandant halted his stride and released me from his crushing hold. He turned me, so that I faced him. I stared at him with the fascination of one mesmerized. His face was an unreadable mask in which the eyes glittered with cold intelligence.

If he had grabbed me then to do his awful deeds, I should have died unable to resist, unable to defend myself. However, part of his ritual involved a cat and mouse game preceding the end. The monster desperately needed to satisfy his perverse impulses by ritualistically, step by step, forcing the victim to experience every detail of his power and lust.

Suddenly he smiled at me, almost benignly. "Let us look at you a little closer," he said. "What treasure is hidden beneath this ugly cloth?" With that remark he pulled off the kerchief covering my hair, letting it fall to the ground. All German women wore the kerchiefs while working. Mine was a plain blue cotton cloth.

"Hmm, pretty hair," he stroked my hair, making me cringe. He felt the knot of my falsie, *die Falsche*, around which my hair was twisted.

"What have we here?" he wondered with amusement in his voice. He removed the wooden comb and pin that had held the knot together and my hair fell to my waist.

"Ahhhh, lovely, lovely," he groaned.

Then he glanced at my false hairpiece in his hand. Looking at the unappetizing, grayish lump with loathing, he screamed, "What the devil is this dead thing?" I almost fainted with distress. His loathing revived me.

"It is a false piece of hair to wrap my hair's length around," I said, forcing the words painfully from my throat.

"Disgusting!" he shouted again and threw the offensive piece to the ground. I swear, it was by divine providence that my falsie was hurled against a stone where it broke open in plain view. And there lay my precious stones sparkling in the rays of the newly risen sun.

"Oh, hoha, what have we here?" roared Kalachnik excitedly. He might never have noticed the stones, but he noticed my immediate downward glance, followed by my dismay. Thus, he followed my gaze down and saw the precious stones still embedded in one half of the broken baked shell.

He was so sure of his complete control over me—so greedy—that he knelt down to see the find for himself. This was the deciding moment. I knew there would never be another. With horror and trepidation I pulled the knife away from my thigh. With every ounce of strength I could muster, I drove the blade into his back, down to the very hilt.

I gasped! I had done this deed that I had dreamed about. I took a step back, then another. I felt like running away, but could not. I had to watch, as if a snake held me in its stare. Ivan the Terrible roared like a wounded bull. His bellow was followed by an unearthly, ghastly noise escaping his throat. Again he screamed with fury, but mouthed only gibberish.

I retreated, step by step, never taking my eyes off him. Then I heard myself scream with horror, for Ivan suddenly raised himself to his knees and stood up, looking like a monstrous bear. And then, oh God, he began to walk toward me. How could he do this? Should he not be on the ground, dead or at least badly hurt? I had plunged the knife deep, surely, forcefully.

I retreated further, stepping backward, never leaving him out of my sight. I tripped, something had painfully grabbed my ankle, and I fell backward into a growth of blackberry bramble. I found myself gripped by torturous vines. They held onto my dress, ensnared my limbs and tore my hair. I struggled valiantly to get free, for the pain was horrendous. The more I struggled, the more I became ensnared.

Now the fiend laughed, a demonic, gruesome laugh. All the while Ivan came closer, his face a grimace of hate. He groaned. He roared with fury as he moved. His left hand was a fist, his right reaching like a talon.

He was so horribly close, and still my frantic clawing and pulling had not freed me. Another step and his clawed hand, only inches away, would touch me, and then he would kill me. My body went slack. I stopped the struggle against the vine.

Suddenly, I saw a bright flash behind him like a thunderbolt from the sky. I stared in disbelief as an axe cut into his enormous neck. The commandant's near-severed head fell to the side. An enormous fountain of blood gushed from the gaping wound and drenched me. The monster fell dead to the ground, his hand touching my shoe.

Salvation

When I raised my eyes from the ghastly bloody hulk reposed before my feet, there stood exposed a man whose person had been hidden behind Kalachnik's bulk. The stranger and I stared at each other in astonishment. We had been turned into statues by utter disbelief. Once again my glance fell upon the dead man between us. As if the grizzly murder finally registered in my brain, my hands flew to my face, to cover my mouth and stifle a scream. Although I saw the gory, almost decapitated body before me, I could not comprehend what had just happened.

The stranger recovered much more quickly from the shock of the kill. From his dress and physical appearance, it was obvious that he was not a Russian, but a native of the taiga. His lightly tanned face with brown, slightly almond-shaped eyes looked at me coolly and calmly, as if we were meeting in a street. Enormous tension vibrated between us as we regarded each other, one murderer sizing up another.

Genady Markov had mentioned that the taiga was brimming with native tribes, herders of reindeer, or caribou, with tribal names like Yakuts, Komi, Yamalo, Nenets and Okrugs. To which of those tribes did he belong?

"Why not run?" he asked in bad Russian. I assumed he wondered why I had not fled Kalachnik's assault.

"I am trapped by bramble. Look at my back!" I motioned behind me. Instead of coming to free me, he bent over the corpse and tried to pull my knife out of Kalachnik's back. I had struck well and deep. The knife refused to budge. Undaunted, the man placed his foot into Ivan's back and pulled with great force. While I watched in disbelief, he pulled the knife from Kalachnik's body, which writhed throughout the procedure like a living thing. Unperturbed, methodically, the strange man wiped the knife clean on a bunch of grass and weighed it approvingly in his hand. For a moment, a satisfied look flitted across his face. Before pulling the knife from the corpse, he had already cleaned and returned his axe to a belt around his middle.

While removing the knife he must have seen something else of interest, for he stopped in mid-motion, and bent over the corpse again. From a holster strapped around Ivan's middle, he pulled a machine pistol, a big, ugly-looking gun, gleaming metallic blue and brown in the sun.

"German," he said. He studied the gun for a moment, and said, "Can you read?"

"Yes," I said, "I can also read German." Satisfaction replaced the look of concentration on his face.

Finally, he approached me. For a moment I thought he would kill me. "What will keep him from slaying me too? I am a witness to murder," I thought. My fears were put to rest when he used my knife to slash and cut the vines holding me. So persistently embedded in cloth and hair were the thorns that even after I was freed large tendrils of vine still clung to me.

Free at last, I stepped away from the brush. The significance, the sheer enormity of the last hour overwhelmed me. I began to shiver. "Thank you! Oh God, thank you!" I sighed. I fell to my knees, weak and overwrought. I looked up at the stranger and said, "You saved my life. This man was evil, a monster."

"I know," he said simply. "You can go."

"Go where?" I asked, aghast. "I cannot go back into that camp. They will kill me."

For a moment he seemed perturbed. Apparently I had not figured further in his plans. Having thought for a moment, he shoved the gun at me and said, "Read!"

"It is a Walther P-38 machine pistol," I said. "Very powerful."

"Good," he grunted, and then, pointing at the corpse. "Help! Make hard for guard!" he smiled, looking young and kind.

We filled Ivan's pants with rocks and tied the greatcoat around him. The native motioned that he wanted me to pull on one arm while he pulled on the other. All the while I just wanted to flee, to be far, far away from the ghastly scene. The problem was, however, that I did not know where to go and what to do. I realized I was utterly dependent on this man of the taiga, that I had to trust him.

As we dragged the monolithic corpse toward the water an electrifying thought came to me: Ivan still held my fortune in his fist! I could not allow him to sink to the bottom of this river with diamonds and emeralds in his clenched claw.

"Wait," I interrupted our process. I motioned to the man to help me open Ivan's fist. We did not succeed. His claw was like an iron trap. Without wasting further time, my rescuer brought my knife to bear upon the wrist and hand, slashing sinew and tendon, wordlessly trusting my reasons for the act. He opened the mangled hand and saw the stones, gathered them, and handed them to me, as if he did this every day. I saw no greed, no avarice in his face.

I instantly returned them to his hand. "I want you to have them. May they bring you good fortune."

He pondered the situation for a moment, said "Thank you," and then, with the same ease he did everything, he pulled a small leather pouch from beneath his shirt, opened it, and placed the stones inside.

We had wasted precious time. Guards could come at any moment in search of their commandant. My hero, I had come to think of the stranger as such, motioned me back to work. We pulled and pushed the body through the brush as far into the river as we could. While performing this morbid, awful task, my heart pounding, my breath coming in great bursts, I asked him, "What is your name?"

He knew the word "name," and breathed back, "Suomo."

I pointed at myself and said, "Katya," which he repeated twice as if to memorize the word.

The moment the commandant's corpse was hidden, Suomo said, "Go," and began to trot down river. Sheepishly I followed, stumbling awkwardly. It was a mystery to me how Suomo knew where to part the brush to reveal a small, delicate, birch-bark canoe. Certainly, if there were marks by which he had found his way, I never saw them.

The canoe rested by half on the shore. He pointed at me to step into it and sit in the front. I followed his orders, whereupon he pushed the light craft into the water and joined me at the last possible moment. He produced a single-blade paddle, which he used to stroke the boat into the middle of the river, where he gave the craft a quarter turn, which propelled us back to the site of the killing. We saw the partially hidden corpse, its half-severed head bobbing grotesquely in the water, between branches of willow and ash. Suomo aimed the boat precisely at this spot.

A hand floated beside the corpse, waxish white, looking more like a claw than ever. "Take hand—pull," said my hero. I understood his design at once; knew I had to be the one, for I could not maneuver the boat. Only by valiantly overcoming my loathing and disgust could I touch that dead, white hand. I was fully prepared to yank my arm away should the corpse come to life again and reach for me.

"Irrational," I thought. "He is dead! Nerves."

"Pull," reiterated Suomo, and I pulled with all my might. The willows suddenly gave up their prize and the body floated free. Not a moment too soon. From afar we heard voices. Men were approaching. The guards were looking for the commandant.

A few well-placed strokes put the canoe in midstream. By now the commandant's clothes, his greatcoat and boots had soaked up enough water to pull the corpse down. I finally was able to release my loathsome grip on his hand—the corpse of Ivan the Terrible sank.

Furious paddling sent the light boat speedily down the river. For the next hour or so we did not talk and barely moved, because that was impossible in this small craft. After all the macabre excitement, the overloading of my senses with conflicting emotions, it was pleasant to sit, to do nothing and allow my tired brain to sort things out.

While I carefully removed painful blackberry pieces from my hair and the back of my dress, I played back earlier scenes. I had surprised myself with the swiftness of my reactions. When the moment presented itself, I had without hesitation become not just a killer but an executioner. Although they would never know it, I had become in this fateful instance all things for the women in my camp—the judge, the jury and the executioner.

The man Kalachnik Bogdanovich had meant to kill me after hurting and tormenting me, of that I was sure, yet I could hardly believe what I had done. Perhaps I would have been incapable of the deed, if I had not defended myself night after night during my frightful nightmares. Did God prepare me for this? What about the knife? Without the knife, I would have been defenseless. Where did it come from? Who had placed it in this particular tree for me to find?

The sounds of machines and voices disturbed the quiet reverie. They brought me back to harsh reality. I felt the man behind me tense a little, almost imperceptibly. His knees, pressed against my back, drew up slightly.

I assumed that we were passing the worksite where my poor sisters slaved, cutting linden, ash and oak.

Suomo used the oar severely, harder than he had before when we progressed with peaceful, measured motions. He forced the boat to the riverside where it bordered the worksite. I understood. If, by chance a person was hidden among the river vegetation, they would be able to see the breadth and length of the river. Their view of the same bank, however, was limited.

I was very much aware that I constituted an impediment, a hazard even, to the man facilitating our getaway. The small canoe was sufficient for but one. Two bodies presented greater challenges for Suomo, pressing the boat deeper into the water as he propelled the craft with limited movements.

After a while we heard no more sounds. As my tension ebbed from the very real chance that we could have been seen and apprehended, hunger pangs attacked me. I had eaten nothing since last night's watery soup and black bread. By now hunger and thirst began their torment. Yet, how could I complain to Suomo? I could not expect him to provide food for me, a stranger.

Imperceptibly the scenery had changed. We were floating through an area where the riverbanks disappeared and the river became part of a great marsh. The river had shallowly spread out and was now divided by small islands and stands of trees into streamlets and ponds. Sometimes the streamlets gathered as one, and then, without discernible pattern, parted their ways again. The scenery confused me, raising awful dread.

As a child of the steppe, I was used to a wide-open view where I could see far ahead and knew where I was going. The conditions of the marsh were foreign to me, frightening me. How would we ever find our way out of this chaotic bog?

"How will we find our way out of here?" I asked Suomo. I don't know if he understood, but he must have heard the worry echoing in my voice."

"Is good. Is good," he said soothingly a few times, steering the boat to one of the bigger islets, pushing it ashore onto tufted grass. We left the craft, stepping onto surprisingly solid ground. My companion retrieved a small leather sack from a space behind his seat and led me toward the middle of the isle.

What was the purpose of this stop? Why did he bring me here? Did this stranger whom I had known for barely a few hours mean to do me harm, assault me? He had, after all, very coolly and without discernible emotion dispatched a man with an axe. If he meant to leave me dead on this isle, no one would ever know. What could I do? I had to trust him. I did not know where I was. I was left in God's wide world without shelter, food, or any other means of survival. Thinking successions of dreadful thoughts, I trudged along behind him.

Without warning, Suomo stopped walking and sank to the ground. Cautiously, I walked a few more paces and let out a surprised cry of joy, so pretty and sweet was the place. Tufts of grasses interspersed with multitudes of other green plants made it a cozy place to rest. I pushed my fears aside as we sat down in the most peaceful place I had known in a year.

A profusion of birds could be seen and heard, especially many kinds of waterfowl. It was midsummer. The birds' young had recently fledged and were preparing for independence and the long migration to warmer climes. Butterflies and other delicate insects had already disappeared. After all, the unpredictable taiga had already surprised its inhabitants with a few snowy nights, ameliorated only by the warm days.

From his leather bag, Suomo produced bread and dry meat. He broke a generous piece off a round loaf of bread and offered it to me. I received it with grateful anticipation amounting to greed. I was ravenous. Unable to control myself, I sank my teeth into the bread. It was, oh, so good. Made with real flour, no sawdust mixed in, it had been fried in oil and dipped in coarse salt. Mmmmm, I savored each bite.

While I ate, I observed that Suomo cut the meat into pieces, with the same knife that had killed Ivan. No matter, we ate with gusto. After the meal, thirst drove me to the islet's edge in search of water. Although the water was tinted brown by decaying vegetation, I was prepared to drink it, because drink I must.

Suomo saw me on my knees, bent toward the brackish tea, and touched my shoulder.

"No!" he said sharply. "Come!" I followed him as he walked the islet. Lo! He found a small pool. In its middle, clear, clean water bubbled to the surface. He knelt, scooping the water with his hand and drank, and I did the same. We returned to our picnic place where Suomo sat down. He indicated he would rest here a moment. I used the calm beauty of the spot to pick the last of the uncomfortable brambles off my dress and out of my hair. The latter had been a bother to me, flying about free and untamed. All my life it had been put up and covered by a kerchief, the *Kopftiechel*, or *Kopftuch* in high German. Using my fingers to fork through the long tresses, I untangled my hair and braided it in a long plait on each side of my head. As I fumbled to secure the braids with a few strands of hair,

Suomo, having discerned my intent, surprised me by twisting together a few dry grasses into twine to bind the ends of my braids.

Then, as if he had spent himself in the process, he lay back, closed his eyes, and was instantly asleep. Seeing him like this I could finally study every detail of his personal appearance. He was tall, close to six feet, I thought. His oval face was pleasingly endowed with large, slightly almond-shaped eyes, dark, narrow brows, a fairly small nose, a round chin, and a generous mouth. I had already observed that his eyes were dark brown; yet, his shoulder-length hair was light brown.

He had worn a round leather cap, which lay discarded beside him. His forest-green shirt, cut in the Russian style, had a v-opening at the neck and long, voluminous sleeves gathered at the wrist. The shirt—belted around the middle with a broad leather belt, upon which loops held an array of necessities: his axe, a pouch, my knife and an object that looked like an awl—fell over soft brown leather pants, which were tucked above the ankles into soft leather boots.

I had only wished to sit and rest for while, but fell sound asleep. A gentle tug on my arm startled me awake. Stretching my arms skyward, I was pleasantly aware that I had not felt this good in ages. For the first time in what seemed an eternity, I was not hungry or tired.

We climbed back into the confining boat and took off, to only Suomo knew where. To my surprise, he had no difficulty finding the main arm of the river again. Not long thereafter, we left the confines of the marsh. Suddenly I observed that the river flowed strongly, pulling us along at a good pace.

After an hour or two—I assumed from the shadows it was late afternoon—Suomo angled the boat toward shore and beached it at a small strip of sand. Here, he dragged the canoe out of the water and, by throwing a rope over the branch of a nearby tree, pulled the slight craft up until it disappeared in the foliage. There it hung, hidden and drying.

He began to walk westward at a strong clip. I hastened behind him. I do not know how he knew where we were going, for we did not follow a discernible trail. The vegetation was minimally, hardly noticeably disturbed. After about an hour or more, my legs grew tired. We had not walked much in camp or at the worksite. Just when I became very preoccupied with my discomfort, the forest opened to a clearing, occupied by a small tent-village.

A few boys and girls attired in fantastic, extremely colorful outfits came running to greet Suomo with excitement. He acknowledged their joyous shouts, but kept walking at a demanding pace until we reached the middle of the encampment, where a group of adult men sat around a large fire. We approached the group. Suomo walked up to an older, impressive-looking man. I assumed him to be a man of power, a chief or an elder, someone with decision-making power.

Suomo began to speak rapidly, addressing the group as one body. He pointed at me. With words and motions, he seemed to explain the terrifying saga of this day. When he had finished, a moment of silence ensued, whereupon a tall man with imposing manner spoke with force and vigor. He pointed at me with threatening motions, which frightened me. It seemed as if he wanted to do away with me, the sooner the better. One after another the men spoke, some with milder oratory than others. However, the argument always came back to the first, greatly antagonistic man.

The sun had set and the temperature dropped so fast that, in a few short moments, I shook violently from cold and fear. Across from me sat a bronze-skinned man who impressed me with his looks and bearing. He seemed to be tall, although his height was hard to determine, because he sat bent forward. A shirt made from deer hide, which was embroidered with colorful designs, covered his broad shoulders and large torso. His face was deeply tanned and creased; his hair, raven-black with streaks of gray. He had a long, strong nose and, most amazingly, deep blue eyes. From his neck hung several leather thongs, each attached to a pouch, while silver bracelets and charms adorned his wrists. He had not taken part in the raging discussion, but had solemnly studied me in great detail.

The arguments about my person had become fierce, when suddenly the interesting man stretched out his arm and commanded silence, in a ringing voice. Without further comment he rose and walked in a semi-circle around the group to where I stood.

Standing in front of me, he looked down at me, forcing me to raise my gaze to meet his eyes. For a while he looked at me thus, as if searching my soul, seeking my spirit. He abruptly closed his eyes. Then he put his hand on my head as if drawing energy from my body and remained in this position for a while. At last, he turned from me to the men who had followed this scene in silence. When he spoke, his words drew a sharp hiss from my antagonist and low murmurs from the others. I intuited the danger had passed. Having passed sentence on my survival, the man I assumed to be the spiritual leader of the village returned to his seat. I could tell by his look of concentration that he was deep in thought—as if he was determining my future.

I heard Suomo exhaling deeply and thought, "I am saved!" This was the second time that day I had been saved. Now, with the danger of expulsion or death dissipated, my senses functioned once more, and I heard soft voices conversing behind my back. I turned my head and saw a most charming picture.

A short distance behind us, a number of women and children were gathered in a group worthy of a master's painting. They were clad in what I assumed to be their summer clothes. They wore long-sleeved blouses and long skirts, also dresses with long sleeves, gathered at the wrist. The peoples of this tribe expressed themselves with color. Yellow, purple, blue, red and orange were used in every combination on blouses, skirts, dresses and flowered scarves. Perhaps the gregarious colors overcame the dread of the long, bitter winters and bestowed upon them a deeper joy of summer.

Over skirts and dresses, every woman and girl child also wore a colorful apron, each set off by a black border. The ample headscarves covering their hair came in multi-flowered designs and seemed to be made from silk. They tied the scarves at the nape of their necks, allowing the long ends to fall over their shoulders and backs as if they were flirty braids. Their shoes were made from hide, some plain, some embroidered.

Having heard the spirited debate over my future, the women looked at me with the same intrigued curiosity I had for their outfits.

Suomo took my hand and led me to one of the men sitting by the fire. "This man speak Russian very good," he said, "will tell all." He noticed that I was freezing. Saying he would return shortly, he walked away. How I missed my coat, heritage from a time long gone by, which I had to leave behind in camp. Cheering me, however, was the thought of the lucky woman who would have my coat during the coming winter freeze, and I was well pleased.

Returning to the present, I found myself looking into the friendly, intelligent face of a man who could have been Suomo's brother. "Welcome," he said. His voice was strong, yet well modulated, "Welcome, to Komi people village. I am Korya. I can answer your questions."

Suomo had returned and draped a fur coat around my shoulders. I noticed that even a few of the men had sought warmer covering. "What will happen to me?" was my first question. "I had the impression that some of the men did not want me to be here with your people."

"Yes," acknowledged Korya, "they know the Russians will find the body of the commandant sooner or later, and hunt in every native village for the killer. They cannot prove anything except for your presence. So the argument went that you must leave."

"What did your leader say that convinced them to let me stay?"

"He is our spirit man. He says that you are a clean spirit, that we must help you because God would like us to."

"Who is your God then?"

"Christ," he said simply. In the days to come I found that the Komi had been taught Russian Orthodoxy, but had sweetened the harsh dogma with their old shamanistic lore. They did not believe, as the Orthodox did, in preordained suffering for every person on earth. Instead they believed in love, forgiveness and righteousness. The kind of spirit inherent in each person was very important to them and, as explained to me, was almost Lutheran in concept. Above all—Christ was love and forgiveness to them.

Bit by bit, I found out what I was burning to know. The spirit man, the shaman, had proclaimed that I was to stay with this Komi group until they could safely pass me on to another part of their tribe, farther away from their camp. Thus, I would be handed from tribal group to tribal group until they could send me down the Northern Dvina to Arkhangelsk, the city by the White Sea.

What a great name for a city—town of archangels—covering both banks of a mighty river, near a sea frozen five months of a year. Yes, only archangels would allow a ship safe berth and passage. Out in the White Sea the devil would seek to crush ships in an icy maw and toss them in fierce storms before they could reach shelter.

Suomo was convinced that they could get me on a boat to England, or, failing that, onto an Allied ship destined for Holland or Belgium. The Germans still controlled the Baltic and the Gulf of Finland. Therefore, the Allies used Arkhangelsk to supply the Russians.

"I think we can persuade someone on an Allied ship to take you out. You might go to Scotland, Holland, England or even America," smiled Korya.

"How do you know so much about the ships in that harbor?" I asked, nonplussed that these simple hunters and herders of reindeer should have such sophisticated knowledge. Compared to them, I knew nothing, knew nothing at all of this part of the world.

The reason for their astonishing wisdom was the fur trade. The Soviets forced the many minorities, of which the Komi, the many groups of Nenets, the Yakuts and the Okrugs were only a few, to part with great amounts of high-grade fur for little money. Once confiscated, they sent the pelts to their controlled factories. There they were turned into fancy hats and coats, which, in turn, the Soviets sold to the Allies for outrageous amounts of money.

No wonder the northern ethnic tribes tried to sell furs and reindeer meat, another commodity the Soviets extorted from the natives, directly to the Allies for much greater profit. Of course, such commerce was strictly illegal and was severely punished when intercepted by the Communists. But one can hardly blame the natives for creating ways and means, through the age-old system of bribes and *baksheesh*—a system alive and well—to barter and sell to the highest bidder. This system was flourishing exceedingly well in Arkhangelsk, a city that hated the Communists by preserving a seething rancor for all things Soviet. This city had fought the Red Army with unprecedented vigor, holding out against the Red onslaught for two years, from 1918-1920, while the White Army was in town.

Among its citizens most still wished the pox on the Reds. While Korya, Suomo and I talked, they walked me to one of many small cooking fires that had been lit. Around these fires, families gathered and were fed hot rich food from the cook pots of the matriarchs of the family.

They had led me to the fire of Suomo's mother, who welcomed me by repeatedly nodding her head and touching my cheek. She was a squat, square woman—someone who could be easily overlooked. With a round, pleasing face, brown almond-shaped eyes and wearing the bright-colored attire of her tribe, she represented the kindness of all mothers: caring, warmth and security.

She served me first as the guest of honor, heaping my plate with meat and vegetables, and added to it a large slice of her delicious fried bread. I ate until I nearly burst. I could not remember when I had last been filled. However, it was not enough that I was provided such a wonderful meal. There was more. The amazing woman then brought me a round pastry filled with cranberries. For a moment I thought that heaven might be found here among these lovely people.

In the back of my mind, though, there arose a nagging question.

"Suomo, why does your mother treat me like an honored guest, as someone very special? What have I done to deserve this?"

"Because you did her a great service," said Suomo. And then Korya translated for me a most amazing story.

Profile of a Killer

Many things that I had not been able to account for, many unanswered questions were suddenly answered in the context of this story, as all fell neatly into place. It had bothered me why a stranger had been so willing, nay so eager, to kill a Russian commandant and help me—an unknown person. And how did it come to pass that this valorous native had been at just the right place during my time of need. Had it all been just a crazy coincidence? How about the hidden canoe—had this been a coincidence also?

"No coincidence," said Korya, "Suomo had been stalking Ivan the Terrible for a long time."

"But why?" I asked.

It was then that I heard the story of the two brothers, of Pavel and Suomo, as told by Korya. Suomo's brother, Pavel, was younger by four years and very handsome. At eighteen he strove to be as accomplished as Suomo was at twenty-two. He competed avidly to be a better hunter, a more successful herder, a faster runner and a better marksman. But despite the constant, sometimes annoying competition, he was a great asset and of invaluable help to Suomo who loved him devotedly.

Suomo was married and had three children. Pavel assumed many difficult tasks, which allowed Suomo to stay close to his family. For example, Pavel would often go alone into the forest to check their trap lines in the worst of the winter—a harsh, dangerous job. After delving into their brotherly relationship, Korya came to the main point.

"Last winter Soviet agents came to our camp. They were accompanied by a troop of soldiers and demanded a large part of our family's reindeer herd. They had come before, stealing from us to supply their camps and cities with meat. This was a reason for us to keep on the move, so they could not find us easily."

Both men silently stared into the fire, pondering the sad times when Soviet forces had invaded their camp and taken away their means of survival. When Korya began speaking again, both their faces were grimly turned to mine. But then, smiling, Suomo said, "Fortunately, the commies could order how many head we had to supply, but they could not control the herd and take from us what they wanted. The animals spooked and ran every which way the moment the soldiers approached them. Therefore, they had to depend on our expertise to separate the stock for them."

Now, both men grinned outright. "Our family quickly sorted out animals that had proved to be sterile or produced inferior offspring; we selected the misshapen and defective deer—animals we would otherwise have used for our own consumption, and rounded up a herd for the commies."

Upon completing the roundup, Suomo and Pavel were ordered to drive the herd to a slaughtering compound in a camp along the railroad, where all sorts of meat was prepared. There the animals were slaughtered, bled, cut and frozen, for consumption at an enormous camp of over two thousand men on the banks of the Northern Dvina. Everyone in the taiga camps had heard about the effort to build a bridge across the Northern Dvina, a tremendous feat that engineers had for many years thought impossible to accomplish.

Flying into the face of expert opinion, Stalin commanded that the railroad line Vorkuta—Kotlas—Konosha was to be completed within the year and that the enormous bridge across the Dvina was the most important link. Therefore, brute force and merciless methods were employed by his henchmen to satisfy the wishes of the communist tyrant.

Even in our small work camp everyone knew of the thousands of unfortunate, hapless Volga German men, the common prisoners and the civil engineers who had been commandeered to the project and given the Herculean task to build this bridge. We knew they lived in terrible deprivation in camps on each side of the Dvina. Flogged, starved, freezing and dying by inches, the men built the bridge.

According to Suomo, even the slaughtering camp, Kopek, aptly named for its worth, was a disease-ridden place marked by torture and starvation.

"And, do you know who commanded this camp?" asked Suomo through Korya.

"Yes, it was Ivan the Terrible." Strangely enough, the inmates at Kopek had also named him thus.

After delivering their herd, the brothers were handed a very small sum in the accounting office, a sum much too small for the amount of meat they had brought and far fewer rubles than they had been promised. Young Pavel, enraged, kept complaining bitterly despite his brother's warnings in their native tongue.

"We have been deceived and coerced. You have stolen our herd," he hurled at the pay officer again and again. Suomo, much wiser when dealing with the Communists, tried to pull him from the room. Yet, Pavel resisted with all his strength. "I am telling the truth!" he bellowed.

This went on until the administrator called for the commandant. Suomo's face sagged with sadness.

"Ivan came! My heart stopped. He listened to the complaint from the administrator, heard Pavel's shouted complaint, and without the slightest sign of anger, his face wiped clean of any emotion, he grabbed Pavel by the front of his fur-lined coat and said, 'I will show you what your animals are worth—nothing!' Suddenly he reached with both hands for Pavel's neck and before my eyes he strangled my brother. He flung the lifeless body at my feet and said with icy calm, 'Take his body and leave before I do the same to you'."

The memory still haunted Suomo. He fell silent. Korya took up the narrative.

Suomo was horror-struck. His beloved brother was dead, and he had been unable to prevent it. He looked into the eyes of the administrators who had witnessed the senseless murder, and their cold, silent stares told him what they thought—they were in league with the killer. Not one of them exhibited even a flicker of pity.

Suomo, a brave man, was suddenly afraid for his own life. He was in the den of wolves. Despairing, he lifted his brother's body. Staggering under the weight, he heaved him over his shoulder and groaning silently, he carried Pavel away. Not knowing what else to do, he dragged himself to the train station and purchased two tickets with the money they had been given.

"No bodies on the train," said the man behind the ticket counter.

"It's not a body. He is drunk," lied Suomo.

"Dirty, drunk natives," growled the ticket man, but he did give him the tickets. On the outskirts of Kotlas, a miserable assemblage of huts and houses pretending to be a town, Suomo found the rough wooden structure in which a Nenets woman ran a cantina. Besides the kitchen and a large service area, the house contained a few small rooms, narrow as monks' cells, which squeezed in just below the rafters above. In the service room, she provided simple stews, fried chunks of bread and potatoes, pickles, beer, kvass and vodka. Surrounded by labor camps hers was one of the few establishments catering to the desperate needs and cravings of men and even women who had been forced to live and work here.

Suomo had carried his brother all the way. In the train carriage, he had propped him up as if he were asleep, shielding him with his own body. Every step he took, every moment he held on to the corpse reminded him of their lives together. He thought of the spring drive and the herds they used to manage; the hunting trips they now would never take; the races they would never run.

He thought of the girl Pavel had courted and wanted to marry in spring—the family that would never be. Strangely enough, the hardest things to contemplate were not the affected living, but the grandchildren for which his mother had so fervently hoped. No children would spring from Pavel's loins.

It was the thought of his mother and father that finally broke him and made him cry. After he'd spilled his tears of bitterness, he went dead inside. It was as if deep in his chest an ice ball had formed, to stay there forever. By the time he reached Kotlas, cold anger had extinguished the earlier hot rage in his breast. In his heart he vowed that the killer must die.

Preoccupied with murderous schemes of revenge, Suomo arrived at the house of the Nenets woman Amuta. Komi and Nenets had friendly relations. They often met at grazing grounds where the young boys were kept busy separating their tribes' animals, sorting them by the patterns cut into their ears. Sometimes they hunted together.

Entering the simple, Spartan tavern, Suomo felt as easy as if visiting an aunt. He had left his brother's body outside in a shed, high in the rafters so the dogs or the wolves could not get it.

Inside Amuta served large, hot portions of stew to a mixed passel of hungry individuals. On rough benches, facing long, narrow, wooden tables, sat men as different from one another as God could make them.

Natives, looking like Finnish or Swedish nationals, sat beside bronze skinned, slant-eyed Asian natives. Dark-haired, bearded Russians sat across from blue-eyed, blond counterparts. Engineers sat beside guards, soldiers sat beside Komi natives. Amuta fed all of them, provided they did not get drunk. A few of her regulars, guards who had guns, ejected the inebriated before they became a problem.

"Ah, Suomo! I am pleased that you come to my house," intoned Amuta the very instant she noticed him.

"Come, come, have food. What would you like?"

"Stew and bread and your ear to talk to," came his reply.

Amuta, in tune with her people, sensed his pain. Realizing that he needed her she removed her stained leather apron. Bringing him food she sat down beside him on the bench.

"Vassily," she shouted to a tall, husky man, "take my place! I must sit with a friend for a moment."

Due to the twin reasons of exclusivity and excellence, the cantina was almost always filled to the last seat. The first reason was that her tavern was one of only three such establishments, the second, that her food was the best tasting in town. All year long she employed the members of her family to scour the woods for mushrooms, nuts, roots, berries and edible seed grass. She received a constant supply of fresh reindeer meat, and the native hunters sold her their best game. Fishermen brought their catch all summer long. Those fish not instantly consumed fresh were smoked and dried for the winter. But best of all, she knew how to season with salt and herbs to ensure her simple dishes were the best in town.

This tall, substantial woman with the friendly moon face was, therefore, the most sought-after woman in the area. She held to standards and enforced rules. Guards and soldiers tired of the wretched slop in the camps were welcome to partake of her largess, for which everyone paid handsomely, but had to follow her gentle restraints. Not too much vodka; everyone was equal and must remain friendly; there was to be no talk about politics, camps and the war.

Now she turned her friendly face to Suomo, and said, "So what has happened. Something in your eyes tells me tragedy has struck you."

Suomo told her his tale unembellished, breaking her rule about camps. She never noticed. "Pavel is in your shed," he ended his narrative, and then added mournfully, "I must get him home so Father can bury him. It will kill the old man."

Another rule was broken at this moment—strangers were not to break into other's conversations. Today, however, the guard seated next to Suomo turned to him and said, "Forgive me friend, do you speak of Kalachnik Bogdanovich? Ivan the Terrible?"

"Yes, why do you want to know?"

"I will tell you why," said the guard, blood rising in his face.

"That butcher murdered my best friend in a camp on the Pechora. Shot him, because he would not bring him a girl he fancied. Just stood there, all calm, and said, 'This is for disobeying an order,' and he pulled the trigger, shooting my friend through the head."

The guard, a grizzled man in his middle years, downed the vodka left in his glass and blinked back tears.

"Yes, that is the one that broke my brother's neck—for no reason at all. Eighteen he was and the pride of my parents."

"Someday someone will kill that murdering swine," said the guard, scratching his stubble. "Perhaps it will be me. He is hard to find alone, always with soldiers or guards." He looked disgustedly up into the space among the beams. "Someone must owe him something big, or maybe fear him up there, in the upper Soviet, where they make decisions. For they move him from camp to camp before someone can get to him."

The cantina had become silent. Other men, soldiers commandeered to camp duty and civilians, too, had made the fearsome acquaintance of Ivan, and uniformly cursed him.

A Komi Tent

At this point Korya's tale was interrupted. Sitting around the fire, we had fed the flames from a stack of wood. Although I wore the warm sheepskin coat Suomo had put around me earlier, my legs were freezing, and I felt drowsy from the day's exertions.

"Time to sleep," yawned Korya, exposing two rows of shining, white teeth. Our group dispersed, but before he left Korya explained to me that I would sleep in the tent of Suomo's mother. That tent, not fifteen feet from the fire, looking more like a yurt than a tent, was made from hides. There were, however differences. For one, there was no smoke hole in the top, for the Komi did not cook inside during the summer. In winter they lived in wooden structures with stoves. These things, however, I learned later.

I was led to a place where a pallet of furs and blankets had been prepared for me. All around me, at the perimeter of the tent, people slept already. In addition to Suomo's parents and me, seven young people slept in this hut. During my short stay with his family I never learned whether some of the children and teens in the tent belonged to Suomo, or if they were his younger siblings.

I made a nest for myself among the furs and blankets, and fell asleep the moment I got warm. Sometime during the night I awoke with a start. I had had a nightmare. I did not know where I was, which frightened me all the more. Lying back quietly among the furs, smelling strange new smells and listening to the soft breathing of the people around me, the events of the previous day came back to me.

I recalled what had awakened me; oh, the horror. I had dreamed that I was chained to a wall. Before me stood Ivan, a boar's head atop his body. The boar's snout opened in a smile—a horrid grin, exposing monstrous tusks. In my dream he leaned closer and closer, smiling his pig's smile and saying with Ivan's voice, "Just a kiss, a kiss on your neck." I knew if he reached my neck, he would bite me with his horrible tusks and drink my blood. He licked his lips and came closer still.

That is when sheer terror awakened me. I began to breath easier again, comforted by the knowledge that I was safe, perhaps only temporarily, but safe for the moment. I relaxed into the soft covers. I prayed and thanked God for my deliverance, safety, warmth and shelter among kind people.

I was extremely lucky that many people in this small tribe were willing to risk life in the gulags to shelter me. It dawned on me that some of the men had been ready to expel me into the taiga, into certain death, because of their deadly fear of the Russians. I understood that if they were to put their lives on the line, it would be for a member of the tribe, not a stranger.

At last I slept again, comforted by prayers, the smell of the heavy, cloying smoke from last night's fire on the coat that covered me, and the deep stillness. Upon awakening in the morning I recalled snatches of other dreams: of rivers, canoes and reindeer, although I had yet to see one of the creatures in the flesh. My dream perceptions stemmed solely from the picture books of my childhood.

Around me people awoke, rose, and quietly left the tent. They donned warm coats; mornings could be frosty. I followed their example. My shabby work boots, scuffed, cut and dirty, were outside the tent where I had left them. Putting them on cooled my warm feet instantly and I shivered.

Suomo's mother, Samea, her smiling face welcoming me, had already made a fire and was heating water in a large can. Two girls in their early teens, their colorful garb hidden beneath long fur coats, helped Samea with her work.

Suomo's father sat on a round of wood cut from a large log. More of these rounds were arranged around the cooking fire as seating for the family. The inscrutable father took no notice of me, preoccupied with fixing what I deemed to be a harness of sorts. I motioned to Samea that I would like to help, but she discouraged me by pointing at a seat. Korya came to join me. I was glad. Being a stranger and unfamiliar with their customs, I was suffering, because I needed to relieve myself and did not know how to act according to custom.

At first Korya was perplexed by my shy questions. Then he laughed. He pointed to the woods and gave me a small handgun. "Animals," he said, "shoot into the air."

Breakfast consisted of meat, bread and delicious herbal tea. It was sweetened, a wild honey treat, they said. Korya, unmarried, had been put in charge of me. Samea needed firewood and we were sent to get it. This was a good task, giving me time to ask of Korya some of the hundreds of questions for which I needed answers. We talked as we picked dry branches and pinecones off the ground and chopped fallen dried tree trunks into chunks.

"Where did you learn to speak Russian so well?" I asked Korya.

"In school. Already under the government of the Tsar, officials tried to round up native children and place them in schools. Later, the Communists forced us to speak their language in order to control the tribes. The local Soviets do their utmost to settle us in villages. If they succeed, they will always know how many animals we keep, how successful our hunts and trap lines are and how best to exploit us."

He laughed a harsh, bitter laugh, "Would you believe, they even sent officials to record how many berries and mushrooms we find in the forest. We need these resources to sustain us, to stay healthy during the long winter months. If we do have a surplus, we want to sell it ourselves to purchase what we cannot grow and gather. The Soviets would take everything. They claim the forest belongs to all Russian peoples and so the food we find belongs to the state."

I said, "I know this kind of reasoning. Where I come from, the Lower Volga, they also said that our land now belonged to all peoples of Russia. First they took all our food, then they forced us off our land, and later still, they commandeered our homes, sending us into labor camps, to the German Front, and into the wilderness."

We had both stopped working and were looking at each other. I assume my face must have been as sad and somber as his. At last he said, quizzically, "So they treat others like the natives, too?"

"Oh, yes," I cried, "they make no distinction when it comes to non-Russians. They distrust and dislike all of us." I began to count on my fingers for him, "Kalmyks, Chechens, Tartars, Germans, Jews, Kirghis, Kazaks, Estonians, Lithuanians, Latvians, Ukrainians," and here, having run out of fingers, I pointed at my nose. We laughed.

"I know," Korya chimed in again. "In school the teachers treated us as if we were too stupid to learn. They often said we were worthless, stinking herders—good for nothing but keeping reindeer." He paused, thinking back, "We had troubles but they treated the Yakut children even worse. They often beat them for not knowing the right terms or uses of things foreign to them—things they had never seen or experienced during the reclusive lives on taiga and tundra."

I understood instantly. "Of course, they would not know electricity, books, pencils—everything would be new and confusing to them."

Korya nodded, sagely, "Yes, Yakut children were even less exposed to civilization than our Komi young."

At this juncture, we had collected large piles of wood and were engaged tying sticks and branches into bundles and sorting kindling into baskets. Our heads whipped around to a loud huffing sound and we saw a large, brown animal ambling by. I was petrified. A wolf was the largest wild beast I had ever seen. Needless to say the beast terminated all talk about tribes and Russian schools.

"Stay still," Korya said calmly. "The bear means us no harm. I think he is after our herd by the river. Every so often a bear finds the herder sleeping and takes a stray wandering about alone."

With the bear far away, we loaded large bundles upon our backs. Korya had fashioned a harness for me from leather thongs, which allowed me to carry two baskets along with the pack on my back. He himself carried an enormous stack of branches on his back and another on his chest.

Like beasts of burden we walked toward camp. I had to stop time and again to rest my arms; the pack on my back bothered me much less. To take my mind off the load, I asked Korya to finish Suomo's story.

"You left off when he was in Amuta's tavern and heard the tales of many other men who had met Ivan and had seen him kill."

Yes, there were many who felt Suomo's burning anger. He, however, had an important, pressing problem on his hands, and told them, "I need to get my brother home to my people." Fired up by beer and vodka, many of the men proposed solutions to convey the body home quickly. Amuta, with calm demeanor, interrupted the well-meaning preparations spun by her guests. She offered the only rational plan.

Taking Suomo outside, she proposed, "My nephew will be here day after tomorrow. He will take you up the Pechora River in a reindeer-drawn sled. Snow covers the ice and you should make good time. Further south, you can leave the river and sled cross country to the winter encampment."

Suomo thanked his wise friend. She always knew what had to be done. "Good, good," she said, "just do not speak of our plan to anyone. Even among my trusted customers might be a spy who would betray you for money."

Suomo returned to his people and buried his brother. Then, the funeral barely over, he said goodbye to his wife and children, left them in his parent's care, and began his pursuit of Ivan the Terrible.

Converging Stories

Suomo's first chance to be close to Ivan came when, apart from the commandant's marches around camp, he saw Ivan leave by the back gate. Not long thereafter, Suomo's and my paths crossed. At that time I had been a prisoner at Yagnodnaya camp, a camp not far from Kotlas, for half a year. In the spring of 1942, Ivan became its commander. Suomo had followed Ivan's reassignments. People were only too willing to talk about him, thankfully noting the moment whenever he was given another command; a command far away from their own lives.

During the months I suffered fear and trepidation inside the camp, watching our women disappear, Suomo had hidden himself beyond the fence in the brush by the river, where he carefully watched the routine in our camp. The first he saw of Ivan, apart from his camp walks, was one evening when Ivan left the camp through the back gate. Suomo recalled, "Ivan came out late one evening carrying a large bundle to the river's edge. He knelt at the riverbank and did something to the bundle, and then pushed his burden into the river."

As Korya told Suomo's story his eyes had the faraway look of a person in another place. Because he knew the camp, the river and the story well, he probably saw before his inner eye what he told me. He looked indescribably sad and forlorn, the way I imagined Suomo must have looked at the moment of his telling.

Performing automatically, Korya spoke again. "When the murderer left the river, it was already dark. The bundle in the water was darker still. Suomo removed his clothes and walked into the frigid water and pulled the heavy bundle onto the shallow bank. He hid it, farther down river in the brush. Next morning, as Suomo furtively moved about, he saw Ivan return to the spot where he had disposed of the bundle. Ivan looked around for a good while, walking up and down the riverbank a bit. Satisfied that the bundle had disappeared, he returned to the camp."

I shivered with foreboding. I had an ominous feeling that I knew what Korya would say next. Unfortunately, my assumption was correct. And yet, I had to hear it from Korya's lips as if hearing was validation of my thoughts.

Suomo removed the sacking covering the solid thing contained therein. He, too, had an inkling that he would find a body. Yet when he saw the bruised and tortured corpse of a young woman, who once must have been astonishingly beautiful, the sight overwhelmed him.

He walked away, his stomach churning. He had seen death; the life of the taiga people was hard. Disease and death were their constant companion. But the demented, heinous torture and killing of a woman was a different thing altogether—an abomination. Oh, he knew of cruel men who treated their wives harshly, sometimes even with such brutality that the elders or the shaman intervened, but this abomination he could not comprehend.

After awhile he steeled himself and walked back to the corpse. He re-wrapped it in the sacking and weighed it down with stones. Naked once more, he pulled the bundle into the flow of the river. What else could he do?

Then the wait began. Day after day, he patrolled the river and watched the camp. He observed how Ivan disposed of another body. To verify his suspicions, he unwrapped the bundle—it was a woman again. He knew then that he never needed to look again. Ivan's new victims were women.

Suomo had prepared for Ivan's execution. His axe was finely sharpened; a leather thong was ready to become a snare if he needed a moment of surprise to overcome Ivan's physical advantage. Now, all he required was an opportune moment.

And then, ruining all his preparations, he saw Ivan bring a living woman to the river one evening. He walked her away from the spot where Suomo kept himself concealed. In the half light Suomo could have imagined that a pair of lovers walked by the river. For a while the couple stood in an embrace.

Suomo remained frozen and silent, unable to approach the monstrous man for Ivan carried a gun and would kill him before he came within killing range. Toward midnight the night descended into deep darkness. Suomo heard bodies fall to the ground. He heard a woman's cry, instantly silenced. From the sounds following the outcry, he knew that the woman was being raped—violently, awfully. He heard slaps, thrashing and then she cried out again.

Suomo dared not approach the scene in the darkness. Everything was uncertain when you could not see. The woman cried out once more. The cry was followed by a long, choking moan. As the deep, profound, awful silence continued, Suomo knew the woman was dead. Ivan had strangled her with his bare hands.

Still frozen in place by the horrible murder he had witnessed, Suomo saw a light. The powerful beam of a flashlight shone down on the dead woman. She, too, had red hair as had the others. Ivan wrapped her in a tarp. He tied her wrapped body with practiced, powerful motions into a package like the others and dragged it to the river. Suomo believed that Ivan was so sure that the body would sink and disappear that he did not bother to wade into the river. He gave a mighty shove from the bank and that was it—the end of another life.

When Korya reached this part of the tale, I asked him to stop for a rest, for my wooden burdens were wearing. I put the baskets on the ground and was about to relieve my back of the heavy bundle, when Korya stopped me. "Don't do that! It feels even worse when you put it back up. Just rest a moment, and we will go on. Camp is quite close now. No need to bother unloading."

To keep my mind focused on weightier matters than the load, Korya began to speak again. "There was another woman after the one I just talked about. Suomo had hoped he could prevent her rape and death, but the commandant had become very cagey, as if he expected detection, or worse. He had once again changed the time for the victim's death, leading her to the river in broad daylight on a Sunday afternoon. Suomo had been drowsing in a thicket when he heard a commotion. He crept to the brush's perimeter to spy on the intruders, only to witness the last frantic spasms of the victim.

Apparently the killer had been unprepared for this encounter—a spur of the moment act of passion, for he had none of his usual paraphernalia at hand. Details, however, never bothered Ivan. He shoved the still warm body into the river, pushing it into the flow with a large branch. He wiped his hands on his military pants, pulled out a cigarette, lit it and smoked contentedly. After surveying the landscape around him, he walked back to the camp, satisfied and content with the world.

Suomo cursed and swore. He called himself a coward, a worthless Komi herder. He bemoaned his incompetence as an avenger, demeaned his own manhood, as one intimidated, incapable of killing. When his rage subsided, he swore an oath to his brother and his parents: next time he would do the deed, even if it killed him.

Korya looked at me expectantly. "You know the rest," he said. "You were the next victim. Suomo said he did not trust his eyes when he saw your knife flashing. He observed in complete disbelief how you thrust the weapon into Ivan. Released from this improbable spell, he began walking toward the two of you, axe in hand. He thought he was screaming: 'Run, girl, run!' But it must have been in his mind—and you did not run. He saw Ivan get up and begin his terrifying lurch toward you, saw you retreat step-by-step, and then you stopped!"

"Now he feared for your life, feared that he would be too late once again. He ran despite his fear that Ivan would turn and shoot him before he could kill him. But God was with him, Ivan never turned; he saw and heard only you."

Korya fell silent. I had relived the scene again. The horror and the fear had washed over me like a wave, only this time I imagined what Suomo must have seen. Yes, hearing this story, his mother must have believed that I played an important part in the drama, avenging her son. We reached the camp. Arriving at the tent of Suomo's mother, we dropped our burden by the fire pit.

The sun was shining, the sky was blue, and the last flocks of birds overhead flew south. Soon the land would be frozen and cold once more. Where would I be then?

Journey to Arkhangelsk

In the evening the shaman, the spirit man, came to Samea's fire. He asked me many questions, which Korya translated. I told him about my family, the village of Schaffhausen, about our sad fate. I even told him about depressed, kind Alyosha when he asked me if I had a friend. What would I do in another land, he asked, a land far from here without support from a family. Would it crush me? Would I allow people to use me?

"No," I said firmly. "I walk with God and He keeps me even when other people seek to destroy me." I sensed that he liked that answer.

"Yes," he affirmed, "walk with the spirit that made you. Only that spirit is truth."

That day, I saw the spirit man conferring with many in the tribe. I assumed that he was making plans on my behalf. During the following days in camp I tried to be as much of service as possible. I played with the children, teaching them games and letters. They had some simple books, so I read to them, and we gathered firewood. At night, I prayed that God might convey me to safety. Here, my presence presented a danger to the people.

Early one morning, after about a week had passed, Korya and the spirit man came again to the tent. "Your guides have arrived. They are camped two days from here. It is time to leave, Katya," said Korya. Samea, inside the tent, overheard and scurried to the fire. Suomo rushed over from his wife's tent. Everyone who had shown me favor and kindness came to see me.

People shyly, sweetly, pulled presents from behind their backs. There were soft, fur-lined boots, a gift from Suomo; a round, mink-lined hat from his wife; warm leather pants, as the women wore in winter, from Korya; but the best gift of all came from Samea: a long fur-lined coat, as warm as the one I had lost—only this one was new.

I could not help myself. I cried, cried with deeply felt gratitude. I was thankful for the care these simple, kind people had lavished upon me, thankful for God's grace and providence. After Ivan's murder, I had found myself alone in the coldest place of Russia. I had lost even the smallest of my possessions, standing at the river's edge in a rough dress, unsuitable for the wilderness, and decrepit, equally unsuitable boots. I had thought then that I could not survive even one night. But then, there had been Suomo.

This man of the Komi had saved me in more than one way. Taking me to his people and planning an escape from Russia for me was so much more than I could have ever hoped for. How could I show these kind, wonderful people how grateful I was?

The Komi were not a demonstrative people. I had observed that they expressed affection only with the most minimal gestures, stroking a child's hair or gently patting a hand. In this way they were similar to my taciturn Volga German relatives, where a father's affection was often measured in belt-strokes, administered to a recalcitrant boy's behind.

I tried hard to express my feelings of thankfulness. Using my eyes and my hands I thanked each person in turn. They understood. We patted hands. Samea patted my cheek. Then it was time to leave. Korya would be my guide and protector—this, the shaman had declared. This man, so much a mixture of pastor and native spirit guide, came and placed his hands on my head, saying prayers in singsong fashion. Thereafter, the spirit man fashioned beaded amulets to my wrists and hung a spirit pouch around my neck. Now he deemed me protected, fortified against any evil that could befall me.

With Korya's translation, I thanked him for his protection and he wished me well. I thought God would forgive me the pagan ornaments on my body for they had been given with the best intentions. I had come to find that anything and everything containing goodness and truth is woven into God's plan.

Time came to say goodbye to Suomo. We had become very fond of each other and he shook my hand until it hurt. I turned away from him and we were off. Suomo's reticent, stoic father had given me a sack made from reindeer hide, the shaved pelt on the outside—shining silver gray—in which to store my precious presents until the time of need. Winter would soon be upon us. I carried this sack on my back. Korya, too, carried a much larger sack with his belongings and our provisions.

We walked at an even, sustainable pace. The morning had been very cold and we wore heavy jackets. After a few hours of walking we shed the jackets, adding them to our packs. We stopped talking after the first hour. Korya concentrated on the trail, which I could hardly discern as such, and I had no breath to spare for talk.

As we silently moved through thick stands of conifers, lovely woods of silvery birches and open meadows, we saw much wildlife: a few single wolves; a bear—thank God, from afar; red squirrels; minks; a hissing wolverine, which followed us for a while; and wild caribou. Neither the wolverine nor the bear bothered me. I knew Korya had a gun in his pack.

"One cannot walk about in the taiga without a weapon," he had said earlier. "One might have to shoot some food." No matter. I felt safe, far safer than in the gulag. When the sun was high, we rested by a small stream. We ate sparingly, some bread, meat and dried berries—who knew when we could re-supply—and we drank the water of the clear, little brook.

Before leaving the pleasant resting place, Korya filled two skins with water. "Don't know if we can find water by nightfall," he said. I had been told that we were hiking to link up with another part of the family group, who were driving a herd south toward the Northern Dvina. We would stay with them until we reached the river. Then we would part company, and go north.

It got dark early. When shadows of the trees fell far ahead of us, Korya said that we must stop and prepare for the night. He told me to gather wood for a fire, while he put up a lean-to with branches and saplings, covering the skeletal structure with conifer bows. He found large stones and made a pit for the fire.

"We must try to keep the fire going all night long," he said. "This time of year the bears need to put on fat for the winter and they become aggressive."

We were glad that we had thought to carry water, because we did not find water close by. Korya made tea in a tin can, which we sipped as we ate dry bread and berries. The thought of sleeping with a man in close quarters made me uncomfortable. I felt strange, unsure of myself, yet I tried to act as if it did not affect me at all.

Korya probably never gave the situation a thought. In a Komi's life, hardships made difficult situations an everyday occurrence. Without being discomfited or embarrassed in the least, he told me to take every warm item from my bag and put them on. "It will be cold tonight. I expect a strong frost and we must keep warm."

He, too, clothed himself warmly. Wrapped in our fur coats, wearing our warm boots and hats, we crept into the hut. Korya had covered the ground with dry grass and lichen to keep the moisture away from us. When we were inside, he closed off the entrance with a few bows. The rolled-up reindeer bags were used as pillows, and as soon as our heads rested upon them, we fell asleep.

I heard Korya get up during the night a few times to feed the fire, but although I tried each time to stay awake until he returned, I never managed this feat. Toward morning, snuffling and grunting awakened me. I felt that Korya was sitting up beside me. Something was out there.

"What is it?"

"Bear! Too close, too curious." I thought Korya had the gun in his hand because I heard a strange metallic click. With one quick movement he removed the entrance cover and crouched in the opening. In an instant he was outside. He made a loud, huffing, warning sound, standing tall. I saw the fire flicker for an instant. I crawled to the entrance, terrified to be stuck in this small hut. If the bear attacked I wanted to be standing, not lying helplessly on the ground. Korya moved toward the fire, making it possible for me to crawl out.

It was velvety-black outside. In the glow of the fire, beyond the pit, I made out the outline of a great hulking form. Korya stood motionless, his gun at the ready.

"Take a branch, put it in the fire, and when it burns throw it at the bear. You might have to do it more than once."

"Why don't you just shoot him?" I complained. In my mind, this would solve the problem.

"Just do it," he said tersely. The beast observed us with the greatest interest, as if weighing his chances. He growled a low rumbling sound from deep within his massive body. My branch had caught fire and become almost fully engulfed in flames. "Throw it," Korya called. "He is getting angry."

I threw the branch; the beast moved away, but not very far. "Do it again," said Korya, and I did. Now the bear rose to his full height. He was enormous. I threw another flaming missile. I threw it better than the first time, for it landed in front of his feet. Lucky for us, a patch of dry grass caught on fire and flamed up between the bear's paws.

The bear was angry, but uncertain, fearing the fire. He roared! Nevertheless, he turned, came down on all four legs, and trolled away. I shook with fear, excitement and, as I realized moments later, with cold. I shook so badly that I walked to the fire and sat down. My legs did not want to carry me any longer. Korya, gun still trigger ready, walked to the patch of grass I had set on fire. Grimly he stamped it out and returned to me. "Why did you not shoot the beast?" I asked annoyed.

"Bears don't die easily," he told me. "If you don't manage a kill shot, they get very angry, and then you have problems. Furthermore, had I killed him—then what? We are in no position to skin and harvest a bear. They are a resource to my people and not to be wasted. We kill them only when we have to, for food, for the pelt, or in defense. Otherwise, we share the forest with them. It belongs to them as much as it belongs to us. This one had an interest in us because he smelled the food I carry." He smiled, "Punishment for my laziness, I should have cached it properly in a tree."

I thought about his sensible words, got up and fed the fire in earnest. When Korya was certain that the bear would not come back, we made tea and ate a meager meal of bread and meat. Though meager, gratefully I still thought it better food than the miserable meals at the gulag.

We began our walk when the ground became visible in the pale light of a morning that had a distinctly wintry feel to it. White, fresh frost covered the ground. It emblazoned the grass with crystals and the early fallen leaves with hoary dust; it lay upon the needles of the conifers like silvery motes, and crunched under our feet. Our encounter with the bear turned my thoughts to an earlier time when another beast had interrupted our conversation. I seemed fated to explore the topic further. Breaking our silence, I asked a question that had lingered in my mind.

"You speak Russian like a native. Your Russian is much too perfect for a grade school education. How is that possible, for you live in the taiga surrounded by Komi?"

"You are right. I had special schooling. You see, our teachers reported to the officials who among their pupils had intelligence and an aptitude for language. Those special children they wished to cultivate further. They tried to design them according to their plan, until they could become officials in their own right, ready to oversee the native people. Who better to spy and report on the natives than some of their own? Those men would be invested with trust, and knowlegeable in the ways and secrets of the tribes." He coughed and spit distastefully, as if clearing away the unpalatable memory.

"Gifted children were taken early from their parents. We were so little, afraid and hurt. We cried for many nights in the communist dormitories. I was five when they took me from my mother and put me in a boarding school. We at least had nice teachers. They slept with us in the large dormitory, ate with us in the dining room, lived with us every minute, forever speaking Russian." For a while he walked silently behind me until we reached a stretch that enabled us to walk beside each other.

"Poor boy! You must have missed your mother and your family terribly."

"Yes! I did; so very, very much. I remember we cried sometimes at night and waited, fiercely desiring the time of our confinement to be over. But they never allowed us to go home, for belonging to nomadic peoples we would surely have disappeared. Our parents would have hidden us well. The officials knew that and kept us like prisoners."

I sighed, "What power these Soviet people have over us, with their guns, their army, and their police. How conceited they are, thinking that they know what is best for all people, yet furthering only their agenda— whatever that may be. In the end, all they want is to enslave everyone and control us for the benefit of a small group."

"You are right," Korya agreed. "The teachers were imprisoned, too. They had to stay for many years with us without the benefit of a personal life. But the officials and the people in the Soviets, they lived well. They had nice houses behind fences, which we saw when we were led for our walks through the city. They rode horses, and some even had automobiles."

"So, did you become an official then, an overseer for your people?"

"No," he laughed. "When I heard what they wanted me to do to my people I ran away, first chance I got. I was in high school then. I looked Russian, my hair cropped short, my clothes Soviet issue, my speech flawless—I was perfect. So when the teachers took us to town one day, I snuck away the moment their attention was otherwise occupied. I calmly walked through the streets until I came into the poorer section of town, where people had stalls and sheds behind their homes. I hid out in a cow barn until night time. Then it was easy—a Komi can become a ghost. I found my family, and the Communists were never able to recapture me."

What else could be added to our laments about communism? Nothing! Therefore, we trudged on in silence. Shortly after the noon break—we had been out of food since the night before—Korya became excited. He stared at the ground and smelled the air. I sensed nothing unusual. But then he also was able to hear things long before I heard the sounds.

"Komi," he said. "A big herd is just an hour ahead of us. We will eat well tonight." Making this promise, he increased his pace twofold. Struggling along behind him, I moved in a running walk, trying to keep up. The extra effort was soon rewarded. Korya stopped dead in his tracks, allowing me to catch up. He pulled me along his side, pointing excitedly, "Look, there is the herd. Nenets, friends, they will take care of us."

For the first time in my life I saw the wonder of a reindeer herd. Their fur shone silvery in the afternoon sun, although some still sported brown patches. "They are changing their look for winter," said Korya. "Silver-white with black accents allows them to blend into the winterscape."

Half-wild reindeer have lived for thousands of years in a strange symbiotic relationship with the peoples of the North. They allowed themselves to be herded, albeit their human companions were destined to follow their migrations from winter to summer pasture and back. Gaining protection from wolves and bears, reindeer became, over time, used to being the willing companions of people. They learned to carry loads, allowed the herders to ride them, learned to pulled sleighs.

Spread throughout the open landscape in front of us, they were exciting to behold. The big bulls were covered from their heads to their shoulders with shining, long, white hair. Their antlers were huge, overmatching their solid, strong bodies. These were warlike deer: even the females had short antlers, because strong, cunning hunters preyed upon them every day of their lives.

Korya did not hesitate. Without fear he walked through the widespread herd of grazing animals. I followed with apprehension. Few of the animals raised their heads to look at us. They smelled us, and our odor must have been agreeable to them or they would have taken off at a fast trot. Meandering, it took us a while to get clear of the herd. Shortly thereafter, we saw the tents of the Nenets.

Two men, small in stature—I think I was inches taller than they—came, smiling broadly, to greet us. They, too, wore colorful clothes, deep green shirts with red and multi-colored embroidered stripes. Korya told me that they belonged to the taiga Nenets, who often intermarried with Komi people.

The men instantly fell into an animated conversation, ignoring me. This gave me an opportunity to study the new people in my life. In contrast to the Komi, who had European features, the Nenets men had bronze skin with Mongolian flat features and eyes. Darling little children, brightly ornamented like Christmas trees, approached our small group. They were exceedingly curious, yet shy. In the background by their tents, reminiscent of the Komi tents, I saw a few tiny women in bright garb.

After a while, Korya remembered that he was not alone. He motioned me to stand beside him, and speaking in what sounded like a squall of syllables, he seemed to explain my presence. The Nenets men smiled broadly and gave short little nods in my direction. I, not knowing what else to do, nodded back.

At last, we were escorted to a large, prestigious tent where their elder or shaman resided. I had learned from Korya that many of the Nenets, like the Komi, were Orthodox Christians. They had also co-mingled their Christianity with spiritual aspects of their old shamanistic culture.

I was ecstatic to know that they knew the Christian God—our God of love and forgiveness. People who knew him and his grace would also be kind, forgiving and protective. I knew therefore that I could entrust myself to them without apprehensions for my safety.

The leader of this band of Nenets was taller by a head than most of his people. Slender, sinewy, with a bright spirit shining from his deep, dark eyes, he coolly assessed me when Korya presented me. He motioned us to sit by his fire. He called for his wife, presumably to bring refreshments. Moments later, my guess was proved correct.

His tiny wife, perhaps four feet six inches tall, brought us water and bread. How did she know that we had been deprived of food and drink for many hours? Korya and the Nenets leader conversed at great length, while I, understanding nothing at all, observed the people of this tribe.

After the newness of our arrival had worn off, the life of the small tent-village unfolded as usual. Men called commands to teenage boys and those called upon loped in the direction of the herd. Korya, noting my interest, said, "Night is closing in and the boys must gather the herd." As our host attended to tribal business—people came and went—Korya gave me important news.

"My tribal group, the one that we were to travel with, left the area days ago. They are far south by now. Therefore, we will be traveling with the Nenets, our friends and cousins. They will provide us passage to the Northern Dvina. We are close. It should only take a few days once they get moving."

As honored guests, we were fed a sumptuous supper. Fresh roasted caribou, the wild cousin of the reindeer, sugared bread with berries, and wild mushrooms roasted in a pan, were our feast. We washed the lovely fare down with honeyed water. Thanking our hosts profusely, we crawled into the chief's warm tent and slept like logs.

We stayed with this Nenets group for four days, traveling leisurely until we reached the Dvina. The next morning we said goodbye to our hosts, and freshly and generously provisioned, we set out down river in a small canoe.

The Dvina is placid but treacherous in her own quiet way. She is used to transport log floats and boats filled with fur and forest produce to Arkhangelsk. Because of her many uses she buries in her body the flotsam and jetsam of the taiga. Old drowned logs and stumps, iced-in boats, dead bodies, peat floats and loamy soil—all of these clutter her sides treacherously on their slow way to the White Sea via this river.

A few times, when we floated too close to the bank, we were snagged by large debris. We tried to stay to the middle of the river. There, however, we were easy targets for the Siberian patrols. The population of Russia was strongly discouraged from entering forbidden zones. These were zones in which the captive population might find a way to escape the regime or find trade unhindered by exorbitant taxation. Arkhangelsk was such a place. Despite the war, during the summer months this harbor was a place where a person might find a tiny hole in Russia's fence and escape. Everybody knew it. Therefore the approach to the harbor was already closely guarded hundreds of miles away from the target.

Korya had instructed me to play the role of a deaf and dumb native. "If we come across a patrol I want you to smile pleasantly and shake your head if asked any questions," he advised me. I thought I could play this role with great confidence.

We made great progress. Our next goal was to reach the city of Podsosanye. There, Korya assured me, were settled Komi who would take us in, allowing us to rest and be resupplied. We slept each night in quickly raised lean-tos. The nights were bitterly cold already. Frost blanketed everything in the morning. Many days the frosty cover never melted, growing thicker at night.

"Soon the Northern Dvina will freeze," said Korya apprehensively. "Before that time we must reach Arkhangelsk, for the White Sea will freeze next. Before that happens, I must smuggle you aboard a ship and the ship must leave soon or it will be trapped in the harbor."

I am cursed with the flaw of incremental inattention, as are many other people. By that I mean that I relax into the flow of the present, forgetting in small stages imminent danger—the big picture of a situation. Since I had lived for so long under extreme tension and abject abuse, the supra-normality of my present days allowed me to slip into a soporific, enchanted state in which I loved every minute. The river, the frost, the taiga and then the tundra, the Komi and Nenets people, Korya and the boat we were riding in—I liked everything and everyone with an all-embracing enthusiastic love.

It was not as if the enchanted state left me in a stupor, no! I experienced every minute fully engaged, sensing the slightest change in the temperature during the day or Korya's mood. Therefore, I responded with every fiber of my being when I sensed he became tense, turning his head often. The way he alertly surveyed the water and the dismal banks of the Dvina bespoke danger. His hyper-alertness returned me instantly to my previous wary, cautious state. My worries returned, flooding me like a black wave. How could I have forgotten, even for a short while, where we were and what we had to do?

"What troubles you?" I prompted.

"River patrols," he shot back. So far we had encountered many boats, large and small, wood floats of hundreds of logs corralled and controlled by barges and men with poles. Some of these rafts were exceedingly large, forcing us ashore where we lifted the boat onto the bank. However, we had yet to encounter one of the swift patrol boats.

"We are getting close to the city. That's where they are stationed, racing up and down the river. They could be upon us in the blink of an eye."

Evening came. We had spotted the city ahead of us, far down river. Korya suddenly asked me, "Can you endure a night of great hardship? I would like to float in the dark to the edge of town. There we can leave the boat on the bank and spend the rest of the night with friends in a real house."

"Of course I can. I have been colder before," I said bravely, although the moist frost rising from the water had stiffened my legs already.

"Good! I thought you would be brave," he said. "Let us paddle harder. Perhaps we can stay warm that way."

As night fell upon the river, surrounding us with its deep, dark, cold cover, we paddled on with forceful yet cautious strokes. We could not afford to make any noise. We strained our eyes, piercing the darkness in an effort to detect floating logs, stumps and other debris. A spill could drown us or kill us with hypothermia. We were lucky. Whatever floating junk we encountered glanced harmlessly off the boat.

Just when I thought my hands might stay frozen forever in their curled position clutching the paddle, we passed the first lights of Podsosanye. Soon Korya found the mooring he wanted to use. Two boats were tied up here already, to which we added ours.

Our bodies creaked with cold and ached with stiffness, the stiffness resulting from cramped positions in close confines. For the first time since I set eyes on Korya, I saw that even he had a breaking point. As he bent to help me climb onto the planks of the gangway, he involuntarily groaned with pain.

For the first steps on shore we clung to each other like a pair of drunks. Our feet ached with frostbite; our backs were naught but agonizing pain. Step by step, we dragged ourselves along the path that led from the mooring onto a lone, dark street, which, in turn, led into the inky, flat tundra.

How I wished I had not answered with foolish bravado that I could endure a hard night. This experience was worse than winter days in camp. Then I had been able to move, keeping my blood flowing. Korya remained silent for the length of our painful trudge. I stumbled along numb to my surroundings. Korya, however, despite his own aches and pains was fully alert to the sounds of the dark.

An icy wind was blowing, another obstacle to struggle against. Suddenly Korya stopped. He straightened his body, standing erect, listening. He removed the earflap from his hat, concentrating on the sound. "My people," he said at last.

We walked faster now. From deep within, I brought forth an energy reserve I had not known existed. A short while later we arrived at a Komi encampment arranged around a village of small wooden houses. Korya led me unerringly to the biggest of the houses, where the spirit man of the tribe welcomed us.

A Plan for Freedom

I slept in a warm nest of fur for a very long time. It was almost dark again when finally I rose from my fur bed. By now the cloying smell of smoke, fur and human bodies was familiar to me. I had awakened at the right time because the smell of a good stew tickled my nose. I was not disappointed, for moments later the mistress of the lodge ladled out stew, broke bread and filled jars with tea.

The wood house was equipped with a stove for cooking and heating. I felt, of course, that I was in the warmest place I had known for a long time. I ate with the women and the children in the back of the room, while the men held court in the front by the door where they were joined by men coming and leaving at will.

The women spoke only a few words of Russian, but the children, once they lost their fear of me, spoke to me in fluent Russian. They told me that they went to school during the winter months. They boarded in town, coming home on the weekends. I asked whether they had reindeer herds, and of course, they did. The young men of the tribe, however, had taken the animals to the southern winter pasture.

"Here," they pointed at their house, "it is too cold. The wind never seems to stop, and therefore the young men move the herds."

Behind my back the men spoke rapidly in the Komi language. Without pretension, I thought that some of the talk was about me. And I must have been correct because Korya took me aside later in the evening and told me that we would leave at first light. The belief prevailed among the men that Korya had only a slim chance to get me passage on an Allied ship before Arkhangelsk harbor froze over.

"The ships," they told Korya, "leave long before the real freeze begins for they encounter fierce storms out in the Barents Sea on their way home." They also commented on our remarkable luck, for the convoys had been running only since 1941. Before that time, the harbor had been more tightly controlled than at the present. The first convoy had arrived in November of that year supplying 79 light M-3 tanks, 59 fighter planes, 1,000 trucks and 2,000 tons of barbed wire to the hard-pressed Red Army under the Allied Lend-Lease Agreement.

Later, I learned that the polar convoys crossed the North Atlantic and steamed along the polar ice of the Barents Sea. Leaving British ports, they encountered an enormous minefield between Scotland and Iceland. Skirting this menace, they would turn south and proceed in an almost straight line to Murmansk or, by way of Medvezhy Island, to Arkhangelsk. Depending on the ice barrier the ships encountered, the passage route could be 1,500 to 2,000 nautical miles long one way and take between ten and fourteen days to accomplish.

"The old men here do not believe that I can get you on an Allied ship. But despite their little faith I think we will be lucky. Our spirit man said that you must be saved because God wishes for you to reach freedom."

"How does he know what God thinks?" I could not help myself, doubting that a mere man, a native at that, could communicate with God. Our pastors were learned men who studied the Bible all the time and led Christian lives, yet they never claimed to know for what God wished.

"Believe it. When our spirit man says such a thing, then God must have given him a special feeling about you. He also said that we must take you to Arkhangelsk—all other ways out of Russia are closed."

"I will pray hard tonight," I said. "Perhaps it would do both of us good if you prayed also."

Korya said simply, "I will."

Travel and Danger

The sky was gray. The sun had not yet risen, yet we were getting ready to leave. From a sheltered corral the elders led out three reindeer, big, strong animals. They were already haltered and had pad saddles on their backs. "This will make it easier for a while," said our Nenets friends. I understood without explanation that we were to ride these beasts—and I did not like it at all. I had ridden horses, but these mounts had huge antlers and I knew not how to control a reindeer.

However, no one cared one wit about my fears. With Korya's help I mounted one of the creatures, and he explained rapidly, in a much too casual way, what he expected me to do. The men loaded our supplies, contained in leather pouches, onto the back of the third creature. Someone behind me made a clicking noise and, before I knew it, we were off at a flying trot.

Once I got used to the reindeer's movements, its rhythm, I relaxed and quite liked the fact that I did not have to walk. The creature carrying me was gentle and followed the cues I gave. But I think more often it followed along in Korya's wake, inhaling the familiar scent of its herd mates. After a while our mounts became winded, they slowed their fast pace, and I rode up to Korya's side.

With minimal exceptions the land was flat all around us. Sparse vegetation shone in frosty silver. A few small bushes, some grass pods and lots of lichens were all I saw surrounding us. Although the sun had risen as a pale, yellow orb far away in the east, a frosty fog diminished her rays' ability from reaching the dismal tundra.

We rode along the eastern shore of the Northern Dvina, keeping the river in sight at all times. "Where are you taking me next?" I asked.

"Ust Pinaga," he said. "We pass another city before we reach it, but that one is a bad place filled with alcohol and despair. Our people avoid it. No friendly people reside there."

"How will you get me aboard one of the Allied ships?" I asked. "The elders seem to think it is impossible."

"Don't worry. Don't think about it at all. I have friends, who have other friends, who have friends on ships where the crews appreciate our furs. Not all of the sailors on these ships like the Soviets. Most of them have heard enough about Stalin that they will take risks to defy him and his henchmen and, in the process, their own captains.

It got terribly dark, long before the day was over. Within minutes a bitter cold wind blew from the east, chilling us. The reindeer were nervous and hard to control. Korya abruptly stopped our progress and sprang from his mount.

"Bad weather," he announced, "we must put up for the night." He threw me the reins of his mount and pulled the leather bags from the pack animal's back. While I held the reins he hobbled the animals. Once they were thus disabled, he let them graze on the poor forage around us.

We put up a small tent. It was made of supple, strong felt and was incredibly thin and light. "Will this soft stuff stand up to the force of this awful wind?" I worried.

"Oh yes, we will be fine." Korya was very sure of himself.

The moment the tent stood erect, the reindeer gathered in its wind shade, bedding down next to it. We sat in the entrance of the tent, ate some bread, drank some water and crawled inside. The tent was incredibly small. If one of us wished to turn we had to coordinate this feat with the other.

Korya was a wonderful person with whom to travel. He had long ago decided to look at me as his sister and treated me with the same respect and care he would accord his blood sister. Although I was very tired, worries kept me awake. The closer we came to the goal, the more afraid I grew. If we were intercepted and my identity disclosed, we would both suffer terrible repercussions.

The death of my poor father came to my mind. He had died honorably fighting men who were without a conscience, without a soul. Could I be that brave? My fears made me think of Mother, Joseph, Arkady and Alyosha. Where were they now? What had been done to them? Were they still alive?

I slept fitfully, hearing the wind abrade the tundra, hearing the animals move about outside as they changed positions for a turn at the inside spot. A few times we woke up because we, too, were freezing on the side exposed to the tent wall and needed to turn.

Next morning, when we awoke, the storm was blowing worse than during the night. "We cannot travel today," said Korya. "We could not survive."

The reindeer tried to graze in the fierce wind. Their empty stomachs plagued them enough to leave the minimal shelter of the tent and hobble pitifully to lichen patches. We only crawled out into the howling inferno to relieve ourselves. The icy, ferocious wind tried to tear the clothes from our bodies, chilling us, driving us back under the cover of the tent in an instant. Korya, however, braved the storm a few times to check on the animals to insure that their hobbles were firmly in place without chafing their delicate legs. "We are nothing without the reindeer," he said as he slithered his way back into the tent.

It was strange to be wide awake and confined with a man in the smallest space I had ever known. We had recharged our physical batteries and were itching to be about—upright and moving. Lying crushed together, shoulder to shoulder, eye to eye, we soon became bored. Korya, I knew, could have sent himself into a hibernating stupor. I, however, was incapable of this feat.

Each time he tried to return to a drowsy state, I kept him awake with idle chatter.

"Tell me a story, Korya. A story which the people of your tribe enjoy," I begged. He raised himself a bit, leaning on his elbow and looked at me a bit peeved. Upon reflection, however, he told me the tales of the witch Baba Yaga. This witch was an old crone with three gaping teeth, a large hooked nose and numerous hairy warts on her pointed chin. Her body was crooked; between her shoulders rose a hump; her legs were bent, her knees were shot. Therefore, she used a sapling to support herself, limping forward with a hobbled gait.

It so happened that this witch Baba Yaga fell violently in love with a young Komi hunter. She had spied him when he set traps close to her wooden lodge. Disguised as a raven, she followed him, and saw him bathe in a stream. The young hunter had shed every thread of his clothing when he stepped into the water. As he rubbed himself with soap plant leaves here and there, he alternately turned his sweet, manly front and strong back to her, who sat in a birch tree. She became so enamored of the young man that she swore a magical witch's oath, which was preceded by a spell. The combination of oath and spell would enable her to possess him.

No sooner had she said her spell, but she flew to her wooden house, where she brewed a strong potion, which she drank in one big draught. As the magical potion circulated throughout her body, she turned into a maiden of such beauty that the trees bent before her when she left her lair.

She had become a girl of seventeen, milk-white and rosy, with raven hair, firm breasts and a waist so small that two hands could span it. Her gown was spun from gossamer; her sandals were made from soft, green, woven grass. Thus, she walked forth, half flying, half stepping, until she came to the stream where the hunter still bathed. She stood upon the stream's bank in her full beauty and gazed with feigned innocence upon the naked young man.

"He would not have been a Komi if he had not seen her with great appreciation," said Korya. "The moment he saw her—and she was a man's dream—the young hunter became bewitched. Nothing would do but he had to approach the fair creature. The young man left the stream as in a trance. He stepped upon the bank, and with burning desire and the sweetest of pains in his breast he approached the enchanting vision." Here Korya sighed as if he could see the scene before him.

"What happened then?" I asked. "Did she pull him into her arms and give way to his desire?" I, too, could see the scene on the bank of the stream.

"Hah," cried Korya, "nothing of the sort happened." It seemed that Baba Yaga had a problem of her own. The moment she embraced the young hunter she turned—oh, how awful—into a horrid, grizzly she-bear, with an enormous desire to kill and eat the young man clutched in her monstrous paws. The young Komi froze in the bear's powerful embrace just long enough for the bear spell to wear off. That, however, became also a most horrifying surprise. Imagine embracing Baba Yaga in her natural state.

Pushing the witch off his body, the young hunter ran naked through the forest in search of his family, while Baba Yaga fell crying to the ground, cursing all of witchcraft and impotent spells.

"That, Korya, is a most unsatisfactory tale," I said. "Don't you know a tale where love wins out?"

"No, dear sister. I don't know any of those." He then said quietly, "If there were one, you would be turned into a Komi maiden and I would marry you."

"Oh," I said very subdued. Apparently my friend and chosen brother had come over time to see me through a man's eyes. I had also, on occasion, seen him for the special, attractive man he was. Korya turned away from me and pretended to sleep.

Around noon, the wind finally slowed its roaring fury. Korya and I both had enough of the enforced idleness with its underlying problematic feelings, wishes and sexual tensions. Deep within me I understood Korya's feelings, his desires for me. I, too, was not made of clay. I, too, had developed a special kind of love for the man who was sacrificing months of his life to my well-being. How could I not love him? But what kind of love did I feel for him? He was another hero person, another knight to rescue me from the clutches of the Russian bear. Was he seeking glory for his soul, his ego, or was he in love with me?

I came to the conclusion that to Korya I was a chimera, a witch's beautiful representation of a young girl that he desired, as much as he was to me the gorgeous young rescuer whom I would like to love. I understood totally, however, the underlying problem. If I loved him today he would expect me to love him the same tomorrow and forever. But this I could not promise. Would I be able to live my entire life among his people?

I knew that between us was a deep chasm of two very different cultures. These cultures were hundreds, perhaps thousands of years apart. When did my ancestors last slay wild beasts to survive? I could not answer that question. When were my antecedents rooted in herding or hunting culture? I could not answer that question either, and yet the impossibility of any union between us lay contained therein.

I knew, without doubt, that I came from a long line of farmers, who had turned the very soil they tilled into a partner. I knew that my religion clothed me with an armor of love and mercy, defying war-like people, the killers, the destroyers. Even with the greatest love by my side, I could not imagine myself living any longer in Russia where the killing of innocents had become so easy, to be part of an unsettled, migratory life. On a common level of thought, we both realized that youth, beauty and romantic wishfulness was not enough to bind for long.

Quietly, thinking sad, sobering thoughts, we passed the morning hours. I assumed by the clamor of my stomach that it must have been around noon when the wind lessened. Outside, the world was frigid and depressingly barren. A weak, pale-yellow sun hung like an icy, sulfuric disk in the gray sky, a sun incapable of imparting warmth.

The reindeer had managed to hobble quite a distance away from the tent and fed contentedly on a large patch of vegetation.

"We will leave as soon as we can eat and break camp," said Korya glumly, letting me know that he too had been thinking impossible thoughts. A little bread and dried meat and the last of the water gave us sustenance. Thereafter, we rolled up our blankets, our spare clothes and the tent, storing them in the leather bags. While I busied myself with the later task, Korya removed the hobbles from the animals' legs and saddled them. A few minutes later, we were moving speedily across the bleak tundra.

It darkened early, yet Korya pressed on. We had not yet found water, which we desperately needed for us and the animals. None of my small jokes and cheery remarks had restored Korya's usually pleasant countenance. It seemed as if, henceforth, he would only think of ways to rid himself of my presence.

It was fully dark when we heard the whine of an engine. A car was coming toward us from the left, the bank of the Dvina.

"Patrol," said Korya. "Small military, truck. They have not seen us yet. Let's get down low and perhaps they will not notice us."

We slid off the backs of our mounts. Korya cued the animals to kneel. "If they see us and approach I will say that we are making camp. Remember you are my deaf and dumb sister." I murmured agreement and prayed away the engulfing fear, which threatened to drown me.

The patrol car drove by us, not a hundred feet away. Its lights did not touch us. The patrol never saw us. When the car was far away, we pulled the animals from the ground, mounted and rode on. Lucky for us, the gray sky cleared to reveal a multitude of bright stars. Korya knew just how to orient himself by the stars, traveling north in a straight line.

Unfortunately, the clear sky allowed the temperature to drop rapidly. Soon we were freezing. My feet felt like blocks of ice, yet we pressed on. Finally, we came upon a small, sluggishly flowing stream, the water already frozen on each bank.

"Is it drinkable?" I asked, for some water sources were not potable. "I think so," said Korya, filling the skins. He handed me one of the water bags and drank from the other. The reindeer daintily stretched their necks from the bank and drank without wetting their legs.

We put up the tent and slept. The next day we had traveled just a few hours when we heard the motor patrol again. My heart almost stopped. A while later, they spotted us, and drove at us with full speed, intercepting us moments later. The olive-brown, robust vehicle had a machine gun mounted on its heavy steel hood that pointed viciously, directly, at us when they came to a halt.

"Get off the animals, stand on the ground!" shouted a deep voice. "Put your hands over your heads!" was the next command. We followed the orders precisely, although we still held our reins. "Drop the reins!" shouted the voice.

"Can't, comrade, Sir," cried Korya, "The animals will run and we will be unable to catch them for days." There was a moment of silence. The man behind the steering wheel giving the orders was burly, round-faced, and bespectacled. His head to the neck was enclosed in a fur-lined, military leather hat.

"Volodya, go hold the reins," he said. A strapping, young man in fur-lined camouflage gear left the car and came toward us. Stepping around us, so his companion always had a clear line of fire, he took the reins from us and told us to step away from the animals. Now the driver too joined us. He told us to take off our coats and throw them on the ground. Then he searched us for weapons.

I suffered throughout the procedure as if pins and needles were piercing me, for I knew Korya had a gun. My heart was pounding. What if they had my description and knew that I was somehow connected to terrible Ivan's death. I tried to control my breath, coming ragged and rapid from my lungs. They prodded us. Searching, they dug through our bags, coats and items of clothing, yet, miraculously, found nothing.

"Papers, show us your papers," boomed the bass. Korya produced his pass, which the driver perused in great detail. Ever since he'd been in school Korya had been registered. Even later, years after he had escaped the school and the search for him had ended, this document had enabled him to receive new documentation and allowed him to travel without problems throughout the lands of the Komi.

I, of course, had no such document, and was worried that this circumstance alone would lead to my detection. "Where are her documents?" asked Volodya, studying my face sternly, "and where are you going?"

"She has no documents," said Korya. "She can't hear, can't speak, never went to school, never got registered. You know very well that most of our women have no documents."

There was a long silence during which the two Russians seemed to assess the situation. I was so terrified I thought I would faint.

"Where are you going then?" asked the driver, who was obviously the person in charge of the patrol.

Without the slightest hesitation, Korya said, "Arkhangelsk."

"And what will you do there," asked the deep voice.

"Get her married to a friend," lied Korya, smiling slyly.

"Poor friend. Deaf and dumb, what a bride!" exclaimed young Volodya.

"It's not her hearing he is marrying her for," grinned Korya. The men laughed loudly together. I took offense on behalf of the deaf and dumb bride, almost giving myself away with a smart remark. However, at this point young Volodya, who had looked me over carefully, remarked, "Well, why not? For a native she is a good looking girl."

I hid my face behind my hands as if to avoid his looks, but in reality I covered the angry blush I felt rising up from my neck. The Russians stepped aside for private consultation. When they returned, they gave the reins of our animals back to us, and the deep voice said, "Fine, you look like upstanding people, so travel on. I will see if I can notify the other patrols that we have cleared you, sparing you the trouble of another search."

"Thank you, comrade, Sir," said Korya humbly. I allowed myself a shy smile, batting my lashes at them.

"I was right," said Volodya, "she is quite pretty." On that pleasant note they entered their vehicle and drove away, leaving us standing in the stink of their exhaust.

"Where is your gun?" were the first words from me.

"Stuck under the lichen patch beyond," said Korya. Following his words he walked straight to the place, pulling the gun from beneath the gray growth.

When darkness fell, we saw an encampment. Coming closer Korya said that these were the Nenets whom he had hoped to find. "This group will soon be traveling south along the river," he said, "but for tonight we will be their honored guests."

We slept warm and safe with the Nenets. We replenished our resources, rested and fed our reindeer well on lichen, moss and sparse, dried bunch grass. But our leisure did not last long. After a day we were off again, with all the speed we could muster.

Days and hours went by, uncounted. Once more we met natives who were helpful to us. Then, one evening, as we tiredly rode across the cold flat expanse, we spotted lights far in the distance. "Arkhangelsk," exclaimed Korya, pointing. "We will be there in another day or two."

We rejoiced. Surely we could survive two more days and nights. We were so close, what could stop us now? Upon awakening though, we were sorely disappointed. The dreadful east wind had sprung up again and brought snow-kernels of a sharp, icy consistency with it, which, blowing at an angle, lacerated the skin.

Once again we had to curb our impatience and hunker down. It was three days later when we finally came within striking distance of the city.

As we cheerfully contemplated how we would spend the night in a real house, with friends and good food, we heard the roar of a motor.

This time, I sensed trouble from the first. Because of the ever-present wind, we had not heard the patrol car early enough and the interceptors were upon us the moment we became aware of them. "Stop, don't move!" a voice bellowed. We froze in position. "Get off the animals!" was the second command. We slid from the reindeers' backs. Korya was in an awkward, exposed position facing the small military car.

I stood behind him, somewhat hidden from the view of the patrol. "Take this and slide it in the cinch under your animal's belly," hissed Korya. Without moving a muscle in his face, he reached back and slipped something into my hand. I felt the cold steel of the gun, the item that could get us shot or sent to a gulag. Gently, ever so gently, I slipped my hand below my animal's belly. The beasts did not like to be touched there, for it was a most vulnerable spot. Carefully, inch-by-inch, without showing movement to the pursuers, I slipped the cold steel between cinch and belly.

I will never know why the big male stood motionless, allowing me to proceed with what was very unpleasant for him, to say the least. Perhaps he, too, was tired and cold and dully accepted just another torment. Or, perhaps he knew that I would never do anything to harm him and therefore allowed me to proceed undisturbed.

As in our first encounter, two men manned the vehicle. They both came at us, their guns at the ready, pointing at us. Both men wore fur-lined leather clothing, topped by long, heavy greatcoats. Lambskin-lined leather army caps, with earflaps and neck rims, topped their heads. One had a young face with dead, cold eyes. The other's face was wrinkled, tired and mean.

The young one ordered us in harsh tones to put up our hands and let go of the reins. As before Korya begged nicely for the deer to be held, but the young soldier, to harass us, insisted that his order be obeyed. As we let go of the reins, he fired his gun at our feet and the frightened animals ran as if wolves pursued them. I, for one, thanked God. The gun was gone. I did not even think of the consequences arising for us should we survive the search. Everything had proceeded at lightening speed.

Korya groaned, while the older soldier shouted sharply, "Vassily, you idiot. All their stuff is on the backs of those creatures. Nothing to look for now."

"I can catch them with the car," said the young one proudly. "I can run anything down."

The older man groaned, and asked rhetorically, "Why do they always give me these untrained morons?" Then, turning to his moron, he said, "You cannot corral reindeer with a truck. Impossible. They are gone by now."

As if to make up for Vassily's stupidity he became very businesslike. While the young soldier held us at gunpoint, the older man patted us down for weapons. He searched our coats and boots, exposing us to the icy wind. Finding nothing, because our knife, which we used for everything, was in the saddlebag, he demanded to see our papers.

"Hers are in the saddle pack," said Korya grimly, producing his own. "Komi," said the older man dismissively. "Worthless nomads," said Vassily the idiot. "We will take them to the station; the camp is getting short on labor." They ordered Korya to go to the vehicle. For me they had another plan. The young soldier had in mind to at least torment the Komi girl, thereby proving his power and manhood.

While the older one watched, he opened my coat and fondled my breasts. He rubbed against me and did other things. The older man never objected to my mistreatment and debasement. He said, however, "Don't stick it to her. These natives are crawling with gonorrhea." I suddenly felt the crushing pain, as old as time, the great, hopeless pain felt by powerless people subjected to defilement and abuse.

My eyes were beginning to fill with tears. "Don't weaken," I admonished myself, "Don't let him see any feeling he can feed on." I thought of Ivan the Terrible, and my hate returned, steeling me.

Throughout the ordeal, I stood still as a statue. I kept my face frozen and replayed the scene by the river, the moment when I sank the knife into Ivan's back. At last, dead-eyes tired of his amusement, and I buttoned my coat.

"Look at her," he said to the older soldier. "These aboriginals have no feelings, no shame. She never moved a muscle. If it had not been so cold, I could have raped her and she would not have objected."

"To the car," he said, "we are taking you in, so you will learn to work." He pushed me toward Korya. I could read Korya's face—it exuded icy, quiet control. My face, too, hid a look of raging, murderous fury beneath the same stillness.

They were about to load us into the back of the truck when the older man hesitated. He thought for a moment, and said, "Damned, Vassily. Today is Saturday. If we take them to the station we will have to go all the way to the other side of town. I want to go home just once. Have a good meal, a little vodka."

Suddenly, perhaps aroused and wanting a woman, Vassily, my tormentor, did not have the stomach to take us in. "Run away, *davai, davai!* You are free to go," shouted the older man. Korya took my hand and we walked away from the disgusting pair.

"They might shoot us in the back," whispered Korya. "If they fire, don't run, throw yourself on the ground." He knew these types of men well. We had walked perhaps thirty paces or less when a hail of bullets came flying, sending us to the ground. We did not move.

"Korya, are you alright?" I cried.

"I am fine," he answered. "They are only playing with us, having some fun. If they had wanted to kill us we would be dead already."

"How did you know that they would not shoot us on the ground?"

"Experience. I am a hunter. Game runs, exciting in the hunter the kill response. I have often seen bears chase a reindeer down, throwing it onto the ground, if the deer lies motionless the bear sometimes walks away. These men are much like the bear. If we had begun to run, they might have killed us."

We heard the high whine of the engine as it, cold and tormented, refused to start. They cranked it a few times; finally it turned over, and they drove off. We got off the ground. I shivered with cold and fear. Korya shook with fury. "Bastards," he growled, "sons of whores and murderers."

He took my gloved hand in his, saying, "What did he do to you? I could not help you. They had the guns."

"I am alright," I lied for him. "He did things just to humiliate me. Does this happen often to your women?"

"That and more. Not long ago they wanted us to join a fur collective. When we refused they came with helicopters and hunted us like the wolves in the tundra."

While we talked, Korya had set us to a running walk. It was almost totally dark and we needed to find our animals, for even if we walked all night, we could not reach the city. If the wind returned with its forceful assault, we would freeze without a tent. Every so often Korya stood still for a moment and emitted a shrill whistle, a sound piercingly high, penetrating far.

The still night had become gray-black. There were no stars to be seen overhead because large gray clouds covered the sky. "That is good," said Korya, "not so cold." But I knew that he was frustrated. Without the stars he could not navigate, because clouds or fog obscured the lights of Arkhanglesk. Lost and forlorn we stood in the vast landscape as, time and again, he whistled for our reindeer.

I was tired, freezing and past caring. All I wanted to do was to sink to the ground and go to sleep. If I never woke up I would be with God, and my ordeals were over. No sooner did I give in to exhaustion, sinking to the ground, when miraculously, I heard the stamping of hoofs and the cautious sniffing—our gentle companions had returned.

"Oh, Korya," I moaned thankfully, "they have returned, the dear beasts came back to us."

"They know what is good for them," he retorted grimly. "Without a herd and herders they would be easy prey for a wolf pack. They know we can protect them." While he spoke he pulled the tent from the pack animal's back. He told me to retrieve the gun from the girth of my mount, and secure the animal with my belt. Fumbling, we hobbled the animals; bumbling and bungling, our fingers unfeeling and stiff, we erected the tent; groping, we found the last morsels of bread, shreds of meat and drops of water, and consumed them.

As I contorted my body into the tent's small space, I shook with exhaustion, drained by fear and the morbid tensions of this day, shivering with the never-ending cold. I was praying, thanking God for our delivery from evil, our delivery from death. Korya lay silently beside me. He was depleted—his abundance of strength and spirit had ebbed away.

Despite the cold, we soon fell asleep and did not waken until late. The morning was gray and yet cold. We looked wan and worn into the day's ghostly light. There was no more food or water. Slowly, dragging our feet, we packed up our small camp. The animals showed less of yesterday's stress than we did. Korya supposed they had found water somewhere after running away and, although hobbled, had grazed all night. Soon we were moving again.

Strangely enough, the closer we came to the city the more the vegetation improved. Shrubs and strands of trees had once again become numerous. "It's warmer close to the sea," said Korya. "Until the river and the sea freeze over, the coast is warmer than the tundra." He explained to me that Arckangelsk was about thirty miles away from the White Sea. The city spread over both sides of the Northern Dvina and a few islands in that river providing a perfect natural harbor.

City of the Archangel

A government big enough to give you everything you want,
is big enough to take everything you have.
—GERALD FORD

We passed groups of frost-covered houses and huts long before we came close to the city. The homes on the outskirts of the icy city were poor, rough, weathered, unprepossessing. One knew immediately that the people living here were survivors—were tough. They would know how to get by, how to make do with little, how to find their way around the obtuse laws of the government, besting it whenever they could.

We were seeking just such a compound of weathered buildings as the approaching night filled our hearts with desperation. We had not eaten in twenty-four hours, nor did we have anything to drink. Our animals were exhausted. They wanted water and rest as much as we did. Korya finally led us to a compound of small wooden homes huddled around a large, weathered, gray structure, where the tribes sorted their pelts and conducted a lively business in natural commodities.

The people greeting us after our long ordeal were Nenets, business-like, brusque, and as sharp as other entrepreneurs. They had left the tents of the taiga long ago; had settled close to the city and learned the Russian way of life. They were, however, still imbued with the honor code of the tribes—they would never wrong one of their own.

They reminded me of my great grandfather, who had the same demeanor. I understood their attitude. It was one of trade and barter—the belief that a good deed or a business deal was to have a favorable outcome for both sides. They were people who believed that to help a member of the tribe meant to enrich everyone.

The head of the compound greeted Korya, ignoring me as one would overlook a mere appendage. I did not care. As so often in the past year, I was tired. The warmth of the large, plain room we had entered penetrated my fur clothes, making me mellow, drowsy, sleepy. The men talked in the Nenets dialect, of which I still understood nothing.

279

Dully, I thought of my reindeer mount. I had left him with the other two in the care of a young man who had promised to water and feed them. On arrival in the compound, a tremendous feeling of gratitude for this dumb beast overwhelmed me. The patient animal had carried me for over a month over tundra and taiga all they way to the edge of *Beloye More*—the White Sea. Arkhangelsk from afar looked like a monastery city. On a quay, above the river, a few grand buildings erected with rose-colored stone rose into the air. Those buildings, the best the city had to offer, overshadowed the crude, rough working districts. However, all this grandeur I would see only later. Approaching, we had seen only the seedy outlying districts and far away the grand upper part of Arkhangelsk.

Upon reaching the city I felt suddenly that without the beast I would still be out in the wild, a small creature unsuited to withstand the cold, the wolves and the Soviet patrols. Throughout our wanderings, the strong buck had willingly carried me without shying or trying to buck me off, had suffered deprivations without understanding why. Upon arrival, I had stroked his soft nose and he had lowered his head. I knew by now what he wanted me to do. More than anything he liked me to scratch his head between his antlers, a place he could not reach with his hoof.

I stood dumbly, as the elders of this tribe once more decided my fate. I wished I could go back to the hard but simple days of riding through the taiga. I was uneasy, nay, scared to death when I contemplated the means of my escape from this land. What would I be expected to do? Where would I go? Who would look after me like Korya had? Would other people be as kind and dependable as the Komi and the Nenets had been?

An energetic, tall, thin woman in Russian dress came into the room. Her ample dark hair was put up in a braid framing her face. She wore a colorful, wide-sleeved blouse, taken in at the wrist, and a floor-length brown velvet skirt, the sign of a rich woman. Obviously her husband, the Nenets elder, had come up in the world. I would make it my business to find out how he had been doing this so successfully in the new Soviet Russia.

Taking my hand, Marina said in good Russian, "Welcome, please come with me. I will show you where you can clean yourself and make yourself comfortable." True to her word she took me to a small bathroom with a basin. There, a ewer filled with water, real soap and a towel awaited me. She also brought me a long, quilted robe, and told me to wear it.

For the first time in perhaps six weeks I had a thorough cleansing. I washed and combed my hair, feeling like I used to feel at home in Schaffhausen. I had barely finished my transformation, when the energetic, rosy-faced lady came to get me. "Here, please wear these," she said, handing me a pair of embroidered slippers, a skirt and a blouse. "I forgot to give you these before."

"Forgive me for prying, but I would like to ask you a few questions," I asked somewhat shyly.

"Ask," she said.

"Where am I? And why are you so very kind to me? You don't know me yet."

"You are in the house of the Nenets elder, Evgeny Okrug, and I am his Russian wife, Marina Vassilyevna. The reason why I take care of you is your condition. We know that Korya and you had a hard time. You both look as if you need rest and food."

Not long thereafter, the interesting woman took us to a real dining room. Beholding this room, I was transported into another world, a world of the domestic normalcy I had known before my village life ended, and I stood open-mouthed in the door. Marina Vassilyevna, who had gone before me, turned around, enjoying my astonishment. This room was something totally unexpected in this type of house. It was a veneer-paneled room with a long refectory table and many chairs.

On one wall, framed by two silver sconces, hung a large, elaborately framed oil painting of a battle scene, which depicted the Russians storming a Turkish citadel. On the opposite wall stood a large, solid sideboard, centered upon which rested a silver samovar of wondrous proportions. The table, covered with a deep green tablecloth, was set with stoneware dishes and pewter cups and ewers.

"Oh, how lovely," I exclaimed, charmed by so much domesticity. Marina laughed, obviously pleased. She motioned me and the men behind me to the chairs she wished us to take. When we were seated, Marina, at the head of the table opposite from her husband, clapped her hands and three beautiful young girls entered. They were obviously her daughters, carrying large platters and a great ceramic pot to the table.

Skillfully, they first served a delicious cabbage soup, followed by potatoes, a roast and pickled cucumbers. They also brought a white, braided bread, beer and tea to the table. After the lovely maidens had served the fifteen guests, they also were seated and became part of the company.

One could tell at first glance that Evgeny Okrug was pleased with his family, his domestic arrangements and his life in general. No one who saw him sitting there at his large table, dressed in his velvet-embroidered peasant blouse, a heavy gold chain with a cross around his neck, his fingers encircled by massive gold and onyx rings, would have taken him for a nomad herder.

It was only his bronze, large, round face with identifiably Mongol eyes that made one think of his origin, made one wonder about the way he had chosen to arrive at this table. In his manner of conducting the conversation around the table, from guest to guest in fine Russian, he rivaled any powerful man, whether they were tycoons, potentates or commanders, anywhere in the world.

The men discussed their various business deals in both languages. I could grasp snatches of their conversation, and it seemed these modern Nenets were engaged in a multitude of legal and prohibited trade. I heard talk of fish: fresh, dried and salted; of caviar and smoked sturgeon; of pelts, ermine, mink, silver fox and bear hides; of leather products and hides that were barely processed. Furthermore, they were engaged in the selling of vodka to the Allied soldiers. "The good stuff—only the best for the Brits and the Amerikis."

They knew who wanted precious stones, coveted icons and who liked art. And, of course, they traded heavily in miniscule lacquered birch boxes, the folk art the Russians had acquired from the Japanese, but which they had imbued with their very own style and spirit.

"The soldiers cannot get enough of the small Matryoshka dolls. We must have more," said a young man who was smartly dressed all in black in the Russian fashion. His pants were stuck into beautiful leather boots, a fact I noticed when he sidled over to Evgeny's oldest daughter. The girl, a raven-haired beauty with a flawless complexion dusted with a tinge of gold, was much taken with the young man, but her father watched him closely.

Evgeny Okrug now pulled the young man's interest away from his daughter. "Yes, we must have more. The ones made from linden wood, not the other versions, for they swell in moist weather. Also, the foreigners like the intricate dolls, with eight to ten others inside them, for they are the best. So why don't you make that your task! It will involve some travel and will do you good to leave the city for awhile."

Only a very dense person could have missed the direct order to stay away from the girl for some time. The young man, without a hint of being insulted, smiled at the girl and said, "Your papa wants me out of your pretty hair for awhile." Laughing, he bowed to her and returned to his seat.

To my chagrin, Korya was sitting far away from me and although I sat close to Marina, I felt constrained from asking any real questions. I commented on her good food and her lovely, well-behaved daughters, and left it at that.

Suddenly, looking at me across the table, Evgeny Okrug said, "So you finally killed him!"

"Killed whom?" I asked, befuddled. I was unthinking in the moment and did not understand to whom he was referring.

"Kalachnik Bogdanovich, of course," he bellowed.

"I cannot take full credit for the deed," I said modestly, "Suomo finished him off before he could strangle me."

"But you plunged a knife into his back—all the way to the hilt."

"Yes, I did do that, Evgeny Okrug," I agreed. Okrug smiled broadly. "Anyone doing this deed deserves our help. Is this not so, friends?"

"*Da, da*," sounded the enthusiastic response from the men. They raised their tankards and toasted this truth. "So it is agreed, we will seek out passage for her and send her to freedom."

A fresh round of *da, da*, confirmed their enthusiastic agreement. And so, before the day came to an end, I had the assurance of help from a most interesting group of people.

The following days were refreshingly carefree for me. The weather had turned for the better with temperatures between six and ten degrees Celsius. The sun was shining, making even this old, weathered compound look pleasant.

As the men schemed, swarmed the city, and tested their partners for willingness to aid in my escape, I was allowed to just be. I helped Marina Vassilyevna and her girls with the running of the household, and found a Bible and two books of Russian history, which I read in snatches whenever there was a quiet moment.

Marina explained to me her family's unusual interest in my well-being. She stemmed from a family of wealthy merchants, who had been targeted by the Soviets to be disowned and destroyed because they represented the so-called reactionary bourgeoisie. Back then, in 1918, she had been eighteen years old, sheltered and protected, a girl who knew nothing of the world.

When the commissars came to arrest every member of her family, her father, discerning what was about to happen, had hidden his daughter atop a tall, old armoire with a fake upper front. Among the commissars making the arrests was a young, extremely large and strong man, whom the others called by name and to whom they all deferred. Marina would never again forget the name of comrade Kalachnik Bogdanovich. He was the man who had shot her brother and father before they even left the house. He then dragged off her mother, her gorgeous twenty-year-old sister and two female servants, pulling them by their hair, and none were ever heard from again.

Marina had escaped the house before the Reds could come back to plunder. With a parcel of clothes and necessities, she set out not knowing where she was going. The thought had formed in her mind that perhaps she could find sanctuary in a church. From the way the commissars had talked, she knew with certainty that every one of her relatives and her family's friends had already been purged, long before the Reds had come to her house.

It was then, as she walked scared to death, sick with grief and tears in her eyes, that she met Evgeny Okrug. After winning her trust, he dissuaded her from seeking out sanctuary in a church. As he reasonably pointed out, the Orthodox Church had begun to make common cause with the Reds in an effort to retain their large land holdings and the wealth they had acquired.

In those days Evgeny had been a slim, serious young man. Forcibly educated in Russian schools, he was filled with hate and distrustful of all things Russian. He had, however, learned many things useful to him and his tribe, and he planned to implement his new wisdom to help his people circumvent the rules made by others. With guile and intelligence, he had established his little fiefdom, helped by Marina, who had married him only months after meeting him.

"He is a great man, Okrug," said Marina, "a man who keeps his word, who manages his tribe's affairs to their advantage, and he is a good husband and father."

She spoke these words as we walked atop the most unusual surface I had ever paced. To this day, I do not know another city in the world where some of the streets and walks are paved with the finely worked trunks of trees. As we strode along, I brimmed with a sense of well-being. It was unusually warm for this time of year, and we did not wear coats but strode along in blouses and skirts overlaid by woolen shawls. The older daughter of the Okrug household had generously supplied my outfit. Held against my will to a starvation diet for so long, I had fortunately retained the slim body of a seventeen-year-old.

Marina advised me how to wear my hair, so that, together with the look of the outfit, I embodied a Russian woman of the lower middle class. We drove by *droshky* into the commercial part of town. On the way into town Marina talked about the city she loved fiercely, a city that had been built around a fortified monastery, named for the Archangel Michael. She pointed out the richest street, Podyarskaya, the only street in town featuring stone buildings. Later, she had the driver take us along the quay for a view of the Naval and Trinity Cathedral, the monastery and Assumption Church. These grand old buildings outlined against the shiny white water of the Northern Dvina left me with an unforgettable impression.

Then we had gone to the large market. This market, although farther north than any I knew, was better supplied with goods than the markets I knew in the towns along the Volga. The variety of fish, game, produce, meat and spices was reminiscent of oriental bazaars. Other sections offered pottery, household items, icons, jewelry, furs, willow and sedge baskets, quilted jackets and other products.

Marina chose carefully. She often decided in favor of quality over quantity. On this day she picked large filets, shining pearly with freshness, of a whitefish unknown to me. She picked cabbages, carrots and beets, ignoring other vegetables less robust and fresh.

As we walked back to the rickety *droshky*, a starveling horse between the shafts, she pointed to the many beautiful wooden houses along the street. As if to defeat the snow and frost that painted their town white for six months of the year, many of the elaborate buildings were painted in brilliant colors: shades of green from lime green to dark forest green, blues, from the palest to the deepest, hues from yellow to gold, together with various shades of pink and red.

I filled my eyes with the joyful picture, which was warmed, enhanced by the rays of the autumn sun. "Enjoy," said Marina, "this might be the last of autumn. Tomorrow we could be in the middle of winter. We live in a clean, clear, cold town where winter reigns half the year."

While in town, Marina bought a dress, a coat, stockings and underwear for me. "We don't know what you will need where you are going, so we will buy what you normally would wear here." What a reasonable thought! I thanked Marina with deep gratitude. For a while, we speculated how my escape from Russia might be facilitated.

"*Och*, leave that for the men," she said, in her practical way. "They will not tell us anything until it is time for you to leave."

And, she was right. Korya came and went with Evgeny Okrug at all hours of the day. Strange men came to dinner; afterwards, the men disappeared into Evgeny's *Kontor*. One day Korya brought a tailor to the house, who measured me for a man's suit. "We might have to cut your lovely hair," Korya said, his voice filled with regret.

"So be it. If we must do it, we will." I said, taking the news as matter of fact, handling it so casually that Korya said with annoyance, "Perhaps you don't even know what a treasure you have there."

"It is hair, Korya, it will grow back," I laughed.

"Yes, and I will not be there to see it," he replied sadly. I knew then that he loved me; loved me more than I could fathom, more than he ever let on. My heart was suddenly filled with a flood of emotions, as though they had slumbered there for years—harshly suppressed. Long ago I had a great liking, or perhaps love, for Arkady. I knew that I had loved Alyosha with a passion that I thought would never die, yet the flame was extinguished, snuffed out by hopelessness, abysmal fear and murder. For Korya, I felt a strange mixture of friendship, love, deep appreciation and attraction. And so, driven by my upwelling emotions and without a thought, I went to Korya, embracing him, kissing him devotedly.

He responded with such fervor, it took my breath away. For a while we stood there, sensually embracing like lovers, until suddenly his face clouded and he broke from my arms.

"No, no more," he said. "I cannot bear it. You will leave soon and I remain here." He turned and left me alone in the room, which had suddenly become cold.

Planning the Flight

A few days later, very early in the morning, Korya and I entered a *droshky* that drove us to a house on the quay. It was the once handsome stone and timber home of a purged merchant. Deprived of the care its former owner had lavished on the mansion, abused by the Red Army and Soviet functionaries, it had deteriorated to the point where the Soviet found it advantageous to sell it off to the highest bidder.

Somehow it became the office and supply house of one of Okrug's associates. In the front rooms, on the ground floor, were the offices of Anton Derevnikov; the back rooms were used for storage. On the two floors above were living quarters, which sometimes, besides the man himself, housed Derevnikov's diverse business partners.

With a heavy heart, I had said goodbye to the Okrugs, who wished me well and prayed for me. Now, with my small bundle of clothes and personal things, gifts from Marina Vassilyevna and her girls, I entered this house. Korya opened the huge, carved wooden door for me. Cautiously I stepped into the impressive old foyer, a neglected yet still dignified room.

From there, a door inset with colored glass panels led into the office. A most unusual room it was. Paneled with fine wood, which still bore the abuse of the Red Army in the form of scratches and knife slashes, hung with precious icons, its wood floor covered by an old Persian rug, its walls laden with shelves of old books, the room looked more like an uncaring man's library than an office.

Across from a large sectioned and curved window, behind a massive table, sat the owner of the place. Anton Derevnikov was an interesting man. At first glance, he appeared to be a charming actor of comedies. Of medium height, with a shock of brown curls and deep brown eyes in an oval, elegant face, he was clothed in a soft, comfortable suit of amber brown velvet and wool. Therefore, he looked on second thought like the prodigal heir to a fortune.

As I got to know him better, I discerned that his unconventional appearance and his forever cheerful, polite and tactful disposition enabled him to accomplish the impossible tasks and the deals for which he was known.

No one else could have satisfied the wishes of the Red Army, the local Soviet, the merchants, the police, the native traders and the Allied soldiers without ending up in prison or in a gulag. Derevnikov, however, could do all that and more.

Korya introduced us, saying, "Anton Antonovich Derevnikov, I am pleased to present Katya."

Here he was interrupted by Derevnikov, who reminded him kindly, "No names, no names, please."

"I am sorry," said Korya abjectly because he had forgotten this important rule of their association. "I know all that I need to know about the young lady," said Derevnikov, reminding us that Evgeny Okrug had apprised him on all important matters.

"We will take care of you, mistress Katya," he assured me. "For now we will make you comfortable, show you to your room, and then we will eat and talk." He told Korya to take me upstairs, "the third room on the left with a view over the river," and then to return for the noon meal.

It was obvious that Derevnikov liked his comfort, liked well-prepared amenities. This craving extended to the preparation of his food. A large, comfortable woman with a white apron and a white, ruffled cap atop graying hair and a happy broad face, greeted us. In the opulently furnished dining room, she set before us a large platter, which displayed the largest omelet I had ever seen. Portions of smoked fish, meat and fowl surrounded it.

To make my day complete she brought loaves of freshly baked bread and butter and cheese, for which my eyes grew large with greed. I had not known how much I missed these simple, everyday foods. Oh, butter, golden, sweet and spreadable! I indulged my eyes, tasted every last morsel, rolling it over and over in my mouth until every smidgen of flavor had fully developed, saturating my senses, appeasing my ravenous stomach.

Everything in Derevnikov's house was larger than in ordinary life. The goblets—he served me wine—and the beer tankards for the men were enormous. The apple cake his cook brought in for his approval was studded with fruit, flat as the tundra, and just as large. I will never know how, in those desperate times, real cream could be served in an average Russian home, and yet here they had a pitcher of cream filled to the brim.

There were only the three of us dining, Korya, Derevnikov and I, and we enjoyed ourselves immensely. At first the men talked and I listened. They were frank about their business deals. I listened with astonishment as bits and pieces of Derevnikov's business acumen and his power in the city were revealed.

Apparently, everyone in the city who needed a favor, whether they looked for food, furs, wood to heat their home, fresh fish, a case of vodka, or tickets for the theater, anything at all, could, for a price, be supplied in no time. Not only was Derevnikov the "concierge" of the mighty, in fact, he helped everyone, even the lowliest, who knew how to approach him. One, for example, was Evgeny Okrug, who had become an important part of his operation.

"How do you do this?" I asked, and he frankly explained how it was done.

The way his business was conducted was very clever. Ostensibly he dealt in vodka—very fine vodka. He kept the vodka in the house, in large wooden cases, which was acceptable to the Soviet functionaries who examined his books and extracted his tax monies. He paid plenty in taxes. Few people ever came to the house. Still he, like everyone else, was watched closely. Therefore, he made the rounds in the cafés and the bars where he talked to his "clients."

He employed three men who made vodka deliveries and could be engaged in an emergency. If the commandant of the naval citadel wanted to throw a lavish party for the British, he called upon Derevnikov to supply the cooks, the vodka, fowl, game, deserts, cigars and beer, and knew that everything would be of the best quality, timely served and handled discreetly.

Derevnikov also dealt indirectly and, on occasion, even directly with the Allies. They would request what they wished to purchase through the Soviet officials with whom they dealt, and he provided those things not available through normal channels. For this unaccounted, under-the-table business to flourish, Derevnikov greased the palms of many. No one else could have run such a shadow empire and gotten away with it. But Derevnikov was liked, even esteemed by everyone. He had no enemies. He was unobtrusive, inoffensive, filled with the best of humor at all times, and knew how to placate the ugliest officials.

"Are you not afraid that they might catch and torture me into giving all your secrets away?" I asked aghast, when I understood the extent of the man's associations, his forbidden dealings.

"My dear, if you were to talk to anyone about my shady life, your life would be extinguished instantly." He smiled impishly, "You see, so many men would lose their heads if anything about me became public knowledge that I am quite safe in their midst."

He filled my glass again with the delicious yellow wine he was serving, and although I should have refused, I sipped. "We shall explore how to get you aboard a ship," he said suddenly. My mellow mood evaporated and I became terribly tense.

"Do you speak English?" he asked, "even just a little?"

"No. I speak French, very well, my mother taught me."

"Hmmm, not one Belgian or Dutch ship is in town, only Brits."

"Why is English necessary?" I asked.

"Were you to speak it, I could stick you into a sailor's uniform and get you on board. Our harbor guards, however, speak English or have interpreters with them. Out of boredom or a perverted sense of duty, they like to challenge the sailors. Also, every group of foreigners allowed on land for liberty is provided with an escort. They are also constrained in their choice of restaurants, bars and areas to be visited. It would be hard to sneak you into a group without English."

"Perhaps she could learn," said Korya. "Just a few phrases to get by."

"Not enough time," said Derevnikov. "The ship I might get her on is the *HMS Intrepid*, a destroyer, acting as escort."

"My God," said Korya, upset, "that will put her in great danger! The escort ships are the first ones to draw fire."

"No matter. The Germans try to send every ship to the bottom. At least on a destroyer she has some powerful defense weapons in her favor. The man I have approached and bribed—which took plenty of favors, persuasion and precious stones, for he wants to marry a rich girl and needs to supplement his poor navy pay—will look after Katya quite well. I told him Katya is a resister, he liked that a lot. He hates Stalin, and if it were not for his patriotism—Hitler after all bombs his country viciously—he would just as well fight Stalin."

Derevnikov, looking like the foil to the ingénue in a play, drank deeply from his glass. He smiled intrigued as if solving a puzzle, and said, "Too bad, I had a very nice uniform made up for her already. Now, to the next plan." He turned to me and asked, "Are you claustrophobic, my dear?"

"No, I am not. I can deal with confined spaces."

"We could try a vodka case. Or a pickle or herring barrel." Korya interrupted him. "They stink. She will pass out and smell forever of pickles or herring."

"I don't mind the smell as long as it gets me out of Russia."

"Good girl. We will try them out tomorrow and see if you can stand the confinement and the smell."

"How about hiding her in a bundle of fur?" contributed Korya.

"They are pressed too tightly. She could suffocate. And sometimes the guards count the furs in the bundles."

"Are any Russians ever going on board to do anything?" I asked, trying to come up with a solution.

"No, no one is allowed aboard. Perhaps with the exception of an admiral or commandant for an official visit."

By late afternoon we gave up the seemingly futile exercise of finding a way to smuggle me aboard the *Intrepid*. Anton Antonovich called for a *droshky*, taking us for a drive through the city. Here and there we stopped at a café or a bar, which he briefly visited, taking orders. Business always demanded his attention and sometimes his presence.

He returned from one of his explorations unusually quiet and deep in thought. "You will forgive me, friends, but I have obligations to take care of. Therefore, you will please excuse me if I leave you now and have the *droshky* take you home."

Back at his house, his cook served us a lovely dinner. Upstairs, she showed me to a bathroom with a wonderful claw-footed bathtub and soft, white towels. I bathed and went to sleep in the large bed in my clean white-and-green bedroom.

For the next two days I was often left to my own devices. Korya and Anton Antonovich went their separate ways, yet each was on a common quest. I read. There were many books in the house and I had been deprived of intellectual stimulation for a long time.

A few times, in search of human contact, I joined the cook in her gargantuan domain. She kindly allowed me in, but only if I refrained from touching anything.

She did, however, tell me tales of her employer, of whom she spoke with the tender love of a devoted mother. "Anton is the kindest, most likable man I have ever known," she said. "He helped my husband when he came home from the front, his leg shot up, and he could not work. Can you believe it, but Derevnikov paid all the hospital bills. Then, when my husband was better, Anton Antonovich gave him a job—a good job."

It turned out that her husband had become one of Derevnikov's runners. "He helps many people. I could give you lists of names of people he has helped."

She shot me a meaningful glance, "He will help you too, dear. This is how he is."

Escape

Early the next morning, all hell broke loose. Korya woke me from a deep sleep. Breathless and fast, his words poured over me like an ice-cold waterfall, waking me.

"There will be no rehearsal as we had planned. It has to be now! Not a moment later."

"What is going on?" I asked, still half drowsy.

"The *Intrepid* is leaving, and you must be on it. The lading began during the night. God only knows how much time we will have."

For the first time since I had met Korya he was in a state of excitement that instantly transmitted itself onto me. Throwing off the covers, I jumped from my warm bed.

My hands shook as I performed the well-known tasks of the morning. Korya laid out two different outfits before me. One was a plain, almost ugly dress, the other an elaborate beautiful costume complete with hat, gloves, elegant shoes and a fancy wrap.

"Put this one on first," he ordered, pointing at the ugly one. "Then put the other one over it." Unquestioningly, I did what I was told, while he explained to me how the men involved in my escape plot had strategized in the early morning hours to implement a quick getaway.

"We are improvising, doing everything as best we can. You must be on this ship."

"Why not another?" I asked stupidly, "There are other foreign vessels in the harbor."

"Don't you understand? The *Intrepid* is one of the escort ships. When she leaves, the entire convoy leaves. Also, we have bribed people on the *Intrepid*—no one on the other ships. So you see, this is it."

While we talked, my hands flew over my body as I tightened sashes, buttons and hooks. I placed the elaborate, large black hat, sporting a white plume along one side, upon my head, fastened the hat to my head with long, pearl-handle pins, and lastly, I slipped into the elegant, high-heeled, little black boots. No time for breakfast. The moment I was dressed, Korya summoned me to leave.

We ran down the steps of the fine old staircase, setting it to groan and creak under our pounding steps. Below, in the hall, Anton Antonovich awaited us, calling out:

"Korya, say goodbye to Katya. We must leave at once."

I hugged and kissed Korya, who looked sad, confounded and forlorn. Anton pulled me away.

"*Davai, davai!* Fast! Out! Now!"

Outside, his usual *droshky* awaited us. As in a play, Anton graciously handed me into the *droshky*, as if we had all the time in the world. He walked around the vehicle, entering from the other side. Instantly, the *droshky* drove off at a fast pace.

"What was the ceremony about?" I asked, "I thought we are in a hurry." I had to ask, although my eyes were still moist with goodbye tears. Despite the sharp pain of leave-taking, I was forever curious about everything.

"That, my dear, was theater for the vicious, prying eyes watching my house at all times. They will think I am taking a lady love home and that is good for us." He looked searchingly out of the window and said, "No one out there! So, take off the fancy outfit and keep on the other."

Off came the fancy hat, the long, soft gloves and the flippant little wrap, while the *droshky* flew along at an extended trot. Anton helped me with the buttons in the back, while I pulled open the sash and the hooks. Throughout my transformation, the driver never turned his head or paid the least attention to us. Instead, he remained tightly focused on the road.

As the dress slid over my hips and onto the floor, the coarse, gray dress of a working girl was now my costume. From his pocket, Anton pulled a cap, as coarse and gray as the dress.

"So, now you are a worker in the potato shed," he said, and then explained the plan. "The British are provisioned by the government with food and water for their voyage home. I, Anton, provide potatoes, vodka and furs. My men have agonized over the best method to smuggle a live body onto the ship and settled on the following: the potatoes are carried aboard in huge baskets, some so heavy that two men shared the load, which then are emptied into a large bin by the kitchen.

You will be in one of these baskets. We will try a diversion when they carry you in. The officer keeping the tally by the potato bin is in on the plot. On arrival inside, you will step from the basket and hide behind the bin. There, you will find a bundle of warm clothing for the voyage along the ice. At some point, when the convoy has gone too far to return you, the men will reveal your presence to the captain."

My head was spinning. "How did you manage to persuade so many people to help me, risking their lives?" I asked, nonplussed by the elaborate plan.

"Jewels, Korya gave me jewels to rescue you. Some I sold as bribery money, some I used directly." He smiled a disarming, charming smile, and admitted, "I myself profited handsomely, by keeping a large emerald for myself. I hope you don't mind?"

"No," I said thoughtfully. Understanding struck me like lightening. Dear Suomo, who could have made his tribe rich, had instead used the fortune to buy me safe passage. By giving the jewels to Korya, he had sacrificed to save me. I was overwhelmed by the generosity of the Komi and began to cry.

"No, no! Do not cry. No breaking down now, my dear." Anton patted my hand and wiped my face with his immaculate white handkerchief.

"It was not all done with money and jewels," he said. "Many people are helping just because they want a plot, representing a strike against the Soviets, to succeed. You see, we are caught in a tragic dilemma. We are patriots who want to win the war against the Germans, but we also hate the brutality of the Soviets and will fight them for the rest of our lives once the war is over."

Amid his explanations, we had reached our destination. Anton's potato and vodka shed was situated in the middle of the harbor quay. The *Intrepid*, however, lay half a mile away at anchor at the very mouth of the harbor. There it was connected to the quay by a long gangway, which necessitated that all supplies had to be trucked to the ship.

Our *droshky* had stopped in front of a large, dilapidated, wooden structure. We left the *droshky* and moments later entered the shed. Inside, similar to most other of Anton's endeavors, the shed looked solid. It was well cared for, chinked, caulked, warm and dry, another miracle of deception.

Anton had learned early in life that perception was everything. People were willing to believe what was ostensibly put before their eyes, without analyzing the incongruities. If the outside was shabby and poor, they assumed the whole building must be worthless. He told me that his innocent deceptions were the result of early childhood discoveries.

"People rarely think," he laughed amusedly. "They emote! This is how tyrants like Stalin can become powerful. People always look for a savior—for one man who will make the difference. They never perceive their own power, their own complicity in historical events." He laughed again, with harshness and anger this time as he spun out his theory:

"In Stalin, they worship the person of the powerful avuncular, elder friend—an act he has so carefully rehearsed that he performs it flawlessly on stage. He makes the masses believe that he will take care of them, protect and feed them, in effect be their parent."

While expounding his theories, we had walked to a large table where women attired much as I was sorted potatoes by size into different baskets.

"The Brits only want medium to large potatoes," he explained. "Our people are happy to get any size if only they can get them at all." I examined the baskets, nervously measuring them for size. Would I fit into them? Possibly. They were quite large.

"Come along," demanded Anton. I followed him quickly into his *Kontor*, passing a station where men washed potatoes in large cement basins by spraying them with pressure hoses. "The Brits do not care for dirt clods on their potatoes, so we wash them," explained Anton as we hastened through the shed.

In the middle of the *Kontor* stood a large old rolltop desk. Otherwise it was an unremarkable drab room, windowless, with plank siding and flooring. Below a green metal lamp hanging from the ceiling, hundreds of official notices were tacked on the walls. Standing in the light of the lamp, two men anxiously awaited our arrival. My eyes fastened on a giant of a man, for it was impossible to look elsewhere first.

At least six feet six inches tall, with enormous shoulders, arms that were attached to a barrel of a chest and legs as solid and round as tree trunks, he was so awe-inspiring a figure that no eye could avoid him. He had a friendly face, bright blue eyes and short, dark-blond hair. In sum, he was a strong, handsome man.

The other man seemed blanched beside him. He was as short as the other was tall. His triangular face reminded me of a fox's visage, and his eyes were as smart and cunning as the eyes of that animal. He exuded an actor's energy and, in the end, managed to draw attention away from his tall partner.

Upon seeing Anton, the giant said, "I have the perfect basket."

"Hello, Gavrilov," greeted the so addressed.

"Shall we try it, and if it works, we make the run?" asked Gavrilov. Anton looked at me, "Do you know your weight?"

"No, I lost so much weight in camp that I do not know anymore," I confessed.

"Nothing I cannot handle," smiled Gavrilov, the giant, confidently.

"Alright then, if it works we will make the run," said Anton, his face serious and tense. Thereupon Gavrilov lifted me as easily as if I were a small child and placed me into the basket in front of him. Standing upright, the rim of the basket came to my waist. There was enough room in the basket to sit down, and so, knees pulled to my chest, I sat.

"Good," groaned Anton, relief in his voice. For the first time I realized how much pressure he was under. He always made everything seem so easy, as if there were no problems attached to his plans. I now knew differently.

"Alright, let's cover her up and do it!" Oh, God! I realized that the moment had come, when our cabal could send many men and me to death or the gulag. I shivered with sudden fear. Someone covered me with cloth and then, covering me, they filled the basket to the rim with potatoes.

"How is this? Can you endure this position for a while? About half an hour?" asked Anton.

Despite my fear and doubt, I said, "Yes, I can! I can do it."

Unceremoniously, without allowing anyone to have second thoughts, Anton said almost harshly, "Good, we will do the thing right now!"

The giant Gavrilov lifted the basket and swung it onto his back. It felt strange, being part of a load, as the basket settled on his back.

"Goodbye and good luck, Katya," Anton called to me.

"Thank you for everything, Anton Antonovich! May God bless you and all the men who are part of our endeavor," I cried, and then the giant began to walk.

Outside Gavrilov lifted the basket high into the air. "I am putting you with other baskets on the truck, which will take you to the *Intrepid*," he said. I heard him talking to the small vulpine man, who was going with us. His name was Butrin. From their conversation I understood that he had an exceedingly dangerous part in the play to ferry me safely on board.

The truck groaned and rattled, spitting fumes into the air as it creaked the half mile down river. Abruptly it came to a stop. We had arrived. Gavrilov lifted the basket with me inside from the vehicle. "Not a sound!" he admonished.

I heard Butrin pick up a basket also. He groaned and complained fiercely. Some soldiers shouted that his large partner should carry him plus his load too. Butrin acerbically returned their abuse, derisive joke for derisive joke. He was extraordinarily comical. I heard the guards roar with laughter, and understood why he had been chosen to work with the giant.

Gavrilov began to walk, shaking me gently with each step. My heart pounded: this is it. This is it! If this succeeds, I will be free at last! Behind us the foxy-faced Butrin whined and complained about his hefty load.

I heard an exchange between Gavrilov and the guards. "They must be at the guard posts stationed before one reached the gangway," I thought, for I had seen earlier how Russians guards were posted at the bottom of the gangways of other ships.

"Stop, giant!" shouted a soldier. "Let us see what you carry so carefully in your basket."

"The English queen! What do you think? Potatoes! Of course! You know damned well we carry potatoes."

The pesky guard, however, insisted, "Let us see what you carry!"

"Damn!" boomed Gavrilov, "my load is too heavy already, and none of you will lift the basket onto my shoulders again once it is on the ground."

I was sick with fear at that moment, for our passage was cut off. I knew with the certainty infused by fear that the guards would find me upon inspection. At that moment of great anxiety, a loud disturbance ensued. Angry shouts erupted. I heard Butrin's voice, cursing and yelling, accusing the guards of harassment, of menacing him, of making the life of a good Soviet citizen a miserable torment.

I heard people scampering, cajoling, laughing, and above the fray, Butrin's cries of retribution. A tribunal he wanted, to adjudge all miserable, no-good, non-working sons of curs guarding the gates of hell who interfered with working men, the best the worker state had to offer.

At the onset of the commotion, Gavrilov had begun to walk again as if no one had challenged him. Throughout the shouting, he walked unperturbed, evenly measuring his steps as if walking through a market in search of bargains. The cries behind us sounded fainter and fainter; fewer and fewer were the words I could understand from the distant commotion.

A heavily accented voice challenged Gavrilov. "Potatoes," he said, and they let him go. I felt how he made his way down a narrow stairway. Narrow, because he bumped and banged into the walls numerous times, before his gait evened out again. I felt him turning to the right, walking steadily.

"You are safe, Katya," he growled pleasantly. He stopped walking and swung the basket off his back onto the ground.

"Is that the illegal cargo?" asked a man's voice in bad Russian.

"*Da, da,*" agreed Gavrilov. He picked up the potatoes that covered me by the handfuls, throwing them into the bin, and plucked the cover off me. "Stand, Katya," he said softly. I unwound my body, stretched upward, and quickly looked around. Beside the basket to my right stood a uniformed young officer. On a tablet he held sheaves of paper. He looked at me and grinned a young man's mischievous grin.

"Welcome," he said in his accented Russian, and then he turned away and ignored us. "Goodbye and good luck, Katyusha," said Gavrilov with deep feeling, the excitement of our escape reverberating in his voice.

"I don't know how to thank you," I cried. "Only God can reward you for your goodness and valor." I kissed Gavrilov on the cheek. He had to bend very low for that kiss. Again he wished me luck, swung his basket over his shoulder and left.

Automatically, I did as I had been told. I walked to the rear of the potato bin. Sure enough, behind the large, wooden crate the curved hull of the ship left a narrow tunnel for me to crawl into. True to Anton's word, at the end of the tunnel I touched a soft bundle of hide and fur. Safe, I fell into a state of collapse. Every muscle in my body seemed to become gelatinous.

"Lord," I thought gratefully, "You have seen me through the most unusual adventures. You have preserved me when hunger and disease should have taken me from this earth. You sent me an avenger when I was close to death, sent me a rescuer and many peoples willing to risk their life to help me. So, Lord, I ask you now, please see me safely to a new homeland where I can live as I know I should live."

I had not prayed with a full heart for a while. Every day my life had been filled with new adventures, sights, experiences, excitements, emotions and knowledge. A wealth of strange, powerful living in a very short time had consumed my mind and demanded all my attention.

I heard the potato men coming and going. One after another they emptied their baskets, their loads tumbling noisily into the bins. Overcome by the emotional turmoil of the day, I must have fallen asleep, for I awoke to the repetitious, powerful pounding of engines. It was totally dark. I smelled oil and the earthiness of the potatoes, and I was cold.

The significance of finding myself on the high seas aboard a destroyer, while cringing with cold, finally sank in. Since the murder of Ivan the Terrible, I had fervently hoped to escape the land of my birth, a land that had become an empire of slavery and death for its own innocent citizens. However, I had not been able to conceive that my hope would turn to reality.

I realized that the odds against flight from Russia had been overwhelming. And yet, I heard the roar of the engines, smelled the oily fuel, and felt the rise and fall of the ship as it broached the swells. The plan, envisioned by a Komi spirit man, and which his tribe had conspired to carry through had finally set me free. Boundless love for those I left behind overcame me. As I remembered each and every one, I cried.

I cried for Suomo, Samea, the spirit elder, Korya, Okrug and Marina, smart, amusing Derevnikov, and the final actors in this enormously dangerous play, Butrin and Gavrilov. I mourned for the wonderful Russian people who lived in this vast country, who endured and by their very decency triumphed. At last, spent, I became aware of my cramped position. I had been instructed to wait for someone to contact me, but I was freezing.

Inching backward, pulling the bundle of clothes behind me, I emerged from my hiding place. Out in the storage room I could finally see my surroundings in the diffused illumination of a few dirty light bulbs, naked in their sockets.

However, that was enough light for me to see the items in the bag. First off, I found a coat and a fur blanket. From a deeper layer I pulled fur-lined boots from my treasure bag. At the very bottom, I found a fur hat and mittens. I would survive!

Quickly I slipped into the boots and the coat, feeling instantly warmer. I now saw the wisdom that had placed me in the storeroom. This was the room next to the kitchen. The temperature would never go below freezing in this compartment where fruits, vegetables, bottles of vodka and kegs of beer were stored.

Looking around, I identified the different storage units. I saw bins of carrots, cabbage and onions. Farther away, in the back, seemed to be a meat and a dairy locker. Metal shelves were studded with claw-like devices, holding bottles in firm grips. There were barrels of beer and oil and cases of vodka, stamped with black ink. I smiled when I thought that here I would not die of starvation—not amid carrots, cabbage and potatoes.

But what would I drink? I was thirsty. Hungry, too. I hoped that someone would remember that I was on board. And where was a toilet I could use? These contemplations panicked me. What if they had forgotten about me? I only knew of one young man, the potato basket counter, who knew I was here.

To put my mind at ease, I said prayers for my mother, my brother, Arkady and Alyosha, prayers for everyone deserving my gratitude. Soon I was plagued by the urge to relieve myself. The more I tried to banish the thought of my need, the more I needed to go.

Finally, in desperation I wandered about looking for a suitable container. I was in extremis. It was only normal that this should be so. Since perhaps four in the morning all my bodily functions had been curtailed. I assumed that now it was eight or nine o'clock in the evening.

In the middle of my search, I heard a sound. The big round lock turned on what I assumed to be the huge steel door to the kitchen. Beside me was a shelving unit. I hid behind it as well as I could. The man who entered the storage room looked furtively around, and seeing no one, slipped over to the potato bin where he peered into my hiding place.

He straightened up and scratched his head. "What the devil," he murmured, "she was supposed be behind the potato bin." I did not understand what he was saying, but his state of utter confusion led me to believe he was searching for me. For a moment I hesitated, but then I took a chance and stepped forward.

"Are you looking for me?" I said. Relief spread over his face, like sunshine over a meadow. "Ah, there you are!" he exclaimed in Russian. "How are you?"

"Happy to be here. But I very much need a toilet."

"Come with me!" He led, and I followed him into the kitchen. "I just got rid of the cook. We need to hurry, because he will be back to prepare sandwiches for the night watch."

With sure movements, he guided me through the stainless steel galley, past huge ovens, counters, sinks and shelves upon which canned foods and seasonings resided, corralled by crisscrossed steel. Having navigated the long, narrow galley, which was designed to keep the cooks within reach of everything in a storm, without being bounced about, we reached another door.

Beyond this door lay a mess room and, thankfully, to the left a head. "I will stand guard," said my new friend, whom I now recognized as the young man with the tally sheet.

"If I whistle do not come out." I worried that we might be discovered. We were still too close to Arkhangelsk. No one knew how the captain would react to the discovery of a stowaway. Close to the city he might call a patrol boat and hand me over to the Soviets.

However, all went well. My friend took me back through the kitchen where he picked up a plate of sandwiches and a pitcher of water. He dared not hang about the storage room a moment longer, but left me with my provisions.

"Stay hidden," he admonished me. "The cooks can come in here at any time looking for supplies."

Therefore, I sat in front of my hidey-hole eating and drinking. At last, quite happy with the world, I crawled back into my space behind the bin and went to sleep.

The Attack

I lived like this for four or five days, in somewhat of a daze. In my head I replayed scenes of camp life, the rescue by Suomo, travel with Korya and the miracles that brought me on board. Twice daily my precious keeper came, lead me to the head and to provision me. Then, during what I thought to be my fifth night on board, all hell broke loose. A monstrous explosion shook the ship, tossing it in the air as if it was made from cardboard instead of steel.

After the ship fell back into the seas, throwing me about, it shook like a dog shakes water off its coat. Sirens screamed, whistles shrilled, the ship ran with greater power than before. Its engines were pounding, howling and roaring like beasts. I crawled from my confinement where, before the explosion, I had almost fallen asleep.

I could barely stand on my feet, when another awesome force hit the ship. The boom and crash were deafening. I thought, "A bomb has struck the ship and we will sink," as I slammed into metal shelves.

A great fear took hold of me: I did not want to die in the icy Bering Sea, hidden below deck. I wanted to live, or die standing on deck—in the cold freezing air with the stars above me. The idea of dying like a mouse in a runnel below deck was so physically abhorrent to me that I became nauseous. Braving exposure to the crew of the *Intrepid*, I began to manipulate the kitchen door lock.

Magically, the door opened. On the other side stood my friend and co-conspirator. It dawned on me this very moment that I did not even know his name.

"I came to get you! We are being attacked by German planes and I want you above, on deck," he screamed. Stupidly, I yelled, "What's your name? I must know your name!" Somehow it had become very important to me to know this man's name.

"Elliot Bromfield!" he cried. "What does it matter? We are being attacked!"

"It matters, Elliot Bromfield! If you die, I want to know for whom to say my prayers! If I die, I want you to pray for Katharina Grushov!" He grabbed my arm and pulled me toward a stairway that led to the upper deck.

Above, everything was dark. Every light had been extinguished. Because the night was clear, I was able to see the organized chaos on deck. Sailors ran across deck in every direction, seemingly aimless. They, however, followed an intricate plan they had trained for. They rolled hoses off wheels, manned guns, ran to take positions abandoned by injured mates.

Elliot ran off to God knows where, leaving me leaning against the superstructure. I looked around and was awed. I had, of course, never seen the ship carrying me across the icy waters of the Bering Sea. The *HMS Intrepid* was huge—over three hundred feet long. I looked up and directly above me was the bridge. Behind the bridge, aft, a huge tower rose into the sky. Farther aft, two tremendous smoke stacks reached for the heavens.

That was all my cursory glances discerned. A hail of bullets raining down upon the ship, sowing death, mesmerized me with fear. Above the ship, squadrons of German airplanes pounded the ship with bombs, which fell around us, roilling the water, and strafed our decks with machine gun fire.

I now was able to discern that the *Intrepid* was a ship on the right flank of a convoy of many different vessels. Some of them, awkward like fat ducks, sat in the water ready to be shot to kingdom come. I heard orders shouted, saw soldiers running—nothing made sense to me. I was gratified to see that everyone was too busy to pay attention to a stowaway.

Another explosion nearby caused havoc among the men. I saw bodies flying in every direction. One of the limp bodies landed right in front of me. I bent over the man, trying to help, and discovered that he was out cold, bleeding and obviously seriously hurt. Right then, my uninvolved observations ended.

I knew about emergencies, knew about taking care of hurt, injured people and creatures. Deeply ingrained, the old teachings came to the fore. I knew I had to get the man away from the firefight into a protected place where I could take care of his wounds. I grabbed him under his armpits and dragged him inside.

In the narrow, metal stairwell I came across a sailor who looked at me in wonderment. He understood that I had a problem. Silently, he helped me get the man below. We opened the first door into a compartment. Luckily for the wounded man it held a few beds. We lifted the sailor onto the very first bed, at which point my helper smiled at me and left. Never having said a word, he acted as though I were a mirage.

I threw off my coat, giving myself room to operate. Suddenly I was hot. I opened the man's jacket and shirt, which were soaked with blood, and found to my happy surprise that his chest was free of injury. As I removed his jacket I felt something hard inside the pocket and discovered a good, sharp knife, which I used to cut a sheet from the neighboring bed into strips. He had a superficial head wound, which bled copiously. I cleaned it with a piece of torn sheet. Finding the wound manageable, I wrapped a piece of sheet tightly around his head and proceeded to look for other injuries.

At this point, he awoke and looked at me dazed, stupidly. He said something in English, which I, of course, did not understand. Before I could stop him he sat up, groaned, and fell back again. A head injury, possibly a concussion, I diagnosed. There was nothing further I could do for him. For now he just would have to lie quietly.

To keep him from hurting himself, I cut some more strips of sheeting and tied him, hand and foot, to the bed. Above, on deck, the horror raged. Although very absorbed in my ministrations, I heard the tumult above and knew there would be more broken bodies and that helping hands were needed.

Strangely, not once did I fear for my life or fear for the safety of the ship. I knew we were in the hands of God and he would protect us or would want us to come to him—it mattered not. The very moment I had my man strapped down, I ran up onto the deck. Not a moment too soon. A doctor and a bevy of medics flew about deck triaging the wounded. I saw a likely candidate with a shattered leg valiantly suppressing his screams and I thought, "I can help him!"

Bolder now, I waved over a white-coated fellow and had him help me move the hurt man below deck. He said something in English and I answered in Russian, and lo and behold, he knew enough Russian to tell me to take care of the man until he could return with syringes of morphine.

I softly talked in Russian to the young sailor who was a study in valiant control. I cut off his pant leg to the hip and applied a tourniquet above his knee. There was nothing else I could do. His leg, with its protruding bone, needed to be set and cast. The medic in the white coat returned. He shot morphine into a vein of the injured man's arm and the patient relaxed.

"You must help me set this leg," said the medic, whose name was O'Shaughnessy, as a badge proclaimed. On closer examination of the wounds he changed his mind. "I will get the doctor for that," he said. "It is more than we can handle." He was almost out the door, when he gave me the order, "Stay with him! I will get more wounded."

It dawned on me that by a stroke of incredible luck we had carried the wounded to a room belonging to the nearby infirmary. The concussed patient lay quietly, held by restraints. The other man was relaxed; the morphine was working. I busied myself, cleaning the blood off the sailors, checking for other wounds and lacerations. Occupied thus, I heard a sound behind me. O'Shaughnessy was back, but not alone. He and Elliot Bromfield carried a large man who was bleeding profusely from a wound in his side.

"Get rags and staunch the blood," cried Elliot in Russian. "The doctor will be here any minute."

"Who is she?" O'Shaughnessy asked, disbelief in his voice. Apparently he had only now comprehended that a strange Russian woman was on Her Majesty's destroyer. This was an occurrence too inconceivable to contemplate, an impossibility.

"Later," Elliot said, distractedly. "Get ready to bring in more injured."

"Listen," I called out. "It is silent above. The planes must have left!"

"Bloody time, too," said Elliot grimly. "We pounded them with four 4.7 inch guns and six machine guns and that's not counting what the other two cruisers put out."

"I am afraid they may have disabled one of the smaller boats. We might have to take on some of their crew," said O'Shaughnessy. Both men spoke Russian more or less well and were trying, struggling with the difficult terms, to include me in their conversation.

Untimely Discovery

A loud shout of, "What the hell has happened here?" had us turn to the door. There, framed by the four by four inch steel bars of the doorway, stood a doctor, his white coat bloody, dripping gore. He was a serious looking man in his fifties. Gray-haired, of medium height, his colorless face closely shaved, his thin-lipped mouth pressed together, he mustered us, ready to administer discipline.

"Sir, I can explain the whole thing a little later." Elliot smiled, trying to placate. "She has been a great help with these wounded in here. I think you should have a look at Wooster here. We need to take him to an operating table. Katya here has stuffed him up well, but only God knows what you will find once you operate."

"Alright, bring him in the operating room and we will have look. Get me a couple units of blood and plasma; we will need it." The doctor's annoyed look had changed to one of tired acceptance. More medics appeared, helping injured men maneuver into the room. In a few minutes every bed and every chair was filled with patients. Most of the men, thank God, had not sustained life-threatening injuries in the German air attack.

The medics left, leaving us with the wounded they had brought below deck. Elliot, O'Shaughnessy and I led and carried some of the patients from the gangway into the infirmary. There we triaged their injuries and directed the seriously injured into the operating room. Elliot had disclosed earlier that he was an ensign, and had no business being here at all, except for the fact that he was looking after me.

"I think I should hide you away now that the attack is over, before you become any more exposed," he said, looking thoughtfully at me. The words had no sooner left his mouth when a short, compact man in the uniform of a high-ranking officer entered the surgery, stopping short upon seeing me.

"Mr. Bromfield," he barked, "would you kindly explain to me why I see a Russian woman on my ship?" The speaker's face had turned purple with anger. I backed away from the operating table until a wall stopped further retreat. I understood nothing of this outburst, but sensed that my presence caused the man's anger.

"Captain, Sir, I can explain," stuttered Elliot.

"No, you cannot. This is a war ship, not a God-damn-it-all refugee ship for Russian whores." Looking at me in my unkempt state, the awful dress, the fur boots, my hair a mat, smelling rather ripe after five days without washing, I realized that anyone might have thought ill of me. Fortunately for me, though, I did not understand the awful slur he had bestowed upon me. The interchanges that followed the outburst, from one who was obviously the captain of this ship, were in great detail later related to me through the good offices of the unshakeable Elliot. Therefore, the drama played out before my eyes with sound and fury left me trying to interpret the content of words I did not understand.

"Please, with your permission, Sir," interrupted the surgeon, "I am about to operate on this man. Can you please interrogate Elliot outside my surgery?"

"I damned well will," shouted the furious captain, seething with anger.

"Elliot, follow me and bring the damned woman," he said with barely controlled fury, leaving us to follow as he strode forcefully from the surgery.

He ran, more than he walked, down a corridor and up a steep, metal ladder to a room filled with charts, instruments, binoculars and a desk heaped with papers. He strode across the room, and turned to face us. His arms were crossed behind his back, as if gripping his hands out of sight gave him control of himself.

"Do you know that I will have your commission for this stupid stunt?" he asked. "After all, you are an officer!" He smirked acerbically. "Albeit only of low rank, but an officer nonetheless, and as such you know any nonmilitary personnel is absolutely forbidden on Her Majesty's ships. Do you understand this? How did this woman get on my ship anyway, and why?"

The longer he spoke the more he lost his composure and slid, almost apoplectic, back into his original anger and outrage. He stopped his tirade for a moment and glared venomously at the two of us. Elliot used the lull in the exhortation, by saying quickly, "Sir, may I explain from the beginning?"

"I wish you bloody well would—not that anything will justify or excuse this outrage!"

"Well, Sir, this woman before you is a real heroine. She is not a Russian, but a German!"

"Oh, for God's sake! Are you insane? Are you bloody well telling me we have an enemy woman on board? You must be unbalanced, crazy, fallen through the hatch, or you could not do this to me. You could not be sane and do this to me!"

"No, Sir! No, she is a Volga German!" blurted Elliot in desperate straits. "Her forebears have lived in Russia for hundreds of years!" Then, with desperate haste, Elliot began to tell my story, and explained how important it had been to get me out of Russia.

"But why on my bloody destroyer?" asked the captain furious, obviously not mollified by Elliot's tale.

"Because, Sir, the people who helped her had only a few days to get her out of Russia. They had no connections to people of trust on the other ships. Do you know of anyone more trustworthy than one of Her Majesty's officers or ships?" Elliot was quite proud of himself that he had come up with what he thought was irrefutable reasoning in his favor, and he paused for a moment.

"No one would have known about her, at all, if we had not been strafed. She would have stayed hidden behind the potato bin until we berthed at Loch Ewe and no one would have been the wiser. You must admit, Sir, how could we have left her behind? You know the gulags. Stalin is a ruthless dictator, killing his own people. How could I have left her there to die with my good British conscience intact?"

Captain Howard had become calmer, thoughtful even.

"Oh, damn Elliot," he said almost mildly, "why me? Why my ship?"

"Captain Howard, Sir, I understand that this can cost me my commission. As much as that would hurt me, I will be able to live with it. However, I could not have lived with the possibility of her dying in a gulag on my conscience."

"Well, what's done is done. Tell the girl I want to ask her some questions!" He faced me, mustering me closely, saying, "So, young lady, where are you going once we reach England?" The question surprised me, for I had been unable, apart from the captain's monumental anger, to understand anything of their volatile exchanges.

"I don't know," I said perturbed, because I did not know what I could do. When Elliot translated this insipid, innocuous remark, Captain Howard was incredulous.

"You mean she has nowhere to go?" he asked Elliot.

"She has an uncle and two brothers who had been long ago smuggled out of Russia into Germany, but, obviously, we cannot get her there. She thinks she might be able to go to America. She knows that sizable communities of Volga Germans exist in America. They are the people who left at the first signs of the Bolshevik tidal wave. Katharina believes that someone from the Lutheran Church of these communities would help her to emigrate."

"More complications, more trouble! How am I going to explain her to the Board of Admiralty?"

"Put the blame entirely on me, sir," said Elliot with blustery valor.

"I damn well will!" erupted Captain Howard again, "but this is my command, my ship, and in the end my problem." Captain Howard lapsed into silence. He looked at us balefully, thinking. At last, after a long, uncomfortably pregnant silence he spoke again.

I had closely observed the man who obviously held my fate in his hands. He was at the lower end of medium height and had small, elegant hands that managed to look strong. His head was large for his size. His face was oval with deep-set, dark eyes. He had a large nose and heavy dark brows—altogether a commanding man's visage. I had searched his eyes for an opening into his soul. Was he a good man? A kind man? Apart from sternness, righteousness and a great sense of duty I could discern nothing in his physiognomy.

"Elliot, now that I know of the girl I cannot and will not allow her to be stuck behind a potato bin. Let no one say that anyone on Her Majesty's *Intrepid* was ill-treated. Find an open cabin for her, but keep her out of sight of the men." His voice began to rise again, "I will not have the operations of this ship jeopardized by inattention."

"Thank you, Captain, Sir. I will take care of it," Elliot enunciated with military precision. After leaving the uncomfortable interaction with the captain, we rounded a corner where we could not be overheard. Elliot faced me and announced with a lopsided grin, "I think you will be alright. The old man is a true gentleman, always on the right side of a problem." He then proceeded to fill me in on the past drama. As he translated he assumed the roles of different parties with such droll skill that he had me laughing despite the trouble we both faced.

Elliot guided me through long, narrow corridors until we arrived at the office of the third officer, a man who filled many roles, including those of quartermaster and purser.

Inside his small, stark office another repetition of my story commenced. After hearing Elliot's account of my troubles, Michael Brubaker, the occupant of these cramped quarters, let go with a loud whistle and said, translated by Elliot, "Bloody hell, Elliot, you got yourself into a fine pickle. The old man will take you apart piece by piece and hang you out to dry." Yet despite his dismal prognostication he proved himself to be very helpful and almost convivial.

He found me an empty cabin and stayed with me to discourage curious visitors until Elliot returned with my belongings, which he retrieved from the space behind the potato bin. Thereafter, Elliot accompanied me to the showers and stood guard while I washed off a week's accumulation of grime. I dressed in the most feminine outfit provided by the Okrug ladies and felt refreshed, clean, wonderful.

Emerging from the showers, Elliot looked at me approvingly and said, "I have never seen you without the drab, gray thing you wore before. Who would have thought that inside the ugly chrysalis lived a butterfly?" I laughed aloud, for I had not thought of myself as attractive in a long time. Suddenly I was transported back to another time, a time long gone, when I had laughed often with the sheer joy of youth, when I had been happy and tried to be desirable.

The room Brubaker gave me was a narrow steel cubicle with four bunks—two on top of each other on each side. All were empty. There was no porthole in the tiny space. All light emanated from two tired bulbs recessed in the ceiling.

"So," I thought, "this is how fighting men live." I was filled with admiration for the men who were braving the icy ocean, always ready to fight off a German attack.

Earlier, as we made our way toward Brubaker's office, Elliot had given me a brief background of the ship. The *Intrepid* had been launched in 1936, running the Arctic route since 1941. She was a most powerful ship, fast, as much as a ship of her tonnage could be. It was her mission to provide protection for convoy ships, a duty she shared with other battle-class destroyers. Most of the ships were much smaller than the *Intrepid*. The convoys were an assemblage of merchant marine and trading vessels; few of these ships had ever been found far from the coastlines of Europe.

Some were slow, cumbersome ships, sitting ducks in a conflict. When attacked, the battleships raced around them like a pack of dogs herding sheep, while at the same time firing deadly cannon salvos, strafing enemy ships and airplanes with their guns.

On September 2, 1942, a few days after Ivan's death, the *Intrepid* had begun a new voyage, chaperoning a convoy of forty-four ships on route from Loch Ewe to Arkhangelsk. They came under attack from German ships and aircraft using the coast of Norway as base.

The battle had been fierce. Although the *Intrepid* fought valiantly, exposing her flanks to the enemy as she flew around the convoy of merchant ships, the enemy had succeeded in sinking thirteen of the convoy's ships. The remaining convoy, however, had reached Russia on September 21. Now it was October, and *Intrepid* was steaming home. She was still twenty days away from Loch Ewe in the United Kingdom where she would be safe.

Of course, she had already been bombed and strafed, drawing most of the fire, for on the home route the Germans were much more interested in sending a destroyer to the bottom of the ocean than the half empty merchant vessels. It was quite the reverse from the runs to Murmansk and Arkhangelsk when the merchant ships were filled with airplanes, ammunition, machine oil, highly refined aircraft fuels and other sundries of war. This time, the *Intrepid* had been lucky to get away with minor injuries to ship and crew.

Lying on the lower bunk I had chosen for myself I thought about the war. The irony was not lost on me that I, a Russian German, innocent of all crimes, except for the act of my birth, was probably equally despised by the Russians, the British and the Germans, who by now had encountered many Russian Germans in the frontline of the war.

I must have fallen asleep when a loud, metallic knock on the door startled me awake. Elliot had shown me how I could barricade myself in for privacy, because on a destroyer doors were never locked.

I opened the door and Elliot bounded inside, smiling broadly. "I was just about to get some food for you, when Captain Howard affably ordered me to bring you to his cabin. We are going to dine with him. Apparently he has become very curious about you, and would like to know more about your life." Sensing an easing of his difficult position, Elliot shone with palpable relief.

I straightened my clothes, a silk blouse with a small cardigan and a flaring skirt, and combed my hair, which finally had dried. It took only minutes while Elliot watched.

"Put your hair up again in that knot in the back—it is very becoming," he said and, to please him, I did.

Elliot led me through the warren of unfamiliar corridors to the captain's cabin where he knocked, deferentially waiting until the captain loudly bade us enter. Captain Howard's quarters were by no means spacious, but very elegant. Instead of the ubiquitous metal walls and floors, veneered wood paneling added warmth and glow to the room. A large oriental carpet covered the wood floor, and a solid, grand desk in the background let you forget that you were on a ship.

In the middle of the room a table had been set with a white tablecloth, fine china, white porcelain with cobalt blue edge, and beautiful, sparkling crystal. Captain Howard, immaculate in his uniform and snow-white shirt, stood by the desk, a drink in hand. He cordially asked us to come forward. Looking at me with astonishment, he said to Elliot, "What a transformation. Is she truly the same girl or do you have two on board?" He laughed at his own witticism and so did Elliot, who translated his comment for me.

We were treated to a drink pored by a tidy, smiling steward who attended to the captain's every wish. Captain Howard offered me a seat on a small settee, its leather upholstery studded with brass nails. He sat in a heavy leather chair, obviously a companion to the desk, and placed Elliot on a chair, which showed by its worn leather that it received all visitors.

I sipped a glass of Mosel wine, and sat back smiling, for apparently wine transcended my difficulties. Robert Howard asked if I had been made comfortable. I answered in the affirmative, and thanked him for his kindness, mentioning that my transformation made me feel so much better. He laughed out loud, "Aha, she noted my double take when she entered my stateroom."

"Yes," said Elliot, "she is very bright."

Thus began another retelling of my saga. Elliot seemed to enjoy embellishing Ivan's death and my role therein; for I saw him act out my stabbing and then, in the later part, Ivan's demise by Suomo's axe. The captain asked questions—Elliot answered. I understood only pantomime, but I enjoyed sitting quietly, studying the room with its unfamiliar gadgets and little personal touches, for example, an elegantly framed picture of what I assumed was Howard's family.

The more Elliot talked, the more Captain Howard wanted to know. I had to tell him about my stay with the Komi and the abominable treatment of the minorities by the Soviets. I told him about the Russian patrols, the Nenets, bears and reindeer—and, of course, about my time in the gulag. By the time I told him what kind of rations were given us for hard labor, his face had darkened with anger.

We had long since been seated at the table and been served a very fine meal, indeed. Although we kept speaking of terrible things, I still managed to enjoy the food immensely. At last, Captain Howard said, "Well, Elliot, I will put in a few good words for you. Can't promise anything, but you are a decent chap."

During the rest of the journey I was the captain's guest a few more times. These were always very pleasant interludes in an otherwise boring voyage. I felt that the sailor's life was a busy routine punctuated by bloodcurdling alarms. Sometimes, always at night, I was allowed on deck to stretch my legs, but most times I had to remain hidden away in my cabin. I had been given a few good books and enjoyed reading again; however, I missed the freedom of moving unhindered. Therefore I was overjoyed when Elliot told me that the lookout had spotted the lights of the English coast.

I had prayed for the safety of the convoy every night, and we had been left unmolested by the Germans. With the coast in sight new worries stirred. What was to become of me? I felt like a small ship in very large seas. I had no doubt that in the end, others would decide my fate, my future. I depended entirely on the goodwill of the British.

Stateless in England

The *Intrepid* did not stay long at Loch Ewe but steamed onward to Liverpool, where she was due for an inspection to determine if she had sustained any damage in her last skirmish. Her crew's shore leave was due, and the ship was in need of refitting and restocking. We arrived in Liverpool late in the evening. The ship pulled into its berth and soon everyone left except for a skeleton crew.

I had to remain on board for another night under the watch of the second officer, who brought me food and walked me to the showers. Late next day, Elliot returned with two officers from the Immigration Service. He told me that Captain Howard had gone with him to the authorities to plead my case and ask for a quick resolution of my status—to a status which would allow me to resume a somewhat normal life.

I was marched off the destroyer between the officers, a tall, handsome man and an equally attractive female. They treated me with cool correctness. Therefore, my heart sank, when we reached the quay and Elliot, my translator and friend, had to leave us. My escorts led me to a large, black official car. The handsome young man, wearing a trench-coat, took the driver's seat, while the pretty, dark-haired woman sat beside me in the back.

By the time we reached the city proper, having driven through dreary, industrial streets lined with machine shops and warehouses, it was late in the evening. Gloomy fog, lifting off the water, drifted through the streets and obscured the features of the buildings, many damaged by German bombing raids. I, however, was unable to converse with my escorts and learn of England's war problems. Toward the end of the ride it began to rain. It was steady, dismally wind-driven.

My guards spoke convivially with each other throughout the drive. I understood nothing of their conversation, which only served to make me feel even lonelier and more frightened than before. The driver stopped the black sedan before a tall building with many windows, fortified with steel bars. I was certain that this building must be a prison. Once, in Moscow, I had seen a prison and it looked just like the building before me.

The officers motioned me to leave the car, and escorted me into the forbidding complex. Clutching the crude leather bag holding my few possessions, I walked between my escorts. Inside, we encountered a bank of cubicles with desks. A sign hanging above the desks must have announced the specialty of the cubicles' inhabitants.

My guards guided me to one of the cubicles, explained my situation in detail to the beefy man behind the desk, and left. I remained standing, clutching my bag, and feeling abysmally depressed and disheartened. Where was I? What was happening to me? Was I to be left in a prison? Elliot had mentioned nothing of the kind. Instead, he had told me that I was merely to be detained until a judge could hear my case and decide what procedures had to be followed to make me legal.

No one, so far, had been able to respond to my attempts to question my situation—and I had tried French, Russian and German. This left me in the dark as far as my current and future situation was concerned. While I stood under the harsh, white light that allowed no softening shadows, the beefy man made phone calls.

After a considerable waiting period, a large, buxom, uniformed woman with hair as bright as buttercups, appeared and indicated by moving her hand that I was to follow her. To emphasize her motioned request, or to keep me from absconding, she held onto my arm, propelling me through a door behind the cubicles and down a long corridor. By elevator, we reached the fifth floor of the building.

Detention

Upstairs we walked past many doors until the matron—I assumed that was her function—found the room destined to receive me. She put a large key into the lock of a heavy, blue steel door and pushed the groaning door open. We stepped into what looked like an institutionalized assembly room. Industrial furniture, metal and wood tables and chairs, lacking warmth and charm, were the bleak appointments of this room.

An open door to the left allowed a view into a large dormitory, which was furnished with steel bunk beds. To the right, a door led to bathrooms and showers, as I found out later.

An assembly of the most extraordinary women walked about in stages of dishabille in preparation for the night. A few wore bathrobes, some wore flannel nightgowns, and others had towels wrapped around their naked bodies and turbans covering their wet hair. They paid us no mind, as if we did not exist.

Only upon the matron's loud call, "Girls, girls! Pay attention, I bring a new visitor," did the women pay attention to us. She stopped speaking until all eyes were on us. "Hopefully Katharina Grushov will not find your company too trying. So be nice and make her feel welcome. She speaks no English, but I think some of you might be able to talk to her. I have been told she speaks German, French and Russian."

"I will translate for her," said a pretty young girl wearing nothing but a towel around her middle and pink, feathered slippers on her feet.

"Good," said the matron, satisfied. "In that case you can tell her that I will have some food brought up for her, together with towels, a nightgown and a toothbrush." After this announcement she left abruptly.

"Welcome to our group of stateless, passport-deprived, or generally unwanted women," intoned the pert French girl. While she spoke, she slipped a cigarette from a pack at the table in front of her. She lit it instantly, deeply inhaling the smoke, which she blew in delicate clouds from her nostrils. Yet smoking did not keep her from introducing me to the women surrounding us. All the inmates of this institutional apartment now congregated in this, the living room. According to their whim, they sat on the hard chairs, leaned against the wall; two even sat cross-legged on the floor.

"What is your name, where do you come from and what have you done to end up here?" were the questions the French girl fired at me in rapid succession. She told me her name was Manon. I told her briefly what I wanted them to know about me, giving my name as Katya. I left out the part about the destroyer. I thought mentioning a ship would be sufficient.

"These two, Katya, are from Czechoslovakia," said Manon, pointing at the girls on the floor.

"Their names are Anna and Marina. They landed here upon escaping from a circus where they were held like indentured servants. They left behind their passports, which the owner had taken from them." She took a deep drag from her cigarette, waving it at two small, delicate Thai girls. "These two, with unpronounceable names, also came from the same circus."

Manon obviously enjoyed the attention paid her. She rose. Cigarette in one hand, holding her towel with the other, she walked about, pointing to the women she introduced. Manon herself admitted to being a prostitute who had been smuggled into the country to set up a brothel in Soho. She talked about her profession, unfazed by shame, as cool as any businessperson.

In addition to the already mentioned Czech acrobats and the Thai contortionists, I was introduced to a German dancer and suspected spy; and a very young black girl from Kenya, smuggled in by her sailor lover. Furthermore, I met two Chinese girls who had sold themselves into five years of servitude, and been smuggled in from Hong Kong by their future employer. British immigration, ever vigilant, had caught all of them in its net.

Just when I thought I had met the entire eclectic group, a strange person emerged from the showers. This was a man of medium height in a short bathrobe, from which two very male, knobby-kneed legs protruded. He had soft black hair, olive skin and a round girl's face, which was disconcertingly covered by a shadow of strong, black facial hair, recently shaved. A surprised cry escaped my lips, "What is this man doing here? I thought this was a women's detention?"

The women and girls laughed with glee. "But this is a girl," squealed Helga, the German girl. "Well perhaps not quite. Shireen had the misfortune to be born with male and female attributes. Because of this circumstance, they placed her into our company instead the center for males with problematic citizenship issues. They thought she would be safer here with us than among possible predators."

Apparently these women had kindly and tolerantly accepted this poor misfit. They treated him, as I saw later, with the indulgence one bestows on a precocious child. At times, they forgot that he could be aroused by their uninhibited behavior, as they pranced about in all stages of dishabille.

I thought that Shireen, a name meaning sweet or sugar, was an unfortunate misnomer, when Hamid or Ali would have served better. During all my days in the apartment, I never saw him misbehave, leering or ogling. Although he was always pleasant and nice, I could never be as free around him as the other women were, because I always tried to intuit his feelings and thoughts.

His history was a sad tale. As a small child, he came to England with his Persian diplomatic family. His father, a strict Muslim, had always been ashamed of the poor hermaphrodite and would have killed him at birth, if he had been present. When his family returned to Iran, the family left Shireen behind in England without a passport, making his return to Iran impossible, thereby, turning him into a stateless person.

In Iran, his family had hidden him under voluminous burqas. Here, in England he had been allowed to wear men's clothes, which were more in keeping with his male appearance.

He had accepted his fate without misgiving, never bemoaned his difficult circumstances. Over the years, he had come to understand his predicament, and his father's immense dislike for him. He missed his mother, the only person besides his sisters who loved him. From birth, she had sheltered and educated him. Now, in his strange circumstance, he was almost happy.

From diplomatic postings in different countries he had become fluent in many languages. However, as he only conversed in English or French I never knew till later of his extraordinary linguistic ability. When alone with me we conversed in French, and so he told me, "The English are nice. In the end they will give me papers and accept me as a citizen." He smiled wickedly, "I can be of great service to their intelligence community, because as a translator, speaking Persian, I will be the only one giving them even the smallest, most interesting details that others might care to hide from them."

I consumed my meal when it arrived. It was sent together with the promised toiletry items. Later, I got ready for bed and was given a choice of one of the bunk beds. The German dancer, whose language was so pure compared to mine, showed me a bank of lockers. "Choose one for your possessions, lock it, and pin the key with the safety pin to your bra. This way you will know if someone tries to steal from you." She rolled her eyes in the direction of the Chinese or the Thai girls. I could not discern whom she labeled a kleptomaniac.

At first, I thought I would be unable to sleep in this most strange place. I had found the simple Komi tents less stressful than being locked up in this prison, but eventually I slept soundly and long.

The following days were dedicated to adjustments, the learning of the routine. No one from the outside world came to interact with any of us inmates. Manon apprised me that many days, even weeks could pass until a hearing before a judge took place. Despite my intense desire to escape this dismal place, I prayed, holding myself to discipline and patience, for good things would happen in God's own time.

A week passed. I read the magazines and books provided to us, played chess with Shireen—Hamid, as I called him. Days ago, while playing chess with Hamid, I had discovered that he spoke four languages perfectly well, among them German, but he had been too inhibited then to claim knowledge of anything but English and French.

I would not have known about this ability, had he not involuntarily replied in German, "*Nein, Du hast mich nicht. Schau mal genau hin!*" when I jubilantly cried, "*Schach matt!*"

To pass the time I also put together complex picture puzzles with Helga. I noted that the other girls shunned Helga. They were not exactly mean, never verbally expressed dislike, but they excluded her from their activities. However, they included Shireen in most of their doings.

"Why do they exclude you from their little circles? Why do they dislike you?" I asked with the directness of the village girl. She smiled with a mixture of sadness and scorn.

"They think I am a spy for the Germans."

"Why would they think such a thing?" I asked, intrigued.

"I came to England before the war with a German ballet ensemble. We performed with the Royal Ballet. When the war began everyone went back to Germany, except for me. My parents had died. I was on my own, and I did not like the beginnings of fascism in my fatherland." She looked directly into my eyes, as if to say, read me, I am telling the truth.

"When my problems began, I had become one of the lead dancers at the Royal Ballet. This engagement continued, until a well-known general wanted to make me his mistress and I refused his very generous offer," she laughed scornfully. "He became very angry and told me I would regret refusing his patronage. It was only a week later that I was arrested and accused of spying. They found what seemed to be incriminating correspondence. Fortunately, there were many people who knew me well, knew the general, too. The intervention of the solicitor they hired for my defense made it possible that I can remain here until my trial instead of being confined in a prison."

After hearing Helga's story, I suddenly did not feel the burden of my predicament with the same crushing weight as before. Most of the women here had stories that rivaled my own adventures. It was amazing how they were able to set aside their troubles, concentrate on the moment and, thereby, extract the most from an untenable situation.

They beautified each other, created hair designs and painted their nails. They reworked their sparse wardrobes, sang, danced and taught each other intricate steps. My mother's old lesson came to mind, "You can begin the day with a smile or a frown, and depending on this attitude the world will create the day for you."

As the days passed, my memories of Elliot Bromfield and Captain Howard began to fade subtly. I felt forgotten, left to a fickle fate like a leaf drifting on the breeze. However, that was all right. I was safe, in a free country, where people adhered to laws. Eventually, I would be free.

I had just convinced myself of this truth, when one morning Matron McPherson arrived to tell me to get ready. "Take a coat," she said, "because you have visitors who will take you out."

I shivered with excitement. Who was here to see me? Where were they taking me?

I took my fur-lined leather coat from my locker. This coat, so befitting the taiga and tundra of Siberia, looked coarse and poorly made in a civilized city. Alas, there was no help for it; I would just have to wear it, for it was bitter cold outside.

The matron, very officious, took me by elevator down to the entrance, where in front of the cubicles Elliot and Captain Howard awaited us. How can I describe my feelings upon seeing these two men? They had not forgotten me! Here they were, my saviors.

I left the matron's side, rushing to the heroes of my adventure to furiously shake their hands.

"Thank you for not forgetting me," I cried.

"How could we forget you?" said Elliot, who went on to translate for Captain Howard.

"You have become my charge," proclaimed Captain Howard, "I would not abandon a person entrusted to my ship."

I cried happy tears and laughed, as I shook their hands at the same time.

"We have come to take you shopping," announced Elliot, glowing with happiness.

"We will meet my fiancée, and she will help you find proper clothes. Things you will need for your hearing before the magistrate. It is important that you cut a fine figure, a figure worthy of the British Empire!"

"Yes," said Captain Howard dryly, "we will make you British, one way or another." He smilingly told me that Lady Howard, after hearing my story, had insisted that I was to have tea at their Liverpool flat one day, so she could vet my outfit for the meeting with the judge.

Liverpool was by no means the equivalent of London when it came to shopping. Of this I was informed by Elliot's fiancée, Beatrice McIntosh. We met this very energetic, young lady in the more exclusive part of town, a part once dedicated to elegance, high-finance commerce and the arts. Yet, despite the effort and pretense, even this part of town could not shed the commercial, mechanical feel that the rest of the city endured with forbearance. Furthermore, there was the damage visited by German air raids upon parts of Liverpool with the names of Wallasey, Wirral and others. I knew nothing of these areas, nor could I imagine the damage they had sustained. I was lucky, to see only mainly unscathed parts of town.

Beatrice, a slender, tall, elegant girl with raven hair and flawless complexion, took hold of my arm and steered me into a large department store the size and magnitude I had never known to exist. I was flabbergasted. My mind turned to mush before the unbelievable selections. And this was in the middle of a war! Yet, like any woman worth her salt, I floated straight into the right aisles, oohed and aahed over the best assortments as if I had done this forever and a day. Beatrice sighed, and remarked that the treasures delighting me were a far cry from pre-war quality.

I was ever so glad to have Beatrice beside me, for Captain Howard, fired on by his wife, would have bought me the first thing at which I covetously glanced. Beatrice quickly put a stop to this, saying, "No, no! This is lovely; however, it does not work as an ensemble. We want to find things that will coordinate into entire outfits and suits. With war-time allotments of coupons, we must be savvy." Her remark reminded me that, depriving themselves, they had pooled their precious coupons to clothe me.

Elliot and Captain Howard meanwhile had a wonderful time talking about cricket scores, battle plans and the refitting of the *Intrepid*.

When our purchases were packed, I cried with horror, "Oh, no! There is no place at the detention center to put any of this. We even have a few thieves among us. What an irresistible temptation this lovely lot would be for them." When Elliot translated my outburst, my companions were momentarily puzzled. What an odd dilemma to have. However, what I perceived to be an insurmountable problem proved to their fertile minds to be a bagatelle.

"Pick a few nice things that will fit into your locker," said Captain Howard. "I will have the rest of it sent to my house, where it will wait for you until you leave the center. Also, this way my wife will be able to meet you as she has wished for."

Beatrice, with a fine understanding for the appropriate, chose a two-piece costume to take with me to the institution, which would serve for the hearings to come.

Outfitted with more clothes than I would have chosen myself, we left the department stores for a "nice luncheon place." As we left the store, with me attired in a new dress, coat, shoes and gloves, I felt like Cinderella going to the ball.

Proof that I Do Not Exist

As soon as next morning the wisdom of the shopping trip was revealed. I had barely finished my breakfast of cornflakes, watery milk and coffee when the matron appeared.

"Dress nicely, Katharina," she said, her voice filled with meaning. "You will be seeing the magistrate this morning." Turning officious again, she sharply advised me to be ready in half an hour. Manon, her eyes filled with curiosity, had translated the matron's commands.

"*Mon dieu*," she exclaimed. "Who is moving the earth for you? Usually we have to wait for months before anyone hears our cases. What makes you so special?" She seemed tremendously disconcerted, so comically irked by my good luck that I laughed out loud.

"Perhaps it is the company I keep," I teased. "Maybe you too must pray—hard—and your fate will change."

"Oh, *oui*! Bring God into the conversation," she fumed.

"It would not hurt you to pray sometimes," I smiled, heading for the showers.

The matron returned promptly at eight thirty with the same female immigration officer who had brought me to this place. Today she wore the British national dress—a gray raincoat, a small, green felt cap and solid brown shoes. Despite this outfit she managed to look stunningly attractive.

Because Manon was still out of sorts, Helga translated the officer's comments to me. A magistrate was going to hear my case. A translator would be provided for the proceeding; however, as of this moment they did not know in which language the translation would take place.

"Take me along!" shouted Manon. "I will translate for nothing but the chance to get out for a while!"

"Sorry," said the officer. "Only certified British citizens can apply for the job."

Moments later we were whisked away in the black official car. After a short drive we entered another large government building. This one, however, exhibited the wealth and power of the Commonwealth. Marble floors, gleaming brass railings and teak wood paneling announced the importance of the place.

We strode up a flight of stairs, went along a corridor to the right and entered the reception room of the Honorable Ian Rutgers. My case officer announced our arrival, upon which we were requested to sit and wait.

When I was finally summoned and beheld the Honorable Sir Rutgers, I was overcome with disappointment. Behind an enormous mahogany desk, loaded with books, files and pictures, sat a wizened, bespectacled man. He wore the ubiquitous silvery wig of a judge to make him look distinguished, a fleeting notion, destroyed when he bent and the wig fell. Then we saw that his round head sported a patch of silvery hair on each side of a bald dome. His face was pasty and deeply lined; his mouth sloped tiredly downward and even his large nose seemed to droop. Only his eyes were alive in his face, gleaming intelligently, almost malevolently, behind the lenses of his glasses. I did not know why, but suddenly I felt deeply apprehensive.

To the left, in front of his desk in a comfortable upholstered chair sat a middle-aged man with Slavic features; aha, I thought—the interpreter. My assumption proved to be correct. Sir Rutgers asked my case officer, Mabel Goodwin, to be seated, but left me standing before him.

Of course, Magistrate Rutgers must have read my file, including the affidavits prepared by Elliot and Captain Howard. They had assured me that they had done their best to describe my situation.

In a raspy voice Rutgers asked me through the interpreter to tell my story once more. The interpreter struck me as filled with self-importance, and I prayed that he would not embellish my story unnecessarily. I resolved to use only short sentences. If he translated long diatribes, it would be obvious that he was adding elaborate verbiage.

I tried to explain myself in a clear and concise manner. Summing up the story of my life, I tried to explain how the killing of Ivan, a concentration camp commandant, had been done in self-defense, and how, later in the story, I had been hidden by accomplices in the larder of the *Intrepid*.

When I finished there was a moment of silence. The interpreter had, so far as I could ascertain, done a creditable job. I was, therefore, overcome with incredulity when the magistrate, who seemed to have been listening with keen interest, said, "So, Katharina Grushov, show me your papers, birth certificate, passport and such."

"My God," I thought, "has he not heard? Does he not understand anything I have been telling him?" I suddenly quaked with fear. Could this man be incompetent? Did my fate reside in the hands of an imbecile? Despite my fear and forebodings, I controlled my voice, keeping it from revealing my growing anxieties, a mixture of hostility and fear.

"Forgive me, Your Honor, but I hope I clearly explained that it was necessary to leave my few personal belongings behind in the Siberian gulag. When I had to flee, I had barely a dress on my body, never mind a purse with papers."

"Well, my dear," said the magistrate with bureaucratic glee. "That might have been the case, but how can you prove it?" He peered penetratingly through his glasses and pointed his bony forefinger at me.

"Without papers you do not exist," he shouted triumphantly.

"But Sir, I stand before you in the flesh, and two British officers have testified to the veracity of my story."

"That might be so," he crowed, "but until I see official verification from Russia as to your existence, I can do nothing."

"From Russia?" I objected louder than called for. "From Russia? Do you believe the Soviets will admit to having locked me up in a slave labor gulag? They will deny my existence! For them I am dead."

"Well then, if there is no official who will certify that the person before us is truly the Katharina Grushov you claim to be, then a woman by that name does not exist."

To the utter astonishment of the interpreter, Miss Goodwin, the officer and me, he declared the hearing closed. He admonished me not to come before him again unless I held the proper papers in my hands.

Mabel Goodwin led me dazed and befuddled from the office. "I must be insane?" I thought. This cannot be happening to me. I had been prepared to face all sorts of difficulties. The possibility of being declared nonexistent, however, had not been one of them.

As we walked from the building, pert, officious Miss Goodwin petted my hand in a show of sympathy and understanding. Her warm gesture accomplished what adversity had not; I began to cry. We had almost reached the car that would take me back to my prison, when we heard a shout, "Katya, Katyusha! Wait for me!"

The caller was none other than Elliot and, as I turned, I looked into his by now familiar, cheerful face.

"Why the tears, Katya?" he cried with instant concern. Momentarily I could not speak. Miss Goodwin took over, conveying in English the gist of the ghastly hearing.

"The magistrate said that you don't exist?" Elliot shouted these words in Russian with such fervor that a few passersby turned their heads and looked at us with interest. Elliot had met Mabel Goodwin before. So now they conversed with the greatest of ease.

"Would it be possible to take you lovely ladies to lunch?" asked Elliot, "I know it would do Katya a world of good, and you, Miss Goodwin, you, too, must eat. Do you like curries and palaus with a bit of spice?" Mabel Goodwin agreed enthusiastically, and I, not knowing what curries were, was ready to find out. Through my harrowing experience in front of the magistrate, Miss Goodwin and I had forged a female bond. Now she asked, through Elliot, if we would be comfortable not to stand on formality and use first names. Young and enthusiastic, we agreed to her suggestion with the same vigor we had agreed to try curry.

"That is it then," smiled Elliot, "I know of a lovely little place that serves Indian food. Somehow, despite the food shortage, they manage to prepare great food, albeit for exorbitant prices. We shall go there presently."

Mabel had the driver take us through Liverpool's gloom to the restaurant. It was a place marked by the life-size statue of a Pathan tribesman, which stood to the right of the entrance. Dressed in baggy pants, an embroidered long shirt that fell below his knees and was held around his middle by a pleated, red sash, and topped by a tall white turban adorned by a foot-high, pleated red fan, the Pathan reminded me of the colorful Kirghiz.

As soon as the restaurant door opened, we were greeted with wonderful, pungent scents, which were unfamiliar to me. I deeply inhaled the warm and welcoming smells. My eyes were immediately drawn to a statue standing before the opposite wall. There, on a pedestal, a martial bare-breasted woman with four arms was riding a lion. She towered over a fearsome creature, half dragon and half serpent, she held impaled on an enormous trident. An elaborately ornamented helmet crowned her head as she smiled, wickedly and yet benignly, upon the patrons below.

Noting my interest, Elliot explained to me that I beheld the Hindu goddess Durga, the warrior form of Devi, the mother goddess. He said, "The entire statue, pedestal and all, is carved from a single block of sandalwood to honor Devi. She is all-encompassing. Therefore, depending on the situation, she assumes the forms of Durga, the slayer of evil and sin, of Kali, the avenger and destroyer, of Lakshmi, the goddess of beauty and wealth, and of Saraswati, the goddess of music and learning."

I was fascinated by the statue, drawn to it by its powerful statement of righteousness and protection. While I still stared at the Asian décor, the proprietor, a dusky, thin man wearing a blue turban, had seated us. With wonderment, I beheld on a wide mantle, running the length of the wall, an array of huge chased-copper plates and coffee pots. On the opposite wall, hung a tapestry stitched with gold and silver threads, depicting a mahout and his elephant; the latter held his leg and enormous foot raised above the head of a prostrate man, ready to crush the man's skull. The Indian owner smilingly told me, as Elliot translated, that this elephant had been the favorite of the famous Mughal Emperor Akbar in the city Fatehpur Sikri, where the animal had crushed the heads of his enemies.

Elliot ordered for the three of us. I had never even heard the names of these dishes, never mind tasted them: velvet chicken, palau, dal and nan. The names alone transported me to worlds far away. While awaiting the food we drank aromatic tea, flavored with cardamom, and of course, Mabel and Elliot discussed my untenable situation. As I did not understand even the gist of their English conversation, I was left to savor the exotic ambiance of the restaurant and relax.

Because we were early for lunch, few people were in the restaurant. Those present were golden or swarthy complexioned natives of India.

Conferring busily, my companions optimistically arrived at a solution to my problem. Elliot turned to me and explained. "We do not know if this will work, but Mabel and I think that if we can find a Volga German community in America, good staunch Lutheran people willing to sponsor and vouch for you, we can find a way out of your dilemma."

Mabel had an idea, which Elliot translated into Russian. "She will get you before one of our judges. I have agreed to pay for a solicitor to represent you. This lawyer is a very smart and very well-connected man who might get you out of detention. In the meantime, I will seek among my American friends, young ensigns and flying aces all, for someone of Volga German descent. I figure there must be a young Volga German-American somewhere, willing to be hero to a damsel in distress."

We laughed at the old cliché. However, I was truly a damsel in distress. The humor did not sidetrack me from my observations. I might have been a "country egg," as they say, but I was not dumb. I knew of the cost associated with lawyers and vividly remembered some of my family's battles with Russian bureaucracy, all very costly. Therefore, I just had to pry, "Elliot, how are you going to pay for the solicitor? You are on an ensign's pay and want to get married. Solicitors cost a fortune—I know that much."

Elliot swallowed hard. He was very serious now. After a long silence, he said, "Don't worry. I know of a way."

However, I was not put off that easily. "Please, you must tell me the truth. I know that because of me you might lose your commission. I don't want to add any more hardship to the trouble I have already caused."

He hemmed and hawed uncomfortably; then he said, "Remember, back in Arkhangelsk I accepted some precious stones from Anton Derevnikov to take you on board. Well, one of these stones, a flawless diamond, was to be the stone for Beatrice's wedding ring. It is the best of the three, and will bring plenty of money for a solicitor."

"No, no! Elliot, you must not do this! You earned the diamond a hundredfold—I cannot let you do this!"

"What are you two debating so hotly?" asked Mabel. We were both silent. At last I said, "Elliot is already sacrificing his career to my cause; now he is about to imperil his financial future." I implored Elliot to explain the story of the gems to Mabel.

"It is the solicitor's fee. Is that the problem?"

"Yes," I said, "that is what we are arguing about."

The food arrived, smelling ambrosial. We served ourselves in silence and ate thoughtfully until I involuntarily exclaimed, "There are silver strips in my food!" The others laughed.

"Yes, the rice is a royal dish and the silver is edible."

How incredible a meal this was! It tasted like no other food I had ever eaten before. Not distracted by culinary delights, Mabel soon spun her web of ideas again. "I know of a solicitor who, if the case intrigues him, might speak for you pro bono, or for just a small remuneration."

Elliot became all ears, and between them they continued to weave the story of my salvation. When we left the restaurant my spirits were high once more. How could I fail to find a home somewhere when God had provided me such lovely guides?

I had learned that Mabel, who despite her officious demeanor was a rather sweet and caring girl, had hopes of marrying the young officer with whom she had escorted me from the *Intrepid*.

That night in the detention apartment I could not help but wonder what motivated Mabel and Elliot to be my advocates? In Elliot's case it was even more than advocacy, it had become an investment in an unprofitable venture.

None of the people working on my behalf were religious, but they all, even Captain Howard, believed in God. Perhaps this alone was enough motivation. Yet, as I mused on the subject, it became apparent that there was more. Among Mabel, Elliot and me existed the connectedness of youth, idealism and enthusiasm. We still believed that we could make a difference in the world by standing on principle, by being of service. Examining my own core beliefs, I knew that I would have risked imprisonment or my life if either of them had required my help.

In our talks together, while my impressions were albeit somewhat hampered by awkward translation back and forth, they had displayed a certain righteousness. Add to that, in Elliot's case, a profound hatred for Stalin, about whom he had learned much from his sources in Arkhangelsk. And there was another incentive to save me.

I knew little of Captain Howard's motives, except that he had two daughters my age. That, in itself, perhaps, was enough emotional ground to take pity on me.

That night, as I lay on my narrow cot, counting my blessings, I heard half-suppressed sobs. They came from the separate cubicle in which matron housed Shireen, or Hamid, as he was inscribed in my mind.

I slipped off my cot, pulled on my heavy bathrobe, and went to his cubicle, calling softly, "Hamid, come out and talk to me!"

The sobbing stopped. After a bit of sniffling and rustling of clothing, the young man-girl stepped from behind the curtain.

I took his hand and led him into the common room. In a corner of the room, on a small table, rested a hotplate surrounded by tea things. It was cold in the dormitory. England was at war and used her resources sparingly, and domestic fuel was scarce. While I heated water and made tea, I talked to the despairing Hamid. I found some blankets, which we wrapped around us. Ensconced in their warmth and steaming cups of tea in our hands, I was able to elicit Hamid's grief.

As I had feasted on Indian delights, he had been before a magistrate to clarify his status. The magistrate had outright refused to issue an asylum permit. "Instead," Hamid sobbed, "despite my desperate pleas not to be sent back into the hands of my awful father, the magistrate will have me deported. He said I would be unable to support myself in England after spending my life hidden under a burqa without formal education."

For a moment I was taken aback. "But you did receive an education, did you not? You learned four languages. Someone must have taught you?"

"Yes, of course, I went to school and was educated by my mother, but I do not want to live as a woman anymore. Look at me!" His last words were a cry of utter hopelessness. "I look more like a man than a woman. When, in jest, you called me Hamid, it seemed right; it fits me better than Shireen—sugar."

"Did the magistrate object to you wearing male attire?"

"He said flat out that I could not succeed in the business world, men would not accept me the way I am made. To make his point, he waved my medical records at me. How could I counter this evidence?" More sobs accompanied this statement. Taking his hand in mine, I told him that our God loves all his children the way they are made, and that he was no exception.

"You must pray, and ask for a hearing in front of a judge," I advised. "In the meantime, we must find a way to make you look even more masculine and, at least in outward appearance, make you totally comfortable." To my relief the tears stopped. There was a newly awakened interest in his eyes.

"Do you think it is possible?" he asked, very uncertain still.

"Everything is possible if God wishes it. Look at me. I came to this land on a destroyer. Have you ever heard of the likes of it? I believe, if you focus on the things you can do well, like translating, and state your wishes and dreams clearly in front of a judge, you might get your wish."

That night I prayed fervently for Hamid. It was hard for me to imagine the combined torments of his body split into two sexes, hard to imagine the ridicule and abuse his dastardly father had poured over the helpless child.

The American

A long time passed, long for the inmates of the detention complex, but perhaps just fourteen ordinary days on the outside. Finally, Matron brought me a message from Elliot. It read:

> *Tomorrow evening put on your pretty dress and all the other frilly things that go with it, because Beatrice and I will pick you up for dinner. I already arranged it with Matron, who requires you to be back at eleven sharp. You will meet a most interesting man, an American pilot and Volga-German offspring.*
> *P. S. Be happy. You are not forgotten!*
> *Elliot*

After reading this missive, I dance-stepped across the floor of the common room, singing a silly, fiery Russian song. For days I had valiantly tried to keep up my flagging spirits. I played chess with Hamid, encouraging him. I listened to Helga's problems, which were hard to sort out, for the man testifying against her was very powerful. I altered clothes with Manon, and received English lessons together with the Chinese and Thai girls from Hamid until my head hurt.

Therefore, Elliot's letter felt like balm. I opened my locker, looking for the perfect thing to wear. There was only one dress and one charming suit. The dress was black, three-quarters length, slim, long-sleeved and high-necked like a nun's habit.

There was nothing for it—this was the dress. I wore borrowed faux pearl earrings and black high-heeled shoes, together with a pretty black shawl to round out the look. Giving myself a critical look in the mirror, I saw a severe, but sophisticated and yes, even elegant young woman. In my mind I thanked Beatrice for her good taste and advice.

I was ready fifteen minutes before it was time for Elliot to pick me up. Manon had forgotten her grudges against me, and piled my hair atop my head in a most becoming hairdo. Because I had no jewelry or other frou frou besides the pearl earrings, Manon dug through her "chest of pretty things," coming up with a faux gardenia, looking much like the real thing. This she fastened in my hair for an astonishingly attractive look.

Elliot whisked me out of the detention center into a taxi where Beatrice was awaiting us. The elusive American, I was told, was awaiting our arrival at the British-American Officers Club. Elliot gave me a crash course about American involvement in the war.

Since 1940, even before America entered the war, American Air Force flyers and parachutists had fought Hitler's and Mussolini's forces under British command. Parachutists from the 8th Air Force conducted their first mission in February of that year. The American pilots fighting with the RAF were housed at a base at Debden, near London. Their Quonset huts later, when I was long gone, became the nucleus of the American Command Center.

The club was far removed from the center of town, close to the military installations. An old mansion had been converted to meet the needs of hungry and thirsty young men, running on excited energy. The grand old entry was filled with uniformed men and their dates, surrounding a grand piano which endured forceful punishment from a good-looking, tall, dark man. He furiously pounded the ivories, swishing across the keys as in a fever, driving his audience into a frenzy.

The men and women stomped, clapped, sang and laughed uproariously. I stood speechless beside Beatrice. We had taken only a few steps into the place, becoming rooted to the very spot. Never ever had I seen anything like it. No doubt, the handsome man on the piano could play. He suddenly stood up, striking the keys with ever greater force, creating amazing, totally enthralling music.

Elliot had begun to move to the impelling rhythm while Beatrice danced in place. I remembered suddenly the German tale of the Pied Piper of Hameln. This story figure had played the flute with such magic that rats, mice and children followed him wherever he led them. The man on the piano seemed to possess the same power, for everyone in the room seemed to be entranced by him.

Finally he stopped and reached for a drink sitting on top of the instrument. He downed half of the contents and turned, facing his enamored admirers.

"Play 'Frenesi,' Herb," called some.

"Please, please play 'Green Eyes'," shouted others.

"'Tangerine'," they yelled.

"No, no, play 'Moonlight Cocktail'!"

But the loudest calls were for a song called "Chattanooga Choo Choo."

"Hey, hey, hey! Have mercy on the music man," laughed the piano player, but he obediently bent over the keys again when he caught sight of Elliot. Relieved, he threw his arms up into the air and jumped off the piano bench, yelling, "Enough already! My party has arrived!"

A roar of grumbling and complaining greeted his abrupt departure. It seemed the crowd claimed him as uniquely theirs. He was their entertainment, their focal point—their soul. Pushing through his admirers like a swimmer parting seas, he reached our small group, heading straight for Beatrice.

"Beatrice! Girl, you look lovelier than ever." He kissed her on the cheek, turning to Elliot.

"Elliot, you lucky guy! How are you?"

"I am fine, and so are you apparently, judging by your audience. I am glad you are in town for a few days, old boy." Elliot seemed to suddenly remember me, because he turned and said, "Herb Baumeister, meet your date for this night, Katharina Grushov."

I was dumbfounded. This explosive powder keg of a man was to be my date for the night? I had anticipated a well-mannered, calm, perhaps even stoic man—one much like men I had known in the past, and so I stood a little statuesque, appraising and cool, before him.

From his height, for he was very tall, he looked down at me and looked me over without even a pretense of propriety. "Well, well, Elliot, you are right, she is very nice." Turning to me, he said in German, "Welcome to the club, Katharina. I cannot wait to talk to you. I have heard you come from Schaffhausen with relatives in Norka. That's where my family is from."

He took my arm and we followed Elliot and Beatrice deep into the clubhouse to the dining room. As he steered me competently through the crowd, I slowly lost my reservation about him and began feeling more at home in the strange surroundings.

"So," I thought, "this is an American? Strange, self-possessed creatures they are. They are also loud, boisterous and captivating."

Although by unspoken agreement I was not a real date but a project—he was to help me make connections—I, nevertheless, had a fine time. Herb, as they called him, pulled a small leather notebook and a pen from his breast pocket. He had heard my escape story in great detail from Elliot, and wanted to know my family history before dinner arrived.

"Family stories can ruin a good steak," he laughed. Yet, he was very businesslike in the way he took notes of the names and places in Russia I cited. I worked my way backward, talking about my parents first, then my grandparents, the Hildebrandts, and my great-grandparents, Alexander and Adela Döring. I talked about Henrietta and Heinrich Baker and before them the Trägers, and proceeded all the way back to the Meiningers, Christoph and Martin, who had been founders of Norka.

"Give me the names of village people you remember." Furthermore, he urged me to recall and recite the names of people who had left the village and emigrated to the United States.

"If someone in Fresno recognizes these names, especially the names of your family, they can vouch for your parentage and, therefore, your existence."

During his interrogation Herbert was serious and focused. His German was excellent, because, he said, "My parents insisted that my sister and I speak both languages fluently." By comparison, my German contained strange bits of idiom that had, over time, crept into a language cut off from the main branch.

The moment Herbert had finished taking notes, he turned his attention to "the steak." I had never had "steak," but found it much to my taste. Of course, all courses were small because of rationing, but accompanied by a plentiful assortment of different bottles of wine. Much of the wine stemmed from the private cellars of British nobility and upper-class citizens as their contribution to the war effort of the fly-boys. Unaccustomed to such ample libations, I grew quite happy and loquacious.

During this evening, which seemed to never end, I learned a thousand things about America, Fresno and California, for that was where Herbert came from: the raisins, the vineyards, politics, the war and new dances. Oh, what a dancer he was. He truly danced divinely. To my delight he led me onto the dance floor for most dances. He taught me new dances until my feet, in their new shoes, ached ferociously.

Even a bit tipsy, I could not fail to notice for one moment that the divine Herbert belonged, not only to his adoring fans, but also to several young women who claimed his attention on occasion. In his easy way, he acknowledged their presence by waving and twice excusing himself to visit other tables.

Elliot and Beatrice danced, flirted and kissed, and so we all had a wonderful time, until Elliot suddenly exclaimed, "Holy Matron, it is almost eleven and I promised I would have you back by that time."

Goodbyes were said in a hurry and the three of us flew out the door of the mansion. Outside, for once, the clouds had been driven off by a freezing wind blowing from the ocean. The sky was clear and filled with stars. We tumbled into the waiting cab, which raced per Elliot's instructions toward the detention center.

We were late! Matron played the dragon for a moment and then tweaked Elliot's ear in a fond motherly display of feigned anger. Elliot, slightly tipsy, did the unthinkable. He grabbed her by the waist, twirling her about a time or two.

To my utter astonishment, the stern woman laughed and twirled quite willingly, tweaking his cheek when he finally let her go. Then she led me to the dormitory, locking the door behind me.

Inside, I found the girls and Hamid waiting up for me. They sat in their nightgowns and pajamas on the hard chairs, drinking tea.

"Well, Cinderella, how was the ball?" asked Manon.

"What did you eat?" asked Hamid greedily. The food served in detention was notoriously bland, the portions small.

"Did you dance?" asked Helga.

Still carried on the wings of an exceptional night, I patiently answered their questions and let them be a part of the outside world.

The Christmas Miracle

Three more weeks passed in worrisome suspense and stretches of boredom. It was almost Christmas of 1942. Matron, with a flock of helpers, had carried a few pine branches, ornaments, candles and bows into our lair. She instructed us how to decorate the barren common room, to create holiday ambiance. We did our best. However, in the large, institutional-looking room warmth was not easily evoked.

Hamid had a meeting before a judge. I had sent him off, his spine strengthened with the Lutheran steel of righteousness, telling him to forge his future by giving the judge concrete reasons, to convince him that he would be an ideal citizen of the British Empire. Lo and behold, he came back grinning from ear to ear, overflowing with the news that the judge had decided in his favor and granted him asylum with eventual citizenship.

"I told him what you said to me." And then, Hamid, because that was who he had become, proudly recounted how he had presented his assets to the judge.

"Who better than I to confound your enemies?" I asked the judge, and he agreed that I would be an asset in any spy operation. "No one can be more loyal than I am, shunned and stateless," I said. Again, the judge agreed with me."

"And here I am, a British citizen in eight more years. In the meantime, I have lawful asylum." Hamid was beside himself with joy. Inquiries had already been made into agencies requiring interpreters. We all shared in his happiness, and I used the good outcome of his hearing as an example of possibilities for the others. Helga viewed me with doubting eyes, but I told her that with hope and prayer her record would be cleared.

On the morning of December 16, 1942, matron handed me another note from Elliot. This one read, cryptically:

> *Beatrice wants you to wear the bottle green suit tomorrow morning. We will pick you up at nine in the morning. Herbert Baumeister will be with us.*
> *What a surprise we have in store for you. Think happy thoughts!*
> > *Until tomorrow,*
> > *Elliot*

How could I sleep that night after reading this mysterious note? I don't know how, but I managed to fall asleep late that night. Promptly at nine the next morning Matron transferred me to Elliot, Beatrice, Herbert and— Mabel. And therein lay the mystery. What was Mabel doing here? Mabel was official. The four people awaiting me in a government car were in high spirits. They greeted me noisily, yet did not let slip out one iota of the surprise.

I was puzzled when Mabel slipped behind the wheel and drove the car. Apparently this was not an official outing. Herbert sat beside her, and the rest of us sat in the back. The streets of Liverpool, for the most part, were grimy and gray, as was the sky above and the triste rain falling from it. The Christmas season in no way influenced the drabness of the town, for the relentless war did not allow for lights and shiny decorations—a dead giveaway to bombers.

Mabel parked the car across from an imposing five-story building. My heart began to pound the moment I deciphered the word "IMMIGRATION" among others written in large gold lettering above the entrance. So, I was to have a hearing, but what were Herbert and Beatrice doing here? They did not have a role in my proceedings.

Mabel led us to the third floor, first by elevator then down a broad corridor where courtrooms beckoned with shining golden numbers to those expected for a hearing. Bailiffs flitted about in their uniforms. They collected the flotsam and jetsam of society and directed them to the correct chambers.

One of these helpful persons guided us to a waiting room and bade us to sit in comfortable chairs beside tables topped by a few magazines. After sitting in the impersonal room for a considerable time, my companions' spirit dampened considerably. Perhaps their lapse into silence was due to the austere surroundings, perhaps they had become bored. They still were not willing to confide the reasons for our being here. I, therefore, could not help speculating.

Foremost, I hoped that the judge might grant me a way to citizenship. Secondly, if that was not possible, I hoped that I would be allowed to leave for the United States, albeit as a stateless person. My last hope was to receive a probationary period, which would permit me to leave detention and allow me to work in pursuit of citizenship. I had heard of such things, but would they apply to my situation? Frighteningly, at the bottom of my mind remained the awful possibility of being expelled from the country, of being returned to the Soviet state as a stateless person, or being dispatched to any country willing to accept me.

Whenever these scenarios played in my mind, I reached a point where the picture froze, and the reel would not turn further because my mind could not conceive of the horrible end. I saw myself handed over to the Russians, walking handcuffed between guards off a ship. The harbor would be Murmansk, free of ice months longer than Arkhangelsk. The Red guards would lead me away and push me into a truck. They would drive me to a miserable prison and throw me into a dirty, icy cell, after robbing me of all my fine new clothes. At that crucial point, my imagination would always refuse to stop, but project further, where I was left between filthy, gray walls, on a wretched, dirty cot in a cell permeated by the smell of urine and blood. I knew this cell so well from the days in the gulag.

Beatrice, whom I imagined must have harbored a certain amount of resentment against me, abandoned for once her superior, cool demeanor and clutched my hand in a hard grip. This wonderful girl had been planning a wedding when her beloved suddenly became Sir Galahad to a stateless waif. I had tried to put myself into her role, had felt some of her feelings, and was grateful that she had set aside base jealousy to act on my behalf.

Now, it was as if she could read my thoughts. Mabel, Elliot and Herbert kept up a low, serious conversation, which by their expressions dealt with the many facets and possibilities of my case. At last, when I began to shiver with anticipation and plain angst, a bailiff came and spoke to Mabel, whereupon she ushered us into the judge's chamber.

My solicitor sat, brown-suited, white-shirted, bowler respectfully deposited upon his knee, before the judge, who was resplendent in white wig and black robe. I had met solicitor McArdle once before and liked him, although the meeting had been very brief. Beside the solicitor sat an interpreter arranged for by Mabel.

Judge Maitland called the hearing to order, and then the magnificent theater determining my entire life unfolded. I devoured the man in front of me with my eyes—how would he decide my fate? The judge's wig framed an ascetic, intelligent face in which large gray eyes dominated. I had to trust that his intelligence would be tempered by empathy—by feeling for his fellow man.

I will not speak of the hearing, of which I understood little. To my surprise, I was to testify in German. I assume this was to certify that I was truly a Volga German. My German, even with the classical training I had received, was far below the language caliber of the interpreter.

Throughout the proceedings I held on anxiously to Beatrice's hand. Her face was a mirror of the hearing. Sometimes she smiled, especially when Herbert testified. She frowned a few times, grew concerned, and then, when I tensed with fear—she grew relaxed.

At last, after what felt like hours of agony, the translator stood by the judge's desk and intoned,

> After reading Captain Howard's deposition and the depositions sent from America, together with the testimony of the witnesses who have appeared before me, I Harry Maitland of Her Majesty's Immigration Service, order that the Volga German female Katharina Alexeyevna Grushov be given by decree the status of legal alien subject. She will receive the necessary papers to live and conduct lawful business in the United Kingdom until such time that she wishes to leave for another country.

I was called to stand before the judge who had risen. He began to speak and, as I heard his words translated, he shook my hand briefly.

"Congratulations, Katharina Grushov," he said warmly, "I hope that your life in the free world will be as sweet as your life once was bitter in Russia."

Shaken to the core by a flood of emotions, I was barely able to stutter my thanks for this generous gift. My vision blurred, obscured by tears. I barely could understand what had happened and how. I just knew that in this one moment my existence had been tossed into a new, wonderful orbit.

The judge left the room. Turning to my group, I stammered my thanks, shook hands, and received their congratulations.

"Off we go," called Herbert joyfully, "let's celebrate!" Of course, he had the full cooperation of everyone. I did not hold an opinion, as I was dizzy with joy and disbelief. Questions rattled about in my head until it ached. The most obvious of questions was, of course, "How could a person who was certified a non-person by a magistrate suddenly be a legal British alien?" I still had no birth certificate—so, what had changed?

In the car, my friends talked up a storm, in English. Since I had remained silent, no one bothered to translate. So happy were they with what was obviously their accomplishment that they had almost forgotten about me.

We disembarked in front of an old Liverpool pub. At that time of day, there was little traffic in the establishment and we took a large comfortable corner with a round table and plush leather chairs for ourselves. The men ordered drinks: ales for the men, gin and tonics for us, the "girls." Alcohol was rationed, as was everything else. Therefore, one drank sparingly and with proper reverence.

The very moment my companions fell silent with their first draught, I spoke.

"Would someone please tell me what happened in the judge's chambers today? A few weeks ago I had been pronounced a non-person, a non-existent human without a birth certificate. And here, today, I am a legal person with all rights of commerce in the United Kingdom. How did this happen?"

They cried out, laughing, telling me the story all at once and in four versions, until Elliot shouted them down. "Order, order. I am the judge and I decree that we tell the story one by one. I will begin!"

He explained in the greatest detail how he and Captain Howard, with the solicitor's help, had drawn up papers and depositions on my behalf. The solicitor had found enough precedent to make my appeal a case of urgency because the applicant needed asylum on humanitarian grounds.

He handed the talking baton to Herbert. Herbert had searched in the Volga German community of Fresno for people from Schaffhausen and Katharinenstadt, which the Soviets had renamed Marx. Lo and behold, he found several families and a few single men who had known my family or known of them. On his last trip home, Herbert had somehow managed with the help of a lawyer friend to depose all these people and bring these legal documents back to England, presenting them to the judge.

"The judge was very sympathetic to your plight," said Elliot, "and could, in good conscience, give you legal status. He knows full well that Herbert's community will sponsor you in no time and that, henceforth, you will be America's 'problem'." They laughed.

Mabel said kindly, "I would wish that this 'problem' would remain in England. We welcome good people."

As the general conversation went on to other topics, Herbert fulfilled my wish and talked about Fresno and its German community. The earliest Volga Germans arrived in Fresno in 1887. They were just ten families originally slated to go to Lincoln, Nebraska. However, their leader, Philip Nilmeier, conversed with a Jewish salesman aboard ship via New York, who painted a picture of a bountiful valley—the San Joaquin Valley. Nilmeier persuaded the heads of nine other families to join him in the California adventure, and—voila!—another German colony was born.

"Some Germans already living in Fresno welcomed the new arrivals from Russia, and you know how hardworking our people are. They saved, bought homes, and later, during the Great Depression, were able to buy land. As they prospered, they sent money and reports back to Russia, enticing more people to leave the Volga colonies. Later, when life became unbearable in Russia, between the years of 1909 and 1920, the Volga Germans came in masses. We had an influx of 35,000 people from the Volga into Fresno."

"I know of this time. My parent's friends left the Volga then. My mother's brother and sister and other family members left. They fervently urged my parents and grandparents to also leave the country. They, however, loved Russia too well. They thought to protect their businesses and estates, but by staying in Russia, lost it all."

I had told Herbert about my brother fighting on the front, that I didn't know if he was alive or dead. I had told him of my mother, who might be alive or dead, somewhere in Siberia. Through these horrid tales, he knew the price most Volga Germans had paid for remaining loyal to the land, the soil, their cradle.

According to Herbert, three people had testified on my behalf. Two men and their wives from Katharinenstadt had known Holger and Victoria, my grandparents, and also my parents. Although, I had been born after they left in 1916, amazingly, they had heard of my birth. The other witness, a woman who hailed from Norka, had known me as a ten-year-old, when I had come to visit Hilda and Reinhart Döring's grandchildren.

I marveled at the stroke of good fortune, or better, God's foresight, placing those people in my path. The plan, as my friends explained to me, was as follows: I would remain in Liverpool and work until the Fresno Lutheran congregation could arrange for the necessary papers and raise the money for my passage to America.

"Tomorrow you will be free, my dear," said Elliot. "After your release papers arrive, Mabel will escort you from the detention center and take you to Captain Howard's home."

The Anglican Queen

On a perfect day in May 1943, I leaned against the railing of the British ship grandly named *The Anglican Queen*. The ship was crossing the Atlantic from Aberdeen, Scotland, to New York. I was aboard because the good people of Lutheran Cross Church in Fresno had provided me passage on this ship, so I could eventually join their congregation as a free person.

As I stared into gentle green blue waves, I did not know why I should feel pensive and gloomy. Had not my Heavenly Father changed my fate for the better? Had he not blessed me with kindhearted, generous friends, who had worked hard on my behalf and overcome insurmountable obstacles?

Since leaving Russia I sensed that every experience had been a pleasant delight compared to my former life. Therefore, I now blamed myself for feeling depressed and unhappy. I realized, of course, that I fretted in part over the uncertainty of a new life. Would I like America, California and its people? Would I be able to find work, be able to feed myself? On self-examination, I realized how few skills I possessed. I spoke three languages. I had kept books for the *kolkhoz*. I could also train horses; however, beyond these few odd accomplishments I had nothing to offer.

As to where I was going, I only knew the name, Fresno, California. But where was Fresno? Herbert had told me that it was a town in a pleasant valley, the San Joaquin Valley. Joaquin sounded to me like *Joachim*—a male German name of biblical origin. Was this a portent? Was I to live in a German, a biblical place? The people certainly thought and acted as did the people I had known on the Volga. They were caring and kind. Look what they had done for me already, without knowing me at all.

This thought raised my spirit. I contemplated Herbert's promise that the valley was flat, dry and warm—hot even in summer. I liked the idea of a warm place after freezing so often in Siberia. Perhaps my new life would be sunny and bright? My thoughts of warmth and freedom reverted back to the cold, the gloom of oppression. Would I ever see any of my people again? If I could make a home there in promised California, would God grant me a reunion with my mother and Joseph? Would I be able to find my grandparents and my brothers, Michael and Peter, again?

Would the Allies be victorious in the war that still raged? My heart knew with visceral certainty that the outcome had to be a victory for us. Oh, I already counted myself one of them, one of the defenders against evil, one of those righteous and truthful. Once the countries of the world were at peace again, might one find one's missing friends and relatives?

In the midst of such profound musings, I was disturbed by the sudden appearance of an American warship on the horizon. As the ship came closer, I recognized it instantly to be a destroyer—had I not lived on one very recently? This warship, however, seemed like Goliath when compared to the *Intrepid*, my David, because I saw for the first time a whole warship from afar in its glory.

My eyes absorbed the picture of power and might, as my heart grew stout. The ship was studded with large cannons and guns as a hedgehog is armored with quills. It was because of mighty ships like these, hunting the U-boats cruising in the depth below, that ships like *The Anglican Queen* could still ply their trade and move people across the ocean. I had learned that at its infancy a destroyer's main arsenal had been torpedoes, which they could fire at great speed before running out of harm's way. However, as the tactics and arsenal of the war changed, especially through the use of aircraft, cannons and more guns had to be added.

From below deck, many Scottish, Italian and Irish emigrants clambered up, all of us hoping to become permanent citizens of the grand United States, the heaven of free people.

Excited, smiling people surrounded me, crushing me to the rail. We all waved, hoping the brave men on the ship would be able to see us, see our outpouring of thanks and love. Voices were raised in song. It was amazing how many operatic melodies were familiar to all.

As the destroyer came closer, we spotted its crew and read its name: *USS Perkins*. The sailors milling about deck were as curious about our ship as we were about theirs. At a signal, the crew stood at attention, as formalities were observed and communications exchanged. Then the magnificent ship moved off. But not before they had warned our captain about U-Boat activity before we could reach American waters. This warning was repeated to us in Italian, French and English.

This encounter reminded us forcefully of our precarious situation. During this war, every ship, even a carrier of civilians, would be sent to the bottom of the ocean if the enemy believed that apart from human cargo war materiel was being ferried across the sea.

As the martial ship steamed on, I was not the only one who recognized this reality. For the previously exuberant mood of the crowd had suddenly changed. The faces of my fellow travelers had an anxious, worried look. Mothers held the hands of their children as they descended the iron stairs to the decks below.

My gloomy mood returned with a vengeance. I was thinking of the war, of the two sides embroiled in the monumental struggle. In the beginning, the sympathies of the Volga Germans had been with Germany. News of Germany's internal atrocities and outrages never penetrated the Volga region. Isolated, and coping with terrible troubles of our own, we paid scant attention to the rest of the world. However, after Germany invaded most of Europe and then began a war with Russia, the Russian propaganda machine deluged us with real and prevaricated accounts of the former ally, now turned enemy.

While lingering in detention, I had finally learned the truth of the conflict. Herbert and Elliot, my guardian angels, explained to me why American descendants of Russian-German parents were appalled by the new militaristic Germany and its mad Führer. They had become Americans with heart and soul and were fighting against the cancer, fascism, which was devouring Europe.

In the detention center, our bizarre assortment of foreign companions had been well informed on things political, for our lives depended on the balanced state of the world. All of us prayed and hoped for a victory of the Allies over fascism and the Axis-controlled countries.

Before I left the detention center, the British had extended temporary passports, for the duration of the war only, to all of my fellow freedom seekers. Therefore when I left, everyone was in a joyful, celebratory mood. For the next two weeks I had lived as a guest in Captain Howard's home in London, guided and helped by his charming, active wife.

Lady Howard was involved in numerous volunteer activities concerning the war effort: raising funds, supervising an auxiliary, preparing special kits and care packages for soldiers, and visiting the wounded in hospital. Before I knew it, I was working alongside this dynamic woman, accomplishing things I never knew I was capable of doing.

Not a fortnight had passed when, thanks to her, I had been offered and accepted a job at St. Swithin's, which had been turned into a military hospital. I became an assistant to the night nurses, a flock of women who were overworked and understaffed. With me in attendance, a few of them sometimes got a few extra hours of sleep.

I had been happy in the hospital, glad to be useful, gratified to ease the painful lot of young, wounded soldiers. When I felt helpless to combat their discomfort and pain, I would pray with them and for them. Not one of the lads rejected my offers to pray. If I had a little time, I would read in my broken English to those with bandaged hands and eye injuries. They waited eagerly for these times when my voice would take them far away from the war, the hospital and their agonies.

I had almost forgotten Herbert's promise to bring me to America. He, too, was fighting the war, providing air cover for British, Australian and American troops in the Middle East and North Africa. Once, he had picked me up after my night shift, bought me breakfast at a pub, and spent the better part of the day with me. Thereafter, though, I had not heard from him again, until one day in April, Lady Howard sought me out at St. Swithin's with a cable in her hand.

"Dear child," she cried, the moment she saw me, "look what great news I have for you." Together we read the long cable, informing me that I had been accepted as a permanent resident of the United States with the right to citizenship after seven years. Furthermore, the cable told of a passage purchased for me on *The Anglican Queen*, which made it necessary for me to travel to Aberdeen, Scotland.

I had saved a few pounds from my job at St. Swithin's, but not enough to purchase a train ticket to Aberdeen. Lodging, food and sensible clothes had consumed most of what I earned.

Now, looking sheepish, I confessed my dilemma to Lady Howard, saying that I did not know how I could get there. Aberdeen was as far away as the moon to me. "Nonsense," said the lady, "we will get you there! This is too good an opportunity to pass up. America, although at war, is free of fighting on its soil. You shall finally have a chance at a normal life." She clasped me to her chest, smelling faintly and deliciously of what I got to know in later years as Chanel No. 5.

True to her word, when the time came for me to leave London, she had arranged a most marvelous passage for me. How can I describe the swirling mixture of feelings running through me, wild excitement, fear and delight when the car she had sent for me deposited me at a small airfield, far out in the country. I learned that, for the first time in my life, I was to fly. Lady Howard, thinking the flying surprise would be a lark for me, had not prepared me in any way for this adventure.

The two young aviators, civilians flying depeches and supplies into parts of Sicily, made short shrift of a greeting. Having no time for great explanations, they told me, "Here put this on!" while handing me a parachute. I must have looked extremely befuddled, for, in an instant, they both surrounded me, strapping, fastening and snapping the device onto my body. To my surprise, the imagined "lofty thing," the parachute, was heavy and cumbersome. "If we need to bail out, you jump, count to eight and then pull the cord. If the chute does not open, pull the second cord here, that should do it." The shorter of the two men, led me, as I wobbled slightly, to the airplane that I judged to be much too small to carry anything. "Hop in, gal," he said, "and sit down wherever you find free space."

I was mortified. Did they really expect me to fly away with them or jump from this woefully inadequate machine, which loudly screamed impermanency at the beholder? However, I considered that I had no other options. Moreover, would Lady Howard expose me to danger? She probably thought nothing of "hopping into" one of these crates and flying off into the blue.

"How cosy," I managed to mock with gallow's humor, when I looked about inside what I termed "the mosquito." Mailbags, made from greenish brown canvas, crates of pristine new wood, stamped with clean, black lettering, and a few kitbags made up most of the cargo. There was hardly any space left amid the clutter for me to sit.

The pilot, Benson, noted my dismay as I stood half bent over—there was not much headroom. He kicked a few things aside with practiced motions and pulled a leather kitbag from the clutter, presumably his, and said, "Here, make yourself comfortable. If the flight gets a little crazy hold on to this." He pointed to a strap hanging from the ceiling. Pointing at a metal bar on the side, he cautioned, "Don't touch this! It will slice your hand in two."

A moment later the pair was in their cockpit seats, turning on the engines, making them roar. Before I knew it, we rolled down the small, dirt strip, pretending to be a landing strip. Benson pulled the joystick back, the plane took a little hop and bounce and lo, we were air-borne. As the plane gained altitude I felt strange, as if my stomach was filled with bees. But soon the little machine found its equilibrium and I began to enjoy the ride.

Mahoney, the shorter of the pilots, suddenly came back into the hold. Grinning wickedly at me, he yelled into my ear to overcome the infernal noise of the plane, "If you like, you can a have look around. Just go and sit in my seat. I will take a quick nap back here. Benson will send you back when he needs me."

Steeling myself against rising fear, yet swayed by aroused curiosity, I crawled forward, and sank into the copilot's seat. When I finally dared raise my eyes past the instrument panel in front of me and looked beyond the cone of the plane, a miracle revealed itself. It seemed as if a secret was revealed to me.

Below us were villages, fields, woods and rivers. Houses, petite and charming, lay clustered together, as if finding comfort in the nearness of others. Approaching rapidly, I saw a magnificent city with grand buildings, looking like castles.

"Cambridge!" screamed Benson over the din. "Our town of famous universities. The river you see is the Cam."

The plane suddenly shook and bucked. For a moment I was terribly scared. Benson adjusted his controls. Seconds later, flying calmly again, he screamed, "Originally you were to ship out of Plymouth, but the Germans have been hitting that harbor hard, and so Lady Howard decided that we should fly you to Aberdeen, which is still relatively calm." He lit a cigarette and bellowed, "Much nicer this way, for you get to see a good part of England and Scotland, too."

Because I did not feel my voice adequate to combat the noise, I shone my sunniest smile on Benson. I hoped, thereby, to adequately express my delight in the sights, more magical than anything I had ever seen before. Benson motioned me to put on earphones. I had no clue what the strange things were. A moment later, however, to my great delight, I could communicate with him calmly and clearly with the din from the manifold reduced. I marveled at the wonders the world had to offer—there was so much an ordinary person would never see.

As we flew on, Benson called out the names of the larger cities we flew over: Huntingdon, Peterborough, Stamford, Nottingham, Doncaster and more. He also named the rivers and the shires. We talked about our families, the war, and what we hoped to do with our still very young lives. Benson hoped he could continue flying. He envisioned a future for huge airplanes, carrying millions of people from continent to continent.

I, on the other hand, could not even in my wildest fantasies imagine what God held in store for my life. If offered choices, would I choose well, choose the right things for myself? Or would I fail? I spoke of my apprehensions and fears, but Benson, with a young man's enthusiasm and overweening optimism, pushed my worries away. "You are young and healthy. America is a great place and so you will be able to do anything you please. Have a horse farm if you wish. You love horses and know all about them, so why don't you?" I had to laugh. Everything seemed so easy for him. Nothing was impossible in his world, and therefore, he made me feel very good about my future.

Over Northumberland we were plagued by turbulence. The little plane shook so badly I thought it would break. "Go and get Mahoney!" requested Benson, and slipping off the earphones, I reluctantly complied. For the rest of the flight, I was relegated to sit among baggage and cargo.

In Aberdeen, we landed on proper tarmac. My flyer friends hastily said goodbye after landing. They put me into a car, explaining that the driver was a friend who would put me on board *The Aberdeen Queen*, which was to sail the next day.

And so, pulled along by events beyond my control, I found myself in the middle of an ocean, on my way to new worlds.

A New Shore—A New Continent

Five days had passed since we had seen the destroyer. Two of these days had been spent fearing for our lives in a tempestuous storm. I knew the awesome, destructive force of storms well. When storms raged across the steppe, she lay below the onslaught, helpless and subdued, as a woman being raped. Arising in the Far East, the storms always brought misery to every living thing. They scorched and desiccated in the summer; they froze and ice-covered in winter.

This storm, however, was a different experience for me. For here, I was part and parcel of a fragile vessel being tossed about like the toy boats our boys launched in the Volga when she was wild with spring thaw. Before, we had endured the might of the winds by burrowing into our homes as wild things burrow into the ground, seeking shelter between the tenacious roots of the wild grasses.

As the wind howled and roared hour after hour, most of the passengers below became violently ill. I did not succumb to the ills of the stomach. But to earn that favor, I had to spend much of my time on the top deck in the fresh air, becoming an integral part of the ocean's chaos.

The Scottish crew seemed to me soldiers at war, fighting an enemy of superior strength. Covered in oilcloth, they clambered valiantly across the wave-scoured deck to their appointed tasks. The helmsman steered the ship straight into towering waves, breaching them, until I thought the mass of water ahead of us would crash down upon our ship, taking us straight to the bottom of the sea.

One of the sailors, who could not convince me to stay in the cabin because I got sick down below, took pity on me. He tied me securely to the mast, where I remained for many hours of the tumult. Whenever I did retire below to a dormitory of bunks where sick people clung to their wretched beds I was, thankfully, so tired, cold and wet that I could sink onto my small, allotted space and fall asleep.

After the storm, the ocean, as if to make up for her terror, showed her most pleasant face. Although the waves were still higher than before the storm, they could be endured. The sun shone bright, warming and drying everything. The captain used full steam and powered the ship toward land, thereby making up for lost time. And then, late one afternoon, the lookout sang out, "Land ahoy! Land ahead!"

Soon the deck was crowded with passengers. Everyone wanted to be the first to have the honor of spying the Statue of Liberty. It was dark when we finally reached New York harbor. To our dismay, we were not to disembark this night, but had to wait on board until morning to clear immigration services.

To mitigate our disappointment, the cooks prepared a special meal to which all passengers on ship were invited. For many poor families this proved to be a great treat. The passengers in steerage were very poor. They had not had a hot meal since leaving Aberdeen. Many slept on the bare planks of the deck, cushioned only by their belongings. They survived on the meager rations they had brought with them: hard sausage, hard bread and cheese, oil, garlic, onions and fruit. The ship's master provided tea and water, which they often used to soften their bread, which was getting harder by the day.

Compared to these poor people, my accommodations had been princely. The good Germans of Fresno had provided for a small cot in a dorm room with thirty others and plain but ample food from the ship's kitchen.

After the farewell meal, many of us walked on the top deck. I had not been very companionable throughout the voyage. Instead I had withdrawn deep into myself, wondering what to do with my life. Yet all I derived from these painful ruminations was a deep feeling of loneliness exacerbated by the fact that no one around me spoke a language I knew. Gradually, I came to the realization that I would just have to bend like the grass of the steppe bends before the wind, and patiently await what God held in store for me.

Early next morning, the ship weighed anchor and pulled into the harbor, where Miss Liberty beckoned. Beholding the cauldron of activity that was New York harbor, I was not the only one dazed and overwhelmed. How could persons find their way amid the chaos of the milling crowd, vehicles, stevedores, and assorted dangerous contraptions I had no name for? Yes, New York frightened me, filled me with such dread that I wanted to hide under the blankets of my little bunk. But I had to leave the safety of the ship. I gathered my few possessions and walked, following much braver souls down the gangway to set foot on the soil of my country of hope.

Fresno

The sun shone brightly in a clear, blue sky when I stepped from the train. I tightly held on to my valise and the small bundle of odd belongings. Anxiously, I scanned the faces of the few people who had come to pick up friends and family. I had been told that someone would be at the train station to take me to the house of the Mehling family, who had agreed to take me in until I could provide for myself.

In New York, Frau Berg, a Lutheran connection and former Volga German settler, had taken me to her home. The following day she had put me on a Southern Pacific train bound for Fresno, California. I realized by now that the good people of the Lutheran Cross Church had invested a small fortune in my person. The ship's passage alone amounted to two hundred and fifty dollars, never mind the rail ticket.

I felt humbled and honored by so much trust. Herbert must have been a good advocate for me to have inspired such confidence in the congregation. During the short time I spent in her home, Frau Berg had told me how most Russian Germans had gone deep into debt in Russia to be able to afford the ship's passage of their families. She laughingly said, "You know our people. Once working in America, they remitted the money in no time. No one in Russia would have refused our people a loan, because their honesty was well known."

Thinking of my obligations, I walked steadily to the exit of the train station. Approaching the exit, I saw a man with a sign that he held very high. He was tall, so there was no need for him to hold the large sign so high that it obscured half his face. I remember thinking, "How odd; it is as if he wants to hide from someone," and then I read the sign. It was in German and said, "Welcome to Fresno, Katharina Grushov."

A small cry of surprise escaped my lips. I hastened to the stranger and said, "I am Katharina Grushov. Thank you for being here." The stranger pulled the sign away from his face and I screamed with delight, "Herbert, oh, *lieber* Herbert!" I instantly forgot that I had tried so very hard to make a proper impression, putting on the bottle green suit with the adorable hat, styling my hair more severely than I otherwise would have done. But now, all concessions to convention flew out the window. I dropped my baggage and stretched out my arms, reaching for Herbert with almost painful relief.

Oh, Herbert! The person I had least expected to see upon my arrival in Fresno—here he was. I suddenly felt weak as tension ebbed from my body. The worries that had haunted me for weeks evaporated like water in the hot sun.

"Well, well," he said, grinning from ear to ear. "You are finally here, *liebes Mädchen*." He embraced me with great warmth and so much vigor that my fashionable hat fell onto the dusty perron. Releasing me, he swept the hat off the platform's ground and ceremoniously placed it on my head.

"I imagined you far away, flying over England or Italy, providing cover for troops," I stammered happily.

"Oh, I was there until three days ago. But then I was given fourteen days' leave."

"So how is it possible then that you arrived here before me?" I asked, filled with incredulity at such a feat. Herbert smiled his wonderful, broad smile, which lightened up the world for those who saw him. It was so engaging; I could not help but smile back.

"I came on a plane," he explained. "I hitched a ride on a transporter, refueling in Greenland, on its way to New York. I could not have done it, but for a general and two colonels who were going home on leave and invited me along. And so things worked out perfectly. From New York it was easy. I know enough fly-boys happy to give me rides."

My mind boggled at the thought of a plane being able to fly from Europe to America, across a continent, across the ocean. My experience in the small two-engine plane had been fraught with frightful moments, leaving me with lasting insecurity. So, how then could a plane large enough to carry heavy supplies, and on many occasions many soldiers, even get airborne? I smiled. However, I was quite serious, saying, "You are making fun of me, are you not? How could a plane, as large as the one you describe, lift up into the sky?"

Now Herbert was in his element. He was positively aroused, expounding on his greatest passion—flying. "*Mädchen*," he said in a tone that suggested I had impugned his veracity, "you don't know what you are talking about." He breathed in, thereby gaining two inches in height and breadth before going on.

"We have fleets of huge transporters, and so have the Russians. You just never saw them. Many of the planes were commercial carriers before the Armed Forces Services commandeered them. Years ago they took soldiers to China and ferried Chinese to the front against the Japanese. These planes are enormous and wonderful, and one day I will show you one."

He picked up my humble bags with one hand, holding onto me with other and led me into the street. Here another surprise awaited. Tied to a lamppost, a perky bay horse played with its reins as it stood between the poles of a small carriage.

Herbert threw my belongings nonchalantly into the back of the buggy, and helped me onto the seat beside him. The moment he held the reins in his hands he clicked his tongue, moving the horse into a respectably fast trot, and began to speak again.

"I came home in a very fine, special plane, the C-75, which once was called the Stratoliner when it flew commercially. Best dang plane in the army." He positively glowed with the memory of this glorious piece of machinery. Although not suitably impressed, due to my ignorance, I prompted him to tell me how he managed to hop from New York to California in one day—a trip that had cost me several days riding in a train.

Herbert seemed delighted that I should ask. "But of course," he cried, "you know nothing about America, nothing of the brotherhood of pilots, and so I am glad you ask."

He smiled devilishly, "Believe me, flyers are crazy. In our fraternity, someone always knows another pilot ready to be of service to a brother. The moment I put out word that I needed a ride across country, the guys in the chain talked. When I arrived in New York, I already had a ride lined up to Colorado with a guy flying important mail. In Denver, I hitched a ride with a guy flying tests of the P-51 Mustang from the airfields of North American Aviation out of Inglewood, California."

My head was spinning. I had not the faintest idea what he was talking about. But being a good sport, I said, "That is fantastic. What a wonderful group of men you are connected to." I meant this wholeheartedly, because, here he was, the knight of my grand rescue. I suddenly realized that I had no idea where we were going. Trusting, like a lamb following the shepherd, I had followed Herbert.

"Where are we going? Where will I be living?"

"You will be living with the Mehlings until you can support yourself. They are a family that came to California in 1887 from the Russian steppe, the *Wiesenseite*, the place that knows all about troubles. When they heard about you and the hard times you endured, they said 'Bring her to us. We can help. We understand'."

He flicked his reins because the horse had slowed its pace. Looking into my eyes, he said, "My parents would have taken you in if the Mehlings had not volunteered." His face grew dark. "Better the Mehlings, though, because my parents must care for my sister, who was thrown from a horse and has been an invalid ever since."

"I am sorry," I said. "It must be hard to be young and be severely disabled."

"Yes, Christina is a bright girl. Once she was bursting with life. It was her exuberance that got her into trouble. She always liked the fieriest horses, the fastest cars and the most scintillating boys best. Now, God is her best companion. You will be meeting her soon because I am taking you home for dinner. My parents wanted very much to meet you."

"How kind of them to welcome me to their home," I said, humbled by the goodness of our people.

We rode in silence for a while. It was wonderfully sunny and warm; the air was heated and dry as during the best days in the steppe. I looked around, taking in the sights. The town of Fresno was not large. By the Southern Pacific's railroad station I had seen warehouses, stretching along the railroad tracks. The dusty street had been lined with commercial, single-story buildings, which later gave way to diners, small stores and the occasional home.

The buggy turned into a side street lined with prosperous houses, which proudly displayed porches, newly planted trees and small flower beds. On we went, down I Street, which would later be renamed Broadway, and soon we found ourselves driving beyond the city limits.

The land was flat, brown as far I could see—green where cultivated—and it seemed to go on forever. My heart beat faster as I beheld the benign emptiness. Oh, how it reminded me of the steppe in summer—warm, open and wide. The carriage turned onto a dirt path, which opened to my surprise to a view of orchards filled with apricot and peach trees and of vineyards. There was so much green, I could hardly believe my eyes.

The dirt road led straight through the orchards. When finally it curved onto another dusty path, the eye was once again free to roam to the horizon. At the end of a small vineyard to the right of me stood a brand-new, handsome wooden house, before which Herbert halted the carriage. Although it was only a one-story house it stood taller by far than the homes on the Volga. Its roof had less of a slant than the ordinary Volga house; little snow and less rain, I was soon to learn. A large, shaded veranda, to which broad steps led, encircled the home. Windows, much larger than any in Russia's villages, allowed the light to permeate the rooms.

As we stepped from the carriage, I assumed that this must be the home of Herbert's parents. I commented on the open design of the house, the quality of the exceedingly beautiful wood and the large windows.

"That is California-style," said Herbert. "My parents and everyone who came here soon found that wood was good, plentiful, and easy to come by. The climate is mild, so there is no need for heavy, tight construction."

We had not yet set foot on the broad steps leading up to and across the veranda, when a tall gray-haired man, who looked remarkably like an older version of Herbert, flung the door wide. Herbert's father, August, stepped onto the veranda closely followed by a handsome woman in her late fifties. A long dark dress covered her from neck to foot and was kind to her full figure. The white ruffled apron she wore nicely set off her still slender waist. Her dark hair, streaked with silver, was gathered at the back of her head.

The pair exclaimed almost simultaneously, *"Na, da seit Ihr ja! Wilkommen, wilkommen, Katharina!"* Hands stretched out, they both came toward me each took a hand and shook it vigorously. I greeted them warmly and thanked them for their kindness. I hoped that my heart was revealed in my smile.

Inside, too, the house was different from our Volga German houses. We stepped into an entry, a small room that was tiled with large, gold-brown squares and furnished with a hat stand and a wooden bench. From there, three framed doorways led to the kitchen, into the *gute Stube*, and would wonders never cease, into a dining room. Beyond that, they told me lay the bedrooms and the baths.

As I marveled at the nicely tiled floor, the way the wood shone and the spaciousness of their home, Margarete told me of the wonders of life in California.

"The floor you admire so much was laid by the Mexicans in town. Many of them just work in the fields and the orchards, but a few of them are craftsmen and they have taught us that the tile keeps the house cool. The woodwork was crafted and finished by German artisans, fellow immigrants."

I learned that Herbert's parents had come to America in 1903. They had been healthy, strong, and twenty-two and eighteen years old, respectively. During their first years in Fresno, they had worked so hard that twelve years passed before their first child, Herbert, was born.

"It must have been the backbreaking work that prevented me from having a child," said Margarete, wistfully, "but then, within three years, Christina was born, too."

I learned that, at first, they had worked in the fields planting vineyards. The work was excruciating but paid well. Soon they could afford to buy a small shack in Rooshian Town, the poor section of town where Russian Germans, Mennonites and Lutherans congregated. Having achieved this small measure of success, independence from landlords, Margarete found work in the food industry while August became the supervisor on a vegetable farm. Tomatoes, cucumbers, lettuce, cabbage and melons sold well. Of the latter, especially the melon variety the Volga Germans had brought from Russia and Americans named Klondike, was in demand while the small, round, native melon was ignored.

The drying of apricots, peaches and grapes was and still is big business in the San Joaquin Valley to this day. Most dried fruit consumed by Americans came and comes still from this sunny valley. The picking, cleaning, cutting and drying of the apricots also was hard work but more benign than the planting of vineyards. Working in the drying sheds, Margarete relaxed and was blessed with children.

As August, a dry-spoken, thoughtful, deliberate man, led me through the house, his greatest pride, he said, "You must always take pride in your ancestry, Katharina, for I know of no other people who were dispersed over the globe and prospered in the same way our people did. When we came to Fresno we had nothing, except the clothes on our backs and a set of work clothes." For a moment August grew quiet. He seemed to retreat into those difficult days, but looking out the window and beholding his acreage, he revived.

"In the beginning we earned a living working alongside Negro and Mexican field workers, while living in the worst part of town, which was known to flood on occasion. By scrimping, saving and working unceasingly, however, we could eventually buy a house on I Street. Not a bad place to have arrived." He looked at me proudly. "Twenty years later, we bought the acreage out here and built this house."

We had aimlessly walked across the broad terrace into the garden. For a moment he grew pensive and became withdrawn, only to comment an instant later, "I always thought that Herbert would take over my farm one day, but America is different from Russia."

"In what way?" I asked.

"Altogether different," he said. "Every child has to go to school, free of charge. And not only that, but we are free to practice our religion. Furthermore, no one in the schools indoctrinates our children to become something other than what they are."

I well remembered the attempts of the Russian Orthodox Church to turn German children in Russian schools away from their culture and their religion, and I told him what I remembered. August explained the wonder that was America further.

"So you see, here, our children loved school. The American children taught them all sorts of new things. Upon marriage, our girls suddenly did not want to go and live in the groom's household anymore, as they had in Russia. No, they wanted a home of their own like the American women; and the boys, especially the smart ones, wanted to go to college. And—there went Herbert: first off to college; then to flight training. God only knows what he will do when the war is over."

I smiled at him and said, "Don't give up on him, yet. He might become a farmer after all."

He sighed heavily, "I don't think so."

At this point on our stroll, we heard Margarete's voice calling us to dinner. Herbert introduced me to his sister. Christina, beautiful of face and upper body, with blond hair and delicate skin, was a paraplegic sitting in a wheelchair, which Herbert now pushed to the table.

I realized that in my honor the usual cold German *Abendbrot* had been replaced by a special cooked meal. Strong familiar aromas from the Volga awakened my senses, and suddenly I was terribly hungry. We sat around a large, oval table bedecked with white linen and set with lovely china. The delicate white porcelain featured a design of rose baskets around the edge. I remembered that my mother once told me German women had one thing in common, no matter their social standing: they all loved good linen and the best china they could afford.

Oozing *Hausfrau* pride, Margarete served us borscht for the first course, followed by roast chicken, *Klösse*, brown gravy, sauerkraut and assorted vegetables. She finished the marvelous meal with *süssem Kuchen*, made with watermelon syrup.

When I finally left Herbert's hospitable family I thanked them repeatedly for making me feel so welcome, at home even. I promised them I would become an American citizen of whom they could be proud.

A New Family—a New Job

I stayed with the Mehlings, my sponsor family, for only two months. To my misfortune, the Southern Pacific Railroad transferred Karl Mehling, the father of a brood of seven, to San Diego, and the church community found me another sponsor.

Bruno Halbig and his wife Else, had emigrated to the USA from Saxony, Eastern Germany, and spoke a heavily accented German dialect. They had no children and appeared to be nice people. Living with them in their spacious house, however, I soon found that they sponsored me not for my benefit but for very selfish reasons.

Karl Mehling had found me a job in the apricot industry without difficulty. Because I spoke hardly any English I did not qualify for anything but the most menial tasks. Right then, I vowed that within six months I would speak enough English to understand and speak the everyday language.

Of course, I knew that living in a family meant I would be treated as one of the members. In the Mehling household, I had cheerfully helped with chores in the morning before going to work and in the evening upon coming home. With seven children there was always work to do. However, the Mehlings gave me most of Sunday off to go to church with them, to look after my clothes and to learn English.

Conversely, the Halbigs expected me to be at their beck and call every hour not spent at work. I cleaned the house on Saturday and cooked and washed for them on Sunday. The Halbigs did not believe that "servants" should go to church like other folks, but were to serve God by doing good works for their betters.

Herbert had flown out of my life again two days before his leave was up. Cheerfully, he had hitched flights again, which he had carefully lined up days before. We had spent some time together, walking the town. "So you don't get lost," he quipped. Of course, he took advantage of his father's carriage to drive me about in the countryside. Bit by bit he taught me additional English words and phrases. We enjoyed our time together immensely, although our relationship was bittersweet.

I was terribly attracted to him, and he seemed to like me much more than was implied in the brotherly manner he projected most times. Every so often his eyes and his hands gave him away. However, we carefully avoided speaking of anything but the present. The dangers of the war and the uncertainty of a pilot's life were mentioned often in our conversations.

Imagine my surprise, therefore, when he kissed me passionately goodbye on our last date, but still said nothing of his intentions, not even that he would write.

Feeling used by the Halbigs, I thought about Herbert more and more. The kiss grew in proportion to my misery. Herbert and this kiss became the one bright spot in an endless, joyless sea of work. My situation soon went from bad to worse, with the result that I felt that I could not allow these two selfish people to abuse me any longer. The food they gave me was terrible. In order to subsist I bought food with my own money, money that I was supposed to save for repayment of my ship's passage and for future independence. I worked every waking hour of the day and fell into what might be described as a gulag state of mind: always bone weary, dull and spiritually deprived.

One day, as I bought a milkshake in the big drugstore on I Street, a bold thought took hold of me. I was overcome by the dreadful realization that I could not go back to the house where the owners, like jailers, robbed me of human contact and life. I knew at this precise moment I would never go back to that joyless house. I couldn't listen one more time to their crude, broadly-accented, commanding voices; knew with deep conviction that I had come to this country of the free—to be free. Well then, I would be free! The moment I made the decision to change my life, I felt better.

I approached the owner of the drugstore and said in my terrible English, "Is possible you have job for me? Work hard, very clean, learn good, fast."

The startled, bespectacled man in the white coat looked at me disconcertedly, as if he saw me for the first time. He mustered me from head to toe, "German?" he asked.

"Yes."

"How long have you been in the country?"

"Six months." He harrumphed, clearing his throat, and thoughtfully surveyed me in even greater detail. I must have looked trustworthy, able to work and learn, for the round, mild-mannered man said, "Good, start tomorrow morning at nine. I will pay you three dollars a day. Do you understand?"

I understood perfectly. With three dollars a day and the amount I had saved from my food-drying job, I could rent a small room and be on my own. I thanked him very much, and managed to stammer, "I need a room for pay. You know rooms?" And, by God, he knew a lady who rented rooms.

When I left the drugstore my step was light. I went to the address the druggist had given me. There, a pleasant, middle-aged woman, who looked like a faded rose, opened the door. The druggist had given me a note, which explained better than I could have that I needed a room, that I worked for him, and that, therefore, I was able to pay my rent.

The thin, worn woman accepted me with a squall of words of which I only understood a few. Her gestures, however, enhanced my understanding. She led me up a set of plain wooden stairs to the upper floor, down a narrow hallway to the last room on the left. Everything, the stairs and the white walls of the hallway, was perfectly clean, and so was the room when she opened the door.

Of medium size, the room was simple and square as a box. Although sparsely furnished, it managed to look cheerful and inviting. A bit of white lace over the large window, which gave a view of I Street, a quilted, mul-ticolored coverlet, and a flower print on the wall made the room seem warm, welcoming. What a change from the drab, windowless closet I had retreated into each night.

"Twelve dollars a month," said Cora Blackwell, who had told me already that she was a widow, raising two children. I heard the price and shrank back; twelve dollars a month. I would only make three dollars a day, and from that I had to clothe and feed myself and, most importantly, save enough to repay almost three hundred dollars accrued in expenses for my passage, papers and food. This was money I owed the congregation of the Lutheran Cross Church.

Cora Black must have seen my reaction. She understood hardship because her life was fraught with problems. She inspected me closely and then looked away. By her furrowed forehead and her faraway look, I knew she was thinking hard. When her gaze fastened once more on my person, she said, "If you help me with the laundry every second Saturday and run some small errands, I can let you have the room for six dollars a month, because I need help with the boardinghouse."

I did not understand fully. With the help of my dictionary I asked questions until I understood what was offered to me. Once I understood the offer, I gladly agreed to the lady's generous terms. I told her I would come back in the evening with my belongings. Then I ran all the way to the drying sheds where I washed, sorted and cut apricots, spreading them onto screens to dry in the sun.

I told the supervisor at the shed that I would not be back as he handed me my pay of four dollars. He told me that he was sorry to see me go, but even he agreed that three dollars in the drugstore was good pay for lighter, less boring work. "If it does not work out for you, I will be glad to take you back," he promised, making me smile with pleasure.

My shift was over at eight and I rushed to the house of the Halbigs to retrieve my things. No one seemed to be at home. I went straight to the dark hole that had been my room, which I was determined to see for the last time. I had barely arrived and was gathering my clothes into my valise, when I heard the unpleasant, screeching voice of Frau Halbig.

"Where have you been? I expected you at six to clean the vegetables and start dinner." The Halbigs had their main meal at night, because they worked too far away to have a hot meal at lunch as the Germans liked.

I ignored her outraged barrage and quickly finished packing my belongings.

"What are you doing? What is this all about?" she cried, her tinny voice vibrating dangerously close to breaking.

"*Papa, Papa, komm mal her. Die Katharina packt Ihre Sachen!*"

Herr Halbig came in a hurry, "What is going on here," he demanded to know, staring at me menacingly.

"I am leaving!" I said simply.

"You can't," yelled Frau Halbig.

"You will stay," he commanded, "because the church put you into our care! That is it! You remain here!"

"Oh, no!" I reiterated, steeling myself before this double onslaught. "I am leaving."

"You will not! I forbid it!" roared Halbig. Suddenly I grew afraid of these people. They acted as if I had no rights, as if I had become their rightful slave. Suddenly the two of them had turned into maniacs. Their fingers pointed at me; their arms waved in front of my face; they made punching motions. Their faces were distorted by malice. At one point, Herr Halbig pushed me onto the small cot that had been my bed.

My fright deepened. I was desperately thinking of a way to get away. As if by divine inspiration, the answer came to me.

"If I do not show up at my new lodging in half an hour the police will come and search your house for me," I said with as much bravado as I could muster.

The Halbigs grew uncertain. They began to think. "You cannot leave without paying for room and board we provided," said quick-thinking Frau Halbig. I, however, was fighting for my life and thought just as quickly.

"I worked for both of you every waking hour, even Sundays, and the pastor told me I was to save my money. You, the sponsors, would provide room and board in exchange for some household help, which you have received manifold."

"You will not leave here until you pay us thirty dollars for your care," bellowed Herr Halbig, red of face and sweating with fury.

By now I was shaking with fright and anger, and, like an animal cornered, I turned to bite. "Wait until the police go with me before the congregation. What a tale I will be telling. The way you prevented me from going to church, the way you used me as your slave, and the terrible food you fed me—they will love to hear all about it."

Then, it was as if I was given a command. I heard it loud and clear in my mind. "Take your things and push past both of them."

I grabbed my bundle, pulling it from Frau Halbig's hands. She had laid hold of it as if she wanted to keep it. As I plowed between them, striding to the door, the beefy, dastardly Herr Halbig struck me across the face so hard I thought I would fall, pass out even.

"Ungrateful monster, defying God's will," he bellowed. I, however, spurred on by fear, kept pushing to escape. He, angered by my defiance, shoved me powerfully toward the doorpost. I fell against his wife, who blocked the door with him. In turn, she lost her balance and fell onto the bed. Suddenly, there was an opening between them and I pushed through and came free. I ran down the dark hallway to the front door with both of them in hot pursuit.

They breathed excitedly, like wolves chasing game. I now fully understood that they meant to keep me here by force if necessary. Perhaps, if they succeeded, I would never see the outside again. I jerked the door open and tumbling over the threshold I reached the front porch. Somehow I found my balance and jumped down the three stairs leading into the street.

My pursuers did not stop at the open door, but came running after me. Although I sped fleetly down the sidewalk, Herr Halbig almost caught up with me when I tried to avoid a collision with a portly gentleman. In desperation, I screamed, "*Hilfe!* Help!" at the top of my lungs. At that, our race attracted attention. Passersby stopped and stared. A large man crossed the street with the obvious intention to insert himself between the furious couple and me. His intervention stopped the Halbigs in their tracks.

"What's the problem?" asked the large man, with concern in his voice.

"I not want to work for them!" I said emphatically with my bad English.

"Oh," he exclaimed, understanding the situation instantly, "and so they want to force you?" His voice had become very loud. An angry rumble came from the small crowd which was forming.

Stopped in their tracks by the intervention of strangers, the Halbigs suddenly seemed to shrink. They turned and walked hastily back to their house. Awkwardly choosing my words in English, I thanked the nice people who had stopped on my behalf and, thoroughly winded, walked on. Although I was greatly relieved that fate had turned the frightening situation in my favor, I did not yet trust the peace. As I walked at a fast pace, I turned often to look back for the Halbigs.

At last, walking at a normal pace, I breathed easily. An enormous weight had been lifted off my shoulders and a poem came to mind:

Poem of the Fallen Man

The deep sunk sinner loves to see
The righteous man give way
And fall into the deep, dark pit
Of avarice and decay.

His own sins, piled high to the sky
Seem petty to his eyes,
Compared to one, but fateful step
Of righteousness' demise.

Professed to goodness, pledged to right
The latter's sins weigh more.
For sinners sinning all the time
Have long ceased to keep score.

These hollow men, vain hypocrites
They walk and pray and sing
But deep inside their song is dead
Their pride is everything.

Don Weidenweber

Life of Freedom

My new life began when I again arrived at the modest house on Willow Street, a cross street to broad I Street. Cora Blackwell was already waiting for me. She seemed relieved to see me, making me think that lodgers were not easy to come by. I found this observation later to be true. Most single men preferred to save their hard-earned money by sleeping in drying sheds and under the stars, which the mild weather permitted.

I paid Cora Blackwell the first six dollars' rent and she gave me the key to my room. My heart seemed to jump a little when I was finally alone in the sweet, bright room. Mine! Paid for with my own money. I felt proud. After years of dependency, I was now my own agent.

Pulling my bundle of clothes and personal items apart and emptying my valise, I saw with astonishment and increasing abhorrence how, prior to my packing these belongings, rough hands had examined, nay worse, viciously searched each thing. The hems of each item had been ripped open, not fully but amply enough to push a wire through in search of hidden jewelry or money. My dress shoes had torn inner linings, and even the chic little hat, the one to match the bottle green London suit, had suffered.

I fell to my knees and thanked the Lord for delivering me from people with evil souls. Thanks to the paranoia, instilled in me by a life under communism and in the gulag, I had never left even a cent behind in the room. At my earliest convenience, when living at the Mehlings, I had sewn a body-belt from stout linen, which lay flat upon my skin. I always wore this belt, unnoticeable to observers. Without this foresight, the Halbigs could have robbed me blind; of that I am quite certain.

The Drugstore

The next day, I wore my dark, rough-cloth work dress, ready to do any kind of work. My new boss, Harry Pillmann—I loved the comic touch that his name in German meant maker of pills, the pill man—was exactly what he had chosen to be. He did not stand on ceremony.

"Katharina, you have to clean the floor before the customers come." He pushed a bucket and mop at me and motioned toward the checkered linoleum floor. By functional design, mops and buckets seem to be the same all over the world. Their purpose is crystal clear. Mopping the floor was an easy task for me. The black-and-white-checked surface was not very dirty, so the job required little effort; soon I was done.

I loved being in the drugstore. After six months of mind-numbing drying of apricots, the store with its lunch counter, soda fountain and rows of shelves stocked with health items and beauty aids was an oasis, brimming with interesting delights. I had seen drugstores in Liverpool and London, but they were boring by comparison. One could not get sodas and lunch in the English establishments; neither could one find there bag balm for cows' udders, treatment for horses' thrush-infected hooves, nor the salves to treat mange in pets. One half of a large shelf was dedicated to the ailments of creatures. I liked that immensely, for I remembered how difficult it had been to gather herbs, wash lanolin from fleeces, and then combine herbs, minerals, lanolin, or balm to make salve to treat sick livestock.

The beauty aisle also held my fascination. There were creams, lipsticks, dark pencils and powders for brows and eyes, bobby pins, combs and brushes, curlers, soaps and creams, and other substances for uses mysterious to me.

After cleaning the floor, I learned to set up the lunch counter and the soda fountain. Patiently, often repeating his words and showing me by example, Harry Pillmann initiated me in the art of caring for the equipment, making sandwiches, mixing sodas and milkshakes. He seemed pleased with my efforts. Thereafter, we both stacked shelves.

My first hour had gone by like a nice dream, before Harry Pillmann opened the door for business. The first customer to arrive was an old lady looking for liniment. I tried to help her, but she let me know in no uncertain terms that she preferred finding it herself. Harry grinned and waved me to the counter, where he stood in his white apron behind the till.

"This is Mrs. Bow. She likes to look slowly through the entire store. It gives her pleasure." I understood. An old man came in. Leaning against the counter, he killed time by chatting with Harry. Other customers came, asking for sodas, cold cream, Epsom salts, emetics, laxatives and cotton balls. I was sent to the backroom in search of odd things: vaporizers, rubber gloves, elastic stockings and, of all things, light bulbs. We had it all; I was impressed.

I made sandwiches and prepared drinks, all the while learning English. I was happy as a lark, rising into the blue of the sky, singing full-throated. At one thirty, after the lunch crowd, Harry told me to fix two sandwiches. "Make them good ones," he advised, "plenty of ham and cheese, because they are for us." He ate his at the counter by the till, but sent me with my sandwich and a drink into the backroom where I could sit down and eat in peace. When we closed at six that evening I was tired, but happy. God had delivered me among good people and I felt deeply grateful.

Arriving the next morning, Harry had a surprise for me. He handed me a prettily wrapped package, in which I found a white, ruffled little apron to wear over my dark dress. With this simple gesture, he made me a part of the store, counterpoint to his own large white apron.

I found out that Harry was in his mid-fifties and married, as the ring on his finger declared. He was round of face, round about the middle, and of course, of German ancestry. He was calm, competent, and as I got to know him better, intelligent and a good judge of people. To those attributes, I must add that he was gifted with dry humor and a keen appreciation for the ridiculous. Without ever seeming to check or intrude on my work, he astutely evaluated my performance, apparently with occasional glances from behind the cash register.

With great difficulty, I had explained to him that every second Saturday Cora Blackwell needed my services. I was worried he might resent my absences, but he removed my concerns by assuring me that his wife would be glad to come in once in a while.

My first Saturday in Cora Blackwell's laundry, a small house in the backyard where she also cooked meals on hot days, was filled with hard work but also with the satisfying pleasure derived from female companionship. Little had I known how much I missed it. In the drying sheds I had worked alongside mostly Mexican and black women whose patois and my poor English made conversation impossible.

Cora told me that she had bought the house from a Volga German and this was the reason that it was endowed with the out-back kitchen-laundry. "Look around town," said Cora. "If you see a backyard kitchen building, chances are that a Volga German built it."

She told me little tales about her boarders and her children, Becky and John—preteens and precocious. I learned that she became a widow at twenty-eight, when the love of her life, her husband of ten years, died of a strange fever. The doctors—she even sent for one from San Francisco—had been unable to diagnose the illness, and the searing fever consumed him within a week. Ever since his death, she had been raising her children alone, supporting herself with the boarding house. Most of her boarders were Southern Pacific Railroad men, who stayed in town for a few months at a time.

"Why stay single; why not marry?" I asked.

She sadly shook her head. "The men I would marry, well-to-do and civil, are already married. And the others would just like to live in the house, becoming permanent non-paying borders." Her voice dripped sarcasm as she said those last words.

We discussed Harry Pillmann. "No one nicer!" was Cora's comment.

"And his wife?" I asked.

"Oh, Helen is very nice too, but often ailing. Something with her lungs, they say."

Chatting thus, we finished the linens that were used in the six bedrooms of the house as well as Cora's and my personal items.

On my first free Sunday, I slept long, dressed leisurely, had breakfast with Cora, whose children were visiting with grandparents, and then I walked to the Evangelical Lutheran Cross Church in the "Rooshian" part of town. The church was a simple, friendly wooden structure. The congregation had planted some shrubs and trees around the perimeter of the church to soften the stark look.

In the large open door stood Pastor Legler, the minister who had welcomed me on my first day in town. He had found me the home with the Mehlings. His warm gray eyes grew in size when he saw me. "Katharina Grushov, where have you been? We have been searching all over for you. The Halbigs told us that you ran away with a man and no one ever saw you again."

"That is not true!" I burst out hysterically. "It is a sad story, but the Halbigs held me in bondage like a serf in Russia. They would not even let me worship on Sunday." I cried unhappily, as bitter tears dripped from my eyes. As I relived my tormented weeks of serfdom, I dissolved ever more. We had stepped aside to allow the congregants to enter the church. Herr Legler held my hands as I poured out my sad story in a flood of tears.

"Now I understand why we have not seen the Halbigs this week. They must be afraid that you will speak out. Never mind that. I am just very glad that you are well. The church members will be excited to see you. They were grieving, not knowing what had happened to you."

"I am just as excited to be here," I said. "I have been working in the drying sheds, making money to repay the congregation, which the Halbigs almost stole." I told him the story of my clothes and the way the Halbigs had torn them to find my wages.

"This is so dastardly, so grievous an offense that I cannot be silent," said Pastor Legler. He led me into the church, down the aisle to the pulpit. As we passed, pew-by-pew, the people grew silent. Most recognized me and were amazed to see me.

When we arrived at the pulpit, the silence had become deafening. The pastor put his hands upon my shoulders and turned me so I stood before him, facing the congregation.

"Dear Brothers and Sisters in Christ, today we can thank God once more for the deliverance of Katharina Grushov from evil. Some of our own have deceived us, taken advantage of our goodness, betrayed our trust and spoken without veracity. All this was done for the purpose of enslaving Katharina, whom they believed to be vulnerable."

A deep sigh went through the congregation. Then voices incredulous with disbelief called out. The pastor commanded loudly, "Tell your story Katharina!" His voice resonated with anger. I did as I was bidden. Still shedding tears, I told the tale straightforwardly without embellishments, but I did not hold back—I told all. When my English deserted me, I finished the sentences in German.

When I had finished, tumult broke out. Most of the people were deeply upset by the callousness of the Halbigs, and for a while everyone seemed to speak at once. Pastor Legler wisely allowed his people to react, to vent their disappointments. However, when he deemed emotions should be cooling, he silenced his flock. "Is there something else you would like to tell us, Katharina?" he asked.

"Yes, there is," I cried joyfully, "Your faith in me was fully justified, because I would like to repay my debt to you and add a small sum for the church." I put three crisp hundred dollar bills into Pastor Legler's hands to the clapping of the congregation.

I have forgotten the sermon preached that day, because while I listened I was lifted by joy so high that my thanks for God's grace interrupted my understanding of the pastor's words. After church, people besieged me. They shook my hands, wished me well, and invited me to their big Sunday dinners.

Herbert's parents came to me. Margarete almost cried as she told me how upset they had been when they heard of my disappearance. Of course, they had sent word to Herbert, who at first could not believe the tale. But after the months passed and I did not come to church, he, too, had begun to doubt. The Baumeisters, too, wanted to take me home for the *Sontagsschmaus*, but Pastor Legler wanted none of it.

"She is coming home with me today," he said. "I feel so bad that we did not search hard enough for you."

"What else could you have done? I moved around from one drying shed to another. After apricots came peaches and then we were drying grapes. We traveled around in a rickety old truck to the locations where we were needed, and the moment I returned I had to work more. Bruno often came to pick me up from work, seeing to it that I did not waste a minute. Most times, I could not even buy a bit of food but had to eat the picked-over leftovers the Halbigs gave me."

Thank God, all that was in the past. That very Sunday I had a most wonderful meal at the Leglers. They owned a cozy, pretty house of medium size on Bakersfield Street, which, branching off I Street, still had a rural feel. Frau Legler, motherly and soft like a pillow, with graying hair and rounded figure, served a meal that Volga Germans dream of. The dish around which the meal was composed was *Broda*, a chicken roasted with vegetables. Of course, there were *Kartoffel Klösse* with brown gravy, and *Berrocks* made with beef, cabbage and onions, baked into an oblong shape.

For dessert, as if one needed or could eat another thing, she served *süssen Kuchen*, special, because it was made with watermelon syrup.

The Leglers had many questions and I told them of the many changes in all of Russia brought about by communism, which in a short time had killed every bit of progress the settlers had made along the Volga and which evaporated the wealth they had created. They, in turn, told me the story of Russian German settlers' arrival in Fresno.

"The first settlers coming to Fresno were all from the villages of Straub and Stahl on the *Wiesenseite* on the Volga," began Pastor Legler. I, of course, knew precisely where these villages were located. Schaffhausen, where I came from, was also located on the edge of the immense Kazhak steppe. "When they finally reached the small Southern Pacific Railroad depot, which the city of Fresno owned at that time, they had traveled for fifty-two days."

"These people were so poor, they only owned the clothes on their backs. They had a few dollars in their pocket for the rubles they had traded in earlier. Of course, they carried their Bible, the *Volga German Gesangbuch* and a few of their most precious personal items," chimed in Margarete, her face filled with pity. "No matter how hard they had worked all their lives, once again they started over with nothing."

Her husband took up the thread again, leaving Margarete to her sad musings. "There were thirty-one men, women and children. They had journeyed from the Volga through Poland, East Prussia and the Province of Brandenburg to the port of Bremen. There they embarked on the ship that brought them to America. You know how hard it was for them to escape from the Russian authorities," he paused looking at me meaningfully. Yes, I knew. Without travel documents one could be stopped by any minor authority figure to be incarcerated, banished to Siberia, or in the most lenient cases, be sent home, where other punishments awaited.

"When the Kerner family, three people; the Karle family, four people; the Metzlers, five people; the Steitzes, a couple; the Bergs, five people; the Nilmeiers, seven people; and the Mehlings, five people, stepped from the hot train onto the hard, dusty cement of the depot, there was no one to greet them, no one to tell them where as much as a drink of water could be found. Stoic, ever practical, and of good disposition, they walked across the tracks to some warehouses where they took shelter from the sun. God is good, because by evening they all had found rooms or homes to stay in until permanent lodging could be arranged."

Furthermore, Pastor Legler told me that within a day every householder had found some sort of a job to earn money, beginning a new life.

John Conrad Metzler's story embodies the spirit in which the newcomers approached life. In search of work, he and a friend went downtown. Everybody in town knew the Germans were eagerly seeking work. Within a short time, the manager of the local water company approached the men, picks and shovels in hand. He motioned them to follow him to a spot in the street. There he marked off a square and set them to digging up the ground within the square.

The two Germans stared and marveled when they uncovered a system of pipes after a few hours of work. They were astounded. Imagine the novel concept of pumping water via a pipe system into houses and business buildings. How deprived they had been in Russia of the most basic amenities, a network distribution of a necessity, which had become common in most of Europe. For their work, uncovering pipes for inspection or repair, they earned silver dollars, twelve a week, a fortune compared to the pittance paid for any labor in Russia, and they were very happy.

As he spoke with great passion, Pastor Legler jumped from his seat at the table and waved us into the parlor, the *gute Stube*. Minutes later he joined us there with a large folder under his arm. Margarete served us cold melon juice in tall glasses. She smiled indulgently at her husband, as he leafed through a thick pile of newspaper pages.

"These are very interesting articles from Fresno newspapers," he enthused, "which I have compiled over the years. They document the arrival of our people and the important impact they have had on the Joaquin Valley. Here are some of the earliest." He handed me a small stack of cutouts, and I began to read. The first was a story headlined "German Laborers," written up in *The Republican*.

> *On Monday, eight men and seven women, immigrants from a colony in Russia, arrived at Fresno, having come for the purpose of securing occupations as farm laborers, like most people from the old country, with the intention of securing land of their own in this country where land is so plentiful and cheap.*

The editor then went on to comment on the appearance of the immigrants. They looked odd to Americans who were free to indulge in any fashion, style and taste. The article notes that the newcomers attracted a good deal of attention with demurely cut, but brightly colored clothing for both sexes, all without modern style, but quite clean and tidy.

I laughed out loud, "If they wore bright colors they wore Sarpinka, because no other material is so colorful as to find favor even in the eyes of gypsies." The Leglers, too, smiled broadly, "Yes, yes, Sarpinka is what they called the material."

I perused yet another article in *The Evening Expositor*.

> *A number of German-Russians arrived in Fresno yesterday from Europe, and are in camp near the depot. The company is composed of men, women and children. They propose settling here, but, we understand, want to secure work until they decide where to locate.*

Time had passed, pleasantly but fleetingly, as we delved into the new chapters of my people. At last, I thanked my hosts and said my goodbyes. Sedately, I walked to my new home and allowed myself an afternoon nap. Later, Cora invited me to take a stroll through the city, ending with a stop at a small, rickety shack, where a Mexican woman together with her older daughters ran a *taqueria*.

Cora bought us some tacos and lemonade, which we consumed at a table flanked by rough-hewn benches. My first Mexican food made my heart sing. It had the spice and flavor of the sun, melded deeply into the tomatoes and jalapenos.

That night, I was in bed early, thinking that today had been a perfect day—normal, like other people's days, joyfully spent with dear people. If only I could have shared this day with Herbert, dear Herbert, so far away. I hoped with all my heart that his parents had redeemed my character, this very day, in letters to him. Did he still think of me?

The Essence of Life

Weeks passed. I adjusted to my new routine, growing comfortable in my job as I gained competence. I loved working with people, helping them, and thereby learning the American way. Oh, that American way! I could only marvel at the boundless freedom the Americans enjoyed, a freedom unimaginable anywhere else in the world, or at least where I had been before. Even in London and Liverpool the citizens were bound and hemmed in by countless rules and regulations, while here, with minor exceptions, everyone did as they pleased.

People moved freely about the state or the country, bought and sold lands, built and removed structures with the greatest of ease. There were no restrictions on professions one could enter; neither did one encounter restrictions on the regions where one could or could not live.

Despite the ongoing war, Fresno was enveloped in most peaceful normalcy. Yet, however much I reveled in the calm, I thought constantly of my poor mother and Joseph. I could imagine the horror and deprivations they faced every day of their lives, if they were alive.

I had often thought of contacting my relatives in Germany, especially Uncle Martin, who had been handed the responsibility of raising my brothers. The mail, however, was the sticking point. We were at war with Germany. As an immigrant, I thought my mail would be scrutinized, and that a simple conversation could, perhaps, be misconstrued as spying. I did, after all, have a most unusual escape from Russia. Considering these and other facts, I decided to wait for the war to end.

Where men and my social life were concerned, Cora had taken me a few times on outings with friends. The young men of her acquaintance were all very nice, some even attractive and appealing, but I could not communicate past a certain level with any of them. They had little formal education, which I did not hold against them, but I resented their ingrained disinterest in books, classical music, art and poetry. Most did not even bother to read the newspaper. To be truthful, my disinterest in the young men had perhaps nothing to do with the flaws I perceived, but stemmed from my deep feelings for Herbert. I dreamed intensively of Herbert. Oh, Herbert; I prayed God he was safe.

This is how things stood when I awoke one day to the realization that I was twenty-two years old, an unmarried old maid. Girls in my society, my Volga German community, were usually married by the time they were eighteen. Only difficult, choosy or handicapped girls lingered past eighteen, whether in desired or unwanted spinsterhood. Examining my life, I came to the unhappy conclusion that every man who possibly could have become my soul mate had been torn from me by fate or circumstance.

There was Arkady Semyonov—where was he now? Was he still fighting in the mad war, or dead in a grave? I had loved Alyosha Kulov, who had been removed from my life by Stalin's forces. There was Korya, a native among whose clan I would have died from lack of intellectual stimulation. Then, there was Herbert Baumeister, who had been told that I absconded with some unsavory, unidentified man. It had become of the utmost importance for me to explain myself to Herbert, to reconcile to him. I had to win him back so the small bud of tenderness we held between us could blossom into true love. The thought of explaining myself to Herbert, of being given a chance to return to the moment of tenderness before he departed, became an obsession.

I will always remember the second advent of 1943. By design I had chosen an aisle seat in the festively decorated church. Instead of the evergreen bows of the old country, an artistic soul had used late blooming flowers, star thistles, grasses and other native plants, in a most charming, creative way. I sat along the aisle, so I could leave without social interaction after the service. Cora needed me to run the boarding house in the afternoon while she spent time with her children and parents.

Sitting there, watching people file in, I suddenly heard a very familiar, dear voice. For a moment I became dizzy with relief, as the blood pounded in my temples. I knew instantly that just a few pews behind me stood Herbert, talking to his parents and friends.
Herbert—he had returned sound and hale. I was overcome with joy. Never mind the awful tale of my elopement with some stranger; his parents would have told him of my sad travails. What remained unclear, I would explain and he would understand.

I rose, left the pew, and went to him. The instant he saw me his face changed to a formal, uncomfortable masque. My grandfather used to call such a face, "waxed fruit."

"Katharina," he exclaimed, with a tortured, forced warmth in his voice, as he took my outstretched hand, "what a surprise!"

"Herbert, I am so glad that you are home, home and well." I smiled with great pleasure, as I tried to overlook his strained behavior.

"Yes, it is good to see you, too," he hesitated for a moment, saying earnestly. "I would like to see you after the service. There are some things I must tell you!"

"Good, I will see you outside, but I must be quick, for I need to go to work."

The service seemed to last forever. That which usually was balm to my spirit became endless torment. What would he say to me? He had been so strange, so unlike the Herbert from yesterday. What had become of the flamboyant, charming, endearing man I had known? Ominously, the picture of our first meeting came to mind: Herbert at the piano—a bevy of gorgeous, spirited, sophisticated girls, drinks in hand, crowding around him. Could it be that one of them got close to him? Oh, no! That could not be! I did not dare to think any further, and yet, he was so strange.

We met out front. Although it was December, the sun drenched the ground of the place of assembly at the church entrance with her warm rays. To the right and the left a few trees had been planted, throwing long, narrow shadows onto the naked ground.

When I left the yawning entrance, flanked by the opened doors, I saw Herbert already waiting in the shade of such a tree. He looked serious, troubled. Suddenly I expected the worst and, to my great pain, the worst came.

"Katharina," he intoned, avoiding my eyes by searching the ground, as if the footprints in the dust were runes for him to study, leading him to a mysterious, profound and painless explanation. "I know, when I left, there was an unspoken understanding between us. You know that I cared very much for you, and I still do. But then, I heard that you left with another man. At first I did not believe it, but when the months passed and no one ever saw you again, then I lost hope."

We stood a few feet apart by now, staring at the ground. I had lowered my gaze, so my hurt would not show in my eyes as naked and painful as I felt it. His words rushed over me like a waterfall, forcefully pushing me under water, suffocating me—pressing the very breath from my lungs. As a terrible darkness encompassed my soul, the sad man before me spoke again.

"What I am trying to tell you, Katharina, is that I am engaged to be married to an English girl, the daughter of an earl. I knew her before I met you, and got closer to her when I believed I'd lost you."

He had stopped his painful narrative and finally looked into my eyes. I read sadness and regret there. I could not speak. An executioner seemed to have laid a garrote around my neck, tightening the terrible noose in increments, and now the stricture was almost complete.

How could I blame Herbert? He had not known me long enough to grow, to establish unwavering trust in me.

"I was terribly upset and confused by what I thought were your despicable actions," he said almost inaudibly. "I was angry at you. I thought that, besides betraying my feelings for you, you had also shown yourself unworthy of the many acts of bravery, kindness and selflessness performed by my friends, my parents and my church."

Hearing his thoughts of groundless, undeserved condemnation, even though based on misinformation—while unscrupulous, greedy wardens held me hostage—finally broke my last vestiges of self-control. I began to cry, uncontrollably. Unable to look into Herbert's face, I turned slightly, looking blindly into a tree. The unfairness of it all vexed me. Sobbing, I blurted out, "You were ill informed. Instead of dallying with a lover, I was held as a slave by unscrupulous people. My life was as sad as in the gulag. The only things that gave me hope and pleasure were thoughts about you and your kindness."

His head sank to his chest. "Evil news traveled fast!" he said regretfully. Herbert put his hand in a comforting gesture on my arm. However, I could neither countenance his pity, nor could I stand to be touched by him.

Abruptly I said, "I am sorry, but I have to work today. Goodbye, and thanks for everything. You did so many wonderful things for me that I cannot thank you enough." Yet, as I was already leaving, I turned back. With the utmost control I could muster, I managed to say, although the words seemed to stick in my throat, "My congratulations on your engagement."

I don't know how I got home. It seemed as if eons had passed. I walked the now familiar streets while my mind roiled with snatches of confused thoughts and self-recrimination. How, oh how, could I have been so foolish to have allowed myself anything other than kind regard and appreciation for Herbert. He had not pretended, made promises, or given me hope for anything else but friendship.

But…most amazing I marveled at my ability to deceive myself. Rationally I had known that Herbert had made no promises of any kind and had reasoned according to these facts. How then could my heart so callously deceive me, telling me sweet little lies, hidden deep down, undetected by my questioning mind? How could this fiend, living inside me, have whispered tomes of hopes, dreams and joys—all false? How? How? I could not stop berating myself for being such a fool, a person so unlike my rational self!

My hands trembled. My pounding heart drove the blood in such enormous gushes through my body that my head felt as if it would explode. Entering Cora's boarding house my mind was still raving with a grand passionate condemnation of self. Cora appeared apparently from nowhere, and stepped into the small entry.

"Catherine, dear God, what has happened to you?" she called out. "You are fever-flushed. Are you ill, my dear?"

I had no desire other than to be left alone. Least of all did I want to speak. However, her kindness and true concern for me made me gather my wits, steeling me. I could at least be, if not loquacious, polite. "I was given sad news in church," I said.

"Not about your family, I hope?"

"No, I still have received no news concerning them because of the war. No, this concerns me," I managed to mouth.

"Oh, Catherine, dear," she always used the English form of my name when addressing me, "come into the kitchen and talk about it over a cup of coffee—it makes it less painful, if one talks."

So, she had guessed my news. I had mentioned Herbert—casually, I thought—but perhaps I had divulged more of my feelings than I had known. Politely, I tried to decline her compassionate offer; politely, I explained my need for silent retreat, but she insisted that soothing solace could be found in shared grief.

Finally, I relented and followed her into the kitchen. At one end, far from the stove and dish counter, a large table with twelve chairs revealed where she fed the lodgers their breakfasts and luncheons. There was no dining room in the house. Therefore, as she once explained to me, she had removed a wall into the pantry, thereby enlarging the room, and been able to use this space more efficiently.

Cora was a simple woman with an eighth-grade education, but she had great tact and understanding. I had been taught that a fine-feeling soul is the basis for all kindness. Cora had such a soul. She gently fussed over me, as I sat haplessly at her table, staring dully at the vase filled with wild flowers gracing its center. She poured me a cup of coffee, stirring in milk and sugar—the way I liked it. She already knew my preferences, because she observed the people in her care.

She put freshly baked cookies on a plate, knowing full well that I could not resist the aroma of warm chocolate and almonds. In this way, saying nothing at all, she worked her magic, and I relaxed. When she suddenly said, "Was the sad news about Herbert?" I relented and nodded my head. Yet I was not ready to talk. "Did something happen to his plane?" she coaxed gently, thinking that he might have come to grief during a mission.

"No," I said. It just escaped my mouth. "Herbert is fine. He just got engaged to a British girl, the daughter of an earl," I said. Hearing the bitterness in my voice and disliking the sound, I laughed. That laugh, however, also sounded bitter and false.

"But he took you to see his parents, so how could he pledge himself to another?" Cora said loyally.

"I cannot fault him," I said, despairing. "The Halbigs told my church that I had absconded with another man, some worthless stranger. Of course, he heard about it."

"And he believed it?" she cried, disbelief resonating through her words.

"Not at first, I think. But when the weeks turned into months, he changed his mind and thought it possible that I had done this thing. What did he really know about me? He had only been with me a total of maybe fourteen days."

"Men!" huffed Cora with evident exasperation. "He should have known you by then. Could he not read the goodness in your face? Men!" she repeated. "They fly from one woman to another without care. Often enough I have seen a husband bury one wife and marry another within a few weeks, giving the first no more thought."

She bustled through the kitchen, returning with a tissue for my tears, growing fewer now, and my sniffling nose. My hurt unassuaged, but capable of functioning, I hurried her off on her visit and began my routine of boarding house work. Later, however, came the long, painful night and no one could help me then.

Over the next few years, I saw Herbert a few more times from afar—fleetingly, sadly. It seemed that fate had condemned me to live my life without love. Would it be my lot to become a spinster? I wanted children, wanted a family. I craved to emulate the very life I had known in the villages on the Volga. However, I could not conjure that life from thin air.

Peace

Two years passed slowly. I came to understand that as long the war continued, nothing would change in my life. I worked. I saved money and enjoyed the attractions Fresno offered. Most were connected to the cycle of our three seasons, because we had no real winters, and our church.

"The Cross" had a great choir. Singing releases the soul from earthly attachment and pain, allowing it to soar, lifting the spirit heavenward. I had a good voice and soon practiced with the choir twice weekly. *Die Proben*, the practices, became on many evenings my most enjoyable experiences. When I sang, my voice became God's instrument. Instead of my will prevailing, God's spirit reigned. Especially when I was singing my favorite compositions—the Te deum, cantatas and classical church music—I became truly aware of life's reality. I, with my free will, my choices, was really not in control of anything, even though I often thought that I was.

I understood during those moments that I was no more than a leaf, drifting in a breeze, my path pre-ordained. What did it matter whether I struggled violently against the world? In the end, everything happened according to a plan other than my own. Whenever I meekly submitted, life flowed best for me, arranged in an orderly fashion, by a design, determined by laws with a foresight that humans do not possess. At this point in my musings, I always thought about the knife, which was stuck in a tree I was destined to fell. How did it get there? Why had I been the only one to notice it? Who had known in advance that I would need this knife to defend myself against Ivan; more even, that I needed the knife to become the avenger of many murdered people? Why had Suomo lingered for weeks at the camp's edge, at the very place where I would try to slay Ivan?

One might say—coincidence! That I found the knife because of my exceptional eyesight. That Suomo waited for a chance to kill his brother's slayer. I grant the validity of these objections, but must question their veracity by reminding doubting souls that Suomo had missed his chance to avenge his brother, time after time, until I needed his intercession. As to the knife, many women in my work detail possessed the same fine eyesight I did, yet never glimpsed even a flash of light.

Lastly, I was thinking of the Russian patrols along the Northern Dvina. Both patrols had acted out of character for such border guards, as Korya told me time and again. Oh, Korya. When I remembered our flight across the taiga and tundra, I felt blessed that I had been saved by innocence itself. Among the natives, as in every population of people, there were many who would have taken advantage of my helpless situation and proved themselves to be rapists, thieves or killers. But I had met only kindness itself. Contemplating these things I sang my songs full-throated with the choir, and received, in return, the grace of bliss.

The year 1945 arrived, and palpable excitement rippled through the grand American nation. We—yes—we, for I had become, heart and soul, one of them, we were so close to winning this war that even the schoolboys, coming to the drugstore for ice cream or a soda, could taste the victory. The newspapers fairly screamed our successes at the front in our faces. Now it was only a matter of time, and we, who had died, bled and conquered fascism, would soon be able to dictate a lasting peace.

I, like all of America, had become impatient for the war to end, the killing to stop and normalcy to return. However, I understood that a lasting peace could only be achieved through total submission by a vanquished foe. Our enemies were godless monsters—without human decency—monsters whose credo was their own superiority and power. Nothing else mattered. Therefore, the fight had to be fought to the bitter end: the total destruction of the fascist system.

Of course, I clearly saw that the same appellation, godless monster, should also have been applied to Iossif Vyssarionovich Stalin. However, at this time America failed to see the communist monster for what he was. It would take decades before the public would fully understand what a horrible psychopath had been their ally.

When on May 8, victory over Germany was declared, the joy in the streets was boundless. Cora heard the blessed news on the radio and came running to the drugstore to tell all of us. Harry Pillman distributed free sodas and ice cream to every person entering the store. He turned the radio up full strength, blasting the good news mixed with elevating strains of music throughout the store.

In the evening Cora came to church with me for a thanksgiving service. Afterwards we went out with a young crowd to celebrate the wonderful news. Like the others, I danced in the streets, drank potent drinks, got kissed by strangers, all-the-while thinking: It is over. If Joseph is alive he will not have to fight anymore. Arkady, Alyosha Kulov, Elliot, Herbert and all the other young men fighting in this war—if alive—would now be saved.

Perhaps I could find the remnants of my family; find my brothers Michael and Peter, Joseph, Mother, aunts and uncles? If I could just locate some parts of the whole family, I would not be entirely alone anymore. There would be someone again of my own blood I could connect to, someone who cared deeply for me.

Although we celebrated with gusto and gladness, the victory was not yet complete. Japan, entrenched on islands such as Iwo Jima and Okinawa, fought horrific battles that cost many American lives. Though Germany had capitulated, Japan fought on until later in the year. On August 6, 1945, the bomber *Enola Gay* dropped the first atomic bomb onto Hiroshima, giving notice that America would not be denied her peace. However, it was only a second bomb falling on Nagasaki that finally broke the will of the Japanese to fight on.

And then—it was accomplished. The people of the world heaved a communal sigh of relief. They slept better at night as dreams of hope, the return of loved ones, and the expectations of small luxuries crept into their minds. In the San Joaquin Valley the farmers once again dreamed big dreams. Their produce had always been in demand but the luxuries, wine, grape juice and fresh fruit, which depended on fast transport, had lagged in development. Now this would change. A growing demand would bring greater prosperity.

In Fresno, which means ash tree in Spanish, young people met nightly in the park-like setting of the old Fresno City Hall. Nearby stood Fresno's old water tower, which had been built in 1894. There youths would promenade, eating ice cream and watermelon. The young girls compared notes on the homecoming of their beaus. Who would be first to be demobilized?

Harry Pillmann was anxiously awaiting the return of two sons. One had been stationed in the Philippines, one in Europe. I was amazed to hear that Harry had boys in the war. He had never talked about them at all.

"Why did you never speak of your boys to me? Why keep this deathly silence?"

At first, he told me, "It's too hard to talk about them." But then he admitted his bent toward superstition. "If you don't talk about them, I thought, the devil will not know where to find them." He smiled sheepishly, and said, "God knew where they were all along, and the devil did not need to know."

"Harry Pillman!" I exclaimed. "You, a man of science, believe in such superstitions?"

He grew serious. "We all must do what allows us to cope, silly as it might be. My wife, she prayed all the time and wrote hundreds of letters to our sons. This helped her get through the war."

He was right, of course. In the end we all have strategies, helping us to survive. I did not talk about Mother and Joseph much either. To speak of their uncertain lives saddened me, depressed me so much that my work suffered. Cora, too, talked nowadays with great enthusiasm about cousins and nephews coming home, where previously a few casual remarks had sufficed.

Not many months later, the soldiers began to come home. There were parties, parades down Main Street, ceremonies and picnics. For all of us, for the returning men and for us who received them, the sky was bluer, the sun shone brighter and the air was sweeter to breathe.

Then it was over. The day came, when bereft of euphoria we returned to our everyday lives. My thoughts, as the thoughts of the country, turned to the future. What was to become of me? I was certain the drugstore job could not hold me forever. I, who a long time ago had been satisfied with the monotonous, quiet lives of our village, had been torn from everyday peace, thrown into deadly adventures, and was complacent no longer.

I had played with death and destruction, had been titillated by danger. The happiness of calm, so much desired by me when I came to Fresno, had slowly turned to boredom. Perhaps marriage and children would have altered my state of mind, fulfilling me; not so my present situation.

My life had progressed with the greatest frugality. I had saved up a nest egg of astounding proportions for one earning so little. For all my extra help with the boardinghouse, I lodged almost rent-free. I bought few clothes. My clothes from England sufficed for most formal needs, and for the warm days in the San Joaquin Valley I donned calico dresses sewn on Cora's sewing machine. I had to buy shoes and sandals though, for I walked all the time in the valley and I soon wore them out.

For a long time I had been curious to know more of California's history. Our area especially roused my interest. What was special about Fresno, about our bountiful valley? As for the valley's name, San Joaquin, and its significance, I researched the historical record. A lieutenant, Gabriel Moraga, sent to explore the valley of the rushes—*Valle de los Tulles*, found a rivulet that he named San Joaquin, which later gave its name to the river. The name is ancient. It precedes the New Testament and appears in the pre-gospel text of James, denoting Mary the Mother of Christ's parentage, with *Joachim* being her father.

Learning the English language, names distracted me often. I still had a lot to learn about the country and its people. I struggled with the intricacies of the language which was so different from Russian and German. It had no fixed four- or six-case structure for nouns and did not require that the gender of a noun be known. From the library, which I often visited with Cora, I brought home folktales and children's stories. There was no better way to learn a language than from the bottom up—like a child.

So near the end of the war, it was not yet my time to go to Germany and seek out relatives. I would begin the process through the mail, as soon as relations with Germany stabilized. I heard from news accounts that Germany had been divided into two parts, the East and West. The eastern part had been occupied by Russian troops and the West by troops of the Allies. My heart bled for the eastern part—poor innocents, they had no idea what kind of a monster had conquered them. My fears were justified, as was proved in the months to come.

On April 27, 1945, American troops had assumed control over the provinces of Thuringia and most of Saxony. However, by order of the Allied High Command, those troops were withdrawn and ordered to hand over those large provinces to Russian troops. Capitulation by the German Army occurred in May 1945, and before the victorious powers had even officially divided the hapless country, the Russians began to seek out all

Russian Germans who had fled the miserable communist-ridden Soviet Union. They dragged their victims off by force, shipping them in cattle cars to Siberia and Middle-Asia. Then, having found their most sought-after prey, the Russian Army concentrated on raping and plundering the civilian population of Germany.

The Russians tore apart every one of the German factories, ripping the machines from the very concrete floors, shipping them to Russia—forgive me—the Soviet Union. Through their communist German spies, they discovered every one of the Nazi food caches. Previously, when the Americans had found such hording places, they had always given up a portion of the spoils to feed the population. There was no such consideration given by the Russians. Every morsel of food was carried off to the lair of the bear.

As they had done in the Volga region and the Ukraine, the Soviet Union sent its troops into the Eastern German villages and confiscated the entire harvest of 1945, sending it to Russia. Smuggled reports told us in America how starving hollow-eyed Germans, their stick-thin children beside them, stood cordoned off from the train stations, watching with despair as mountains of wheat, potatoes, sugar- and yellow-beets, carrots and corn were loaded onto railroad cars, leaving for Russia filled to the brim.

Through church members who had relatives in Germany, I heard of the horrible things the East German population had to endure. Besides pilfering the food supplies, the Red Army raped the women in the miserable Russian sector. Stalin had given orders that the punishment of the Germans must include rape to make the victory for the frontline troops all the more satisfying, more poignant.

Safe in America, there was nothing we could do but pray and cry over the accounts of the worst crimes. I had become restless, frustrated that I sat here safe and well-fed while Germans were raped, starved, and dragged into the Soviet Union to be exploited for their physical labor or their brains. Whole laboratories, departments of universities and research stations were dismantled and relocated in various parts of the Soviet Union, people and all. Hearing the accounts, I fretted about Mother, Joseph, Arkady and the people of Schaffhausen. Those people, left behind without homes or land, so poor that even the Soviets had not found them worthy to be torn from the *kolkhozes*, lived near starvation throughout the war years. The plunder and the bounty of the German harvest were shipped to Russia to be divided among Moscow's elite, Stalin's yes-men.

Amid the chaos, the uncertainties of our lives and the destruction wrought upon Eastern Europe by Russia, my church was a beacon of sanity. Our Lutheran Cross Church was only one church of many such beacons in America, collecting money and supplies for those left behind in the miserable old country. My mind boggled at the grand amounts of money collected from people earning some of the lowest wages in the country. And yet, these very people owned homes, had prospered, and gave generously to the cause of those held hostage behind the Soviet border.

I marveled at the sheer determination and problem-solving ability of my church, whose leaders found creative ways and means to get funds to our Russian German people inside Russia. Later, much later, we were to hear through witness accounts how many lives had been saved through the goodness and material sacrifice of Russian Germans living in America.

Cora noticed my restless fretting. She startled me one day with the revelation, "Why don't you go to college? You are plenty smart, you can get a degree." Her simple statement hit me like lightning. However, there loomed before me enormous obstacles. Education was expensive and would my previous education be deemed good enough in this country to let me enter a university? These were certainly obstacles; but the real problem I faced was inherent in the constraints put upon women. Not many women in these days received a higher education. Many fathers still refused to fund their daughters' higher education.

Here, I could be different, for no one would give me anything—I would give it to myself. The California State University campus in Fresno had been founded in 1911. I passed the site often. Now that the seed had been planted, my fertile mind sprouted the idea into a promising plant.

I discussed the idea with the Leglers. They were cautiously optimistic, while other people in the congregation were downright discouraging. "Don't waste your money on an uncertain thing. Why don't you get married and have a family," said some.

"What would come of education? Do you really think they'd give a man's job to an educated woman?" warned others. There were, however, two people in the mix who never wavered in their support of my dream— Harry Pillmann and Cora.

"Do it," said Harry Pillmann. "I will always have work for you whenever your schedule allows. One of these days my boys will be back from the war and perhaps one will take over the store. Whoever it is will need all the help he can get."

"Oh, do it!" sighed Cora. "I will be ever so proud of you. You are lucky. You have no one who depends on you, no one to hold you back." Her eyes were bright and wishful, "I would—if I were you." She backed up her worthy rhetoric with promises of help: Sunday work in the board-inghouse, which would keep the rent affordable. Affirmed thus, I made my decision suddenly. It was July, and based upon my inquiries, I was already late with enrollment. Most of the students had already been chosen, hav-ing applied upon graduation from high school.

My greatest impediment to enrollment was the complete lack of any paperwork to certify the thorough education I had received, not only from the very good school in Katharinenstadt, but also from my home. My grandparents had been educated to superior levels for their time. My par-ents had contributed to my education with their knowledge of the history of Russia and Germany, math, geography, poetry, philosophy and the lore of the many peoples of Russia. Though eclectic, I admit, it was a very solid education and better rounded than the knowledge the high school chil-dren in our church had demonstrated to me.

Undaunted, almost stupidly intrepid, I went to the office of the Dean. The campus consisted of low-slung stone structures neatly surrounded by trees, lawn and flowerbeds. A concrete walk led up to a few curved steps and a large double door, one side of which stood open in a halfhearted way as if to indicate, "No one is doing much in here and we don't expect anyone either."

Despite this far from welcoming feel, I passed through the door, entered the foyer and found myself standing on a polished marble floor amid walls of plaques and notification boards. So many announcements were displayed there that I got confused. I saw a sign for the admissions office, and suddenly felt intimidated, overcome by a deep sense of futil-ity. Gently pushing open the door labeled admission, I crept in. Inside, a distinguished older lady with blued, permed hair asked the purpose of my visit. I explained that I was here to see the dean, for I wanted to enroll.

"He is not the person to see, dear; we have other people who take care of enrollment." I sighed, and began to explain my rather peculiar situation.

"Oh, my dear," said the lady, "have you really thought this through? Few girls are enrolled here, and those we do have, are well known for their scholarship or are independently wealthy."

"Oh, yes, I have carefully thought about it all," I said in my best newly-learned English. "It seems all the more important that I gain ad-mission, because there are so few women enrolled." I shone my brightest, slightly cheeky smile on her. Did I imagine it? But I thought that a rather peculiar, intrigued expression came over her face.

"Tell me something of your background. Better yet, give me your personal history, flaws and all," said Helen Cumberland. I had detected a sign with that name on her desk. I began telling my story. Numerous times we were interrupted by people seeking her expertise, so that, a bit annoyed, she called to a young man to cover her desk, while we retreated to a small backroom.

When I had completed my narrative, she called for coffee, cookies and orange juice. While we sipped beverages and nibbled on cookies, like ladies at a tea party, she asked me many questions; about Mother and Father, the *kolkhoz*, Stalin, the Reds, the gulags and, of course, about my escape on the *Intrepid*.

"Did you really kill a man?" she asked point blank at one juncture in the conversation. "Yes," I admitted candidly. "Someone else finished him off, but it had been my intent to execute the monster."

"How do you feel about the killing today?" she asked, and I sensed that there was a deeper meaning to her question than just idle curiosity. "I cannot say that I ever regretted what I did. Neither can I admit to sleepless nights while fretting over his death. Quite to the contrary, soon after what I like to call the execution, I had the strongest, most righteous feelings of having been directed to rid the world of evil."

On Helen's face appeared a satisfied expression as if she, too, had been a part of the deed. I surmised that in her life she must have felt many times the desire to eradicate something evil or despicable, without having the opportunity to act. She glanced at me with a measuring look, as if judging my attributes, the very traits God had bestowed upon me in the cradle, as if she could discern my spirit.

At last she said in a motherly tone, "Come back tomorrow at ten in the morning, my dear, and you shall have your interview with Dean Broward. I will prepare the ground for you. Sometimes he listens to me and takes my advice." I sighed with relief.

"How can I verify your story? You understand that it is a most amazing, unusual story."

"I understand," I concurred, sighing deeper yet. Then I wrote the addresses of Elliot, Captain Howard of the *Intrepid*, the British Immigration Service and Pastor Legler on a sheet of paper for her, saying, "Any of these people can verify large parts of my personal history."

New Dreams and Hopes

I sang all the way home. "Cora," I cried the moment I entered our simple, well-ordered house, "Cora, I think I have found someone at the university willing to help me." As words spilled from my mouth, pushed forth by overflowing happiness, I told her about Helen Cumberland and her promise of intercession.

Cora was the perfect foil for my unbridled joy. "I knew you would find a way," she cried, her face reflecting back my excitement.

We splurged that night, went out to dinner at the Italian restaurant and ordered red wine with our delicious lasagna. It seemed to me that Cora was vicariously living a cherished dream through me. Who would have thought that the mother of teenagers, consumed by worries about their daily bread, frazzled by the vagaries of lodgers, still harbored dreams. I knew Cora loved to read, but I had never guessed at ambitions beyond the books she read.

I returned the very next day to the campus, sparkling with hope and the excitement of the challenge to win the dean over to my side. When Helen ushered me into his inner sanctum, I found a distinguished man in his fifties, brown haired with becoming gray temples. Dean Broward had the most disconcerting green eyes. Below strong brows, they reminded me of marbles when the light fell into them. His face was long and aristocratic, and so was his nose. He wore a dark suit of excellent cut and a crisp, snowy-white shirt.

Dean Broward scrutinized me with as much interest as I directed at him. He began the conversation abruptly without much ado. "Cumberland told me an interesting tale about you," he intoned, after Helen had barely introduced me.

"We did some checking. What you say seems to be true—mostly. We will verify the rest later." He motioned me to be seated on one of the plain chairs in front of his oversized desk, behind which he retreated and settled down in a comfortable, heavily padded chair.

"Pray tell me, how do you imagine joining our institution without any record of your academic achievements?" he asked.

I sent Helen, seated beside me, a lost look, and she quickly translated the gist of his words into simple English.

"See," he crowed triumphantly, "You cannot even follow my words."

"But sir! I am completely self-taught. I have learned much English in just two years, while working two jobs."

"So, what did you learn in Russia," asked Dean Broward. I could see that, so far, I had not made a favorable impression on the man.

"I learned mathematics—algebra, geometry and trigonometry. I was educated in the history of Russia, Europe and Asia, although very little of America. I was also taught geography, biology and a small amount of physics. I am fluent in Russian, German and some French, and know the literature of the first two languages extensively."

"You practiced to say this litany, did you not?" he wanted to know.

"Of course I did!" I exclaimed, "I know what I am still missing in English."

"Well, well, well," said Broward. Beside me, Helen Cumberland made little placating gestures with her hands, moving Dean Broward to say, "Mrs. Cumberland, would you please arrange for Professor Huber to meet with me. It seems that before outright rejecting this young woman, we should test her, giving her a chance to display her scholarship in her own language."

We were dismissed by the wave of his hand, and a firm, "Good day!"

In the hall, in front of Dean Broward's office, Helen Cumberland squeezed my hand and said, "Well this was more auspicious than one could have hoped for. If you can pass the test, he might very well let you register."

I thanked kind Helen Cumberland profusely for her intercession. She, in turn, promised to alert me the moment a date was set for the tests.

Henceforth, I fretted. I bemoaned my audacity, my inadequacy, my hubris to challenge academe. Now I had to prove that I was possessed of the necessary knowledge, that I had the grit to perform under pressure.

My friends were happy for me, while the doubters remarked that the test would prove the wisdom of my decision. So, they, too, thought that women were inferior in thought and knowledge. Perhaps they secretly hoped that I would fail! Somehow my detractors and their negative reflections put fire into my soul. If I failed, fine, but before that could happen I would give it my very best effort.

1992

The sun pleasantly warms my back. I am sitting in my garden, having turned the chair against the southwest rays. I am wearing my comfortable Panama hat, a present from my ex-husband, a man long since gone from my life. He went south—somewhere into Mexico with a flame that somehow ignited his cold, miserable ashes. A blessing on her, more even—prayers, for she set me free. She would need the prayers!

Here I am in my seventies, as happy and free as I was in my youth. Death threatens me every so often, swinging its scythe; I don't mind. The doctors say that my gulag time and the following adventures with all their deprivations had been hard on my physical systems. "Circulatory problems!" they say. "You have a heart strained by hunger, hard work and freezing cold. Combined with psychological stressors, this has rendered you susceptible to stroke and heart attacks."

"Nonsense," I say. "That was written into my genetic plan. If my time comes, I will go. Gladly, for I know where I am going." I laugh at the doctors and do as I please, not as they say. As my mind revisits the many events in my life, I am not displeased, perhaps disappointed at times, but also profoundly, fondly, glad that I have experienced what is unknown to most people in a lifetime. From the deepest fears to the highest joys, I have lived it. I remember gratefully the tremendous relief I felt upon being saved from enemies or other harm. I do not regret anything in my life, but would I willingly repeat it knowing what I know now? No, emphatically, no! I am grateful that I am old—that the struggles, the emotional storms, the worries are a thing of the past.

It is wonderful to sit in the garden with my favorite book without a care. Dinner will be the great accomplishment of the evening. Perhaps a salad and a baked potato with cheese? One must love microwave ovens—five minutes and it is done. Speaking of innovations and things I would repeat, I would surely go back to university again in another life.

Once I passed the tests to enter university, pushing through anxious hours of stress and worry, I became a student to be reckoned with. I spent every waking hour studying and rehearsing texts and lessons. I would have graduated summa cum laude if I had followed the precepts of my classmates and played it safe, choosing professors only by the weakness of their grading. Instead I chose with gusto those teachers maligned as terrors. They were men who thought with razor-sharp logic.

Speaking of men, we had only one woman professor. She taught English literature, a favorite subject of mine. Elena Morgenthau was a poetic soul who enthusiastically embraced me and all my poetic baggage. As we became friendly, I told her of Alyosha and my heartbreak with Herbert. She, in turn, told me of Joshy Rosenberg, her fiancé. He had flown planes like Herbert and was shot down over a bomb-making factory in Thuringia. She still grieved years after the event and would not look at another man. I knew that telling her my troubles would not ease her pain. However I wanted her to know that we shared grief. Therefore, I told her a little of my life; told her that I did not know where my loved ones were or if they were still alive or dead. We grew close; shared grief; divulged painful emotions; drained our heavy hearts. Elena remained my dear friend until she died much too soon, at only thirty-eight.

Having crammed all my requirements into three years, I graduated in the spring of 1949. I held a double major in English and Library Science. Thinking that the latter would at least feed me, I was unpleasantly surprised, for no one wanted to hire me. Young men had returned from the wars, deserving the available teaching and librarian positions.

Here it was almost the middle of the twentieth century, I had a university degree, and I still worked in a drugstore and as boardinghouse help. Suddenly, my complacency burst like a giant soap bubble. Harry Pillmann had his sons back, unharmed by the war. Soon he would not need me anymore. Cora was dating a returned Marine, who began running the boarding house with astounding efficiency.

Perhaps this was heaven's sign that I must locate my family and look for a life elsewhere. I asked Cora if she would save me my room, renting it out only short-term to allow me to move back if I returned from Germany. She promised me a roof over my head whenever I should need it.

I got my papers in order and applied for a visa. But most of all, I assured myself of re-entry into America. I was not a full citizen yet. Then I spent almost every last cent I had on a ship's passage. My Uncle Martin in Germany, with whom I had begun to correspond, had promised to pay the return passage. Could it be that he hoped I would stay there forever? What was Germany like? Would I like the country? Would I like the people? Although they were my people, the monstrous reports of concentration camps had tainted the whole nation with infamy. However, I was driven to find a connection to those who were mine, of my blood, and whom I knew to be innocent of participation in inhumane crimes.

As I was musing about those days of yore, the sun was preparing for its daily demise. I suddenly felt cold. The sun's fire died, having burned itself into rosy ashes which did not warm. I rose from my wrought iron chair and ambled slow-footed toward the house.

What a charming abode it was. Made from native stone and wooden beams, with a wide, matronly loggia, my house was an American-Italian hermaphroditic mélange and I loved it. I had built it with the man I married before we both returned from Germany.

Germany-Bavaria-Franconia

Oh Germany—the Punished! Aggressor incarnate—diminished, vanquished, destroyed! I perceived the punishment, and it was just. The justice of the horrific punishment, however, did not make me grieve any less. The vanquished were my people, my cultural and genetic heritage, which I could not dismiss or set aside as if it did not exist. I suffered as I observed the ruins—places where hell had held a party. I suffered, seeing the incendiary collateral, the blackened shells, which enfolded the ashes and burned bones of ordinary people.

Burned to cinders, no one knew or cared anymore whether they had been fascism's adherents, innocent bystanders, or active resisters. In death, they lay united by one truth—that man does not control destiny—God determines the outcome of lives. The only control a human being has is the choice of whether to live within the constructs of God's laws—honor, decency and kindness—or to live by depravity, deceit, scheming and un-truth, by accruing power and riches, by treading upon the souls of others.

Another phenomenon I had observed was man's inability to confront evil when it approached in pretty speeches, disguising the veracity of its intent. I saw this phenomenon in every one of the three countries in which I had lived. People were split almost evenly into two groups where beliefs were concerned. One group, filled with grand emotions, judged people, history, and their fellow man not by the facts laid before them, but by the emotions they felt. Whether the emotions were true or false, supported or unsupported by facts and knowledge, it mattered not. They would choose a cause because, to them, the emotional content of that cause felt right.

In Russia, we had seen how every new wave of Pan-Slavism turned the hearts of the Russians ever more against their minorities, especially the Jews, Germans and Ukrainians. Even those Russians who were closely connected to those minority populations, and who, therefore, knew the facts full well, allowed themselves to be subverted by the sheer emotional onslaught of hatred.

In America, basically good, decent people fervently defended Stalin, the Reds and their actions on no other basis but slogans. It was the propaganda put forth by the Reds, promising that communism would improve the lives of the underclasses. Thus many American citizens based their estimations on nothing but the emotional content of these words, for the facts and the reality of the Russian people bore no resemblance to the claim. It seemed to be such a shining, heartwarming goal to enrich people's lives by making everyone equal. When confronted with the facts of the Communists' mass killings, the gulags, the torture, the sheer monstrous inhumanity of the new system, these idealistic people ignored the thousands of examples and facts piling up in front of them and persisted in their flawed beliefs. Furthermore, they assisted the communist governments of Europe with money and speeches.

And in Germany, the anointed "Messiah" had come to the hungry, disappointed masses with speeches of hope and change. Trumpeting his message, he had promised to eradicate the old broken political system and the failed strategies and create a new nation. "I bring hope," he had sung in his Siren Song. We need *Lebensraum*; an end to the tyranny of the European nations, which heaped impossible reparations upon the nation. And, of course, he roared: I will procure a better, exalted life for the common man. "Give me a chance! Give me the power and I will make Germany great again."

Oh, I had read *Mein Kampf* at university. I had even found a few of Hitler's speeches. I remember thinking, why would anyone believe such empty words, such demagogic rhetoric?

Such thoughts plagued my mind as the ship docked in the destroyed Hamburg harbor, where ruined cranes stretched skeletal arms into the blue sky. With superhuman effort, parts of the docks had been cleared, for the harbor was the heart of the region. The people had had to clear it if they wanted to live. American and British troops had opened portions of the harbor to ensure docking space for their own vessels. Despite these efforts, one could not help but be depressed by man's monumental capacity for destruction.

Germany! Such hopes, such wishes and dreams of being surrounded by loved ones, of finding kinship. From Hamburg, which looked beaten and destroyed, I traveled by train to Würzburg in Bavaria. At the train stations, too, the effects from many bombings were evident. The train cars suffered from heavy use, old age and neglect. I found a window seat in a compartment occupied by three hungry and worn people. The train gathered speed and I saw more of Hamburg's destruction, the result of a firestorm caused by an attack of more than seven hundred bombers. The old engine, sending enormous black clouds of smoke into the air, pulled us through large sections of town where the skeletons of burned and exploded houses created an eerie cemetery. Some standing house fronts, five or six stories high, their windows blasted, melted and crisped, seemed to look at us with macabre curiosity.

In another block, far away from the center of the destruction, I saw broken furnishings inside apartments with missing walls. Torn, shredded fabrics dangled from upended tables and chairs. No one had been allowed to enter the unsafe buildings to look for possessions. Forty thousand people had perished here, paying with their lives for the fascists' war, whether they had been part of the Nazi regime or had resisted it. One million people, I was told, had lost their homes all in a single night.

Once in the countryside we breathed easier. I shook off the gloom and tried to think of better days for the country. But as soon as the train rolled through another town of substance, the picture of destruction and horror repeated itself.

Whenever the train rolled through the open country, I was given glimpses of Hitler's Autobahn, now facilitating the flow of American Army convoys, their vehicles painted olive brown or camouflage green, and a few civilian trucks.

Sometimes the view included a rustic scene, peaceful and undisturbed by mayhem, only to change instantly to a nightmarish picture, where burned and splintered trees stretched tortured, blackened limbs upward, or bent like weeping women at a grave.

I shared the compartment with an old man, gray and wrinkled, yet with sharp, piercing, alive eyes, his equally shriveled, hungry and dejected-looking wife, and their obviously retarded adult son. The latter obsessively opened and fastened the buttons on his suit jacket, as if this process conferred security upon him, assuring him that everything still worked.

As we passed another wooded section of countryside devastated by conflagration, the man pointed at the destruction and said, "You are not from these parts, are you?" When I shook my head, he said, "There were bombs falling all over the land. Thousands fell on nothing at all. The fields, the woods and even the rivers are full of craters. Many bombs never exploded. They are the inheritance of the next generation."

"And yet we must be grateful to the bombers," said his modest, little wife, flicking soot off her gray, worn summer coat. She turned directly to me, explaining, "Without the bombers it would never have stopped, and we could not have kept Karl,"—she motioned to her son—"hidden any longer. They would have put him away like the others, and he does no harm." I murmured in sympathy; however, after this exchange we all fell silent again. What was there to say?

Leave it to the Germans. The trains were running again on time, and I arrived punctually at eleven in the morning in Würzburg. Uncle Martin had advised me to hire a cab, which he offered to pay for at the house, because I would not have any opportunity to exchange money.

As we drove into the city proper, I stared astounded at the monumental damage Würzburg had sustained. The train station, plain and gray like others I had seen, had also been damaged and a section was cordoned off. From the moment I set foot outside, this section of town presented itself, bathed in sunshine, as pleasant and *bürgerlich* as any city I had ever seen. That image was sustained until one turned the corner. There one saw another area of ruins in the process of being cleaned by a corps of *Trümmerfrauen*, the famous German *Rubblewomen*. I had learned that these women had taken on the backbreaking task of making Germany whole again after the war, for few men had returned. Many soldiers, although alive, were in prisoner-of-war camps, including untold numbers toiling in Russian gulags.

The cabs were horse-drawn carriages, because the town had barely enough gasoline in its reserves to run the few buses I saw. Many farmers, stung by shortages and joblessness, had pulled their horses from their stalls, beginning a thriving transportation business. The first carriage, in a line of waiting conveyances, was a small open *landau*. The owner, dressed in the *Landestracht: Lederhosen*, checked shirt, knee-high socks and *Gamsbart* hat (mountain goat hair-tufted)—sat proudly upon the driver's bench, reins in hand. Looking at his thin little bay horse, I assumed that feed was scarce. I soon found that this was true. For man and beast, all food was rationed.

Uncle Martin's house was not far from the train station. He resided in the *Altstadt*, the center built during medieval times, where fine, ancient homes had once presented faces of meticulously cared-for polish. However, now there was little left. I stared with horror at the skeletal remains of former homes, where zigzags of half-burned walls pointed at the clear sky. Rubble was everywhere except for the streets, which had been cleaned and readied for use. I cried out with anguish, when I realized that my uncle must live in the middle of this destruction. It was a miracle that the family was alive.

"Yes, my lady, look, and look well," said the coachman. "This was done to the city on March 16, 1945. The British came with 225 bombers and destroyed three-fourths of the city in seventeen minutes. The old town was almost totally destroyed in a conflagration in which 5,000 of our townspeople died." He turned, facing me with a grim smile, only to laugh deprecatingly, "I think they wanted to destroy the munitions factories in Schweinfurt and instead destroyed some of the finest buildings and greatest art in the world."

However, I was not so certain the British had committed an error. I think everyone had been sick of the war and the Allies were determined to destroy the German population's will to resist. Hence the cruel attacks on Dresden, Hamburg and Würzburg.

Although the buildings had been destroyed, the remaining walls and the rubble confined traffic in the streets as much as the houses had done in peacetime. The streets were so narrow that my rattling old cab, taking me through their confines, had to back up twice into the remains of someone's entrance or garage to let another vehicle pass.

Fortunately, there was not much traffic. After making our way through the sad remains of people's homes, we came upon a section of almost untouched houses. They were situated close to the ancient *Julius Spital*. Once a hospital, this baroque building with its medieval wine cellar had been the first and largest winery in town.

The cab stopped before a large home. It was large only by comparison with other houses, and was distinguished by grand beams containing *Fachwerk*. A few of the windows featured ancient panes of stained glass; others looked as if they had been damaged and replaced with whatever glass was available. The massive, gleaming wood front door was beset with ironwork. I rang the doorbell of the fine distinguished house, and a moment later

Uncle Martin himself opened the door. I knew in a flash that this had to be my mother's brother. He reminded me so strongly of mother—as smiling he stretched out both hands to greet me—that tears sprang from my eyes.

"*Na, na, mein Mädchen. Schon gut, schon gut,*" he cried heartily. He clasped me to his chest, patting my back. Muttering endearingly, "*Willkommen, willkommen, komm mal herein,*" he ushered me into the *gute Stube*.

Inside, the house surprised me with its modern look. The kitchen, the bathrooms and other rooms, too, had been refitted and modernized. There were large windows out back, overlooking the small garden, allowing the sunlight to stream in and brighten the charming old rooms.

Uncle Martin wore the comfortable Bavarian gray pants and a green jacket with handcut *Gemsenhorn* buttons that were the civilian's uniform in Bavaria. Never having seen anyone in such garb, I had to smile. Uncle Martin's wife, Gudrun, bustled in. Over the years, thoughts of this woman had occupied my family for countless hours, for she had become mother to my brothers by default. We had often wondered whether she liked or resented them, and whether they had been the reason for her to remain childless.

Gudrun was a motherly woman in her fifties, rounded, yet firm, who wore her blond hair blunt-cut halfway to her shoulders. She wore a blue and gray paisley housedress and black slippers, golden earrings and a golden wedding ring on her finger, all very simple and straightforward— not at all like a rich man's wife. I soon heard that her expensive jewelry had been used to buy food some time ago when the family was starving. My family, had they only known, could have rested assured in the knowledge that my brothers had been delivered into the hands of the kindest woman, endowed with a heart to love them dearly.

After greeting me, welcoming me into her home, she exclaimed, "Oh, the boys are so excited that you have come. They will arrive in the afternoon with their wives and children."

Oh! Heavens! I had almost forgotten that wives and children came as my brothers' entourage. I secretly dreaded the thought of being engulfed by a clan; so many new people with emotional claims. Uncle Martin and my brothers, although I had never known them in the flesh, were not enigmatic strangers because of the oft-repeated tales about them. I had seen their few photographs and their letters. Their families, however, were another pot of tea altogether.

Gudrun, with *hausfraulicher* officiousness, went to bring in *das Mittagsessen*, which was waiting to be served. I knew, of course—having heard it during the Atlantic crossing on the ship and later from accounts on the train—that all of Germany was suffering from a food shortage which, in some parts, bordered on famine. The tales of how oriental carpets, precious jewelry and grand furniture pieces had been parted from their owners for a few pounds of meat, a chicken or two loaves of bread echoed through the land. So, when I saw Gudrun's feast, I understood instantly that my uncle's family had deprived themselves for days, perhaps weeks, to afford me the pleasure of a grand meal. They could not fathom how thoroughly I, the gulag survivor, appreciated their sacrifice.

Sparing nothing, Gudrun had set the table with her finest linen and china, upon which she presented a veritable feast. After meat dumplings in clear soup with parsley came roast chicken and potato dumplings with gravy, carrots and cauliflower, followed by butter lettuce with vinaigrette, a cheese platter and Marzipan tartlets in almond crust.

I felt tremendously honored, knowing that my arrival had been anticipated with great love and sacrifice. Partaking of the feast, doing it justice by slowly savoring each bite, we talked—talked about the old Tsarist days, which, bad as they had been at times, most people now fervently wished would return. Together we gave thanks. We marveled at the grace they had received, for their house, content and all, had remained intact. They told me gently that my grandparents were dead. They had not lived long in Germany after leaving Russia. It was as if, deprived of the searing sun, the freezing cold and the steppe wind, they had withered and died.

During the short time left to them in Germany, they had lovingly kept the bond alive between my small brothers and the rest of our family stuck behind Stalin's Iron Curtain. They had painted verbal pictures of the villages, the Volga, the steppe and the icy winters; they evoked our culture: how we lived, who we were—united in God and church, assuring them that our love for them would last forever. It was because of these vivid, rich communications that my brothers grew up with their parent's pictures in their hearts and a strong connectedness to our poor Volga German relatives.

After the meal Martin and Gudrun showed me Würzburg. Or better put, they showed me the parts that were untouched by the war. Würzburg was an arch-Catholic town, filling the valley of the beautiful blue, strong Main River. It was at its liveliest best along the riverbanks. There were over one hundred churches in town. They rang on Sunday mornings for different services at different times, creating a cacophony of bells. Uncle Martin told me there had been more, but many were damaged and silent. "There are some who say the silence is a gift, but the rest of us would rather hear all of the bells ringing again."

The grandest bridge across the Main, dominated by larger than life statues of bishops, cardinals and saints, was aptly named the *Heiligen Brücke*, the Saints Bridge. Standing among the overpowering statues of holy men, Martin directed my gaze upward into the western hills where the *Marienberg Festung*, the enormous fortified fortress, overshadowed all other buildings on the mountain. It overlooked the entire town and a large part of the river running through the area.

Every hill and mountainside was covered in green—vineyards, they told me. On many of the mountaintops still stood ancient castles and *Burgen*, fortified by heavy walls. They looked down into the vineyards which were terraced, enclosed by solid stonewalls and crisscrossed by narrow, walled-in paths, barely allowing oxcarts to drive through for the grape harvest.

We walked through a wonderful park. In its midst stood the *Bischofs* residence, a complex of buildings commissioned by two prince-bishops. Their home, the magnificent residence, was a receptacle for some of the finest artwork in Europe. Not far from the residence arose the *Hofkirche*, the interior splendidly appointed with winding marble columns, angels, statues, paintings, frescoes and much gold work.

Here, too, we were grateful that this part of town had not become a target of the bombers. Had the bombers been instructed to spare this treasure? Or, we wondered, had God intervened, saving what was truly great and beautiful? Although so much of the city lay in ruins, I was touched by Würzburg's gentle beauty, its sweet, light mantle of joy, put upon it by a people who loved a good, gracious life.

When the time came that the rest of the family would be released from work, we slowly walked home. Uncle Martin had proudly told me that Michael had become a physician who worked in the famous *Luitpold Krankenhaus*, a university hospital. Peter had used his share of the money invested by Holger for the family at a time when everyone had hoped to emigrate, and bought into a wine business.

It was late afternoon when my brothers arrived with their families. Michael, his pretty, dark-haired wife Charlotte, and their three pretty girls came first. Strangely, but today I cannot remember the childrens' names—I am getting old and forgetful. Why do I feel so strongly that I should remember? Perhaps I should remember because I inscribed their names in our family Bible, which I gave to my children.

They were darling girls—very thin, with big dark eyes like their mother's, wearing little sundresses, makeovers of their mother's old wardrobe. Their coltish legs were bare, and sandals that caught my eye enclosed their small feet, because the sandals, too, were imaginatively cobbled together from older shoes. They were shy and so well behaved that they alternately delighted and depressed me. I think this depression arose because they evoked in me the pictures of our village children in the last days before the deportation. In them, I once again remembered the enormous, hungry eyes, the grayish skin and the thin faces of Schaffhausen's smallest citizens.

Peter arrived, bringing in tow his wife Margot, three little boys and a five-year-old girl. This girl, Renate, I remember well. She was the third in a row of four children. She was as different from her other female cousins as a wild rose is different among tulips. Already strong-willed at age five, she had made it quite clear to her mother that she would not wear anything frilly.

"She is my only girl and I wanted to put a ruffle on her dress, when I made a pretty nightgown into a dress for her," complained Margot, a vivacious blond, "but she wanted no part of it." She laughed, "Look at her! Plain as a sheet."

Tall for her age, thin, with large hands and feet, Renate was dressed in a simple, white sheath. It was a narrow-cut creation, slightly flaring at the bottom, leaving her knobby knees in plain view. On her long, narrow feet, she wore the same sandals as her cousins. Renate was the only one of my nieces and nephews who did not feel strange meeting me. The others treated me to different degrees of shyness, discomfort and avoidance. She, however, walked right up to me—her hand stretched out to greet me.

"Papa says you are my aunt and that you are from Russia. Are you?" I smiled, enjoying her straight approach. "Yes, I am your aunt, and I am from Russia," I said.

"So, why did you stay in Russia when Papa and Uncle Michael came here?" she wanted to know, and with this question she set the tone of the conversation for all of us.

I recounted for my newly-found family the years after Michael and Peter had been sent out of the country. I told of the famines, the takeover by the Reds and their regime of horror; told of the *kolkhoz*, disease, murder, the disappearance of people and our people's quiet resistance.

My brothers were handsome men. Michael looked so much like Father that I had to control myself valiantly to hold back my tears. Peter looked more like Mother, but he was as tall as Michael. Their personalities were the reverse of my parents'. Michael was serious, studious and

reserved—so much like Mother it was astonishing, while Peter had inherited Father's Russian exuberance. As they sat before me, I was terribly
drawn to them, but I controlled my desire to hug and kiss them.

"So tell me about the *kolkhoz*. How was this system supposed to
work?" asked Michael. I told him how Mother and I had worked in the
calf barn, how we were paid like factory workers for an eight-hour day, but
that the work, however, required many more hours because cows do not
calve on government time.

"They eradicated the demarcations and the hedgerows separating the
fields, making monstrously large plots. Then they sent in one man with a
team to plow a field a mile wide and perhaps a mile long. The men would be
all alone out there with their beasts, often without food and water. Everything
that a man raised on this soil would not be his, it belonged to the government.
If the land did not yield, the government still took the little that was raised and
left us nothing. When famine struck, it was our fault, not the government's."

"How can this be? They cannot take everything that belongs to you
and give you nothing to survive on!" cried Peter.

"Oh, yes, they can," I averred.

"They are beginning to do this in the East now, I have heard," said Michael. "There are speeches foreboding that they will do to East Germany and
the other communist vassals the same as has been done to their own people."

"Oh, those poor people," I exclaimed. "The hardest thing for us was
the confiscation of our animals. We had treated them as living, feeling
creatures, our partners in the fight against fickle nature. The Communists
used them like machines, as if you could keep them going with a little oil
in their joints and a gallon of water once a month."

Peter, who was active in the *Landsmannschaft* of the Volga Germans,
told us of some statistics compiled by avid members that described the
Red rule. These statistics were still incomplete, for many people could not
be accounted for. However, from reports by those who had escaped the
tyranny, it was ascertained that the entire Russian-German population had
been uprooted and sent into internal exile east of the Ural Mountains. This
region was undeveloped. The report stated that no proper housing or even
crude shelter had been provided in this wilderness. Neither had the people
been supplied with food, clothing, or medical care.

"I think Mother was sent with the others to the Urals when they took
us to the gulag," I said.

Peter's eyes were filled with tears as he continued the daunting report.
Between 1945 and 1946, a quarter of a million Russian Germans died of

malnutrition, typhus, scurvy, exposure, exhaustion and tuberculosis. Here we were safe and wondered silently if Mother was among the dead. Although we believed that we had to keep hope alive at all cost, sometimes the facts just overwhelmed hope.

Long ago, as we conversed passionately, Gudrun and my sisters-in-law had set the table with dishes, sandwiches, beer and juice. We had partaken of the simple meal, the table had been cleared. Long ago, the children had tired of playing in the street, falling—sated and bored with adult conversation—sound asleep wherever they found a cozy place. At last it was time for my brothers to leave. Finally, after having talked at length, evoking our lives for each other, I felt close to them. I was able to warmly embrace them. I could touch their "thick Russian hair," and hug their wives. In small steps we were becoming a family again. Although we had used our first visit to forcefully debate, after all we were trying to make sense of a monstrous world—we slowly began to grow the ties that bind families together. They heard and saw me as their sister and at the same time as a part of Russia, a representation of the Volga Germans.

When my brothers left that night, they and their families had become a part of me, our connection had been restored. Now, as they were leaving, I could freely clutch them to my breast and cry over them—the tears were bliss; and they, also, could show affection.

We met often during my allocated four weeks. I visited their homes—simple, clean, sparsely furnished abodes—which made me think of a painter's spare canvas, before heavy oil paint brush strokes fully define the master's intent. One day, I hoped, my brothers' wives would have the wherewithal to imprint these places with their personalities.

I stayed for four weeks in Würzburg, then my visa was up. However, these weeks ranked among the most important weeks of my life. I saw the ravages of the war, and heard the German citizens' side of history. I heard about the fascists, Hitler's takeover and the feeling of total helplessness by many in the face of his brutal regime.

During one of our dinners, Uncle Martin said, "Hitler came like every tyrant, promising every man everything: hope, prosperity, supremacy of race, *Lebensraum!*" Martin laughed, "Of course prosperity, hope and power were just for him and his adherents, as we saw in retrospect. Never believe a politician who claims to be able to change your condition, for the only one who can do that is yourself."

I understood the progressive takeover by the fascists perfectly. I understood how it had affected the people, for had we not been

eclipsed by the same evil in Russia, been blinded by the same rhetoric? Was the difference in these monstrous "isms" in any way different? As I pointed out—a bit truculently—in practice, the simi-
larities between communism and fascism were overwhelming.
I quoted my brothers a much bandied-about cliché: "Fascism is communism in patent leather shoes instead of combat boots." A true statement,
for both regimes were totalitarian systems to benefit their adherents only.

Both "isms" had descended upon the populace in the disguise of pol-
iticians promising benevolent relief for the oppressed and hungry masses.
Both espoused fervent belief in the indoctrination and re-education of
whole segments of their population. Both believed in unmitigated force
to achieve their goals and exerted might until death befell their hapless
victims. And both systems, directed by their psychopathic leaders, cleaned
out their own ranks mercilessly with the vigor and expediency of paranoid
schizophrenics.

At first my brothers tried to argue that the Nazis had foisted a greater
plight upon the Germans than the Soviets had upon Russia. That was the
moment when my Uncle Martin joined me in the debate like a frigate with
filled sails and ready cannons: "If you cannot understand Katharina's arguments and the reports of her suffering, or the horrific tales of the German
immigrants arriving from Russia, perhaps you can be persuaded by a good
look at East Germany. Look and see what the communists have wrought
there! Just take the misery of the East Germans and multiply that a hundredfold and you experience the horror of the villages of Lower Volga, the
Ukraine and every other minority in Russia!"

He paused for a minute and, totally incensed, continued even louder,
"Hell, even the simple Russian *muzhiks*, for whom supposedly the Revolu-
tion was made, lived in a nightmare we cannot even imagine here!" Enraged,
I joined his angry oratory.

"How can you forget that your mother and father risked everything
to secure a better life for you here? How can you forget that your father was
dragged off to Vorkuta, where he died, by the mere word of a communist?
Even then, in the beginning of the Red regime, the daily terror we endured
was enormous." I never knew if they fully understood my point.

When they told me of the Nazi concentration camps, I spat, "What of
the gulags? I was starved and worked to death in one of those, but the European and American press never mention Russia's horror. Instead of analyzing
the war as a whole, seeing all sides, they cry guilt-ridden mea culpas. Facts are
simple—emotions complex. If you allow feelings about vague intentions to

dominate reporting, you arrive at wrong conclusions or one-sided reportage. They are blind in one eye and only see what they are forced to see in the other!" My brothers had no answer to deflect my fury.

Through the following weeks we often discussed the power politics of our time. At times we parted, subdued by deep, painful thoughts and feelings of division. I could not help but be angry sometimes. However, through the difficult discourse we learned to understand each other better as we learned one another's reality.

The Breaking Apart of Germany

Each time we met thereafter, walking along the mild, mellow Main River, having a picnic at its banks or meeting at their homes—small, clean and efficiently furnished—the enormous problems of our time arose. We debated vigorously, as if we could personally change the ills of totalitarian governments. We argued fervently about the means required to rectify the enormous wrongs. As we examined the other, the Russian-occupied part of Germany, I pointed out the many differences between capitalist and communist entities.

The division of Germany into two parts had taken place recently. While the western part, administered by the American, French and British Allies, was constituted as a Federal Republic, the eastern part, bordering Poland, the Baltic, Czechoslovakia and West Germany, adopted a constitution creating a Democratic Republic.

From the beginning it was plain to see that in East Germany one party, the SED, a communist-organized entity—an alliance between home-grown German communists and German Russian exiles, who returned protected by the might of Soviet tanks—had taken control of the faux republic through force and intimidation. Uncle Martin had many business associates who fled Russia's budding communist satellite at that time for West Germany because the SED had instantly confiscated—for various trumped-up reasons—all large businesses, factories and utilities, making them *Volkseigen,* supposedly belonging to the people.

The same fate struck large, rich farms. Uncle Martin told us, "In 1949 so many former land–owning families, often accompanied by an entire village of disillusioned farmers, fled East Germany that they created another food shortage." He smiled grimly, "I wonder what kind of a harvest they will have over there this year, for not much was planted during spring and summer."

"It won't be long now, and the Communists will expropriate the land from the rest of the farmers," predicted Michael. Those were prescient words, for it was only two years later that the rest of the small farms were appropriated by the SED-led government.

As we talked, I studied my brothers' faces. I still had not gotten over Michael's strong resemblance to my father. His strong Slavic cheekbones, his bright eyes, overshadowed by exquisitely shaped, strong brows, his generous mouth—so like Father, that he made me ache for the gallant man who had died too young. I noticed my tendency to stare and, therefore, consciously avoided gazing at Michael too often.

Peter had taken up the thread of the conversation, "They take away all civilian rights of the people over there. For the last two years, we have been watching how the Communists curtail freedoms. They proceed under the guise of *Entnazifizierung*, the cleansing of nazism.

"What in particular do they do?" I asked, as if I did not know already.

"The first act of the Soviet Army, after peace had been declared and the treaties had been signed, was to go from one mayor's office to another and confiscate the lists containing the names of legal weapon holders. Not only the weapons of soldiers, the SS or other military groups, no, they also took the weapons of forest masters, hunters, watchmen and policemen, until only the Soviets and their ilk remained in possession of weapons. Then, when they held elections, their thugs tormented the other, newly-formed democratic parties with a reign of terror until these besieged entities gave up posting placards, posters and holding meetings."

"That's exactly what the Red Army did in Russia. First the weapons, then the torment," I chimed in.

Peter, with Russian vigor, spat, "Next came the purges of teachers and intellectuals who could have exposed the power grab and started a counter movement. The Nazis had already been purged."

The words had hardly left his mouth when I chimed in that it had been the same in Russia, where teachers and professors had been replaced with untrained party *Bonzen*.

"We are lucky to live in the West," said Uncle Martin, as if reciting a prayer. "The Americans have freed us from the Fascist ilk and left us those freedoms a populace at peace should enjoy. They look for Nazi criminals, take apart the old network, but they leave the ordinary man alone to clean up the war mess." He took a large draught of his beer and added, "The *Amis* are our *Besatzungsmacht*, our owners by might, but they do not act that way."

"They feed the children in the schools with cottage cheese and ham sandwiches because so many were desperately undernourished," said matronly Gudrun, emoting so much warmth that her face reminded me of an icon I had seen in Russia.

I soon understood Gudrun's feelings for the Americans, for being virtuous victors, they behaved unlike any other nation on earth. For one, they displayed none of a victor's arrogance. To the contrary, they did their utmost to create a normal life for the population.

American churches vied with each other to marshal the most aid, expressed in care packages, sending them to the defeated Germans. Not only did these marvelous, good people aid the churches and social services in the West; no, they also gifted the repressed churches of East Germany. They cared for the peoples in a territory which was soon to become the new, implacable enemy of America and the free western world. Stalin had already begun the cold war of annexation through local communist operatives within countries like Greece and Turkey. Seeing this silent war of attrition, Truman would soon have to make a stand.

But I was still young then, in a country new to me, in a new city. My tall, handsome brothers wanted me to have good time. There were times when we wanted nothing better than to forget—to forget the war, to forget Hitler and the bloody fascists, Stalin and the murderous communists— everything! After what seemed an eon we just wanted be at peace, normal! Unafraid, undisturbed, unthinking, innocent! Würzburg had little bread then, but they had wine, very good wine, indeed. Therefore, my family arranged for hikes, boating and small parties, all with wine.

One of those parties they had arranged took place in a delightful, small castle, the *Steinburg am Steinberg*. This castle sat upon an audacious promontory at the end of a long, narrow mountain, filled from top to bottom with vineyards, overlooking the Main River and most of the city. Its owner presided over one of the best wine cellars in the region, and we were fortunate to be invited to try last year's vintage.

As always when going to a party in those days, the guests brought as many victuals as they could decently spare. On my sea voyage, I had helped a young GI, Eddy Bronson, with translations, as he made his way to the Leighton Barracks part of the *Hindenburg Kaserne* in Würzburg. His company had been shipped out earlier. He, however, had been laid up sick in hospital in the States, and now was catching up. "Call me if you need anything over here," he had said. "They don't have much of anything in Germany, and I will get whatever you need from the PX."

The US Army's 3rd Infantry Division had liberated Würzburg and was now stationed at Leighton Barracks on a mountain ridge, which soon became known to everyone by the English name The Skyline. True to his word, before our party, Eddy took me shopping at the PX. After my purchases, at the checkout, we were in high spirits, kidding and joshing. Suddenly an authoritative voice put an end to our jollity.

"Stand at attention soldier when a superior officer is present!" The voice was matter-of-act, not so much reprimanding as teaching. However, Eddy snapped to attention; clicking his heels he saluted smartly. "Beg your pardon, Sir! I did not see you, Sir!"

"I know! Just wanted to make you aware."

"Thank you, sir!" Eddy was glad to get off so easy. Some officers were terrible taskmasters when it came to new recruits.

While the little interlude transpired, the officer, a tall, handsome captain, had paid me more attention than the hapless Eddy.

Thanks to Eddy and to everyone's surprise, I arrived at the party with bags of marvelous things. There were foods in the bags they had not seen in ages. Surrounding me, the guests ooohed and aaahed as I revealed my treasures. I had brought ham, ice cream, white bread which was then a delicacy, mayonnaise and cheese—all I could afford. I blew all my money, for Uncle Martin had promised to contribute to my passage back to America. "I have money," he said. "We were able to exchange a percentage of the old Marks into the new currency, but at the moment we cannot buy much. So I will be able to purchase a ticket for you." His promise allowed me to act in spendthrift fashion.

My moment of glory was rudely interrupted by the arrival of an American officer, around whom the party rallied like archeologists around the Rosetta Stone. In the starring role one moment, I was suddenly left at the outer edge of the circle surrounding the familiar-looking uniformed man. From their excited exclamations, I gathered that he was a Captain McKenna, and highly popular with the natives.

Even my brothers and Uncle Martin grinned from ear to ear while they shook his hand and slapped his shoulder. My sisters-in-law, together with the rest of women, were all agog over the man, eyeing him with what we used to call on the Volga *Kuh-Augen*. Soon I found out that the "cow-eyes" were not just for the handsome captain, who reminded me very much of Herbert Baumeister, but also for the presents he brought. It seemed to give him unmitigated joy to bestow upon the women nylon stockings and Nivea crème. The latter items held the power to turn loose women into prostitutes. Captain McKenna also brought whiskey for the host, chocolate, coffee and cigarettes for the guests.

Cary McKenna was fair-skinned, freckled and had auburn hair. Harmonizing with his freckles, big, brown eyes looked with amusement upon the world around him. Despite the feminine attributes of fair skin and freckles, he managed to present a very masculine picture. He was tall, well-proportioned, in fighting trim, and looked as if he could hold his own in any skirmish, never mind the army's demands on him.

The moment he had bestowed his last favor upon the ladies, he turned around and saw me standing at a distance from the excited crowd. "Well, if it isn't the girl from the PX!" he called out. "Where is your young enlisted man?"

"I have no idea," I retorted pertly. "He is probably being reminded by one of your high caste to stand at attention right now."

He grinned, "Peppery, spicy are we, eh?" I laughed. He reminded me so much of Herbert, it was comical.

"Do you play the piano?" I asked.

"No, why do you ask?"

"Nothing in particular. You just remind me of a piano player I knew in the States."

Our host, Hans Spaltzer, presenting glasses filled with last year's vintage, fortunately interrupted our silly conversation. Würzburger, or Main, wines are in a class all by themselves. Grown on steep, chalky, stony mountain-sides, often enduring cold winters and hot summers without the benefit of much rain, the wines derived from grapes on such hills are strong with special mineral notes, and I sipped slowly, trying to do it justice.

Someone had discovered an old record player, and in no time we were listening to pre-war dance music. To my surprise, my brothers were the first to lead their wives to the middle of the room and begin to dance. Soon everyone danced lustily. Lately not much fun had been had in Germany. And so, if the moment allowed a little joy, people sought it eagerly.

I danced with Michael, and it was as if I danced with Father. As I rested my head on his broad chest, I told him, "Father resides within you. Do you know that you look and even smell like him? I love you for this familiarity, this intimacy." He squeezed the hand by which he led me, saying, "When I look at you, the picture of a serious young woman comes to me. She is wearing a heavy sheepskin coat and hat as she lifts me into a train compartment. She looked so sad, as if her heart were breaking."

"Yes, Mother told me the story many times. That was the day when she sent you off to Germany, out of the Communists' reach. You were better off here than in Russia where you would have been cannon fodder on the front lines against the German Army."

"No one was safe anywhere," corrected Michael. "Peter and I were almost shipped to the Russian front by the Nazis. Toward the end of the war we were forced from our jobs to fill the Army's decimated ranks. Until then we had been protected. I was safe, because the Chief Surgeon would not allow necessary staff to be deployed, Peter by his position as Home Front Warden. However, toward the end, 250,000 of us were forced into Field Marshal von Rundstedt's Ardennes offensive. We had no training, were green as fresh-cut wood, and faced General Patton's seasoned troops."

Michael led me to a seat. Our host had placed tables and chairs under the stars, on a broad stone platform edged by a battlement of enormous square stones which, during the Middle Ages, allowed defenders to rain death upon foes. There, Michael told me about his and Peter's short war experience.

"Our hapless company was hopelessly surrounded by Patton's tanks. Having been barely given enough ammunition for a good hunt, we gladly surrendered. No reason to die for a bad cause," he added, laconically.

Peter came, asking for a dance. As he twirled me about I could not help but say, "You have Mother's good looks but Father's Russian exuberance; you are a lucky man."

He laughed loudly, like Father always did, and said, "Margot tells me that I am the favorite son, that the family bestowed the best upon me."

"That might be true," I teased. "I, however, was the one they kept."

Peter was instantly serious, "Don't laugh or fret about that. I know they would have smuggled you out, too, if they had been able."

The moment Peter released me, Cary McKenna claimed me for a dance. Someone had changed the record and now a strange, wild tune rent the air. Sounding much like many a Russian folk song, the music spoke to my soul.

"What kind of dance is this?" I asked McKenna.

"Hungarian gypsy music," he replied.

Violins sent trills of joy skyward, a cymbal popped a rhythmic melody, violas wailed and bass players harshly, wildly plucked their strings. I danced, not knowing the steps. My body swayed with the rhythm, somehow following McKenna's lead, and I was wildly happy.

"Do you like this music," asked my handsome captain.

"Like it? I love it," I exclaimed with exuberance.

"I am glad," he said, "for I love it as much as I do Scottish and Irish music."

The magic dance ended. We feasted on an unusual array of victuals: a few bites of sausage, a slice of white bread, a dab of ice cream and plenty of wine to wash down the offering. Since it was Saturday night and no one needed to go to work the next morning—even Michael was off duty from the hospital—we celebrated under the stars, looking upon the sleeping city with happy eyes, until my eyelids drooped and my feet hurt from dancing.

McKenna announced his leave. "I have duty at seven. With luck I will get four hours of sleep." He kissed me on the cheek, and said, "I will call you." With this intangible promise he left.

"How can he call me?" I asked Peter, "He knows nothing about me."

"He will find you," my brother assured me.

Marriage

And so it was. McKenna not only found me, but not long thereafter he married me. For three years, I was an Army wife in Würzburg. Lucky me! I was able to remain close to my family and yet have a life of my own. We often traveled in Europe, and I saw with amazement that Europe's industrialization was light years ahead of Russia. America's industrial development I had expected. But to my surprise, even small countries like the Netherlands were rich and civilized compared to Russia.

It depressed me, extraordinarily so, to realize that here, even small villages experienced the scourge of war, exhibited a standard of living unknown to Russia. In Europe, even the most insignificant spot I visited was blessed with electricity, good schools, paved roads, piped clean drinking water, and often, indoor plumbing. I came to find later that this was not always the case, but for most of the countryside this was true. Compared to these villages our rural areas in Russia had suffered from age-old neglect. Katharinenstadt had been endowed with a few such advancements, but our small villages were not.

My Own Family

Our first child, Fiona, was born in Würzburg at the end of Cary's tour of duty. I pleaded for a permanent home in America to raise our children. I asked that we might live in Fresno where I felt comfortable. I knew then that I would be forever a small town girl, and Fresno was just that to me. It was a place where life flowed calmly in well-ordered ways. I knew the kind members of the Cross Church. I had a true friend there in Cora. But above all, the land was flat like the land that had raised me, yet the climate was mild.

Cary, however, was an Easterner. He was born and bred to the Atlantic coast, and Connecticut beckoned, drawing him home. Suffice it to say, when the time came we boarded a ship for New York and then drove to Stamford. There, outside the city, his parents owned a fabulous old home, surrounded by three acres of prime ground groomed to park-like perfection.

His family was numerous, opinionated, bold and sophisticated. Soon after we arrived I noticed that Cary, too, fell easily back into their refined but loose, witty but sarcastic, intelligent but often cuttingly hurtful ways and patterns of speech. It was obvious from the start that his parents were not happy with his choice of bride.

Cary's mother, auburn haired, delicately skinned, slim and tall, embraced her son with great warmth, while spreading coldness upon me. "So, you are a German from Russia," she intoned, as her nose rose upward on her face, withering my soul.

His father, a silver-haired patrician with a long nose and water-clear green eyes, also espoused a grand show of welcome for his war-hero son, and then looked down his nose upon me.

"Intelligent fellow, this Stalin," he grinned at me.

To which I snidely replied, "Yes, quite good with gulags, into which he relegates everyone with whom he disagrees."

"So, you grew up in a small Russian village," he pursued the line of my inadequacies. I, however, stupidly eager to make any contact at all, told him where Schaffhausen was located on the Volga. At this juncture he cut my verbal thread, "So you went to a village school?"

Again I tried to connect with him. "Yes, for eight years. After that I received an education in a private school in the city."

He said nothing but sounded a long drawn-out "Hmmm!" upon which he was finished with me, paying full attention to his drink, ignoring my presence.

The welcoming party for Cary, and supposedly for me, was held on a large terrace overlooking the park. Chinese lanterns, hanging upon tree branches ,scintillated like fireflies in the still night. I marveled at the beauty, the elegance and sumptuousness of the affair, which impressed me like a good fairy tale. At least eighty people were present, talking, laughing and drinking in groups. Most of them, of course, surrounded Cary.

Soon, after the barest introductions had worn off, no one paid me any mind. Not one of those present exhibited even the slightest curiosity in me, in Russia, or Germany. I understood that they might have no interest in me. But even so, why would they not have an interest in the country that I knew would soon become a bitter enemy of so much freedom and prosperity? For capitalist success, combined with enormous democratic advances for the population, ran counter to communist philosophy, nay communist doctrine.

Standing there alone, looking upon the lively happy crowd, I suddenly was painfully aware that I had married the wrong man. I tried valiantly to suppress knowledge of this hurtful epiphany. Had he been beside me during those initial moments, had he protected me from the raw stares—they looked upon me as if I was a Russian bear—and given me support, I could have endured the rude treatment without discomfort.

Cary, however, played the role of the homecoming hero from the beginning and to the hilt. Soon, he was surrounded by schoolmates, old friends and a bevy of girls. I felt terribly alone among this group of boisterous people, who, although hard drinking and noisy, managed simultaneously to appear elegant and sophisticated. In my entire life, I had never experienced an event like this, and wondered whether the parties of my parents' youth could have compared to it.

Left to my own devices, I strolled into the park where small lamps seamed the walkways. When I returned, Cary greeted me with reproof. "Where have you been? I have been looking all over for you!" he said angrily.

"I doubt that very much," I contradicted him. "I was only gone a short time. No one noticed my presence, no one noticed my leaving. So, what is the urgency now?"

"I want you to meet some of my friends from way back." His speech was fast, slightly slurred, and whiskey emanated from his pores. He must have been drinking hard and fast. I had been looking forward to this event. In my innocence, I had believed that it had been planned for us as a married couple, to introduce us to family and friends. I had dressed in my best summer gown, one I had bought in Italy, sighing over the many lira spent. I had elaborately swept my long hair in a classical style atop my head, a style Cary had very recently complimented.

Yet, earlier, when the guests arrived, I had noted with dismay that I was sadly out of fashion. Every one of the assembled beautiful girls sported either short, vamp-style haircuts or blunt-cut glossy bobs. I, of course, had no idea what these styles were, but I realized that I was outmoded.

Cary, pulling me along, seemed excited, as if I was a prize frigate in tow. "Here she is," he cried gaily, approaching a group of young people. "Here is Catherine. Look and marvel, who would ever believe that this dainty girl killed a guy who probably weighed 250 pounds?"

There was moment of shocked silence. I almost fainted. How could Cary make me a vulgar object of curiosity, an object of lurid, macabre interest?

I pulled myself together. "I did not kill him," I smiled, a smile that caused me physical pain. "Another person, a man, did the killing. I just tried to keep an attacker from raping and killing me."

"What did she do?" shouted a tall fellow, whose eyes, behind glasses, appeared to sit on stalks like a snail's.

"She stuck a knife into his back!" said Cary, with the gusto of the inebriated.

"Damn, buddy! You better watch your back, and don't make her angry, Cary," shouted a bland, pasty fellow, throwing his arms around the girl in front of him. Suddenly I felt as if someone was draining the blood from my veins. I felt weak. The party scene had taken on a ghostly cast. In the eyes of the people around me, I beheld a grisly curiosity. Especially the women were casting judging, impertinent, curious eyes upon me. Underlying their curiosity throbbed an unhealthy, morbid tenor. Their eyes suddenly seemed to be facetted, as those of flies, looking upon me as if I were carrion to be devoured.

"I am sure, if attacked, you, too, would defend yourself," I said mildly, facing them. "Or is violence so abhorrent to you that, rather than fight, you would instead succumb to being raped and murdered?" I blurted out with hot passion.

Indistinct murmurs greeted my words. Debate was not a sport they had in mind; baiting a German-Russian was more to their liking. I looked at Cary. As he stood there beside me, slightly befuddled because his lark had gone awry and turned serious, I felt for him the twin emotions of pity and disgust.

In my earlier epiphany, it had become clear to me that Cary was a man defined by circumstance and company. Like a chameleon changes color in different environs and backgrounds, Cary rose to the expectations and the culture of the people around him. Thus, having been expected to be an exciting young American officer in Germany, he became just that.

Here, at home, he instantly fell back into the role of hometown boy. I now remembered vividly that during our travels in Europe he alternately charmed French, Italian and Dutchmen in turn. In Europe I had deemed this trait an asset, an endearing part of his personality designed to please people and put them at their ease. However, I now came to see a shallow side to this trait.

My new perceptions of Cary struck me with the cleaving force of a sharp knife. One knows that one is cut, but does not yet feel the pain. I was, therefore, able to say with composure, "Excuse me, but I have to leave." Walking away, the truth of my situation hit me. I felt ill. A few days earlier it had become certain that I was pregnant again. This bout of nausea, however, was not caused by my condition.

The farther I got away from the party, the faster I walked. Soon I almost ran. Tears were streaming down my face, unbidden, without self-pity. Tears for the realization that the beautiful life I had hoped to have for my family would not be. I was not crying for myself but for my children. What kind of a father would this vacillating man be? He had not stood up for me to his family or friends. Nay, worse, he had made me the object of ridicule.

Perhaps I could salvage the marriage, perhaps save him from himself, by leaving this place as soon as possible; leave before the pervasive, cold arrogance of these people could destroy us. In Europe, Cary had acted and thought in different patterns. He had been a truly great guy or I would not have married him. Under a different sky, might he not become that man again?

I repeated this hopeful thought over and over, comforting myself, thereby killing the nagging voice telling me, "He is what he is, and you can't change him." As I stumbled blinded by tears through the park, a strong wind had begun to blow. The dark canopy above me shook, moaning and sighing with alternate gusts. Something large crashed through the brush ahead of me, halting my steps.

Sanity returned to my tormented self. Where was I? I needed to get back to the house, to my child. I considered that perhaps it was best for me to go back the way I had come. Although the path I had chosen should have led me to the guesthouse in the park, the house was nowhere in sight.

It was pitch dark. I could perceive the path beneath my feet, for the light pea gravel reflected the sparse light falling through gaps in the canopy. I wiped away my tears with the backs of my hands, and began to retrace my steps. It was not long before I once more walked on a path lit by lanterns. Then I saw the fork leading to the guesthouse, which I had previously missed.

Moments later, I was able to dismiss the nurse who had watched Fiona. I sat in the darkened room and looked sadly at my child dreaming in her bed.

Next day, when Cary was sober, I tried to explain to him my profound hurt and disappointment concerning my treatment at the hands of his family. More, I expounded on the even greater grief his uncaring exposition of a violent part of my life had caused me.

"You had no right to present a traumatic part of my life in such a sensationalized manner, to use me like a freak to popularize yourself. Titillating your audience with tales of a horrible, dangerous wife got you an exceedingly large amount of attention, while marking me forever in the minds of these people as 'the gruesome Katharina'."

"Come, come, Kate! You are melodramatic. It was just a good story, showing that you are a strong girl, with plenty of grit."

"Is that why your friends admonished you to watch your back and mind your step?" I mocked him: "Ha, ha, Cary! You'd better be on your toes all the time! Ha, ha!" I was furious. My husband seemed incapable of extracting empathy from wherever he kept his emotions, or was it possible that he did not want to understand my experience? I tried again with milder, more objective, words to make him understand my feelings. Alas, I could have addressed a wall.

For a week I faced my predicament. I contemplated every aspect of my situation, concluding that I had only one way open to me. I had to leave Stamford, with or without Cary. I agonized over the most minute, dire details of so drastic a decision. If I remained, I would lead a stifled, bitter life and come to hate Cary. That would be the end of our marriage. If he refused to go with me, the marriage would also end, but my soul and spirit would remain whole. I considered Cary's chances of earning a living in Fresno and concluded the chances were quite good. He was an electrical engineer who could find a job anywhere in the world. I thought of little Fiona and the child in my womb, and I knew beyond the slightest whisper of a doubt that their future did not rest amid their grandparents and aunts, for these people denigrated their mother. I could not allow my children to grow into the kind of people they were.

They were Catholic. They went to church each Sunday, yet Christ did not reside in their heart. I am not implying that their flaws found nurture in their church; no, these flaws stemmed directly from their class-driven arrogance. The exchange of words between Cary's parents and me had been bitter, not a good beginning. Henceforth, the situation grew only worse. Cary had four sisters, all married to rich men. Two were married to businessmen, one to a senator and the fourth to a city councilman. None of their husbands had seen combat. Those who had been in the service had seen sinecure assignments in the procurement of food, ammunitions and, yes, tires.

Although I spoke presentable English by this time, they marked my slight accent for ridicule. It was gentle ridicule, but cutting just the same. Cary's oldest sister Leonora reserved the most scorn for me. "So, darling, do you play bridge? It is important, for I would like to introduce you to the right people."

"No, I am sorry, I don't play bridge," I answered.

"But you should, you know." Her voice had risen half an octave, "It is a very intellectual game."

By now I had endured enough stings to feel a little demon raising his head inside my throat, and the next moment he said, "Do you play chess, Leonora?"

"No," she said, "why should I?"

"Oh it affords even greater mental gyrations, always testing the intellect," I smiled sweetly.

And so it went. They were not happy with me, and I heartily disliked them. For Cary's sake I tried to be pleasant and make things work. However, it was as hard a task as felling trees in the gulag, even though the labor performed was mental and emotional. To add salt to my wounds, our adorable daughter Fiona could not please the family either, because they already had so many handsome, cute "grand-boys."

My worst torments were our living arrangement. The patricians wanted their homecoming hero close and were, therefore, determined that we should live in the guesthouse in the park. "Until you find something better of course. First you must find a position to feed your family!" they said. And, at first glance, this was a fine and generous sentiment. However, inherent in this offer was their encoded right to come and go at our house as they pleased.

At first I demurred. I murmured my objections to Cary. Then I groused, jokingly, but much louder. Until I burst one day, after his mother and a sister with three little boys in tow, finally left, having kept me prisoner for three hours during which they consumed urns of tea and the dessert I had planned for that night's dinner. That day I screamed at him. Screamed in anger at the man who had been so dear to me before coming to Stamford.

Then came the day when after a walk in the truly magnificent park I confronted Cary.

"I am asking you to make a very hard decision," I began. "I have agonized every minute of my time in Stamford about our lives, about the things we must do. I have come to a conclusion, which is this: we must leave Stamford, must leave your parents, and begin life elsewhere. Here, I am unhappy, sickened to death." I chose strong words, for only they could convey what was in my soul.

"I will go with you anywhere, endure anything, but I will not stay here! I still think we should go to Fresno. I have friends there, a church filled with loving, kind people; but most of all, I know you would fit in and could be happy."

It took weeks of debate. Yet, when I finally set a date for my exodus, Cary relented and we left for Fresno. I will spare posterity the clamor and anger of his family when we told them of our plan. There were times when Cary weakened. But I stood strong, reminding him that I would leave without him. Perhaps I should not have coaxed him and pushed him so hard. Perhaps I should have foregone the dream of home and a whole family and immediately forged on alone. Only God knows what should have been done. Therefore, I refuse to take responsibility for all the events that later transpired. I tried. I thought. I planned. Like a sibyl I tried to foretell the unknowable.

In Fresno Again

We arrived in California at the end of September. It was my favorite time of year. Out in the country, at the outskirts of Fresno, drying raisins filled the air with a sweet, fermenting aroma.

During all my years away, I had always faithfully corresponded with Cora and the Leglers. I had always kept them apprised of the changes in my life, and in turn knew the important events in their lives. They were enduring friends, for when we came to Fresno, they had already found us suitable lodging, a small house not far from Cora's boarding house.

Once the pressure of the McKenna clan was removed, Cary became again the man I had married. In short order, Cary found a job with the Fresno Electric Company; I delivered a healthy boy, Keenan, and became a full-time mom. I loved being a wife and mother. At last I had family again. Sometimes, at night, when I had time to reflect, the very realization brought tears of joy to my eyes.

However, that did not mean I had forgotten my family in Russia. I pined for my Russians, my unfortunate loves, trapped behind Stalin's perfect fence—trapped in the largest gulag on earth.

Uncle Martin was as determined as I was to find Mother and Joseph. We also searched for Arkady Semyonov. Martin's lengthy inquiries finally uncovered the facts of my mother's death in a labor camp in the foothills of the Ural Mountains.

According to an inmate's written report, she died there in the winter of 1941. The man, Heinrich Bach, in addition to knowing her name, precisely described my mother after he had escaped the camp. Bach had reached the front and was lucky to become a German prisoner of war. He described my mother as "an angel," for she had selflessly taken care of others, to the point of neglecting her own needs. That description fit my mother well, and we believed his account of her death during an outbreak of typhoid fever. "Almost half of the women and quite a few men in this camp died in this outbreak," he had written in his report.

Heinrich's story itself was an incredible saga. Petrovka gulag was a mining camp in the Chelyabinsk oblast. Although segregated by sex, the men would daily see the women who ran the mess hall, the kitchen and the laundry. Everything was designed to allow the men maximum time underground, mining high-grade precious ores and minerals. Vanadium, titanium and tungsten were much in demand for the war effort, and the men spent day and night in never-ending shifts underground. By a lucky coincidence, mineral deposits containing ilmenite, yielding titanium and vanadium, and ores of sheelite yielding tungsten, were found in different deposits of this mine.

The horrid typhus episode with its resulting death toll, frightened, nay, terrorized Heinrich. Having been one of the unfortunates employed in the burial detail, his waking moments were haunted by the grotesquely distorted bodies of the women, which they had to fling into a panned-out part of the mine. "They did not allow us time to dig proper graves. It was the norm that had to be fulfilled—always the norm," he told the sympathetic German officials who debriefed him and wrote his report.

Heinrich had long ago decided to escape the camp if he ever got a chance. The very moment he saw a likely possibility, he took the risk and fled. Astute and observant, he had noted that one of the soldiers on the detail, which escorted the trucks loaded with mineral treasures, paid one of the women to wash his uniforms for him together with the regular wash. The man, a sergeant of medium stature and build like Heinrich, lived in barracks where the soldiers had to do their own laundry. His unit provided safe passage for the mining trucks from the mine to Stalin's best-loved city, Magnitogorsk.

Heinrich had always wondered why the trucks were so heavily escorted. He had assumed the Reds had total control of the country. This, however, was a misconception. Resistance still existed in isolated pockets of the Urals and other wild places, steeping every communist in paranoia. A foul up, like the capture of a truck filled with precious ore, would be severely punished. The officials in charge faced a quick death or banishment to a gulag.

The amazing city, Magnitogorsk, had grown mostly along the left bank of the Ural River because of a geological anomaly: a mountain, the Magnitka, of almost pure iron ore. No wonder Stalin paid special attention to this spectacular gift of nature. Along the river, a sprawling iron factory connected to enormous cleansing lakes provided much of the steel needed for Stalin's war effort. To smelter iron ore and make steel, one needs admixtures of vanadium and titanium to create alloys, or additions of tungsten for super alloys. Therefore, the trucks fed the refinery on a regular basis.

Heinrich had ferreted out the special details of the truck route. His Russian was fluent and pure. At every opportunity, he cleverly engaged the soldiers in small talk. Some, inured to boredom, would speak, while others just grunted at him with disgust. Thus, he learned where the barracks of the escorts were located, knew the schedule of the trucks, and knew most of the escorting soldiers.

To set his plan in motion, he stole the Russian sergeant's uniform. It fit him like a glove. He polished and pummeled a discarded pair of boots until they looked like a soldier's. Then he waited patiently.

His chance came when enteritis in the barracks of Magnitogorsk laid flat an entire escort detail. When the new escort detail arrived, none of the men knew him. Fortune dealt him great cards. His shift had just ended when the new company arrived. Heinrich gambled that the new men would not know each other well. He reasoned they had been assembled in a hurry to fill a void. With a mixture of trepidation and audacity, he put on the Russian uniform and the pampered boots.

He stood inside his own barracks where the men of his shift slept the sleep of the exhausted, staring out of the window, watching the loading of the trucks only a hundred meters away at the mine entrance. And then, Fortuna smiled on him again. For a moment, thinking themselves safe in camp, the soldiers left the trucks, while looking for food, drinks and a quiet place to piss.

His heart pounding, Heinrich stole from the hut where he had existed miserably for the last three years. As he calmly but quickly covered the hundred meters to the first truck within reach, he marveled that he was still alive after months in the gulag, thin but left with some strength. A little voice told him to be brave and sit in the cab, to brazen it out when the driver came back.

It seemed impossible to imagine, but more luck came his way. The trucks were filled and ready to leave, when an infuriated mine official on the run screamed and whistled for the escort to get a move on. "*Davai, davai!* Move, you lousy bastards!" Soldiers came flying from the cantina and the privies, still buttoning their flies, as abuse was heaped upon their heads. Helter-skelter they jumped into the vehicles and onto the running boards behind, and the trucks took off.

Along with the driver, another man had crammed himself into Heinrich's cab. "What the devil are you doing here?" asked the driver. "You did not come with us."

"I just jumped in when the *bonze* whistled and screamed. You know how it is! Do first and then sort it out later, or they punish you," said Heinrich, who had served in the army with Russians and knew the drill. The soldiers grinned and became positively sunny when Heinrich produced *machorka*, which he had assiduously, bit-by-bit, purchased with food rations and saved for an emergency. Well, he needed it now.

Arriving in Magnitogorsk with a detail of legitimate soldiers, no one questioned him or paid him any mind. He had carefully removed the sergeant's insignia from the uniform, replacing them, and was now just an innocent private by the name of Kravotkin. He did what the other soldiers did, following their lead. When, the empty trucks took off for another run he rode at the back of the truck, ready to make his escape. While two other soldiers with him talked and joked, he carefully examined the landscape for a likely spot to depart.

His moment came during a difficult ascent on a winding, narrow stretch of road. Where on one side the mountain rose steeply, the land fell precipitously toward the Ural River on the other, Heinrich's side. He spied a small promontory below the road thatched with shrubs and wagered his life in a desperate gamble. He jumped, fell flat, knocking the wind out of his lungs, and grabbed the first piece of vegetation to hit his hands.

The bush held. God had saved him. He moaned a small prayer. It seemed the other two soldiers had not seen his jump. As he gathered himself into a kneeling position, trying not to look over the edge of the outcropping, a saying of his mother's came to his mind. "*Unkraut vergeht nicht!*" Weeds never die. Ha! He was such a weed, he would not die, he would get away.

At last, stable, he knelt, afraid to stand and topple into the abyss. In increments he crawled toward the road. When he reached the end of the small outcropping, he saw the road above. From the rocky promontory up to the road was a sheer rock wall of twelve to fifteen feet that had to be overcome. To be saved, he would have to claw his way upward, dangling above the dreaded chasm. There was, however, no other way out. The climb upward was what he had to do—nothing else would serve.

Heinrich viewed the seemingly insurmountable obstacle and felt defeated. He sank to his knees. Looking up at the rim, he began to pray. He had not followed the Lord's teachings for a long time. As a matter of fact, he had only prayed in the gulag when times became so desperate that, like a small child, he would break and call out his pain to the parent above. However, like a child, he had resented and cast aside the offerings of the deity, just as he had thrown off the advice of his parents.

Yet, here he was at a crossroads. Climb up without a fall into the abyss and live, set a foot wrong, slip, and your life ends in the depths of the Ural River. Finally Heinrich knew which path he was to take. "Take my life and do what you will!" he prayed. "Your will be done! I am yours to command."

Thus, he prayed, and lo, without seeking, his hands felt the tiny recesses of the rock, and his fingers were exerting a power he did not know he possessed. His feet sought the places designated by the seeking fingers; his muscles tensed; his knees thrust upward; his body, like an arrow, uncoiled upward.

Suddenly, looking up, he saw the sharp edge of the gravelly road surface. One more grand effort, and he propelled his upper body onto the road. Seconds later, he was sprawled flat upon the narrow mountain path. With gratitude, he realized that he was saved. But although saved from one evil, the other problem was palpably present. He was desperately aware that, for the Communists' inquiries to be satisfied, he needed to disappear, truly vanish without a trace.

At the end of his exhausting adventure, he looked into the day's rosy end. Below in the Ural's valley the sun had set a while ago, while up on the cliff the setting orb was still visible. Once more, Heinrich felt gratitude. His tracks would be hidden for another day, perhaps forever. Standing upright, he began to scramble down the mountainside road as fast as he could. Hours later, in the coal-black dark, he decided he needed to rest. He climbed the steep side of the mountain, found a strong tree, and made a nest beneath it. The temperature dropped precipitously. He, however, was used to hardship. Covering himself with the leaves and debris of the surrounding shrubs and trees he kept the cold at bay. Thinking himself fortunate, he fell asleep.

He awakened at dawn to the sound of falling rocks. An avalanche of pebbles swept by his nest under the tree. He roused himself and stared up the hillside above him. What he saw filled him with terror. Stuck to the slope, as if glued to it, was a huge brown bear. Holding on to fragile vegetation with three of his paws, he used the fourth to tear apart a decaying log.

Heinrich was struck with fear by the enormous size of the animal and the realization that any shift in the wind might bring the hungry giant, looking for a more substantial meal, to him. As quietly and unobtrusively as he could he eased himself from his puny shelter and allowed his body to slither silently down, onto the road. Not for one moment did he dare take his eyes off the preoccupied animal. Once he felt the road beneath his feet, he gently trod along the gravel-free, dirt edge, increasing his speed with distance gained. He progressed in this manner for a good while. Then, believing himself safe, he began to run.

He walked most of the day, stopping only to rest and to drink from an occasional streamlet, flowing fleet and clean. With the exception of a few rickety carts driven by ill-clad, weary peasants, who informed him of a village where the road branched off, he had not seen any traffic.

He had almost reached the valley floor, cleaved by the rushing Ural River, when an army patrol car intercepted him. With machine guns trained at his chest, he was made to approach the car. The officer in charge, a big subaltern with sergeant's stripes, challenged him, "What do we have here? Where to in such a hurry? AWOL, friend, are we?" he laughed delightedly, and the rest of the lower-ranking men in the open car laughed derisively with him.

"No, no!" averred Heinrich, "I am trying to rejoin my unit. Look at me! I fell out of a truck and am barely alive." He decided that he could not lie too much; veracity was his better friend. So he named as his unit the detail he had escaped with, told them how the unit had just finished an escort run when the accident happened.

"So why are you running down when your unit is way up?" asked the big man, whom Heinrich, by his bearing and looks, believed to be a Cossack.

"I barely escaped with my life. I am tired and hungry and hoped to find a ride at the bottom. I have not eaten since yesterday morning."

"A likely story," said the Cossack. He turned to the other soldiers, "He is AWOL I bet. What do we do with him, consign him to the gulag or shoot him right now? We have that power." A flood of advice poured forth from his men who had been bored to death all day. Two men, making a criminal impression, advocated for instant death, the third begged for leniency. "He looks honest. This could happen to any of us! Would you like to be shot for falling off a truck?"

Secretly Heinrich harbored the hope that the Cossack was one of the dispossessed, angry members of his tribe, one always on the lookout for a chance to subvert the system. He now looked deep into the man's dark eyes, trying to forge a connection. After a long silence, during which the men slapped at the stinging flies with their hats, lighting cigarettes, their leader said in a meditative vein, "On second thought, I think the devil sent you to our advantage. Since your unit thinks you dead and gone, I will take you into mine. I am required to send fifty men to the German front. You can die there more usefully than being shot here."

Inside his scraped skin, Heinrich rejoiced. He made a feeble attempt at protest. "You cannot do this. You are required to take me back to my unit," he demurred. But the soldiers liked the idea of sparing one of their own from combat on the German lines. Without further ado, they pulled him into the small truck, telling him to comply or die on the spot.

Later Heinrich was to tell German authorities how three weeks later, under yet another name, he was assigned to Alexei Kuznetsov's defenses in Leningrad. There he languished for a year in the freezing, beleaguered, starving city during the Axis power's siege, until, in December 1942, he was sent with a reconnaissance party to forge a connection to the Volkov Front. Everyone in his group was promptly caught by German troops, and sent behind the lines to a prisoner of war camp. There, he finally revealed his real, his Volga German identity.

Having learned of Mother's fate by means of Heinrich's report, we avidly pursued news of Joseph and Arkady. We found neither Joseph nor Arkady, nor heard tales of their fate. Our inquiries went nowhere, and the Communist Iron Curtain efficiently shut away those left behind, in what they now called the Soviet Union.

Family Life

I was never busier than during the early years of our family. The children were our joy, or so I believed, for Cary acted as if he enjoyed being a father. He brought home a fine salary, leaving me comfortably at home to take care of the family. As soon as the children started school, I found a most satisfying position as a librarian at a public library, a job very suited to my personality and my needs. I cherished books and order—two attributes necessary to be successful in this job.

With two salaries we finally saved enough money to buy a piece of land at the outskirts of Fresno. The ten acres were still very inexpensive in those days. A vegetable field bearing different crops during different seasons and, of course, a vineyard bordered our land. Bit by bit, as we could afford it, we constructed a delightful house.

As the structure grew, I marveled at the size of the rooms and the opulence of the materials which clad the floors, the walls and the large loggia. I, of course, compared my castle to the village home of my mother, while Cora, who came to visit often, urged me to choose even better, newer and more extravagant building materials.

Cora had married her wonderful marine. She bore him two children, two boys, who became the playmates of our children. They had sold the boarding house and built a home just for their family. Within a few years, her husband was able to buy the hardware store, which he had managed for an absentee owner. They were on their way to becoming very well-to-do.

On weekends our families often picnicked on the San Joaquin, on a special stretch where a small sandy beach had formed. We visited with the Leglers, most often after church for meals. Having integrated my family into my Lutheran church, living in blessed peace and more than a modicum of comfort, I felt safe, content and happy.

How deluded I must have been. What I perceived to be reality must have been utter denial. Although I sensed that Cary did not love us with the same abandon and adoration we lavished on him, I believed that he loved us in a quieter, less obvious way. I was wrong.

After fourteen years of marriage, when Fiona was eleven and Keenan was nine, I came home on a cold day in November to find a note on the kitchen desk where I paid bills and wrote letters. Separate from the rest of the correspondence, a lonely white sheet caught my attention. My heart grew colder than my hands, as I read with disbelief.

> *Kathy,*
> *I don't know how to say this, other than to say I cannot take it anymore. For the longest time I have valiantly tried to live the family life, be an everyday ordinary Joe. I cannot do it anymore. Joy has left me; I am depressed. I hate the electric company, the church, Cora and her "Marine." Don't take it hard. It is not your fault that I am leaving. I don't know where I am going or what I will do.*
> *Cary*

I read the note. I did not weep, although the room had suddenly become dark and I could not breathe. I could not think, and so I sat there by the wretched little desk, staring dully and numb at the large patterned Mexican tile floor. Of all my attempts at love, this had been the only one allowed to flourish. All others, even blossoming romance, had been snuffed out. My innocent adoration of Arkady came to naught because of the Red Army; my passion for Alyosha died in agonizing grief when they led him away to whatever tragic fate awaited him; my sisterly flirt with Korya was doomed from the start; my true, mature love for Herbert Baumeister was rejected.

I had found Cary to be sometimes lacking in substance. But we had children and I cared deeply for him. I had worked hard to make him the center of our family, to allow him to feel wanted, nurtured and loved. However, I had failed, for one can never feel all of another's feelings, never discern all their thoughts. Perhaps I had projected my own love, my wants and wishes onto him, conjuring up a man who was not there? I must have done just such a thing. For the man I thought I had lived with would never have walked out leaving a bland, bare note. That man, although willing to end it all, would have confronted me with passion, anger, unhappiness or sadness, but never with a six-line note.

When the children came home that afternoon, Fiona from piano lessons, Keenan from baseball practice, they sensed the tragedy immediately. As I looked into their sweet faces, Fiona's an oval with clean Irish skin, dark eyes and auburn hair—so much like Cary; and Keenan, so much like my father, strong, gray eyed, thatched with brown, "fat Russian" hair, the tears came after all.

"We will be alone from now on," I said hoarsely. "Your father has gone to do other things."

"What other things?" asked Keenan, imbued with the firm belief that aside from himself there was to be nothing else in a father's life.

"Are we divorcing then?" asked Fiona, with terrible certainty in her voice.

"What do you know about divorce?" I asked, appalled at her adult demeanor.

"I know what it is," she said grimly. "We have two children in class who got divorced."

"You mean their parents divorced," I corrected, breathing deep to keep my voice controlled.

"No, believe me, the whole family got divorced. Emily told me how it is. The dad moves out. He says that he will see the kids often, but then he does not. So he divorced her, too."

Keenan had followed this dialogue silently but with growing horror. "So where will Dad live then?" he asked, his face piqued, the eyes enormous and accusing.

"I don't know," I answered. "He did not say."

"So what did you do to him?" asked my little man, infuriated. "Were you mean to him? Did you yell at him?"

"Nothing of the sort. I think he might be just a little tired of all of us, especially of me."

Fiona began to cry. "It is all my fault," she sobbed. "Yesterday he told me to clean up the mess I made in the kitchen, and I did not. So he got angry and made me do it later on. He was so upset and now he is gone."

I had pulled both of them into a tight embrace and calmingly assured both of them that they carried no blame. "Nothing you could ever have done would lead to such a terrible thing as his leaving," I soothed. "Grown people sometimes feel very bad about their lives, because they carry much responsibility, as for example, making money and working for the electric company. It seems Dad hated his job. It had become hard for him to work there. You know how much you hate to help me in the garden. You hate the weeds, the dirt and the heat. Well he must have felt like that going to work."

"Yes, but we do the weeding anyway because we love you. And he should do the work, because he loves us," determined Fiona with grim righteousness. What was I to say to such a reasonable summation? I could not orate away the human condition, the psychological gyrations of the heart and mind.

It seemed to take forever before my children were reconciled to their fatherless fate. At first, we hoped daily that he might return. Forever they asked upon returning home, "Did Dad call today?" He never did. As the days passed by, we accommodated one another, pouring love and attention upon the one most in need. I got a divorce decree and it was over. We survived. As we shed the stain of abandonment, we grew healthy again, grew stronger, closer.

Then came the day when Cora returned from a vacation in Mexico, in Baja California, and surprised me with the salacious story of Cary leading the loose life of a fishing, drinking man, playing his days away with a senorita, whom Cora simply described as *puta*. Strangely enough, her report did not hurt one bit. I hoped Cary was happy.

Cuckoos in the American Nest

As I went about my daily life, I encountered a multitude of different foreign people. I met them during visits to San Francisco, visits to Los Angeles, the opera, and even at the local grocery store. To me the strangest, most haunting of the foreigners were the girl children of the old KGB bosses. Whether they were the children of Russian KGB, Rumanian Ceausescu adherents, or East German SED-offspring, I could spot them from a mile away.

They were always dressed in the latest American fashion, trying to blend in; they always seemed uncomfortable in their skin, while looking beautifully perfect. They never answered questions openly, straightforwardly, and I smelled the stench of death and French perfume, in which they were raised, from a mile away. This odor still clung to them years after invading America, announcing their privileged, enclave upbringing which had been bought with the blood and broken bones of their fathers' victims.

What creatures they were! Still defending the monsters who had enabled their elite upbringing in the gated elite enclaves, complete with schools, servants indentured by the party, and direct delivery service from the fabulous shops in West Berlin, Paris, London and New York. They had been loosed upon an unsuspecting public, unused to pretty masques carrying hidden death. I know of a few men, unsuspecting, rich sacrifices, who died upon the altars of these very special women.

These men, enamored by youth, beauty and old-world upbringing, died soon after tying the knot with one of the Eastern charmers, leaving their considerable fortunes to the young wives and the families who controlled them.

Although I could detect the poisonous substance oozing from their pores, they, to my amazement, never detected me to be the gulag survivor I was. Hearing me speak Russian or French with friends, they'd flock to me in a desire to reminisce about home. Taking me for one of their own, some divulged their wishes for a return of the full communist power under which they had lived, while others told me of their roles, subverting senators and congressmen with sex or money to vote for certain socialist measures.

One of the girls said candidly, with a sarcastic note, "Communism and Islam have one thing in common. Neither one will stop agitating until the entire world is of their persuasion."

"Do you think that can be accomplished? Would not Islam fight communism, too?" I asked.

"Once America is a communist country, we will take on Islam. So many poor people in their realm will listen to our promises." She spoke these words with utmost certainty, her eyes filled with a zealot's gleam. She had been programmed well.

Epilogue

The years passed. My friends, the Leglers, died. We miss them sorely. They had become the grandparents our family lacked. My children finished high school and went to university. They were handsome, of course, smart, and self-reliant. They were my beloved picture of the new American. Yes, they together with millions of other émigré children were the new Americans.

In time, they found wonderful, suitable mates, better choices than their mother's. They had children—three for Fiona and two for Keenan—who rounded out our family and imbued me with the greatest feelings of joy. Does not the Bible call our grandchildren the crown of our old age? What better to fill a grandmother's heart than to know that her darlings can have that of which most children in the world don't dare dream? No hunger, no famine, no unwarranted searches of homes with its accompanying state-sanctioned robberies.

Here in this country of unfettered freedom guaranteed by an unparalleled Constitution, one was left in peace to pursue happiness and children could become whatever they aspired to be. I had reached with both hands into the depth of opportunity offered by America and found them filled, my wishes granted. Nothing was asked of me in this haven of opportunity but that I apply myself, and use my mind to shape my own destiny. What a difference, what a chasm lay between America and the land of my birth. Hearing the reports that seeped through the pinpricks in the Iron Curtain, I could only say prayers of thanksgiving to God for my deliverance.

For the short time still accorded me, not a day shall pass separating me from the soil. As I kneel on arthritic knees, weeding between lettuce, carrots and white cabbage, I crumble the soil between my fingers and feel once more the connection to the land of my birth. I stem from tillers of the soil and the soil is in my blood. Breathing in the mineral pungency, I am removed to the Volga.

There, my forbearers civilized the steppe for the "Great Catherine." Strange that the meekest of lambs accomplished with Christian endurance what regiments of Cossacks had been unable to do: tame the savage frontier.

No one knows the total extent of their endeavor, although many have faithfully labored to account for their existence and travails. I know how the Volga Germans loved the land, land often so poor that it only defiantly yielded crops; how they alternately cursed and blessed the soil, and nourished it with their blood, sweat and tears.

I think of the simple times, my earliest years. I remember our unpretentious house, the dirt roads and our humble church. We could have lived there happily forever if granted peace. My brethren, who had lost all in Russia, began anew in America, using their bodies unsparingly, suffering hunger and disease once more, never shirking responsibility for their own lot. They became all they are now through their own spirit, their will and God's grace, the grace that had seen them through untold torment.

As I look back, being German—or for that matter any minority, be it Jewish, Cherkess, Abhor, Chechen, Ukrainian or Kalmia—one suffered the lot of martyrdom in the Soviet Union. The record of the hunger, deprivation and oppression suffered by these unfortunates has largely been consigned to weighty tomes that no one reads. I despair that their torment has been forgotten or worse, ignored.

One of the most important things I learned from my communist experience is that if a government takes from its citizens, whether it takes money in the form of taxes or the grain from their cellars, and, rather than create an equal benefit for all, distributes the spoils for the benefit of certain groups from which it benefits politically, then it is merely robbing one group and giving to another.

Indoctrination through class envy was the first act of the young socialist agitators. I remember vividly that, although poor—everything my parents and grandparents had worked for had already been taken by the government before I was born—we had never envied anyone. We had never wished for what others had created through their labor, with their mind, or their business acumen. The socialists changed all that. Through their propaganda, in a very short time, every class hated every other class and coveted their neighbor's success.

The communists then used the discontent of the masses to create the chaos needed to overthrow the established order. And, in the ensuing anarchy, "all sheep were fleeced together," as the farmers say. Albeit the wool spun from these fleeces was not apportioned equally or evenly "according to need" as the Red sheep bleated. Quite the contrary, the poor serfs were even poorer and died even quicker than before, while the spoils were the reward of the Red elite and their communist hangers-on.

My ancestors had been allowed to prosper under the relative freedom of the tsars. But under the authoritarian regime of the Soviets, they were first branded as kulaks for their prosperity and then personally punished for their successes by having their possessions, their livelihoods, and even their lives taken from them. Stalin proclaimed that he intended to lighten the load of the common man, but those who dared question his motives were subjected to immediate horrific retribution.

Amid the members of my church, we discuss over prayer the history, the hardships and destruction of the Volga Germans. We, those saved from the jaws of death, have thanked God a thousand times for the common grace granted us: America.

I am old and prepared to depart this world. All I can do now is to tell my story and trust that those who hear it will learn from the messages it brings. And I pray. I pray for the safety of my grandchildren. I pray for their fortitude against those who seek to deprive them of their strength, their faith. I pray for sanity and honesty in governing minds, for wise thoughts and actions free of the moral turpitude that I witnessed in Soviet Russia and the gulag. I pray that my new country's political leaders have learned about good government by studying governmental failures of the past.

In my darkest hours, when worry and despair about the future of my family blankets my soul, I hear my father's voice, giving me hope. On the day they dragged him to the gulag, he had looked at my mother with courage in his eyes, and said, "They can singly destroy us, but they can never destroy God and our communal soul. We are eternal; our faith, like the Volga, flows forever."